THE EIGHTH
DIVINITY

J. Martin Lutece

scribe for the latest on *THE EIGHTH DIVINITY* at

://www.theeighthdivinity.com

an the QR code above.

Preface

The thirty chapters to follow represent the first volume in a trilogy of stories, all of which are a sum total of four years in the making. A science fiction thriller, *THE EIGHTH DIVINITY* explores the lives of seven individuals in contemporary times as they discover their role in a much larger multiverse. This polyptych approach to storytelling appears in many genres, but it works particularly well in science fiction and horror, where isolation of individuals can serve the voyeur and the humanist alike.

The seven (called Vesiks) are Janet, Frankie, Mayak, Boothby, Conique, Shigeru, and Olga. Each section indicates the point-of-view with the character's first initial, followed by asterisks. Their stories are interdependent, and thus you ought read them like notes in a chord rather than separate threads to complete one at a time.

In the promotional material, I've underscored the origin of this story with the term ***brainscribed***—it means human-generated without the use of large language models. We've entered a period marked by heavy dependence on vast networks to generate text with increasingly believable precision; in such a world, the biggest consumers of text will be the machines used to create them. Therefore, human-generated books will rise quickly in an ocean of bland mockups. My books will never rely on this technology—I spent thousands of hours writing this story, and I hope fellow humans enjoy it in the spirit it was created. Fiction can move mountains, after all.

A work of this scale doesn't happen in a vacuum—the acknowledgments could run the length of the trilogy. I am enormously grateful to family and friends for their encouragement and support. I would also thank Daniel Schmelling for his outstanding cover art and Oren Eades for his edits and input on the early drafts.

To you all, and foremost to Kelly, Robin, and Clyde—I dedicate this novel.

I

Summons of
THE EIGHTH DIVINITY

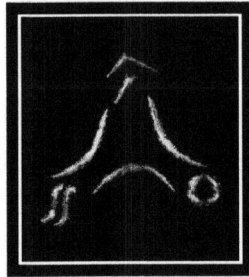

J. Martin Lutece

Prologue

It was a world of secrets. The **Falterrans** named their verdant birthplace **Earth** for the rich soil that sustained them. Evolving over thousands of millennia, these once tree-dwelling primates migrated to the plains, mountains, deserts, and ultimately both sea and sky, achieving global dominance even before **Ghyan** explorers discovered them. In the 21st century by **Falterran** reckoning, documentarians among them examined their long history to identify **Gemyn, Dynax**, and **Otofos**: three fractures promised in early **Ghyan** myth.

Gemyn (*Mind*) blessed these animals with language, and they excelled in many things; first, toolmaking to improve their hunting and gathering skills, second, agriculture to organize peaceful tribes, villages, and nations, and third, weaponry for the gluttonous to conquer and the meek to protect. As it was with such things, the creatures passing through the schism could never return to the world they abandoned.

Instead, they honed their craft, triggering the second fracture: **Dynax** (*Flame*). Wielding power once reserved for the stars, the **Falterrans** marveled at their greatness. Once more, they abandoned the old order, never to return.

The second fracture heralded the third **Otofos** (*Biome*): to better prepare themselves for the ravages of their newfound strength, these intelligent creatures turned their awesome powers on themselves to tease and refine the very blueprints of life.

The **Falterrans** had gained the power to destroy themselves, and it was then that the **Ghyans** found them. In the eighty solar revolutions to follow, the three known fractures would bless them once more, but this time in reverse. **Otofos** promised to loosen nature's shackles to create supermen: age and disease were its intended casualties. They called this *genomics*. **Dynax** would allow them to manipulate the smallest things of the universe to reconfigure matter and energy. Their name was *nanotechnology*. **Gemyn** would, if successful, imbue ageless machines with ghostly intelligence—their processing speed outstripped the organic counterpart by factors of a trillion. They called this *artificial intelligence*, and its proponents insisted it would usher them to utopia.

But darkness descended as the specter of extinction grew: the superstitious among them prognosticated fire and brimstone while scientists predicted ecological collapse. All could agree that a great decision rested before them, and many foretold the worst.

And yet hope persisted. Like **Ghya** before it, **Falterra** housed treasures left from long ago. The **Arkivar**, **Ghya**'s chief curator of history and records, devoted himself to studying **Falterra**. His contemporaries sought power through knowledge and resources, but he understood that **Falterra**'s true strength derived from the **Vyrvesikon**, a psychic structure comprised of seven key vertices within **Falterrans** sharing an ancient bloodline. These people—the **Vesiks**—could embody the first seven virtues: empathy, power, courage, truth, love, advocacy, and knowledge. But each component of the **Vyrvesikon** bore its shadowy vice: selfishness, impotence, fear, falsity, hatred, exploitation, and ignorance. Each Vesik could choose a path, and though any seven of the permutations would activate the **Vyrevesikon**, the world to follow, if any, depended crucially on those choices.

The **Vyrvesikon** contained an eighth and final vertex—the keystone embodying both wisdom and malevolence. At long last, these **Vesiks** would hear the **Preskamon**—a summons commencing in gentle whisper but concluding in clarion brass. The eighth **Vesik** would dare universes to assemble and empower the others. To answer this call, he must follow in the footsteps of the primal architect—a **Monagar** by **Ghyan** designation—but most called him **THE EIGHTH DIVINITY**.

Ghyan Conspectus on Falterran Incursions, 1071.1 Epoch of Light

Part One: Preskamon (the Call)

1. First Vesik: Janet and Her Planet in Twenty-Two Rules

J***

Silence. Sly so. The girl, if she were to perceive herself at all, smirked with a knowing look— was this another dream, like so many before it?

"Mona," called a resonant voice, both of authority and compassion. From within her head? She opened her eyes, spying a familiar enclosure. Something cylindrical, dark, rusty. All too familiar. A dream she'd experienced before.

Again, an entreaty sounded. "Mona." It was somehow familiar. *Moyolitlacoani*?

Above her head, she glimpsed open sky, stars. Too bad she hadn't paid attention in astronomy. Problems here on earth were her priority, not stars. Despite scouring books on constellations, she couldn't find the ones above.

Between the dark terrain and the sky were spires of ice and snow, all strange to her considering she was warm. Around her was a circle of dark, heavy stone seats. Seven, she counted. In the center was a circular altar with a stone piece protruding. Behind her was a three-sided pyramid—a tetrahedron, she remembered from geometry. The place was so familiar, recurrent, common.

"Mona, return to me." The voice beckoned almost lyrically, splashing into her mind a dazzling rainbow of tendril energy, the sketches of a man in the center. Stars streaked by as she hurtled amidst a striated iridescence. She'd read once that scars from the Big Bang were visible in the heavens. These mighty wounds indicated when and where the universe had been born. The universe was big enough, but were there more?

She couldn't recall dosing herself with acid, nor had she sought entertainment of the illicit sort since joining her noble profession. What was it again?

The surroundings dissolved away, replaced by a spectacular cosmos of nebulae, planets, and stars. Her consciousness suffered an eclipse in this place, despite her acquisition long ago of a unique power to rebuff the strange, recurrent apparition she knew only as *Arkivar*—the one companion, bound to her childhood dreams, imparting golden insights. She'd learned the meaning of his name many times, but she rarely remembered it once returned to the waking world.

But something inside of her, deep within her core, pushed her towards hope. Or maybe despair.

"Yes, I am Mona. What do you want, now?" The admission seemed right, yet the waking world called her by another name. What was it? Could this be her reality, and the other the dream?

Amid brilliant flashes of light not unlike those she knew to reside within the human brain, and thus perhaps indicative of some incredible consciousness, the gentle voice eased her uncertainties, saying, "You, *Yolteotl*, are the first Vesik. The Preskamon has sounded. You must follow the trembling desert, where you shall find the second."

She struggled to focus, but she asked, "First and second of what? Vesik? What is Presh…" She couldn't repeat it.

Arkivar answered in poetry, so she listened with more than a little frustration.

Seven seeds, planted well,
Do sprout life, this world will tell.
Gifts bequeathed; power untold.
Each of Seven, power behold.

The short poem led her to believe this might be incomplete. She closed her eyes, muttering to herself, "Rule number twelve: Don't trust riddlers." Whatever good it did here. She could not abide enigmas, purposeful puzzles, and the like.

As the words manifested, so did images of extraordinary design. Opening her eyes, she watched six stars merge close by, yet she could bear to see them. She could not see *Arkivar*, but she knew, somehow, that a firmament beneath her coalesced. It was earth, that blue and green and sandy marble that she knew to be so precious.

She directed her attention to North America, noticing a luminous red fire spurting from it, landing in Texas. The fire spurted once more, flailing itself far to the east—somewhere in Asia. Bouncing once more, it found its way to California. Next, the southeast of America, and Japan. Then, she followed the flare to one of the Scandinavian nations. She knew geography well, and somehow, she retained those faculties.

It appeared, then, that these seven points along the projected surface flashed a brilliant white, connecting somewhere in Asia once more.

Next, a tremendous rumbling obscured all light and color, washing away as though water drenched, diluted, and cleansed the spectacle; it was as though all fire in the universe had been extinguished in haste. She felt cold, dark, alone perhaps more so than ever before. Must she endure this? Who was the dreamer? If there was no dreamer, was there no dream?

Somehow, she understood that to end her solitude, she must follow the plumes of fire. Sixth sun? A new world? She insisted on understanding. "Please, why show me these things? You haven't visited me here in years."

His voice echoed, bleeding across time and space. "Should Falterra die, Ghya will follow. Look for the second Vesik and protect your brother. Oh, Mona, the things we'll do."

"Fal…? Terra? Why your words, now? What do they mean?" she asked, shaking heavy fatigue within her dream.

"You will understand, little Mona. There will be help." His voice died.

Janet Yazzie found herself free of the dream as she awoke with a start, sweaty and winded. Glancing to her cellphone resting on a simple but elegant nightstand, she touched the screen, noting 2:33 AM, a time preceding her usual waking by nearly two hours. She darkened the screen with a second touch, then lightly shoved the phone somewhat away. Burying her head into the cool side of her pillow, she brushed aside her fine black hair with annoyance. "Fucking insomnia," she muttered, drawing a heavy breath.

Closing her eyes once more, she spent some time searching for the nightmare leading to this morning's rough landing. Dim, sketched outlines, more a contrast than an actual thing, came to mind. "Trembling in the desert?" Deserts didn't tremble, at least not anywhere she'd lived.

She rubbed her eyes, then shook her head. "Fuck, just say what you mean."

Rule number three: Don't dwell on the past.

Dreams within that strange setting had plagued her from early life. They were hard to isolate and address. The *Arkivar* had guided her to pursue the nursing career in which she now found herself and now he'd returned, to tell her to chase flames on the globe? It seemed more likely those flames would destroy said world before she could respond. Par for the course, or so the expression went.

She shook her head, casting away any concern for the nightmare. After all, no nightmare could compare with each day of nursing, laboring within the practice of an infectious-disease doctor. Diseases weren't uncommon, but some patients were more difficult to treat than others. She was too young for cynicism, but too old to question it.

Shaking her head, she huffed, "Another sleepless night." Tossing the bedspread and sheets off, she swung her legs from the bed, stretching for the pull chain of the lamp sitting on the nightstand. Light exploded into the room, the halogen fixture sparing no sleepy head.

Within minutes, she had showered, dressed into her black—aptly colored, by her estimation—scrubs, and prepared for a light breakfast. As she nourished her body, she tried to do so likewise with her mind, watching news on her small phone. Listening to the current statistics on vectors and fatalities among the poor and underserved, she ground her teeth, placing the grapefruit back to the table.

Rule number seven: one should share strength with the weak.

Pushing the thought aside, she listened to the female news anchor say, "In other news, a research group from Cambridge suggests that we should consider a post-human world. Professor Luke Kemp warns that the temperature rise projected in 2100 exceeds all other predictions, with emphasis on what they call the four horsemen of the apocalypse, namely, 'famine and malnutrition, extreme weather, conflict, and vector-borne diseases.' Kemp goes on to say that we are approaching the point of no return."

Janet realized she'd held her breath for the duration of the ill omen. It was apparent that the end of the world couldn't sell enough tickets for this to appear in corporate media. "It can't get much worse," she sighed.

Goodman continued, "Ten died and thirty-two were injured after a gunman opened fire within LaDonna Lillinghilly's, a popular LGBTQ nightclub in Vegas. Justin Murphy, 24, died at the scene after exchanging fire with Las Vegas police. In a rare move, the comedian and nightclub's owner Miss Lillinghilly herself spoke with reporters. 'When will saner heads prevail? I'm not a statistician. But water will be wet no matter how many times we touch it. Hearts and prayers are with our beautiful patrons and their families, but let's strive to keep overkill weapons out of the hands of lunatics.' That was LaDonna Lillinghilly—she announced a public vigil outside her Summerlin North estate. We have journalist Karna B. Dune from *Rearmount News* to report on this and other issues later in the broadcast—she also tended bar there at Miss Lillinghilly's club."

Janet burned with anger, silencing the little hell portal of her phone. She slapped the table hard, fighting the tears—only for the infernal thing buzzed, indicating an unblocked call. Shaking her head at the name on the caller ID, she took a deep breath to level herself. After a good ten seconds, she answered, "What is it, babycakes?"

The male voice responding corresponded to her foster brother and forever sidekick, one Adam Baumgartl. He answered with energy, "Morning, sunshine! Doctor T says we need to come early to the hospital." She was silent, and he spun into song, either to irritate or wake her, "*Promise you'll never go away again!*"

Smiling, she swallowed a bite of grapefruit. He did so often cheer her with his song and dance. She asked, "You know, I still don't know why you don't get out of nursing. Go sing on Broadway."

He laughed, singing, *"You made me love you, I didn't want to do it, I didn't want to do it. You made me love you, and all the time you knew it, I guess you always knew it.* Okay, who would help you tend to all the sick if I left you?"

Chuckling, she asked, "What's the story?"

Adam responded, "Triage is supposed to be up like thirty patients. Overflow from Sierra Vista."

Janet closed her eyes. "Fuck, that's so many. I should just go back to sleep."

He asked, "Did you have another one of your visions?"

She rested her fork next to the grapefruit half, finished with it. "I wish you wouldn't call them that. And Jesus, baby, how the fuck do you know that?"

He laughed as though it should have been obvious. "I've known you your whole life, girl."

She eased herself back in her chair. "I wish you wouldn't call them that. I don't want to talk about it, Adam."

He responded jocularly, "Well, I'd share my dreams if you wanted to hear them."

She pinched the bridge of her delicate nose, pushing her thumb and pointer finger into the inner corners of her almond eyes, retorting, "Nope."

His voice was a comfort in tone, if not content. "Well, we were walking along the yellow brick road, and my baby blue checkered skirt blew up in the wind, and—"

She cut him off. "Adam, I swear I could clobber somebody. Don't make it be you." She stabbed the grapefruit with her fork.

He offered conciliation with, "Hey, it's your rulebook, even if it sounds more and more poetic with your, umm, revisions over time. Number five: bottling up means poisoning yourself if I got it right. I didn't mean to make you feel bad."

Her fork clicked against the plate as she sliced into another chunk of the grapefruit. He asked, "What happened this time?"

Janet cocked her head. "It's funny. I don't remember much, but I saw, well, fire."

"Fire? Where?" he asked.

She nodded. "Everywhere. The world was on fire. The continents, like a map or globe."

He had stopped munching whatever mass-produced garbage of the day. "Good God, that's terrible. Was it nuclear fire?"

She snapped in fury. "Jesus, I don't know. I can't remember. I don't *want* to remember. Dreaming about that same place all these years, and for what? What does any of it mean? The world is already fucking on fire."

Adam sounded as though he understood completely. "Shit. I'm sorry, baby. *I don't wanna set the world on fire,*" he sang.

She smiled a smidgen of anger away, answering, "It's okay. You know I don't want to think about the past. Or the present. Or the future."

15

He chuckled at her. "Well, there isn't much space leftover."

She closed her eyes. "I guess then you haven't heard?"

He asked, "About the earthquake in Texas?"

She shook her head. "It was another nightclub shooting."

He was quick to say, "Hang on." He paused, likely running his fingers over the face of his smart phone. "Fuck me—LaDonna's place? No wonder you were upset."

She said, "It's another hate crime, I'm sure."

He lost his cool. "I'm one faggot that shooter should try to kill—I would break him into pieces."

She wept at that. "Adam, be serious. There are people who want to kill anyone they think is different. What if we're treating those people? Militant anti-science? You can know all the martial arts in this universe but can't stop fucking bullets."

He said, "I am serious—they'd hafta see me coming. And I have my sis."

That hurt even worse. "I just don't know," she said as her fingers grasped the phone. "I think I'm just fucking worn down by our job."

There was silence. Perhaps the call dropped? No, Adam was hesitating, preparing her for a question of great discomfort. "Janet, are you thinking about your test results?"

She pushed the grapefruit aside, exhaling slowly. "Adam, I don't want to talk about that. We have work to do, and—"

He paused her mid-sentence and said, "Babycakes, no one would fault you if you took a leave. I'll take one, too. We'll go to Europe."

She tossed the fork to the table, the clattering arresting Adam. "No, I will not abandon our patients just because of some stupid test. Rule number thirteen: We deserve exactly the care we give."

He didn't wait to argue, even if it risked angering her, "I thought your rules made life easier. You don't have to kill yourself. ALS isn't just 'some stupid test.'"

She closed her eyes, pushing from it images of those suffering in the final gasps of the disease. Loss of motor control, speech, and more awaited her. The voice instructed her, as was routine, to protect her brother. But she'd soon be incapable of protecting anyone, let alone Adam. She just sighed. "I really don't want to talk about it. It doesn't make sense."

He prodded her, knowing somehow, as he always did, that she needed to say more. "Say, did you hear back from Codeka?"

Her eyes flapped open at that, so she thumbed through apps on her phone until landing on an icon of a C and a G interlaced. Opening it, the screen read, "Welcome to Codeka Genomics, Janet Yazzie."

She waited while he said, "But it really is creepy, ya know, letting them slither around in our double helixes. I'm still waiting for my results. At least we'll know what kind of mutt I am."

16

Her screen indicated that her own sequencing had yet to happen. She muttered, "I'd welcome the attention to my helixes, I'll have you know. And remember Rule Number Seventeen: Mutts are smarter than purebreds."

He brightened as he said, "Hey, speaking of your rules, I found your oldest rule book the other day."

She was delighted. "OMG where did you find it? I thought Beaumont and Orthenia trashed them." Even the sound of their foster parents' names nauseated her.

He answered, "In a box of my old papers. I guess they had other demons to pray out of us."

What a funny thought, the two morbidly obese Jesus freaks failing to destroy something so representative of her rebelliousness. She chuckled, "Hey, they're the ones who wanted us to believe in commandments and magical thinking. Mine make more sense."

She let her mind wander, visualizing the slovenly pair. They were hyper-religious zealots, concealing their extremism from the Arizona government so they could adopt. She didn't fault the religion itself, for she knew the foster parents would have found justification anywhere they looked for the cruelties they inflicted upon the two of them. It was bad enough that her skin was dark; when they'd learned Adam's sexual orientation, all hell had broken loose. Scandalized, they'd compelled him into conversion therapy, something both children knew to be morally wrong. The Ten Commandments and other rules were capricious, stupid.

So, she'd decided to rebel and to build her own rules, starting with rule number one: God was invented by the power-mongers. Scrawling one after the other, Janet kept them in a locked journal called *Janet's Planet*. The night they broke into it had led them to the most vicious attack on both her and Adam over the course of their time with them.

Adam crinkled the wrapper of whatever junk food he was eating. "You won't get an argument from me, but they weren't so sophisticated sounding back then. Rule number thirteen said something like 'don't expect people to be nice when you're not.'"

Janet cracked a smile. "I still think that's pretty sophisticated for a twelve-year-old." She inhaled a deep breath, then said with a shrug, "The people we treat refuse to take their vaccines, but I actually believe science. I want to live, Adam. I give them good care, even though they don't deserve it." She thought she ought to cry, but her tear ducts burned, as though so dry they could no longer support this basic emotion. It was appropriate, considering her compassion had cooled to indifference.

Adam was pained. She'd known him since childhood, the first person to whom he popped himself from the closet. She knew he loved her. He finally responded, "Well, I'll help in any way I can. Just know you have me, okay?"

In clear defiance of the mood he'd set, he munched on something Janet could only assume was his junk food du jour. While he paused, she pondered just how unfair it was that he could maintain such a good physique while stuffing himself full of the worst of processed foods. The mood lifted as he said, "Besides, I can hope you just can't live without me. I know I can't live without you."

She took the bait, replying, "Suicide pact?" Adam belted a laugh, answering, "All the way, baby." They shared a chuckle, followed by a brief silence. At last, she asked, "What time does Doctor T want us to appear?"

Adam giggled, "Zero three thirty, baby."

She reached for the phone, speaking quickly. "Then I'll see you then." She disconnected the call before he could respond.

Pity for Adam flitted across her mind, albeit transiently. He was her closest friend—more than a friend, in fact. Hell, more than family. Few knew of the special gift she'd discovered in childhood–frightful: opaque nightmares followed by some slight clairvoyance. What it meant was beyond her curiosity now, considering the dire state of her world.

Rule number eighteen: In the face of the impossible, rage against the dying of the light.

God bless Dylan Thomas, even if she didn't like most poetry.

Pandemics had ravaged many populations, and she had more than once almost cast aside her nursing shingle because of the sheer stupidity of those bathed in conspiracy theories. She, like her favorite scientist, Carl Sagan, enjoyed satisfying wonderment in the richly complex natural world to the tragic and self-defeating obsession with conspiracies.

A question often came to mind, one she placed in rule form: "Rule number nine: Imagine what Carl would do."

In any case, time was wasting. Placing otherwise-healthy young individuals on ventilators in triage remained a horror unlike any other she had personally endured. The sounds, the smells, the fragility of the human form effaced by this tiny invisible foe—it all leeched life from her soul.

Janet glanced at a wall clock, muttering, "It's showtime."

J***

The flicker of sunrise greeted Janet as she parked her small convertible into the clinic's lot. Stepping out into the chilly air, she waited for the sunlight to touch her face. Muttering a curse at herself, she fished a mask from above the sun visor over her seat. Attaching one ear after the other, she chuckled at her preoccupation, worried that even the slightest mechanical efforts resisted her; could it be the dreaded disease she'd discovered would claim her? God, she hoped not. Not now. Not this soon. Damn, even in Tucson the winter proved little better than a torment to her.

To her relief, yet embarrassment, Adam popped through the main entry, prepared to greet her. "Babycakes, I'm so glad you made it." He reached out to embrace her, something she only stiffly returned, causing their identification-badge plastic sleeves to clatter against one another.

She sighed, shaking her head. "I'm not sure I can do this anymore."

He cast a furtive glance about the empty lot, and, with a hushed voice, placated her. "Look, this is a tough job. We got into it to help people; to be here when the going gets rough." His bright blue eyes widened as he spread his arms and hands. "We passed *rough* some time ago."

She remained still, staring into the sidewalk. He placed his hands on her shoulders. "Janet, what is it? Was the dream worse than usual?"

She met his eyes with her own, a dread from within her welling up. "Let's not do this here." She pointed to a car approaching, maybe a patient or temporary admin.

He stepped backwards into the reception area, motioning for her to follow.

J∗∗∗

Janet sipped coffee from a styrofoam cup, drawing a chuckle from Adam as he scratched his chin. "You're the ecological queen, and here you are, drinking from the devil's own chalice."

She darted her eyes down to the cup, looking at the a reflection of her round, rather lovely face. Adding to his chuckle, she raised an eyebrow and said, "Who the hell still says *chalice*? Anyway, you do know me well, Nurse Baumgartl."

He opened a thermos, drinking from it. After a courteous pause, he angled his head, and the fluorescent bulbs caught the gray and silver flecks in his eyes. "Have you seen Sylvia lately?"

Janet plopped into hard-as-wood, uncomfortable staff chairs Placing her cup on the table before her, she shook her head. "I haven't been to the shrink in months." She sharpened her eyes at him, a flash of frustration erupting in her. "Why ask what you already know, when what you really mean to say is, 'Janet, you seem especially bonkers today, so go see your crazy doctor?'"

Adam leaned into the counter behind him, firing reassurances. "No, no, babycakes. You know your limits." He paused, cuing her that he was most certainly taking care with her feelings. "Maybe just try to respect those limits. The dream used to make you feel good, and—"

She interrupted him, interjecting, "This wasn't good. The fire destroyed everything. And *he* was there."

Adam's eyes betrayed despair as he repeated her, "Everything." Regaining himself, he helped her along, rolling his hand with, "The man was there? *Arkivar?*"

Janet gulped, squeezing her eyes shut for a moment. "She was. Her voice was the clearest I've heard it in a long time. Whatever else was there didn't make itself known to me."

Adam placed his thermos next to the sink basin. "Could you see him? What did he say?"

She twinged at the consideration. "She was there, hidden in the darkness and cold, but her voice soothed me." She crossed her arms, bringing herself from the reverie. "Adam, I will NOT engage with the dream and its hokey bullshit. I've been in therapy for eight years—"

Adam interrupted her. "Mother Orthenia forcing you into church counseling wasn't therapy, babycakes."

She tossed her hands. "Whatever. Three years with Sylvia, and there is nothing there to gain. Dwelling on it makes it too real. And it isn't."

She closed her eyes. "I wish I understood why this happens to me."

Adam reached for her face. "Rule number fifteen: Why isn't always the right question—errm, I think that's right." She just stared, amused that he tried to remember her rulebook. "Babycakes, you used to think *Arkivar* cared about you. Maybe that's the helpful way to think about it. Maybe that's why you can hear him. He's given you premonitions before. We should call Sylvia so she—"

Janet ran her fingers through her shoulder-length hair, pulling it lightly. "Two shoulds, sir? You don't get any more of those today." Shrugging, she finished, "Besides, Sylvia wants me to believe the dream isn't real, and I don't need a premonition to say the world has gone to shit."

Adam pulled a chair quickly aside Janet, then seated himself with an arm about her shoulders. "I don't know that you, umm, ought to care whether the dream is real, imagined, or telegraphed into your brain by some alien civilization, but all I care about in this is you. If forgetting it makes you happy, I want that."

She saw past his face, her mind wandering as words appeared to her. "*Arkivar* said something distinct this time. Something about following the 'trembling desert.'"

He pulled back as the door to the break room opened to reveal the tall and stout director in charge of them. Adam looked to him deferentially. "DT, good morning."

Director Thompkins smiled, making his way to the coffee dispenser. "Good morning, people. I hope the early wakeup wasn't too disruptive for you."

Janet sipped more coffee from her cup, brandishing a smirk. "Not at all, Director. The Hippocratic Oath protects hypocrites and civilians alike."

Adam laughed, "Add that to your rulebook!"

The physician pivoted towards her, asking, "Oh, right, what did you call it?"

She felt her cheeks flush, but it was Adam who chose to answer, "Janet's Planet in Twenty-Two Rules."

Their boss cracked a smile, "Only twenty-two? What's it all about?"

Janet clicked her tongue, then pushed Adam's shoulder in playful rebuke. He answered for her, "It's something she made up when we were kids."

The physician peered over his glasses at her, raising his eyebrows, "Well, you're adults now."

Janet stewed, replying a forced, "It's that attitude that led me to make them up in the first place."

Their boss eased back, dazed by her pointed comment. Glancing from Adam to Janet, he conceded, "Yeah, we all had our triggers. Don't let me be yours."

Adam intervened, as he so often did when her temper popped, "It really is okay. Our time in the orphanage led to her trying like hell to manage a world spun out of control."

Janet closed her eyes, wishing she were still asleep. Instead, she quipped, "It's still out of control."

Director Thompkins smirked, "Maybe the twenty-third rule would be about futility." Kicking the cavalier aside, he said consolingly to her, "People, the world will always be out of control, especially in our line of work. And that's work that won't do itself."

Adam touched Janet's shoulder to engage with her, "Isn't that rule number nine?"

Compassion in her friend's sparkling eyes did much to cut the temperature, so she answered, "Fair enough. Let's get to it."

She turned to grab her cup of coffee as two admins, one fat, the other thin, entered the break room while clutching their phones. The fat one, Kate, or maybe Kathy, said with urgency, "Are you seeing what's happened in Texas?"

Adam took a sip of his coffee, offering, "Meh. What have they done this time?"

The thin admin, nameless in Janet's memories, shoved her phone into their faces, tapping the screen as a news anchor spoke, "Breaking now, Big Spring experienced one of the worst American earthquakes recorded so far from the pacific fault lines. For more, we go to correspondent Ben Ramirez."

The screen shifted to a man standing amidst rusty oil refinery equipment, something Janet wouldn't want to see up close and personal. Adam pointed to it, chuckling. "Can you spell *tetanus*?"

The nameless admin shushed him as Ramirez said, "Thanks, Rudy. The quake here measured five-point-two on the Richter scale, leading to damage along several fracking sites, all the way to the refinery six miles away. As you can see behind me," he pointed to plumes of smoke and ash along the flat horizon, "EMTs and firefighters are struggling to contain the damage and treat injuries among the exposed engineers and mechanics in the field."

The fat admin rubbed her red hair, huffing, "It's the end of the world."

The thin one answered, "Oh give that a rest, Kay." Janet winced that she'd memorized the wrong name.

Kay laughed her off, "You'll see. Signs and wonders like deserts trembling and bushes burning."

Though Janet understood the words before he responded, Adam jerked his head to her in surprise while the director shot back at her, "I don't know that trembling deserts appear in the good book. It looks like Burning Man." The correspondent coughed a few times from the soot and dust, then continued, "I have here two employees of Dasher Petroleum." The perspective pulled back to reveal a thick man with a shit-eating grin, the other a fit young man sporting a killer beard and intense blue eyes.

The heavier man corrected the reporter, "I'm George Dasher, *owner* of Dasher Petroleum and Affiliates. This is one of my technicians, Frankie Putnam."

Adam watched the screen, whispering to Janet, "I'll take Blackbeard there home with me." Her stomach turned when she decided he'd saddle her with the obese one, as thick in the head as he was in the gut.

Kay shushed him once more with, "He said his name is Frankie." Adam shushed her in return with a dismissive roll of his eyes.

The reporter Ramirez asked, "What did the two of you see?"

With a striking Texan drawl, Blackbeard answered, "I was checking the pump pressure to calibrate flow sensors when the ground shifted under me. I ended up on the ground, and it felt like a bad roller coaster."

George Dasher interrupted with a painfully slow enunciation of words with more than two syllables, "My sub-ord-inate here means to say that he didn't see anything."

Ramirez pressed him, "There's talk that fracking could be responsible for the quakes—"

George Dasher pounced with no small degree of hostility, "Not that I expect the fake news to report what I say accurately, but this isn't anything we did to the Earth. We can't destroy it, even if the fake news wants us to believe it. It's you people," he pointed to Ramirez, "You're the bad guys." Ramirez shook his head in dismay while the fat man continued his tirade, "First, you make us wear masks to restrict the amount of oxygen we can breathe, then they force us to take vaccines, which will sterilize and kill us, and then they plan to take our guns and make us follow Sharia law."

Director Thompkins broke his silence, exhaling, "Too real, man."

The reporter, absolutely unflappable in Janet's estimation, gently commented, yet probed, "Well, those are serious claims. May I ask what proof exists for any of them?"

The Texan seemed genuinely unprepared for the question. Stalling, he answered, "You mean you want me to tell you why these obvious things are true?"

The Texan responded, "Look, I told ya what I believe, and nothing can change my mind. My man Putnam here and me will continue doing what we do to keep people's lights on, and you can naysay all you like. Earthquakes caused by drilling? What a hoax."

He stepped away, leaving Ramirez a bit shellshocked. He looked to the camera to finish, "Well, that's it for Dasher Refineries. We'll keep you posted with new developments, and back to you, Rudy."

Janet had fixed her eyes on the screen, not noticing that Adam was watching her. She turned to catch a knowing glance. He had to agree with her that the earthquake had been a premonition. Could she trust the *Arkivar* of her dizzying dreams? Why did this trembling desert matter?

As she stepped from the small group, Adam captured her attention as he followed. Whispering, he asked, "Anything else?"

She nodded towards the huddle grouped around Kay's phone. "Blackbeard. There's something about him."

Adam grinned. "Yeah, he's fucking hot."

She cut him off. "No." She shook her head. "Well, maybe. But there's something about him. I need to find out more. It's as though..."

The director raised his voice above the din to gather their attention. "Shift's starting. Let's get to work, people. We have triage on the floor above—fifty new patients, most of whom likely need intubation." He pointed to the door. "So, let's move."

Janet tossed her styrofoam cup into the trash, following the physician. Adam whispered to her, "Probably all that Thankstaking turkey time. Shall we?"

She acknowledged, but her mind remained fixed on the trembling desert. Was *Arkivar* trying to connect her to this fracker? She tried to form a picture in her mind, watching him operate the dirt-covered junk passing for refinery equipment. The redneck was important, but she didn't know how. Then again, rule number eleven said it plainly: even a stopped clock is right twice a day. Maybe she was the fool.

2. Second Vesik: Frankie the Fracker

*F****

The heavy thrumming of the behemoth drill obliterated all other sound, but Frankie Putnam would not complain, left to the privacy of his thoughts.

Something was wrong with this world, he'd long-since decided. Fracking gave him the solitude he wanted to ponder just how far south of crazy all people had gone. He thought of himself as principled, moral, and sane. Not everyone walking his path would want salvation. And most of the billions of people wasting space and resources would not amount to anything more than sinners in hell, so he would avoid them as much as possible. Breaking the sweet quiet of deafening equipment was a nails-on-chalkboard yodeling, "Puddnuhm!" At once, he found himself plucked from what little serenity he found in his work, returned to the madhouse of reality where his least favorite childhood friend George Dasher now supervised him. He knew he'd never hear the end of the interview in which he and George had participated.

A plump, ruddy hand encroached within eyeshot, snapping its jewelry-covered fingers, and a familiar anger welled in him.

He turned his attention to the fatass bully he couldn't shake. Frankie sighed, easing off the heavier intensity of the drill. George reached him, at first recoiling from the heat in the equipment. "Fuck me, Putnam, your drill is almost on fire!"

Frankie couldn't hide his delight. "Heat never bothers me, George."

Without regard for personal space, he crammed his greasy smart phone into Frankie's face with a heaving laugh. "Look at what those antifa fuckers said about me on my feeds!"

Frankie blinked, removing a heavy leather glove from his left hand, then slid his bare fingers into his stocking cap to scratch his thick hair. "George, I needing to finish this bore hole before my shift ends."

George teetered back and forth in amusement, pointing to his cellphone. "Look at this! They said my IQ is low since I'm fat. I think fat people are smarter than thin ones." George leaned into Frankie with a laugh too loud and breath too terrible.

Refusing to look at the cellphone, Frankie stewed a little. "George, they already think we're morons. It doesn't help to push them further toward believing it."

The obese supervisor retracted his phone, huffing. "Says the guy who never liked ye ole Rush." He touched the phone, darkening the screen. "You *wanted* to tell them it wasn't our drilling causing them quakes."

Frankie glanced upward, sunlight catching his blue eyes. "On principle, man. They just don't know what the cause is. But you made it about everything else under the sun."

George fumbled with his phone, making a big to-do of holstering it to his belt, then placed his hands on his hips. "Sheila said I made her wet when I told him off."

Frankie closed his eyes, shoving George's grotesque wife from his mind with as much force as he could muster. He locked one of the gear manifolds into place, then removed his remaining glove. "George, now they won't believe you either way. Why do you try?"

The hefty supervisor scratched his gleaming bald head, guffawing. "You're always listening to your talk radio heroes. Don't they say what I say?"

Frankie sighed, weary of this particular dance and the can of worms inevitable to spill. "Some say we should just mind our own business, George."

George guffawed more curdled milk breath into Frankie's face as he reached again for his holstered, now-ringing phone. "Yeah, Sheila says it should all be my business." He lifted up a finger in Frankie's direction, as though he was too stupid to be silent while his superior fielded some important call—or, at least, important in the imaginings of one George Dasher.

Frankie amused himself by thinking of the nickname George had earned himself in their shared youth: Porky Georgie without the Dasher. God, he detested this man. Why did he ever agree to work for him? If anyone was to blame, it would have been Pastor Chet. George bullied Frankie when they were children, but their pastor thought it was important that Frankie work with George. His ways were not Frankie's, he supposed.

The fatso amended his tone sharply, demeaning the hapless caller. At least Frankie's shared history with George offset the sham smugness with which the bastard smothered his other employees.

George shook his head, repeating the word "No" so many times that Frankie fantasized, if only for a moment, of spit-roasting that pig on the gear manifold. "No no no no no no no, that's not right." He withdrew a spacious breath, exhaling, no doubt, to buy himself time to color his next words. "It is not for you to det-er-mine that. You should never have been allowed to decide that."

George then covered the microphone, mouthing with floppy-lipped talking horse affect, "I gotta take this."

Frankie decided to hell with it; his sister was planning to meet him for lunch, so he stepped away.

Walking to his truck, his ears rang. There was no such thing as true, noiseless quiet for him. Doctors called it tinnitus, but could they be wrong? He even heard it in his sleep, despite claims that he should not. His pastor Chet Avery often called it the Legion of Locusts, a burden God had placed on him.

Perhaps he did hear locusts, but even the ringing was better than listening to George the windbag.

In town, he'd find his sister's choice: the Hotel Settles, a strikingly beautiful landmark filled with Victorian and French provincial furniture. Decor didn't interest him, despite having a brother Tyler study interior design.

No matter the interior, the hotel featured a cafe he hadn't tried, so, again, what the hell?

F***

As Frankie drove his Ford F-350 into town, the heater in his cabin furnished a welcome change of temperature. Passing along the open road, he scarcely noticed the fields mottled with both functioning and derelict oil pumps, tanks, and loose scrap, for machines rusting into the earth were commonplace throughout Big Spring. Most of it withstood the quake from the early morning, though he wondered whether it would mean more expenses George would rebuff, even in the face of all reason.

Instead, he considered the event itself, and the claim that no such tremors had occurred in the long history of the region. Perhaps that was a lie? But why would his parents and his late grandparents never talk about them if these quakes had been happening all along? Hell, in his own twenty-five years of life, he hadn't known them to happen.

He was too tired to fuss over it, for fracking was difficult work, with long hours and not much respite. He'd normally take lunches of a half hour and no more, but this was the rare extended variety. His little sister planned to move out of state soon, so he felt compelled to spend time with her, even if she drove him nuts.

Tuning out the tinnitus, he listened to his favorite author, S. K. Varnum, someone as high above Porkie George in intellect as a monkey is a flea. Varnum spoke deliberately, saying,

"On the topic of communism, we learned the hard way over one hundred years that too many died for it. Lenin, Stalin, Red China—all killed for Marx." The speaker remained silent for applause. Continuing, he added, "Those who attack me on social media are just more of the same. Social justice warriors wanting to make us all the same, just as Marx did."

He slowed his speech to deliver the words to follow most deliberately. "Make... no... mistake... They want the same things Stalin wanted. And it'll be our heads. The heads of thinking men. Young men like yourselves, unwilling to take whatever branding they put to you."

The crowd applauded, but he could hear some women booing Varnum. Frankie could imagine the types: tattooed, body-pierced girls with purple hair, doing just about anything to make a spectacle of themselves. They had no idea how difficult women made life for men, Frankie decided.

So, he muttered to himself, "This is why I stay off of that grid."

The voice persisted. "It could be as bad as any threat from the nearby bushes, as poisonous as a mother's resentment and the chaos she represents. Extinction of thinking people such as ourselves."

Frankie's eyes flared, flashes of his deceased mother materializing before him. Yes, her rage and anger seemed forever with him. Maybe Varnum's words could comfort him.

"There are people here in Canada eager to run me out of the country on a rail— whole social media campaigns to banish me to America, where I probably would enjoy a better reception."

Frankie flashed a smile, answering, "Come to us, Professor Varnum." Noting the dusty turnoff to reach his destination, he seized a brief moment further from this heroic truth-teller.

"Why must we face social consequences for refusing to call kids by their confusing self-chosen pronouns? I was born a man, and I could never convince anyone otherwise."

Shocking Frankie, a member of the professor's audience blurted, "I'm surprised people think you're a man to begin with, eh?!"

At the clash of voices, Frankie suffered a heightened buzz of the locusts. This torture angered him. He imagined a bloodbath of Canadians in his wake, beginning with the removal of this prankster's tongue and genitals.

The recorded talk erupted into a mixture of applause, booing, and catcalls, with Varnum answering, "You see, he just prefers we all accede to bland uniformity, where nothing matters. Words don't mean anything anymore, so why bother using them in favor of grunting and snarling?"

Frankie nodded hard, answering, "Of course he's a man, you fucking faggot."

Silencing the playback, he pulled his truck into the quaint downtown blocks of the town, where he next found the gravel parking lot of the hotel. His sister's azure bumper-sticker-covered EV rested nearby, so he sidled his enormous pickup alongside her little blue box. Frowning at what passed for her transportation, he zipped his thermal vest closed over his plaid flannel shirt, then pulled his gray winter cap back over his ears for comfort. The weather hadn't delivered on the chilling forecast for the day, but a respectable temperature of fifty-five degrees Fahrenheit still proved enough for him to require the thermal wear.

Entering the spacious hotel, he noted the grand staircase flowing outward, walls adorned with spectacular paneling of varied colors. He'd never in a million years pay a decorator for anything resembling this place. Filling the space behind the stairs' landing was a tremendous color portrait of a native woman on horseback—well, the woman, at least, was something to behold. The rich dark wood of the staircase featured elaborate carvings, drawing, oddly, a smile from him. His brother would love it indeed. Well, he could have it.

A mousy girl stood near a small podium to the left of the entrance. She seemed immediately excited and embarrassed to see Frankie, something he'd long ago discovered sharp features and blue eyes would net him just for showing up. He greeted her, saying, "Howdy. My sister Myra probably already got us a table?"

She exposed shining braces on her teeth with a cutesy smile as she pointed through an entry informally separated by batwing saloon doors. "This way, sir."

Flipping them open, he decided he might like that part of the hotel after all. He nodded, offering, "Much obliged." In the noisier, more contemporary cafe, he spotted his sister in the corner at a booth, her pink-and-green hair a showstopper—and, to his thinking, not a good one. She hopped to her feet, beckoning him to her table with an enthusiastic wave.

Once he reached her, she grabbed him with a hug, exclaiming, "Frankie!"

He returned her affectionate gesture, then motioned that they should sit. As he pulled his winter cap from his head, he bobbed his forehead towards her hair and probed, "What's this mess all about?"

She touched it, answering, "I just wanted to try something new."

He frowned in rebuke, blistering her with, "The piercings aren't enough? And the tattoos?" He gathered himself with a sigh, then asked, "When are you taking that fugging Bernie sticker off your toy car?" He regretted the remark as soon as he said it until his thoughts met the locusts once more.

She gave a laugh of discomfort, her first response to any rebuke he had for her. But her reply pissed him off. "When you decide to get the vaccine."

He intended to counter, but the waitress interrupted him as she asked, "What would you like to drink, sir?"

He answered, "Just ice water."

The server shifted on her feet uneasily, responding, "Umm, the City of Big Spring sent out a notice that the tap water isn't safe to drink, so we can only do fountain drinks or bottled water for now."

Myra pointed to her brother while remarking to the waitress, "Frankie here could tell you about that, considering he's into the fracking that's wrecking the water table."

Frankie further co-opted the poor, uncomfortable server into the argument by reading her nametag. "Yeah, Helen should agree that painting your head into an Easter egg, stapling yourself, and stamping stupid pictures and gook letters and words all over yourself and your little wind-up car don't entitle you to complain about everything. You take no responsibility while the rest of us with jobs do all the work."

Myra glowered at him, then shot back to the hapless waitress, "Because destroying the fucking environment is okay if it's your job, right? If it were just a hobby, then you might be guilty of mass murder." She tapped the bottle of water sitting before her. "It's okay to poison me if I don't have a job, and I don't have a right to say anything about it."

She gestured above her. "Catastrophic climate change is the sixth extinction event, you dummy. And guess what? You having a job won't save you from dying with the rest of us in the next Great Flood."

He paused, watching her, then answered, "Maybe there needs to be another to clean up the Devil's mess."

Helen the waitress appeared pained, so she quipped, "I'll give you guys a minute." She vanished.

Frankie eyed her shrink away, after which he tapped the table, exasperated. "Why the fuck did you even want to have lunch?"

His sister's eyes swelled, tears forming. "I wanted to see my big brother before leaving town. Is that so wrong? Why do we have to agree on everything?"

Frankie narrowed his eyes. "Fine. You're the one who brought up politics."

Myra returned fire, escalating. "You attacked me for my appearance. That's just cruel, and you're probably the only person in a mile radius who cares about it."

Silence followed as Frankie watched his little sister blot her tears with the brown recycled-paper napkins. He recognized his anger, but feelings remained a difficult thing for him. Even when he was quite young, others and their behavior had perplexed him plenty. This small person before him, his younger sister, seemed foreign, disconnected. He didn't hate her, not as he did his foolish fat boss. But he couldn't *feel* her feelings. Why did she care so much about things that shouldn't be her business?

Varnum was right about one thing: women were sheer chaos in the flesh.

Helen at last crept back to the table, asking Myra, "Are you okay, hon?"

His sister shook her head. "I'm just trying to say goodbye, and he's being an asshole."

Frankie's temper seared, so he asked the waitress, "Don't you think too many tattoos and piercings are ugly?" He turned his eyes towards the server, only to notice at last that she had full arm markings and nose and eyebrow piercings. He felt his own cheeks surge with heat, reddening. "I mean—"

The waitress twisted her sunbaked face, wagging a crooked finger. "I tell you what, why don't you just find your lunch and work out your family drama somewhere else?"

Myra tugged on her pastel hair, pleading, "I'm sorry he's such a dick. Please let us stay."

The waitress stared daggers deep into Frankie, waving her finger once more. "You're paying for your little sister's meal. And not another peep of that negative shit, or you're outta here. Comprendeme?"

He touched his face, feeling the heat. He wondered if the insects filling his head caused the blush; no matter, they screamed when someone dared rebuke him. As the waitress scurried away once more, they quieted, leaving him to examine his sister. Her face bore no anger, just wistful disappointment. He knew his agitation followed more from his earlier interaction with George than anything else, so he sighed, offering a dejected, "I'm sorry, Myra. But what you do is just weird and hard to understand."

She drank from her glass, spurting back to him, "Well, I think the perverted shit pumped out by the orangutan is weird and horrible, but you follow him. Yet I'm frustrating because I care about the world around me?"

He squeezed his eyes closed, the locusts thrumming behind them. He measured his words, "You'll see. In a few years, MAGA will be remembered as our most important movement. The Democrats and Black Lives Matter will turn us into communists, and we know—"

Myra interrupted, "According to queeny little Skillet Varnish, we'll all become slaves? Do you have any idea how insane that fucking sounds?"

He unzipped his thermal vest as the debate increased his blood pressure. "Just look at everything the libtards do in the world. Give billions to people who don't work. Teach kids that it's a sin to be white. And anyway why do you call Varnum that? He's not gay. Even if he were, wouldn't you like him more?"

She laughed, unable to sugarcoat her response. "My God, Frankie, watch him mince around the stage judging everyone else from the closet. He's a creep and a fucking moron, Frankie. He's like that airhead guy out of Voltaire, thinking the world is better left alone, all positive and wonderful as is. Only he's cruel to his students, and he says it's okay for bullies to do what they do."

Frankie fidgeted with his napkin and place setting, anger increasing yet again. "He just doesn't want to be forced to call a boy a girl and a girl a boy if he doesn't want to. And he was just saying that guys become pussies if they're not pushed by bullies to become strong."

He huffed a small laugh, adding, "Like our brother." The buzzing sharpened as the Legion descended. He laughed more, adding, "He could use toughening up."

She cocked her head in disgust. "That's so fucking mean, Frankie. You bullied him at home, just like Porkie George bullied you, and he's still himself." She paused, then flapped her hand in his face, asking, "And why should it be up to Skillet Varnish? Even if he *were* being told what to say, which he isn't?"

Frankie tossed his napkin to the table, biting the inside of his cheek until he tasted the salt and iron of his own blood. Seething, he answered, "He's just standing up to the cultural Marxists attacking him. They want to control what everyone else can say to them and about them. He's just arguing against political correctness."

His sister began to weep. "What would he say about the shooting?"

Frankie asked the most obvious question, unprepared for her response. "Which one?"

"Fuck, Frankie—even the fact that you hafta ask should spell it out. There was one at an LGBTQ nightclub in Vegas."

He shrugged at her. "Again, with all the letters. Just call 'em steers and queers."

Her face turned red. "You mean to say that's the part of that sentence that offends you?"

He said, "Because some guy shoots a bunch of dykes and queers, I'm supposed to turn in my guns? God says—"

She almost spit on him. "Nothing about guns. But a lot about loving your neighbor."

He shook his head in disapproval. "No, Myra. That being gay is a sin. They weren't going to heaven, anyway, and they're not my neighbors."

She bit into her lip, causing it to bleed. "Jesus, Frankie, you need to be more careful about what you say. You want freedom to say what you want, but you don't want the consequences." She looked up to Helen the waitress approaching, timing her words, in his estimation, to ensure she could complete the thought. "Your brother is gay, and I'm bisexual. How does your love-in with Magadom and Professor Skillet Varnish fit with all that? Do we deserve to die?"

Stunned, Frankie leaned forward. Now he could feel something: genuine surprise. Almost speechless, he asked, "What did you say?"

She rose to her feet, looking to the waitress. "I'm fucking outta here. No more inbred Big Spring, no more goddamned Texas. No more motherfucking family!"

Frankie traded glances with the waitress, the server blistering him, "Oh, what in the mucky undercroft of hell have you said to her now?" The waitress craned her neck to spy a look at Myra as she left, then turned to him, shouting, "You're a terrible brother, treating your sis that way. You should get the fuck outta here now. NOW!"

She continued shouting as the Legion drowned this shrill cunt out of his mind. He remained silent as he watched his baby sister storm her way through the flapping saloon-style doors, several patrons throughout the cafe monitoring her dramatic exit.

Good God, could it be true? He had gossiped some with his father on the possibility that his brother, a fashionista obsessed with decor, lighting, and the like, might prefer the firmer sex. True further still, George had demeaned Tyler as fairy-folk for years, but Frankie had just ignored it, though they had speculated on what manner of creature his sister Myra might be.

All of this left him with too much to consider. What would Pastor Chet say? What would Porky George think to hear the truth he'd claimed for so long? He avoided the topic of Myra with George, thanks to the sordid, lusty fatso asking whether Frankie had seen piercings in her box. Good God, who would care about something so awful?

F***

Frankie reached his small apartment around eight in the evening, exhausted in more ways than one. He couldn't think of burdening his father with the current news; his mother had passed only six months prior from a short but horrible decline due to bone cancer. His dad remained frail, and Frankie, along with his younger brother Tyler and sister Myra, were all that remained of their family here in Big Spring.

Damn. With her leaving so suddenly, just the three remained, though Tyler did have a roommate.

Jesus Christ, a black roommate! Were they an item? Was Tyler not only dating a man, but a black one at that? What was his name? Marvel, like the comics? Marvo

The thought of a black man touching his brother left him with retching. Pushing it out of his mind, he unlocked his front door, pushing it open with a twenty-pack of beer. Ah, beer—a thing that would set him right as rain.

He dropped his keys into a brass bowl just inside the doorway. The drab little house held little in the way of furniture, yet it wasn't at all cheap, thanks to the fracking boom. Tyler had threatened on more than one occasion to decorate the place, but Frankie had refused, assuming—now rather correctly—that his friends might think Tyler was gay. Fuck. Pastor Chet had been right when he said that demonic influences were attacking the Putnam family. When their mother was ill, the pastor had only negative things to say to Frankie's father, crippling the old man's faith. Even Frankie had resisted Pastor Chet during those dark days.

Porky George believed he himself had convinced Frankie to continue attending church, thereby saving, and, by boneheaded implication, owning his soul. But he had his own reasons for sticking with the straight and narrow: what the pastor called the *Korobskron*, a thing he could never let George know about. Not that Frankie hadn't fantasized about sharing it with him. But Pastor Chet exacted total discretion on it, and Frankie felt he owed his spiritual mentor both in this life and the one to follow.

His thoughts exhausted him, so he pushed them away, then pulled free the heavy boots from his tired feet. Slipping off his vest, he collapsed into an evening chair, twisting the cap from one of the beer bottles. The taste refreshed him.

What was the beginning of this chain? He wanted to ask Tyler whether Myra was telling the truth. But he already knew the answer.

Sleep sounded like a better plan.

32

F***

"Frankie, are you there?" The sweet, warm voice was weak, cruelly drained of vitality.

He took her hand. "I'm here, Mom. I'm here." He wasn't sure where "here" happened to be, for all he saw was his mother upon her deathbed, with all light gone save a spotlight on the crumbling, feeble form before him.

She had withered from the beautiful golden-haired angel of his boyhood into a hairless, gnarled skeleton stretched with ashen, bruised, and breaking skin. He held her bony, crooked hand, remembering the perfect, smooth skin long gone. She squeezed his own hand as best she could. "Frankie, sweetheart, I know this is hard, but you need to be there for your father and your brother and your sister."

He perceived great dampness in his eyes and about his face—he was unaccustomed to crying or feeling much of anything. "Mom, I don't understand. How am I supposed to take care of them?"

She smiled, reaching for his wet cheek. "Your father can't find his way without you. Your brother needs love and support. And your sister needs you to see past whatever she's done."

He shook his head. "She's a drug user, Mom. She's done terrible things."

His mother squeezed his hand harder. "Jesus teaches us to forgive as He forgives us."

He sighed. "I'm not sure how I can help Tyler. He's off in his own little world."

She chuckled, observing, "You'll know what you need to do when you need to do it."

He kissed her hand. It was cold and damp, as though the grave had already claimed her. "I love you, Mom."

Her eyes widened as she spoke somewhat more sternly. "There's another thing you must do—a man you must find." Her voice transformed rather suddenly to that of a man with brilliant tendrils of light surrounding the form upon her hospital bed. "Look to the old enemy. Mayak. Find Mayak and the doomsday weapon."

He tried to release her hand, only to find himself inseparable from the spreading luminous energy. "Mom?" he said as he struggled to release her, or it.

The voice repeated, powerfully resonant, now male, with his mother's voice overlaid upon it. "You, birthed of *Dynax*—the power— must find Mayak. The old enemy. Doomsday." Then, as she always said as she lulled him to sleep, "Poof! Next stop, and you'll be there, little Frankie."

F***

Frankie awoke with a start, drenched in sweat. The television before him showed nothing but static. Surrounding him were empty beer bottles. He looked to a clock across the room and saw that the time was exactly 2:15 AM. He sighed, wiping sweat from his brow.

"Mayak. Dynax? Who makes up this shit? Old enemy?" He shook his head. "What the fuck does that mean?"

He pulled his notebook computer into his lap, swinging it open. The screen brightened with a request for login information. With the appropriate keystrokes, he pulled up a browser window, with the search bar awaiting him. He typed "MAYAK DOOMSDAY" to no avail, though a link to the doomsday clock, a book by someone named Daniel Ellsberg, and a *Star Trek* episode title appeared. He squinted at the cover of Ellsberg's book, wiping some sleep from his focusing eyes. "Hmm, *The Doomsday Machine?*"

He typed "WHAT IS THE DOOMSDAY MACHINE?"

A list of links to articles about nuclear devices appeared before him. He typed, "MAYAK NUCLEAR," and this time, found a listing for Mayak Chernovsky, a former technician at Los Alamos. Clicking the profile link, he read aloud to himself, "*Miracle child* studies in Russia from 2005 to 2010, nuclear engineering and field analysis at Los Alamos from 2010 to 2017, then what?"

Nothing. The profile ended rather sharply there. He searched online for the name once more. Nothing. No obituary, no record, save a marriage notification in Voltkinsk.

He rubbed his beard, inhaling deeply. What did it mean to be a miracle child? Was he a product of virgin birth?

He decided he would call Pastor Chet.

3. Third Vesik: Mayak and His Skrytyypass

*M****

Mayak Chernovsky rested his fingertips, eyeing the panoply of knobs and buttons along the ancient panel. With a quiet sigh, he imagined Moscow's stingy bureaucrats hoarding money while the equipment controlling the world's most dangerous weaponry disintegrated alongside the once proud Union. It made a kind of sense to him. Trained to be a nuclear engineer, he *chose* to safeguard these engines of extinction. No one who touched the technology would argue against the name. His father would say he'd squandered a beautiful mind, but if the weapons were a fact of life, Mayak wouldn't let them destroy themselves because of deteriorating tech. Discipline might not be within the bureaucrat's wheelhouse, but Mayak had received enough military training to deny self whenever it was needed.

The young lieutenant did support flag and country, not that his superiors and peers would tolerate open discontent. Nuclear engineers, technicians, and even the paper-pushers supporting them bore heightened scrutiny, and Mayak had long been capable of recognizing the Federation Security Service's exhausting ubiquity.

Not that they could understand why. Mayak's life skill level-ups remained hidden even from the masters of secrets. He knew the score, even if it meant refusing both marriage and fatherhood. The ever-watchful eye of the state could exploit these for both handed over footholds to the operatives he knew surrounded him.

35

It was true, though, that the reason he knew where to look might indict him of madness, first for following the reason, second for believing it. So, he soldiered alone, left to his work first and hobbies second.

But the human animal, party member or not, thirsted for companionship. Again, why would he choose such a profession? A penchant for physics, an uncle dead to Chernobyl, and a deep dislike for the technology's implications, if not the tremendous beauty of its theoretical grounding—a trap, a snare, with no escape now. A resignation letter may as well be a suicide note, and the bulky panel before him offered no comfort, each speck of decrepitude capturing the state of the whole of Mother Russia's nuclear arsenal.

As his thoughts returned to the problem before him, the integrity of fifty missiles competed for his attention. A wave of alert indicators flashed, reflecting across his narrow features, and a fellow technician burst into the maintenance pod, droning as was his custom, "We seem to be in trouble, comrade."

That captured the whole of Petrov Posk, at least as long as Mayak had known him. A burliness and sturdy affect sheltered a funny, loyal, and sometimes insubordinate soul. He was close to a best friend as the young lieutenant could permit himself. A supplier of much humor and even more vodka, Petrov offered neither now, supplanting them with alarm.

Mayak's hands danced across the dated keypad. His security-issued laptop provided an interface into the rust-kissed status and control panels. Though it wasn't a sleek and sexy device, his computer appeared in sharp contrast to the mass of circuits and machinery below it, like grandchild and grandparent, or maybe great grandparent. He fidgeted in his seat, cold blue eyes fixed on the screen. "Perhaps this is drill, no?"

Petrov pulled a squeaky, tattered chair over to the panel, plopping his heft next to the lieutenant. "Why would stage two be flashing? I don't remember simulation that could touch stage two."

Mayak huffed. "Be still, Petrov." He scanned along the command interface on his computer screen, one line after the other.

Petrov watched the screen, then looked to Mayak's unbroken attention. "What does diagnostic say?" He paused, waiting for response. "Mayak?"

Confused, Mayak answered, "How can administrative commands be issued spontaneously?"

Petrov shook his head. "It is not possible. Again?"

Mayak raised a single eyebrow as Petrov's cologne scent filled his nostrils. He preferred distance, social or otherwise, but the emergency before him took precedence. Refocusing his attention, he asked, "You've seen this before?"

Petrov studied the security board while the flashing lights traced his face, then replied, "Check second channel. Maybe this is malfunction."

Mayak entered commands into his keyboard as he tried to slow his breathing. Answering, "Second channel reads fine. Checking third." The text output to his commands waited as the klaxon sounded above them. Petrov glanced at the flashing lights above while Mayak fixed himself on his laptop's screen. The results were clear. "Dammit, backups not in malfunction. Checking sensors." He waited, cursing under his breath at the command-line interface's glacial response. Gasping in relief, he reported, "No issue there. This is real."

His friend cursed, then looked to the emergency wired telephone hanging just over the right of the panels. "I must call it."

The world shrank at those words, a surrender to the doomsday Mayak and others like him were charged to prevent. As he made his way to the receiver, Mayak touched his arm, asking, "If strike has been ordered, why have we not been told?"

His friend pulled himself free, answering over the increasing alarms, "Our job is clear: confirm launch." He picked the receiver, speaking carefully into it, "Tier two monitor, confirming launch. Is drill? Confirm, no malfunction." He turned from Mayak, then reiterated with brimming frustration, "We detect no malfunction. Repeat, no malfunction." Mayak turned back to his screen, hoping a second run of diagnostic commands might reveal this elusive malfunction. Muttering, "Nothing wrong here." Turning to Petrov, he asked, "You know what is happening?"

His friend turned back to him, his face drained of all color. He spoke to their commander with care, "Understood. Yes, sir. Understood." Replacing the receiver, his eyes conveyed a torment Mayak could not mistake for anything less than the genuine article. He whispered, "Mayak, it…" Interrupting him was a blast of alarms, more deafening than any of the sirens already splitting his eardrums.

He shouted to Petrov, "Did someone order strike? Against whom? What is happening?!" Before he could answer, a security sergeant and armed escort burst into the diagnostics room. The imposing figure shouted over the alarms, noise joined with hollers and screams coming from the corridor. "Mayak Chernovsky, Petrov Posk, you are to come with us."

Mayak pointed to his computer screen, protesting, "With respect, we are running important tests on weapons. They may be in danger." Frustrating enough, he evoked no sympathy from the guards. He tried once more, insisting, "Please, firing mechanism may be compromised."

Petrov intimated worry to his friend, whispering, "Not here, comrade. Not here."

The leading soldier shook his head hard. "You are to accompany us, Chernovsky." He cocked his automatic rifle, raising the barrel in Mayak's direction. "However, we grant you choice in manner of accompaniment."

Petrov spoke quickly. "We'd best do as they say, comrade."

Disgusted and angry, Mayak complained, "Sure, goon squad ordering me at the tip of a rifle to abandon my post, right when alarm sounds. Security genius at work."

Once to their feet, he and his good friend were met with yet another insult: guards on either side of the squad's lead goon held black hoods ready for each of them. Mayak shifted his icy gray eyes to the sergeant. "What fresh hell is this?"

The guard twitched one corner of his mouth upward into a smirk, nodding. "You will place these over your heads."

Pissed off, Mayak sneered, "This is fun for you? We could be at war."

Mayak's computer terminal sounded yet another alarm, pulling his attention away. He saw root commands appearing in sequence, only to feel the hood fall and quickly tighten over his head. The guards shoved him into his friend, so he complained, "Petrov, my terminal appears hacked. Root commands run…" A blunt object struck his head, causing him to see flashes of light.

This drew a rare, fevered response from his friend: "What are you doing, you fools? We cannot solve problem through goddamned blindfolds!"

The sergeant answered, "We want you silent, Posk." Another whack sounded, this time Mayak's friend fell silent to their blows. Even without struggling, Mayak felt a pair of muscular hands seize each of his arms.

Mayak felt terrific pain on the back of his head, confident he was bleeding. With a clearing head, he rebuked them, "Please, understand. If my terminal is hacked, someone could spoof launch, or, worse, force one." The guards said nothing, so he insisted, "ICBMs are on my monitor. They can strike NATO and beyond."

The sergeant warned him, "I can hit you harder, Chernovsky."

Mayak could taste the sour shock in his throat as a gun butt was thrust into his upper back muscles. Petrov pleaded, "Why are you attacking us?!" Grunting in agony, he gasped, "Do not hurt him."

Part personal concern, part the need for contemplating their plight, Mayak hushed his friend. "Petrov, just be still." Cool-headed, reasonable, careful all appeared in his staff dossier. Even if the apocalypse was under way, he would process, then act. Brain-trauma from overactive goons would not serve any end.

Their captors moved them from their station into the connecting corridor while Mayak thought through the commands, each with highest privileges. Log erasures, changes to system commands were the sum total of what he could catch before being pulled from his chair. He wouldn't venture a word for fear of reprisal, but no one from government or security could hack his terminal. So he turned his mind to the guards shoving them along the corridor. He was certain they'd traveled toward the common area thirty meters from his station. Once there, he heard ten or more pairs of boots clattering and squeaking on the hard floor. One heavy shove sent he and his companion to the deck. Shots discharged in the distance maybe even outside. The guards handcuffed his right wrist to a handrail lining the hallway, then ordered him, "Stay here." He pulled at his shackle, only for the restraint to dig into his hand. The guard repeated, "Stay here, I said!" His vision flashed once more as his captor thumped his skull. He fell unconscious.

*M****

He called out, "Petrov?" The din continued somewhere nearby, but he could not hear his friend. He could hear the disorganization and fear among the voices of guards and staff, all arguing about contradicting field positions. He whispered louder, "answer me, Petrov. Are you okay?"

He reached up to the dark hood the guards had placed over his head, slipping it up with care to draw as little attention from his captors as possible. He pulled the hood over his jaw, then higher. His eyes struggled to adjust to the corridor light, but one thing was clear: guards and others surrounding him lay motionless. Were they dead? An attack would explain much, but there was no blood. Petrov wasn't next to him, so he yanked the cuffs in frustration. To his surprise, they pulled free from him, clattering to the concrete floor. He rubbed his wrist, wincing at the burn. He kicked the cuffs, watching them crumble as if exposed to acid.

Listening to the mayhem in the distance, he couldn't find Petrov in the corridor. Swallowing hard, he stepped over to the floor-to-ceiling windows. A whiteout of heavy snow blanketed the nearby countryside, and a flashing red light from the periphery grabbed his attention. Perhaps a nearby aircraft or helicopter?

His first instinct, as was with any good Russian, was to call for some help—don't do the thinking, just the informing. But the bastards did cuff him, and for no reason he could imagine.

So, deciding to ignore the instinct, he crept closer to the window, scanning the terrain as best he could. Nightfall without the moon often was blackest of blacks, and public lighting for secure facilities such as this wasn't a priority of the Russian government.

There was another red flash outside. What could this be? The bedlam he heard seemed to be distancing itself from his position, though the alarms remained in effect. He didn't like the sound of them. Launch sequences had activated on several weapons. Petrov would panic, so perhaps it was good he was nowhere to be seen. After all, running wild while the missiles launched was sheer futility.

Nope, it was Mayak's job to diagnose and neutralize the cause.

Sprinting back to his station, he knew he needed to search the logging vomited onto his terminal. Even through his even temperament, he found it most appalling that the Federation Security Service would scoop him from his post during an emergency like this. Turning his laptop to face him, he verified the connection he'd made with the legacy equipment. Hell, yes, it was a legacy alright—a legacy of ineptitude. At least the fools hadn't confiscated his only means of understanding and reversing the possible disaster.

Suspending the log readout, he entered commands to obtain the launch status. His jaw dropped as he read the striking alert issued from the command output: "LAUNCH SEQUENCE ACTIVATED. STRIKE IN THREE MINUTES."

Petrov would have colorful expletives ready to launch, but Mayak would operate in silence. The world about him shriveled, faces immediately popping into his head. His friend Petrov. His parents. His advisors and team from Los Alamos. His neighbors. Would all end here? Between the blast, the fallout, and the all-powerful smoke, the ICBMs within this facility could handily erase a continent's worth of people.

His head pounded from the blunt-force trauma, so he strained to focus. He restored the logging to the foreground to read a new alert. Because launch stage had activated without intervention somehow, the missile-locking clamps had not released. So, the missiles would only *attempt* to launch.

Mayak permitted himself a small chuckle. The countdown had begun. He would die, along with everyone in this facility and the nearby village, but the weapons would not reach their targets in western Europe and the Americas.

And then the thought reformed in his head. What the hell was the red light he'd noticed outside the windowed corridor?

Knowing his death to be imminent, he followed his curiosity, abandoning his post, this time under his own initiative. Did the light have something to do with the launch activation? He'd worked in this facility long enough to memorize, at smoke breaks in particular, each and every light and detail of the facility's long winter night presentation. This red light was no aurora.

Upon reaching the corridor, he rushed to the staff exit he used daily for his doses of nicotine. Flinging the heavy door open, he stepped into the biting, numbing chill. Snow was all about, with minimal lighting from the facility, and yet, in the sky, he watched an elaborate dance of five to seven flashing red lights. They swapped positions with sharp directional changes, snapping here and there like hummingbirds or dragonflies. Some maintained a repeating pattern of seizing four or so separate locations, jumping at speeds Mayak couldn't fathom.

The alarms behind him became unimportant as he watched these things. Could they be rescue craft? Invaders from the west? Illusions?

But these could not be crafts of earthly design. He hadn't studied much aerospace, but he knew these flashing dots were operating with trajectory and maneuver dynamics outstripping any secret research he could imagine.

And why were they here? To sabotage and destroy the facility? He couldn't believe their fantastic dance was some coincidence with the inadvertent activation of the ICBMs stored here.

He now spied eight of the moving lights, one of which seemed to grow in intensity as the others persisted in their dance about the sky above the facility. He watched, though his apprehension spiked when the lights focused upon the missile's actual silos.

Sabotage came to mind, but without time to consider further, he recoiled as one of the lights approached him. He squinted to see it better. He would have expected fear, but there was no time. Instead, he felt his muscles freeze.

Struggling against them, his eyes locked onto the coming object. The cacophony of guards and staff, the blaring alarms, his own fear, all quieted before this red apparition. Was it all that mattered here? The whining increased, and an understanding pieced itself together before him. His long fear of the devices he maintained seemed dwarfed by an overwhelming compassion, not for himself, but for the... peacemakers, was it?

He found himself speaking, as though reading a page before him. "Blessed are the courageous peacemakers, and you, too, are a peacemaker. You will find the one who seeks me out."

He saw a vision, a variegated tapestry alive with animation. First, he watched primordial rodents leaping from tree to tree, then morphing into apes, then to humans hunting and gathering, farm-fields filled with corn and wheat, then railways, ships, technology dwarfing all to come before. It resolved into a vast, complex, interdependent infrastructure, and he perceived connection, evolution—the intricate, almost crystalline Tree of Life. The hum resonated in his jaw, and he felt a powerful pull from the red light. He could trace the story from beginning to end. Images flooded his mind, and he recalled tripping on psychedelics back in America's southwest desert.

But this thing, this light, somehow controlled his perception. He no longer feared, nor worried, though his thoughts were becoming heavier. Whatever the red light was doing, it... would... be... OK...

As quickly as one might flash a camera, all the lights pulled away, screaming off at speeds Mayak knew weren't possible. As his red light released him, he collapsed hard upon the concrete walkway, fresh snow crunching underneath him. Incapable of stirring, he lay in the cold, watching fat snowflakes float to the ground about him. His lungs sucked hard, and his mind was exhausted from whatever binding the light had over him.

The alarms around him no longer made sense. How could others not see these lights had meant no harm? But alone, he could not understand.

No sooner had the thought crossed his mind than a voice spoke from within him—a voice he hadn't heard since late childhood. As distinctive and familiar as it always had been, the voice called to him, "Mayak, my Podopech. Can you hear me?"

Mayak gasped, his muscles slow to stir after the light released him. Knowing the answer he'd hear, he asked, "Sargon?" He felt himself tense more, knowing he'd reached the conclusion of the years-long rest since he'd last spoken to his hidden passenger, the *skrytyypass,* as named by his doctors. Perhaps he had simply hit his head upon the concrete?

The resonant voice answered, "Yes, Mayak, I have returned to you."

Mayak closed his eyes in pain as the screeching klaxon faded. And then the darkness of unconsciousness claimed him.

$$M***$$

Awake now for three hours, Mayak decided he must've hallucinated the return of his *skrytyypass*. His last words with Sargon were Christmas ten years earlier, a separation which could not have wounded him more had it been the death of his parents or loss of his eyes and ears. Could it all have been a dream? Compared to his most recent experience, he couldn't care less that the loathsome Federation Security Service chose to interrogate him. The red lights he saw may well have been a hallucination, so he could determine no justification for revealing the vision, or whatever the hell he saw, to anyone. After all, his past invited too much scrutiny even in the best of times.

Two Federation Security Service agents, one fat, the other thin, paced before him, a table separating them. Mayak, a master of stoneface, would not tip even a thimbleful of anxiety to these goons; he understood their training all too well, and the possibility they could break him would spell disaster.

His schizophrenia had left him quite capable of concealing his feelings. The doctors had insisted that Sargon didn't exist, but he'd taught a very young Mayak the careful art of chicanery. Hope and despair refused to leave the room, but he would share neither with these clowns.

Fishing him from his thoughts, the fatter of the two interrogators rapped a baton on the table where Mayak sat. The glare of the blinding lights flickered along its onyx-like surface. He grunted, with no small amount of anger, "Chernovsky, you will answer."

Mayak folded his arms in defiance. "Look, I've told you this story as many times as you've asked. For final time, I have no idea why weapons activated." The thick interrogator laughed, then adjusted the reflected glare to shine into Mayak's eyes, who complained, "You try to agitate and deplete detainee with light? Your technique is rough, Comrade."

Annoyed at Mayak for his comment, the toady encroached on his personal space, grunting, "Weapons activated, then deactivated. Comrade Chernovsky, did you sabotage our weapons?"

He shook his head, emoting nothing. "No, I did not." Leaning forward, he shot back, "Why not tell me why your friends in security dragged us from my station? Treat us like prisoners?"

The interrogator pointed to the exit of the chamber. "Yes, speaking of, how well do you know your friend Petrov Posk?"

Mayak scratched his blond whiskers. "Since academy. Should be in my file unless you cannot read." He paused, then added in spite, "Comrade."

The interrogator struck the table with his fat fist. "Then you choose your friends poorly, Chernovsky. Posk plans to cooperate with us. We know you tried to launch missiles with no authorization. Who are your accomplices? You escaped custody handily."

Mayak scoffed, "You believe I overcome ten guards and break my handcuffs? You are fools. And you're not very good at interrogation. Petrov couldn't think that, primarily because I cannot unilaterally launch weapons, even if I so wanted." He firmed himself up, adding, "You're simply telling me anything you can to catch me in some lie, just like good KGB dog."

The interrogator responded sternly, "We're not KGB anymore, and you have no idea how miserable I can—" One of the other security officers stopped him, whispering something imperceptible to Mayak in his ear. The interrogator bobbed his head in acquiescence.

Mayak took the opening, if just to irritate this stooge a bit more. "You can change name of your organization all day long. Swine still stinks, either way."

The interrogator appeared stunned, as he predicted. In haste, the man struck Mayak with the back of his hand, sparking his field-of-vision as the fat hand impacted his right eye. He turned the other cheek. "You'd feel better if you struck me second time, no?"

The thick interrogator raised his hand again, only to freeze at the sound of a woman's stern voice. "Enough."

Adjusting his officer beret, the heavier agent stepped back into the shadows as a door opened into the chamber, contributing some additional light. A silver-haired female officer entered, calling to the interrogators, "Sayek, Kalke, you may go now." They saluted quickly, then disappeared through the door. Mayak couldn't help but permit himself a laugh at seeing the high made low, as it were.

The senior interrogator stepped closer to the table, light illuminating her cold, yet elegant features. "I am Andreva Kierkov, commander, Federation Security Service."

Mayak glanced about the room as the other guards left, then his gaze settled on her, a fit woman of fifty with confident carriage and a harsh beauty, though the lighting presented confusing silhouettes. "It isn't often that KGB identifies itself."

She smiled, placing herself before the table across from him, though remaining just in shadow. "As my rather dimwitted associate suggested, we operate under different title now. Besides, I myself am operator, not agent. My identity isn't all that important, in any case."

She cocked her head, her silver hair flowing over one shoulder. Pointing to his head, she remarked, "I trust they did not injure you too much." Studying him with her chilling eyes, she slid her fingers over his face. "It is true you possess tremendous resistance to physical pain, no?"

Ignoring her, he said, "Never mind me. Is Petrov okay?"

She folded her hands. "Your friend is fine, though we had some difficulty catching him. We did not"—she paused—"injure him too greatly."

His tone revealed his alarm as he asked, "You hurt him?"

She acknowledged, almost with embarrassment, "True, Posk is more susceptible to physical pain than you." A deliberate smile crossed her face as she whispered, "I would be interested in testing your own tolerances."

He sighed. "You need not detain me to read my file, Comrade."

She eased off, adding, "Sometimes my agents become too, shall we say, zealous?" She extended a gloved hand in his direction. "I assure you, he is safe and protected." She nodded, leaning back in her chair. "We are debriefing him, as we are you."

Mayak slowed his breathing. Cognizant that his concern for his friend might serve her untoward intent, he refocused his inquiry. "I'm guessing you know we did not activate weapons."

She chuckled. "Of course." She pointed lightly behind herself, smirking. "Accusation precedes confusion. Effective on the simple-minded and weak-willed."

Mayak straightened his spine in the chair, permitting himself a stretch after many hours of sitting. "So, I'm not either of those things?"

She laughed. "Of course not." Her stern features hardened as she stepped a bit further into the light. "What did you see outside observational corridor, Mayak?"

He shook his head, noting immediately the striking beauty of her eyes—gray, yet hollow, sad. "It's as I told your comrades—I lost consciousness in corridor with hood over my head. I only heard alarms and security officers shouting." He paused, shifting in his seat, still watching her eyes as she shifted back into shadow.

Shocked that he didn't think to ask until now, he proposed, "You have checked surveillance footage, no?"

She nodded with a smile. "Very good." Crossing her arms, she continued, "As it turns out, Comrade Chernovsky, all surveillance cameras malfunctioned simultaneously during period in which you claim you saw nothing. More than a coincidence."

He met her eyes. "How is that possible? Cameras are redundant."

She chuckled, remaining locked in a stare with him. "We had hoped you or Petrov would tell us. Security around you were unconscious."

He waited, watching her eye him. Shrugging, he asked, "What happened to them?"

She then pulled papers from a small table just outside Mayak's field of view. Without removing her eyes from the pages, she answered coldly, "They appear unaffected, though they are under examination."

Switching topics, she asked, "You were diagnosed with schizophrenia at age ten?"

Pained, he bowed his head. "That's correct."

She smiled, permitting herself a brief glimpse of him as if to enjoy the sting of her observation. "And it abated all on its own when you were seventeen, after which you exhibited a tremendous surge in mathematical skill?"

He met her gray eyes once more, finding himself lost in them, despite their cold sadism. "Yes, and yes. Ancient history," he groused. What the hell was wrong with him? Why was he showing this strange woman so much emotion? His anger swelled, very much so against his usual steely mind.

She chuckled, reading, "*Miracle child*, hmm." Replacing the papers, she asked quickly, "And so your parents dispatched you to America for school? To shield you from local publicity?"

Mayak's impatience appeared to outpace hers. "You know all of this. Why does it matter?"

He expected scorn, yet she laughed almost playfully, her pronounced jaw and nose transiently exposed as she moved about the fluorescent light. "You have been…" She paused in thought, casting her eyes about. "Shall we say, *person of interest* to us at Federation Security Service for some time."

She approached him, a pronounced scar across her forehead appearing. He felt shocked, though he tried to look elsewhere. She smiled, touching the scar. "Wound well-earned, my young friend." She seated herself before him, folding her fingers together. "We only want to help you."

He felt himself undone by her, attraction replacing his usual placid constitution with a hideous chimera of fear, rage, and lust. She reached for his face, and the feelings almost overcame him. Traces of moisture beaded in his eyes, then fell down his cheeks. Was he crying? At this woman?

A booming voice pierced the unbearable silence. "She is lying, my podopech." The *skrytyypass* spoke!

Kierkov twisted her face, then jerked her hand from Mayak, releasing him from the torment of emotion. She gasped. "How?" She seized, eyes shutting hard.

Sargon boomed, "You know whom you must seek. The truth-seeker in the west."

Mayak stretched his neck to see Kierkov; she remained in shock of some kind. He whispered, "You are back? What did you do to her? How has she done this to me?"

Sargon replied with strain, "She is stunned for now. She is a *haligscriosta*, insidious in her mind control. You must tell her you saw nothing, Podopech." After a brief pause, the voice continued with strain, "She will now release you. Exit, then find the man. Hurry, and we shall speak again soon."

Kierkov opened her eyes, then touched her right temple with discomfort. She exhaled, "You will tell me, Chernovsky."

He answered with a low but firm tone, "I saw nothing. You must release me."

She droned,. "You saw nothing, I release you now, but, young Chernovsky, You remain person of interest." Regaining her expressiveness, she traced her finger over his hairline, then whispered, "Great interest." Recoiling, she ordered, "You may go for now."

Mayak breathed, glancing about the room; he wanted to ask after his friend, so he started, "Where have you—"

The voice interrupted him. "Podopech, there is no time. Go now!"

He collected himself, stopping once more to behold the exotic beauty of Kierkov before heading for the exit in the adjoining corridor.

*M****

Mayak reached his apartment late, his mind aswirl from the shift, the ordeal with the weapons, the red lights, the ensuing interrogation, and on and on. Exhaustion nipped at him, and he couldn't wait to serve himself chilled vodka, straight-up. Approaching the latched door of the refrigerator, he opened the old behemoth, grabbing a bottle from his parsimonious supply of groceries. Holding the clear liquid to the light, he sighed. "Nectar of gods, maybe?"

Pouring a shot, he downed it quickly, then imbibed a second, a third, and even a fourth. But this nectar gave no comfort. Anger and shame flooded him when he reminded himself that his friend Petrov might be in trouble, as well as fear in knowing his *skrytyypass* had somehow reemerged after so long a hibernation. Had his illness returned?

The doctors and his parents had beaten into his head that Sargon lived only within the illness, but his passenger had come to his aid many times, whether in his scholarship or the interpersonal difficulties they blamed on his disease. They seemed to fear his friend, so he also feared him and the tests, the pain, the torture. Why had Sargon come to him in the first place? He was his best friend, his mentor, his tutor, his helper, yet Mayak suffered horrors because of him.

So, Mayak hated him. He'd loved him once, but now hated him. Petrov often said love and hate were inseparable, but that was rhetorical nonsense to Mayak. One must make up one's mind, but he couldn't in this mess.

He rapped the glass on the countertop, waiting as long as he could bear, then, at last, demanded, "Are you back, Sargon?" He thought it over, then quoted, "Blessed are the truth-seekers." He knew this to be some maxim, but from where?

He grabbed his small phone, typing the phrase into the search engine. Something from the Christian mythos.

Pondering, he recalled that the voice had told him to seek someone—the one who searches for what? The lights themselves?

He typed into the search bar, "Blessed are the peacemakers, red lights in the sky."

A website floated to the top—a page for a publication called *Blessed Are the Truth-Seekers*, a curious reversal of the scripture. A name, E.G. Boothby, popped up under the link. Mayak clicked, opening a picture of Boothby, a rotund man of sixty-five with snow-white hair, a gray beard, and bug eyes so expressive they seemed to confirm some insanity.

Tipsy, he chuckled at a picture, clearly staged, of the man pointing to a saucer inserted into the sky scene. The image carried a small animation, the man's arm pointing from the saucer to the camera, pronouncing in a raspy New Jersey accent, "Falterra ain't alone, friends! I believe!"

Farther down the page was a blurb:

Ufologist E.G. Boothby publishes his quarterly journal on strange sightings and occurrences at no cost to you. Can you afford ignorance when the visitors are upon us? Find out in our pages what the U.S. government knows but won't say, what a UFO actually looks like, and where to go if you want to see one. Are aliens real?

Someone once said, "Blessed are the peacemakers." We say, "Blessed are the truth-tellers."

Mayak sat in silence. "This is bananas," he whispered.

Backing out to the search engine's results on the quaint little man, Mayak couldn't help but see a canned search called 'Boothby crazy pics.' Clicking it, the screen filled with a dozen or so wild-eyed pictures snapped of the ufologist, and none were particularly flattering. One had a twisted expression, others just looney google eyes. His hair spread in all directions at times, as if a wind-storm caught him just as the photographer nabbed the image. Others caught Boothby baring his teeth, as if he growled at the would-be paparazzi. Sighing so loud it snapped him from his click-bait hypnosis, he found a video of the poor man in action. Playing it, Mayak watched an especially insane, bespectacled Boothby shouting in an auditorium as bouncers escorted him out. "You know you're lying about it! I've seen the aliens—Falterra ain't alone! Stop denial! Stop denial! Truth!"

The speaker then said, "And that, ladies, and gentlemen, is why we have lithium." To resounding laughter, he asked, "Any other concerns?" and the video ended.

Sitting in silence, Mayak next entered 'Falterra' into the search engine, but nothing happened. Trying several variations on spelling, he still struck out.

Discovering he'd held his breath for several seconds, Mayak exhaled. Rubbing his eyes, he returned to Boothby's site to click, reluctantly, the contact link.

Sargon manifested swiftly at his search, booming in Mayak's brain. "Podopech, have I taught you nothing?"

He froze, staring at the computer, understanding at once his sophomoric mistake. "Fuck me," he muttered, for he'd searched in an ordinary, unsecure browser for this crazy fellow. He could have screamed his action from the rooftops more securely.

Sargon answered, "There is no time to dwell on errors. You must contact him, but only through a secure channel. Now, listen carefully."

4. Fourth Vesik: Crackpot and Journalist

*B****

E.G. Boothby reclined on a plush couch. Nightshades shielded from him the light of day, a suggestion by his analyst to help him concentrate. Concentrate on what?

Her voice interrupted his thought. "Mister Boothby, I'll ask again: What was it about the older lady that bothered you?"

He rolled his eyes, though he knew Doctor Tremont couldn't catch his gesture. He rasped, "It wasn't her, good God. It was her, umm, ferret."

The voice was quiet for a moment, just as he expected. "A homeless lady with a ferret?"

He nodded, adjusting his purple nightshades to cut out the glimmers of light sneaking underneath them. "Yeah, it's San Francisco. Cats and dogs are old hat."

The analyst flipped pages in her pad, continuing, "Okay, the ferret, not the old lady?"

He scratched his gray curly beard, protesting, "Oh, Christ, this isn't a mother issue, Doc. I wrote in my paperwork that I never knew her."

The doctor scribbled something down while he listened carefully. As he wondered whether the notetaking was genuine, she remarked, "Alright, Mister Boothby, describe this ferret."

He frowned, holding his tongue while thinking the ferret over once or twice. At last, he answered, "Well, hell if I know. He was a ferret. Like roof rats we have back east."

The shrink seemed unable to let this go. "Mister Boothby, a roof rat and a ferret are two different things."

He cleared his throat, though he knew it was futile in clearing the rasping. "I'm not a goddamned zoologist, Doc! It looked like a squirrel or maybe a rat. Three clicks, three clicks."

His therapist asked, "Three clicks?"

He muttered, almost under his breath. "Something your predecessor suggested. Click my heels, and I'll be somewhere else."

With a little more than the acceptable amusement, she asked, "Does it ever work?"

He exhaled in a dramatic finish. "I'm still here, ain't I?"

She chuckled. How dare she?! He'd paid out of pocket—not quite so much thanks to the Affordable Care Act, but cash burned gaping holes through his pants. Before he could utter the words aloud, she asked, "Okay, why did this animal frighten you?"

He ripped the nightshades from his face, the light adjustment stunning his eyes. "That's why I'm here, Doc. I don't why it scared me. Dalian, twisted." He paused, eyeing her paper. "Just what are you writing?"

She clutched her papers with her left hand, her right hand motioning him to recline back into the couch. "Case notes, Mister Boothby, so we can determine a course of care."

He shook his head with a sigh. "Geez, I haven't been to a shrink in a long while. Look, the goddamned pest chewed on my things before I could pull them away."

She paused her noisy scribbles, piqued by this. "What things?"

Did he really want to share his secrets? He quipped in frustration, "Just notes. Stuff for my work." He cringed, expecting her inevitable query.

More scribbles followed, then another question from her, "Your work?"

He pointed to his tan satchel he'd left near the door, answering on reflex, "It's a lot of research. I thought I might have a huge lead to follow."

Her voice wasn't unpleasant but he steeled himself as she asked, "And the ferret?"

His head amok, he gasped, "It chewed on my brochure."

Another pause made him think she'd laugh. She swallowed her jasmine tea, the sound loud. At last, she said, "Surely this brochure is something you can copy?"

He pulled at his hair, then complained in a low growl, "It's the principle. I used to keep paper leads all the time. Files online can change and be corrupted. Everyone is watching. Anything is possible."

The therapist acknowledged while he squirmed under the silence. "This brochure. What is it?"

He exhaled, debating whether she should hear his lead. Then again, if she thought he was a madman, she wouldn't believe a word of it. So, he explained, "I saw this brochure at a bookstore downtown. I couldn't stop thinking about it. The name caught my attention. Something called the Plowshares."

She fidgeted with something, so he peeked from his shades while she pursed her wrinkled mouth. "I'm not familiar with them. Are they farmers?"

He answered with no small melodrama, even for him, "They ain't farmers. It's a nuclear disarmament outfit."

This drew a swift question, leaving him to worry how one might perceive his taking such a thread forward. "I thought you studied UFOs."

He decided he couldn't chance her knowing the connection, so he fibbed, "I might join up. I can search for aliens until hell freezes over, and if we blow ourselves up, it won't matter. Maybe I'll take up piano in hell. If they have them in hell."

"Interesting." Seeming to take the answer in stride, she redirected, "So the ferret wanted that brochure? May I see it?"

He bristled, "Umm, you'll think I'm crazy." He removed his shades, then pulled the tattered brochure from his satchel.

She took it from him, peering through her reading glasses. Gentler than any therapist he'd had so far, he wasn't as defensive as he could be. But he watched her eagerly as she scanned it. Pointing to a torn part, she asked, "This is the ferret's handiwork?"

He rolled his eyes, answering, "The lil' bastard tore the group photo."

She traced her fingers over the team of five pictured on the cover. The image one on the front row and right-hand side was mottled with teeth marks and tears. Pointing to the woman's missing face, she asked, "What do you know about these people?" She tapped the group photo's caption, remarking, "Conique Voyant. That's not a name one hears everyday."

He watched the brochure, unable to take his eyes off of it while it rested in the care of this comparative stranger. He growled, "Umm, yeah. Maybe it's a professional title, a stage name? I don't know anything about them. They are retired people who get themselves arrested for mischief on nukes."

She handed him the brochure, then removed her glasses. "That's a dangerous business. This might not be a great way to manage your anxiety."

As much as he hated it about himself, he often blurted his thoughts without really thinking. "But if the nukes attract the lights."

His therapist asked, "What do you mean? Why would UFOs want to be near nukes?"

He tried to change subjects. "Well, it's not like this Conical Clairvoyant woman would know how to turn them on and off."

Doctor Tremont crinkled the brochure, adding, "You're referring to the reports suggesting UFOs, if they're real, appear over nuclear stuff? *Mister* Boothby, that's a dangerous game you shouldn't play. I need you to promise me you won't be trying to sabotage nuclear devices."

Shrugging with more than a little disappointment at her mechanical performance, he stared at her certifications conspicuously covering the wall behind her. Missing his previous shrink, he stuffed the pamphlet into his satchel. "Umm, gotchya. You are the doc, Doc."

She motioned for him to replace the shades, then lie back onto the davenport. Once he blotted the light out of sight, he listened as she continued questioning him: "Let's get back to the ferret."

With satirical exasperation, he shouted, "Of course. It's a bestial conspiracy to undo me and my work." He listened for a response, then he followed up with, "Just kidding, Doc. That mangy rat had to be a rogue agent."

This elicited a chuckle from her, so she dropped it. "Okay, how long have you suffered from anxiety?"

He kicked his head back, falling into the couch. That part of analysis and psychotherapy he'd definitely missed. He answered, "Since I was a boy. Lived in an orphanage. Lots of bullies there."

She crossed her legs—astonishingly long legs for a woman. Perhaps she stood a head higher than he? Tapping the pad before her, she asked, "And how about the adults?"

He replaced the nightshades on his face, the world about him dissolving away. "They let them do it. Sometimes encouraged it. Headmistress Sagini said it was good for me."

She seemed to tense, then she said. "Francesca Sagini, The Miracle of Honor Grove Orphanage."

He sat up, removing the shades. "Wait a sec—you know of her?"

The analyst pursed her wrinkled mouth, then replied, "Few who've studied child abuse would not know her name."

Boothby was floored. Perhaps this analyst was not interested in his ufology, as were so many others. "Oh, Jesus, you wanna know about her and Whore's Grave, and not the lights in the sky?"

The analyst removed her glasses, locking eyes with him. "I've treated many adults who were child victims, and the worst of orphanages are fertile grounds for research. But"—she paused, glancing away—"if you don't want to talk about her, we don't have to."

He heard a few more scribbles as he replaced the shades, and she asked, "Okay, then, how long have you been interested in the supernatural?"

He shook his head. "Lady, I'm a reporter and a journalist. Not a..."

"Ufologist?" She seemed relieved to say it, though he'd still heard it too many times.

He winced with a slow exhale. "Look, I report things about the natural world, things governments would prefer kept secret." He wagged air quotes in what he hoped was her direction. "There's nothing 'supernatural' about it. Besides, they admitted they'd seen 'em. We had a big discussion over at MUFON on the AATIP program and how it ties to the MJ Twelve."

Sorting notes on her paper, she asked, "What are these acronyms?"

Feeling grazes with indignance, he explained, "Mutual UFO Network has studied the lights since 1969. The Majestic Twelve was Truman's investigative arm into Roswell. The Advanced Aerospace Threat Identification Program is a forcover for their true motive: locate and control the lights."

She said nothing. Did she think him nuts? He said, "For Chrissakes, lady, you are supposed to be searching for the truth. Can you not see it?"

She shifted in her chair—or at least, he thought she was shifting. He lifted his shades to check, then dove back to safe blackness. His surroundings stayed in his mind's eye. Like something taken from a Norman Rockwell calendar, the office featured creaky floorboards and aging antiques. Even the therapist seemed to belong, but Boothby, like the floral couch on which he parked himself, appeared out of place. It was the story of his life.

At last, she countered him with a question. "Okay, so what interested you in UFOs?"

He bit his lip, frustrated. How many goddamned times must he tell this story? Every new doctor, every new friend. He'd given up dating so many years ago, he'd lost count. "Good grief, I wrote about this in my newsletter, and I have to tell it at every book-signing." He rolled his eyes, regretting the last few words—what signings? His last book had been a failure, commercially, critically, and personally.

Put-upon, he answered, "I experienced a close encounter when I was a kid."

The voice didn't bear enthusiasm. "And what was that like?"

He laughed, drawling, "You care about my abuse story, but this one isn't interesting? Christ, am I this much a joke? Crazy, a total zoodoraphobic?"

The doctor's tone shifted to one of reassurance. "Boothby, we're all crazy in some way or another." She tapped her pad once more, remarking, "I like your neologism."

He liked the compliment, replying, "Thanks. I scored well in writing."

She placed the pad aside, asking, "So, will you tell me about it?"

He closed his eyes—not that it mattered under the nightshades. "I was eight years old." Jesus, sixty years earlier, he realized. He continued, "A man came to take some of us from the orphanage on a field trip."

She asked, "Did you know this man?"

He shook his head. "No, met him only that night."

"Continue." She flipped another page in her yellow pad. "Where did he take you, and why?"

He wracked his brain, picking over the memories as he'd done so many times prior. "I still don't know why. Headmistress Sagini must've let us go, though I don't remember her talking to him. We knew him as Mister Ephyr."

Enlivened by this new thread of narrative, the shrink asked, "Can you describe this man?"

Boothby chuckled. "I've done this several times, including for my first book. He was probably thirty, a colored man who wore eyeglasses and carried a black briefcase." He held a finger in her direction. "No, I don't know what was in the briefcase. Only that he had one."

Her chair creaked again as the analyst reached for her tea. "So, what happened?"

He reached under the collar of his shirt, scratching his neck. "Mister Ephyr took us to a farm somewhere, promising to show us animals and husbandry. Equipment and the like."

The doctor whispered with a little surprise, "A plowshare?"

Boothby stopped, thinking it over. "Yeah, come to think of it, he did show me one of those." He paused, then quipped, "It must be a coincidence."

She seemed keen to write more, based on the scuffling of the pen point on her paper. "Interesting. Can you imagine why the headmistress would've permitted this? If you were eight, it would've been a different time for an African American to take white children from an orphanage."

Boothby corrected her with a higher rasp, "He wasn't no American. An accent I don't remember, but he weren't from here. No matter to the headmistress, she was always happy to get rid of us. The orphanage was Catholic, and we *Messianic Jews* weren't her cup of tea."

The scuffling stopped. "The other children were Jewish, also?"

He laughed. "Jesus, she had it in for us. And back then, they could get away with anything, no matter how brutal. You already know about what she did."

She sighed. "I'm so sorry, Boothby." He heard her pouring more of her drink as she asked, "Would you care for some jasmine tea?" He shook his head, content to enjoy the aroma alone., Moving them along, she asked, "What happened to you and the other children on this farm? Anything uncomfortable or abusive?"

He smiled. "From Mister Ephyr? Oh, Lord no. He was very kind to us. He showed us animals, equipment." That part of the remembrance was a delight. He giggled. "I really liked him, enigmatic as he was. No matter the digging, I've never been able to find out who he was. Or the addy for this mystery farm."

She slurped a small bit of tea as surreptitiously as she could, after which she creaked back into a resting position in the ancient chair. He wondered whether it would crumble under her weight, though she was a delicate thing. "You looked?"

He adjusted his eye cover, scratching his beard. Goodness, he'd answered this too many times. With a huff, he responded, "Honestly, it was cold as a coal miner's G-string, like tundra cold. Snow everywhere."

He jerked his head towards her, the eye drape momentarily sliding from his face. "I'm an investigative reporter; I've looked all over the eastern seaboard." Fidgeting with the drape to shield himself from the prying light, he added, "If it's there, it's hidden."

She leaned towards him as the chair crackled beneath her. "Hidden? For what purpose?"

At last, he had to rant, if for nothing more than to wrest the session back from her incompetence. "Christ, lady, I dunno. Why does anything happen ever, good or bad? It's not like anything keeps score on this. We reporters look for truth. Others believe lies. Is this really helpful in treating anxiety?"

She placed the pad on her table, then said, "We're here to understand your story, good or bad. Truth is relative. I need to know these details, even if you've told the story before. You still suffer from anxiety, whether anyone else keeps score is beside the point. Perhaps in this recounting, something new will emerge—some detail you've overlooked. A way to connect this memory to your current difficulties."

He turned to face her, as though he could see her through the nightshades, then fell back into the cushy couch. "I've been over it a thousand times. We all went to bed in pallets along the barn floor, and I woke up, hearing my name. I got out of bed, or pile of hay, or whatever, and I followed the sound outside."

The analyst asked, "Were any others with you?"

He laughed. "I was always alone. Always. Almost no one cared to be my friend, even amongst us Jews. Headmistress Sagini wouldn't allow us anything to do with our heritage, and this was before 1967, when America suddenly gave a damn about Israelis." Pausing, he finished, "Anyway, they knew I was even more different than the others."

She scrawled a bit more. Damn, she must've been drawing the Sistine Chapel. "Because you're gay?"

He bellowed, "So what gave that away, huh?!" He calmed himself, trying to focus. "I was asleep, alone, and then was a light outside. Bright light. I moved towards it, hearing a voice calling." He turned his face towards her, touching his temple with his pointer finger. "Only inside my head. Not through my ears."

She stopped him. "How do you know it was inside your head?"

Tickled, he pointed around himself, as though his bunkmates were there with him. "They couldn't hear it, so it must've been in my head. Some sort of induced hallucination."

The scribbling had ceased, Boothby now wondering whether his ludicrous ramblings strayed so far from her neat and tidy reality that she could not bear to sacrifice a scrap of paper more. No, instead she remarked with intensified attention, "Insightful for an eight-year-old."

He quipped, "I've had a lot of time to consider it, live it over and over again. It was cold, but when was it not in rustic New Jersey?" he mused, imagining the barn. "I remember the colors of the wood, red and white. I stepped outside, and eight lights appeared overhead."

The psychiatrist wrote something else, then asked, "Eight? You're certain?"

He complained in genuine surprise. "Lady, even an eight-year-old can count to eight. I ain't no numerologist, but it was eight." Calming himself, he continued, "There was eight lights, all white."

Tousling his hair with a spare hand, he gestured about the room as though the setting had changed. "The voice said to look to the lights in the sky. The voice told me that answers would come from outside the world."

He paused, so she interjected, "Answers? To what?"

Squeezing his hands together, he replied hoarsely, "I'm not sure. I guess we all want to know certain things."

She sat back into her chair, remarking, "We're running short on time, so, so let's continue this next time. For now, I want you to focus on how..."

He blasted her, "You don't believe a word of it, do ya?" He flung the shades from his eyes, then glared at her.

The slight but firm lady retorted, "Mister Boothby, I think you should dwell less on what others think of you and your work, and more on what specifically makes you anxious. Trauma often refers one to hallucinated memories, a brain's way of shielding you from the worst of it."

He locked eyes with her, complaining, "Isn't the advice-giving a little premature, Doc? Besides, that's, umm, reductionist and obvious, right?" He rolled his eyes around the room. "I mean, come on. The headmistress hated me in particular, her little sissy boy project."

Unfazed, her icy blue eyes met his own. "You've always looked for acceptance, meaning, satisfaction. This hallucination made you think you could find it from outside the world, so you've shirked away from human relationships."

She removed her bifocals, tapping them with her fingers. "Sometimes, Mister Boothby, it's as simple as that."

He stood, angry. "This was no hallucination, Doc!"

She watched him carefully, unfazed by his defiance, and made a few more scribbles. "Okay, before time ends, let's get back to the old lady and the ferret." Without glancing up from her notes, she asked, "How did the headmistress punish you?"

His ears flashed hotly with embarrassment as he conceded, to himself at least, that small mammals plucked his nerves. "Jeezus, can we move off that already?" She wouldn't budge, so he confessed, "Yes, she tortured us with rats. Me especially."

She placed the notes aside, and with manifest compassion, said, "Mister Boothby, that is truly terrible."

His eyes watered, a medley of anger, shame, frustration swirling within him. "I don't like talking about it. I want my life to be about finding answers that matter, not about how a crazy bitch liked to torment children. I don't want to relive the past. I don't want to hafta think about her, that hell hole, or anything else. The lights, Mister

Ephyr—that speaks to me. The future, not the freaking past." He'd had no idea he'd weep, but the tears burned his eyes.

The therapist placed her pen on the table, head cocked. "Please, go on."

He somehow found himself seated once more, wiping his face with tissues she must've offered. "I seek reasons. I investigate. Understand."

She found an opening, adding, "Understanding your past is important, maybe essential, in understanding your future. Where you've been is as important as where you're going."

He'd heard this too many times. The clock showed three minutes till the hour. At last. "I know, I know. But my own past is so uninteresting to me. And painful." His eyes swelled with tears as he blotted at them. "I've had a dozen therapists through the years."

"Mister Boothby, you came to me to treat you for anxiety that has worsened, not remained constant. Though these memories may offer some comfort, remember that they fade, real or not. Without hard evidence, I wouldn't dwell on it." She removed and folded her spectacles, then offered, "Now, let's review your medications?"

Pulling the shades from his face once more, he jumped upward. "Medication, Lord yes!" He withdrew himself, referring to her with respect. "Umm, please, Doc."

*B****

Seated in the dusty corner of an empty waiting room, Boothby watched the pharmacist behind the counter package his clonazepam.

In the spare moments, he felt sorrow for his therapist, hapless though she may be. It wasn't her fault. Boothby knew himself to be a goof, taken less than seriously by others. If he mentioned the poetry, she'd have had him committed. He did have irrefutable proof of his experience, however. But his freedom and likely his life would be forfeited if he shared it with anyone. He wanted no such bullseye on his back. No matter. Separation from each therapist, be it retirement, move, or death, led him to a fresh shrinker, and despite his protests, nearly all tried the non-pharma route first. But with patience, he expected fresh opportunities to thank science for the little chemical helpers to still his torment.

At last, the pharmacist called his name. He gathered himself, stepping toward the young woman. It was remarkable that working professionals nowadays were young enough to be his grandchildren. Her facial mask barred him from seeing more than her almond brown eyes, but he often marveled at how the brain assumed greater beauty under the mask than was actually there on average.

As she crinkled the paper bag containing Boothby's little helpers, she asked, "Have you taken this medication before?"

He chuckled. "Honey, I've been on this med since you was a kiddo." Her eyes twinkled, so he added, "Well, you still are a kiddo to me."

She darted her eyes to the label. "Oh, I see a new doctor is prescribing this."

He shrugged. "Yeah, the prior shrink decided to retire to Maui, so cursed a life." He sighed again. "And the new one sent me to a new pharmacy."

The girl responded, "Well, we'll try to give you our star treatment here, Mister Boothby." She paused, staring at the label, then his face. "Wait a sec, you spoke at my school a few years ago! E.G. Boothby, the flying-saucer chaser! Oh, my God! I wanna post on my insta!"

He blushed, "Well, I haven't caught any of 'em yet. I'm no Jacques Valle, though this ole' queen can try."

She rounded the counter before he could protest, pulling a phone from her coat pocket. She said, "My friends will flip when they see this!" While situating her phone at arms' length, she whispered from the corner of her mouth, "Your voice is dope, man. Why so raspy?"

He rolled his eyes. "Oh, good Gawd. They call it too much of a vestibular fold, or something like that." He scrunched his face up with a smile.

While snapping pictures, she said, "It's as amazing as the fact the government pretty much just admitted they really exist! No one seems to care, though."

He bared his teeth for the selfie, ribbing her. "Oh, my vestibular folds are as real as can be. I'd be glad to show them to ya." He winked. As she laughed, he tore into his prescription, following with the a sober remark. "I'd been saying it, along with other experts, for years. No one listened, though we knew the Air Force had the footage."

He popped a pill, the bitter taste presaging good things. She seemed mesmerized, holding her phone on him. "So, what do you think will happen now?"

He drew a deep breath as the pill dissolved in his mouth, watching his face on her screen. Jesus, he looked fat to himself. Ignoring it, he answered, "Well, the trick really is to understand where they go and why."

He turned his head to see a new customer entering the pharmacy. Lowering his volume, he whispered, "I'm working on it." He winked at her, then collected his bag. "I'll see ya' next time."

She clasped her hands together, calling, "Have a wonderful day, Mister Boothby. And thank you so much!" In a chipper, sing-song tone, she added, "I'm getting hits already!"

*B****

Boothby reached his apartment at dusk, the day spent. The building's layout seemed absurd, at least for any purveyor of privacy. The front gate opened toward the landlady's front window, and the temperate weather led her to leave said cursed window cracked. He had yet to sign a new lease, and though Miss Tutog harbored icky obsessions with him and his work, her new plan would see his rent increased by five Benjamins a month, a number near his breaking point. He'd just as soon move, but when would he find the time?

So, avoiding her had to be the tactical solution. Oiling the hinges of the gate to sneak in undetected might've been prudent, but he wasn't all that handy.

He was fatigued, with the ferret, the therapist, and the wait for his medication sapping him for the day. He was in no mood for Miss Tutog, so he unlocked, then eased the rusty gate from its closed position. Squeak followed goddamned squeak, and the thick burgundy window dressing betrayed a dreaded rustle. There, between the shades, sat her solid black devil of a cat, Archie Bunker. Startled, Boothby took a step back only to collide with the landlady's iron gargoyle partly obstructing the walkway. "Fuck," he muttered as one of its horns poked his haunch. The statue's icy stare pissed him off, but the living creature concerned him more. He quickly whispered, "Nice kitty, please be quiet."

The emotionless face and emerald eyes watched him, then the animal yowled, leading to more racket from behind the window. The little panther disappeared beneath the thick drapes just as a voice hollered, "Mister Boothby, dearie? Is that you?" With that, out popped a round face pounded hard with the worst drag queen makeup getup that he'd ever seen, including his own renditions. Wreathing the swollen face was red hair, pinned with green curlers, all dressing for beady eyes, suffocating perfume, and an annoying nasal cannula owing to her morbid obesity. "For a moment, I thought you were my Franklin Mint delivery—oh, my next porcelain masterpiece is out for delivery, or so the website says."

He muttered, "Imagine the disappointment. Another lynx statue for your cabinet?" He could muster no particular pretense to his weariness. Passing through a settling cloud of smoke, he waved at it. "Smoking and oxygen tanks don't mix, Miss Tutog."

She said, "Oh, that would be Rhoda."

He shuddered at the name. "Your sis should know better. Besides, you have a nonsmoking policy."

Miss Tutog giggled. "For tenants, dearie, not the landlady and her company. Besides, I want her to feel welcome." She withdrew a snappy golden cigarette lighter from her robe. "Does it scare you?" she said as she flicked the flame off and on.

His rasp buzzed his own ears as he shouted, "Jesus Christ, Miss Tutog, are you insane?!"

The flame illuminated her clown makeup. "You would know, Boothby. Rhoda tells me you used to be in an insane asylum." She extinguished the light before dropping it in her robe pocket. With a chuckle, she cranked the dial on her oxygen tank to reopen it.

He shook his head in disgust. "It was an orphanage."

She drew a deep breath of satisfaction. "That used to be an insane asylum, so I bet you weren't there by mistake."

He grumbled under his breath. "Just stay away with your fire and oxygen."

Looking at her repugnant statue, she asked, "Did you move Mohgra?"

"That ugly thing shouldn't be in the walkway, Miss Tutog. It's a tetanus epidemic waiting to happen." He put a little distance between him and the whale of a woman.

"Beauty is as beauty does. Mohgra watches over my property, and more than one bum off the street falls over her." She patted it, stretching a doughy paw from the window. Looking below, she then laughed as the cat emerged from the low bushes. "Oh, what a good kitty."

He groused, "Please keep that animal to yourself. Nearly gave me a heart attack."

She laughed, "Oh, sweet Archie, letting Miss Tutog know that grumpy old Boothby arrived." She rocked her head left and right as the gate fell shut behind Boothby, then said, "Stay there, and I'll meet you in the courtyard." She disappeared, the collapsing drapes revealing, for a blessedly brief instant, gawdy and tacky crap crammed from floor-to-ceiling. Golden lamps, chandeliers, clawfoot fern stands and prayer benches would be in short supply as long as Miss Tutog was around to buy them.

Snapping himself to the path before him, he decided he would dash to his apartment rather than wait for further harassment. He had the advantage, considering her morbid obesity and reliance on tube-fed oxygen. He readied his key, imagining the ferret to give his legs an even greater reason to hurry him along. As he reached the door, he could see she had yet to reach the special hallway connecting to the foyer. He felt relief, only to fumble his keys while aiming one for the lock. They fell to the sidewalk, leaving Boothby gasping. "Fuck!"

He bent, his lumbar arthritis playing no fair as he stretched his right hand for the errant keychain. Grasping it, he pulled himself upward with a yelp, only to jump at seeing her shiny clown face pressed to the glass of the front door.

Laughing, she pointed to the fallen keychain. "Poor truth-seeking Boothby." She clicked her tongue. "Maybe you should write about how locks require keys. I'll open it for you."

He stepped inside, where she and her hellcat were waiting; a meow from the beast frightened him. Leaning away from her, he pleaded, "Can you just keep that mangy thing away from me?"

The lumbering woman reached to scoop up her cat, tugging her enormous pink bathrobe to avoid dragging it to the floor. "Poor Mister Boothby is afraid of the big, bad kitty?" From a free hand, she took a sip from a wine glass she'd carried from her creepy dollhouse of a lair.

He pulled the door closed while gesturing towards his apartment at the end of the hallway. "Miss Tutog, I'd really just like to go lie down."

Miss Tutog scoffed with a burp and pained swallow. As she spoke into his face, he felt dizzy at the mixture of vomit and cat urine on her breath. "Now, Boothby, you know it's time you renew your lease. It's been a few months, and we need to discuss the rent."

She turned her face to that of the cat held in her arms. Twisting her cheeks and mouth, she spoke to the beast as though his was an indispensable part of the conversation. "Yes, we do, Mister Archie!" Boothby felt queasy as she kissed the cat's face, then turned both her and the cat's face to him. "There are just a few others interested in renting, and they want to pay more. And there are always the direct-rent and vacation apps hounding me."

He shrugged, protesting, "Jesus, as though housing costs aren't bad enough?" He walked away, and she pursued, shuffling her oversized house shoes and clanking pair of green-wheeled oxygen tanks along the wooden floor. He tried hard not to catch the occasional peek of a swollen red foot under the robe.

She kept the threats coming, needling him, "Language, dearie. Well, there were three people today who came by asking about the apartments, and they seemed a little gauche."

He shook his head. "Miss Tutog, they only come because you advertise the apartments online. Would you please consider not bringing them here?"

She cast her head backward. "Oh, goodness, did I do that? Well, my sister Rhoda says I should just go to direct vacationers on the web, like that air bomb place." She beamed. "There's more money that way." She swigged a bit more of the noxious fluid from her glass. Peering into it, she remarked with affected contrition, "And we know what my sister thinks of you, dearie the truth-seeker. I just don't like to repeat it." She took a deep, labored breath.

Replying on reflex, he said, "Then don't say it, Miss Tutog." She didn't answer, and instead, huffed and heaved in her pursuit. Perhaps her tank was low? He could only hope. Monkeying with his lock, at last, he opened his door to ecstatic escape.

He entered in reverse, facing her down with his own rebuke, "Rhoda is a MAGAt and an idiot." He flung his bag inward, huffing. "And as for the apartment, fill it with more ugly mail order furniture, rent it by the hour to the grifting prostitutes, or just burn it to the goddamned ground. Just let me have peace."

She stopped suddenly, her brown eyes darting away. "Hmm, worth considering. Insurance money might be good. Well, I want to play the system. See if I can make some money. Unless you wanna take up piano and entertain my guests."

Wanting to have no more of it, he pushed his door shut as he sighed. "Good night, Miss Tutog."

She bellowed from behind the door, "Well, Rhoda says you're crazy, Mister Truth-Seeker. Keep chasing little green men, if you can't catch a real one, man!" She gave a triumphant hiccup, then waddled away from his door, her noisy oxygen tank in tow. He heard her speaking to the cat, but it stayed near his front door for a few minutes, yowling.

Thank God for medication. He found himself seated at his desk, a comfortable setup for the 100 percent remote work of reading and writing. The day drained him, events sufficient to derail a lead too attractive to pass up, too important to share prematurely with others.

He knew, just as intelligence agencies the world over, that the lights' appearances documented over the past century corresponded to nuclear sites.

He pulled from his satchel the torn Plowshares pamphlet, then opened his phone to scan a code from it. Rising to the top of his screen was an article titled, "Plowshares Members Sentenced to Jail." Doctor Tremont asked the right questions, but he didn't dare reveal his true purpose to her. Nuclear weapons didn't capture his imagination, but the lights he sought tended to congregate around them.

To that end, any of the members of the elderly troupe could help him find his answers. But the federal government held all of them incommunicado. Well, almost all. Buried deep in the article was the detail he needed to move his plan forward: the name of the one not in jail. "Conique Voyant." Per the article, "…Miss Voyant received a suspended sentence, owing to a combination of medical circumstance and a sympathetic jury."

Muttering to himself, he thought of the therapist and her skepticism. But he had inescapable proof of his encounter, something he'd held back from all of his retellings. He didn't know why, but this proof calmed his anxieties. Falling to his knees, he pulled a rug from the floor under his desk. He pried open a loose board, revealing a box below, wrapped in a towel. He lifted it with care from its resting place, then unwrapped it. Within it was a chunk of metal and mineral, beautiful in its imperfections, a substance for which there was no natural explanation. Touching it, his nerves steadied, his resolution solidified. Mister Ephyr called it a focus stone, a gift offered to him during the encounter, and Boothby just knew he would help him understand it all once he could return the chunk to him. What a simple, if ludicrous plan—even the government admitted that nuclear sites attracted UFOs, and this woman knew how to reach a nuclear site. So Boothby would find this woman. Sure, it could get him killed. But not knowing the truth was a death of its own.

5. Fifth Vesik: The Evangelical Activist

*C****

Keys. Dammit, where could they be?

Conique Voyant reached her plump hands into a pile of things on her kitchen table. Bills, privacy notices, credit card offers, and endless charitable entreaties existed just to frustrate her. Lighting a match to it seemed appropriate—a bonfire finish reminding her of her Woodstock days. She had more stories than minutes left to tell them.

Glancing at a mirror, she paused to watch herself. Touching her short, silver hair, then her white face, she smiled, mystified. "Conique, who are you? No wonder you can't find them." She recognized the blouse, which was variegated in her usual flamboyance, but the face seemed so old, so strange.

Her husband appeared. A robust black man of seventy-five, he was more attractive to her now than when they'd first met. "Dear, are you looking for these?" He jingled the keys.

She sighed in relief. "Oh, thank goodness." Reaching for them, she beamed. "Now, let's go do this meeting."

He nodded, his rich voice bringing a wash of comfort over her. "Connie, dear, we only have to do this if you want."

She grinned, touching his trimmed black-and-silver goatee. "Reuben, you can talk this girl into anything."

After some last-minute preparation, the couple settled into their small sedan. They had been early adopters of the more advanced electric vehicles, though the range didn't matter now. The meeting was close.

She glanced at him. "I really am safe to drive, Reuben."

He shook his head with a start. "Now, Connie, dear, we talked about this. I can drive you wherever we need to go."

She pulled her clubmaster sunglasses over her face and fastened the seat belt. It seemed a bit of overkill given the news they had received recently. That was right. Dreaded news. Everything seemed to return to that these days. And yet, she'd faced worse.

She buried herself in thought as they pulled from the garage into the street, then into traffic. It was a sunny day, with verdant trees all about. Atlanta was a good place to settle, and it was where things were to end. Fair enough.

She turned to her husband. He had not aged much since they'd met twenty years prior. Black don't crack, or so the expression went. She wished that it were so for herself, but he seemed no less a fan of her face now.

They crept into the parking lot of their destination. The sign read, "Philbert Nivens, M.D." Reuben smiled, offering, "I think this'll be good for us. He specializes in—"

She stopped him, sighing, "Picking out the casket and the flowers?"

With a gentle grin, he squeezed her hand, replying, "No, he'll help us navigate this, together, just like always."

His voice soothed her. She paused, watching his face, then went back to the business of unbuckling her safety belt. "Then let's navigate."

C***

After what had seemed an eonian wait in reception, an assistant appeared at last. "Miss Conique Voyant and Doctor Reuben Hamora? Doctor Nivens will see you." Reuben had already replaced the copy of *National Geographic* on the end table and reached his feet by the time Conique could stir to the edge of her seat. Dammit, cooking good food had led her in many wrong directions. He delicately helped her to her feet with pure affection and warmth.

They passed into a connecting hallway—a distance, to be sure. How many shrinks could one building hold? She'd been in many therapy groups over the years, but this would be a first. Or a last, rather. Her husband did residency with this particular psychiatrist at Emory decades prior. So, some connection, along with a healthy dose of anonymity, perhaps might make this venture fly.

They reached the door, and the assistant opened it for them. She smiled. "You all may go on in."

Inside the office, she found the customary couch and chairs assigned to patients and their plus ones, or plus twos, or whatnot. With plain design by her own thinking, the room smelled of the musty mold plaguing so many older buildings throughout the humid southeast.

Behind a desk sat a slight gentleman, dapper, bald, with gold-rimmed eyeglasses. Seeing them, he stood with a smile. "Rube! Good to see you again."

Her husband, towering over the tiny figure, clasped the man's outstretched hand with both of his own. "Good to see you, Phil. It's been too long." He turned back to Conique, placing an arm about her shoulders. "This is my wife, Conique Voyant."

Doctor Nivens shook her hand. "Very nice to meet you, Miss Voyant."

She looked to her husband with an uneasy smile. "Rube?" She turned to Doctor Nivens, whose happy face at least put her at some ease. "I've never heard anyone call him that."

Doctor Nivens waved her off with his spare hand, chuckling. "It was the very definition of irony. He was no rube."

She adjusted her bracelets, then pointed her forehead in his direction. "You know, we protested together during the Freedom Rides." Reuben squirmed, attempting to interrupt her, only for her to get the sentence out that she knew he hated to hear repeated. "And he got a nice, hefty concussion at Selma."

Doctor Nivens bobbed his little head in recognition. "Yeah, I heard about that at the time. Brutal stuff." His skull wouldn't have survived Selma, she decided.

Noting the clock behind the patient seating area, the doctor craned his neck a bit. Melodramatic, this one. He bit his lip, then whispered, "Well, let's get started."

They found themselves seated together on the couch, which was softer and plushier than she'd expected. She might never get off once she planted her rear there. Reuben turned to her after he crossed his legs. "Are you ready, dear?"

She inhaled a deep breath, then smiled at this shining knight, his black skin almost sparkling under the lighting. "Yeah, let's do it."

The doctor began, "So, Miss Voyant, tell me about how you and Rube here met."

Interesting tactic, not asking about the problem now. Could she flow with this one after all? She answered quickly, "We met in a bereavement group in 1999." She looked to her husband, and he nodded, offering her permission to say more. She hated discussing this, but could agree that the whole picture might be more important than more recent fragments. "My daughter Angie was killed by a drunk driver. She was walking home from a college class."

She turned back to her husband, hoping he would add the next few details. He obliged, speaking with no small measure of pain. "My son had been killed by the police. Unarmed, no threat."

Doctor Nivens steeled himself, moved by the two revelations. "That is terrible." His blue-grey eyes met her blue ones. "For both of you."

Reuben exhaled, adding, "It was very difficult. Rashad was our only child." He squeezed Conique's hand. "My wife then took her own life."

Conique couldn't stop the tears, knowing the pain her sweet Reuben had endured. She blotted her face with a tissue, and, knowing her eye makeup would most assuredly run in all directions, did her best to minimize the mess. "Yes, we were brought together by trauma. All God's plan."

Doctor Nivens' face beamed compassion. He said, "It's hard to imagine God would have caused those things to happen."

On reflex, she answered, "I learned a long time ago that praying against something that would happen no matter what didn't help. Instead, I asked God just one thing."

Nivens pursed his lips with a nod. "And what is that?"

She caught his eyes once more. "To bear it. To change my attitude."

"That's laudable." He held fast. "It's actually quite profound. And healthy." He checked his notes, then looked back at her. "So, you would call yourself—"

She broke into his sentence, completing it for him. "Spiritual?" She tapped her fingers on her thighs. "Three months ago, I was diagnosed—" Her sentence trailed off as her disjointed mind pulled together fragments of the whole. Reuben squeezed her hand, the warmth of his touch quickening her broadcast.

She redirected her eyes to this rather small therapist. Could he really help her? "Three months since they diagnosed me with that terrible disease." She paused again, searching for the words.

"Please take your time, Conique." The listening doctor did project compassion, so she continued, uncomfortable with the vulnerability accompanying personal disclosures.

Love, that was the key. Moving in her gifts, she remained a tremendous force in her community of fellow evangelical outcasts. To help this man do his job would be the way to love, and to minister.

Her thoughts coalesced at last. "In the past year, I started losing things." She cut her eyes to Reuben, his beautiful brown eyes, even for a man of seventy-five, furnishing her a security capable of dissolving her worldly worries. Glancing back to the clinician, she continued, "First, they were minor things—nuisances, really, like notes, household hardware, and the like."

The therapist seemed to receive her frailty well. What did God want her to do for this man? First, though, she felt compelled to continue. "Next, I lost more important things—car keys, medications. God, my medicine cabinet looks like a pharmacy hit by a twister."

Doctor Nivens cracked a smile, unburdening her a little in this wretched self-directed discussion. Reuben chuckled. "Well, getting old does that."

She could bask in the booming of his voice for all the ages. She thought a small prayer of gratitude for him, then spoke more of her truth. "More recently, I started losing time. I might discover I'd wandered into the small park near our home."

She sought some refuge from Reuben, beckoning clarification. He followed her unspoken request, adding, "Sometimes, she'd disappear for a few hours, then have no memory of where she'd been." He, too, seemed reluctant to depict her terrifying plight.

Doctor Nivens rescued them both with a more direct inquiry. "So, Conique, please tell me how this diagnosis makes you feel."

This she could answer, even if she confessed a disconnect in her faith. "I've been a minister for forty years. I've seen people in all stages of emotional, physical, and spiritual disarray, and I've had my own tragedies, too." She shook off some doubt, doubling down on her past. "I've watched the sick be healed, the broken mended, and connected people with the unconditional love of God through His Son."

Doctor Nivens cocked his head slightly, piqued by this. "You speak of miracles as if they're real."

This proved easy to field. "In 1983, I lived in San Antonio, working as a waitress. I didn't know who I was or who I was supposed to be." Reuben beamed, always eager to hear a retelling of an old tale. "I heard about a couple ministering at a church."

Images flooded her in reverie. "I was raised in the Methodist tradition up in Gainesville. I never really thought that much of faith or God. I'd already married and divorced, my first husband dropping me for a strumpet with a waistline for days." She watched the expected smile from her listener, then continued, "I went with a friend to a meeting. And this man playing a piano sang me a song."

She turned to Reuben, then back to Doctor Nivens, feeling fatigue in her cheeks as a smile stretched across her face. "I'll never forget it. The song was extemporaneous, telling me my story about my ex-husband, the tall, dark, and handsome man I'd meet one day, and the ministry I would soon undertake."

Doctor Nivens scribbled a note, then leaned forward in his chair. "Please, do continue."

"The minister told me that I would do what he was doing. He could pick someone from the crowd, then speak directly to that person about the motorcycle accident he'd had two years prior, or how her stepfather had caused her terrible pain, or how a financial reprieve might be imminent, or whatever."

The therapist took great notice of this, though she couldn't discern skepticism from fascination. Maybe it was both. "You mean he could read people's thoughts?"

She laughed, folding her fingers together with a bit of confidence. "It's more than that. Past, present, and future are the same to God."

Doctor Nivens eyed her now with growing suspicion, or so it appeared. He asked, "So, God gave him visions, or thoughts?"

She nodded, delighted in shining her truth wherever she might. "We call them gifts of the Holy Spirit—prophesy, words of knowledge, healing, and the like."

Doctor Nivens looked to Reuben. Could he think he'd appeal to the other scientist in the room? Her husband laughed. "Phil, it's the real deal. Nothing contrived about it."

Doctor Nivens planted his gray eyes back on Conique, now invigorated. "The minister told you that you could do these things?"

She remembered him so well—he'd had a black beard and a gorgeous wife with a voice that was manna from heaven. "Yes. He pushed me off the cliff, as he called it. Told me I had a word for a person down the row from me."

Doctor Nivens shook his head slightly—disbelief, or confusion? Reuben chuckled, adding, "The person he pointed her towards is still a good family friend now."

Conique closed her eyes, recalling the scene. "I prayed over her, just like the minister said, and I could immediately see an alcoholic sister who'd nearly died several times from alcohol poisoning. My new friend had not seen her sister in months, or so I heard and reported. The word of encouragement was that Jesus held her sister close, and that within two months, she'd call for help, then enter rehab for the first time." A flush of warmth permeated her as she recalled the moment. "I made a great friend that day. Karen just bawled her eyes out as I prayed over her. Every detail was exactly correct, even though it felt so ordinary to me that I thought I must be making it up as I went."

Awe surrounded Doctor Nivens now. "Did you start working with the minister?"

She shook her head in frustration. "No, I moved back to Atlanta not long after." Noting a small cardinal land on the sill of a nearby window, she sighed. "I think they're in Arizona now, retired. Forty years is a long time."

Doctor Nivens watched her as she lost herself in silent reminiscence, though she listened to his probe for Reuben. "You're still Islamic in your faith, aren't you?"

He nodded. "Yeah, my father was pretty specific about following Allah, though my mother was from Harlem."

Doctor Nivens nodded in recognition, asking further, "So, how do you reconcile evangelical Christianity with Islam? As a couple?"

Conique laughed, answering easily, "There's no real contradiction. I don't have many friends in the neoevangelical movement, since I don't put any stock into hell, torment, and all that crap."

Reuben shifted in his seat next to her, leaning a little into her, much to her delight. He persisted in the thought with, "My dad just wanted us to live right, and following his faith led in that direction. Conique finds Jesus to be compelling. I find Mohammed." He turned to her, winking. "The point is that we believe the world will be saved, whole."

She grinned at the small man, delighted at his confusion. Tossing him a bone, she remarked, "I once heard a teacher ask, 'If the disciples had found that Jesus did not resurrect on the third day, does that mean we shouldn't love our neighbor?'" She shifted her focus above his balding head, searching for the exact words. "To me, following the tenets of Christ literally means emulating the virtues he presented."

She paused, waiting for comment. None came, but her mind wandered along a passage she favored when someone might question her faith. *"Now we see but a dim reflection as in a mirror; then we shall see face to face. Now I know in part; then I shall know fully, even as I am fully known. And now these three remain: faith, hope, and love; but the greatest of these is love."*

She chuckled, considering them, then understood that once more, her mind had wandered from the social template. Such a long quote was inappropriate. Reuben's face conveyed love, while the therapist watched, noting her every symptom. She felt her face had fallen into a neutral expression, so she smiled. "I don't need a badly translated book to tell me what He placed in my heart. Maybe He's just a manifestation of all that is good in the Universe."

Doctor Nivens eased himself back, saying, "So, you're not a fundamentalist?"

Braying with laughter, Conique responded, "Jesus, no. The eternals and forevers weren't translated correctly from the ancient dialects. There are obvious contradictions between books. They spoke in parables and hyperbole, making much of it somewhat difficult to apply today." She rested her hand on Reuben's thigh, adding, "It's something my misguided moral minority may never understand."

The therapist checked his watch, prompting Reuben to ask, "Are we running low on time?"

Doctor Nivens nodded quickly, then smiled at his old school chum. "Let's go a few minutes long." He looked to Conique, adding, "If that's okay with you, Connie?"

She exhaled in glee, even rapture that she could share her truth with another. "Absolutely!"

Reuben corralled her somewhat, suggesting, "Phil asked you how the diagnosis made you feel."

There it was. Back to the pain of it. It was a long story of marvelous feats, and yet she knew she'd be incapable of recalling them within a short timeframe. "Anger." What else could she say? Faith, hope, love mattered most, but what would happen when the phrase itself left her decaying brain?

Doctor Nivens pointed to the ceiling with the most obvious and relevant question. "Anger at God?"

She looked to Reuben, then back to the therapist. "Yes, I suppose so. There's so much left to do, and now, someone has put a timer on me."

He placed his notepad aside, then gestured openhandedly. "We all live on a timer. We just don't have it in front of us very often. So, by 'much to do,' you mean your ministry?"

She answered without a thought to whether he'd understand. "Because of the Plowshares."

A delayed cognizance covered the therapist's face. "The nuclear-weapon activists?"

Reuben snorted a chuckle, placing a warm hand on Conique's left leg. Oh, how she loved this man. He answered, "The same. I'm surprised you know about us."

The therapist appeared piqued, adding, "Oh, yes, I know of the general principle. Marring nuclear weapons with blood to make a statement politically. You have to know it's been in the papers' I didn't think you had it in you, Rube."

Reuben beat her to the next question. "Do you disapprove?"

The therapist's eyes sparkled. "Not at all. It seems risky."

Reuben looked over at her as he said, "Yeah, there've been a few near misses for her and radiation poisoning. Miraculous, really." His eyes said it all—rebuke and pride, all wrapped together.

Blushing, she pointed to the sky as she winked. "Mysterious ways, dear."

Reuben clicked his tongue. "It still seems too good to be true. But, anyway, that's one of the things she's been up to."

Nivens shrugged at that. "I just can't believe I haven't read either of your names among those recently put in jail."

Conique laughed. "Well, Reuben didn't participate in the fun. And the prosecutor's office knows I have dementia, so they decided the disease made me do it."

Doctor Nivens grabbed his notepad to jot a bit down, asking, "What made you decide to get involved with the group?"

Conique searched her thoughts, then said, "I met my first Plowshare buddy eleven years ago. I prayed over her, and I told her that Jesus approved of the risks she took on behalf of her brother, and that those actions would save lives, even if it cost her freedom."

Reuben rubbed her thigh a little in playful recollection, then completing her thought. "We spoke to her after the meeting; her brother had been a marine assigned to the cleanup on Runit Island—"

Doctor Nivens tapped his notepad, asking, "Runit?"

Conique supplied the answer, testing her memory. "The nuclear tests in the south Pacific led to widespread death among indigenous peoples, and the US government decided to gather the nuclear waste scattered about the region and store in one great big concrete basin on Runit Island." She shook her head, recalling photographs of the tragedy, anger rising in her voice. "They sent Americans, greenhorn Army and Marines, to gather the materials with absolutely no protective gear."

Reuben patted her to stay her anger, after which he completed the story. "Many died, riddled with cancer. The lady to whom Connie referred lost her brother in the ordeal. It was a grisly death, so after hearing her spiel, we decided that this was a place where we could make a difference. Connie even visited Runit."

70

Doctor Nivens peered over his glasses. "You were allowed? Isn't that dangerous?"

Conique felt a wash of pride, though she didn't want to delve into it. "It was a joint thing sponsored through Peace Corps. I wasn't worried about me. The peoples there suffered horribly, and I wanted to help them. That's all."

Reuben squeezed her with a hug. "She's awfully humble."

She touched his arm, offering unspoken succor for the torment of his trauma. He returned her kindness, then prompted her to continue. "I'm actually writing a book about our time with the Plowshares." She stopped cold, recalling the reason she was speaking to this man. The disease was hell-bent on robbing her of the precious memories vital to assembling a memoir. "Anger is damn accurate."

She calmed herself a little as Reuben started to weep. She squeezed her eyes shut, then reopened them with a start, though with greater calm. "People need to hear the truth."

Doctor Nivens cocked his head once more, presaging another line of inquiry around her illness, or her self-burdened expectations. "And you believe you must deliver this truth?"

She nodded hard. "I'm just one small piece of His will. Thousands of artisans, scientists, moralists, every kind of 'ist' wants to fight this battle. Some people will listen to me who won't listen to anyone else."

Doctor Nivens chewed at an earpiece from his glasses, then he asked, "So often, the lens we see the world through says more about us than the world might say itself. I think it's actually pretty healthy to try this, even if ambitious. Voices are important."

She decided she might like this doctor after all, even if he would be accompanying her to the gates of death. But his point made her think of something she knew to be important. "Yes! I want this story to be about more than just old ministers slapping blood on nukes. There are soldiers, doctors, politicians, and everyone else aiming to make a change. I'm reaching out to so many, and maybe you can make recommendations."

Reuben touched her arm, suggesting, "Maybe we let Phil do his job here."

Doctor Nivens corrected him, "It's okay, Rube. Yes, if I can think of anyone."

She clicked her tongue, asking, "Have you heard of Shigeru Nakamura?"

Doctor Nivens shook his head, replying, "The name is familiar. A professor?"

She could hope, quipping, "He's one of the most important medical doctors working on what happens to people exposed to radiation. I've tried to reach him, knowing he could help me build a better case for laying down these evil weapons. His secretary got a little bent out of shape when I kept on calling."

Reuben's puppy dog brown eyes melted her so easily, and they spoke as much as his words, "Connie, he might just not want to talk to a minister."

Doctor Nivens followed his comment, asking, "Why do you think you need his perspective?"

She thought about the question, then it hit her like a bolt from the blue. Shrugging, she said, "I just get the sense that as much as he thinks someone like me needs to listen to science, maybe he needs to hear me. I think we could reach more people together than separately, even when you add it all up. I get the sense he's in need of a little enchantment. I've been praying for him since I read an interview of his from the *Atlantic*. I keep seeing him alone, confused, angry."

Doctor Nivens shot a glance to Reuben, then reconnected his eyes with hers. He said, "So contacting this person isn't just about what you need from him?"

Reuben muttered, "Another lost lamb." He then smiled, "It's my Connie's thing."

A decade younger, she'd have been angry with him. In the now, she answered in play, "So the big doctors will gang up on me, huh? Look, I get a sense about people when I meet them, read about them."

This time, Reuben did piss her off, muttering once more, "She could love a rabid porcupine."

Nivens sought to pacify, intervening with, "No, Rube. I want to be clear about our goals with these sessions." He measured his words, then consoled her, "Miss Voyant, working could be a healthy thing, so long as you understand your limits. Maybe this sixth sense should be something you keep under your hat?"

She prayed silently for strength in the face of skepticism, then it hit her. The gift flowed. "By the way, God seems to be telling me that your son will abandon the warhawks and come back to you, asking your forgiveness."

Doctor Nivens stopped in mid-scribble, his eyes flashing with something new— uncertainty, or loss of control? He peered over his spectacles. "I beg your pardon?"

She saw it clearly—a younger man with familiar-yet-ugly trappings. "Your son has listened to the white supremacists for years, and the last time you spoke with him, he told you he wished you were dead."

Doctor Nivens remained frozen, listening as Reuben smiled and nodded in his direction. "Any of this ring true?"

The therapist's body language shifted as he nodded slowly. "What else do you see?"

"He told your daughter, his sister, that he planned to go to the next capitol riot."

His gray eyes bulged in surprise, letting her know she was correct. "How could you possibly know that?"

Reuben placed his arm around his wife, holding her close, and answered in her stead, "This is how the gift works."

Conique sensed that the appointment would soon end, so she tacked encouragement onto her message. "God wants you to know that your son will soon free himself from the circle of friends poisoning his mind, and that he absolutely will not participate in any future riots."

A knock at the door interrupted the therapist as he started to speak. The receptionist poked her head into his office. "Doctor, I am so, so sorry, but you've kept your next patient waiting for thirty minutes into her time, and she can't stay past three."

Doctor Nivens said, "Just a moment." Then, he looked to Conique, commenting, "I won't pretend to understand what I just heard, but I want to hear more. And please schedule your next appointment with my assistant."

Reuben rose to his feet, then helped her push off the couch. Damn the masks they wore for protection. All she could see was the man's eyes. Maybe that was sufficient to peer into a person?

C***

As Reuben and Conique settled into their sun-warmed car and prepared to drive home, he decided he would chide her. "Dear, you know that you were there to get help from him, right?"

She placed her large sunglasses on her face, a smidgen dissatisfied that they muted the vibrant green of the moss, kudzu, and big Georgian trees all about them. "I go where the Spirit leads, Reuben. Doctor Nivens needed to hear those words."

Reuben seemed content with the answer at face value. She had no trouble recalling that he'd lost all arguments on the subject, considering the apparent good she spread through her gifts. Whether she'd remember in a month was opaque to her, but her pressing concern, as she directed the air conditioning vents to cool herself, remained her manuscript about the days she'd spent among the other Plowshares. Since she wouldn't be writing the book from the hoosegow, her loyalty to her fellow members had prompted her to write the memoir as quickly as possible so as to publish ahead of any sentencing for the others. She doubted it would make a difference, but what the hell? At the very least, it could pass for a manual on antinuclear activism.

But she needed an expert's opinion. She fished in a bag sitting in the floorboard behind Reuben, muttering to herself. He asked, "What are you looking for, dear?"

She fixed herself on the bag, searching by touch alone. "I need my notes."

He pointed towards the open road ahead of them. "Dear, you know you'll get car sick if you try to read anything now."

She laughed, musing, "Well, I won't remember it tomorrow, you know."

He frowned, responding, "It's strange you can joke about it so easily." He patted her as he pointed to traffic ahead of them. "Dear, it'll be forty-five minutes at least before we're home. Why don't you try to nap if you can?"

She huffed a laugh, pushing hard on the bag to dislodge whatever annoying obstructions were within it. It seemed like even the simplest of tasks had become Herculean. Could that be a sign of the illness? Snickering, she said, "Reuben, I'm not an invalid yet. I'm not out past curfew." Closing her eyes, she added, "Then again, I am really tired."

He squeezed her hand in his. "Plenty of time to read when we're home. Just relax."

She drew a deep breath, taking her mind off of the car, the interstate, and even Reuben. Conique was not one to dwell within the problem. She decided she'd ask her Source for help. With a sigh, she closed her eyes, expecting forty winks. Gently, she whispered, "I am thy vessel. Tell me Your will, Almighty."

*C****

Conique found herself standing in the snow, and though she wore only her night gown, she felt no cold.

Looking up from her bare feet dusted by snow, she examined her surroundings. An old wooden fence, reminiscent of what she might find back in Texas, sat behind her, stretching far in both directions. So far, she couldn't make out an end to either. Looking up, she saw that the night sky was clear, beautiful, the stars crisp, and though she'd never known that much about constellations, the Big Dipper was there. Illuminating the snow was the full face of the moon, grand and beautiful.

Before her lay an estate of unclear age—a large fortress of a house, a barn, and a handful of other buildings and sheds. Where this was, she couldn't say, but she did notice at last that she was holding hands with someone. To her left was a fellow boomer—a shaggy, unkempt man with a gray beard. To her right was the unmistakable if elusive Japanese doctor she'd sought. Conique looked further, seeing a much younger man beside the shaggy one, a blonde with cold blue eyes. Beside the Japanese physician was a white woman with blonde hair, as well. She seemed maybe fifty, as best Conique could determine. There were two others beyond the young blonde man, but she couldn't see them.

So, seven in a line, it seemed. She tried to speak, but none of the others shifted their focus from the estate before them.

So, she directed her focus to the same, and a man materialized before them, a form of perfection. His brown hair and sapphire eyes captivated her. She found herself smiling, thinking, *Well, if God is this good-looking, I might ask for the express ticket to check out from life.*

The two holding her hands tightened their grasp, as though the presence of this eighth figure upset them. She looked to either side, wanting to suggest they calm themselves, yet nothing came out of her mouth. She eyed the figure before them and saw that he had stepped closer to them.

A woman's voice boomed with conviction and certainty. "You Seven Vesiks are the culmination. Watch—Preskamon and Verafaj—you are summoned, and you must answer. Through you shall I rise. I am the culmination."

"God the Father is God the Mother?" Conique chuckled at that. "Am I dead? Are you the Messiah?" Turning to the strangers, she asked, "Where are we?"

None of them stirred, but the woman's voice from the heavens said, "Rejoice. I await your arrival—this world must be saved, but only *through Me.*"

She looked to those next to her, but the details were cloudy. Unable to move, she shouted at the sky. "I have served you all my life, Lord. What must I do?"

The voice replied, "Each of the Seven Vesiks shall seek the next in the chain. The *Otofos* dwells within you—the power of life itself. The eighth is the catalyst, dispatched to begin your awakening."

She decided her resentment deserved some attention. "My daughter? Where is she? Is she in heaven?"

The stars flickered, but the voice didn't address her question. "This world, the third planet from its star, can be saved when you find Mirrum."

Though she would receive no reply, Conique asked, "Who is Mirrum?"

A frightening thought hit her: the Antichrist would appear beautiful, considering Lucifer was the most beloved of God's angels. She studied the eighth's face, finding in it no love or warmth. "What evil is this?" She prayed, "Lord Jesus, a thousand can fall at my right, ten thousand at my left, yet it will not come near me. You promise life of the ages; this pretender comes to pillage. Banish him from my sight."

Explosions shocked her. Reopening her eyes, she watched the estate burning around them. The woman's voice boomed once more. "Usurpers and false prophets may hijack this rite. Do not permit it, for none can find Me save those I have ordained. Without Me, this world shall fall."

Conique's dreams darkened, and she beheld the Earth as though she were in space, high above the cerulean and emerald jewel. Soon, the surface was burning, disintegrating, the lives of billions erased by the fires. Their energies grazed her, and she felt anguish.

Behind this world, there were more shapes. More Earths? A line of them, though they differed. They all burned alongside it, however. She heard the screams of people, scorching, melting, sizzling, dying. Soul-chilling terror, flesh-burning flames moved over the Earths, omnicide of life, all life, all places, as though she saw the hell she'd been raised to believe awaited the unbelieving—blackening sun, bleeding moon, burning Earth, rivers of fire and blood, the once-fertile lands of the world undone, choking with smoke, ash, and searing radiation.

She could not scream, but she knew she wept. This could not be the past. Was this the future?

The voice sounded once more, warning, "All life known to us faces extinction, unless you pursue the Seven. You must follow a faith—a peace passing understanding, as the fable goes."

She felt air wash over her, and the heat abated. She squeezed her eyes shut, then opened them to see all fires extinguished. The moon seemed to fall towards the earth, chilling the air. The cold face approached, rumbling, and the dream ended.

Conique's eyes fluttered open as Reuben shook her. "Connie, can you hear me, dear?"

For a moment, she didn't know him. But it dawned on her that they sat in their car, parked within their garage. She said, "I understand what I'm supposed to do."

He held her shoulder, his face full of concern. "I couldn't wake you up. Are you okay?"

Conique was quickened by the dream. "Dear, I need paper and pen. I need to write it all down while I can remember it."

His soulful eyes bore pity. "Babe, you don't need to stress yourself. Let's get you inside."

She couldn't accept this. "This isn't my senility, Reuben. I think I'm in contact with angels." He reached to unhook her seatbelt, so she grabbed his wrist. "Dear, I'm as sane as ever. Believe me. Please."

He didn't resist her, though God knows he probably wanted to. Instead, he answered, "Okay, I'll believe you. Tell me what you saw, and I'll remember it."

She concentrated, but the details dissolved faster the harder she tried. "Dammit. I can't remember it all. But there was a large farmhouse. And seven people. And—" She balled her fists, planting them into the dashboard. "Shit, it was all there. A woman's name."

Reuben hugged her as tears welled in her eyes. "C'mon, dear. Let's go inside."

She stopped short, recalling, "That Doctor Nakamura was there! I have to speak with him."

6. Sixth Vesik: Physician Heal Thy World

*S****

"Professor?" There had been question from the audience. What was it, again?

Shigeru searched the notes before him, then darted his eyes to the familiar frump of his colleague Madeline. Moderating the talk, she pressed her face a little forward, then bounced her eyes from him in the direction of the spectators, hinting that he was keeping the questioner waiting. He took a moment to adjust his black bolo tie.

The young girl from the student listeners had posed the broadest of pro-nuclear questions. He'd fielded the question so many times, the variations were irrelevant to the meaning. He knew of the girl, a visiting student from America. She had not missed any of his special lectures, despite her own interests in robotics, computer architecture or some other nerdy interest he couldn't recall. Most questions from differing disciplines intrigued him, but nascent academics turned provocateurs incensed him. Especially the female ones, a resentment he didn't try to cover.

The girl repeated, "Do you believe America should've developed the atomic bomb to stop World War Two?"

He scratched his black goatee, then shook his head, picking as good a response as he could muster after spending the last hour dissecting the human price exacted by the weapons she appeared to see as justified. "Miss, I have spoken about the hibakusha and similar survivors about the world—namely, to address the tremendous uptick in cancers, birth defects, and so on. You have picked the more general question of whether the bomb ought to have been dropped on this country, my home, as a means of saving other lives."

She bobbed her head. "That's right, sir."

He inhaled in pause, considering that her vehemence was aimed to assuage a sort of national guilt he found among the more dovish American students. Rather than cut to the heart, he would respond to the question as clarified. "What is missing is a genuine counterfactual."

She cocked her head, beckoning a less-technical term.

He opened his hand, gesturing a scale. "Experimental statisticians, and thus anyone who requires their expertise, are profoundly interested in the counterfactual, the outcome had we chosen the alternative path." He fought a grin; the term seemed a whimsy. "On one hand is the outcome by deploying one strategy." He raised the other hand. "The other is that corresponding to the alternate choice. Nuke a city, or don't nuke a city."

Reaching for his jacket flaps to rest his hands, he squinted at the ellipsoidal spotlights aimed at the podium. The girl would not budge from her stony impatience. She was a pretty girl, though her hostile blue eyes couldn't recover from a tall forehead. Even the slightest flaw in appearance irked the shit out of him. "Whatever one calls it, dropping the bombs stopped the war. Whatever would have happened afterward had to be worse than what happened here."

He planted his palms upon the heavy rostrum before him, his frustration rising. "Counterfactuals, Miss, are incredibly difficult to assume."

He moved his eyes aside to limit the light, then continued. "I have spent sixty minutes explaining to you the plight of those who suffered, be it Hiroshima and Nagasaki, Chernobyl, the testing in the South Pacific, or the testing in your own country. Your own American treasure John Wayne died of cancer early because of testing upwind from the location filming of *The Conqueror*."

A bit stunned, she shook her head with a struggle to say, "That can't be true."

He redirected her. "This seminar is about the genetic abnormalities cursing the survivors. My mother and father were downwind from Nagasaki on August 8 of 1945, and they, too, along with all of their natural children, suffered greatly." The girl froze as he continued. "There was pain, hair-loss, utter digestive collapse, death of internal organs from the inside out, and a desperately shortened lifespan—for those with milder symptoms."

He spied tears welling in the girl's eyes. She responded, with some care, "I didn't know your family was part of this." She wiped a tear, pulling her sandy red curls from her rounded face. "But you??"

He replied "No, my parents adopted me much later." Sympathetic to her own tender expression of compassion, he softened. "If you want my geopolitical analysis of the situation as it was in 1945, I do not believe it was necessary to deploy nuclear weapons. There was talk of surrender, so long as Japan might retain her emperor, who was nothing more than a religious figurehead."

She shook her head. "No, America would have allowed that if Japan had been willing."

Shigeru deemed the remark absurd. "Miss, I would entreat you to read your very own Air Force History. They boast of washing away Korean villages by bombing dams, all in contravention of the Geneva Accords. Read the *Pentagon Papers* leaked by your own Daniel Ellsberg. Better yet, read his recent book on nuclear threats, *The Doomsday Machine.*"

With volume that surprised him, she responded, "Your people bombed Pearl Harbor, murdering hundreds of our servicemen."

He laughed. "Your government conducted military exercises a couple hundred kilometers from Japan's shores, and they stymied supply lines in Manchuria, actively participating in the war with no formal declaration." He reeled in his irony somewhat, hoping maybe to project professionalism. "If Iran conducted war games two hundred miles from your state of Virginia, I believe you'd have a problem with it."

She piped up in anger. "You're just anti-American, like everyone else outside the country."

Shrugging with an irrepressible smile, he said, "Well, technically extra-American, considering I'm not an American." The crowd laughed, after which he continued. "In any case, the Allied forces had firebombing at their disposal, which was easily as destructive in the short term, and with far fewer long-term consequences. The firebombing of Tokyo was, in many respects, equally or more devastating than what was wrought by the nuclear weapons."

She shook her head in defiance. "But the nuclear bombs were easier."

He raised a finger, almost interrupting her. "Not at all. You suppose a world in which you have hundreds of conventional weapons or a nuclear bomb ready to go. But the cost of developing nukes was overwhelmingly more." He noted Madeline letting him know that only five minutes remained in the discussion.

He leaned into the podium, hushing his voice somewhat. "Again, the problem here is that the counterfactual is missing, and almost certainly exaggerated. Would so many more civilians have died? It seems to me that your government simply wanted to test its new toys, and my people were the Guinea pigs."

She didn't react, so he continued. "There were physicists at Los Alamos concerned that deployment of the weapons would ignite the atmosphere, consuming the biosphere in apocalyptic fire. Yet they continued the work, despite these possibilities being raised to ranking members of the project. The bombing of Dresden, and, again, Tokyo, demonstrated that conventional weapons were sufficient in murdering civilians and eliminating strategic targets."

He turned once more to Madeline, raising a hand to request slightly more time. "Since my research aims to understand genetic changes due to radiation, I don't discuss the greatest risk posed by nukes. It isn't the fallout."

He paused, the audience hanging on his next words. Madeline cast a look of rebuke at his showboating, so he continued,. "It's the smoke. When ash and soot reach the stratosphere, they sit above the troposphere, away from all things weather." Gesturing his hands as a falling sheet, he said, "Rain normally would bring the soot downward, as is the case with volcanic eruptions. But nuclear weapons are far more powerful, and once the stratosphere darkens, plant life dies, followed by almost all animals, ourselves included."

Another voice from the audience asked, "But couldn't we live—"

With no time remaining to address particulars, he interrupted, "Without the sun?" He rapped his knuckles on the pine lectern, shaking in resolution. "No. We die."

He pointed in the direction of the American student. "Incidentally, your military leadership of the 1950s knew this, and they persisted in building more weapons."

She answered sharply, "But the Soviet Union..."

He laughed, then preached, "Was never as credible a threat as your policymakers argued. Does it seem so hard to believe that your grandparents and parents were told fiction to convince them that bloated defense spending was good national security? Your military was more powerful than the next ten combined, and yet they couldn't prevent the September 11 attacks, and they couldn't bring order to the Middle East. Instead, six figures of civilians are dead, and seven figures are maimed, displaced, and in utter ruin." He flung his hands up. "But at least your corporations continue to roll in the fat."

The girl shouted, "So, what, we're supposed to sit around feeling sorry for ourselves that people died forever? I didn't drop those fucking bombs!"

He snarled, "I am no priest, little Miss America. I offer neither absolution from your sins nor affirmation that you're a good lily-white."

Madeline put a stop to his tirade, interrupting with firm bordering hostile, "Well, with that, we should conclude by thanking our speaker, Professor Shigeru Nakamura, jointly appointed to the Okinawa Institute of Cancer Research and Nagasaki University."

His heart slowed as the crowd applauded, though he could see the American girl had already sliced through the group to reach the auditorium exit.

Gathering his papers, he decided that if slide after slide of grisly, charred, mutated adults and children had proven unpersuasive, little Miss America would be morally beyond reach. He stewed, only to hear the moderator whisper as she approached him, "Shigeru, did you really need to go so hard on that girl?"

He turned to her—an aging flab of a woman he'd known for twenty years—and answered, "Madeline, she deliberately baited me." He returned his eyes to his disheveled mess of papers, lowering his voice to say, "Besides, she needed to know her flag-wiping bullshit is just that: bullshit."

Madeline admonished him as she removed her glasses. "Don't make this about her, Shigeru."

He jerked his head towards her, repulsed somewhat. "My seminars aren't about nuclear disarmament. I don't bring it up. What am I supposed to say?" Trying to avoid keeping her in view, he fumbled with his briefcase.

She touched his arm, and he felt revulsion. "Come on, Shigeru, she's just a child. They learn from the beginning that their military is the core piece of culture."

Madeline paused, smelling him with an accusation. "How much vodka have you had today?"

His attention snared, he scanned her lined face, her eyes surrounded by distasteful breakage. How could she be the same age as himself? Yet those hazel eyes penetrated him, the scrutiny enraging him. "I can do my job whether I'm drinking or not. You know, if you want to act like you're a nagging wife, you could at the very least get a chemical peel." He slung a hand to the air, mocking her, "I would have to be drunk to see your face everyday."

She sneered, "Jesus Christ, you're an asshole. My God, you need to grow up, Shig. You owe your fit physique to genetics, not to fate and certainly not moral character. And that girl isn't an ex, a colleague, or an acquaintance. She's a student from America, and words matter."

Looking down to his papers, he muttered, "Mad, pardon my French, but she was a cunt. And you're not different." He met her eyes resolutely at the last word, a word he knew would scatter her.

As he hoped, she stiffened, responding, "That's deeply offensive, Shig, especially to say to a woman."

He forced the case shut, then buttoned his jacket, "Well, Mad, I'm happy to call a man a dick, if that makes you feel better."

He pulled the briefcase to his side and turned towards the stage exit. She called to him, "Shig, they're not going to cover for you forever."

He stopped, turning to face her. Slapping his briefcase, he boasted, "Mad, I'm on to a discovery that could revolutionize the way we treat radiation sickness. I could fuck every student in every university in this country, and they'll still give me the Nobel prize before I'm done."

She scoffed, "Jesus, you really haven't changed one iota. This hubris will lead you to ruin, Shigeru Nakamura."

Reeling to the blessed reprieve of a stage exit, he marched away with a laugh, "Hide and watch, Madeline Dukarn. Crow pie to go with crow's feet."

S***

Riding the train home, Shigeru stared at the mighty Mount Fuji, its upswept arcs of snow and ice reflecting the long rays of winter's evening sun. Deep in a mixed drink, he ruminated on his feisty young critic, noting the quickening in his chest and the flutter of warmth when he found a girl attractive.

Shaking his head, he pulled out his phone to check his e-mail and social media feeds. The girl's face appeared again and again to him, so he decided he might creep the school's pages to learn her name. Alcohol emboldened him, so he thought he'd try his usual tack: a conniving apology for his behavior.

But Mad's aging countenance also floated in his head. Could she be right? Private and state sponsors of his work wouldn't want to pay off another burgeoning scandal, and even he, darling and star in his field, wouldn't survive #MeToo. He didn't think of himself as an abuser. A tacky dog, at times, but not one of the evil ones.

Sex was his obsession, and his unnaturally slow aging ensured a wider range of conquests. Conquests, yes, they were.

Mad called him a misogynist. How could he hate something that never left his thoughts?

Earlier therapists had connected his female love/hate to the abandonment by his true parents. But why didn't he hate men? He certainly didn't want to fuck them.

Later therapists had called him a nymphomaniac, leaving him with seething resentment. Yes, he lost count of his lifetime sexual partners after five hundred. He'd tried every variation he could think of, but first world white girls perched at the top of his list.

Madeline reduced his escapades to a desire to punish American girls, a reversal of colonialism. But his desires were deeper, buried in some part of the brain untouched by the neocortex and its need to explain. No, the urge to plow, then ditch, possessed him.

Why? He thought the reason was plain. Carnality, pornography, vodka, all numbed a soul drowning in sea of autopsy reports and images depicting pure horror: babies born with no faces, children whose gangrenous limbs broke off, men and women robbed of their genitals, scalps baked to the bone, eye sockets fried shut. Jesus, no wonder he drank.

He closed his eyes, feeling shame for his compulsions. It wouldn't last long, thanks to the vodka. He seldom spent any commute time on business, knowing that prying eyes might try for academic espionage. But Mad's comments left him angry, humiliated, and, as usual, horny. The briefcase contained research not known even to his dimwit assistant. It never left his person, but a compulsion to dig into the particulars pressed him. Concentrating on his breathing, he tried to relax. In his mind, a woman appeared, delicately featured, porcelain-white skin, and shining gold hair. For him, appearance mattered. A physicist from Norway, she'd become an obsession for him. Her expertise could help him complete his top-secret project: a bang capable of rearranging the way people treat cancer. He chuckled at the irony—this woman played hard-to-get with him, the role he preferred. Who would postpone speaking to someone of his reputation? Instead of opening his case, he placed it aside, then drank his beverage.

Lifting his head as he saw the bartender making rounds about the car, he asked for a refill on his martini. The bartender was attractive, but his type was white, western. She winked at him as she returned with a freshened drink. She spoke English, surprising him. "You are Professor Nakamura?"

What the hell? He'd break his rule on speaking English to his own people. "I am. Do I know you? Why do you speak English to me?"

The bartender cracked a smile, answering, "Your American English accent is pretty much right on the money. I'd swear you grew up there and not here. But no, I don't know you."

He touched his glass, then slurred, "My work often requires English fluency— fluency upon which my parents insisted, in their unassailable prescience."

She withheld the drink in her hand a moment more, remarking, "That's lots of words."

He frowned at the drink she held, then asked, "Why did you bring that?"

Motioning with her head, she replied, "The American wishes to buy you a drink." He followed her gesture to see, much to his angry anticipation, the agitator from his seminar. Here, on his train? If he believed in Providence, he might thank It for this fortune.

He waved her over while the bartender hovered. "Is there—"

Fixed on the American, he blurted, "No, thank you."

The girl proved exquisite—ample where he believed women ought to be, with a silver dress, sheening, that captured each of her contours and curves. Her clear blue marble eyes met his with a clear voracity, and the importance of anything else in this train car vanished, replaced by transcendent beauty. He would triumph against this creature.

Motioning for her to sit, his heart skipped a beat. He'd slept with so many students and research assistants, they blended in his head. This one presented a new challenge for him: slay the American arrogance.

With the aim clear, he thought through de Angelo's recipes for seduction. He'd start with feigned indifference and inappropriate cruelty, making the bitch work for it. Social justice charlatans could deride the man all they want, his technique worked for Shigeru, at least in pubs and bars.

The girl stepped over to his table, eager yet confident in offering a hand. "Professor Nakamura, I'm Mary Simmons. We spoke—"

Remaining focused on his drink, he muttered, "More a spat than a discussion."

Frustrating his pecking order, this defiant sprite said, "You were accusing my country of genocide." She then pointed to the table, asking, "Aren't you going to ask me to sit?"

He waved her off, then growled, "You must ask to sit."

She glanced to the seat, then back to him with unease. "Umm, I'd like to sit with you."

His abdomen fluttered, a flood of erotic images filling his mind. To reel her in properly, he needed to further her discomfort. "Get the fuck away if you don't want to be polite."

She shifted from one foot to another, the heels of her stilettos no doubt augmenting the burden. Surprising him, she leaned forward, planting a quick kiss on his mouth, and he tasted the tropical drink she had toted with her to his table. Whispering, Mary asked, "Please, may I sit?"

He pulled his head away from hers in protest. "No, no, no, this is way too fast for me. Manners, first." He pointed to the empty seat across the table from himself.

Sheepish and demure, she lowered herself into the seat, the dress catching every jot of sunlight from the windows. "Thank you." She flashed a smile, positioning her drink before her. He opened his hand, motioning towards her body. "Why the fashion spectacle?" He laughed in sneering derision. "Did they open a whorehouse near campus for students?"

She reddened, just as he'd hoped, cutting a reply, "Since when can a girl not gussy herself up?" She pointed to the window, then traced a finger across the firmament. "There are always parties and fun times, if you know where to go."

He crossed his arms, answering, "Like I said, whorehouse."

Delight lilted through his drunken brain when she appeared offended, protesting, "I am not a prostitute, you dick."

He laughed, tightening his arms, "I've struck a nerve, haven't I?" He pointed a finger behind her, grousing, "Then, by all means, seat yourself alone. I'm sure somewhere on this train you can find a dolt sufficiently inebriated to entertain your little rosebud."

She shook her head, clearly dismayed by his brazenness. Rising from her chair, she spat, "Screw you, Professor Dick."

He laughed, sinking backward into his chair, recognizing the imminence of his objective. "That's the idea, girl."

She stopped, leaning a small bit in his direction, a smile emerging. "You're just playing with me, aren't you?"

God, she tickled him. Masking his emotion, he answered, "Slow down, girl. I'm sure you're down to fuck, but we're not even done with our drinks."

She dropped into her chair, frustrated, as he straddled attraction and revulsion. Sputtering, she rebuked him. "Why did you invite me to your table?"

He sipped his drink, the burn of alcohol stinging his tongue and throat. Why indeed? He snapped, "To ascertain whether you're worth the trouble. You showed your big mouth at my seminar. I wanted to know what else it could do." He glanced from her outraged expression to the marquee bearing the names of stops to follow, noting his was the next. Nodding for it, he remarked, "I'm off here. I don't think you have any interest in continuing this conversation."

She answered quickly, "No, wait. I do want to come with you."

The conductor announced over the speaker system, "Shinjuku stop next. Shinjuku."

Triumph! Tonight, he'd tap this slut. "I don't know that you're attractive enough for me, so"—he paused, eyeing her—"let's call this a probational fuck." He shot up, not waiting for her to collect her purse. Leaving the girl far behind bolstered his appeal, at least for the right kind of slut. Plodding into the misty mire outside, he held his back to her.

She clicked her heels into the concrete walkway alongside the train car, yelping, "Wait up, sir!"

He reached a row of turnstiles, then swayed with as much indifference as his pickled brain could muster. He pointed to a darkened lot across the street. "I'm parked there."

As they plodded for his black sedan, she motioned to the passenger door, staggering a bit, smirking, "You wanna be a gentleman, open my door?"

He huffed, knowing that giving her nothing she wanted would court desperation on her part. "Open your own goddamned door. America doesn't ask, it just goes for it." While she shook her head and wiped the budding moisture from her face in dismay, he unlocked his door with a finger touch, refraining from pressing a second time to unlock her door. He pulled his door open, placed his briefcase between the seats, then settled himself into the vehicle. Oh, how he suppressed his laughter at the young girl's growing predicament.

He pulled his safety belt over his chest as he started the engine, aware of her as she tapped the passenger window. "Professor Dick, open the door." He chuckled at her cutesy fury, at last hitting the unlock button. She tore it open, plopped next to him, and slammed the door. Running her fingers through her shimmering hair, she complained, "Look, that was unnecessary. Now I'm wet."

He laughed, answering, "Yes, I have that effect on women." She grabbed his face, forcing hers on it, kissing him with some force.

He liked this girl, and he admired her fierce temper. Yes, he could make use of her, though in his own time. He pushed her away, brushing his hand against her lips. "Slow down, America."

She grazed his leg and his groin with her acrylic nails, and he, or rather his body, felt obliged to respond as nature dictates—it was betrayal, so he wrested, then wrenched her hand from the delicate region. She responded with greater strength than he expected, her hand almost a magnet, the attractive force undeniable. The girl pleaded, "You know you want it, Professor."

She slammed her fist down on the briefcase resting between them, releasing the latches. The case broke open, papers spilling. He snapped, "Goddamnit, clumsy bitch!"

A printed article dropped to the damp floorboard, showing a blond woman behind a carved wooden dais. The girl clawed for the article, mocking him, "Call me a bitch? Oh, is this your steady squeeze?"

He pinched the pages from her, tearing the foremost across the blond's face. "Fuck, leave it." The woman in the photograph reminded him that a world existed beyond his private conquest.

She read the title, laughing. "Quantum Mechanics Guardian Angel" Olga Kunskapsen Discusses Prediction and Random Numbers?" She released the papers, snorting. "You're so anti-American, but you go for the blonds? And an angel, at that?"

He folded the article, stashing it in the opened case. "For the last time, girl, I am not anti-American. I'm not American in the first place." Trailing off, he pointed to the window, resoluteness forming in his gut. "You know what? Get the fuck out of my car."

She glanced out the passenger-side window, heavier rain drops now rapping the sedan's roof. With a face full of contrition, the girl pleaded, "Let's just have a good time. Please?"

He watched her, disgusted, delighted, appalled, attracted. Exhaling in affect, he said, "Very well. Let's see if you're as good a fuck as you think you are." He crammed the magazine back into his briefcase, keeping an eye on the physicist's image as it disappeared. She would have to wait, the student before him ripe for the picking.

This had played out so many times he'd lost count. Her earlier insubordination granted him, at least from his perspective, dibs on bedroom punishment. He'd see to it she had her fill, after which he'd hurl the dirty slut from his condo, disrobed and humiliated.

7. Seventh Vesik: The Noble Physicist

*O****

Olga Kunskapsen stared at the ring of incandescent bulbs wreathing the makeup mirror. She counted thirty-two, fixing her attention on subsets of them while discarding the others, imagining shape after shape. She set aside a pad of paper filled with her notes.

A cowlick along the crown of her golden hair resisted her, so she confessed, "There is nothing to be done." Her younger sister Janna sat beside her at the dresser mirror, grabbing the brush from her. Olga huffed. "Why does appearance matter so much?"

Janna pulled at her older sister's hair with a rebuke, remarking, "It's irrational, but it's reality."

Olga winced at the pain, muttering, "Media and news crave spray-painted mannequins." Scanning the reflection before her, she felt the smell of burned rubber soak into her sinuses. She shook her head, hoping it would clear.

Janna laughed, answering, "You cannot say that your academic conferences somehow are beyond jawlines and curves."

Olga sighed, but her sister spoke the truth. In her research, she knew the pretty ones ascended fast. The two strikes rule, Janna had called it: any two of ugly, stupid, and rude would sink you, with the first being the worst offender of all. It wasn't the way the human race was put together, but it was the way one moved forward in the corporate and even the research communities.

Merit-based success could be an illusion, one she'd prefer to ignore. Her research was novel—valuable, in fact—but without performing song and dance for the unaccountable comptrollers of high-level research, she may as well burn her papers in effigy. Janna had always been the prettier one, and it was fortunate Olga had her to play beauty consultant. "An interview on a science book, and I have to be concerned about my hair?"

Janna didn't smile, reminding her, "Sis, remember, women have to worry ten times more about their appearance than men."

Her sister was right; peacock men could strut, whether they had any beauty to share or not. Olga quoted, "*Is there in truth...*"

Her little sister laughed. "*No beauty?*" Pulling Olga's hair, she answered, "You're always saying that you can find the beauty in truth if you're willing to search." She pointed to the mirror. "It wouldn't kill you to smile."

Olga looked at herself, frowning in the mirror. It did age her when she frowned. Resting bitch face, her sister called it. So, she gave a cheesy grin, asking, "Good enough? Is this how you pick up the guys?"

Janna pulled her hair hard at that, causing Olga to yelp. "Ouch! Dammit, be careful!"

Her sister laughed again. "I look pretty to find handsome guys, yes. You have to look pretty to convince other people to listen to your ideas. Is it different?" Janna covered Olga's eyes with one hand, dousing her in hairspray with the other. Olga coughed as the sweet chemical burned her nostrils. Taming Olga's cowlick, her sister the hair-whisperer told her, "You can't get hair to behave just by adding force. Didn't your physics education teach you anything?"

Olga adored her sister's astuteness and wisdom. Cracking wise remained a favorite pastime in family reunions, so she returned fire in equal measure. "I was learning physics when you were playing with dolls. And I work only on the smaller than small. Forces do strange things on the—"

Janna interrupted her, offering little patience for her elder sister. "On the quantum level. Yes, yes, yes." She finished brushing, then directed Olga to inspect her efforts. She stiffened a little, then asked, "Sister, what does it mean, a Doctor Norcross?"

Olga's eyes found her notepad, the name written eight times in succession. She frowned, replying, "Nothing. Just nothing." She flipped the pad over.

Janna rebuked her. "You understand sabbatical, do you not?"

Olga shrugged, "I'll stop working when I'm dead."

Her sister pulled at her golden hair, admitting, "You hold still or you may get your wish."

She knew Janna wouldn't believe her. Even if she did, it was more likely a symptom of the disease destroying Olga's brain. So she changed the subject with a gesture towards her own reflection, quipping, "I think it is some improvement." She pointed at herself in the mirror. Golden waves crowning a white-skinned figure donning, per Janna's insistence, a pink polyester suit showcasing her figure. Yes, she thought the figure genuinely attractive, even if she were closer to fifty than forty. The thought chilled her, a certain knowledge of her physical and mental decline.

Janna curled her arm about Olga's shoulders, squeezing her tightly. "Go knock them dead, sister."

Knock Olga dead, instead. She had traipsed around Europe to promote her new book, a work she hoped would inspire others to join her field of research, and so far, she'd met with confused anchors and hosts.

She breathed with care, understanding the importance of respiratory technique and relaxation of the mind, though it remained easy to forget. Her mind had not been the same since contracting a respiratory infection a year earlier. Her casework had been light, but the lingering cognitive difficulties pained her as a scientist, and as a human being.

At least, that was what she told Janna. Her sister had helped her a great deal of late, and she'd permitted herself a sabbatical from teaching and research, at Janna's insistence. Nonetheless, her recent professional discoveries had shaken many worlds. Editors and reporters from popular journals craved opportunities to probe her them, even if hoping to sensationalize the conclusions.

Would this be the same? She'd discover soon.

A knock at the door led Janna to open it, revealing the meek liaison this pulp rag had hired to handle the guests. "Professor Kunskapsen, we're ready for you."

Olga nodded, then turned to the mirror for one last look. Janna pulled her to her feet, cheering, "You got this, sis. You'll do fine."

She moved towards the door, Janna following. The liaison wore a small headset, reminding Olga of how fast the world seemed to be changing—or technology seemed to be shrinking, or both.

But for her career choices, one might think her a Luddite. She'd never used social media, nor had she ever considered the internet to be more than a communications-and-research grid. For her, it had become a means of easy recall in the face of her secret-but-steady cognitive decline. Even Janna was unaware of her health misfortune, and she intended to keep it that way. Were it not for the circumstances, she'd never consider speaking to popular journals about her work. But these appearances supplied Janna some enjoyment, and she needed to see her sister happy. Goodness, how so much could cross a mind in just a few seconds amazed her.

The liaison—Suzie, was it?—extended a hand while whispering into the earpiece, as though conversing along two or more threads were natural. Olga looked to her sister, who was watching from the seats reserved for spectators during a live show. The immensity of her discoveries ensured some deference, so they agreed to her request to film the discussion offline and without a live audience. Given the severity of her decline, she wanted to avail herself the editing room for patching together the meaningful bits with as few gaffes as possible.

The rag's hostess Angelique seated herself before Olga, offering the pitcher of water with an open hand.

Accepting the host's offer, she studied the youthful face. Were she more into social media, she might recognize the young millennial seated before her. Alas, she seldom bobbed a head away from her books to observe popular culture. Janna had promised, however, that this internet show could reach the major networks from time to time.

The hostess reached for Olga's face to rub beneath her lips. She recoiled, stunned at the impropriety, and Janna rushed over to wipe her sister's mouth. She laughed, "Oh, sister, you have a little lipstick smear."

Olga frowned, miffed at the snafu. "This is why I do not care for makeup."

The hostess remarked, "You look rather lovely with or without it." She winked at her assistant nearby, then leaned toward Olga, whispering, "Not everyone has your features."

Silly woman. Then again, her medium demanded obsession over appearance. Olga tolerated her sister rubbing along her face. Her mother had done the same thing, dabbing her finger on her own tongue for moisture before erasing recalcitrant foodstuffs from her children's faces. Janna's time as a mother had wrought the same behavior, though Olga still felt reviled by it.

She looked at the square tiles along the floor, relaxing her brain by imagining various two-dimensional curves along the grid, each with vivid colored images superimposed over it. A capability since childhood, she leaned into it whenever she struggled with emotion. Janna held her face tight, then offered a bright smile and said, "You're good to go."

Olga gave a reluctant nod, then faced the hostess. Cued, Angelique turned her eyes to a camera ahead of the stage. "Angelique Jerst reporting from *Veiviseren Vitenskap*. Today, it is my great pleasure to introduce Professor Olga Kunskapsen of the Norwegian University of Science and Technology, Department of Quantum Physics, to discuss her latest discoveries and her book, *The Giant World of the Little*." Turning to Olga, she opened a hand, her bracelets jingling.

Olga could parse the social graces, though it still required work to follow them. Her mother had identified her as suffering from a mild case of Asperger's syndrome, meaning she would find human behavior more perplexing than most. Neurodivergent, the more recent generations called it, and there remained debate as to whether it was a defect or natural difference. She didn't care for the debate in a world that celebrated antisocial impulses like jockeying and manipulating. If that set her apart from others, she would accept the conceit. She knew the same held true in the world of social and television media, so she preferred to play to her own strengths.

But, because of her sister's endless attempts to "Get her out there," she would try. Seeing Janna smile was important to her. Media circuits for her book had proved one means of "Getting out there."

Snapping herself into the present, she smiled, meeting Angelique's green eyes. "Thank you, Miss Jerst."

Angelique laughed, touching Olga's arm. "Call me Angie!" Olga disliked being touched, but she dwelt on it for only a moment before scrawling a smile across her own face.

"Okay, Angie." This venue might as well have been in a foreign language. She wasn't sure whether her face begged for a rescue, but the hostess retook the floor without missing a beat.

Angie grinned an expression reminding Olga of cat pictures she'd seen online in animal clickbait. It made sense to her why this young woman would find popularity in cyberspace. She then announced, "Today, Professor Kunskapsen will share insights from her work and new book aimed at we"—she gestured air quotes—"the little people."

Olga snapped in reply, "We are all"—she added her own air quotes—"little people. It would be irresponsible to claim certainty when more knowledge makes one feel more ignorant, at times."

Angie rapped her knuckles on the hard cover of the book, then leaned towards Olga. "The conclusion of your book says you're planning something revolutionary with time crystals. Do you know where to mine them, and whether they make good earrings? Any chance you'll share that here with these"—she led with air quotes—"new results?"

Olga knew, as did her publisher and closest colleagues, that she shouldn't risk her work with a premature reveal, but they'd counseled her to hook readers and investors with hints. "Time crystals aren't precious gems in the literal sense. We'll go only as far as my book here, Angie."

Angie tapped the book, asking, "So, why did you spin a yarn aimed at the general public? Fiction reaches more people, though it would be madness coming from you."

Olga had many variations of answers for that question, having fielded it a few times already. But the gist was the same. She said, "That could be true. But the general public needs outreach. We can't spend our world's time and resources on scientific pursuits opaque to and disconnected from everyone else."

Looking back from the camera, she nodded to Olga, asking, "That's dope. What is this golden thing on the cover?"

Olga tasted the water poured for her, then said, "You see before you a visualization of the quantum wave."

Angelique laughed. "It looks like a melting rose, only not the right color."

This left Olga confused, but she attempted to right the discussion. "Well, it is aimed to depict the wave without artificial cosmetics applied."

Her host shook her head. "You mean like showing us without makeup? My viewers need no more reasons to tune us out, Professor!"

Olga found herself glancing to Janna, pained. Her sister gestured hand-over-hand that she should continue, so she said, "Well, I wrote the bulk of the book during a lull in my professional work a few years ago." Angelique had done her homework, asking, "When you contracted pneumonia?" Olga was a little stunned, giving her the chance to needle further. "How was it for you?"

Olga sighed, "It is personal, and I'd prefer to leave it that way."

Burning rubber struck her once more, coinciding with moments of anger. She glanced to the table between them, hoping the spell would pass.

Angelique settled into her seat, a little satisfied.

Angelique smirked, her audacity further miffing the tired professor. "I'm sure my viewers very much want to know what you are selling."

Olga closed her eyes, counting numbers—this time, perfect cubes. She felt relief when Janna broke her silence for the first time since the interview recording had commenced, shouting, "Would you just let her tell you what it's about?"

The hostess cast her head back, laughing, "Miss Kunskapsen, this venue needs sensation." She pointed to Olga, nodding. "We're already recording offline, per your request, something we don't offer."

Olga cocked her head, reviled. Maybe a weep or a strip-tease might entertain her? Instead, she just spoke, unimpeded at last, "Quantum physics explains strange things we see on the tiniest scales. Newton discovered numerics for gravity, planetary orbits, and phenomena at the macroscopic level. Einstein analyzed the astonishing tradeoff between space and time when velocities approach that of light, a scale telescopic, if you will. The quantum physicist studies the fascinating world of the micro/nano/picoscopic—a world in which objects exist only probabilistically, flitting here, there, anywhere."

Strange, it seemed, that Angelique now didn't interrupt. Instead, the hostess listened as though a child. Olga continued, "It is a world where two particles can be separated by half the universe, and yet if they are entangled, one tells the other, and vice versa." She smiled as best she could, though her enthusiasm could, on occasion, puncture the shield of no affect. "Instantaneous transfer of information, breaking the cosmic speed limit."

The hostess tapped her glass with exaggerated intrigue, asking, "So, you mean to say I could call my agent, even if I were on the moon, and there would be no lag?"

Olga cheered Angelique's apparent awareness, clasping her hands together as she answered, "Precisely. Right now, NASA and the European Space Agency grapple with mission control when body occlusion and distance lag might mean the difference in preventing a crash of a satellite, for instance."

Angelique set her glass onto the table before her, asking, "Body occlusion? That sounds like a problem we might have when trying to film something."

Olga nodded, forgiving as best she could her interviewer's ignorance. "Occlusion as in the body blocks the line of sight, causing a disconnect of the control signal."

The hostess nodded in understanding, and Olga decided she'd proceed before another damned interruption. "In any case, this entanglement, as I mentioned, transcends space. It appears the entanglement may also transcend time, a topic my book discusses, along with popular metaphors, fit for mass consumption, on other quantum quirks."

Angie was delighted, asking, "You mentioned them before. I still want to see whether they glitter."

Olga actually laughed at that, answering, "No, they aren't crystals in the conventional sense. They retain order and energy through time, despite movement in ways we still don't understand. It could mean communication across time."

Angelique touched the copy of Olga's book, then asked, "So, if I entangle a particle in one of these crystal things, I can use a time machine?"

Olga deemed the term crude, but she bore it to continue the discussion. "Well, for information, perhaps." Angelique stirred, so she added, "Time and space may very well be the same thing. Both are dimensions within the larger universal framework. Particles exist both in space and time." She gestured to the copy of her book sitting between them, adding, "These are not trivial things to understand, even if the implications sometimes can be. I spend a good deal of the book explaining quantum mechanics to popular audiences, without the sensationalized fictions one sees coming out of production studios everywhere. I want readers to yearn for greater understanding."

Angelique slid her fingers over the book's spine, not taking her eyes from it. "You don't want to mislead, and I get that. I read that you believe computers do weird things before a disaster. Is that the same thing?"

Olga cast her eyes askew, wondering whether Angelique had, indeed, read the book after all. She answered after pausing only a moment. "Before the September eleventh attacks in 2001, it was claimed random number generators in place throughout infrastructure seemed to move away from their uniform design."

She noted quizzical faces, and for a moment, she could imagine still being in a classroom. "Though independent scientists reviewed the evidence, concluding that the fluctuations could be expected, the technique of prediction using qubits, or quantum bits, is sound. It is my belief, though I'm not representative of a majority of my scientific peers, that quantum entanglement can provide a means of mitigating disasters, and that such a technology is feasible."

Angelique jumped after a bit of a pause, demanding, "You mean with more expensive supercolliders? Permit me to gauge your reaction on a quote from Picoveer's CEO Carlyle Demmings—"

Olga stiffened at the name. "I thought we were here to discuss science."

This delighted Angelique, so she shoved forward. "He is your former classmate, is he not? Anyway, he says, 'Dumping public cash into sinkholes underestimates the true profitability of science. Colliders, exorbitant labs, and lucrative book deals for an incestuous troupe of scientific elites squander the awesome optimization of markets.'"

Olga shot back at her. "Demmings would know, considering his opulent pedigree. He is an opportunist, a grandstander, and a playboy. Like others, he manufactures headlines to maintain relevant in the twenty-four hour news cycle."

Angelique narrowed her eyes as though she heard Olga, but it was a ruse. "Don't we all wish to remain relevant?"

Olga clicked her tongue. "Relevance applies to ideas, not to personalities. We can discuss science according to experts, not dimwits calling themselves *luminaries*."

Angelique smiled, sated with Olga's strong-arm. "Continue, Professor."

Olga shook her head quickly. "The form of entanglement may be unclear in some respects. It is possible, as I speculate in my book, that nontrivial extrasensory perception is evidence of such technology, emergent in our own biology."

The hostess would have none of it, complaining, "You mean to say that you believe people can tell the future?"

Olga frowned, then felt her face return to neutral as she repeated, "Speculation. In any case, we know there is predictive power in the human brain. Radin of the Noetic Institute has demonstrated it, and it's been replicated elsewhere."

Angelique replied, "So, you're not alone in believing that?"

Olga folded her arms, nodding. "I'm saying there's a great deal we don't understand, and my speculation is just that." She pointed at the book resting on the table, continuing, "But if the human brain somehow can identify particles entangled across time, it could explain part of the mechanism underlying what we've observed."

Angelique laughed, though whether in derision or confusion, Olga couldn't decide. She answered, "But if we can tell the future this way, why wouldn't we help ourselves out of the enormous mess we're in as a world now? I mean, why couldn't I have known my ex-husband was an asshole earlier on?"

Olga watched Angelique, then asked, "Did you know he was an asshole before you married him?"

She darted an answer. "Well, yes, but—"

"Then you wouldn't need quantum mechanics to make a good decision." She stared into Angelique's scandalized expression. Olga continued, knowing now that at least the hostess could follow the hypothesis to a logical conclusion. "Perhaps we're living the best we can, and anything more is a step too far. Perhaps the more distant the future, the harder it is to consider. There's good psychological evidence of this."

Angelique was engrossed, leaning forward. "You mean we bury our heads in the sand like the ostriches we are."

Olga reached for her book, open-handed, adding, "My book is aimed at drawing more people into the beauty and majesty of the unknown. Science furnishes a light if we're willing to see it. That light, if my guesses are correct, might also shed itself upon both the future and the past."

The hostess smiled and beckoned to her assistant Suzie. "Well, that's all we need to put together something. Olga Kunskapsen, world-renowned quantum physicist, tells us how to tell the future and why the rest of us are ignorant wretches in her new book *The Giant World of the Little*. One last chance to share what's next? Don't be stingy, Professor."

Olga couldn't smile. "Good to be with you."

Anything else might have been the truth.

*O****

The car ride home proved caustic. Janna could be protective past a fault. She groused, "She's an attention hog and a bitch. I'm sorry."

The older sister held her cool, replying, "It was fine. She wouldn't have understood anything short of fireworks."

Janna refused to surrender just yet. "It's my fault. I wanted you to go on. I thought it would be good for you." She slapped the steering wheel.

Olga looked outside her window, watching the first snow flurries descend. "Truly, Sister, it is fine. I'd rather just go home. A hot bath and some decent tea will work wonders."

Her sister sighed, letting Olga know that she soon would drop the entire affair. She said, "There were two calls for you earlier today. One was from a Doctor Michal's office, another from the university."

"What did they say?" Olga asked.

"The doctor just needed a call back on lab results. I don't recognize the name Michal, so who is he? Your assistant Ingrid said to tell you she'd found a lead on NCL."

Olga jumped at the letters. "Did she say more?"

Janna shrugged, "Just that she'd found something out. Who is this Doctor Michal?"

The car's interior swayed as Olga sick. Unable to feign patience, she shouted, "Please, Janna. This is important. What about NCL?"

Her sister looked at Olga with dismay at her outburst, then darted her eyes back to the road. "Look, sister, I don't know what that even is. Ingrid said you can call her. But this doctor—are you still sick from the pneumonia?"

Olga exhaled hard in exhaustion, the foul odor of burnt tires causing her to vomit onto her legs and the dashboard. "I am sorry," she whispered as she coughed. Trying to speak, she froze. Her left eye dimmed in an instant, the world spinning. Her consciousness bubbled from her, punctuated with regret and remorse. Janna deserved to hear the truth from her. Darkness swallowed her, and that was that.

8. Physics and Physician

*O****

Swirling around her was a tumult of color, scattering fractals, a fantasia more heavenly and alien than any she'd heard or seen.

If she were, in fact, a her. She could not remember who she was, but the unease dissipated almost as soon as it manifested. Where, when, and why tended to be means of coping with the bothersome peculiarities of the world, yet she sensed no trouble here.

Perhaps she was dead? It would be a relief in remembrance of the suffering awaiting her as her peerless brain betrayed her, falling to genetic damage and drift.

She must still live, for she believed no afterlife followed, any more than a beforelife preceded. No dream she'd had before resembled this one. The spectacle of light and sound caused no alarm, though she was concerned a little about knowing, well, so little.

The one name sounded—a name she believed she'd heard both always and never, extremes her finite mind could not bear. *"Arkiyan Norcross."* Spoken words suggested a voice, yet she could not determine gender, age, or any other empirical measure to ground the utterance.

What was wrong with her that she could not wake? She recalled her philosophical studies. *Existence is empirical, unproven to utter certainty.* Was she real? Had she ever been?

The colors coalesced into a shape. A form. Resplendent, extraordinary. She could imagine no more beautiful angel. He was beautiful, with wavy hair of onyx sheen, green eyes, and olive skin. If she were to confess a type, he'd fit the bill. But something was wrong. Where there was one, now two stood before her. Similar, yet different, two of a type. The colors bled together, as though one doused a painting with thinner. She hungered for him, for them—by no base or, at least by her assessment, untoward impulse, but instead, a thirst for the completeness to follow. He represented her need to know all things. It was an entreaty, a calling. This man would help her find what she sought: knowledge. Words grazed her, imploring she answer her part of the calling. She was not alone in this calling, but no other face was clear to her, save the raven-haired man.

Her sister often told her she'd regret living alone. Sister! Where was her sister? Her sister's name? Jesus, this proved too confusing.

Sketches of the life she believed must be hers formed before her. Yes, she had a sister, though she knew her not to be her own.

Connection. The six before her?

Christ, this reminded her of the time her sister had offered her psychedelics. Why would confusion interest people?

And, at last, consciousness seemed to manifest once more.

*O****

Irksome beeps and noises surrounded her. The lights proved hard on her eyes, but as she opened them, she could see her sister Janna sitting in a nearby armchair, reading her e-book.

With parched lips, she attempted to squeeze out a word or two, then noted the intubation obstructing her. Without speech, she'd try something different.

As she told her right hand to move, it became clear that no strength of impulse could stir it. Dear God, could the tumor have already damaged her motor cortex?

With relief, she stretched her left hand and felt her impulses moving where they ought to go. And yet her left arm remained tethered with medical torture devices she'd expect to see in intensive care. She heaved her arm in Janna's direction, severing one of the myriad wires connected to monitor her vitals. A feverish alarm grabbed her sister's attention from the screen where she read.

Janna jumped to her feet, coming to Olga's side. "Sister! You're awake!" She held a hand up to Olga, signaling she should wait, then disappeared through the large wooden door behind her. "Nurse, my sister is awake!"

She returned to take Olga's hand. Pleading with tears, she said, "Oh, sister, why didn't you tell me you were so sick?" Olga laughed a little, though the tube irritated her throat.

Two nurses and what appeared to be a doctor entered, and the doctor approached her with the light they so enjoyed flashing into patients' eyes. "Miss Kunskapsen, I am Doctor Erickson. Can you understand me?"

Olga nodded. Did he believe she was a simpleton? She couldn't see his mouth through the precautionary mask, so maybe he was smiling. It didn't matter, for she would do no smiling.

"Can you follow the light with your eyes?" He watched, at last satisfied with the results. Sitting back on the bed where she lay, he nodded.

He turned to Janna, then back to Olga while the nurses reconnected the wayward sensor to her left arm. "You had not told your next of kin about your condition, so it took some time to determine your condition. And it doesn't explain everything." His eyes met hers as he prepared to deliver what she knew must be the worst news. "You suffered a seizure, and what I suspect is a stroke."

He paused, then asked, "Do you understand what I've told you?"

Olga watched her sister cry, yet she couldn't muster a tear. Her emotional responses had always been blunted, leading their parents to believe she was suffering.

Returning to the present, she nodded to the doctor. She needed no bracing for the inevitability of death and disease. The universe proved to be as cruel as it was majestic, as cold as it was enticing. She was wise beyond her years, her father would say. Others believed her to be a hardened woman, but to her, knowledge was the end for all means.

Janna asked, "What doesn't it explain? Why is this happening?"

"Her autonomic functions shouldn't be affected, yet she isn't breathing on her own. Something else is happening in her brain stem, but I can't determine it without a scan. I've never seen a case like this." He touched Janna's shoulder as she heaved.

She then snapped, "Then do it. Please, just fix her."

The physician drew a deep breath, adjusted his mask, and offered, "We should discuss likely outcomes, Miss. That is, even if we determine the cause, we won't be able to reverse it. The inoperability of the tumor will only worsen the symptoms."

"Jesus, this cannot be happening," she replied. "I don't understand—she was just fine!"

He turned to Janna, then faced Olga again, his white eyebrows at least offering her a refuge outside the coldness of his gray-blue eyes. "We can take steps to make you as comfortable as possible."

"Oh, God," Janna uttered.

The doctor glanced at a chart as one of the two nurses handed it to him. "Your order is DNR, with palliative care options specified." Returning the chart to the nearby nurse, he added, "We'll establish a morphine drip, and, certainly, anything you wish to see or hear, we can make possible." He touched her right hand, and though she believed she could feel his warm touch, she could not respond. Erickson rose, then motioned for Janna to join him outside.

Olga squeezed her eyes shut, frustrated that her work could no longer continue. When diagnosed with the tumor, she felt she'd made peace with the finality of it, the return to darkness when the physical body could no longer function.

But while her floundering mind wandered, she struggled to see the man once more. It was strange—her death would leave Janna and her children without the most stable thing in their lives, but all of Olga's remorse landed at the failure to locate the man called Norcross. Doctor Michal said she had more time than this.

Janna returned as one of the lingering nurses fussed about Olga, poking and prodding, moving her about. She couldn't protest, even if she'd desired to. "Olga," her baby sister said with a greater emotional calm than earlier, "the doctor says we'll make you comfy. He'll return shortly to remove the intubation." Stoicism proved trying for her sister, though Olga appreciated it. Janna touched the device connecting her to the respirator, looking to the nurse.

The nurse shook her head, pointing to the heavy door of the room. "Doctor Erickson must do it. I'm so sorry." Not as sorry as Olga.

The doctor reappeared with the other nurse, reaching at her face. "Miss Kunskapsen."

Janna spoke, "Professor Kunskapsen, not Miss."

He nodded to her with compassion in his eyes, answering, "Apologies, Professor. This will be a little uncomfortable as I remove it." Olga nodded as best she could. He unwrapped tape from the mouthpiece, then tugged the tube from her. Her throat burned from the friction, but she was happy to be rid of it. The doctor handed the device to his assistant nurse, then asked, "Perhaps you'd like some water?"

Olga finally spoke aloud, though she wasn't sure what her ailing brain could produce. "Yes, yes, yes," she said, realizing whatever other words she'd intended would not materialize. Christ on His ever-loving Throne, could she no longer speak?

Janna rushed to her other side, grabbing her left hand. "Sister, you only need to answer yes or no. Don't try to talk too much."

The doctor gave her a sip, the chilled liquid salving her inflamed throat. She smiled with gratitude, though what she could draw along her face remained, happily, a mystery to her.

Pain stabbed in her head. Strange, she had not noticed it until now. The doctor tapped her arm, then pointed to the intravenous fluid bag next to her bed. "We'll be giving you some morphine straight away for the pain."

The nurse twisted a knob on the drip, and Olga felt as though she had been bathed in warm water. Her cares diminished, replaced by...could it be? Joy?

Death wouldn't be difficult for her, but her sister would be alone, with no husband, her parents dead, and left to raise her children alone. Janna had insisted that Olga could be a good influence on her nieces and nephew, though Olga wondered whether her lack of instinct suited her for anything more than the lifestyle of the ascetic scholarly monk. It was moot now, considering the sudden advancement of her terminal condition.

But what of the vision? The morphine cocktail encouraged her to ponder it and the exquisite beauty of both this angel and the light show about him.

Ingrid! Yes, her research assistant had recovered some evidence of such a person. But without her speech, how could she begin to ask?

Maybe it no longer mattered, for there could be no more mysteries for her. As if taunting her, her phone buzzed from the side table to her left. She motioned for it, so Janna, with some reluctance, plucked it from the table. "Sister, do you really want me to answer?" Curious as ever, even in her final days of life, she nodded.

Janna summoned a shaky greeting. "Hello?" There was a pause, then, "Yes, this is Olga Kunskapsen's private line, but she cannot answer at the moment. Can I, umm, take a message?"

What an amusing predicament! She may never be capable of communicating again, but the morphine left her carefree.

Her sister looked to Olga, then away, saying, "I'm sorry if this is an emergency. She's not available. No, I do not know when she'll be able to speak to you." Her eyes full of uneasy pity, she looked to Olga. "Do you know a Doctor Nakamura in Hiroshima?"

Olga's heart sank, knowing that Norcross and Nakamura were not the same name. She shook her head in the negative. Frustration replaced joy. But she felt herself heave with a laugh. Good God, this was great stuff!

Janna spoke into the phone, "I'll just have to take a message." She grabbed a pen and paper pad sitting near Olga's purse, then wrote a few words. "Yes, I'll tell her. No, I'm not her secretary, I'm her sister." She paused, then continued, "What? Am I on social media?" She tossed the notepad onto the table, grousing, "Why the hell does that matter? No, don't look me up. I don't care. Look, I'll tell her you called. Goodbye."

Replacing the phone on the table, she shook her head. "That was very strange. I've never been propositioned by a total stranger on a phone call."

Olga laughed, thinking of how Janna's extroversion must've sometimes been a curse she was happy to avoid. She wanted to tell her so, but only a laugh popped from her mouth. Janna would probably always receive propositions. Truth be told, she liked the attention, and Olga was happy to see her get it.

Janna settled into the chair next to Olga's bed, then held her hand. "I don't know what the hell that was about. He was insistent on talking to you. Something about radiation and your paper?"

Those words were enough. Olga squeezed her sister's hand so tightly that Janna yelped.

Janna's eyes widened as she responded, "You can't speak to him, Sister. I don't know whether you ever can talk to him."

Dammit. Maybe she could write? She pointed to the pad and pen, and Janna brought them to her. She had been a lefty early in school, though the headmaster at her academy had demanded all students write with their right hands. She'd maintained her left writing on the down-low, and now, this was her best hope.

Scrawling, she wrote, "FIND OUT TYME KRISTOL." The spelling was wrong, even to her, but she couldn't quite recall the right arrangement of letters. She giggled with her sister at the spelling.

Janna touched the paper, then looked into her sister's eyes. "Olga, you don't need to keep working." She motioned around the room at the many medical monitors about them, weeping somewhat. "I don't think you could, even if you wanted to do so."

The universe had cracked the door only a bit, and now, Olga struggled to stay awake and vigilant. Maybe Norcross was a hallucination, but her work on time crystals was paramount. She fussed, and Janna called a nurse to increase the rate of infusion.

At that, the sensory bizarreries accompanying the death sentence abated. Touching Janna's hand, Olga rested her head as warmth covered her. Thank the universe for morphine.

And soon, she would no longer require the universe. Had it ever required her?

What a funny thought.

S***

Shigeru was pissed at the woman he'd reached. Her voice caused him an erection, so he'd thought he'd try to make a connection. After all, it was a wicked waste to pass interactions, professional or private, without some tacit stab at seduction. But the call had to be professional.

Placing the phone on his desk, he sighed, angry. Why would this woman refuse to connect him with Doctor Kunskapsen? His discovery meshed with her own research, and, no matter her prestige, she should have been interested in associating herself with someone of his academic reputation.

But a stirring from behind captured his attention. Delicate hands touched his shoulders, and he shrank from them. "You're still here, Miss America?" he derided.

The girl pressed her hands into his shoulders, giggling. "Are you going to throw me out? Is that how it is?"

He shook free of her, repelled. "Absolutely. I need to work."

She settled behind him, placing her hands at her sides. "So, that's how it is? Pump, then dump?"

He refused to look at her. A girl clinging to him caused his guts to wrench. Opening a file folder, he shook his head, sighing. "Yes, or no, or whatever you choose to believe. But I must work, and we're done."

She laughed, reaching over his shoulders to place her hands on his toned chest. "Aww, all work and no play makes Shiggie a dull boy?"

He pushed her hands from him. "I said, get the fuck out of here." He poured a whiskey, downing a shot at once.

She grabbed his chair, swiveling him about to face her. "You can't tell me you want me to go." She smiled, breasts and vagina on display. "You can bomb this America again."

He found himself snarling, for no amount of alcohol could restore an attraction once he'd had his fill. "Why would I want another slice of this fatty white loaf of bread?"

Her eyes narrowed, and she slapped him harder than he would've thought possible. "You're a bastard, Nakamura! Ass to mouth for you, and then criticize my figure? Dude, you're a dick."

The whiskey did dampen the pain, but he captured her hand the second time she aimed for his face. She attempted to wrench her wrist free, and he clamped down hard, repeating himself, "I told you, GET THE FUCK OUT OF MY HOUSE!" He shoved her back to the door of his office.

She swung for him once more, missing him, and he grabbed her by red curls, dragging her to the entrance of his apartment. Tearing the door open, he hurtled her into the night, slamming the door and then bolting the latch hard. By now weeping, she screeched, "What about my things, you asshole?!"

He scrambled into the apartment, searching for her clothes. The trail of articles they'd left on their passionate path to his bed took a little work on his part, but he plucked each piece of clothing. Grasping for her purse, he lost his hold, the infernal thing flipping open onto the floor. Several small objects clattered around and below the nightstand, prompting him to groan, "Jesus Christ." He collected each object— many recognizable makeup items, some unknown trinkets, and, with some importance, the girl's telephone, and as he scooped the crap with her purse, he recognized that he could not recall her name, despite Mad making such a big to-do of the seminar.

Who cared? He needed more whiskey, but his mission to gather her junk intensified as she started beating on the door. With the items all in hand at last, he could unfasten the lock, crack the door, and push her clothing and purse upon her. She dropped most of it, but he shut the door to spare himself her indignity, as much as he thought he might enjoy seeing it. Alas, knowing she would feel like the trash he knew her to be would have to suffice.

She screamed, pounding on the door with three final thumps. "MOTHERFUCKER!!!

He floated back to his office, his satin robe brushing against his body. Oh, to be an eligible bachelor. He grasped the whiskey bottle, swallowing more firewater. The burn in his throat and his gut signaled greater relaxation to come.

And, with that, a call came on his phone. Could it be the physicist? No, instead, his secretary was calling. He answered, "Hello, Tie."

The gentle voice hummed, "Doctor Nakamura, sorry to disturb you so late into the evening, but I must let you know that we've received an interview request from an author in the United States interested in discussing radiation sickness and nuclear weapons."

He chuckled, answering, "An American wishes to learn from me about their weapons?"

Tie's voice answered quickly, "Some activist interested in the precise details of radiation damage to DNA."

Shigeru laughed. "You sound exasperated, Tie. Why upset?"

His assistant paused, then with greater calm, responded, "You should speak to her. She apparently is somewhat famous for her work, and has spent much time in jail for it."

The physician tapped his forehead, conflicted. "Very well, schedule time to discuss. But I'm no cult leader." He heard keystrokes typed by his secretary, freeing him to taunt, "Tapped any sexy tail lately?" He knew the answer, but ribbing his overweight secretary remained a delight.

Tie waited to answer, then squealed a peep of laughter. "No, I'm working for you."

Shigeru's mood had improved a little, the whiskey at last tipping his enormous wall of tolerance. "Then go tap some ass." He clanked the bottle on the desk.

Tie huffed, "The only ass I'm tapping is my own, because I'm sitting on it." The typing stopped. "Okay, you're scheduled to speak with her on Friday. She had requested an early appointment, though she did not say why."

Shigeru's mind had wandered as he flipped through photos of exotic women on his dating app. "Hmm? Oh, yes, that's fine." He shook his head, flipping the phone to the table. "Is she hot?"

Tie's voice offered no delay. "She must be in her seventies."

Ugh. Well, maybe that box needed a check as well. No matter. He glanced to the diplomas and books visible from his desk, then exhaled with some shame. "Well, if an American student tries to contact my office, just ignore her."

Tie didn't wait for a pause, interrupting him. "Sir, what the hell have you done now?"

Anger snapped in him. "Oh, fuck you, Tie! You'd do well to remember respecting your elders."

Ignoring his challenge, Tie shot back, "You cannot cause more trouble with the international students. Especially the American ones."

Shigeru tried to pour another shot but missed the glass by a few centimeters. Whiskey splattered about his desk, a small amount hitting the screen of his computer. America the bitch had it coming, but his secretary responded better to contrition. "I know, I know, Tie." He recalled her curves and features. "Tie, you had to see her. She was uppity, challenging me during the seminar."

Tie muttered away from the phone, yet Shigeru still could hear him. "Christ."

Shigeru blotted the errant whiskey with a towel, continuing his own defense. "She was so smoking hot, and gave me lip, then gave me lip, if you know what I mean." He'd force his secretary to appreciate his joke.

No such luck. "Shigeru, I don't care if she gave you a Kuroneko lapdance. You're just breaking things that others have to fix."

Anger snapped in him again. "Fuck you, Tie. I hired you when no one else would, so you don't have any room to judge me. You're no angel, either. If you weren't raised by wolves in America, you'd know your goddamned place. You're a pervert." That was right—Shigeru may be no angel, but neither was Tie.

Tie raised his voice, at last bringing some satisfaction to Shigeru. "Sir, my parents aren't wolves—they taught me that respect is earned."

"They raised you wrong, then." Shigeru surged with strength as he cracked the whip on the whelp. "You're a pervert and a mulatto, and I didn't have to help you."

"Jesus, Professor. You know I was drunk and needed to piss while walking home from the bar." He paused, then shouted, "I'm sick of you comparing that to what you do. I don't need this."

Shigeru pressed, slurring, "Well, you… you… you're in no position to judge me. If you were important like me, flashing yourself to strangers wouldn't matter. Stardom has its privileges."

His secretary slammed a door, maybe to conceal his voice. Shigeru insisted Tie remain at the office as much as possible, though he himself preferred the comfort of going home in the evenings. Tie whispered, "Look, sir, all I'm saying is that these messes have caused enormous trouble in the past, and that—"

He interrupted, now slurring to the point that he himself could hear it. "I got this, Tie. I got this. I got this. Don't worry." He downed more of the whiskey as he repeated the words.

Tie sounded as though he had sat back into his chair. Drawing one slow breath, he answered, "Fine, sir. Why don't you just go to bed now?"

Shigeru did like the sound of that. Making a little conciliatory conversation, he asked, "And what is the American activist's name?" Might as well investigate an interested party.

Tie inhaled. "Yes, let me see. Conique Voyant."

Shigeru laughed, shooting whiskey into his sinuses. Through a few uncomfortable coughs to clear the fiery drink, he asked mockingly, "Seriously? What a name."

Tie touched some keystrokes, then announcing, "Oh, I located the draft by Kunapsken. I'm sending it to your email.""

Shigeru spit a small bit of whiskey at that, exclaiming, "Holy shit! Why didn't you say so? I didn't expect you to find it."

Tie remarked, "It was not easy to come by. One of the staff in her department and I go way back."

Shigeru opened his email on his desktop as he chuckled, "So, I hope you fucked her." He didn't say anything, so Shigeru said, "Anyway, this is huge. I knew you could perform."

His assistant asked, "You really think this connects to your research?"

Shigeru's deference had its limits. "That's not your paygrade, Tie. Now, I'll say good night." He disconnected the phone after letting Tie try to speak—he couldn't let him think too much of this success, even if it helped him immensely. Fuck that pervert, even if he had his uses. He'd not expected the portly guy to nab the draft, even if he'd heard of its existence through assistant-to-assistant gossip.

Wishing he'd not spent the evening drinking and fucking, an utterly spent Shigeru opened the email attachment containing a paper called *Time Crystals May Exist in Biological Systems*. For now, he'd settle for the draft, even if he couldn't reach the author. But maybe he'd catch some sleep before diving into its details.

9.Forget Me Not

*C****

Conique rummaged through papers, sending dust spreading throughout her office. Sunrays beamed through the windows, sparkling each particle to perfection. Mystifying, indeed. The swirl had always entranced her, and she'd loved playing in it as a girl.

Returning to the present, she knew she needed to find something she had printed referencing this Japanese professor. Her husband had left to run errands, and she'd promised to limit her troublemaking. But her longing to commit life to paper had proved impossible to ignore, and time was the one thing she was fast depleting.

The dreaded news of cognitive decline could be easy to forget, but from time to time she felt her stomach drop. The road through dementia would not be an easy one. She trusted her Lord Jesus to lead her as He always had. He must have a plan for her, and this challenge should be no different.

And, thanks to extensive experience in the community, she did understand that there may come a point in the progression of the illness after which she'd no longer fear. But the feral mind could be a tricksome thing.

What was she doing?

"Japanese doctor, yeah," she muttered. She grasped a copy of the March issue of *Medicine Today*, the cover of which exhibited this smart physician. "Doctor Nakamura." She said each syllable of the name with care. Fidgeting with her purple-framed reading glasses, she muttered, "No wonder I can't see. Now, let's see why I'm looking for ya."

She carried the magazine into her hallway, back to her armchair. Yes, the tea she'd prepared would go well with cookies and a reading of the article. Plopping into the chair, she read aloud.

"Professor Shigeru Nakamura of the Okinawa Institute of Cancer Research has long documented the longitudinal and transgenerational effects of radiation exposure, with case studies now numbering in the hundreds collected from ground zero of Hiroshima."

Tracing the text with her fingers, she read his biography and later work, more certain than ever she could help him. She then heard the door into the garage open, interrupting her. "Is that you, sweetie?" she called to him.

His powerful voice reverberated, saying, "Yes, dear." He rounded the corner, placing a brown bag of groceries on the countertop. "I found makings for a salad."

She frowned. "Yech. I'd rather have fried chicken tonight."

He grinned, his white teeth gleaming in the natural light of their kitchen. "What's that supposed to mean? You mean you want dinner with a black man? You might as well ask for waffles."

She laughed, pulling the reading glasses from her nose. "I always want my dinner with a black man, darling."

He noted the magazine she held and pointed to it. "Did ya learn anything else about the doctor you want to interview?"

She sighed, folding the journal shut. "Well, I should get to talk to him." She paused, trying to recall the appointment time Shigeru's secretary had approved. "Well, I wrote it in the calendar. Hell if I remember when."

Reuben approached her, leaning in to steal a kiss. Then he touched her shoulder, offering, "Connie, you don't have to do this. You've written books before on our work, and—"

She touched his face, shaking him off. "You're kind to me, darling, but I need, if not have, to do this." She looked to the magazine cover, touching the physician's photograph. "Besides, there's something about this young doctor that I need to find out about."

Reuben cocked his head, just as she would have expected. "Ah, so this is one of your feelings."

She nodded. "Yeah, I think so. This is a story needing to be told. It's not just his expertise, though I want to know more about what happens to the people working around the weapons and reactors."

Bending the magazine, she adjusted her seat. "This young man and I need to talk, or that's the impression I'm getting."

Reuben stepped back to the grocery bag, pulling items from it. "Well, I didn't get salad materials, after all. I got some chicken for the frying and some batter for the waffle iron." He cheered, pointing to a white-and-red apron hanging on the oven towel rack.

C ✳ ✳ ✳

Sitting down to a candlelit dinner, Conique poured herself a small measure of wine. It was less than she'd prefer, but under the medical constraints, what could she do? At least she could enjoy Reuben's phenomenal cooking, and fried chicken, he cooked to perfection. The asparagus, corn on the cob, fried okra, and waffles were also all delicious. Comfort food may've been hard on her arteries, but it was good for her metaphysical heart.

She and Reuben both prayed silently so they could personalize their respective blessings to their spiritual tastes. She prayed that Jesus bless the amazing food, the hands preparing it, and the nourishing of their bodies. Her late mother had taught her to respect the beliefs of others, so she'd caught flack for her tolerance. Hell, it was bad enough that she was a woman preacher.

Her husband reached for her hand. "Penny for your thoughts?"

She smiled, squeezing his in return. "I'm just thinking about the mess we're all in now."

He sipped his wine, then pulled meat from the bone with a splatter of grease. She laughed while he scraped a glob of oil from his chin with a cloth napkin. He asked, "You mean the mess you and I are in, or more globally?"

She found it quite funny that he'd think she was complaining about their own predicament. Years had passed since she had given much thought to her own challenges. She'd traveled as a missionary to the third world many times, and the problems there had forever etched gratitude upon the tables of her heart. She sighed. "The world is in trouble."

Passing a bit of chicken to Aurum, he chuckled, "The world is always in this trouble or that." He wiped his gray mustache once more, then conceded, "But you remember what it was like in the 1960s. We couldn't even have gotten married in most states. Consider the lilies, dear." With that, the telephone sounded. He laughed. "Always during dinner. Never fails." He rose to his feet with a groan, muttering, "Goddamned sales calls, I'd bet."

They had agreed she should not answer the telephone, knowing she might misremember or outright forget important particulars. On the other hand, she'd hoped this might be that Japanese doctor. What was his name again?

Frustrated, she listened as best she could to the conversation between Reuben and the mystery caller, hearing him say, "Yes, she lives here. Can I ask what this is about? Well, she's not been feeling too well, so I don't—"

He paused, clearly facing rapid interruption by this caller. "Yes, sir, I understand that. Well, you should know that—" Another pause. "Well, yes, she'd wanna talk if she knew what the urgency is." Silence, then her husband spoke once more. "Well, I tell you what: Gimme your number and name, and I'll see whether we can fit you into the schedule."

He sighed with deliberation, then answered, "Yes, I understand you may think it's an emergency, but she's a retired, elderly person with health problems. Now, wait a second. That don't mean we—"

He gasped a little. "Say what? What the hell do missiles and immigrants have to do with each other? Oh, little green men? Umm, we don't believe in that nonsense. I'm sorry, Mister what? Boothby? Oh, just Boothby. Okay, I'm hanging up now."

She heard a thump against the wall, indicating he'd remounted the portable house phone. Returning to the dining room, he laughed, relaying, "That was bizarre. He seemed to know about the Plowshares, but then he went on a jag about aliens and nuclear missiles, and how you could get him close enough to the weapons to see these UFOs. Jesus, I wonder what he was smoking. Sounds like horseshit."

She shrugged, adding, "The calling is different for everyone, I guess."

Reuben pulled himself to the table to resume his meal. "Some people hear voices in their heads. They feel *called* to do all sorts of things."

Conique said, "Then I probably need to talk to him." She found his consternation amusing, so she added, "To get him straight to the point, that is."

Taking a bit of fried okra, he snapped, "The only straight needing to happen there is a straitjacket."

Conique adjusted the burning candle sitting before her and responded, "Plenty of people say the same about me, darling."

He removed his tan jacket, hanging it on the brass hat rack next to the kitchen door, then leaned in to plant a kiss on her, something she welcomed, along with the accompanying mustache tickle. Touching her face, he whispered, "Well, I guess if you feel *called* to talk to him, be my guest."

*B****

Boothby tossed his cellphone into the heap of paper scattered across his desk. Miss Tutog had declared him a certifiable hoarder, but it took one to know one. Still, if this woman, this weird faith healing guru sort, could help him access a nuclear launcher, he'd convert to the cult she represented, no matter how crazy.

Strange as it seemed, his longstanding crusade to find the enigmatic Ephyr and his accompanying lights had graduated past obsession to outright mania. The Westall incident in 1966 had affirmed his own experiences, given his exposure to the devices at such a young age. His imagination on fire, he'd often thought Ephyr's focus stone must have had psychokinetic powers.

He had considered speaking to Jacques Valles about it, knowing that the senior scientist had collected bits believed to have been crashed bits of the sky devices. Valles had analyzed his fragments with electron microscopes in California, uncovering a metallurgy many decades, if not centuries, ahead of the twenty-first century state of the art. However, the impeccable scholarship of the statesman ufologist could not overcome Boothby's fear of publicity, theft, and interference by intelligence agencies.

Besides, the recent revelation that Air Force pilots had observed devices capable of impossible aerobatics could draw unwanted attention to ufologists like Boothby. It wasn't that he would mind an uptick in book sales, but he didn't trust vandals and spies who might steal his relic.

Boothby sighed, his mind stuck in a rut over his many concerns. He knew this was part mental illness, but the words were cold comfort. He didn't care why he was anxious; he just wanted answers. He slurped some coffee sludge—a brew so powerful his endocrinologist had warned he'd abbreviate his lifetime by years by drinking it. But nothing tasted better than the bittersweet cocktail of his own making.

Jittery, he downed extra clonazepam, closing his eyes, counting aloud. Once the benzo hit his system, he'd be right as rain. Feeling his breathing, he waited. Rinse, lather, repeat.

At last, the comfort did come. He opened his eyes, and the room appeared brighter, more comfortable, than it had just a moment ago. His Berber carpet, just a moment earlier grungy and faded, now had become colorful, catching the long rays of evening sun with a sparkle, and the air seemed less stale. *Thank fucking Christ Almighty for these drugs.*

Freed from the perpetual torture for a time, he knelt on the floor, pushing the chair away to reveal a small fireproof safe. The combination remained simple—a series of numbers Ephyr imparted during their encounter: six, ten, thirteen, seven. Was there some other significance?

He recalled the frigid air that night, yet he'd felt no sense of cold. How could it have been so cold? It was a winter wonderland, with great fir trees tufting against the brilliant, clear night sky. Had there been an aurora fantasia that night? It seemed true.

He touched the safe's dial, operating the four stages. Pulling the handle, he heaved the door open. Inside sat papers, along with a misshapen hunk of metal—the relic, the prize. Pulling it from the safe, he passed it from hand to hand, testing its weight. He snorted, remarking, "Like it might change."

He passed his fingers over the rough edges, whispering, "How can I not believe?" The object, bearing no obvious design or utility, nonetheless proved his encounter had happened. His residual anxiety diminished, but was it the drugs or the object? He chuckled at himself. "You awe such a sad old queen. Anxious for what?"

Why wouldn't the object yield to him? Why did Ephyr gift it to him? All his bright imagination could conjure were stone walls. He mused at the irony, muttering, "Stonewall Riots changed it all."

Drawing him from his common trance of inner thought was a rapping at his door. He heard rustling, so he grunted and he stood, shouting, "Miss Tutog, I don't want to see you! Can't you leave me be?"

The rapping continued. It was strange, considering her overblown need to proclaim herself to her subjects dwelling in her little castle, but this rapping increased in frenzy.

He puttered to the door, whisking the bronze cover aside to reveal the peep hole, and gasped at the sight—two black suited men with sunglasses. He shook his head, exhaling. "Christ, Boothby. Guantanamo here I come."

One of the figures darted his attention behind them, booming, "Ma'am, please return to your domicile."

He heard Miss Tutog protest. He couldn't quite make out what she said, but the phrases, "I have rights" and, "This is my property" rose above the din as she rushed them, bearing her oxygen tank. Dropping it to the ground with a clank, she shouted, "I'm a disabled taxpayer and an American citizen. I demand you tell me what you're here on my property to do!"

The agent boomed further, "Ma'am, we are NSA, and we insist you return to your dwelling." He stepped away from the door, leaving just one agent, who pounded the wood to the point it creaked and crackled.

Boothby shrank from the sight. What in the hell would the NSA want? He dashed to his safe under the desk, placing the focus stone among the papers with some care. The pounding continuing, he cursed. "Christ on his throne."

He paused, glancing at the sandy brown door barring these invaders from his small apartment. Would the safe be a dead giveaway? These men could be here for any number of reasons, he imagined. They couldn't know the focus stone existed. Perhaps they knew he had tried to reach Miss Voyant. Or maybe his horrible landlady had called them to harass him out of the neighborhood. But then, why would she seem disturbed by their presence?

He deemed the safe unfit to shield his treasure, so he eased to his knees with a groan, arthritis slowing him.

He planted himself upon a thick iridescent rug, emblematic of pride and an unlikely gift from his former boyfriend Barney. Pulling it back to reveal the wooden boards of the floor, he slipped a finger into a knot hole, detaching a board to reveal a tiny crawlspace below. Dropping the alloy lump into it, he replaced the board and flattened the rug. It was an advantage to live in a dilapidated condominium—the ordinary furnished countless hiding places.

More pounding scraped the last of his nerves raw, so as he pulled himself to his feet, he shouted, "For Chrissakes, I'm coming! Stop beating on the goddamned door!"

He waddled to the door while the numbness subsided, and then with a flip of the deadbolt, he pulled it open a crack.

A sole figure stood before him. The other, he speculated, was off to harass Miss Tutog. Served the bitch right, for sure. Dapper in his officious suit and Brilliantine black hair, the young man spoke with cold calm and resoluteness. "Mister Boothby,

I'm Special Agent Jason Axley of the National Security Agency. Are you Edward Gamaliel Boothby?"

Boothby tried to shake the distraction, volunteering, "Yes, I am Boothby, but I know no NSA agents." He motioned past Axley, adding, "And where did your partner go? And what's her name?"

The agent refused to surrender focus, save a mighty sneeze. "Sorry, goddamned allergies will be the death of me. Agent Carolina is tending to other matters."

"North or south?" Boothby blurted without thinking, though this stone-faced man ignored him. Emboldened by the benzos in his blood, Boothby channeled his investigative journalist, pivoting to righteous outrage. "I know my Mirandas. Whatever you're selling, I'm not buying. What business do you have?"

Axley cracked a winsome smile, filling Boothby with hope that this might be less than a staged assassination. He removed his sunglasses, unveiling blue and red eyes, and with a chuckle, he replied, "Mister Boothby, I'll be asking the questions." He then sneezed again.

Boothby laughed off the small warning, pushing the agent a little more. "Gesundheit! I'm a journalist, sir. I'll just answer your questions with more questions. But if ya'"—he eyed the figure—"wanna know more, you gotta start with flowers."

Perplexity splashed across the agent's face, forcing him to shake his head. "Mister Boothby, we're here in an investigative and counsel capacity only."

Carolina approached, though she cursed with a thud. "What is fugly thing doing in the walkway?"

"Okay, Agent?" Axley asked.

Boothby was quick to answer. "That would be Mohgra."

Axley appeared perplexed as Carolina rounded the corner to join her partner. No taller than Miss Tutog, she was a tank of a woman. Her short, neat hair encircled a round face with makeup, all against a suit so similar to that Axley wore that one could believe they cosplayed the same character. She endured a silent rebuke from Axley as she replied, "The super would NOT let me go. She wanted to go on and on about her constipation and her cat, and that disgusting gargoyle—"

"Mohgra," Boothby volunteered without thinking, just as it hit him that Carolina, like himself, hailed from the northeast.

The taller and more senior agent shook his head to silence his young partner, answering, "Miss Tutog and her oddities are not part of the investigation."

She ignored him as Axley said, "We're visiting you, Mister Boothby—"

Boothby rolled his eyes with dramatic flair, laughing. "Please. Mister Boothby was my father; at least, that's what they said at the orphanage. Call me just plain ole Boothby."

Yet another small smile crossed Axley's face, and he replied, punctuating the name, "As I was saying, Boothby, we're here because we believe a foreign agent may try to contact you."

Journalist or not, he felt a wash of intrigue at this. "How very cloak and dagger." Chortling, he asked, "Whyever would someone foreign wanna talk with me?"

Carolina's reply was swift and disrespectful. "Don't play coy with us, Mister Boothby. You travel in all sorts of circles, and if foreign agents known to be dangerous to the security of the United States try to contact you, you have a duty to—"

Boothby laughed him off, responding, "A duty to tell the likes of you whether I hear from some spy? COINTELPRO, PRISM, algorithms do that for ya. I ain't saying nothing.—"

The more senior agent intervened, offering, "Look, Boothby"—he glanced to his junior, then returned his eyes to Boothby—"we just want to tell you that you may receive a request for information from a Russian POI, a Mayak Chernovsky. This person could offer data critical for the security of your government. If he contacts you, I want you to call me."

"Yeah, yeah," Boothby said in a snip. "Flag and fatherland."

Carolina was quick on the rebuke. "Mister Boothby, this is very serious. We have reason to believe others may contact you, and they bring tremendous danger."

Boothby frowned as he felt his throat tighten. "What danger? From whom?"

Axley handed him a business card as he raised a hand to silence her. "Look, just call me should this Chernovsky person or anyone else reaches out to you, and please keep the details of our inquest to yourself. We'll be watching."

Boothby took the card with a growl. "That's what I thought. You just wanna scare me. So I'll keep it in my black book." Flipping it over, he shrugged. "Fine. If a Russian contacts me, I'll kiss and tell."

Repelling his sloppy charm, the agents vanished through the iron gate. Relieved to be alone again, Boothby stuffed the card into his pocket and muttered to himself, "Jesus, what could that be about? When is there not danger?"

He started to close his door, only for his landlady to appear, her enormous pink bathrobe flowing about her. He shook his head at her as he counted fifteen—no, twenty green curlers in her hair. He started again to shut his door, with her calling to him, "Boothby, dearie, who were they, and why were they here?"

He said, "I have no idea, Miss Tutog! I'm gonna retire for the evening." He pushed the door shut, only for her, with momentum behind her, to stay his force. Good Lord, she moved fast.

The thick Tammy Faye makeup this woman wore disgusted him, and it was even more painful close-up. He'd seen more attractive drag queens sporting full beards. She placed her plump hands in the doorjamb as her oxygen tanks rang like a pair of bells. "If they're here because you've done something illegal, dearie, that would abrogate the terms of our lease."

He felt his eyes race about the room, offering a frown. Closing his eyes, at least sparing one of his senses from the assault that was Fat Hog Miss Tutog, he continued, "An investigation that has nothing to do with me, and that's all I can say."

She raised a Joan Crawford eyebrow, then sprayed acrid breath into his face. Easing from the jamb, she aimed a wicked acrylic nail in his direction, beaming a Cheshire-cat smile. "I'm keeping an eye on you, Boothby. E-commerce realtors would be happy to take your apartment."

Disgusted, he pressed the door closed, muttering, "Just go home, Miss Tutog. I'm sure Mohgra could use a polish."

She tapped her nails on his door, evoking images of raptor claws in his mind as she finished, adding, "Don't make trouble, dearie. I'd hate to be forced to evict you. And stay away from my gargoyle."

He flipped the lock, then waddled to his armchair, plopping into it. This woman stirred up nausea and repugnance in him, so why not think of the young agent who may or may not care for his well-being? It was easy to believe he had been genuine in his concern, but Boothby was no fool. He remained certain that parties within the U.S. government were interested in both his lifetime research and the object he had omitted from all accounts of his encounter those many years ago.

He collapsed into an armchair, next to which sat a small table where he had placed his cellphone earlier. More interesting to him was the small bottle of Irish whiskey given to him at one of his book signings. If ever there was a time to drink, perhaps now was that time.

But first, he decided he should check his electronic messages through the browser. Pulling a small pair of reading glasses from his vest pocket, he plucked his phone from the table. Navigating to his private mail server, he found a message that was somewhat odd in character. It requested information on his research, though the return address seemed like that of a spam generator.

The email read,

Long time you have felt called to seek truth. I cannot reach you conventionally because of precarious condition. However, I can offer you means of contact invisible to those who obfuscate Truth. Lights are real, and I can help you make sense of gift. Wait for another message.

He scratched his gray beard, placing the phone back on the table. Grabbing the whiskey bottle, he popped off the cap, pouring some of the fluid into a small shot glass on the table. He swigged the first drink, then poured another.

The intriguing visit from the NSA, followed by the almost-staged email with details he'd never shared with anyone, had primed him. This would prove most interesting.

10.Nukes to Knives

*M****

"No rest for wicked," Mayak whispered as he tossed about in his bed.

The return of the *skrytyypass*, along with the extraordinary events of the past week, had rendered him incapable of sleep. Not that his insomnia needed much encouragement. A lifetime of it had led to his voracious appetite for literature, though Sargon, hallucination or not, had schooled him better than any tutor he would ever meet.

The returned Sargon remained true to this, sharing with him the requisite acumen in combinatorics and cryptography to contact the American ufologist unnoticed. Still, he dreaded the consequences of his earlier search. Who might suffer?

If this Boothby was as crazy as he appeared, wouldn't it be just vanity traffic to the picky intelligence zealots? On the other hand, hearing a disembodied voice hidden from all others didn't exactly situate Mayak among the sane.

He didn't need Sargon to tell him how foolish this line of thought would be. Kierkov would excel in her duties now that she had been loosed on Mayak and his poor friend Petrov; Boothby, too, would now fall squarely into her cyber crosshairs, and Mayak had imperiled the hapless fool, an innocent. Considering the vicious cruelty the Russian government inflicted upon the gay community, Mayak would never have contacted a known homosexual in America if he'd believed the government could capture his communication.

The technique had proved clever, enabling him to conceal a message in a handful of links he'd searched in the online research bank of *Wikipedia*. Following revelations by whistleblowers, governments the world over closed ranks on their respective intelligence agencies.

Mayak had not thought much on the subject, so he claimed no special insight into the philosophy of government or sociology. The human race exhibited all manner of evil he could imagine, and so the existential risks obvious to insiders presented him no moral quandary. If the human race must die to herald a simpler, less-destructive apex animal or vegetable on this planet, he'd concede that nature had selected humans for extinction by natural right.

Not that Mayak could abide the totalitarian snare. The mass-surveillance complex, cabals of power-mongering bureaucrats, subversively gilded technocrats, and politicians-for-hire, all benefited from human creativity. He'd heard in early life that the American experience was no less invasive and controlled than that in his home country, but his time at Los Alamos had suggested otherwise, even with the security clearance necessary to study nuclear physics. He'd understood that all memoranda, email, and even in-person conversations were logged and recorded somewhere, and yet it was freer than any of his life in Russia, so he understood his return to be a mistake.

But Sargon had abandoned him. His return to Russia contravened his passenger augur's wishes, an act of rebellion to coax his *skrytyypass* out of hiding, if he was honest. It didn't work out that way, though, and he'd found himself once more under the control of Mother Russia. Mayak had been lost without Sargon, a separation leaving him in doubt of his sanity.

Kierkov was symbolic of the allure, sinister but sensual. Increased scrutiny probably meant he couldn't talk aloud to himself in his own apartment. It wasn't the first time he'd considered it, but maybe that was why Sargon had gone dark earlier. In any case, he would have to commend the all-seeing, formidable Federation Security Service in dispatching an agent so compatible with his attractions. Could it be possible Sargon had appeared because of her? Mayak seldom dated, for he assumed schizophrenia would lead to women interested in caretaking an ill man.

His mind raced, keeping him awake. He swung his legs over the edge of his bed, and, missing the house shoes he'd placed on the hard tile floor, his bare feet suffered the cold. "Fuck," he cursed. Poking his feet about in the dark, they found their soft shoes, and he pulled himself up to stand.

Maybe more reading and coffee would help him. His textbook collection filled him with joy. There were few sights so beautiful as hardback spines gleaming by moonlight. Physical paper copies also limited his need to research the internet, a decisive shield against the vast surveillance apparatus.

He stepped into his kitchenette, pulling an electric pot from a floor-level cabinet. Filling it with water, he pictured the lights once more. They could not have been fireworks, for no firework could possibly negotiate the rectilinear paths they traced. And, if his recollections from aerospace were correct, no technology could accomplish such course changes—not at those sizes. Even insect navigation, apparent in its discontinuities, featured smoothing difficult to perceive with human eyes.

Turning to the kettle, he heard the boiling water pop as though he were microwaving popcorn. He located cream and sugar nearby, his mouth watering a little as he anticipated the drink he'd soon mix.

Why would Sargon explode onto the scene, then vanish just as quickly? He seethed, sensing a betrayal he thought he'd long put behind him. The voice had proved so much more than a hallucination, educating him, helping him through his academic testing, though he'd concealed this as best he could, leading the expert clinicians to believe he was a boy genius with schizophrenia, rather than an oracle with access to a dimension theretofore unknown.

The pot caught his attention again, so he poured the steaming liquid into his insulated mug. Scooping instant coffee, which was never any less delicious to his maybe-unrefined palate than the more complicated ground-and-filtered counterpart, he mixed the powder into the water, then added the other ingredients. Oh, how the smell invigorated him.

There was a knock at his door just as he tasted the liquid. Late visits were rare, so his heart rate picked up. He dragged his feet the three-meter walk to the front door, almost half the width of his apartment, asking "Who is it?"

Petrov's voice answered. "Your friend, comrade. Let me in before I freeze."

Mayak pulled open the door into his entry to reveal his friend smiling. He himself almost never smiled. He'd always been introverted, and both his parents and Sargon had insisted he keep his feelings to himself, but he did smile a little as Petrov quipped, "Well, they did not tie you to chair and whip you"—even if for no other reason than that he could see himself enjoying a spanking from that woman Kierkov.

His friend stepped beyond the door's threshold as Mayak motioned for him to enter with haste to retain as much heat as the small apartment could on this bitter cold night.

He pulled a second cup from the cabinet, nodding to his friend. "So, you wish for some as well?"

Petrov found one of the kitchen table chairs, a cracked ice design from the 1970s, plopping himself into it with a bit more of a thud than Mayak's smaller frame. His friend groaned a little for melodramatic flair. "Absolutely. You think I would brave snow to see you, then refuse your charming hospitality?"

Oh, what a delight this friend was for Mayak. He often noted it when he smiled internally, even if his face remained static. As he mixed Petrov's drink, he said, "You should not have walked so far, my friend. So, have you been requested at work?"

His friend reached for the cup as Mayak handed it to him. "Not yet. I had hoped you would know something."

Mayak pulled one of the aging chairs from the table, a hand-me-down from his parents. Sitting, he let the flavor and aroma of his coffee perk him back to life and shook his head, answering, "Nothing yet has come to me. With spy agency meddling into it, I'm guessing we may be furloughed for some time."

Petrov laughed, motioning to the cabinet, asking, "Perhaps you have something extra for coffee?" Mayak hopped to his feet, knowing his friend meant vodka. The mix was intolerable, but worth it for the intended consequence.

He opened the top cabinet, reaching far into it for the bottle of clear fluid, a powerful drink, Russian in origin, and, by necessity, the favorite. And what the hell? If they wouldn't be working the following day, why not surrender the night to a sloppy finish?

He pulled the cap from the bottle, and the powerful vapors filled his nostrils. Pavlovian craving overcame him, the scent improving his mood. Of course, Skinnerian behaviorism remained a discounted cognitive theory, save the most basic responses, but he couldn't shake the impression, and he didn't mind the comparison to dogs.

He moved to his friend, pouring into his cup a most generous portion. As he lifted the bottle away, Petrov grasped the neck with his plump fingers, protesting, "Stinginess isn't becoming, Comrade." Mayak offered no physical response save relenting and giving his friend a bit more. He then poured a double shot into his own coffee. It was grotesque, but it would do.

Sitting in his chair, he raised his mug to his friend, offering, "Cheers." He sipped, then pursed his lips, querying, "What brings you here, Petrov?"

His friend touched his shiny red cheeks, scratching them in thought—or, at least, Mayak believed some thinking was occurring in the brain of his ne'er-do-well buddy. He replied, "Well, Jergan called me to ask me whether I'd seen you."

Mayak thought for a moment, then replied, "Our boss has my cell number. Why would he ask you?"

Petrov swigged his drink, then cleared his throat of the alcohol burn, offering, "I think he wanted me to check on you in person."

Mayak blinked several times, signaling frustration, or so he'd learned after the extensive psychoanalyzing he endured as a child. This seemed absurd. He bit his lower lip and shrugged. "He is goddamned laziest person I know."

Petrov raised his mug high in approval, piling on. "Absolute truth you speak, comrade Chernovsky." He slurped a gulp of his concoction, then continued, "I'm guessing he is buried under paperwork."

Mayak crossed his arms, hoping the added warmth would serve him as he listened to the wind outside the window. Looking into the swirling mixture before him, he sighed. "Why does it matter? The government buries the paperwork in any case."

Petrov nodded in greater approval, answering, "When aliens come to look at how we blew ourselves up, they might be interested in paths forged by drones such as ourselves."

119

He did smile a bit at this, the vodka easing his emotional buffer. Raising the mug, he added, "You should've been poet, no?"

Petrov bellowed with laughter in agreement, causing Mayak to cringe, if for no other reason than that a grouchy man lived next door, and he'd sooner or later announce his disapproval of the noise. "Truly, I could wax on blizzards, bombs, and babes."

Agent Kierkov returned to Mayak's consciousness at the word "babes." Conjuring her would be fun, despite Sargon's stern warning.

Wow. He hadn't considered Sargon for a bit, and what a relief.

He drank more of his potion, his muscles and mind relaxing. It occurred to him then that if Jergan had contacted Petrov, he might benefit from anything he might repeat. "Did old man offer any explanation for our furlough?"

Petrov smiled, his cheeks stretching so much, Mayak wondered whether they might burst. He chuckled. "Not much information. He said our division would remain closed while intelligence investigates." His smile drooping, he leaned into the table, probing. "Speaking of which, what did you see?"

Could Kierkov's reach extend all the way to Jergan? He might have dispatched Petrov to question Mayak, but it also might just be honest curiosity on the part of his friend. He reflected the query, answering, "I had planned to ask you same thing."

Petrov watched him, angling his head away while fixing his eyes on Mayak. He responded, "they never said what happened. They asked about our actions leading to event. And about you. They dragged me to conference room, then left me awhile"— he paused, looking to his mug, then back to his friend—"you were found unconscious in courtyard."

Mayak nodded, flat-faced. "I know where I was found. But I saw…" He studied Petrov's face while he paused, considering the situation. He couldn't risk that either Petrov was playing for Kierkov and her crew of fascists or that Petrov's very safety might depend on what he knew about the event, so he responded, "I saw nothing, comrade. I fell unconscious, and what happened next is impossible to say. Except they accused us of sabotage."

Petrov drew a deep breath, running his hand over his gleaming bald head. He spoke with a lighter tone and voice. "Well, we are not sent to stockade yet. Why would they think we would do such?"

Mayak scratched his chin, finding more stubble than he'd like. With a sigh, he answered, "Misdirection, as is often their piece."

Petrov shook his head. "Malfunction? They need fall guy?"

This frustrated Mayak, though Sargon's return loomed, at least in his head, above any political paranoia. "Could be. Equipment is ancient, but our protests for upgraded hardware would reflect poorly on leadership. Leadership refuses to fall, so we wait instead." He looked at the digital clock on the wall, which read 3:17 AM.

Yawning, he spoke. "Well, I should return to bed. Feel free to take couch if you do not wish to go out again."

Petrov rose to his feet, plodded to the door, then replaced his thick cap with a laugh. "No, no, no, my friend. Erna would be unhappy, so I should return home." He downed his last swallow, then handed Mayak the mug. "Thank you for drink and conversation, comrade."

It was just as well, for Mayak preferred his solitude. After closing the door behind his friend, he leaned against it, exhausted yet wired. Perhaps he should dare to check his professional email accounts, though he knew the intelligence people would be watching his access times. It did anger him, but he thought it might also be a means of grabbing Kierkov's attention.

On his cellphone, he opened his old Los Alamos email account and discovered something unexpected: a message from Texas.

```
To Mr. Chernovsky,
     Its weird to write this, but I'm feeling the Spirit is
asking me to. I don't know why God wants this, but your
supposed to feel called to tell me something, or give me
something. I'll pray more, but maybe you know what I'm
talking about.
     I'm Frankie Putnam from Texas.
     P.S. Please don't think I'm crazy.
```

Mayak darkened the screen of his phone, then thought a bit. How in the hell would he know what to say to this redneck from Texas? Could it be a spoof or phishing expedition orchestrated by Kierkov and her goons?

He reopened the cabinet containing his precious vodka, leaning down to replace the bottle, and then, like a bolt from the blue, Sargon spoke to him. "You do have much to tell this American."

It startled Mayak so much that he straightened his back too soon, connecting the back of his skull with the top of the cabinet. "Fuck me," he cursed as pain radiated to his neck and the crown of his head. He whispered, knowing the alcohol had loosened his tongue. "Why have you come back? Why did you leave me in first place? And why—"

The voice of his *skrytyypass* interrupted him, booming, "All very valid questions, my young Podopech, as are the very instincts motivating you to ask them. But you must act quickly, without a verbal response."

Mayak rubbed the back of his neck, seated on the cold floor. He was uncertain what to say to the being, "You left me all alone..." His head burned, as though he were staring straight into the sun.

Sargon answered, though the voice paused sporadically. "Please, Podopech. Allow me time to explain. But you must follow my instructions exactly. Think blue or red, blue meaning you understand, red, you do not." The voice paused while Mayak imagined a color, then it laughed, "Leave it to my young Podopech to think *purple*! Ha!"

Mayak settled on blue, though he was furious. The voice continued inside of him, commanding, "You must grab some paper and a pen, then go to your lavatory."

Grasping a pen and a pad of yellow lined paper, he entered his tiny washroom. The voice continued, "Activate the exhaust fan, but leave the door ajar. Sit on the toilet."

Mayak followed his companion's instructions, understanding at once the concern that Kierkov or others could be listening. Once the fan rattled to life, he felt a little more secure. He then whispered, "Where have you been? What is happening? There are no bugs in my apartment."

Sargon sounded a little pained when he answered, "I confess that my sorrow in this matter may be only a small comfort to you, my dear son. I do wish we had the time to explore each of your questions, and I promise you, I shall answer, but here and now, I cannot, for others are listening to you."

In flat affect, Mayak answered, "That is impossible. There are no bugs in my flat. Besides, they already believe I am insane."

Sargon blurted, "Circumstances have changed. Your friend Petrov played complicit, installing listening equipment just now. And you should not underestimate the reach of the surveillance state."

"No." Mayak cursed under his breath, recognizing the inescapable logic. Not that he blamed his friend, knowing that Kierkov would have threatened Petrov or his family with torture.

The voice echoed in his thoughts, consoling him with, "My dear Podopech, do not blame your friend. He has yet to cast his lot, but it shall be for good."

Mayak felt for his buddy, whispering, "They hurt him because of me."

The voice didn't wait, answering, "The window is closing, and you cannot sit on the toilet for much longer without tripping their protocols."

Mayak answered in deadpan, "The shit police. Astonishing. A scatologist's dream job."

Sargon chuckled in Mayak's head, quipping, "I have missed our conversations. Now, I cannot communicate for long, at least not in this format. You must rest, for a journey awaits you. I shall vanish for a time, but the steps ahead of you will soon be clear."

He waited, then flipped off the fan and flushed the toilet. Dare he hope? Faith wasn't his thing, but he didn't fear Kierkov or her cronies. Despite his neutral emotions, something on his cheeks caught his attention. Tears, he discovered. When was the last time he'd cried? The unflappable Mayak Chernovsky, no less.

And these were tears of joy.

F***

Frankie pushed his computer aside, rolling his clumsy cheap chair away from his makeshift office desk, a worn, vinyl-topped card table he'd inherited from his grandfather. It was worthless, but why squander money on a replacement? He so hated George's extravagance, recalling him pissing and moaning about the size of Frankie's house. This from a man who owned three Teslas, an Escalade, and two houses.

He amused himself, picturing George forced to ingest a mountain of filthy coins. Locusts buzzed in his head.

Pulling a bottle of beer from the refrigerator, he couldn't fathom why he would send such a message. An electronic message sent to a Russian nuclear technician would expose both him and his recipient to the Deep State. Would he face an inquiry from the feds? The NSA? FBI? CIA? Much of the fracking operation in Texas depended upon cash-only transactions, so, hell, even the IRS may try to crawl up his ass.

As he twisted the cap from the beer, the hissing release of carbonation caused his mouth to water. He might be thrown in Guantanamo, but he'd go drunk.

If only he'd reached his pastor. He owed Chet James so much. Here was a man who moved powerfully in the Spirit, cared about the white race, and took an interest in Frankie's immortal soul.

Frankie's faith floundered when he considered the mess of his family. They had carried out God's will as they believed it to be, yet his mother had still rotted away with cancer. His brother was a mincing fag, and his sister a, well, whatever the fuck she was. And he was playing second fiddle to the dumbest fracking manager in all of Texas. Would his mother have been happy for each of them? Frankie had heard through the church that homosexuality was often the fault of a distant, cold mother. But theirs was neither. A longtime music director for Pastor Chet, she was as talented as she was beautiful. Frankie could fault her for little, even if she tolerated Myra's addictions and enabled Tyler's girlish hobbies. Cancer destroyed her, and the loss reverberated through those left behind.

Frankie was grateful for Pastor Chet, even if he had grown a little distant of late. Maybe George's lavish tithes had led the pastor to focus his spiritual guidance on the fat ass and his unruly, feral children.

So, even without hearing back from Chet, he sent an email. How unlike him, for he didn't trust the internet one bit.

George did him one better by claiming Kamala Harris watched him through his microwave oven and the air conditioner in his car. Whether Frankie approved of Harris or not, he could not imagine that such a woman would give a fatass like Porkie George a second thought. And why in the hell would George continue to use those appliances?

The moron also claimed Biden stole the election by brainwashing people just like the communists did in the 1950s. George loved Steve Bannon and Adam Jones, and though Frankie could imagine trusting some of what they said, some of their claims were so crazy that he thought they ought to be locked up somewhere. Jones pushed that the U.S. government perpetrated the September Eleventh attacks, even though George W. Bush's solicitor general, Ted Olson, had lost his wife Barbara on one of those planes. Fuck, he and Porkie George were dumber than a box of hammers.

Sitting and thinking, stewing on the many things that angered him, Frankie looked down at his table. He'd had eight beers, much more than his usual. Breathing into the locust buzz, he saw himself pressing the bottlenecks into George's eyes.

He'd long fantasized about killing the bastard. Sabotaging the equipment wouldn't be all that difficult.

Why was he thinking about this? Why now?

He calmed himself by thinking of Pastor Chet, the only person who understood him.

He knew what would help him shake the locusts—what always had helped him: hunting.

He'd stalked game since he was ten years old, and he could still smell the blood from his first kill. His brother and sister had wept like little girls the first night he, their father, and Pastor Chet had returned with said kill, a buck of impressive stature. Frankie reeked with the metallic scent of blood, having smeared the precious fluid on his face while the animal still lived.

What a thrill it had been—the most powerful, forceful erection he'd ever experienced when he fired his rifle to take that very first life.

His bloody thoughts returned to George. And the stupid, fat little shits he called children. And his shrill cunt of a wife, Sheila. She annoyed him no end with her rants about things like how a Walmart cashier didn't wipe her ass with his bare hands. He wanted so badly to sew her mouth shut before burning her alive.

Pastor Chet warned him that these dark thoughts were Satan's doing, that the fallen spirits wanted to claim his soul for their own. But why did the thought of such violence invigorate him? Horror movies empowered him; when other boys watched pornography, he had watched mutilation.

Pastor Chet was the only person aware of his bloodthirst, though he knew of it long before Frankie shared it. When speaking only to him, the minister had called it the *Korobskron*, the black heart, insisting that all black people held such violence in their hearts, and that he must bear this Mark of Cain. He knew he'd been adopted by his parents, so maybe he had some black blood in his veins.

He didn't care. He was white. White power. "Man hath dominion over the earth," as his pastor said often. And white men were the true men.

He sighed, scooping up the empty bottles with his arms. As he carried them to the trash, one slipped from his grasp, shattering on the creaky wooden floor.

"Goddamnit." He tossed out the remaining bottles, then reached for the pieces. With care, he gathered three of the larger pieces, only for his cellphone to shriek George's obnoxious ring tone suddenly. Jerking, the biggest glass fragment sliced the palm of his right hand, causing him to drop the gathered bits. He reached back to the floor, noticing the pool of liquid about the errant pieces, which appeared silver in the moonlight. Blood was among his favorite things to see, albeit not his own.

The phone continued to ring, flooding his mind with images of George being quartered, ripped apart by horses. Or being doused with sulfuric acid. The screams would please him to no end.

Grabbing a towel, he wrapped his hand. He reached for the phone, then stopped himself. Why did violence fill him so? Why was he so angry? George was no more an ass than usual. Sometimes, he couldn't control his wrath, and things needed to die for him to feel better.

He answered the phone, and George's stupid laugh belted through the speaker. "Haha, there you are, Frankie. Why'd ya take so long?"

Touching his forehead to wipe the perspiration, Frankie recognized that he'd bled much more than he'd thought, unintentionally swabbing of his hairline and face with the coagulating sticky gunk. He tightened the rag to slow the bleeding, then answered, "I didn't know I was on call, George."

His friend chortled. "I'm your boss, Frankie boy. I own you."

Oh, the picture of George upon the guts table where he would eviscerate hunted prey. He'd never eat him. Or would he? Was the running joke about human flesh tasting like chicken correct?

Answering without changing tone, Frankie said, "I'm not your slave, George. Just get to the fucking point."

Porkie George giggled. "Now, now, Frankie. I'm just kidding. I was wondering whether you ran the numbers I asked—"

Frankie was having none of it. "I sent them to your office three days ago, George."

After a few moments of blessed silence, his boss replied, "Well, can you text them to me now?"

Frankie sighed, looking to the clock. "It's three in the fucking morning."

George stiffened with an inhale, signaling that he was donning his manager hat. "Frankie, you're awake anyway. The IRS is all up my anus like a big moldy hemorrhoid. Just send me the data."

Frankie watched the blood drip from his fingers, then sighed in revulsion. "George, no one wants up your anus." He unfolded his laptop, the light from the login screen forcing him to squint. "Okay, George, but don't make a habit of calling me this late."

The bellowing laughter to follow sickened him. George said, "You need to walk that back, Big Mister Frankie Putnam. Don't forget, I can fire you, and no one can say a goddamned thing about it."

Frankie disconnected, then emailed the spreadsheet. How could this person ever have been a friend to him? And what had ever possessed him to agree to work underneath him, an unreliable, disgusting mess of a person?

He moved to the kitchen sink to wash his hands, noting the spiral of ripe blood disappearing into the drain. The water in Big Spring was a problem, but with enough antibacterial soap and bleach, maybe it would be fine.

Tightening the cloth on his hand, Frankie swallowed more beer. He wiped his face with a damp cloth, then walked to his table, above which sat his bulletin board. Schedules, a map, and other professional notes covered it, the regimen of it all the more important in a world so far out of order.

But the items behind it were what interested him in this moment. He placed a hand on either side of the board, his right bringing him searing pain as the wound bore the weight. He winced as he freed the board from the support pins, placing it with care on the floor next to the card table.

The board concealed a great treasure: a wall safe containing some of his favorite things. Twisting the combination lock, he unlatched the face, swinging it open to reveal a collection of guns and knives. He slipped his left hand into the safe, drawing from it a heavy survival knife. It was his favorite, sporting serrations and teeth which did more damage pulling out than pushing in.

The visitation by his mother and the email to a Russian had to signal the end times. He felt as though all of this had been to activate him.

His phone beeped with a notification, though he thought it strange if his message to the Russian had already triggered a reply. He placed the knife on the table and switched tabs within his open web browser.

It was a message. From a girl? Enclosed was a small social media note from someone called Janet. He didn't know a Janet, though the profile picture of her was interesting to him. She had straight black hair, bronzed skin, and deep almond eyes—arousing.

```
Hello Frank (Frankie?),

You don't know me, but I feel drawn to contact you. I
vehemently disagree with your politics, but I feel you
are supposed to help me. Or me you. I'm not sure.
Does this make any sense to you?

Thanks anyway if it doesn't,
Janet
```

The message was strange. He read more of her profile, learning she was a proud Azteca and infectious disease nurse. Why would she reach out to him?

He rubbed his beard, then considered the possibilities. He had felt impressed to contact a Russian, and now, a sexy redskin wanted to talk to him. It was interesting that, even while clutching his survival knife, her image and message vanquished the violence within him. The locusts dropped from him, that is until another message from the pissant George popped on screen. He was probably too stupid to understand the spreadsheet calculations.

Frankie slammed the laptop shut, and as his eyes adjusted to the diminished light, he smiled at the dance of the moonlight upon the blade of his knife. He touched the blade's teeth, images of horror filling his mind once more.

A man could dream.

11. The First Angel Appears

J***

Janet dropped her phone on the end table next to her couch. For ten nights in a row, the dream repeated. Mother Orphenia insisted the dreams were demonic, Satan placing her foster children squarely in his crosshairs. Sylvia had said more than once that *Arkivar* could have been a representation of Janet's birth parents—she needed someone in place of the parents who abandoned her, so her brain obliged. Sylvia also suggested that *Arkivar*'s disappearance signaled Janet's coping capacity with said abandonment. Adam would add that her terminal prognosis could have triggered those struggles once more.

But the latest run of dreams suggested something else to Janet. The young Texan's face persisted, like an afterimage burned into her head. She rebuked herself for feeling arousal at him; he was, feature for feature, a pretty man. Rule number nineteen: Looks are skin deep; ugly is to the bone.

Why would *Arkivar* tell her to contact this psychopath?

And she'd passed the topic of her illness in cold silence, too.

The test result had followed symptoms she'd experienced: clumsiness, slurred speech, and loss of strength in her hands. Amyotrophic lateral sclerosis would rob her of dignity, parodying her life into a pointless charade.

Rule number ten: A mental health crisis is a failure of imagination. It was strange that it brought only a little comfort. As though her baseline cynicism was insufficient, youth taunted her with health and vitality. What a crock of shit. Adam ridiculed her perfectionism, rewriting the rules every few years to appear intelligent, even logical.

She developed her rules to counter a sense of separateness, as though she were a spectator in her life. Curtain call didn't frighten her, but she feared leaving Adam alone. He alone knew of her struggle, and he seemed to be taking it as well as she could expect. He'd promised to cover for her at work as long as she felt capable of being present.

Thank goodness it was Saturday, her day off. She could cook a lazy breakfast, read a little, then force herself to exercise. She assumed that in the months ahead, she'd do more than enough lying in beds, so to hell with sleep. Pulling herself up, she listened to doves outside her window as the sun crawled into the sky. Her home was warm, nestled between two hills near the foothills of the Catalinas. Surrounding her were beautiful hiking trails, one of the biggest reasons she bought the property.

Considering that her hiking days could be coming to an end, she wanted to spend so beautiful a morning outdoors. Slipping into loose exercise clothes, she tied her shoes with a little difficulty—a noticeable change over the past weeks. Pulling a bottle of water from her refrigerator, she uncapped it, squirting the chilled fluid into her mouth. Dry Tucson, indeed.

Stepping outside her house, she locked the door, then placed the key in her shoe. She listened to lovebirds congregating around her birdfeeder. She liked to believe they lived in serenity, unified in their optimism and egalitarianism. But the gentle calls of these birds carried an uglier truth: they would injure each other over territory, mates, and food. Humans could be better, and they could be worse.

Maybe reincarnation could happen? She'd choose a less intelligent animal than herself. She wanted to fly, free of care. Maybe they were smarter than people.

Lonesome, she loved sharing her thoughts with Adam. But he wasn't always awake early after spending most of Friday night clubbing. He always brought a smile to her face. If only he were heterosexual, they'd make an even greater team.

They'd been inseparable since childhood, meeting in an orphanage. Adam had already lived with the foster family that adopted her. She was twelve, he thirteen.

As soon as Adam could drive, they'd run away together using a friend's car. They'd orchestrated an elaborate ruse, convincing teachers to hide them for a time, until they were adopted by a much saner family. Grades had never troubled her or Adam, so they'd both gained scholarships and chose to study nursing together.

Returning to the present, Janet pondered why her history was passing through her mind on this morning. The crisp, cool air did improve her mood, though, and the love she carried for her friend did help her, as did the shadows of the saguaro surrounding her house. It was a lovely place to be, and she often took walks.

Walking. Sighing, she tied her hair into a ponytail. Just one more thing the universe would take from her.

Her property was remote, just as she preferred it. She cared about people, especially Adam, but she also loved the unspoiled desert, with its many smells, the sunshine, and the critters. She'd tried to convince Adam to live with her there, hoping to gain some help with the mortgage. With the confirmation of her illness, he'd join her without reservation.

But she didn't dwell on it. A rustling caught her attention, so she glanced at one of the towering saguaros, a testament to life's implacable will to survive and thrive. Within its trunk sat a small hole, out of which a gray-and-yellow carpenter bird popped its head. She delighted in its orange cheeks, quipping, "Someone got gussied up just for breakfast." She knew the bird would feed from her stash, then bring its spoils back to any babies within the nest.

Her cellphone beeped, catching her attention. She removed it from her pocket, smiling at Adam's beaming face on the screen. She answered, "Hello, handsome."

He giggled, "Well, I'm glad you're up. I was thinking of getting some brunch."

She looked at the carpenter bird as it scuffled within the cactus hole, then answered, "So, why is it you call it brunch?" She looked at the long shadows cast by the cactus. "It's early."

He answered, "Brunch excuses the mimosas I'll be drinking."

She laughed, "Maybe it should be a screwdriver." Twisting to look at her pueblo-style house, she said, "Okay, I'll be ready in half an hour."

J✳✳✳

As Janet waited for Adam's typically late entrance, she watched cars come and go. A black van had entered the lot just after she sat on one of the waiting benches. It struck her as strange that the van just sat in the lot with the engine idling. Even the windshield was tinted, obscuring the interior from her view. Glancing at her phone's clock, she guessed she'd been waiting fifteen minutes. No one got out of the van, so her thoughts returned to Adam. He'd been the youngest In his family, the whole of which had been claimed by a car accident when a long-haul driver fell asleep at the wheel. Cars were dangerous things, and there were lots of cars in the world.

Adam was probably nitpicking the minutia of clothing that no one else would ever notice. would ever notice. She didn't trouble herself. "Natural beauty" was the way others described her. She just didn't have time for the silly and the frilly. Adam, on the other hand, knew the latest styles and which wardrobe arrangements were best. He turned heads, for all sorts of reasons.

At last, Adam appeared—and did he ever His hair was spiked, and he wore a tight baby-blue ribbed turtle-necked sweater that showed off the muscles he tortured himself to build, very nice khakis, more than a few gold necklaces, and that adorable smile.

He leaned over to kiss her cheek, then plopped himself next to her. She sized him up. "To think—I planned to wear the same thing."

He laughed, pointing to her pants and shirt. "I could do something about that." He looked around them, as though he were to utter universe-shattering truths, then whispered in full voice, "But it'll cost you!"

A hostess called from inside the café. "Janet, party of two?"

They stood, but Janet lingered to watch the black van. Adam touched her shoulder, then asked, "What is it? They're ready for us."

Janet looked back to him, then said, "Nothing."

They settled into their table as the server brought an orange juice knockoff. Adam grabbed it, starting with a sip. "That's a good mimosa!" He leaned forward, then pointed in her direction. "You should have one."

She shook her head, replying, "No thanks. Did you order ahead?"

He grinned. "I think they're telepathic here. Anyway, booze would do you some good, babycakes. Trust me, it's more fun to be drunk."

She thought a moment, then sobered. "Earlier, on my walk, I saw a carpenter bird in one of my saguaros."

He gulped his drink and added with a shrug. "You have lots of saguaros. And lots of carpenter birds."

She pointed at him with a finger. "I was just thinking, the bird is a creature capable of making its home in an inhospitable thorny plant, and the plant itself is capable of thriving in an inhospitable desert. The world, the earth, is one planet thriving in an inhospitable solar system."

He finished his first mimosa, flagging the server to bring a second round. Cocking his head, he answered, "Galaxy, local cluster, universe? So, what's the point? The universe is inhospitable?"

She shook her head, gesturing above her head. "No, no, Adam. What I mean to say is that each level seems inhospitable to the last, but maybe we're just seeing it through the wrong lens."

The server arrived with a second mimosa. Adam took notice of him, then motioned to Janet. "Check out his ass, baby."

She furled her brow. How could he be so unconcerned with the world's predicament? "Adam, come on. I'm trying to be serious here."

He sipped with caution on his second drink, offering contrition. "Okay, I'm sorry. What do you think is the point?"

She flipped her menu, signaling she'd decided on her meal. Doing the same with Adam's menu, she responded, "To the bird, the desert is inhospitable, but the plant protects the animal. The cactus would die outside the dry desert, and the desert wouldn't exist outside Earth. Earth protects the desert, and the magnetic field protects Earth. Who knows how far this goes?"

He frowned. "That's complicated, baby. What are you trying to say?"

She closed her eyes with a laugh. "Well, it made more sense in my head. I guess my point is that two layers up is danger and death, but one layer makes things okay. It's perspective, I think."

He appeared unmoved, then cracked a smile, "So, you think maybe there's a perspective from which all of this makes sense?"

She flashed her eyes to the server as he approached. Pointing to the menu, she asked, "Can you get me the country-fried steak?"

Adam reached for her hand, more than buzzed, adding, "We'll make it easy, hot stuff. Just two of those."

The server nodded with a wink, answering, "Sure thing, guys."

Adam raised his mimosa glass with that smile Janet so loved to see. "So, you're my sister the philosopher now?"

She fluttered her eyelids playfully, cheeks reddening. "Now you're just poking fun."

He contradicted her. "No, baby. You've always been the smart one." He spread his arms and hands open to the sky. "If you believe that being able to see the world from the outside makes a difference, then—"

She interrupted. "That's exactly what the astronauts say when they see the world from space for the first time. Rule number seventeen: We won't miss Mother Earth until she's gone."

He finished his second drink, then asked her, "So, have you thought more about the sexy redneck?"

She frowned, pouring herself hot water. "Why do you ask?"

Adam flagged the server yet again, remarking, "He made an impression on you. Didn't your dream talk about the earthquake?" He sat back in his chair while the server brought him a third drink. He pointed in her direction, tracing a circle with his fingers. "Dish, baby. Did you reach out?"

"Well, I sent a message on social media. But I can't imagine talking to him." She fiddled with her napkin.

Adam laughed, "Well, just ask him not to talk about politics while you're in the bed with him."

She returned the favor, asking, "What about you? Any interesting guys? That one fellow? Umm—" She concentrated, then asked, "Tim, wasn't it?"

He shook his head hard. "No way, girl. He wanted to play the disharmonica morning, noon, and night. I would be crazy. Well, crazier."

"Ermm," she stammered.

At last, the food arrived. She had been famished. Unfolding the setup, she dropped the napkin into her lap.

He did the same, then leaned forward, asking, "So, how've you been feeling, Janet?"

She knew this question had been a long time coming. It reminded her that she could forget all about the illness that would claim her. She looked into her foster brother's eyes, knowing the burden to come soon enough. She was struggling to guard her feelings, if only to protect him from the tragedy it might be to live in a world without her, so she lied. "I haven't really felt all that bad. A little cognitive fog, but that's about it." She felt weakness and pain, clumsiness, and the like, but he'd be shouldering it, so she saw no need to trouble him at the moment.

He didn't change his facial expression one iota, but he did say, "Baby, you don't have to protect me. Maybe I see you from the outside of the cactus, and you see yourself only from the inside."

Wisdom from Adam. Bless that boy.

"Fair enough. It's a struggle, and it's only going to get worse." She fought tears. "And I won't let it get very far. I don't need to live just for the sake of being alive."

His eyes watered as he reached for her hand. He whispered, "I'll be with you every step of the way, however you want to handle it." He squeezed her hand. "Why don't we watch a movie at your place? Something upbeat?" She smiled, returning his affection with a nod.

J***

The drive was quiet, but serene. The Catalina Foothills were lovely at that time of day, with snow gleaming from the mountains' dusty caps; winter in Tucson was ideal, if not perfect. She loved hiking the canyon—one more thing she'd surrender when her condition worsened.

The turn-off to her home wound about one of the hills, furnishing expansive vistas across the canyon and valley. The crevices shifted to purple as evening crept upon them. Adam sang, *"When the deep purple falls—"*

He paused as she noticed construction vehicles obstructing the road. She pointed to them, complaining, "There wasn't anything about this in the HOA email."

Adam laughed. "Babycakes, you're the only person on this planet who reads the fine print. Maybe they're building a homeless shelter."

She turned the wheel to angle her car onto the side road. "They're in the street, Adam."

He laughed again. "That's why it's for the homeless. But moderates only. No milds or severes."

As she squeezed between orange cones and pickup trucks, she noticed a black van among the vehicles with strange plates. "Now that's weird. That van was at the café."

He said, "Maybe they like the food."

She disagreed. "They never got out. I think they're following me."

Adam twisted himself around to see the van as they passed it. "I can't make out the plates. There are a lot of black vans in the world—I know, ticky tacky."

Clear of the work zone, she hurried along the road to reach her driveway. Adam hopped out of the passenger seat, rounding the car to offer her a hand up. She was touched by his kindness, but she resisted. "I want to move around on my own, at least while I still can."

He patted her. "Sure thing, babycakes."

Unlocking her door, she led them into the foyer. Adam pranced to the kitchen, shouting, "Now you can't refuse a drink."

She set her keys and wallet onto the entryway table, smiling at her brother. "Fine. Rum and soda, please."

As he rummaged through her fridge and wrestled with the icemaker, she sat near her door, her muscles weakened. As she caught her breath, intent on hiding any infirmity from Adam, she heard from outside the unmistakable sound of gravel crunching under the wheels of a car. Stretching her arms, she brushed open the drapes to see the black van pulling behind her car. She yelled, "Adam? Can you come here a minute?"

He shouted, "Yo ho ho and a bottle of rum—you'll be a dashing first mate shortly, babe!"

Janet watched the van, so she pulled out her phone to snap a picture of it. As she held it up with the camera image containing the mystery vehicle, the Codeka Genomics app flashed onscreen to block it. As the app opened, her phone died. "What the fuck?"

Adam appeared carrying two drinks. "Your wish, fair maiden, is my command."

She shook her phone, unable to rouse it from its slumber. Shushing Adam, she whispered, "Outside, that black van is parked outside."

He set both drinks on the coffee table, then he peered through the bay window looking out into the front yard. "That is strange. I should see what they want."

Janet tapped her phone. "Is yours working? Mine just died. That Codeka app crashed it, I think."

He whipped his phone from his pocket, dancing his fingers on its touch screen. "That's double strange. Mine isn't working."

They heard doors open and shut, so Adam focused. "Two people are getting out of the van. They're coming to the front door. What are they wearing?"

Janet strained to see, noticing they wore white suits. "Hazmat? What could they want?"

The doorbell sounded, with Adam meeting her eyes. "Well, I guess we should find out."

He stepped into the foyer as she pulled herself to her feet. She whispered, "Wait up."

Adam leaned into the door, shouting, "Can I help you? What do you want?"

One of the visitors answered, "We are searching for Janet Yazzie. We wish to speak to her."

Adam didn't waste a second. "I'm sorry, she's not here. Who are you? What do you want with her?"

She could hear them mumbling to each other, after which the visitor said, "We know she's inside. Please, we mean no harm. We'll take good care of her."

Janet replied, "I'm here. Look, I've called the cops, and my brother is a black belt."

The visitor said, "Can we just talk? You can trust us."

Janet motioned for Adam to move off the door, after which she opened it to see through the external iron gate the two visitors.

She could hear her own breathing increase, the dread pooling. "It's kinda hard to trust a black van stalking me, and you're in radiation suits?"

The visitor replied, "It is to avoid contamination. You are in need of our help, Miss Yazzie." He then removed his helmet. "I'm Doctor Gar with Codeka. Your illness is progressing, and we want to help."

She scrutinized the visitor's face, pockmarked but warm. Adam didn't waste a second. "Haven't you guys heard of the phone? Funny invention making it easier to ask before trying to kidnap a person."

Gar's face was blank, so Janet said, "I know I'm sick. Do you show up like this for everyone who uses your services?"

The second visitor removed her helmet. She said, "Gar, maybe we should tell her the truth."

He snapped at her without taking his eyes off of Janet. "Ferris, do not speak to the asset."

Adam postured. "Okay bitches. Explain yourselves before the cops get here."

Gar shook his head. "There can be no police, Mister Baumgartl. Your devices won't work now."

Janet understood, even if she couldn't imagine how they'd accomplished it. "Your app did this, didn't it?"

Gar answered, "Miss Yazzie, we are authorized to collect you. We prefer you be conscious, but that isn't required."

Adam turned to open a nearby closet. "Let's dance, then," he said as he pulled a baseball bat from beneath the hanging coats. Returning, he tapped it along the grating of the exterior door.

Concern spread along Ferris's face. "Janet, we're here because of your genome."

Gar reeled on her. "Ferris, return to the vehicle."

Janet clutched the bars separating them from the visitors. "What do you mean? What did you find?"

Ferris said, "Extra chromosomes."

Adam didn't take his eyes off her. "She doesn't have trisomy—"

Ferris shook her head. "No, it's a twenty-fourth pair, something we've never seen anywhere. Please, it could be why she's sick."

Gar shouted, "Goddammit, Ferris. Stop talking to the asset. Enough of this." He pulled from his pocket a Taser, shoving it between the bars into Adam. He seized, dropping the bat to the tile floor. As he fell back, Gar reached into the door to unlock it.

135

Janet scooped the bat into her arms, then struck Gar's arm as he finished turning the deadbolt handle. Screaming, he wrenched his arm out of the door. With his other hand, he pried open the gate. Janet swung the bat once more, only to miss him. He caught it, pulling it from her. Clamping his arms around her, he said, "Come away quietly and there will be no more violence." Shouting at his cohort, he said, "Ferris, sedate the asset, now!"

Ferris pulled an injector from her side kit as she whispered, "I'm so sorry, Miss Yazzie. But you won't feel pain for long."

Janet struggled to hold the injector away from her body, but her arms were sluggish. Adam groaned as he rolled onto his back. "Fight them, baby!" She kicked Ferris in the shin, causing her to recoil in pain.

Gar spat in fury as he tried to hold Janet still. "Ferris, hurry!"

Adam sprung to his feet, grasping Gar's wrists. "Let go of her or I'll snap your arms like twigs."

Gar shrieked as he released Janet. She tumbled to the floor while Adam forced Gar against the wall. "Start talking—and don't fucking lie to me."

Ferris cried, "Please, don't hurt him. We're just doing our job."

Adam shot a glare towards Ferris as Janet tried to stand. "Yeah, what's your job?"

A voice sounded from the yard. "A good question, indeed."

Ferris turned to face the stranger as Janet made her way to the open door. Gar availed himself the distraction by kneeing Adam in the groin. Shoving him to the floor, Gar made his way to Ferris's side. Janet knelt to help Adam to his feet while Gar asked, "Who are you? Are you with Codeka?"

The voice replied, "Nothing so trivial."

Gar wasted no time in answering. "Then this doesn't concern you, sir. Please do not interfere."

Janet peered out the door to see a man at the end of the driveway. His clothing was iridescent, as though he had wired fiberoptic lights throughout the material. It throbbed a cool shift between blue and green against a white base. His eyes were blazing sapphires, a deeper blue than Janet had ever seen. His eyes met hers, so he smiled. "My business is with this girl. You've served your function, and you should leave."

Adam hollered, "They're here to kidnap her. Please get help! Please—"

Janet grabbed her brother as she saw the figure, whispering, "No! Something is wrong. I feel sick."

Gar continued to argue with the stranger. "Sir, you're in the wrong place for Mardi Gras. This girl is our asset."

The stranger was amused. "I was under the impression that slavery was no longer permitted in this wellspring of freedom and empowerment." He stepped closer, directing his gaze at Janet. "Young Mona, the things we'll do."

She gasped as the world spun hard around her. Clutching Adam's arm, she whispered, "*Arkivar* said the same thing to me." He got to his feet.

Gar moved to the van while Ferris pulled the stranger's attention away from it. She asked, "Who is Mona?"

The stranger spoke with growing agitation. "What is in a name? Your database tells you so little, though I am grateful you led me to her." His expression hardened. "Nevertheless, your part ends here."

Janet peered through the screen mesh. Gar called to the stranger as he cocked a pistol. "Whoever you are, we're authorized to take the asset by force. Stay out of it."

The stranger turned to face him, then opened his arms. "Little Mona, do you know who these people are?" Without taking his eyes off Gar, he continued, "They covet what they can never have."

Janet fell to her knees as the stranger stepped towards the screen door. She answered, "What is that?"

He smiled at her. "Your genetics differ from the local species, and they plan to understand it with their stone knives and bearskins. One would call them Black ops? But I can explain it without placing a finger on you."

Gar shouted to Ferris. "My phone is dead." Switching targets, he shouted his warning. "I have orders to shoot if necessary!"

Janet heard Adam groaning behind her as he struggled back to consciousness. Focusing on the stranger, she asked, "Who are you?"

His face was cold, but his smile genuine. "My name is Norcross, and I'm here to save you."

Though her legs were sluggish, she pulled herself to her feet using the bars within the screen door as leverage. Ferris rushed to Gar's side while Norcross paid them no mind.

Janet met Norcross's vibrant eyes, causing images to flash in her mind. Behind her eyes. She hungered for him, though it was attraction usually requiring careful dates and conversations. Perplexed by her body's response, she asked, "Save me from what?"

Norcross gestured to their surroundings. "This world. Surely, you've never felt at home here. No belonging. I can show you another place, a world deserving salvation. Unlike this one."

Gar shouted, "No more warnings."

He fired three shots into Norcross, blasting sections from him. Janet screamed, but sand rather than blood poured from his gaping wounds. Ferris shouted, "What the fuck is it?"

Gar answered a full-throat scream. "Get the goddamned asset! Now, Ferris!"

As his body shuddered, a tendril of sand shot from Norcross's chest, forcing itself into Gar's mouth. He thrashed, choking as the tentacle hosed sand into him. His throat and ribcage expanded, inflating his hazmat suit like a balloon. At last, he popped, gushing clumps of blood-drenched dirt and viscera.

Ferris froze, vomiting at the horror. The missing bits of Norcross had filled, completing him. He moved like no other human Janet had seen, dashing into Ferris. Clawing his hand into her hair, he tossed her into the jumping cholla next to Janet's king saguaro. The needles pierced her suit, causing her to shriek.

Janet tried to stand, deciding that Ferris, good or evil, didn't deserve to suffer like that. Her body resisted, as though she was trying to wade waist-deep in water. Shouting at Ferris, she said, "Don't struggle—it'll just injure you worse. I'm coming! Adam?!" She unlocked the screen, pushing it open with a creak.

Her brother was behind her, answering, "Baby, he'll kill you!"

Norcross stopped short of Ferris as she screamed in agony. Turning to them, he met her eyes once more. "Mona, you would risk yourself for this one, despite her intent to capture and torture you? And seeing what you've seen? Your compassion is a thing of wonder." He kept her eyes fixed, and she stumbled to one knee.

Adam grabbed her arm to slow her fall. "Hang on, baby."

Ferris managed to stand, though copious blood mattered all over the white rubber of her suit. She dashed for her van, distracting Norcross from Janet. He glared at her as she climbed into the driver's seat. The van's fuel tank exploded, rocketing the vehicle five feet into the air. The shockwave hurled Janet and Adam to the ground. Ferris's burning body emerged from the van. The mass of melting flesh screamed before collapsing just off the driveway.

Janet was dazed, a hiss in her ears blocked the sound as she struggled back to consciousness. She looked around her yard for Norcross, but he had vanished. With a weak voice, she said, "We should help that woman."

Adam helped her to her feet as he pointed to the mess. "She's dead, baby. And we need to get the fuck out of here!"

Janet was numb as she watched the fire explode over her yard, one cactus after the other catching fire. It spread to her house, and she fell into Adam. "I can't move. Adam, my legs won't work."

He flipped her back, heaving her into his arms. Grunting at the exertion, he said, "We're leaving!" She felt as if her lungs would explode as Adam bunched his sweater up to cover her nose and mouth. He said, "Hold your breath until I get you in the car."

He poured her into the passenger seat as she watched a tsunami of fire consume everything in its path. She focused on it, and, as though time paused, the wall stopped, parting like a curtain. Norcross stood within the part. "Do not fear, Mona."

She wasn't sure what had come over her, but she yearned for him once more. He was beautiful, powerful, magnetic. As though her actions were not her own, she pulled the door handle, then pushed her way from the car. Her legs could bear her, though she didn't know how. Adam screamed as he followed behind her, "Janet, stop!"

Norcross smiled at him. "So great a courage for a Falterran."

She spoke slowly, as if the air was water. "How do you know that word?"

Somehow, she knew her recognition of it surprised this adversary. He replied, "Then it is true—the old fool did find you." His eyes returned to her. "He deserves a visit, after all. But first to you, little one."

Adam clutched Janet, wrenching her from the monster's draw. "I'll die before I let you hurt her," he said through fevered breath.

Norcross laughed as the wall of flame wavered in cadence. "No, Falterran. I do not intend to hurt her. I intend to make her whole." He caught her eyes yet again, and her body stiffened. As she looked at the broken remains of the Codeka team, he said, "These others meant to harm you."

She couldn't understand why, but she needed the stranger. Adam grasped her, shouting, "We have to go, Janet!"

Annoyed, Norcross flicked his fingers at him. A searing jet of blue flame shot towards Adam, snapping Janet from her daze. She grabbed her brother, tearing him out of harm's way. The bolt of fire struck her home instead, splashing energy over the adobe and glass. She climbed on top of Adam to shield him.

Norcross snarled at her. "Mona, this human is not your brother. He isn't your tribe. Your home is with me." He stood watching her as the fire consumed her home. "Come with me, and I'll spare him." He flagged for an instant. "You'll come either way, little Mona. Wouldn't you be happier knowing this degenerate survived our encounter? Time is running out. Mona, the things we'll do."

In that instant, she heard *Arkivar* say the same in her head. But this man was not the figure from her dreams. She gasped, the smoke choking her.

Norcross smirked at her. "I'm not the first to say so, am I? No matter the source, I can help you understand your place in these things. No more conflict, no more confusion, no more suffering."

As he reached for her face, her body gained strength. But his proximity showed her flashes of violence with no parallel—acts far more brutal, more violent than the deaths she'd just watched. His heart overflowed with malice, and she recoiled from him. "You're a liar! Stay away!"

He shuddered at her outburst, his form appearing to melt for an instant. Janet shut her eyes, wondering whether she hallucinated him. Opening them, she saw the figure reconstituted. But his face no longer projected confidence. "Mona, this world will end. It's written. Fire clears the wilderness, and these Falterrans can play no role in the new order." He extended his hand for her once more with caution. Janet gasped as a calm smothered her. The grisly spectacle horrified her less as she focused on the small hope his face conveyed. "That's it, Mona. The calculus is crystal clear: one life doesn't matter when compared to a trillion. I can heal your disease."

Her brain ached as she asked, "Why do you want me?" She managed a squeal with her next plea. "Why call me Mona?!"

"A heresy, by reckoning of some. You are imbued with *her* light." A smile erupted over Norcross's face. "And I only wish to free it, and you, from the prison that is this world. You are Vesik, one of seven gems hidden all too well in this sewer. You have tasted mere wisps of the power accorded you. I can teach you how to focus it. I can share truth with you."

Janet could feel the heat increasing, though it didn't frighten her. "What are you?"

He smirked. "The form you see before you is shadow, a mechanism under my power. My physical form possesses powers you can only imagine, all things of wonder." He pointed to his body with pride.

She felt the desert spin around her. "Power? You killed these people!"

He glanced at the burning body of Ferris. "Their fate was easier than that they intended for you. Not so if you join me. I come to fulfill you, to show you the things we can do together."

Adam groaned in pain as he tried to stand. "If you think she wants any part of murder, you don't know her. You can't have her!"

Norcross seemed to stiffen as Janet shouted back to her brother, "I need to know why he wants me, Adam! What is a Vesik?"

He extended a hand to her. "Vesiks open the way to order—you represent a destiny planned thousands of centuries ago. Others, like the fools lying dead here, covet your genome, and your powers. Gifts concealed for the larger truth."

She positioned herself between Adam and the stranger. "What truth?"

The Norcross avatar answered as he turned his eyes skyward. "Seven Vesiks are trapped in this world, and once together, we can unshackle the most powerful piece of technology ever conceived. With it, we can remake this and other worlds. We can *save* this world. But you must come with me, alone, now!" He extended his hand, even if it was just sand beneath it.

Adam groaned in pain as he tried to push Janet off him. "You have to go, babycakes. I'll keep him away from you."

The fire changed colors, turning white-hot. Norcross fixed his eyes once more on her, as a tousle of brown hair dropped on his forehead. He shot a jet of fire in front of Adam, warning him. "No ape can stop me, boy."

Janet's instincts were no longer in turmoil. "I'll give you what you want. Just don't hurt him." She closed her eyes, whispering, "*Arkivar,* if you are real, please help me."

Norcross gave an almost comforting smile, betraying the maelstrom surrounding them. "That's better. Come, child, and I shall give you—" He stopped, casting his eyes back to the sky as Janet's surroundings dissolved around her.

Adam's body tightened, his clutch on her strengthening. Yelping, she turned to look at him. His face appeared as though he were in a seizure, and dabs of blood beaded on his nostrils. She sank as her strength vanished, as though he were drawing power from her.

He pulled himself to his feet while holding her in his arms. His eyes opened, staring at Norcross. He spoke, but the *Arkivar*'s voice boomed alongside Adam's own. "Your treachery is known to me, Arkiyan Norcross. You cannot have the Vesiks."

Norcross replied in budding fury with a name Janet had never heard. "*Arkivar* Ephyr, you still live! Do not interfere, old man. You know the distances I've traveled to be here, and my part is clear to me. You cannot refuse the Preskamon. Your service is a pantomime, signifying nothing, *Arkivar*."

Adam/Ephyr replied with questions. "Why seek them? Revenge? It always fails, Arkiyan. Do you not remember the simulations? A quadrillion outcomes, and our home burns in every one."

He said, "Believe me when I say this, decrepit—I have achieved the solution."

Janet sensed revulsion as Adam and Ephyr's voices joined with no hesitation. "Impossible. The taint of your father dwells within you, Norcross."

The enemy burned with rage. "How dare you, you fool! I am Monagar, heir of Divinity."

This rankled Adam/Ephyr, and Janet somehow knew that the enemy intended as such. The two voices shouted, "Heresy—you are no successor! This world and its powers belong to its people, not to tyrants."

Janet tried to speak, but no words came out. Adam/Ephyr whispered to her, "Do not fear for Adam. He is here, but I require his body for this moment." He shifted on his feet as she fell completely into his arms. He continued to whisper, "Listen carefully. Norcross has betrayed us. He intends to wield your power as his own."

She strained and mumbled, "What is happening?" She turned to see Norcross approaching, flames following on either side of him.

Adam/Ephyr said, "You summoned me with a power unique to you. With it, you can slow him. But I must assume control of you, if only for a moment."

Norcross called to her, "Hear me, girl. I can answer your questions, even if your precious *Arkivar* will not. You are one of seven powerful seeds planted from beyond the firmament. This world is broken, and we, together, are called to restore order and balance." Pointing to Adam, he continued, "Do not mourn the weak. You understand only the smallest fraction of your power, hoarded by senile fools and craven leeches. You are as far above the monkeys raping this world as they are the rodents they torture and kill for their 'science.'" His eyes locked with hers, and she struggled. "You understand me. Ephyr would relegate himself to the sidelines. He is a self-loathing recluse, mired by his myriad weaknesses—sentimentality, asceticism, bah!"

His gaze hypnotized her, pouring images into her mind depicting death, war, murder, cruelty. Burned babies squawking next to their mothers' corpses, internment camps, bombings. She gasped as he waved his hand, dissipating the images. His face calmed her, and he beckoned her with his arms, exhibiting seduction. "Mona, these creatures have not earned salvation. Long have I watched over them, their depravity and ugliness an even match for their ignorance and stupidity. But there are billions to save, people who would choose righteousness over the petty disorder plaguing Falterra. Come with me, and we shall answer the call together."

"Falterra?" she asked.

"This world, little one." His anger was palpable.

She felt as though her head would explode. But she would save Adam, even if the world was too far gone for rescue. Adam/Ephyr held her tight as she turned away from Norcross, her face wet with tears and sweat. As though he could sense her conflict, he spoke in stressed staccato, "Do not listen to him, Mona. His aim is extermination. What you see around you is just a drop in an ocean of evil. He means genocide, and it is not his to command." His arms tightened about her.

Norcross shouted to her. "I promise you and your foster brother a place among kings." His eyes blazed hard. "This is my final offer to you, girl. Or your brother will burn alive."

Adam/Ephyr ignored Norcross's entreaty as two voices whispered in her ear. "He fears you, little one. I am almost prepared. Nod that you understand." She pushed herself as hard as she could, offering a slight nod into his chest.

He placed a hand on her head, and her body convulsed to life, nerves on fire. Her feet slammed to the ground, placing her between Adam/Ephyr and Norcross. Her body twitched, responding to commands she didn't issue. Moving faster than she'd ever, she flung herself into the monster, her palms connecting with his chest as his face exploded with surprise. For the instant there was contact, she could see herself from his perspective. The world appeared much different in that moment—all matter and energy around her resolved to fine detail. She had no words for what happened next. A struggle between titans ensued, each seeking some foothold over the other within her thoughts. There were shapes, colors, and blasts of light, all happening within the dream world where she had met with *Arkivar*. The enemy was violent, coercive, primal. Hatred flowed from him—rivers of fire erupting from a black heart bursting with malevolence. It terrified her, even with the cool calm of *Arkivar* blanketing her mind as he struggled against him.

She felt her mind return to the real world, her hands burning into the monster's mighty chest. The solid figure gave, dissolving his body into breaking sand. Ephyr's voice boomed with her own, her mouth engaging without her control. "Fractal cipher lock engaged! You are finished, traitorous Rapaxis." The name meant something as she said it, but she couldn't recall.

Norcross screamed as the complex images pouring through her brain resolved to Frankie Putnam, eyes fiery sapphire with a chest full of orange embers. Behind him appeared two strangers. First, it was a blonde man of thirty, handsome if depressed. Next flared a plump little man, face full of fear. Janet's field-of-view retained these persistent images as she disconnected herself from him. She dropped to the desert sand with all strength erased. Exhilaration appeared to flow from the creature, replaced by shrieks of agony. They morphed from bestial to mechanical as the fires about him fizzled.

Adam/Ephyr scooped her into his arms once more while Norcross staggered back. The devil fell to one knee as he gasped with foul laughter. "I see them! Ever the imbecile, Ephyr, I must thank you for this revelation. You should not have intervened. After seizing the Vesiks, I will destroy you, old man!" He fell, slapping his claws on the sand as the flames died over crystallized blocks of desert sand.

The *Arkivar*'s voice echoed above them. "These are not yours for the taking!"

The devil's eyes ignited with glee as he laughed. "We will see!" He then spat to Janet, "Run away, little girl! I shall catch you, even if I must find the other Vesiks first." His body convulsed as he shouted, "I alone possess the solution, Mona! You cannot stop destiny! When next we meet, I'll have their strengths. You cannot—" He clutched his head as the glow of his clothing writhed about his body in a kaleidoscopic explosion. His cries raged, deafening in their roars. He seized in one final convulsion, just before his body dissolved into crystal and sand.

Worn down, Janet asked, "What the fuck is he? Is he dead?"

Adam/Ephyr pushed her into the car before plopping hard into the driver's seat. He started the engine, then squealed the jeep away from the fire. He said in overlapped voices, "He cannot die so easily. That was a simple avatar, controlled by the true Norcross. With your strength, your virtue, we have crippled him, denying him access to our technology. He was wise to fear you, indeed." He patted her. "When he appears again, he will be himself, still a force too great to confront." Glancing to her, the familiar face of Adam conveyed love and compassion. "I know you have many questions, but your safety is my sole priority. Your brother Adam rests securely within his mind, a surprisingly strong one for a Falterran."

She steadied her breathing, but the world dimmed about her. She asked, "Falterran? What is this 'Vesik?'"

Wiping blood from his nose, he answered, "It is one link in a chain of individuals selected for virtue, for strength." He coughed, and blood stained his beautiful teeth. "It is difficult for me to reach you this way, and your body and mind are ailing from the connection. Our time runs too short; the avatar spoke truthfully, that this intervention has exposed the others to him. It was the price I had to pay to save you." He sputtered, a bit of blood dripping from Adam's mouth. God, she wanted to help him. He said, "Unfortunately, Norcross knows where we must go next. I can only hope we're not too late. But you should sleep now to regain your strength. The other Vesiks can help once we reach them." He struggled to breathe as he wiped blood from his nose. "I have work to do, as does your brother Adam," the twin voices spoke. His voice moved from her, as though he had shouted to her from a distant hallway. "Soon, I'll be unable to reach you directly. But intertwined throughout the whole is the Katafaj, defensive systems implemented long before we reached this world, systems even Norcross cannot control yet. We are enroute to rescue one who knows how to summon the Katafaj, and you must help him accomplish this. For now, rest."

Unable to keep her eyes open, and unable to protest, she drifted to unconsciousness. It was as though the ALS progressed months in minutes, every muscle refusing her control. She felt as though horror and worry would have been appropriate, but she was content that Adam was with her and the danger was behind them. She found it funny that the *Arkivar*, named Ephyr it would seem, dispatched her from the waking world to that of twilight. She had to wonder which was which.

12. Korobscur Unmasked

F***

Frankie found himself in a church sanctuary, carpeted in red, surrounded by intricate stained-glass windows. Gospel, as performed by the blacks, sounded around him. The organ played and tambourines rattled, black spiritual music flying high. Repulsed, he muttered, "Fucking jigaboo niggers can dance all they want. They aren't going to heaven."

He looked down to see his favorite fully automatic rifle in his hands—a weapon he'd named Nelda. Stranger still, he wore only his underwear. Why the hell would he bring a gun to a church without getting dressed?

It didn't matter. The jigaboos dancing before him weren't real people, so they had no real souls. The spics, the gooks, the ragheads, and the redskins were vermin—rapists, terrorists, thieves, fat, lazy, gas huffing featherheads. He hated them all. They coveted his money, his race, all white jobs, ingenuity, and the like. Mexicans invaded America, breeding poverty, disease, and crime. They were filth, trash, propped up by ivory-tower eggheads who knew nothing of the real world.

The gun in his hands trembled. The singing stopped, and ahead of him, a monkey pastor stood, shucking and jiving his play-Christianity. He couldn't know the Jesus Frankie followed, for only true human beings could find salvation. The rest were animals.

The preacher shouted, "God created us equal, not different. Whitey don't own God! God own whitey!" The congregation greeted his words with applause. He continued, emphasizing syllables along the lines of a typical sermon. "We should work together to help whitey understand what he done. We all will go to heaven

145

eventually, but he need to know what he done is wrong. He know what he done, but he don't know it wrong. Black lives matter, my beloved!"

The crowd applauded further, men and women screaming, "Amen," and, "Preach it brother!"

Frankie felt enraged, the gun burning his hands. These fucking niggers weren't going to tell him what he'd done. He didn't own slaves. He didn't kill blacks in the 1960s.

Black lives matter. He hated them. They just wanted to riot and destroy.

Now, he felt his turn had come.

He stepped down the aisle, aiming his weapon at the pastor. Squeezing off several rounds, he loaded that dancing monkey with lead, blood spurting from the exit wounds as he crashed to the pulpit. A fat black woman in a green dress screamed, so he lit her up next, pumping bullet after bullet into her until her brain-scrambling shriek ended. He left her a mountain of black shit wrapped in green and red like a toppled Christmas tree.

Others within the crowd scattered, trying to escape, so he fired round after round, mowing them down to the ground, where they belonged. He killed so many he lost count, but he continued, feeling a powerful release coming. He felt drenched in their blood, and the warm, sticky fluid invigorated him, just as it had on his first hunt.

After he'd fired many shots, the sanctuary about him was littered with dead and dying bodies. He came over to a crying child, a black girl wearing a yellow dress, pushing and pulling what must have been her mother. She cried, "No, Mama, no! Please wake up!"

He stood over her, aiming the weapon. She turned to face him, crying. He hesitated, trying to remind himself that she wasn't really human. She couldn't be.

He heard his heart pounding and the locusts screaming in his head. This was it. Could he prove he was man enough to kill just another animal?

Before he could react, she said, "Beware your dark heart, the *Korobskron*."

How could she know that term? And she called him by it—a name?

She infuriated him, so he squeezed the trigger, causing the world about him to disappear in a flash.

*F****

Frankie opened his eyes, his lungs heaving. He looked around, recognizing his bed. Drenched in sweat, he checked his clock. Four-thirty in the morning.

He exhaled, wiping the sweat from his face, and lifted the covers to check whether the ejaculate accompanying dreams of great violence had appeared. Yes, as usual.

He rolled himself out of bed, ready to hit the shower. Why did he dream of killing blacks? He didn't feel the hatred for them in his waking thoughts that he had in the dream, but it had felt so good to kill them.

146

To kill. He wanted it so much he could taste the blood.

He carried his phone to the bathroom, checking to see whether Pastor Chet had contacted him. The girl in the dream had called him by the name given by Chet to the dark monster inside of him. Maybe his dream self knew better than his wakeful self. He hated black churches, so it didn't surprise him that the same dream recurred again and again. And Nelda was a very real gun he'd bought at a show in Oklahoma. Guns meant freedom, and no one would take his without a fight.

After finishing his shower, he fried a few eggs and strips of bacon, following the carnivore diet encouraged by S.K. Varnum. He hated the PETA types, granola-chewing potheads wanting to control what he put in his body, just like the environmentalists. He hated to agree with Porkie George on any topic, but he did believe they could not tolerate the success of others, including those working in energy, such as himself. He worked hard for his money, so the others could go fuck themselves.

Saturday would be a light day for him. He tended to spend weekends visiting his dig sites to inspect the equipment, leaving the heavier duties for the weekdays. The pay had once been excellent, though he believed the pandemic's disastrous impact on logistics had been oversold, overblown, and maybe a hoax altogether. George thought the disease itself was a hoax, though Frankie knew better.

After breakfast, Frankie settled onto his couch for another round of coffee and a quick check of his messages. The bronzed girl who'd contacted him earlier stayed at the top of his messages. He wasn't certain what exactly to write, so he hesitated. She was a redskin, and though he felt aroused at her pictures, he couldn't imagine pursuing it further. Her kind had caused enough trouble for America.

On the other hand, he'd hoped the Russian would have responded, but no message had followed. Was it possible the NSA had intercepted and blocked the message? Why would they care about his correspondence? What did he even expect the Russian to say? He didn't know why he'd reached out to him, only that the Russian was supposed to tell him something—answers, but to what questions?

And what the fuck was keeping Pastor Chet from answering his phone? He would provide better answers, so Frankie decided he'd pay him a visit before the morning vanished.

F ***

The drive to Odessa wasn't one of the prettier ones America, or even Texas had to offer, but it reminded Frankie of the wonders of energy. The equipment along the interstate told a story of America he thought was important: Energy. Power. Throbbing machines. Oil and blood. His heart quickened at the sight of it all.

It wasn't all that likely that George would be visiting the pastor at the same time, but Frankie did text him to suggest he resist any meeting requests with George until he could see him. Chet understood discretion, though he hadn't answered his texts. Maybe he'd lost his phone.

Pushing that aside, he considered listening to another podcast by Varnum, but he couldn't clean the images of the slain parishioners out of his head, and he didn't have much interest in doing so. They brought him a strange sort of comfort.

Why should nappy-haired blacks pretend to worship a white God? They'd only learned of Him when the white man lifted them up. And to pay back the good deed, they'd raped the white woman, stolen the white man's possessions, and murdered the white man in his bed. Maybe this was to be the Christian's last stand—a holy war against the darker races. Sometimes, it was all clear to Frankie, and he'd fight for his place in God's kingdom.

Signs of the End Times surrounded him. In the last podcast he'd heard, Varnum pointed to the wickedness of socialized medicine, and said that having the government control healthcare would turn them into China or Russia. Someone, as usual, had interrupted the professor, arguing that America already had a largely subsidized healthcare system. Frankie couldn't believe that liars like that were allowed into schools in Canada, but then again, Canada as filled with French fruit loops and traitors against the Founding Fathers.

As he passed the exit for the Odessa Meteor Crater, he chuckled at the brochure he'd read as a child, which proclaimed that the crater was fifty thousand years old. Pastor Chet had told him that the earth was only six thousand years old, and that only the atheist evolution activists claimed otherwise, though Frankie did wonder about the geology studies he undertook to qualify for a fracking job. The classes had argued that the fossil record was something scientists didn't contradict. But God never chose to make the path of the faithful an easy one. He forever tested His elect.

Within a few minutes, Frankie would arrive at the pastor's home. The houses here followed a southwest flavor, though neater and tidier than the blast zone that was Big Spring. It was ugly country for certain, but Frankie chose to live there to cut his commute to nothing. Not that he minded driving, but living away from George eased his peace of mind.

At last, he saw the pastor's simple ranch-style home. Chet wasn't flashy-showy, like the prosperity folks. He'd often said, "A good Christian waits to have his mansion in the sky." Frankie had to wonder why there were so many Georges and so few Chets.

He pulled his truck into the driveway behind Pastor Chet's trailer and boat, a frequent fixture in the city. Frankie wouldn't waste his money that way.

But Pastor Chet deserved so many things. He understood Frankie, promising to intercede for him and stand before the Throne of God with him on Judgment Day. No one else knew him so well—not his family, not that lardo George. No one.

He sat for a moment in the truck, finishing his thermos of coffee and screwing the plaid lid back onto the container. Then, pulling the door latch, he stepped down onto the pavement, closing his door. He locked his vehicle, even here in his pastor's neighborhood. Gang members initiated the young by coaxing them to steal from others, and his truck might be an easy target.

His boots knocked on the wood flooring of the front porch as he headed for the door. Ringing the bell, he waited. The pastor usually rose early, so the delay seemed strange to him. After waiting a few minutes, he rounded the house to peer in the garage door windows. Yes, Pastor Chet's van sat in the garage, which meant he either was home or had taken alternate transportation somewhere.

Frankie made his way to the front door to try again. Still no answer, so he called once more. He figured most people would fear what he might find, but he wasn't most people. Fishing out his keychain, he found the spare key the pastor had given him some time ago, and inserted it into the lock.

Unbolting the door, he pushed his way into the entryway. The house was dark, and his eyes took a moment to adjust. The air reeked of something putrid, like rotten sandwich meat had been left out. No, it was worse than that. The smell took him back to a hunting memory, one instance in which he and Pastor Chet happened upon game which had died days earlier. It wasn't something he would forget.

Returning to the present, Frankie wondered aloud for Pastor Chet's dog. He whistled for her. "Edith? Here lady." Frankie didn't like her all that much, but it seemed strange that she didn't appear to greet him. He called, "Pastor? It's Frankie."

There was no answer.

He decided he'd investigate. The pastor, a divorcee, lived alone with his collie. Frankie always thought Edith was a strange, gay-as-fuck name for a dog. Mounted on the wall was a deer bust, one of the more impressive of Chet's hunting trophies. Frankie had been on that expedition with him. Guns wreathed the trophy, along with wooden crosses, something Chet collected. Frankie had given him some of his better pieces over the years.

He stepped into the hallway, dark and cold. Reaching his fingers to the light switch, he snapped the appropriate knob, only to receive a respectable shock as it remained dark. Fuck! He'd told the pastor that he'd fix the short in the circuit himself. Instead, he would remain without light. It didn't matter all that much; he knew Pastor Chet's house as well as his own, having known the place since his childhood.

Halfway down the hall, as the smell worsened, he could discern a buzzing not unlike that inside his head. At last, he reached the pastor's bedroom and rapped his knuckles against the door. The rattling caused Edith to bark a greeting to him. She whimpered, but the door was locked.

What if the pastor couldn't answer? What if he was sick? Pounding the door, Frankie called out, "Pastor! Are you in there?"

Dead silence. On reflex, he stepped away from the door, and then, gathering all his might, he hurled himself into it, breaking the latch from the door frame. The door swung open, casting Edith away from it into the room.

The sight awaiting him was more horrible than anything he'd ever imagined. Chet lay on his bed, the color of ash. Flies covered much of him, and large chunks of his legs and arms had been torn away.

Frankie looked to the dog. Her face was soaked in the blood of her master. He kicked her aside, cursing, "Get away, you fucking bitch!" She cried, scrambling out the bedroom door.

Frankie extended his hand to Chet's face, touching the cold, hard truth of the matter: his best friend, mentor, God's appointed protector for him was dead. As his fingers touched the pastor's hardened flesh, his brain hurt, hewn by a terrific buzzing sound, as if a swarm of ten thousand locusts were descending upon him.

Did Edith kill him? It didn't matter. That animal needed to die, if only for feasting on Pastor Chet like some savage cannibal.

The buzz diminished when Frankie disconnected himself from Pastor Chet's corpse. Something snapped in Frankie. Not sorrow for the pastor, nor for himself. Anger welled up, as though he could destroy the world himself. Maybe the pastor had been Frankie's only hope at salvation. He found his way back to the foyer, where he pulled open the folding door concealing a large safe. It was pointless to take a weapon from the wall; none functioned, for Pastor Chet did place great value on safety when it came to firearms.

Frankie had known the combination for the safe since he was a boy, taking the responsibility of cleaning the guns for Chet and his father when they returned from hunting. Now, opening the heavy door, he grabbed a magnum pistol, imagining a dynamite finish for that stupid beast. Loading the weapon, he called, "Here, Edith. Come here, dog." He knew the pastor wouldn't want him to hurt the animal, but whatever restraint there had been seemed to have disappeared.

The animal rounded the corner, tail between her legs. He took aim, knowing he'd feel better afterwards, but just as his finger touched the trigger, the doorbell sounded. He and dog alike were startled, causing him to jerk the gun. She moved faster than his reflexes, so he fired a bullet into the sheet rock where Edith had been. She ran toward the dog door at the rear of the house, and he chased her, taking shots as she ran. Fuck, he couldn't hit her.

He took a shortcut across the dining room, intercepting her at the dog door. He grabbed her hind leg just as she almost cleared the door, causing her to yelp. Before he could pull her back into the house, she managed to twist herself so she could sink her teeth into his forearm, tearing it open. He shouted in pain, "Goddammit!" He released her and couldn't stop her from darting into the backyard. He clutched his arm, which was searing with pain, while he watched her squeeze through a pair of boards in the fence. No punishing her now.

Oh, God, that buzz—as though locusts carved his head from within.

Punctuating the swarm, the doorbell sounded again, this time ringing several times. Who in the hell could it be? Of course, whoever it was would not leave after hearing shots fired.

Frankie grabbed several paper towels, wrapping them around the open tears in his arm. He'd never seen so much of his own blood at one time. Fuck that dog!

The doorbell interrupted his thoughts once more, so he shouted, "I'll be there in a minute, for fuck's sake!" He wiped some of the blood from the floor. Blobs of it fell onto the adjoining rug, and they wouldn't wash out easily. Not that Chet could care at that point.

After stashing the weapon on the kitchen countertop, he plodded to the front door. Peering through the peephole, he saw George. Why in the hell was he here? He pounded on the door while Frankie leaned into it, sending a jolt into his head. He shouted, "Just a goddamned minute!" He flung the door open.

George's eyes widened and his ugly little mouth opened. "Frankie boy! What are you doing here? That sounded like a gun going off."

Frankie stepped back to let George pass into the house, nodding to him. "Yes, I fired a few shots, since—"

George eyed him, then grabbed his nose, protesting, "What the hell is that smell? Like something fucking died." Looking at Frankie's injured arm, he raised his eyebrows, asking, "What happened to you?"

Without giving Frankie an opportunity to respond, he shouted, "Chet, are you here?"

Frankie shook his head with no feeling. "Pastor Chet is dead." He motioned with his head towards the bedroom, adding, "I found him in there a few minutes ago." Frankie pointed once more when George hesitated, holding his hand over his nose. "See for yourself, George." He gestured that his boss should follow.

Frankie broke from him to collect the gun from the kitchen counter while George disappeared into the dark hallway. The gun was still warm from the prior discharges. What he intended remained a mystery, even to himself. Was he still within himself?

When he was halfway into the hall, he heard George gasp and scream, "Oh, my fucking God! What the fuck is this?!" He escaped from the master bedroom to find Frankie waiting.

George froze, shivering and sweating, when he saw Frankie. "Umm, what are you doing there?"

Frankie thought it a good question. He couldn't answer until he recognized that he was holding the weapon trained on Porkie George. The buzz was deafening him.

Power. Power over life and death.

The hallway disintegrated around him, instead burying him into childhood memory. Young Frankie had been so happy to win a medal at school for spelling. So long as he could spell the names of the books of the Bible, his father didn't care, but this was an achievement all on his own, and his mother was proud.

Yet, returning home that afternoon, young Frankie discovered Porkie George and his family squatting, as they oft did. George's folks bounced between the homes of varied parishioners, saving money where they could, and they never refused a free meal, bilking Pastor Chet and the whole of his flock. Chet even took up offerings for the Dasher family; blessed in money matters, George did not repay the generosity to anyone. He and that bitch of a wife would complain about a dollar charge in error, fighting for dirty pennies.

In his memory, young Frankie encountered George in the driveway. The oaf snatched Frankie's medal, demanding Frankie tell his mother that George won it fair and square. It was simple, yet stupid. Frankie's mother promised to bake a cake for whomever took the prize, and the pig wanted that dessert. She, like his father, tried to do right by their fellow church-goers.

None save George, Frankie, and Pastor Chet knew the extent of the fat one's bullying. He was a few years Frankie's senior, even though he'd been held back in school so many years that they were classmates. But he proved larger and stronger in any contest. He'd ferret away Frankie's desserts, steal toys, break others, and coerce unpleasant brutalities. Once, he'd forced Frankie to swallow three cockroaches, promising that he'd cause endless trouble for him if he squealed.

Frankie could've recalled any number of these instances, as if George's scheming and lying in their shared time as adults were not enough to disentangle himself from him. He promised the moon, then delivered manure.

George's cruel vices left Frankie wounded and humiliated. But Pastor Chet had seen it all, Frankie learned later. His father believed the bullying would toughen him, even though he didn't consider himself to be weak. When he spoke to Chet about his problems with George, the pastor told him, "Frankie, God has a plan for you and George. You're supposed to stay near him, for God doesn't want George to fall. His soul will face peril without you to guide him. God tests us all." Frankie's throat tightened. Chet was dead, unmooring Frankie from his channel to the Almighty. Fuck him. Why did he leave? Just when his sister confessed her bisexuality whatnot, just when he learned his brother Tyler was a mincing little fag. He needed answers, and the man he trusted most in the world was lying stone-cold dead.

George's voice pulled Frankie back to the present. "I don't understand. It looks like Chet died days ago. Why were you shooting?"

Resolute, Frankie could see his face reflected on the polished magnum barrel in his hands. After a pause, he answered at last, "Pastor Chet knew me, George. Knew me better than anyone I've ever known." He looked to the gleaming weapon in his hands, then back to the cowardly sack of shit standing before him.

George held a finger to him with growing concern. "Shouldn't we call the police? Was there someone else here? You should put the gun down." He gestured his hand in Frankie's direction, a gesture he used all the time to dismiss anyone he decided was beneath him. It infuriated Frankie, so he trained the weapon on him. Delicious panic spread like wildfire over George's greasy fat face. His finger became a hand, shaped to betray desperation and shock. He pleaded, "I'm your friend, Frankie. I've known you since we were kids. Don't you remember?"

Frankie answered, "Yeah, George. You and I played together, but were we really friends?"

George pointed to the weapon, asking, "Well, we can talk about anything you want, but will you put the gun down?"

That amused Frankie no end. Here was a crook, a liar, someone who professed the ways of Christ, yet would skin his grandmother for the dirty pennies in the couch. He was a narcissist, hellbent on running roughshod over Frankie and anyone else save that shrew of a wife Sheila. God, if only she were standing in George's spot. He'd forfeit his legs for the chance to burn her alive.

He shook his head. "No can do, Georgie. We're playing now, just like we did when we were kids."

George smiled, then laughed. It was not his customary guffaw, but something even more forced, artificial. He replied, "Oh, that's funny, then." He took a step forward, freezing when Frankie raised the weapon.

The locusts continued within him as if devouring his soul. The sound was overwhelming, but upon training the weapon on George, it lessened.

Shifting his weight from one foot to the other, Frankie smiled. "It is funny, Porkie George." Bobbing the weapon in cadence with his words, he continued, "Do you remember that time you wanted to show me how you could throw a rock to knock an apple off my head?"

George winced in unease, stepping back. Oh, the joy this was for Frankie. He pointed to his forehead with his free hand. "You remember how many stitches I needed? The scar is here, just in the hairline." He smirked. "Do you remember how much blood there was? It was everywhere, all over the place."

George rattled a hoarse and weak breath, replying, "We were kids, Frankie. We were—"

Frankie shook his head as the swarm dizzied him. He answered, "You injured me a whole lot, always promising some trick that would keep me safe. Think about it."

George took another step forward, compelling Frankie to fire the weapon into the ceiling, spraying the two with sheetrock. The swarm vanished at the crack of the firearm.

George's eyes reddened, tears forming. He pleaded, "Frankie, we were just kids."

With no small resentment towards the thousand insults of this coward, Frankie admonished, "No, George. You're still the same fat bully—a squatter, a phony."

The fat one replied, "How can I fix this, Frankie? You want money? You know I have lots—"

At this new insult, Frankie roared, "Fuck you and your bribes, George!" He pointed to Pastor Chet's bedroom, screaming, "That man there is the only reason I've put up with the likes of you all these years! He told me that I was responsible for your soul."

The swarm screamed at this, as though it could discern truth from fiction.

Without removing his eyes from Frankie and the gun, George angled his head towards the pastor's last resting place. "Then you can't hurt me, if you're supposed to guard my soul."

Frankie laughed, at last furnishing the blob with his reasoning. "I understand now that I'm supposed to do right by your soul, and that doesn't mean saving it."

This fool quivered in fear, answering, "But Pastor Chet—"

Frankie interrupted, "Pastor Chet is dead, George. Now, I need to confess." He watched his prey squirm. "You see, Porkie George, he knew I'm a killer, with a demon inside me. He called it *Korobskron*, or the black heart."

Oh, the relief he felt in speaking the term aloud. The locusts respected it.

Exhaling, he continued, "I've wanted to kill since I was a kid. Other kids, teachers. You. But Pastor Chet stopped me, teaching me to hunt animals instead of people." He looked above George to a buck head mounted at the end of the hall, musing, "But I now know that you and the rest of the stupid-ass humans are nothing more than animals." He pointed to George, whispering, "You know it. Else why would you be sweating like a whore in church?"

Before he could complete the thought, George begged, "Frankie, that's not who you are. Can't we just pray about it?"

Frankie snickered, "Prayer can't save you, George. I know your sins better than you know yourself. I know what I'm supposed to do."

George said, "Frankie, the police will come. The neighbors…"

Frankie laughed at him. "George, I haven't seen a neighbor here in ten years. I could burn the house down before someone would call for help."

George begged him, "I can give you anything you want. Just tell me what you want."

Frankie tilted his head, popping his neck. He pointed to George's head, smiling. "Okay, then. First, I wanna check my aim. Let's see if I can hit a paperweight on your head." He pointed to a silver cast of hands, meant to be God's own. He himself had given it to Pastor Chet for Christmas some years earlier.

George wept, sobbing. "Please, Frankie. I have a wife and kid."

Frankie laughed. "That shrieking cunt is next, Georgie. And those feral little piglets are better off without you." He hardened his eyes, raising the weapon. "Now put that fucking paperweight on your head." He paused, then screamed, "Put it on your head!"

George bawled, reaching for the weight. He set it on his sweaty bald head. He sniveled, "Please—"

Frankie fired a shot into the paperweight, shattering the metal in an explosion of sparks. George squealed and writhed as the shrapnel cut into his scalp. Blood washed down his face as he screamed, making sounds Frankie had never heard from him.

Frankie felt as though he were leaving his body. The ecstasy was too great for him to bear. "Well, my aim is pretty good."

George dropped to his knees, crawling away from his executioner. Frankie trained the weapon on George's left, then right wrist, firing at them. George screamed as each shot severed a hand. Frankie stomped a foot onto his back, holding him down. "Second, I want to shut your mouth." He pressed the barrel into George's cheek, then he blasted away George's mouth and teeth. The bloody mass wailed and groaned, leaving Frankie to finish. "Third, Porkie George, if you have an honest-to-goodness soul, I want to send it to hell where it belongs."

George quivered, moaning, so Frankie knelt before him, firing a shot at the fat man's right elbow. "It pisses me off when you don't listen."

He swabbed his left hand in the blood, then spread it over his own face. He smiled, looking down to George, offering, "There, there, George. You'll be roasting soon."

He pressed the barrel of the gun into George's temple, and the fat mound of flesh shivered in shock. "Now, fat mother fucker, I wanna wish you a Merry Christmas."

He fired three shots into George's brain, causing his bloodied body to quake.

As he stood over his victim's corpse, Frankie experienced perhaps the most powerful orgasm of his life, as though God were releasing another Great Flood from him to wash away sin. Never with a woman had he experienced this.

The blood, the flesh, the power—it wasn't the same as an attraction. He howled, stretching his arms to embrace the cooling darkness. The locusts quieted, as though even they, now, needed to give him his due.

How could Pastor Chet have denied him this experience? Killing animals was nothing like this. He could conquer the world in this euphoria. To hell with shooting that fucking dog. Chet may have done more for him in death than in life.

Jesus said that committing adultery in one's heart was tantamount to the real deal. That elevated Frankie to mass murderer. So, why not do the real thing? Didn't God need a Champion to scatter the nonbelievers? The baby murderers? The fags who thought God's definition of marriage should be upended, along with all of nature? The greedy? The gluttonous? God killed all the time. Drowned all of the earth. It may brand Frankie a murderer, but wasn't God the author of holocausts? Yes, God had first doused the world in water. Now, he would douse it in flame! What a wicked waste. Had he burned George alive, he'd be off to an even better start.

There was always Sheila.

But doubt smoldered in him. Could he, a crusader, escape martyrdom? Now, the confusion worsened, his fear of death sapping him. It was fear not for his soul, but that this would end. He collapsed to his knees, heaving oxygen as if he were breathing soup. The buzzing resounded in the distance.

Then he remembered that Pastor Chet had told him how God would test His believers' fidelity. If he stayed the course, God would not abandon him in his hour of need, but he must commit himself to God's crusade.

So he prayed, "Father God, You see all things, and You make all things new. Help me to do Your will."

After waiting a bit, Frankie rose to his feet. He remembered that even the dumbest of cops could determine who had been where with cellphone-location data. He wiped blood from his own injured hand and arm before he pulled out his phone. His location data had been active, meaning his time would be limited.

But the Russian had responded.

```
Hi Frankie,
I am Mayak, and I'm interested in your message. I do
not know whether I can help you, but I have experienced
things of late that are unfamiliar to me. If you choose
to speak to me, let me know a phone number. I can reach
you then.
```

Mayak was a real person, and now, Frankie had his attention. Had he miscalculated? Hadn't he followed God's will? He squeezed his eyes shut, breathing slowly. The locusts returned, thrumming behind his eyes.

Belief. Unbelief. Faith. Doubt. Two sides of a bloodied coin.

If God wanted him to pursue the Russian, He would have to show up first. Instead, Frankie would stay his course. And, of course, this meant a few more had to die.

13. Ruby Slippers and Archie Bunker

*M****

Daytime in Novosibirsk this time of year was a joke. The sun chose to appear only here and there, and never for long. Mayak thought that its tiny song and dance always looked better through the bottom of a vodka bottle.

December was resplendent if one could tolerate darkness right at sixteen hundred. Christmas decorations were frequent, and Mayak welcomed them. They were bittersweet to Mayak for a much more personal reason: it marked the tenth anniversary since Sargon had vanished without a trace.

Mayak had spent twenty-two years with Sargon, befuddling his parents, teachers, and doctors. The wall had fallen not long before his birth, and a cold war, like any other war, eased not with a single date but a slow bleed. Thus, the state meddled in his childhood, scrutinizing him and his mysterious *skrytyypass*. In the decade following his disappearance, most stakeholders had decided Sargon was a property of Mayak's creative genius, nothing more. It was better that way. Crazy people might have interested the state apparatus, but psychic contact with a polymath such as Sargon was the stuff of the most dangerous intrigue. It helped that he was a learner, fashioned to sponge knowledge from his books, his education, and his mentors with great ease. His parents knew the truth, for placing Sargon to a probabilistic test affirmed his existence.

The setup was simple. His father would flip coins in one room of the house, and Mayak would ask Sargon to tell him whether the flips showed heads or tails. With a single toss, he could guess the right answer fifty percent of the time. With two tosses,

157

that probability was one in four. With ten tosses, he would have to be lucky enough to hit one in a thousand. Twenty tosses would require close to one in a million. He guessed all three hundred tosses, certifying his capabilities to a degree anyone would accept. In fact, it would be simpler to select a single atom from the whole of the universe.

When government officials asked him to tackle the same problem while they monitored, his parents had convinced him to fail the test, hoping to prevent the capture and torture he would have faced had they known the extent of his gifts. They'd shipped him to America to live with their friends so that he could focus on mathematics, and, in the words of his father, "Wield Sargon for good."

But Sargon had left him. He'd already gained tremendous skill and reputation as an applied mathematician, so he succeeded at Los Alamos, so much so that the Russian Ministry of Defense had asked for his help on maintaining and modernizing the nuclear arsenal. He'd disliked using his gifts on weapons, but his greater concern was that age would introduce faults into the controls, almost guaranteeing another Chernobyl.

And yet here he was, once more at the center of narrative controversy with his schizophrenia laid bare. He stayed in bed, watching the daylight fritter to naught outside. Sargon had remained silent for a time, and Mayak responded in kind, knowing that somewhere in his apartment there were surveillance bugs.

When he was a child, he'd found a way to chat with Sargon without opening his mouth. For some reason, organizing his thoughts proved more difficult since he'd seen the lights. So, he focused, imagining himself in a chamber, alone, just as Sargon had taught him those many years ago, and asked, "Why are you back?"

He repeated the exercise several times, each chipping a little more of his energy and patience. It was as though his *skrytyypass* couldn't answer. Mayak wondered what an imaginary friend did in his downtime. He'd asked before, receiving the not so satisfactory reply of "Fulfilling important, albeit imaginary duties." It worked on him when he was a kid. Maybe that *was* the difference—adults sometimes had less of an imagination than did their child counterparts.

Close to surrendering for the night, Mayak decided to try one last time. He relaxed himself, stretching his arms, legs, and back. His mind quieted, and he found the chamber. Inside, he asked, "Sargon, can you hear me?"

It worked! The voice replied, "My Podopech. I am here."

Mayak felt himself breathing harder, the frustration impossible to mask. "Sargon, why are you back? Why did you leave me? What hell is going on?"

Sargon's voice didn't sound strong. He said, "I have been detained by matters not separate from your own. This was not the plan I'd intended, but even my energies are limited."

Mayak tried to calm himself once more. "Was there plan at all? Last ten years have been hard, and—"

158

The voice cut him off with a chuckle. "You've put them, along with your skills, to good use, my Podopech. Your frustration is expected, and appropriate, though I am quite proud of the man you have become."

Mayak shouted, "You don't know frustration, whoever, whatever you are. For twenty years, you spoke to me, then you leave without trace. You left me feeling insane." Tears were rare for him, but he felt them trickling down his cheeks. "They thought I was crazy. They poked and prodded, examining me every way possible. All because you spoke to me. You fucked my life to pieces, and now you just show up—"

So loud that Mayak thought it would injure his brain, the voice shouted, "I am here for a purpose, just as I left you for a purpose. Indeed, I wish there were time enough to explain even the pieces you could comprehend."

Mayak replied in his mind, "What does that even mean?"

Sargon paused, then returned with a soothing tone, asking, "You remember *The Wizard of Oz*?"

Mayak nodded, whispering, "I don't understand. Why would that fucking matter?"

Continuing, Sargon said, "Do you remember the ruby slippers, how they gleamed?"

Mayak rubbed his eyes, squeezing the impressions left in his nose by his glasses. "Yes, I recall."

Sargon continued with the same deliberateness, "Glinda the Good Witch told Dorothy that the shoes could have taken her home at any point during her adventure in Oz, so naturally she asked why the good witch had not told her."

Turning on his side, he stared at the opposite wall in his bedroom, looking over a poster of Sigourney Weaver as Lieutenant Ripley in *Aliens*. He had loved fantasy and science fiction as a child. *The Wizard of Oz* had remained a favorite of his, though his poster for the 1939 film had long ago deteriorated to a point of no return.

But he understood Sargon's point, answering, "She told Dorothy that she wouldn't have believed her."

The voice electrified Mayak as it answered, "Precisely, young Podopech. Do you understand the lesson now?"

Mayak pulled himself upright, sitting on the edge of his bed. "You are saying that even if I hear truth, I won't believe it?"

Sargon articulated the point well in Mayak's estimation. "If you are ill-prepared to receive knowledge, truth and falsity appear equally plausible. You would not understand, and that is understandably disappointing for you, I know. I admire your courage."

Mayak chuckled. "Ruby slippers principle." He grabbed his glasses, placing them on his nose. "But surely you can explain why you left me and why you're back in some way I can understand. And who or what you actually are? You've treated me

159

like child, only helping me perform parlor tricks, then leaving me. I'm child no more."

There was another descent of silence, so he added, "Ten years have passed."

Sargon soothed him with his voice, inducing some sort of physiological response he recalled from his earlier years. "That is true. I have returned for very important reasons. In the events to follow, you will understand how I appear, the origins of your affliction, and the Calling."

Mayak scratched his head, stood, then slid his feet into his house slippers after feeling the very cold floor. Closing his eyes, he asked, "I feel you say that with special emphasis. 'Calling?'"

Sargon replied, "You are one of seven who have received the Calling, the third Vesik in a chain. I am a Herald, here to help you answer it."

Mayak rubbed his temples. "Calling for what? Why all this?"

Sargon's voice gained intensity in reply. "The only Calling which has ever mattered. The most important Calling there is. You represent an evolutionary leap forward, called to save worlds and all known civilization."

Mayak sank as he considered this. He whispered, "I am alien?" The room swam about him as he fell to his bed.

Sargon replied, "Of a sort. I'd prefer to have relayed that differently, but you need to know that with or without me you are unique, a man with a destiny to save worlds. Does that help?" After a pause, the voice continued, "After all, when have you felt human?"

Mayak frowned. "I am crazy man, Sargon. How can I possibly save anyone?"

Sargon answered, and Mayak felt as though the being were embracing him. The feeling was transient, though substantial. He heard a logical and efficient explanation he himself could not improve. "You are a creature from elsewhere, broken only because of where you are now. You've spent years alone, and though it pains me greatly, you could not have evolved had I remained. Besides, your affliction is the very reason I can communicate with you." He paused, then continued. "Our connection requires tremendous power, and we could no longer continue as we had."

Mayak cupped cold water from the faucet in his hands, washing his face with it. He grabbed a hand towel hanging nearby, wiping his face dry. The chill vanquished any remaining fatigue. He asked, "Power, as in energy? You've used some technology to reach me?" The voice failed to answer, so he asked the most logical question he could muster: "Are you here now because of lights in sky?"

To this, the voice answered in haste, "Yes to both. Because of events happening out of order, the Calling I mentioned has been triggered ahead of schedule. All I can impart for now is the next step. You are the most easily reached, but every intervention I make risks betraying you to the enemy."

How could Mayak not laugh? He replied, "What enemy? World is in peril no matter what I or anyone else does. It's amazing that we haven't died yet." Speaking to the mirror, he asked, "What is next step?"

The voice paused once more, giving Mayak time to splash more water on his face and hair. The answer came at last, though distant, weakened. "You know two others within the Seven Vesiks—one who contacted you, another whom you felt pressed to contact. For each of you within the chain, it is the same. You are third. The second contacted you. You reached for the fourth. He, like yourself, is in grave danger from a creature more fearsome than any this world has seen."

Mayak scratched some words on a pad before him, inhaling deeply. "But how—"

Sargon interrupted him. "My son, I cannot maintain our connection much longer. As I said, it requires tremendous energy, and we have little to spare now. You must simply do as I say. You must trust no one else with what I've imparted. Beware the *haligscriosta*. She is a flaw in the design, and you should fear her." The voice strained. "My dear Podopech, another faces danger, and I... must... reach... Please be... careful... my... son..."

Mayak's brain roiled in tumult, a flash appeared in his vision, and he fell to the cold floor.

Silence followed once more, but it was of a different character. Mayak couldn't articulate the difference, but he sensed that Sargon had, indeed, disappeared, maybe this time for good.

And yet, he didn't feel abandoned. Just piqued.

When Sargon had supported him, shaping him into a mathematical prodigy, he'd felt empowered by the entity, though he resented being an outcast; his profound capabilities had very much isolated him. His parents had feared him, and despite their best efforts to conceal their discomfort, he could sense it. His teachers and peers at Los Alamos had offered acceptance and trust, but the loss of Sargon was as real as losing one's best friend, mentor, confidante, parent, and teacher all at once. It crushed him.

But again, this time it was different, and it was more than just a change in how Mayak processed his own emotions. There was an urgency, a fear in Sargon's voice that he'd never heard before.

The stakes must be high. Though the world was in chaos, there might be order to follow. Yes, Mayak might believe once more.

So, he reached for his computer, opening it to search for the two he now understood to be of some importance, careful to follow the security protocols Sargon taught him. He felt fear when considering the American journalist, as though he needed to send the message soon.

Accessing the tunnel, he typed.

B***

Boothby fumbled with his papers, struggling at organization. Hallowed organization, per Headmistress Sagini; she'd complained at one deficiency or another among her charges, and he had been among her favorite whipping boys. He hated that he could still hear her shrill, smoky voice lambasting him for his confusion at so much of what life handed him. The heartless bitch had abused the children in her care in ways no orphanage today would tolerate. Closing his eyes, he saw her smirking, ugly face.

He hated that he couldn't forget. One can delete files from a computer. Why couldn't he do the same with his bad memories? Obsessive compulsive disorder, anxiety, and depression were all his bailiwick.

His encounter with the domestic intelligence officers had left his nerves in disarray. He'd encountered more than one set of agents representing governments he'd irritated through his writing. The American government cost him the most sleep, though his travels through Brazil and the Middle East had fueled his paranoia, leaving him gun-shy about international travel.

But the convergence of the two new contacts he hoped to nurture suggested that this particular situation presented more danger than most, if not all of his earlier scrapes. After all, he'd tried to reach one of the central figures within the Plowshares movement with the intent to position himself close to a nuclear weapon, and, like a bolt from the blue, a Russian wanted to connect with him—a Russian who happened to work on nuclear weapons.

How could both happen? Along with a visit from the domestic intelligence groups? Coincidence wasn't in his vocabulary: all co-occurrences were connected on some level, be it string or quantum and whatnot. He knew that the lights he'd chased all his life fixated upon said weapons, devices powerful enough to destroy the biosphere of the entire planet, so gaining access could place him closer to ground zero of a type three encounter—how he related, often believing the Estate where Ephyr imparted the chunk was Boothby's very own Devil's Tower. It was a psychic summons of some sort, leading him to wonder whether his childhood experience that cold winter night had impressed upon him the importance of uncovering the truth. He had studied journalism pretty much to do just that. But the steadily paying gigs constrained his editorial content, so he couldn't investigate along the paranormal avenues. It didn't do, though, to investigate the spigot feeding him with stories, and he'd done his share of ill-received reveals of those in power. Paper poison, they called him; his venue would have to be book tours, royalties, and infrequent paid lectures. He had a few admirers, including a few not-so-sane celebrities, so he could offer reform while not panhandling in the streets.

Speaking of panhandling, Christmas time lined the streets of San Francisco with drifters and derelicts. He shared what he could, but his inkwell didn't help those enslaved by drugs or insanity. He himself hated Christmas, though his was as personal a vendetta as one could have for a holiday. Headmistress Sagini had seen to it that the holidays were the worst time of the year. It was bad enough that she would tell Boothby that his more effeminate demeanor caused God to hate him. But the animal torture had been the worst of all. The orphanage was overrun with rats and God knows what else, and the headmistress had captured the vermin to torture them. She'd then place them on the faces of the children at night, justifying her cruelty by comparing the rodents to the demons surrounding them within the spiritual plane.

Jesus, why was he thinking about this now? Most of the time, he believed he'd succeeded in burying those horrors within the past. But could anyone ever be totally free?

Closing his eyes, then reopening them, he laughed. "Boothby, ya stay stuck in ya head too much. Stop it." Of course. Thinking too much tended to lead him nowhere useful.

Action—action would have to be the solution.

He flipped his computer open, and, to his delight, a message notification popped up along one of the tabs. He opened it, and at last, another message from the Russian awaited him, transmitted through encryption Boothby knew to be called tunneling.

"To Truth Seeker, I believe you possess item you must protect at all costs. I do not know what could be so valuable, but I believe you'll understand my words. For now, I cannot communicate further without endangering myself, so this will be final message for now. I've been told that there are seven in our chain, and that you are trying to contact more in said chain of Vesiks. I see plow when I imagine your contact. I'll reach you again as soon as I can."

Boothby eyed the screen before him. To what 'chain of Vesiks' did the Russian refer? And could plow mean Plowshares? If so, how in the hell could he know about Conique Voyant? Was this a Russian spy watching him? How could this Mayak know about the artifact Mister Ephyr had given Boothby all those years ago? He had been so careful all throughout his life to conceal this one thing.

On reflex, his breathing increased. Feeling an electrical charge of worry from his throat to his gut, he tossed his computer aside, hopped to his feet, and pulled open his safe. Inside, he found the metallic chunk, and he exhaled, closing his eyes as he held it to his face, running his fingers over the uneven surface. He'd long understood the need to safeguard this treasure, but the Russian's warning seemed to indicate new threats. The visit from the intelligence officers must've been a part of this.

Dammit. He had to reach Conique Voyant one way or another. Who could the others be? Seven people. Conique, Boothby himself, this Russian. Why seven? It was almost mythic.

Boothby was a student of mythology, though he'd detested the crap Headmistress Sagini force-fed him and his fellows at the orphanage. Tossing her aside, he focused with a sing-song. "One little two little three little Vesiks. Four little five little six little Vesiks. Seven, seven, seven," he repeated as he counted his fingers.

Seven in numerology suggested the need for meaning, connection, and whatnot. There were seven deadly sins, as the headmistress had eagerly reminded him. "PEWLAGS," Boothby muttered. Pride, envy, wrath, lust, avarice, gluttony, sloth. Maybe seven was just a number. Seven virtues, vices—who could know?

His anxiety spiked, leading him to rummage through the paper bags on his table. Somewhere among them were the medications prescribed to help him manage it. Maddening was the burden this disease this disease had been for so many years. He located his clonazepam, downing three small yellow pills. He felt old, tired, afraid. "Damn, damn, damn," he muttered, exhaling after swallowing hard. It would be a few minutes before he could get some relief.

Pulling himself from his thoughts, he sprang to his feet after hearing a clatter from outside his apartment. "Christ, what could that be?"

He squinted through the peephole in his door, conflicted that he would see Miss Tutog, her little hellcat, or even a vagrant dopehead known for wandering in the dark. Instead, he spotted a muscular stranger clad in peculiar glowing garb.

The figure stared in Boothby's direction, but a scratching noise behind him broke his attention. He reeled to spot Archie the cat coming from the bedroom. "How the hell did you get in here, ya monster?" The animal trilled a meow as the light caught his amber-emerald eyes. Boothby decided they were a way the little predator could disarm his victims. Noise outside caught his attention once more, so he peered through the peephole to see the man staggering. Boothby felt conflicted, wanting to help, but wanting to stay alive. The man was very good-looking, but that wasn't an uncommon thing to behold in San Francisco. He wondered whether Miss Tutog hired an escort.

The stranger had moved closer to Boothby's front door as the cat yowled. Boothby shushed, "Quiet devil or he'll hear ya."

Able to see him better, Boothby made out fatigues one could expect to see clinging to a martial arts instructor, though the fabric exhibited colors and patterns that changed fluidly, as though he carried under his clothes a mess of fiber optic emitters.

A mixture of interest and anxiety had frozen him, robbing him of his voice and motor coordination. Maybe he was an assassin, bent on silencing ufology. Even Boothby found the idea so preposterous that he blurted a laugh. The figure must have heard him before training his eyes towards Boothby's flat. "Jesus," he whispered as he bit the inside of his mouth to stifle all sound. He feared that the stranger could see through the door.

The figure took a step towards him, only to jerk his head away. Miss Tutog burst from her apartment while wheeling her twin oxygen tanks. She called, "Excuse me, dearie, but you shouldn't be here." She laughed, pointing to his clothes. "Just who are you supposed to be? The cosplay freakshow convention is downtown!"

The figure answered, and though Boothby couldn't understand him, his attitude was clear. Miss Tutog tensed up. "Do you have some official business? Is dear ole'

Boothby in more trouble?" She watched the man, then she pulled her pink robe taut about herself and fluffed her hair. "I'm a lot more fun than that silly little man. Is there something I can help you with? You're not one of those officers here to interrogate our resident crackpot, are you? He's not right in the head, you know. I've been calling doctors at Langley Porter for weeks about him."

Boothby whispered, "What a bitch."

At that, the figure darted his eyes back in Boothby's direction. Clutching his abdomen, Boothby groaned at the rumble of his sensitive colon. The stranger ignored the lumbering landlady and her vulgar invitation, so she dogged him by rounding the decrepit bird bath a few feet from Boothby's door.

She switched on the exterior lights, then headed for the figure. "If there's trouble, dearie, you'll need to tell me. I'm a taxpayer and an American patriot, you know." Stopping next to him, she complained, "You're not well, young man. Goodness, is it communicable? I'm already almost an invalid, after all."

The cat tugged at Boothby's corduroy pant leg, the ribbed fabric providing a meager protection from the beast's claws. Boothby shivered as he shook the animal free. Leaning into his door, he checked out the man again. The stranger appeared sickly—his flesh was ashen, and his blue eyes were swollen and bleeding. Picturing friends lost to AIDS in the 1990s, Boothby felt fleeting compassion.

But his timidity had helped him survive this long. Untreated HIV wasn't common, but the stranger ailed all the same. Was it SARS or Ebola? Boothby could use neither.

Miss Tutog seemed to think the same thing, shouting, "My immune system is weak. I can't your have your homo plague here! Get off my property and I'll call you an ambulance." She pointed her swollen hand to him. "I mean it, sir! You must go! I can get the cops!"

The cat sank his claws into Boothby's left shoe, pulling him a step away from the door. He yelped as Archie sprung onto a bookcase at eye-level. Locking eyes with the animal, he heard a voice in his head. *Dangerrr, hiss. Monsterr.*

Boothby responded, as though chatting with a feline were the most common thing in the world. "But he's clearly sick, and—" His eyes widened as he looked back to Archie. "You can talk?"

Commotion from outside grabbed his attention. He peered, seeing the figure snapping towards Miss Tutog with snakelike reflexes. She was startled as the first of her oxygen tanks lifted itself into the air before being drawn to the stranger as though he were magnetized.

Boothby held his breath as the figure shot a smile in his direction—he pissed himself as he bit his tongue, filling his mouth with the metallic taste of blood. Helpless, he watched the tank rise until the line connecting it to his landlady was taut. The figure snapped his fingers and the tank ignited. With one flick of the stranger's hand, the tank rocketed into a screeching Miss Tutog. Shrapnel buried itself into her fat rolls as the explosion slathered her with flesh-bubbling flames. She wailed, scurrying as fast as her gobby legs could carry her.

But the oxygen line caught her foot—she stumbled into the fence enclosing her courtyard. Shrieking, she slid to the concrete as her swollen burning hands left trails of smoldering flesh on two posts. Pulling herself to her feet, she started for the gate as the oxygen line snapped apart under the heat. But the god-awful gargoyle statue was her undoing: Mohgra's protruding horn gored her right side as she howled herself out of breath.

She swung around the statue, and her twisted expression was more horrible than anything Boothby had ever seen—her nose and cheeks were scorched away, and her blotchy hair and scalp smoked like the end of a cigarette. The courtyard reeked of barbecue and singed hair, causing Boothby to vomit once more.

Pulling herself free from Mohgra in convulsions, Miss Tutog tore free clumps of hair from her head. She moaned in horror, falling back as Mohgra's horns skewered her. She let loose one final scream as the second oxygen tank exploded over her, and there was no more sound from the roasting heap she became.

Boothby was so horrified that he had taken his attention away from the stranger—he, too, had watched the spectacle, unwilling to miss the details. With Miss Tutog was no longer on the board, the monster turned to face Boothby's door once more, as though the door provided no barrier at all.

Boothby's bowels and bladder evacuated a second time, the smell not making a dent in his fear. He vomited hard as he fell into his door. The room darkened around him.

The cat screeched, capturing Boothby's attention. He turned to see the small animal sitting in the doorway to the bedroom. Entranced by the beast's eyes, Boothby was petrified. He heard a voice through the morass, with words unspoken but heard: *No fearrr. Purr. Scarrred feeds him. Hiss. Makes him strong. Look at me.*

Boothby gasped, "Good God!" He wondered whether he really had lost all hold on his sanity.

The words continued to flow from the small animal. *Must flee. Breathe, then follow me.*

The cat jumped into Boothby's arms, cramming its snout into his cheek. With a bite and lick, it dropped back to the floor. He protested, "Christ, what the hell are you doing?!"

Archie stared into Boothby's eyes, the voice saying, *Calming drug. Purr. Breathe.* Boothby obliged, his attention focusing. *Trrruth is important to you, purr. Try see.*

This stirred Boothby to his feet, and he peered through the door one last time. The scene was grisly, but he only saw the stranger. Something inside of the figure blazed, an otherworldly energy. He stood, arms pointing towards Boothby's door. A

166

line of energy connected them, and Boothby knew immediately it was a siphon. Recalling the cat's words, he knew the man was growing in strength.

Behind him, he felt the words of the animal once more. *He weak. Needs you. Hiss. We flee.*

For an instant, clarity burned away the fear—somehow, he knew this man had coveted something he had. Could it be the chunk Mister Ephyr had given him? That didn't resonate to him. There was something inside of Boothby that this man wanted. It was a hunger. He felt the energy tether pull hard at him, so he resisted, pushing himself back from the door. The energy overlaying his ordinary sight vanished, and he knew he had separated himself. Archie vaulted into his bedroom, and he understood him to be safety.

A sweet voice called from the courtyard, entreating him. "Edgar Boothby! Do not despair. I come to answer your questions. I can help you find the lights that have eluded you these many years." Boothby froze at this, his insatiable curiosity nagging at him.

Archie let out a loud hiss. *No trussst. He liess!*

The voice from outside boomed louder. "I can give you truth. There can be no more darkness for you. Only acceptance and empowerment. But you must choose this!"

Boothby was tempted. Miss Tutog's ghastly end didn't enter his mind. The cat clawed into his leg with a screech. *Look! See hiss evil!*

He obliged, and the blaze in the figure's chest illuminated his face. Whatever he withdrew from Boothby was strengthening him. There was glee in this man, a vicious, creative whimsy behind his mayhem. Worse than that, even. It was a compulsion, something even the monster himself couldn't control.

Boothby turned to follow the cat as the small animal yowled in succession at his getaway bag, the safe containing the alloy chunk, then the window above his bed. Boothby felt numb, but he could follow directions. He pulled his bag out, grabbed Mister Ephyr's chunk, then opened the window.

He tossed his bag into the night air, then wedged himself into the window. Despite agility and strength leaving him feel decades younger, he was too fat to squeeze all the way through. He muttered, "Oh fuck me." At once, he felt three hard shoves into his rear end. He grunted. "Jesus, I'm trying!" The last push broke his body through the wooden frame of the window. He found himself dumped onto the concrete. Turning back, he saw that the cat had done the shoving. Fire jetted from the front of his flat, clear to him even from the sidewalk. He rolled onto his knees, fishing hard for the keys in his pocket.

Archie screeched as he ran to Boothby's car, a beat-up, rusty Civic from '94. The cat growled while Boothby unlocked the door. As he tossed his bag into the backseat, he watched the cat climb into the cab through the top part of the door.

Boothby shook his head. "Of course, you wanna come with me."

The cat eyed him, meowing, beaming into his head, *Drug wearrss off soon. Baddie wants you.*

Choking on the odors all around, he slammed the door. "My car is gonna smell like a goddamned litterbox."

Looking into his rear-view mirror, he saw the figure in his bedroom through the window he'd used for his getaway. Their eyes met just as Boothby tried to start the engine. "C'mon, goddammit, you can do it." He tried and failed a second time, just as the cat meowed a protest. He looked up to see the figure approaching. "Oh Gawd!" He tried a third time, and the engine roared to life.

He floorboarded the pedal, pulling the car free from the parking awning. Hurtling the car into the street, he narrowly missed an oncoming pickup truck as it swerved into a newspaper stand. Horns honked, tempers flared, but Boothby's terror would keep him alive.

He turned to the cat seated next to him as they sped from the apartment. "Chrissakes, what are we doing?"

The cat meowed, and he heard in his head, *Stick to rrroad, hiss.*

He banked the car off of the sidewalk, back to the street. He shot his eyes to Archie once more, asking, "Just how are you talking to me, cat?"

Words came to him as though on a page this time. *Atlanta.*

Boothby asked, "Cats talk in Atlanta?" The cat motioned with his snout towards the interstate. "Oh, you want me to go to Georgia?" He shook his head, looking at the odometer on his aging car. "We'll be lucky to make it out of San Francisco in this junk heap. Good God, why me?" he drawled with a croak.

The cat purred, meowing at him with the message, *You imporrrtant. Can't say much now.*

He breathed hard, digging his fingers into the steering wheel. "Who are you?"

The cat collapsed next to him, falling sound asleep. With a grunt, the words sounded: *Me frrriend, sent by frrriend. Purr. You must find others. Devil chases. Hiss. Frriend can help.* The cat collapsed, surrendering to sleep.

Boothby thought hard, as though he were driving on autopilot to Interstate Five. There was only one answer that made sense, the inevitable end to his quest. He whispered, "Friend. Mister Ephyr?" Boothby could hardly think through the horror he just saw, but something told him his fortunes were changing.

14. Second Angel and Enchanting the Disenchanted

*C****

Conique mussed up her hair as she stood before her bathroom mirror, fussing. "Oh, the tangles. Mirror, mirror, on the wall. Who's the most forgetful of them all?"

Reuben called from the other room, "Are you saying something?"

She laughed, placing the brush onto the cosmetics platter on her bathroom counter. "No, dear." She straightened her night gown, then flipped off the light, stepping into their bedroom, where Reuben sat reading a magazine through his reading glasses. Oh, he remained so handsome, even at seventy-five.

She grabbed her laptop, opening it and seating herself next to him in their queen-sized bed. She typed her password to unlock her system, then inspected her email. She sighed at the disappointment—no response from Doctor Nakamura. She rubbed her eyes, complaining, "By the time he responds, I won't know who I am."

Reuben removed his reading glasses, turning to her. "Conique, you've done more for others in one lifetime than most could do in twenty. Maybe you don't need this fellow's help in writing your book."

She shook her head. No, this wouldn't do. "His perspective is important, and I really believe he needs to be heard. At least, that's the impression I keep getting from God."

Reuben smiled, patting her cheek. "Well, then, keep trying. Just don't be heartbroken if he doesn't answer."

She chuckled. "He probably thinks that I'm an eccentric phony. Truth is, it always feels phony. I always feel like I'm just saying whatever comes to my head.

Maybe that's all there is to it." She fidgeted with her lamp, pulling the chain to switch off the light. "Who was that man from California, again?"

Reuben laughed, setting aside his magazine. "Oh, some loony who chases UFOs."

She furled her brow. "UFOs, as in the flying saucers?"

He nodded, then paused with a playful, knowing glance, adding, "No, no, no, Conique, this isn't another charity case for you to take on."

She laughed, pointing to the ceiling. "He thinks the saucers are connected to nuclear weapons, I'll bet."

He nodded, chuckling. "Maybe they are. But that's a dangerous business."

She tapped Reuben's arm, pushing with small aggression. "The Plowshares have been dangerous for us for years. So, he thinks he might see an alien if we take him along, I suppose?"

Reuben frowned, shaking his head. "Out of the question, young lady. We don't do that now. The judge was just being kind by saying you were too confused to be held liable."

Conique thought this strange, though she appreciated his protectiveness. She answered, "Well, maybe my insanity plea—"

He interrupted her. "Dear, you're not insane."

She laughed. "Same kettle of fish. Anyhow, this is the time to do what we Plowshares do best. They can't hold me liable." She glanced about the room, mocking her confusion. "'I don't know where I am or what I am'."

His demeanor changed, his laugh subsiding at the reminder of her impending deterioration and demise. He looked away, his eyes watering. "Oh, Connie, how are you so glib?"

She patted him, knowing he needed some reassurance. "Dear, it will be fine. God's plan for me has always been His plan."

She knew this was cold comfort for her husband, his relationship with faith being more complicated than hers. She knew from her childhood that the greater plan was more than she could know, and through each turn of events, God remained true to her.

He cried a little, then laughed. "I've never asked you to prove anything to me. But I need to believe there's a reason for this. Taking you out of the equation seems like a loss for the world, rather than a gain for creation. That is, if we're keeping score."

She smiled, touched by his respect and love. "It isn't for me to say what's supposed to be what. Besides, you've been the one saying I don't need to fight anymore. Maybe my visions are more FYI than DIY. Anyhow, God won't abandon us. And we'll be together forever, whether in this life or the next."

She saw him smile, and she knew he wanted so much to believe her. The truth was, as usual, more complicated. Her own faith wasn't as strong as she hoped. Her greatest fear was to burden and hinder her husband, though he'd been an unflagging support in the ordeal.

As a mercy, he murmured, "Goodnight, dear." He turned to switch the light off on his lamp, and she closed her eyes to reach for sleep. Rest did sound good to her.

"Goodnight, my love," she whispered. Like a goldfish rounding its way in a bowl, she guessed the morning would be novel. At least for her.

*S****

Shigeru woke dripping with sweat. What sort of nightmare could he have faced leading to this state? He often woke in a mess of perspiration, the alcohol causing a mess of his system. He reached for the warm open beer sitting next to him. Ugh, it tasted rancid, but he swallowed it anyway.

He squeezed his neck, easing stress from it, then bumbled his way to the bathroom. Half-awake, he tried to urinate before realizing he had aimed for the trash bin rather than the toilet. Fuck. The maid would deal with it.

Stepping to the window of his bedroom, he pinched open the blinds to get a look at the street below. Wet with snow, the street bore a few tire lines. He hadn't known that snow was in the forecast, but he wouldn't refuse it. He accomplished his best lays when the weather outside forced folks indoors.

He reached for his black phone, a phone he'd purchased with the exclusive aim of hooking up with women. His administrative staff at the university, along with leadership, insisted he keep pornography and the rest of his "sordid escapades," as they called them, off university equipment. Fucking prudes.

He thumbed through some profiles of women, seeking the usual blonde girls of European ancestry, his favorite. He'd landed on a profile he liked, only for his work phone to buzz. He looked at it, and an image of his assistant Tie appeared. "What the fuck does the perv want?"

He plucked the phone from his marble-top nightstand. "Hello, Tie."

His assistant responded, "Sir, I hope I didn't wake you."

Shigeru lied, if for nothing else, to coerce guilt from Tie, "You did, but it's okay."

Tie answered just as Shigeru intended, offering, "I'm very sorry, sir. I just wanted to get back to you on a few things."

Shigeru stretched his arms, yawning, as he flipped through more profiles on his black phone. "Yeah, what are those?"

Tie replied, "Well, Doctor Kunskapsen is dying, I've learned. Her sister tells me she's suffered a stroke brought on by a brain tumor." Shigeru turned his black phone face down, plopping it on the bed next to him. He paused, not knowing what quite to say. Tie broke the silence. "Sir, are you still there?"

He answered, "Yes, Tie. That's…that's really too bad." He paused, recalling his mother's battle with cancer. The physician combed his fingers through his long black

171

hair, sighing, "She could be instrumental in the next phase of my research. Is there a means of contacting her?"

Tie replied with some agitation, "Sir, she's as good as dead. She can't help at all."

Shigeru found his assistant's frustration irksome, so he replied in kind, "Watch your tone with me, Tie." Silence. Good, Tie should have known his place. At last, Shigeru inquired, "What was the other thing?"

Tie was quick to answer, "The American woman, Conique Voyant, still is trying to reach you. She said it's urgent."

Shigeru shook his head. Who was this crazy lady trying to contact him? What could she possibly offer him? Not sex. She was fat and old, neither of which interested him in the least. He returned to flipping profiles of dolled-up women on his black phone, forcing Tie to wait on his reply. At last, he offered, "Well, do you have her contact info?"

His assistant answered with eagerness, "I do. If she's really crazy, you might have to be the one to set her straight."

He snickered. "Sure, send it, and I'll deal with her."

Shigeru disconnected the call. Tie had become tedious to bear, and he had plenty on his plate. He opened the text containing Conique's phone number, then searched Google for her name. The first listed was a news item about her and her group. The preamble read:

Reverend and Plowshares Face Jail Time

A group of self-described nuclear activists face felony mischief charges for defacing nuclear warheads with their own blood. Reverend Conique Voyant, 75, pleaded no contest, though Judge Dean Harris decided to commute any sentence following her dementia diagnosis.

Shigeru laughed with some volume at that, saying, "American evangelical and liberal? Strange world." Checking the time difference, he dialed the number provided.

A man's voice answered, marred by a drawl Shigeru found tedious. "Hello?"

Shigeru poised his lean frame forward, propping his jaw with his fist, asking, "Yes, I am Doctor Shigeru Nakamura, responding to Miss Voyant's call. To whom am I speaking?"

The voice bristled, but, considering his own track record of treatment of strangers, he wouldn't project aspersion. Yet it led somewhere fruitful. "I'm Reverend Voyant's husband, Reuben Hamora. I know she's been trying to reach you."

Shigeru found this even more interesting. "I must confess my surprise that an American evangelical would be interested in my work, let alone marry an Arab."

The man claiming the name Reuben didn't seem to care that much for Shigeru's political commentary. "Well, we Americans are full of surprises. And I'm African, though mostly just an agnostic physician in the happy exile of retirement, so go figure."

Shigeru liked this fellow straightaway. He asked, "So, what's your specialization?"

Reuben answered, "Psychiatry." Shigeru intended to ask more questions, but this woman's husband cut to the chase. "So Doctor Nakamura, you should know that Conique recently had a diagnosis of Alzheimer's disease, and she is fragile. She's still in the early stages, but they're noticeable."

Shigeru had been so overjoyed at her flagrant disregard for America's war machine that he hadn't really considered the dementia component. He asked, "Why is Miss Voyant interested in interviewing me?"

Reuben's voice lowered, his answer measured. "Because she's writing a memoir and book on nuclear activism. She knows you're one of the world's foremost researchers in radiation sickness, and she also knows a good deal on your own personal history in grappling with it within your family."

The Japanese physician smiled, gratified that she had read the piece explaining his parents' ordeal. "I prefer not to talk too much about that part. I can describe the consequences of the disease in any detail she wants, but I don't know that she'll want to go into the grotesque."

Reuben paused, mulling it over, then conceding. "She's aware of the evils of it. We've had friends and acquaintances whose family members were tricked into the Runit Island cleanup, with terrible consequences. Many of them met with Marshallese affected by the testing in the South Pacific. Connie herself has met with victims, including many from Hiroshima and Nagasaki."

This touched Shigeru, causing him to fight tears. "I had no idea. I didn't know about her, though I've known of some activists and scientists at the *Bulletin of Atomic Scientists*. But I did not recognize this."

Reuben replied with what Shigeru assumed must've been a smile. He couldn't help but envy the belonging. "She is an amazing woman. She defies expectations, and has a greater love for others than I've ever seen."

Was such a love real? Shigeru had long decided the answer was a resolute no. But this person aroused a need within him he'd long forgotten. He asked, "Well, is Miss Voyant available?"

Reuben replied, "Unfortunately, she's stepped out for her morning walk. But she'll return in an hour or so. I can have her return your call then if your schedule permits."

Shigeru smiled. "That would work."

They disconnected, leaving him alone once more. After hearing the love in Reuben's voice, he hated being alone—alone in a world he wanted both to conquer and to save. And yet he could not find anyone with whom he might share himself, thanks to his appetites and idiosyncrasies.

He thought of his lone foster sister who had survived, all the rest succumbing to Little Boy's ripple across space and time. Trauma, to him, was as a great a force as gravity, a forge in which human bonds were both sealed and broken.

He'd ruined so many relationships by this escapade or that, earning him the nickname "dog." He thought it funny, for the canine was a noble creature.

He felt dirty and gross. A shower would help, and then he'd wait for Miss Voyant's call. Perhaps he could leave one bond stronger than he'd found it.

O***

Olga's mind once was a refuge, secure from the insipid whims of the world. Now, it was a prison. Frozen and in pain, Olga longed for the end. For a hospital, the facility housing her was pristine, but it was cold, sterile, and empty, as though she were ripening for the morgue.

On the other hand, the sounds about her evoked technology—a desperate technology. The machines whirred, burping beeps, whistles, and intravenous dripping sounds, all devastating reminders that she could no longer rely on her body to make good decisions.

But her mind remained conscious. Why? Consciousness was an emergent property of a biological system she found enchanting. Now, her consciousness was nothing more than a suffocating, cruel albatross. What irony.

She couldn't even ask for someone to end her suffering, to snuff her out. She and her sister had discussed death throughout the years, but neither had given sufficient details on how to proceed under the current circumstances. Her neurologist knew her preferences, but Doctor Michal was nowhere to be found, at least as much as Janna had been able to make her understand. Maybe he'd gone to a theme park with his family?

For exhibit A in her defense, she hadn't envisioned this predicament. Exhibit B for the prosecution was her reckless failure to share the grim tidings with her sister. The doctors had not spoken with her, but what would have been the point?

Janna sat vigil next to her, leaving from time to time for bathroom and food breaks. Time—the arbiter, the all-encompassing universe eater. Its amoral calculus deemed her unfit to continue, so Olga Kunskapsen the devout physicist would heed its judgment, even if it were capricious.

She'd leaned into her mental preparation, viewing this problem much as she did all others, by flowchart. A simple prescription, it defined the constraints under which she'd pursue euthanasia. It was illegal in Norway, as it was in much the rest of the world, but she knew better. Her father had died once his hospice nurses had administered the right dose of morphine. True, his bone cancer had ravaged him inside and out, so hefty pain meds would have been standard, notwithstanding the very much intended side effect that he stop breathing. It was the way of it most everywhere in the western world. Her cancer would lead to greater horrors, at least until the staff could locate Doctor Michal. Her end-of-life flowchart failed to account for it, so she couldn't even ask for them, let alone administer them herself.

Breaking her thinking, a doctor entered the room to speak with her sister; Olga fluttered her eyelids, hoping to capture the attention of either. Neither acknowledged her, and her sister refused to hold conversations on Olga's dispensation within the hospital room. The doctors knew she was conscious, but Janna should have known that Olga would want to know the details.

Details would have distracted her from the horror. Despite the conscientious nurses and staff, the pungent and odious smells of bed pans and catheters bothered her delicate olfactory organs. She could not bear this, and wondered whether it might be hell itself, retribution for her atheism. The respirator tube itself smelled like burned rubber, but then again, her tumor made it difficult to discern fiction from reality.

Janna returned to the room, a welcome reprieve from the anguish of her thoughts. She approached the bedside, caressing Olga's face with her warm, soft hand. "Sister, they're coming to take you to a room where they'll give you relief care." The long rays of the evening sun shone through the windows, Janna's red-brown hair catching glints; she was a beauty, and Olga loved her.

She tried to nod, but nothing happened. She did feel tears streaming down her face. She supposed Janna understood the love she felt for her, despite her having no clear means of expressing it.

After a few moments, orderlies appeared to unlock the bolts on the wheels of the bed to push her out. She wouldn't miss her roommate, and just hoped they didn't find the same wing in hell to share. She watched the lights along the hallway ceiling pass above as the doctors moved her along. Janna moved in parallel, asking questions to the staff, though Olga couldn't understand what was being said. Again, what did it matter?

At last, she found a place in a room for a single patient where the lighting was low and warm, the temperature comfortable, and an older nurse waited for her. She touched Olga's arm, telling her, "Doctor Kunskapsen, my name is Destine, and I'll be your comfort nurse."

What a fitting name: an Angel of Death by the name of Destine!

Olga fluttered her eyes, hoping the nurse would know she heard her. God, she prayed for a megadose of morphine to deliver her across the River Styx.

Janna stood along the other side of the bed, weeping. She said to her, "Sister, we'll make you as comfortable as we can. They reached your neurologist on holiday. He gave them access to your records and your wishes. I wish—" She paused to sob, and then, regaining control, she continued, "I wish you'd told me about your illness."

Olga cried along with her, saddened that she hadn't shared the burden. Not for herself, but for whatever survivor's guilt Janna was bound to feel.

The nurse whispered, "Doctor Kunskapsen, we'll give you something for pain, then we'll remove the respirator."

Good deal. She couldn't die soon if they continued to force-feed her oxygen; the sooner the better, she thought. Her sister patted her and said in a hushed voice, "I'll be back, sister."

Olga understood. Removing the respirator wouldn't be a pretty sight, and Janna need not endure that atop the remaining challenges.

Nurse Destine placed a small injection of morphine into the intravenous line in Olga's hand, and she felt a flush of warmth and peace. Next, the kindly nurse said, "I must remove the respirator, and it will be uncomfortable only for a few moments."

She placed one hand under Olga's head, adjusting the angle, then she pulled the tube from her throat. It scraped and hurt, but she couldn't seem to cough. She couldn't swallow, either. At once, she felt her weakness in her lungs. Without the support of oxygen, and with enough morphine, these organs desperate to keep her alive would surrender, and the rest would follow. If she were able, she might laugh.

The world flickered like a façade, a projection within the multiverse of a dimension higher than any she could imagine. Behind that superficial facsimile, the fabric of her universe must have lain in wait. And she aspired to it, hopeful that if there were to be answers, death would provide them, as though the experience of living was by definition one of dwelling in darkness, separate, ignorant.

She decided this musing was positively Eastern in orientation. Again, she almost laughed.

Janna reappeared, pulling a chair close to her sister and seating herself. Destine spoke words to Janna, but Olga neither understood nor cared. Even the details lost their allure. After all, what was life when one expected death? Janna reached for her hand, and with a squeeze, she asked, "Are you comfortable, sister?"

Olga blinked her eyes, reminding her that she and her sister would pretend to be cats as children, smiling at each other with their eyes. Janna wept, but she refused to turn away from dying, even if it was the hardest part of living. Olga would never have asked her, but she was glad her sister was with her.

Janna started singing the melody to Grieg's "Strange Music," maybe Olga's favorite piece of music. The words had been added for a film adaptation of his life, and Janna always carried a torch for the leading man. God, her soprano voice was sublime. The girl missed her calling, derailed by an ugly marriage with an even uglier divorce.

But the time for worry had gone, if ever it had come. This could be a beautiful death, graced with lilting. Consciousness melted from Olga, and each time she closed her eyes, she thought it might be the last. She knew no fear, felt no sorrow. Time had been her master, though maybe there was a place where, per the lyrics, time couldn't change. Janna didn't seem able to sing more.

A lyric baritone voice roused her, singing the lyrics. It could have been Olga's hallucination, but it captured the attention of both Janna and the hospice nurse. Still more perplexing were the strings and brass wreathing the masculine croon.

176

"Soft breeze, whispering dreams.
The summer winds are sighing.
The leaves are lullabying.
Violins are all around you,
I can hear the calls' resound of bounding brass
That seems to say
I've found you, I've found you, I've found you."

The sounds were intoxicating (as were the opiates!) Janna and the nurse didn't move, as though time were slowing to a crawl. Olga couldn't see the man since the door was just outside her peripheral vision. She was not frightened as the sweet voice continued the lyrics.

As his voice and the orchestrations washed over her, the man reached her bedside. Janna remained fixed, glancing to the open door through which this man had passed. Resolved in Olga's vision, she studied him. He was as beautiful as any angel she could imagine, with black-as-coal hair, emerald and amber eyes, pale flesh, and square features. He wore a strange tunic of onyx with rivulets and currents of crimson, organic in their movements throughout the whole of the tunic. Reaper or no, he wasn't grim. If she had hallucinated him, she'd have to commend the doctors for the cocktail.

His sweet voice stopped singing, even as the orchestra continued. He whispered, "No worries, Olga the Knowing. Your sister and nurse are entranced for a short while." It was strange; he was a stranger, yet she knew he meant her no harm. Was it something below the rational mind, an instinct? The morphine? Maybe Janna, at last, had rubbed off on her.

He seated himself next to her in the hospital bed. The closer she was to this man, the better she felt, as though she were a little girl, basking under her father's nurturing. He traced her cheek with his fingers, speaking with warm reassurance. "My name is Zephyr. You've come so far, admirably so. And—" He said as he placed a finger above her left eye. "—let me search for it." The white fluorescent light shifted to gold, then red.

Fixing his eyes on her forehead, Zephyr covered it with his left hand. With empathy, he whispered, "I see it. There, affixed to the parietal lobe." He met her eyes with a nod. "It's metastatic, leeching from the surrounding tissues." He sighed. "Yes, not a moment too soon. I've traveled too far to lose you, Olga Kunskapsen." She couldn't respond, save a plea with her own eyes. He continued, "No sentient creature ought to suffer this way. I can repair some of the damage now, but you must trust me." She blinked in response, just as she had with her sister.

Placing his hands upon her face, fingertips electric against her skin, he bowed his head in what she thought must be hallowed genuflection.

Her mind flooded with images of a world so unlike hers—a civilization of phenomenal technology, airships, space elevators, incredible transit systems, orbital rings, vast space stations, and a flash of the earth, or some planetary doppelganger, only with a ring much like that of Saturn. The images overwhelmed her, one after the other, all of a world both similar and different.

Soon, her muscles tingled, starting to extend and contract. The man seemed to be expending great energy in this act, as though he were transferring his own life energy to her. She could soon move her fingers and toes once more. He concentrated, pressing his fingers hard into her face and head, sending shock surges passing into her.

She felt as though electricity were hurtling along every nerve and ganglia. More images flashed in her mind, but she couldn't articulate them—swirls of color, vast technological complexes housing what?

A woman's voice called, "Seven seeds. Seven calls. Seven ciphers. Seven fractures." The voice was urgent, as though the import of her words might move mountains.

There were doors leading to stranger-still worlds—and doors within doors. These were whole worlds! Variations on Earth. Paradise described many of them, perdition others.

She tensed for the last few seconds of their bond as a shadow covered the worlds, cast from an unknowable thing.

Olga knew—these were two words which had the totality of her life. But this knowledge proved too heavy a burden, even for her. She gasped for oxygen, her cells dying in the vicious extermination of people—all people everywhere.

As though neither could suffer another instant of it, Zephyr disconnected himself, slumping from the bed onto his knees. Olga sucked soupy air into her lungs, then pulled herself up to a seated pose. She reached for him, brightened but parched. "I can speak. My God, I can move!" Her words rang and echoed, reminding her of a time Janna had talked her into trying mushrooms. Trembling, Zephyr heaved.

She touched her savior's shoulder as she asked, "What have you done to me? What is happening?" Shifting gears, she added, "Are you okay?"

He righted himself before her, answering between deep breaths. Taking her hand, he said, "Considering your predicament, you're charitable to ask about my welfare."

She touched her head, but it had numbed. "My predicament? The tumor?"

He grinned while replying words between breaths. "Ever the *Gemyn*, you have questions at the ready. I haven't cured you completely. That must wait for the proper tools."

She touched his clothing, tracing the luminescence with her fingers. "What is happening? I feel strange. What is *Gemyn*?" Her thoughts shifted to her sister. Glancing to her frozen form, she asked, "Janna? My nurse? What is happening?" The lighting had become the color of blood.

"Forgive my indulgence—I did not properly translate it. It is arcane, even in my world. *Gemyn* loosely means curator of knowledge." He looked at them with a nod. "I have tapped an ability unique to you. We sit within a temporal distortion—you might call it a timeslip."

The words landed hard. "That's not possible."

Another smile graced his elegant features. "Well, for most. But not you. Besides, you should recognize the redshift your own Doppler described."

Olga tried to straighten her back, but her body resisted. "I don't believe you. This must be a dream. You can't be real."

His expression was playful. "Then it is fortunate you possess so rich an imagination." He firmed his features. "You were literally moments from irretrievable expiration."

She touched her own head, looking at him in puzzlement. "You make it sound as though I'm a canned good. I want to talk to my sister."

The whimsy left his emerald eyes. "There isn't time now. This place is not safe. Further, if we pull her into the distortion, it will permanently damage her."

This miffed Olga. "This is insane. I don't think I like this dream."

He glanced at the open door with worry. "I assure you we are in agreement, Professor."

She folded her arms. "Call me Olga, please. Now, three things—one, start by telling me what you did to me."

He sat back on his knees to gather steam. "In short, I've released into your system a nanoswarm to triage your brain and supporting systems."

She touched her head. "The doctor said I suffered a stroke. How?"

He managed to stand. "Neuronal and subneuronal polyplasts are holding your connections open, sweeping you free of necrotic tissue. It's delicate work, and I am no physician. Please, your second thing?"

Olga asked, "What is a polyplast? A nanobot?"

He nodded. "Smaller as needed. Polyplasts are multipurpose machines capable of manipulating matter at the molecular level. This sort of work isn't in my training, but we'll manage until we find better help."

She thought it over, then said, "Two, how is this temporal distortion possible?"

He stood to his feet, but she held his gaze. He answered, "Irony isn't lost on me, but that will require more time than we have. But you are, at least in this world, a physicist. If my information is correct, you've been thinking about this for some time." He then produced a small black pouch. Pointing to it, he said, "Inside, you will find clothes fitting you. Thirdly?"

She opened the container, finding a material resembling Zephyr's fittings. "Why are we in danger?"

He motioned for her. "That is simple. Another of my kind is searching for you, and his intentions are dire."

She stiffened at that. "Doesn't sound simple to me. The shadow? What did I see?"

Zephyr gestured that she stand as he replied, "The images are a combination of our Synax—" She cocked her head, beckoning he explain. "—the psychic bond we shared as I transferred the nanoswarm to your body. The shadow could be him."

He pulled the material from the pouch as he answered, "May I?" He took her hand to help her stand. The material exploded over her, fitting her in a handsome suit. He placed his hands on her arms, locking eyes with her. "Skepticism marks a good scientist, but, as one to another, I can answer many questions you've yet to imagined." As blood moved to her head, she felt woozy. He caught her, whispering, "The treatment will leave you intoxicated. Besides, the distortion is ending." His words buzzed, as though they reflected from the walls but widened in frequency. Zephyr continued, "I do not wish to be indelicate, but you are in danger. The shadow—"

Olga reached for her sister's face, gorgeous if statuesque. Something connected within her head, so she spoke the name in completion of his sentence. "—Is Doctor Norcross."

The name pained Zephyr. With a drawn stare past her, he said, "Whatever you learned of him, Norcross means to level this world. He was intended to be Falterra's, or Earth's, eight angel, but, instead, he has abrogated his oath. His betrayal runs deep, flaunting reverence for vulgar avarice." She watched him as he seemed to become lost in thought. At last, he turned his face to hers. "There are others we must find, all in danger. Please, the local distortion field will destabilize soon, and we haven't the time to correct it."

She looked at her sister once more, noting the shift in the light's color. "I can't believe this. If you and your abilities are real, why wait until I'm almost dead to save me? And why do I matter?"

He breathed an almost imperceptible sigh before answering. "I know you have nothing but questions. But we do not have access to the full suite of tools if we are to maintain a lead over him. Your neurologist sequenced your genome to help better understand the cancer inside of you. More than Norcross will come for you should agencies within this world see those results."

She asked, "What results?"

Zephyr touched his arm as though he read some invisible notes. "The distortion is collapsing."

She crossed her arms. "Doctor Michal sent that lab to some genomics service. Codeka, I think. What did they learn?"

He answered at last. "They will know you possess two chromosomes not native to this world. We call them zed-24, left and right. I accessed Codeka's internal data to locate you. Norcross would have done the same."

She felt a flutter within her at this, as though it couldn't be anything less than true. But skepticism was unshakable. "Polyploidy would almost always kill a human being. This is some fantasy concocted by my dying brain."

Zephyr touched her face, leaning his head towards hers. "Then reason it logically. You If I am genuine, you should follow me on the strength of what we've accomplished here. If I am mere conjecture, a dalliance in speculation, you have nothing to lose."

Olga wasn't satisfied. "If Norcross is going to endanger my sister, I refuse to leave her."

He nodded back towards the hospital bed. "He will forego this stop if he and your sister both believe you died. You are of no use to him if you're dead."

She wheeled to see her pale, frail body lying near death. Nauseated, she demanded, "What trick is this?"

He touched her shoulder. "It is a ruse, designed to convince your sister that you have died. I must supply this facsimile so that your sister will not interest him."

She found herself weeping once more. "I do not wish to say goodbye to her."

His eyes filled with pity. "It would be goodbye either way. But believe me when I say that your sister and the other inhabitants of this world will face extinction if Norcross gathers you first. This is an opportunity to save them all, and to claim your birthright. Yours is the gift of knowledge. It neither appalls nor defeats you, Olga. I am loathe to invoke more of the arcane, but the moment demands piety: the **Preskamon** was issued, and we reply with the **Verafaj**. The summons and the reply. With it, you may advance your governing intent—know the knowable, relying only on dispassionate logic."

He was right. Hers was the cool intellect committees and research symposia preferred; even her cancer diagnosis scarcely touched her emotions. But Janna was a different story, even if she thought Olga was too much of a stick in the mud. That made her smile, so she remembered Janna: Embracing her five-year-old sister after bumping her knee. Wiping her tears when a fifteen-year-old Janna's first boyfriend rejected her. Holding her hand during their mother's funeral. Spending hours on the phone with her during her separation from her husband. Playing with Janna's children. Watching her from Olga's deathbed.

The copy of herself lay in peace. Janna would mourn her, but she would go on.

Olga turned from all this, leaving a life behind. Zephyr led her by the hand, and strength shot into her legs. They left the room, entering the hallway as all the lights intensified to a blinding white.

Unaware of what was ahead, she found herself relying on faith. Funny that all it took was reaching the gates of death.

Part Two: Verafaj (the Answer)

15. Trusting the Navigator

*B****

Boothby drove his car into the late-night hours, hopeful that inclement weather wouldn't delay him. He had decided, whether the cat agreed or not, that he would drive to Atlanta with few fuel stops. The small animal appeared contented, sleeping in a roll. "You've gotta strange way of showing loyalty. She was your owner," he muttered.

Her grisly sacrifice meant he'd survived the encounter. So little in his life had ever made sense, and he didn't like furry little creatures one bit. But this cat was something more; maybe he was supposed to learn a lesson of some sort? The sight of the sleeping thing comforted him, even if someone or something was playing puppeteer to the feline.

Archie's golden eyes opened, and he craned his neck in the direction of Boothby's hand. Attention seeking? With hesitation, he touched the small head, his fingers brushing over the soft fur, causing little Archie to stretch, yawn, and purr. Boothby felt all warm and fuzzy, as though the two had been synchronized somehow. Chuckling, he said, "You don't miss Miss Tutog, I guess."

Archie looked up to him, meowed, then situated himself to sleep again. No words, thoughts, or whatnot.

Boothby cursed as he tightened his hands on the worn steering wheel. "Shit, I forgot my medications." The cat peeped, so he looked to see him staring up at Boothby. "Well, I'm crazy with 'em and without 'em. Right, cat? Talking to a cat, hrrm." Hundreds of miles lay between him and his destination.

As he passed into northern Arizona along the interstate, dirt and snow clouded his windshield. He pulled the wiper control to clean his windshield, but the motor hummed without spraying even a drop. "You piece of shit," he mumbled. Paper towels weren't something on which he'd ever skimped. Or glass cleaner. Or masks. Or gloves. The pandemic had affirmed his germophobia, a quirk his nagging former beau could not tolerate. Archie proved a better traveling companion, remaining silent rather than needling him on his eccentricities.

Archie stirred a little with a small meow, pointing his head to the steering wheel. He then dug his claws into the upholstery, prompting Boothby to shout, "Chrissakes! Why are ya tearing my car—" He couldn't complete the protestation before the engine sputtered and seized. "Mary full of grace, now what?" He struck the same steering wheel as the car lurched, bounced, and fizzled. Archie had been anchoring himself to the seat with a clear premonition.

He struggled to maintain control of the car on the icy freeway, cajoling his vehicle to limp to the shoulder. Smoke billowed from the engine, and Boothby slammed his eyelids closed. He slapped the steering wheel hard, shouting a stream of expletives.

Archie struggled, projecting words into Boothby's mind. *We're where we need to be.*

He pointed to the snow-covered fir trees gleaming under the moon. "This is the spot? We're in the middle of nowhere!"

The cat collapsed into his lap, drained by the communication. Boothby clutched the feline's head and neck, caressing him. So, he closed his eyes, exhaled, and waited.

C***

Conique had returned from her morning walk rested and alert. Reuben, bless him, permitted her a solo exercise jaunt on the condition she carry her cellphone, which was location tracked by his own. She was also required to take their golden retriever with them, given that the dog wouldn't forget the way home. She was grateful for his devotion, even if it was infirmity that caused it to bloom. Then again, upsets amused her after the fact, considering she now might forget why or even that she felt this way or that.

Entering the kitchen, she unfastened Aurum's purple leash. The dog groaned, panted, and accepted a few pats on the head. The old girl had been an inexhaustible source of love, entertainment, and fun. At least Conique knew she would die before she'd lose another friend, pet, or, God forbid, Reuben himself.

Her husband must've been in the back of the house, so she sneaked a peek at the caller identifications on their landline. Rapture—E.G. Boothby appeared in the list!

She decided she'd call him now. Situating herself in a chair at the kitchen table, she entered the number. Aurum nuzzled her hand with his velvet snout, then groaned.

She held her breath as the phone rang, and, after a brief wait, a scraggly Bronx or New Jerseyan voice answered. "Hello? Is this Conique?"

She found him amusing at once, leading her to have a little more fun yet. "Yes, sir. Are you the party to whom I am speaking?"

A pause came. At last, the voice answered, "I guess I can't imagine how I'd not be."

She giggled. "So, Mister Boothby, why have you reached out to me? I can't hear you well; it sounds like you're in an automatic carwash."

His voice was frantic, skipping her jokes. "I dunno what's happening, Miss Voyant. I'm on the run from someone trying to kill me."

Conique fixed her attention on the clock face before her, then sat forward with start. "Oh, dear, what kind of danger? By whom?"

Boothby replied, "Oh, Jesus, Charles Manson meets Jonathan Groff."

This sounded much like the man in her vision. She asked, "Can you describe him?"

The frightened voice rasped, "Sandy brown hair, pale skin, piercing eyes."

"That's specific," she said. Coincidence no longer crossed her mind. She asked, "Are you one of the Seven Vesiks?"

He replied in earnest conviction, as though he'd never heard anything differing from that truth. "I believe I am. The monster on my tail burned my super just by looking at her. Pyrokinesis, I'm certain. I have no idea how he did it, but she's ashes."

Conique gasped at that just as Reuben popped in reaching for the receiver. She resisted, instead pressing the conversation. "Where are you now, Mister Boothby?"

The voice responded, "I'm stalled out near Flagstaff in Arizona. My goddamned car, pardon my New Jersey, is broken down."

Reuben wrenched the phone from her, frustrating her enough to ball her fists. He asked, "Who is this?"

She pointed to the speaker option, so Reuben activated it with reproach. Boothby's voice clamored, "Whatever that person is, he's coming for all of us. He's a murderer."

Reuben shook his head at Conique, answering, "Whatever is going on, it isn't Miss Voyant's responsibility to fix it. I'm sorry if you feel you're in danger, but she is ill, and cannot help you. You should dial 911." He gestured in condescension.

Boothby retorted, "Oh, Gawd, they are prolly in on it."

Conique stood to her feet, pulling the extension from Reuben's hands. Aurum whimpered as she shouted, "Reuben, I know you're trying to protect me, but my vision has already confirmed what he's said."

Boothby's voice bounced from the speaker. "'Vision?' Well, I guess Archie was telling the truth!"

Conique blinked, then asked, "Who is Archie?"

The voice answered with bald conviction, "Miss Tutog's cat."

Reuben and Conique exchanged glances of confusion. The word "cat" caught Aurum's attention. Reuben's face burned with frustration. "Now see here, Boothby. You shouldn't call elderly infirm people to spread this malarkey."

She answered, "God works in mysterious ways, Reuben."

His expression twisted as he whispered in anger. "Connie, remember that magical thinking and irrefutable truths are dangerous."

She hushed Reuben, knowing it would incur a rebuke. "What cat is this, Mister Boothby?"

The voice replied, "Oh, Christ, never mind. If the monster catches me, he'll get Mister Ephuh's chunk."

Reuben leaned into the speaker, eyeing Conique, asking, "What chunk, Mister Boothby? Who is 'Ephuh?'"

The voice remained silent a bit, then answered, "*Ephuh*, not Ephuh. With an ah." He continued, "Anyway, I don't know what the hell is going on, Miss Voyant. But I've chased the lights all my life, mainly because Mister Ephuh gave me a hunk of metal when I was a child."

She looked past a flabbergasted Reuben while Boothby's words cued images in her head. She asked, "Was this gifting in a snowy location? A farm or estate?"

Boothby gasped. "No one knows that! How come, Miss Voyant?"

Reuben lightened some at that. He said, "If you've read about my wife, you know she sometimes gets impressions."

Conique nodded. "I somehow see a man offering you this gift in the snow. Lights? They were there, were they not?"

There was another gasp—melodrama at best or terror at worst. "They were there, Miss Voyant. So can ya help me out?"

Conique looked to Reuben, asking, "Can't we call triple A for him?" He resisted, so she pressed further. "If he is really in danger—"

Reuben replied, "Then he should call 911."

She could tolerate no more, waving her finger in his face. "Reuben, I follow Christ. He says to give your life up for your friends, and this man is a friend. I know it. I feel it."

Her husband sighed, unhappy, but not unyielding. "Very well. Mister Boothby, where precisely are you stalled?" The scraggly man didn't respond for a few moments, so Reuben asked once more, "Mister Boothby, are you still there?"

Boothby rustled a bit, then replied, "Oh, Jesus Christ, he's found me! He's gonna kill me!"

The line then disconnected, with Conique shouting into the extension, "Are you there? Mister Boothby? Please answer!"

Reuben placed a hand over the phone extension, if for no other reason than habit. "I think he's gone, dear." He tried to redial the number, and the call went immediately to voicemail. His brown eyes met her gray blue ones, and there was fear on both faces. Reuben's fear stemmed from something else, Conique knew, but she held concern for this odd stranger, not thinking of herself.

Reuben tried to mask his concern, bless him, to project confidence and courage. He said, "Well, it may just be that the guy is running from shadows."

Conique decided she was no safer, complaining, "Dear, whatever is chasing Mister Boothby is also after me. I know this to be true. So, it will have what it wants if we choose not to fight."

Reuben replied, "How do we fight? What the hell are we fighting?"

She pointed out the window, replying, "A new evil that has risen. I am one of the Seven, though I don't know much more than that. Someone means to kill us, and there is an angel here to help. Somewhere."

Her husband shook his head, frowning, his deep voice resonating. "Connie, dear, are you sure this isn't just part of the"—he paused in pain—"dementia?"

Aurum whimpered, pushing her nose into Conique's wrist. She looked beyond their canine to consider it.

Patting the dog's soft golden head, she answered, "Reuben, I don't have the answers. But I need to know."

He closed his eyes, sighing. "You're frailer than you think, dear. You've done enough for the world."

She laughed, "That's never true, dear. The world will always need the faithful."

He reached for her hand with delicate contrition. "It just doesn't make sense. Why now? Why give up what good time we have left?"

Conique squeezed his hand, replying, "Dear, the time left is spoken for. Faith rarely makes sense, but I can't ignore it. Righteousness often demands more of us than we think we can give. Will you trust me?"

He wiped sweat from his ebony brow. "Okay, tell me what your righteousness demands."

*B****

Boothby struggled to breathe, watching the figure approaching his car. How in the name of hell could this person catch up to him on foot? He must have been otherworldly, capable of bending space and time—a quantum traveler, maybe?

The lights along the interstate where his car stalled betrayed the coming shadow. He glowed blood orange like an ember, an energy silhouette through which Boothby could make out his form.

In all of Boothby's years of investigative reporting, he'd never faced this sort of danger. And he'd experienced some hairy run-ins with governments and organizations. In fact, he would have considered it an insult had they not harassed him for one disclosure or another.

Truth was his flag, and people deserved to know it. Governments could threaten him, but they did so only because they feared him.

His assailant wasn't afraid. Killing Miss Tutog was incidental and reckless, disregarding the attention he would attract.

Boothby struggled to breathe as he looked to the small cat seated next to him. He squeaked, "Is there anything you can do, cat? I think he means to kill us!"

Archie flashed his green eyes, then offered a sympathetic meow. Maybe he had nothing left to say.

Boothby looked to the rearview mirror in his door, shivering at the shadow's approach subtitled with "Objects in mirror are closer than they appear."

When the enemy was a few dozen feet from his car, Boothby realized he could hear an engine in the distance. The shadow stopped, and Boothby watched as a vehicle with no headlights tore towards them along the interstate.

The shadow attempted to dodge the vehicle, but it had stepped aside too late, and the convertible Jeep collided with him. His body seemed to break as it bounced into the flailing car's windshield, rolling over the top, then crashing onto the hard asphalt. Boothby vomited into the console as Archie leapt to dodge from the grotesquery.

The Jeep screeched to a halt, then reversed to crush the figure once more. Boothby thought he'd evacuated his stomach, but more sprayed forward, striking the interior of the windshield. The cat yowled in protest as some of the vomit hit him, then snapped around to clean himself, incapable of tolerating such filth.

Boothby gasped for air, discovering that he'd screamed his breath away. He choked and sputtered, having inhaled a small bit of vomit into his trachea, burning him like the fires of hell. He couldn't help but shout, "Jesus Christ!"

The Jeep squealed its tires, pulling toward his car as Boothby watched the fallen shadow, hoping he was dead.

A young man jumped from the driver's seat. He moved to Boothby's window, gesturing that he lower it. Gulping, Boothby obliged. The man said, "Mister Boothby, I see you need assistance. Please come with us." He beamed a smile at the cat, calling, "Hello Archie. It's been too long."

The beast leapt into the young man's arms while Boothby muttered, "Traitor." He muttered, "Betrayed by a cat. Imagine that."

The young man darted his eyes back to the shadow. Boothby followed his gaze, horrified that the form stirred. "Please, Mister Boothby, time is short."

Boothby nodded without taking his eyes from the form. "You don't hafta ask twice. But who are you?"

He strained to see this handsome young man, noting beading of blood in his eyes. "This human, called Adam, serves as a conduit for now. I am the one you've sought since your childhood, and it pleases me to see you."

Boothby froze with excitement. "Oh my freaking God, Mister Ephyr?! Archie was telling the truth!"

The young man grabbed Boothby's bag as he pointed to the Jeep. "We haven't long." Archie hurtled himself into the cab of the vehicle while Adam/Ephyr opened the back door to help him.

An unconscious young woman rested in the passenger seat, so Boothby asked, "Is she okay?"

She coughed, asking, "Adam, did you just let a hobo into the car? He smells like vomit and piss!"

The driver situated himself, announcing, "This is another member of the Seven. Mister Boothby, meet Janet. Janet, this is Mister Boothby."

Archie the cat yowled, leaping over his lap to break eye contact. Boothby said, "No mister required. But Mister Ephyr, where have you been all these years? How are you inside this young man?"

Janet spoke with a slur. "I'd like to know that, too."

Adam/Ephyr replied, "Janet possesses a capacity for psychic tunneling. We'll come to the particulars when there'

Boothby felt his heart leap as he sputtered, "Psychokinesis! Of course!" The cat meowed at him as he continued, "It's a time-saver, little kitty. Besides, you picked quite the handsome puppet, Mister Ephyr."

The driver convulsed, confessing, "Control from such a distance is challenging and not without its risks. First-order problem is to escape."

Boothby turned to see the glowing figure heaped on the pavement. Janet spoke with difficulty. "Can we get the hell out of here?"

Adam/Ephyr burned the tires, pulling away. Boothby turned to see that the figure had risen to its feet. He shouted, "How did he survive that? You crushed him with this car."

Adam/Ephyr replied, "This is the true form of Norcross, formidable even among our people."

As the Jeep swerved along the curve of the intersection, Archie leapt upon the dashboard, anchoring himself with his claws. After sliding across the back seat, Boothby struggled with his seatbelt. He hollered, "Christ, why are back seatbelts so goddamned difficult to buckle?!" The curves left him nauseated, and he gasped, "Oh, God, I'll throw up!"

He unrolled the window to feel the cold air on his face, and he got a look at the creature giving pursuit. This could be no human; it was iridescent, fiery, ruthless, yet bounding at a clip faster than a cheetah. "He's catching up!" Boothby shouted. He turned to face Adam/Ephyr, and the young man shivered, blood running from his ears and eyes. Archie yowled as he tore the polyvinyl with his claws.

Adam/Ephyr fought to say, "He will not catch us!" He diverted the car just as the malevolent form lobbed at them a fireball resembling lava. He hurled more, and some struck the back of the Jeep, burning through the aft window, melting into the back bumper.

Archie jumped from the dash into the backseat next to Boothby, pointing him to the fire extinguisher behind the seat. Boothby fought out of his seatbelt, then pulled the can free. He doused the flames with white chemical foam while he screamed, "He's almost on us!"

The cat clutched him after he extinguished the fire, and he heard, "You have the meanss to sstop him now. Hiss."

Boothby's eyes widened as his thoughts connected. He fished Ephyr's chunk from his pocket. He turned to the cat, pleading, "What must I do with it?"

Adam/Ephyr shuddered in pain. "Throw… it!"

Boothby turned to face the smoldering gape, broadening as an energy melted its periphery. He was anguished at the thought of parting with his prize, his possession. His eyes watered as though it were a part of his very soul.

The cat squealed at him, and he felt a shiver within his core while Archie's voice boomed in his head, "Trrusst, and thrrow!"

Boothby's surroundings faded as he focused on the creature vaulting himself in vicious pursuit. The chunk grew heavy in his hands. The deafening sound of air tearing through the cabin of the Jeep and the splashing explosions of magma being thrown at the vehicle were a crescendo, yet he could, in that moment, only see and hear himself, his object, and the creature chasing them. He gasped, knowing somehow that his prized possession would reveal truth, even if he must part with this thing.

So, he tensed, drew a deeper breath, and then tossed the alloy.

To his surprise and enchantment, the object sparkled, igniting, as though the molecular fabric itself shivered, winked, and expanded into a spectacular light show. The object slowed in flight, generating a variegated pulse of energy of solar brightness. The vehicle lurched forward at the incredible power.

Boothby shielded his eyes while the multicolored energy dissipated. He strained to see, his retinas recalling the blinding flash. He lowered his hand to reveal the creature had vanished.

He gasped, falling into his seat as the Jeep sped along. Despite the cold air, he found himself sopping with perspiration. He exclaimed, "Oh, my God. I think he's gone."

Within the rear compartment of the Jeep, a white-hot ball of energy formed, cooling and spinning until the alloy materialized at its center. The light vanished, and the piece fell onto the seat next to his. Boothby felt his eyes bulge as he grabbed it, lifting it to his face. He felt himself bare his teeth in a reaction of surprise.

He scanned the rest of the vehicle, and though Archie meowed, the others in the car remained in place, offering no reaction. Easing himself into his own seat, he wrestled once more with the safety belt, cursing and muttering.

Once he heard the click, he closed his eyes and sank into the seat. His mind raced as he tried to make sense of what he'd just seen. "Mister Ephyr, what does this thing do? Molecule-sized control? EM scrambler?"

Adam/Ephyr squeezed words with tremendous strain. "You wielded the focus stone with adroitness, young Boothby. But I cannot answer your questions now, for this conduit body requires rest. You and Janet must rest, as well. The journey ahead is long, and Norcross won't remain behind for long."

Boothby started to speak, only to find Archie leaping into his lap. "Where did you come from? And where the hell are we going?"

The cat slumbered, stirring some, but the interaction must've drained the little beast. The girl called Janet struggled, a little awake for the moment. "Hopefully, we're taking you to get a shower."

Adam/Ephyr said deliberately, "We cannot stop. Boothby, you should dispose of your phone. This world's technology can be commanded by Norcross."

Boothby responded without question, tossing his phone through the gape at the Jeep's rear. It burst onto the highway behind them. He sighed in relief. Stroking the cat as he purred, Boothby realized he was exhausted. But he knew he would have the truth he'd sought these many years. A few more hours wouldn't make a difference.

16.Faith and Fire

M＊＊＊

A knock at his door stirred Mayak from his cat nap. Slumped over his computer, he straightened his back, reaching for his coffee mug in the futile hope it was still warm.

A heavy pounding startled him, causing him to spill the cold coffee onto his clothes. "Fuck," he muttered. Brushing the liquid from his pants leg, he called, "Give me moment, dammit!"

Looking at his login details, he cursed to himself. Slamming shut his computer, he craned his neck to see the time of day. He knew the problem confronting him: he had been logged into his system long enough to attract the attention of the near-omniscient surveillance state. He couldn't remember the last time he'd forgotten to log out from his computer, but he did recall receiving a visit from the zealous Federal Security Service proxy.

He stood, tied his robe, and walked to the door. Hunching to prepare for a cold blast of air, he leaned into the door. "Who is calling?"

The voice he'd hoped not to hear said, "Administrator Kierkov for Mayak Chernovsky. You will now open door."

He unfastened the locks, wrenching the door out from the rubber insulation coating the jamb. And there she was, dressed in a smart noire leather coat, sporting short silver hair surrounding a face colder than that of the moon. Even amidst the chill, her form excited him. He wasn't happy when his hormones and his judgment parted ways.

Kierkov's expression remained flat, as she said, "I thought I'd stop by to see how you are doing after your ordeal."

He leaned aside, motioning her to enter. "Please enter, Agent. I have little to offer, save coffee and vodka."

She flashed a disarming smile, responding, "Sounds like challenge for me. By the way, once more, I am not Agent; I am Administrator." In what he was convinced a deliberate move, she brushed along the front of his body with hers, sparing him no indecency.

He started the coffee maker, then placed two cups on the counter. She pointed to them and said, "Please fill mine with half vodka."

He found this, to his surprise, a little amusing. Was her intention to loosen his tongue with alcohol, pretending she might tolerate hers less than he his? The KGB rule of obfuscation died hard, if at all. It was clear to him that she had come for one purpose: to discover his plans in the aim of eliminating him with cause.

Mayak knew too well the culture that spawned him. He understood that if he didn't drink as much as she, she'd assume he'd just broken his oath of service by espionage. So, he poured even more vodka into his cup. She did take note, chuckling, "Quite a drink for Sunday morning."

He answered, brushing his blonde hair from his forehead, "You cannot have head start over me, Comrade Kierkov."

Her smile widened as she asked, "Comrade, is it? We are no longer Soviet, young Mayak."

He shook his head, replying, "We are little better, considering restrictions and legal constraints."

She laughed as he handed her a cup, musing, "You say communist by any other name would control so well?"

He brightened, asking, "Shakespeare?"

Sampling the liquid, she laughed. "We are not savages, Mayak." Correcting herself, she added, "He, or maybe she, was no longer banned after 1977."

Mayak poured the rewarmed coffee into her mug, then into his. Swirling the liquids together, he tasted the singeing burn of high-proof vodka on his lips and in his throat. He ignored the need to cough, hoping to shield any weakness. Besides, he wanted to play her game, only in reverse.

Lifting his cup, he nodded his head. "To Shakespeare, then." She chugged her drink—a tactic to further disarm him, he decided. Instead, he planned to short-circuit her script, saying, "I can imagine you are here for something more than common interest in classic theater. Why?"

She placed her ceramic mug on the tabletop, watching the steam rise from its surface. With a small laugh of understanding, she said, "Very well, Mister Chernovsky. We are aware of your unusual usage of internet, and, given your recent encounter, we must perform routine checks for your safety."

He refused to change his tone. "Such benevolence from Federation Security Service."

Kierkov corrected him. "Their principal motivation is to safeguard those who control WMDs."

He ribbed her. "And your 'principal' motivation?"

A grin crept across her face. "My motivation follows king and country, higher duty."

He tasted his vodka, giving himself to the searing liquid as it touched his tongue. "'Agent' Kierkov, perhaps I should renounce citizenship, then. Americans might grant me asylum."

Her cold eyes hardened, betrayed by a smile. "It would be pity if Ministry of Defense takes greater interest in you. Such threats do not entertain me."

He leaned back into his chair, answering with a mocking tone. "Perhaps I no longer wish to entertain you, Comrade Agent."

She pointed a finger in his direction, scoffing. "Well, in that case, I am authorized to take you into custody."

This drew a rare laugh from him. He asked, "Take me into custody? For what charge?" Of course, he knew she didn't have to tell him one, and even if she did, it would probably be a lie.

Kierkov's face grew colder still, with her gray, lifeless eyes leaving him to wonder whether she was a zombie. She sipped her mixed drink. "For revealing state secrets to foreigners, namely Americans."

His stomach turned a flip, but his fear lasted only a moment. He asked, "What evidence do you plan to submit for such charge?"

She laughed, the wrinkles about her mouth spreading. It seemed she enjoyed this, and she retorted, "Your messages to Americans."

Shaking his head, he replied, "You have no evidence. Messages I've sent are completely harmless."

She opened her small, jeweled purse, producing a tiny file folder. Inside of it was a picture of the shaggy ufologist named Boothby. She pointed to the photograph, asking, "Have you not sent this man message about your work?"

He touched the photograph with a grin. "This is crackpot, not taken seriously in America or anywhere else. I asked him for information on UFOs, nothing more." His finger touched hers, electrifying him for an instant.

She placed the folder back into her purse, asking, "Then why is message encrypted?"

He shrugged, saying, "I encrypt all my correspondence. I am trying new method."

She traced her eyes along his body, then swigged more of the mixture. She was careful to exhibit only what she chose. In the pause, he tried to recall what Sargon had called her: *haligscriosta*. Qualifying as agent demanded a hefty dose of psychopathy, but Sargon's warning was incommensurate with the evidence.

Kierkov finished her cup, then broke his concentration with another question. "So, why reach out to man from Texas?"

He replied, "He contacted me. About what I do not know."

She clicked at him in admonition, adding, "You know you must report all foreign contacts immediately to Federation Security Service."

He downed the remainder of his cup, blurting, "It was harmless person interested in my mathematical work. Besides, since you see all correspondence anyway, why should I care? I am efficient, Comrade Agent."

Kierkov fidgeted in her chair, crossing her arms in disapproval. "You do not define efficiency, young Mayak. Surely, you know that you must report it."

Grinning inwardly, he replied, "How else may I persuade you to visit me? You did not share phone number, Comrade Agent."

She rounded the cup's lip with her finger, then touched the liquid to her mouth. Her lips spread into a smile as she whispered, "I can be persuaded to supply it."

He forced a smile. Intimacy intrigued but vexed him. He asked, "How so?"

Her wistful answer surprised him. "You think old woman isn't lonely?"

Mayak reached for her hand, whispering, "I understand lonely."

She touched his face with her hand, her cold fingers stimulating his cheek. "Seduction isn't unwelcome, but it is against regulation."

Mayak nodded. "Then you join me in circle of suspicion?" A gamble, but he couldn't decide the angle. He rose to his feet, bending towards her, kissing her, and she untied his robe, sliding her frigid hands into his pajamas.

Death by hypothermia was still death. Oh, well.

S✳✳✳

Shigeru sat a vigil next to his phone. The snowfall outside discouraged him from heading into it, sparing him, he conceded, an embarrassment at a bar or strip club. Both scenes had grown tedious, and he could apply his dating tactics in other ventures. The online apps had furnished a universe of opportunities, but in this moment, he needed to focus.

He hoped a conversation with this woman might help ground him. He tightened his silk robe, then puffed his cigarette. True, the vice might cause cancer; the word itself made him miss his long dead parents. He wished they could see the progress he'd made in treating the diseases that killed them.

There was something about the Voyant woman that reminded him of his late mother. She, too, was a follower of the occult, though Buddhism was her trade. He'd always thought that Buddha and Christ were so similar that one or more were facsimile—a copy of a copy of a copy.

He swallowed a hefty swig of whiskey and puffed his cigarette, then put it out in the ashtray on his desk. He knew he wasn't supposed to smoke within his apartment, but he was Doctor Shigeru Nakamura, not a slack-jawed social leech. He breathed a heavy sigh, watching the smoke plumes billow from his nostrils.

And then, the phone sounded. It was, at last, the Voyant woman. An honest-to-god medium, the internet said. What a joke. Americans would believe anything, no matter how insane.

But now, he'd made her wait too long. His dating tactics teachings remained so ingrained in him, he used them unscripted, all on instinct. Assuming control, he answered, "Hello, Miss Voyant?"

The woman's voice sounded as backwater as any southerner's he'd ever heard. She responded, "Doctor Nakamura? Yes, I'm Conique Voyant, and I've followed your work for a while now."

He found this amusing. An elderly evangelical, thought to suffer dementia, yet she was interested in his academic work. "So, what part, Miss Voyant?"

The voice shook somewhat, but then, regaining her footing, she replied, "Well, originally, I'd intended to interview you on the consequences of nuclear testing in the South Pacific and the injuries sustained by those people through the lens of your scientific study, among other things."

He smiled, though he wasn't clear he could help her more than just reading his damned articles. But he reminded himself that sans training, she likely wouldn't understand his technical work, if even the implications. Lighting another cigarette, he probed, "What is the new reason?"

She lost steadiness again, suggesting to him that her memory loss might be worse than he'd expected, but then she once again rebounded, asking, "Have you felt any unusual impressions or had any unexpected, difficult-to-explain dreams?"

He answered with frustration, "Who doesn't have bad dreams, Miss Voyant?"

Her voice strengthened as she replied, "Doctor Nakamura, this may sound quite bizarre, but I do receive certain visions—premonitions, fragments of knowledge."

He chuckled. "Yes, I read about the spook shows you put on."

She replied with what seemed like it might be a smile, "It doesn't matter whether you believe, but I recently received a vision indicating that you and I, along with five others, constituted something called the Seven Vesiks."

Shigeru belted laughter, critiquing, "Whoever sends you these visions can count, at least. The Seven, is it?"

Conique's voice persisted, unflagging, and she reproached him, saying, "I don't bring this to you for jest, sir. We are in danger by the eighth—"

He interrupting her with slightly repressed laughter. "Because he didn't get to be in the seven, right?"

Her voice strengthened with an even louder rebuke. "Belief or not belongs to you, but it doesn't change the state of the universe. I know you've sought a woman with blonde hair, though I couldn't see her as clearly as you in my dream. If I'm reading the vision correctly, I believe you seek her for a reason specific to your own life, just as I have sought you, and another has sought me—and not for carnal purposes, as those are your own. A chain of the seven, if you will."

Shigeru was dumbstruck. He waited, and she said, "I take your silence to mean I've struck paydirt. Can you trust the evidence, Doctor Nakamura?"

He took a sizable swallow of whiskey. then asked, "How can you know that, Miss Voyant? This is some hoax."

Conique cut into his sentence, announcing, "I've been called worse. The woman seemed hazy in my dream, leading me to think she's in some medical trouble." He didn't answer, so she spoke with determination. "Doctor, we can play this game all day. Tomato tomahto. But lives are on the line. So—"

He huffed, answering, "Yes, yes, yes, she's in critical, likely terminal condition. I couldn't reach her."

Conique's tone remained unperturbed, a surprising comfort to Shigeru. She continued, "I didn't get the impression that the Seven Vesiks would not be whole when we join for the Communion, or at least, that was what the angel called it."

He jumped to his feet, shaking the ashes from his cigarette. Skepticism left his hope to flounder, leading him to critique her. "You could've learned who she was through my assistant. Maybe this is just a joke that little shit is playing."

Conique was on a roll. "Shigeru, you've been with twelve different women this month, and though you don't know it now, you have gonorrhea from one of your encounters."

He froze, clutching his phone hard. "Who the fuck told you these things?"

Conique replied with what sounded like a smile. "God, or at least, God as I understand Him. More likely a Her."

He scratched his scalp and pulled at his hair. "You could still learn those things with the right spy tools."

She laughed him off. "Years ago, I was asked to participate in a test to determine whether I really could see beyond my eyes. They flipped a coin several times, asking me to predict it. Out of one hundred flips, I answered eighty or so correctly, and they calculated something called a p-value to describe how likely it was that I get that many or more correct if the coin were fair. It was astronomically low."

Shigeru could hardly believe this. He said, "Why have I never heard of such an ability?"

Conique answered, "Because we're persecuted by a community of thought leaders insistent that our gifts aren't real. I believe mine is a Gift of the Holy Spirit. Very few risk their safety or reputation, but mediums appear in all cultures, all religions, all places."

He asked, in lieu of any other rational question, "Why do you tell me this, even if it were true?"

199

She blew his mind with her response. "To a scientist, the question isn't whether you can detect truth. The scientific method tries to discern a likelihood that something you may believe is, in fact, true. It's statistically possible that I could guess every coin toss correctly just by chance, but that becomes exponentially harder the more trials you undertake. I've told you several things, all of which I could guess correctly with some probability. But what is my p-value here, Doctor Nakamura?"

He was dumbfounded. A hick evangelical woman from America had schooled him on the scientific method. It wasn't so much that he disbelieved all paranormal hoo-ha; he just couldn't believe an American evangelical would have access to any special insight about the universe. But he wasn't immune to her charm. "Well, you have a point, Miss Voyant."

She replied, "Okay, in any case, you need to trust my warnings. There is a place where we Vesiks are to meet. I don't know where it is."

He laughed. "Is there any other place that matters other than those whose locations are unknown to us? Is it Shangri-La, gauzy camera work and all?"

She remained on task, ignoring his growing inebriation. "This place is an estate somewhere in the snow. I would know it to see it, but it's otherwise a blank."

He polished off the last bits of whiskey in his decanter, clanking it down to his desk. "So, we're the Seven Vesiks, but what does it mean?"

Her response was quick. "The fallen wants what we have."

Shigeru lost his footing for a moment, then giggled. "So, the devil is after us because we're so moral?"

Conique became frustrated. She concluded her call by saying, "Doctor Nakamura, this may sound quite crazy, but you're quite drunk. Sleep it off, and I shall call you tomorrow. okay?"

The phone disconnected. He was furious. "What a bitch." How did she know what she knew?

He knew enough about neuroscience to know that some people exhibited traits so outrageous that they were often believed to be of supernatural origin. That had never sat well with him, considering that the natural world furnished any student with endless opportunities to learn, be puzzled, and be surprised.

Well, he decided to hit the hay. But he couldn't resist researching her abilities. Some humans exhibited remarkable capacities. Replicated tests by Julia Mossbridge and others had suggested a presentiment effect of statistical significance, and he'd heard of other odd occurrences, such as random number generators flipping wildly off the uniform expectation if a catastrophe were to occur. He did remember reading about a Russian student capable of guessing coin flips, though he couldn't remember the name. But search results led him to Olga Kunskapsen once more—her work on time crystals was connected to the coin flip oracle, in more ways than one. But the search also revealed her death, as of morning that day. He felt as though he couldn't breathe as he read the news item.

There could be no seven with only six. Could it be that he wanted to believe Miss Voyant? Shigeru thought he was past caring about what happened to the world. He jotted a quick note to remind him to see his infectious disease specialist. He was saddened, exhausted, drunk, and ready for bed. No hooking up tonight. Just sleep.

*F****

Frankie found his way home from Odessa, ignoring call after call from George's wife Sheila. He had texted her once with an outright lie, indicating that George's phone had died and for her to meet them at Frankie's loft. The locusts screamed for her flesh, a necessary sacrament for him.

But would God accept his soul? He knew of many from the Bible who murdered under directives from the Almighty. Who else could see His will to completion than a man with nothing left to lose? George didn't deserve to live. Sheila deserved death even more. She was shrill, petty, and cruel, but more than that, she annoyed the ever-loving fuck out of him.

The world wouldn't understand him. They would murder him, just as they did Christ for setting about His Father's bidding. He knew Sheila couldn't count herself among God's predestined few. He could write volumes on those he'd lump into that category. Did he dare to dream so big? Pastor Chet explained to him that no matter the reason, Frankie would die should he rampage against his enemies. It smacked of prophesy, though he didn't care whether he survived.

The world was in disarray. Men were women, women were men. Looters were celebrated. Christians were demonized. White men were the enemy.

God would exact His due, and if the world fell, that would be that—freedom to crusade, to burn, to purify.

Frankie wanted freedom, but without Pastor Chet's guidance, such a jingle would ring hollow. Killing George had filled him with feelings of relief, power, and even sexual gratification, just as it was when he hunted a buck, but it was a greater response than any he'd ever had. God, this was Freedom, capitalized. Would he surrender this ecstasy?

The world was full of cattle, and he was the Butcher. When needed, he would kill, and it wouldn't matter if he did it for his own reasons, separate from those of others. He'd often thought of working as an executioner, a mercenary, or an assassin, but Pastor Chet had discouraged him from similar vocations, including law enforcement and the military. He understood that his spiritual guide just wanted to protect him, but he no longer needed the cloaking anointment cast by Chet.

Maybe killing himself would be too easy. He hated grocery store clerks, the cross-eyed lady at the bank, the uppity faggots teaching school down the road, and so many more. Myra was right—there was something wrong with him. But it wasn't the thing she thought.

The road before him had darkened, plucking him from his thoughts. The long stretches of highway in west Texas comforted him, yet the *Korobskron* grumbled, squealing for release. He was sweating in anticipation, his entire body ready for the release Sheila's murder would bring him.

Maybe he dared too much. He'd be caught, imprisoned, and executed by the holy state. Then again, they'd have to catch him. Frankie had squirreled away fifty thousand dollars in cash, hidden under his house. He could go off the grid. Maybe he could hide among Myra's weirdo hippie friends, a wolf in the fold.

His phone rang over his truck speakers, the umpteenth call from Sheila. He got a little ahead of himself—he would have to finish the job at hand before he would flee the town. As his erection throbbed, he considered rape. But not her. Sheila was dirty, sloppy, and obnoxious. Frankie hated all of those things.

The plan was simple. He'd lure the bitch Sheila into his home, leading her to believe her fat sack of shit of a husband had joined him there, then torture and kill her. Maybe he could face the police in a final showdown. He had weapons galore, many hidden in his house.

His thoughts returned to the Ruskie and redskin pair who'd contacted him. What was he to make of them? Pastor Chet couldn't tell him. Something lingered just beyond his brain, like a name or a place he couldn't recall. He focused, but the memory wouldn't yield. Though he knew there was something to it, he couldn't discourage his *Korobskron*. It demanded its due, and he knew more internet searches would help enforcement agencies locate him once they discovered George's decaying carcass.

The life he led would soon end, whether by a firefight with the police or his disappearing from society's watchful eyes. Once the cops put it all together, he wouldn't be able to speak with his family. Lunch with Myra had been a disaster, but Frankie decided he should call his father. He and his late wife adopted Frankie beyond his earliest memories. They had been good parents to him, so his father deserved one last conversation before the news would label Frankie a serial killer.

He ordered his phone, "Call dad."

The accompanying beeps, then the artificial ringing filled his cab. His father answered, "Hey, Frankie, what's up?"

He felt some comfort at this man's voice. He answered, "Hey, Dad. Just wanted to say hello. I know it's not time, but I wanted to say it anyway: Merry Christmas."

His father's voice cracked a little. What an emotional man he'd always been, a nurturer with the softest heart. "Aww, Merry Christmas to you, too, son. Say, did your sister reach you?"

Frankie winced at the mention, embarrassed by his outburst. "I saw her just on her way out of town."

His father pressed a little, something Frankie always expected. "She tries, Frankie. She just wants your respect."

Frankie caught himself in his mirror, the blood on his face and in his hairline catching the moonlight to crimson perfection. What a thought. She wanted his respect, and he was a murderer. He answered with a joyless smile, "Myra will always be her own person. She don't need my respect."

His father switched subjects. "So, you're still coming to Christmas? Tyler will be there."

Frankie asked, "Will his roommate be coming?"

His father paused once more, then replied, "Yeah, I think so. They're thick as thieves, really."

The thought sickened him. He adjusted the temperature in his cab so that a little cool air might steady his nausea. "Sure, I bet they are. Listen, Dad, I just wanted to say I love ya, and I'll see you at Christmas."

What a lie. He'd be long gone, disgraced, and too taboo for decent folks.

His dad's warm voice consoled him as he said, "Frankie, is everything okay?"

He didn't hesitate to answer. "Oh, yeah, things are great. Work is great."

"Okie dokie. Just know you can always talk to me, son." His father was perceptive.

Frankie felt a twinge of guilt, but little else mattered other than the kill he was preparing to execute. "Love you, Dad. Bye now." He shut off his phone.

The turnoff was at hand, and he felt butterflies buzzing about in his abdomen. Soon, he'd send that bitch Sheila to hell. It took little thought to stoke his rage. He recalled the many times he'd sat at a meal table with her, listening to her whine and complain about the price of jellybeans, or that a waiter had offered mustard to put on her salad. She was inane, haranguing customer-service reps over the most trite and trivial of things. She was embittered and unforgiving, incapable of moving past anything. She went for forty-five minutes at a clip, complaining that one shoelace was longer than the other or that the bread had come too late, too cold. George cheated on his wife, and Frankie never faulted him for it.

Pastor Chet had always admonished him to make the kill a merciful one. He saw no reason now to follow that protocol—Sheila deserved no mercy.

He approached his house, hoping he'd have time to knock back a few cold ones before killing the cunt.

But two cars awaited him—Sheila's ugly gray Lexus and Tyler's small sedan. Frankie heard himself say, "Oh, fuck."

He slowed his truck, looking into the mirror to examine his blood-covered face. The thought of Tyler seeing Frankie this way made him sick. He grasped for the wipes he kept under the passenger seat, ripping open two new boxes. Plucking one after the other, he scrubbed his face. He must've used twenty or thirty wipes before the red faded to pink. He decided his black beard hide some of the spatters, and he could explain anything else as an accident at work.

But the more complicated quagmire was how he would explain George not being with him. He had lured her by explaining that George's car had broken down, and that she should meet at his house to pick up her fat husband. Then again, he hadn't really lied. George was with him, just not in a shape Sheila would appreciate. Then again, maybe she would. She often threatened him when she was angry, insisting she'd bleed him like a stuck pig.

Frankie had mounted the corpse in his truck bed, and he still had big plans for the body, along with Sheila's future corpse. But Tyler could play no part in his plan. He'd have to think of something.

17. The Haligscriosta Passing Through Walls

*M****

Mayak opened his eyes, aware of the cold, vampiric body of Agent Kierkov intertwined with his own. She was asleep, and he glanced to the window—no sun in sight.

He felt some remorse, his mother and father having discouraged illicit sex. But it stalled the danger his *skrytyypass* insisted she posed.

He'd also committed an even greater sin, having not availed himself of birth control. What a thought—a child with this monster? He could only hope she was too old to bear a child.

Sargon was right to show concern. Kierkov oozed cruelty, beyond what he'd seen firsthand. The Militsiya's legacy in Russia had led to Mayak's parents pushing him out from his homeland, a diaspora, and his mother had warned him dating back to his earliest memories that the uniformed may present one threat, but those slinking in the shadows without uniforms were much more dangerous.

His parents—were they safe? The happenings kept him too busy to check on them, though he doubted they would serve much utility to the intelligence or security agencies. Mayak himself was the prize, even if he didn't have the answers he sought. Game theory had been among his concentrations. State, action, and utility were the main components to any interaction. But no party enjoyed perfect information. He knew Kierkov possessed secrets he wanted unearthed. Sargon probably had the best information, but he meted it out glacially.

Locked in his own head, Mayak noticed only now that the weather outside had worsened, with a massive snowstorm on the move—the state was grim. Maybe Kierkov planned to stay at his side. Then again, hardy Russians weren't troubled by inclement weather, but neither would he permit her to risk her life—not if he could stall her. He needed answers, so if he could leverage her, this storm, or anything else to discover the truth, he'd do it.

He looked at Kierkov just as she opened her eyes. Responding to him, she breathed a comforting sigh. Her long silver hair covered much of his chest, so the cold air replacing it left him uncomfortable as she rose to sit. The snow and wind outside captured her attention at once, so she turned to Mayak, and for a moment, he sensed genuine confusion.

Then, she beamed smile as she caressed his chest with her nails. "Well, I may be staying here."

Mayak nodded with a smile. "Same offerings of coffee and vodka are on order here at Motel Mayak."

She touched his face, adding, "Motel has more amenities than just that." She floated from the bed, reaching for his bathrobe to stay the cold. Pulling a cigarette and lighter from her purse on the table, she asked, "May I?"

He sat forward in the bed, nodding. "If I may join you." He hadn't had a cigarette in a long time. He dashed to grab his spare robe from a closet. Bundling himself, he accepted one smoke, lighting it from hers. He choked at the menthol, complaining, "You prefer these?"

She laughed at him. "Average lifespan isn't far from me. World's expectation is even worse."

Pointing to the apartment about them, he remarked, "It is rule we are not permitted to smoke inside."

Kierkov poured herself a cup from Mayak's vodka bottle. "We all have our vices."

Mayak drew a deep drag from his smoke, filling his lungs and irritating his throat. Now that he'd shared a bed and a cigarette with this woman—a woman stuck with him until the storm passed—he planned his action. Situating himself at the kitchen table opposite of her, he asked, "So, Miss Kierkov, since we know each other better, perhaps you can answer my questions."

She swallowed some vodka, then answered, "You may call me Andreva. You may ask your questions, but I do not guarantee answers."

Clarity became his priority, so he lifted a solitary finger into the air. "And since you had opportunity to torture or kill me, I assume my safety is among your priorities."

She cast her head back with a laugh, answering, "You learned more than mathematics from your *skrytyypass*, it would seem."

He leaned forward a bit, disturbed she'd used the term. He answered, "Sargon is his name. He is not simply figment of my mind."

Her smile, beautiful yet caustic, chilled him, and she focused her eyes upon him, replying, "It does not matter, Mayak. Since we are here together, let us not squander chance to learn."

He nodded. "In movie based on Arthur Clarke's *2010*, Russian ambassador suggests to Doctor Floyd that he will speak truth only for two minutes. Since we must remain here, and since you have done no harm to me, let us tell truth only, if nothing more, for two minutes."

The overhead lights blinked somewhat, from which he guessed the snowfall was weighing on the powerlines outside. The flashing caught her silver hair and timeless face, evoking arousal. Whoever had sent her knew his sentimental attractions too well.

She inhaled a drag from her cigarette. "Very well, young Mayak." Blowing smoke in his direction, she grinned, "But only because you are stallion in your bed."

Flattery wasn't a weakness for Mayak, but he knew that if he couldn't extract answers from her, he'd need to keep her busy until the path before him cleared. It had been years since he'd shared intimacy with another person. He tried a smile, conjuring a swift and angry rebuke. "Oh, Mayak, do not attempt to emote with me. You respond as sullen boy-man, and nothing more, if we are to play your game."

Then, as if a wand had waved away her frustration, she played to the sultry and sordid, giggling. "Very well. You drink for each answer I offer, then we fuck."

He recalled Sargon's sharp chiding when he tried to seduce one of his high school teachers, one of the most uncomfortable of his feeble acts of social outreach. This woman wanted him, so neutrality reigned on his face once more. He hesitated, then said, "You are here to protect me on whose order?"

Hearty laughter bellowed from her, and she answered, "Obvious answer, young Mayak. I follow chain of command."

This wouldn't do, so he said, "I cannot believe Federation Security Service would dispatch senior agent—"

She interrupted both his sentence and a chug of vodka to say, "Administrator."

He closed his eyes, offering a quick nod, then continuing. "They would not dispatch you solely for carnal enticement." He pointed to the bed, then asked, "Why interest in me?"

She chuckled, answering, "Truth, dear Mayak: you remain inestimably important asset in understanding phenomenon. This should be obvious, so I happily say so."

He drank a shot, per her motion, then asked, "Why? What of said phenomenon do you know?"

Pulling her hair somewhat, she blew a juvenile raspberry with her glistening lips. "You researched it. Lights appear above nuclear sites all over world. Under soviet regime, I chaired task force for KGB on these lights."

He leaned towards her, placing his elbows on the table. "I do not understand. You've known about them?"

Kierkov tapped her cup, motioning that he take a drink. He obliged, and she answered, "Numerous events are recorded. United States government studies are verbose, but, like Soviet government, they prefer secrecy."

Mayak nodded. "It all makes sense. Why do lights appear? Why do they concern me?"

She cackled. "If I answer your questions, we run out of vodka."

He chuckled as he pointed to the pantry behind her. "We will die of alcohol poisoning before my supply is gone."

She finished her cigarette as she spoke matter-of-factly. "KGB believed lights were terrorist in nature, aimed at undermining Soviet global posture. CIA feared similarly. Neither agency believed they could come from Earth. Their conclusion is same: prelude to invasion."

He waited, deciding she was telling him the truth. Drinking the vodka was easy for him, for his mind was clear. "You disagree?"

She clicked her tongue at him. "Hammer sees only nails. Lights forestall our extinction. Creators of light could destroy us with thought alone. Now drink, young Mayak. I am ready to fuck."

He folded his arms. "Not yet. Why do lights care about extinction?"

She lit a second cigarette, drawing a hefty puff. "I believe it is immune response. Biosphere of this world is imperiled, so devices appear to slow ruin."

Mayak swigged more acrid liquid, the latest shot of which started to erode his focus. But he needed to understand. "They are benevolent? Who sent them?"

She tasted her drink before flashing a smile that seemed to de-age her face. "This is your part, young Mayak. Your dark passenger knows truth."

He gulped more vodka, choking on it as she blew smoke towards him. "Why would he know?"

She chuckled. "How much do you know of your birth family?"

He shrugged, glimpsing images of him pictured with his adopted parents. "I know nothing of them."

Her smile faded as she replied, "Do you not find that peculiar?"

He refilled their cups with reluctance, then answered, "Seldom do adoptees know their origin. Why?"

Kierkov watched him with eager eyes, as though she needed him to understand her obsession with him. "Would it surprise you to learn that we possess no information about your birth family?"

His heart skipped a beat. "That's impossible," he said.

She took another gulp from her cup as she exhaled more smoke. "Night you arrived at hospital, local villagers reported lights appearing."

Mayak could hear his own breathing. "My parents never mentioned this. Could you be mistaken?"

She cast her head back with a laugh. "To question Mother Russia is to invite death sentence. No, I am not mistaken. No records of you existed. Lights presaged your arrival. Your dark passenger, I believe, is key."

He closed his eyes for a moment, trying to reach his companion. Reopening them, he said, "Sargon? How?"

She swigged her drink, then gestured to the sky. "Crash sites and sightings in Siberia suggest point of origin somewhere deep in tundra. You present mystery, connected now to at least two sightings, with supernatural capabilities provided by Sargon. I believe he is here, coordinating immune response." She leaned back into her chair. "Immune response must be stopped if we are not to lose."

Mayak looked at the bottle—there was still maybe a third of the vodka remaining. He knew he'd vomit his toenails for this, but he drank more. He asked, "Lose what?"

She hardened her expression, as though the game and its joy now bereaved her. "What matters most in all of this world: control."

He huffed, suggesting, "Perhaps we ought not have control. Perhaps control is illusory."

"Order of world is essential, my stallion. Your becoming nuclear engineer confirms my statement." She smiled, leaning back, offering, "Yes, as you cannot ignore, we know all about you. You are optimist." She pointed a cold, slender finger in his direction, punctuating each word with a bend of her digit. "And optimist must believe order can be attained."

Mayak protested with indignation. "I am no optimist, Madame Kierkov."

She wagged her finger at him once more, eyes tracing his form. She retorted, "You assumed your career to furnish some order and precaution to Russian weapon stockpiles. You believe world is to be saved."

He shook his head, pointing to her. "Your presence would suggest otherwise. I cannot prevent our destruction, try as I may. If lights have come to stall our suicide, you mean to stymie them, and thus, world will fall."

Her voice seeped of cruelty. "Young Mayak, world will fall, no matter yours or my actions. Either ecological collapse, nuclear devastation, or global pandemic—we will forfeit this world."

He refused the drink this time, demanding, "Why would you devote yourself to such nihilism? Why not simply surrender? Vanish?"

She laughed hard. Then, licking her lips, she replied, "Because I relish simple pleasures too much." He remained unmoved at her answer, so she added, "World will be destroyed, but some, such as myself, shall enjoy life until twilight. Besides, new order shall rise from ashes of old, like phoenix. But old must burn in destruction."

Casting his eyes askance, he considered his *skrytyypass*, recalling and uttering, "*Haligscriosta...*"

She asked, "Holy destroyer?"

He met her eyes, asking, "What?"

Kierkov extinguished her cigarette, smearing the orange embers and burning a saucer from his grandmother's heirloom china set, *Royal Albert Old Country Roses*. He winced as she answered, "Old Irish for destroyer. Why say so?" Her tenor shifted at this, as though he knew more of her purpose than was her expectation.

Mayak's nausea crescendoed, and he jumped to his feet, vomiting in his kitchen sink. Coughing, struggling to regurgitate aspirated alcohol and food, he answered, "You are destroyer, then?"

She patted his rear end as he clung to the kitchen sink, answering, "I know my kind. We need not offer saccharine apologies to ease understanding of foolish cattle."

Lighting yet another cigarette, she smiled. "Man has always sought apocalypse. He has devoted literature, myth, Hollywood film after film fantasizing final moments. If any among us may persevere, it is those who dispense with"—she paused, then rocked her head in cadence with her words, as though she were in prayerful, cruel repose—"petty sentimentality, prudish myth, crude altruism, and delusions of morality."

Mayak hacked, feeling a terrific burning and scraping in his throat. He felt the room spin about him, and he critiqued her with a faltering voice. "How can one be so unabashedly reprehensible? Do you care nothing for—"

Grabbing the booze bottle, she chugged, and the vivid sound of her swallow forced Mayak to retch. With a huff, she said, "For the human race?"

Finishing the drink while he spewed more vomit into the sink, she tossed the glass container aside, shattering it on the cold floor. She cackled. "Think, young fool. We live better than one in ten thousand, maybe one in one hundred thousand people who've dwelt under our sun. Life for majority is simple misery; animals aping"—she twisted her mouth—"*human* values. They live, they die."

He wiped his mouth, pleading, "What of conscience? Do you feel remorse that they—"

She laughed in further derision, her blinding lily skin and ghoulish grin freezing him hard. "That they must die? I no more apologize for my freedom from remorse than you do for your freedom from ignorance."

Flinging ashes, this time on the floor, she said, "When you were child, others feared you for your remarkable mathematical gifts, to say nothing of your"—she giggled, air quoting her hands—"'*skrytyypass*.'"

Pointing her finger into his back, she continued, "Have you considered that those of us unclouded by morality have also received evolution's next gift? You and I are both feared because we, from the vantage of the feeble peasantry, may pass through solid walls."

She mulled it over, then remarked, "I do not know how you or your friend came to know this word *haligscriosta*, but I shall gain your understanding, and your respect."

He felt his eyes water, though he couldn't determine whether the vomiting sputum or this anti-paragon creature's words were the cause. He asked, "Why would you care for my thoughts, if you regard others as being of so little value?"

Laughing as the power flickered once more, she answered with haste. "Because you interest me, my young stallion. I understand proficiency in your gifts, but not the passenger you carry. And, despite your desperately ill-formed ethics, you bring me some joy."

She seemed annoyed he could not muster more than a heaving despair, brought on either by the coughing or the ghastly tidings or the weather or the evil spirits, so she ran her fingers down his back, clicking her tongue. "Bewildered herd serves prosperous, as they always have."

Dropping her cigarette to the floor, smashing away the flame with her foot, she let her smile fade. "And I, as *haligscriosta*, am inquisitor, butcher, investigator, torturer, executioner."

Pulling him about to face her, she clutched his jaw with her hands, brushing her lips over it. "Normally, discussing this with cattle would be tedious, but you are something else. You," she said as she reached for his genitalia, "are outside, foreign, dangerous, just as are the lights and your mysterious Sargon."

He struggled in pain as she applied pressure, and she guffawed, the powerful combination of vodka and tobacco sickening him. "Natural order demands we eliminate cattle so that those of us deserving may inherit our reward."

She scraped his cheek with her nails, he guessed to punish him for turning his eyes from her. "Pay attention, young one. We must gain control, not just of our weapons, but of lights and their origin." Patting his temple, she smirked at him. "Your reward is place in new order as my pet."

He shook his head, struggling to answer. "But either Russia or America attacking will destroy entire world, so where will you live, crowned in your new order?"

She applied crushing force to his scrotum, but the pain didn't register. Her right hand tightened around his throat, and she whispered, "We who pass through walls unseen shall ascend." Kierkov gestured to the windows, hissing. "Cattle will sustain us with sweet meat in new order." She eyed him, casting her head back with a laugh. "Oh, yes, so you cannot feel pain?" She squeezed him with greater force, a malevolent flicker crossing her face, as though she were a child pulling wings from an insect.

Mayak wanted to vomit again. He shook his head at her. "Sargon will never help you."

She tightened her grasp on him. "He will expose himself to protect you. This I know."

He felt torn between resisting her cruelty and guarding his vulnerable body, so when injury was imminent, he struggled. Huffing, he complained, "He will not appear on command, and I haven't heard from him in years."

She released his throat, pushing him aside in disgust. "You are poor liar, Mayak. Recent events have already forced his appearance, despite your collusion to conceal simple fact. Your scientific refusal to suffer faith disgusts me." She released him from her claws, and he collapsed against the sink, dizzy from the alcohol. Kierkov laughed. "Science is faith, too, young fool. Now, take shower, for I wish to fuck."

C***

Conique rustled a pile of papers in an increasing annoyance, for she was struggling to recall why she had chosen to search a pile in the first place. Reuben had discouraged her from concerning herself with the tedium of paper heaps, but a gnawing notion toyed with her: Why would God offer odd revelations at this stage of the game? Diagnosed with mild dementia, she knew she might imagine things more ludicrous than her past prognostications, most of which had come to pass. But the Seven, the Fallen, an angel—it all troubled her. Remaining present to her conversations, she experienced clarity, or perhaps no confusion, but once completed, she felt as though God were a cosmic prankster, upending the puzzle table just as she tried in earnest to give the combination of pieces some semblance of sanity.

Reuben, ever her protector, must've sensed her frustration, so he entered her office without her noticing. She slammed a balled-up fist upon one disheveled heap, and his ebony hands stilled her wrists. His resonant voice soothed her as he said, "Connie, dear, you're agitated. Let's go have some tea and relax."

He pulled the stack away from her, shaking his head in gentle reproach. Peering over his gold-framed reading glasses, he leaned his head to hers toward hers and said, "C'mon babe, teatime." She tried to refuse, but he held her arms, consoling her with a low voice. "When you're feeling better, you can look at the papers. But remember what the doctor said about the disease: when you're upset, it'll be worse."

She removed her spectacles, letting them drop to her chest, tightening the ribbon tethering them to her. Conique trusted her husband, but she didn't trust the hand she'd been dealt by the Almighty.

He squeezed her hand, his own eyes reddening with anguish, and he assured her, "Dear, your faith is built on your love for others. That isn't going anywhere anytime soon." He took a bottle of pills in hand, unscrewed the cap, then produced two canary yellow capsules. "Your meds, dear."

She shook her head. "You my pusher, now?"

Reuben's infectious smile spread over his face. "That would be funny. Down the hatch, Connie?"

She took them in hand. "They're supposed to make me feel better?"

His smile faltered. "Well, that's the aim. The doctor said it would make things easier."

She shrugged with a smirk. "Absotively posilutely." Placing them in her mouth, she sipped from her tea. His bright brown eyes watched her. She chuckled, "Oh, would you fetch me the paper outside. I heard it delivered earlier."

Reuben stood, placing his hands on his hips. "We're probably the only people in this neighborhood still getting a physical one. Fine, but you stay put, missy."

After he left the room, she spat the capsules into a tissue, bunching it together for the trash. "Sorry, dear, but I want my mind to work a little longer," she whispered.

Standing, she reached for her everyday coat near the door leading outside. Aurum nuzzled Conique's hand. Looking down to her, she could see that the dog carried the purple leash in her mouth. She laughed at the sight. "Okay, you can come along, beautiful."

C***

Conique wasn't sure how much time had passed. All she knew was that it was dark, with mist and fog all about her. There were buildings around her, with garbage littering the sidewalks, with vagrants moving along them. One old man coughed with a phlegm-filled rattle that nauseated her. She knew these were derelicts abandoned by society, and she took pity on them. But she didn't know why she was there.

She checked her pockets for her billfold and phone, but neither were there. She couldn't find a key to her house. The thought crossed her mind that she might belong among the lost souls surrounding her. She decided to walk, but her right leg screamed in pain. Looking to it, she could see blood staining her pants and coat. "Dear Lord," she whispered.

One ancient woman pushing a grocery cart exchanged glances with her. "You're new here, love."

The cockney accent caught Conique by surprise. She answered, "I really don't know."

The woman gave a toothless grin. "I know everyone here. And you—I don't know you."

"I'm Connie. You are?"

Tucking tufts of white hair under her stocking cap, the elderly woman said, "Albeda is my name, love. Wait—" she pointed to Conique's leg, "—you're injured. Dear me, what happened to you?"

Conique tried to think things through. "I can't remember. I think I was heading out the door to take—" She trailed off as she lifted her left hand. In it was Aurum's leash. Threading it through her fingers on her right hand, she pulled to the end. It had torn, and the tip was damp with blood. "Oh, God. Where's my dog?" Her eyes swelled with tears.

Albeda reached for her. "Oh, love. Don't cry. I'm sure there's some explanation. Let me help ya look, what?"

Conique flagged in exhaustion. "Reuben was right. I don't know what I've done."

A man wearing a trash bag with holes cut for his arms sidled to her. With a deep drawl, he asked, "Are you from the Carter Center? Maybe I can help."

Albeda snapped at him. "Shove off, Maurice. She's in need of help, can't ya see?" Placing an arm around Conique, she asked, "Where's home, love?"

She shrugged. "I think my husband is looking for me. He's Reuben."

Maurice caught them as his garbage bag vest rustled. "Like the sandwich? I could use a good sandwich."

Albeda swung her free arm at him. "This isn't the time, Maurice. Now piss off!" She patted Conique. "Sorry about that. Maurice is a little touched in the head."

Conique nodded. "Aren't we all?"

Albeda pointed ahead. "Loretta up ahead has a phone we can use if ya need to call someone. Truth is, I was worried 'bout ya when I heard shouting from down the road."

Conique felt a throbbing in the pit of her stomach. "What did you hear?"

Albeda said nothing for several seconds, making the squeaks from her cart's rusted wheels the prominent sound. At last, she answered, "You said the name Mirrum several times. Is this someone ya need to find?"

Conique stiffened. "What exactly did I say?"

She shrugged. "I don't think it made a lick of sense, to be honest. Something about her being asleep and needing to be awakened."

Conique squinted at the woman to study her prune face. Maurice followed them closely, waddling his disproportionately large hips next to Albeda's cart. "What's strange about that? I need to be woke up everyday." He licked his lips and bit the top of his mouth with an underbite.

Albeda bristled at him. "She next said Mirrum was in outer space."

Maurice played tit-for-tat. "Astronauts have to sleep, too, Albeda."

Conique recalled the name, but not the meaning. She asked, "Did I say where in outer space I can find her?"

Albeda slowed to examine Conique. "Did ya get knocked on the head, too? How many astronauts do ya know?"

Maurice chimed in. "I had five concussions before I could hear them." He pointed to the sky with an arthritic finger. "Now I know what they're doing."

Albeda postured against him. "I swear, Maurice, ya best be gone. I'll help her home."

Conique stopped in her tracks. "No, it's alright, Albeda. Tell me Maurice, who are *they*? And what do *they* want?"

He looked away with an uncertain look, as if his emotions landed on delay. He replied, "Mating with us, of course."

Albeda shouted, "Maurice! Poppycock! We're trying to be serious, love."

He bowed his head in shame, but Conique asked, "Did I say anything else?"

Albeda patted her. "Come on, love. It doesn't matter what ya said. He's not right in the ole' lump of lead."

Maurice was distracted by the meow of a cat, so he duckwalked away.

A few minutes past, and Conique couldn't tell where she was. Albeda held to her arm, patting her. "Almost there, love. Loretta can call for help." She looked ahead, but fog obscured her view. The scene was surreal, making her doubt she was even awake.

A chirp and lights from behind snapped her attention. She turned to see a police car. Albeda clung to her, saying, "Never fails. We'll see if the grasshoppers are here to help."

A policewoman hopped from the car, calling to them, "Stay where you are. We're responding to a silver alert."

Albeda caterwauled, "I found her for ya, governor. Safe and sound."

The officer held a flashlight to Conique. "Are you Conique Voyant?"

Albeda beamed. "Oh, what a name! Wish I'd thought of it meself."

Conique nodded, but the confusion distressed her. "I'm Conique. I don't know what happened."

The officer spoke into her shoulder radio. "Tremont here. Found her on an alley at Peachtree and Peachtree." She extended a gloved hand to Conique. "Miss Voyant, please come with me."

Albeda held her tight, and, despite her bewilderment, she found it comforting. "This lady is lost, governor. She needs her hubby."

Tremont replied, "Thanks, Albeda. We'll take her to him. But she needs medical attention. We believe she was the victim of a hit-and-run."

Conique held up the leash as her heart pounded. "Aurum," she whispered.

The officer answered, "We couldn't find your dog, ma'am. But we think she was injured, too."

Sirens followed her words while Conique mouthed, "Injured?"

Albeda squeezed Conique's shoulder. "Be well, love."

She looked into the elderly woman's face. "I'll find you to help you out. I'm sorry you're homeless."

She grinned. "I have a place to stay, and Jimmy Carter himself helped build it. You're loved, and what is a home if there isn't love, love?"

Officer Tremont offered an arm to Conique, so she limped to the squad car just as an ambulance appeared. The lady police tapped her arm. "We'll get you all fixed up, Miss Voyant. Not to worry."

Two paramedics, one black and one white, who couldn't have been older than twenty-five took her in hand, placing her on a gurney. A third spoke to the officer, but she couldn't understand what they said. As they lifted her into the patient compartment, she said, "Sorry fellas that I'm a bit heavy. We eat too much fried chicken."

The black tech answered without a pause. "You're fine, Miss Voyant. And that sounds yummy—maybe you'll make us some? I'd help around your house."

He flirted with a wink, but she guessed correctly that he was gay. "Honey, don't be writing checks you can't cash." He laughed hard, and the banter distracted her, just as he'd intended.

The medics were polite and professional. One checked her eyes and reflexes while the other tended to her leg. He examined the wound before administering a shot of pain medicine.

Tremont called to her, "They'll take you to Emory. Your husband will be there waiting for you."

"Thank you, officer. I appreciate your help. I hope I didn't cause too much trouble." She waited as they connected her to oxygen.

Tremont answered, "It's not trouble, Miss Voyant. It's all part of the job."

She was afraid, confused, and worried about Aurum. She knew Reuben would be livid that she wandered off. It was a mercy—the techs had covered her with a warm blanket, and the meds relaxed her, so she closed her eyes as a third tech sped the ambulance on its way.

The ambulance ride was short and sweet, though it could have been hours and she wouldn't have noticed. The techs pushed open the rear doors, revealing the intake ramp at Emory's emergency room. Reuben was standing outside the ambulance among nurses in green scrubs. She teared up at her husband and said, "I'm so sorry, dear. I don't know what happened."

His beautiful brown eyes carried no judgment, just worry and comfort. "Don't worry about any of it, dear. We'll get you treated and home."

The techs eased her out, and they pushed her through large sliding glass doors. Flashing in her mind was the hospital where she said goodbye to her daughter. She shut her eyes, praying silently for peace.

Opening them again, she could see that she was in a hallway where other patients on gurneys had been parked. Above her head stood Reuben; his physician shingle helped him walk through those particular walls. His voice caught her attention as he fussed with one of the nurses. "Look, if you don't have space here, you don't have it. Check her out to go, and we'll be outta your hair."

A doctor spoke with him. "Look, we need to get x-rays before we can release her."

Reuben replied, "Well get them done." He could see she was watching him. "Don't worry, dear. We won't be here long. They just have to do some imaging."

She said, "I don't know what happened. I think Aurum is hurt."

"Hush now, Connie. You won't do you any good." He shouted to the nurse, "Also check for DVTs."

She said to him, "Mister Hamora—"

He corrected her. "Doctor."

She answered, "Okay, Doctor Hamora, you shouldn't even be back here. Maybe you should wait."

He refused. "Look, I'm her medical power-of-attorney, and I'm also a physician. I'm not leaving her." The nurse gestured futility with her arms before disappearing among the chaos.

Conique said to him, "There were some indigents who helped me. They might know where Aurum is."

He patted her. "We'll find her."

She asked, "What happened?"

He said in a low voice, "A car hit you and Aurum, then they sped away. Cops are looking for the driver, and they're on the look-out for our old girl."

She asked, "I did this, didn't I?"

His face was in torment, but he answered, "Just rest. We'll get through this."

She shook her head in despair. "Dear Lord, help me bear this."

18. Vyduaion in a Dream

O***

Olga awakened. Consciousness was still an onerous thing. From her vision's periphery, she could see Zephyr. She bristled at the word "savior" as it floated across her mind, but he was nothing less than that. He reversed her terminal illness with medicine outstripping the state-of-the-art in the twenty-first century.

He spoke to her with a sweet voice. "Do not strain yourself, Professor. You are safe."

She stretched her arms, and they tingled to life. "Where am I? Did I die?"

Zephyr answered without looking away from whatever had his attention. "One stratum to another, do you remember watching your avatar's death? You are alive. Do you recall our encounter?"

Opening her eyes a bit more, she examined her surroundings. Gleaming chrome, silver, shining—resplendent came to mind. It was an impeccable layout, with walls lined with onyx paneling and a fluidic scatter of crimson and cerulean. Were they instrumentation? Decorative? Maybe both.

And then there was the man.

He stood vigil with his eyes fixed on his console, manipulating what appeared to be some sort of holographic interface; the sheen of his clothing, she did remember. Zephyr—he had said his name was Zephyr. Zephyros the westerly wind?

With a light laugh, she said, "Zephyr?" She smiled, recognizing that she was altered, either by the drugs administered in hospice or the new strange treatment provided by this person.

Zephyr did not shift his eyes from his controls, though he returned her slow nod, replying, "That is correct." He paused, then turned his exquisite eyes to her. So powerful were they that she felt she might weep, and with gentility, he remarked, "You have many questions, likely more than most would share."

Stretching her arms, she whispered, "What you've accomplished, and what I see now, is impossible. Therefore, I must be dead."

A faint smile caressed his elegant countenance, and he said, "Flawless logic, Professor Kunskapsen, though you'll recall that, 'Any sufficiently advanced technology is indistinguishable from magic.'"

She laughed—or at least, she tried, with a cough replacing it. "Anyone saving my life should call me Olga. Arthur C. Clarke? You know of him? You quote him reverentially."

He turned his face to hers, nodding with a wide smile. "From a stratum of reverence?"

Her eyes widened. "I was thinking that very term. Telepathy?"

His face returned to the console, and he chuckled playfully. "In a way, though limited. Strong, dogged thinking I can hear. Probabilistic pathways. Some excel more than others." He could see her trying to rise to a seating position, so he cautioned, "Olga, you must rest. I shall answer your questions to the extent possible, but we must wait for your condition to improve."

After a pause, the light catching his raven-colored hair, he adjusted his stance, adding, "And, if you believe this is a dream, note that you may touch, see, hear, smell, and taste—each something rare while unconscious. The questions drive you, and this is no vice."

She lowered herself back onto the bed. The surface was soft, translucent, supporting her, warming and cooling her where needed. She'd never felt such comfort from any bed. Moving her flaxen waves from her face, she said, "I've always told my students that knowledge is a sphere of light, along whose surface are questions." She struggled some, adding, "Beyond which is ignorance. Questions we've yet to encounter."

As she touched the surface with her fingertips, the material gave, shining and shifting.

He asked, "Where do you find yourself now?"

She exhaled, lying on her back. "Beyond the firmament."

He was playful. "Starting at the beginning might make the most sense. Query away."

Olga placed her hands at her sides, too tired to gesture. "Basics then. Why save me? Who are you? Where are we? Where are we going?"

He left his console to reach her side. "You ask the most important question of all—why." By instinct, she tried to tense her muscles, yet they refused. But this differed from her earlier experience of the body-wide tingling, burning, and loss of sensation she suffered under her illness. Even as she was now, she felt better than before her diagnosis. And she couldn't ignore the overwhelming splendor of this man, augmented by mercy and gentility. He reached for her face with electric fingertips.

She met his eyes. "Everything follows from why."

Zephyr took her hand into his own. "You thought about strata. Tell me."

She replied, "I was thinking about how the world differs, depending on the discipline. One must add rules to explain randomness. From mathematics to geometry to physics to chemistry to biology to medicine to psychiatry."

His smile was infectious. "One of your own scientists concluded that the literary critic might be the final arbiter of truth. Deep breaths, please." He touched her chest as she obliged.

Between breaths, she asked, "What stratum is this? What you've done outstrips any technology I know."

He pointed to the chamber surrounding them. "A world fashioned by the power of thought."

She looked away from him. "Cryptic," she said.

Zephyr patted her shoulder. "What is thought, if not cryptic?"

Reality hit her as she imagined Janna's face. "My sister?"

Beneath him, a seat materialized from the floor. He sat down next to her. "Forgive me. I too easily stray from the topic at hand. Your sister is safe. Grieving, but safe."

Olga clenched her jaw. "Will I see her again?"

He glanced from her, moved by her request. "In truth, I do not know." She didn't answer, so he continued. "Olga, the world you know is only one of many. Your peers and colleagues call this the multiverse."

Her heart raced. "You are not from this world?"

Zephyr nodded. "That is correct."

She shot her eyes around the chamber, its etched onyx paneling clearer to her now. "These are self-organizing surfaces?"

Zephyr waved a hand, causing a wave of shifting colors in the displays. "They are responsive to my physiology."

Olga frowned. "With this technology, why save me? Surely, your world doesn't need a twenty-first century physicist."

He appeared to marvel at her. "Your humility is a lovely thing. But there is more. You share heritage with my world."

Olga was stunned. "What are you saying? I am an alien?"

Zephyr answered, "You are one of seven, engineered from both my world and this one." He lifted his hand above her, and with a flick of his fingers, images of seven people coalesced, though only the last, taken from Olga's web page on the university site, was in focus. She raised her hand to the images, and the sixth focused.

Pointing to it, she said, "That is Shigeru Nakamura, a physician specializing in radiation therapy. He reached for you."

Zephyr touched Shigeru's image with delight. "Bless me, your mind unlocked his identity! We can reach him."

She touched the five unfocused images, but nothing happened. "I don't understand—who are these?"

He turned away to dance his fingers among holographic consoles appearing next to him. In haste, he answered, "We call you the Vesiks, placed here to nourish a legacy of our people. When the time is right, one after the other receives some indelible psychic drive to locate the next in the chain. Each of you suffer because I couldn't reach you sooner." He watched her as she reached for the images. Her fingers caused the faces to shimmer.

She touched her head. "My tumor?"

Zephyr slid his fingers over her scalp. "Yes. The others suffer similarly, and so we must find them."

She pointed at the five missing silhouettes. "Why don't you know who they are?"

He turned his attention to her once more. "For their protection, and for ours. The joining of the Vesiks opens the way to an awesome power."

"More awesome than this? What is this place?" She watched energy pulse through the surfaces along the walls, as though they contained blood vessels which disseminated vital energy to each console.

He gestured to the surfaces surrounding them. "This is a vessel designed with my world's technologies. It is among the only functional tools we have here."

She felt light-headed, though she fought to stay awake. "I want to understand."

Zephyr placed a hand on her face once more. "I am truly sorry you have suffered so. Because of this, you must rest. I can answer more when your strength returns."

She closed her eyes, and clarity struck her. "Because of Norcross," she whispered. The name visibly pained Zephyr. Olga continued, "I sought him. Who is he?"

Zephyr closed his eyes and closed his fists, appearing almost to pray. His voice lowered. "Norcross is the reason this, and all other inhabited worlds, are in jeopardy. He was intended to be the eighth in a sequence, but he has gone rogue. The hope is that his lead on us isn't too great."

She took his hand. "Why?" At the touch, a face materialized, becoming a hub for the other seven. The face wasn't unlike that of Zephyr, though colder, with lighter hair and fiery blue eyes. "Who is he?" Fear and sadness overcame her, causing her to sob, then to seize.

Zephyr disconnected himself from her abruptly, as he wiped the eight images away. His eyes flashed pain. "Please, you must rest. I dare not risk further emotional transference. For now, understand that recent events have jeopardized civilizations beyond your reckoning. For now, rest assured that your health shall return to you soon, and your senses shall explode as though operating for the first time. I must attempt to contact the sixth."

He turned, stepping to his console. Around him and his station, a sheen of black materialized, flowing like a viscous liquid. It shielded him and his actions from her, leaving her alone. His emotions had overpowered her, coercing her to experience feelings an order of magnitude beyond her own. Her brain did her the courtesy of siphoning her consciousness. She fell to the blackness wondering which strata she'd encounter next.

*S****

Shigeru crept between trees in a wooded glade. The sun shone brightly, its gold rays piercing the calm air. The soothing, discordant ringing of wind chimes caught his attention. Listening more, he heard the chirp of birds and hum of insects—almost a random orchestration supplied by nature. Were there voices contributing to the sounds?

No, he found himself alone, and, worse yet, incapable of uttering a sound. Where could this be? He had no memory of booking any nature tours. Christ, he'd never plan a recreational nature tour, for he despised camping in the outdoors. It must've been his assistant's gaffe, dispatching him into a cesspool of mosquitoes, mugginess, and dearth of creature comforts.

He'd have words with Tie. On that, he staked his life. Well, maybe not his life.

He pushed through towering grass to a clearing containing a few tree stumps. Lumberjacks had been here, though he thought it strange that they'd work within a space not in proximity to a road. But he heard no cars.

On closer inspection, he saw that the stumps were burned, charred by some unseen force. The smell struck him; this was no smell of ordinary rot in nature, but rather, that of rotting flesh. Fetid, foul, as disgusting as the *parts bag* he recalled from medical school. Such a bag—containing arms, legs, and organs reeking of turkey sandwich meat—awaited dissection by often-none-too-eager students.

He retched, forcing himself to press onward into more underbrush. He heard crickets, frogs, and other woodland beasts slithering, climbing, and swinging around him. Damn, did he have an itinerary? He fidgeted in his pockets for his cellphone, but each were empty. Double fuck on Tie for this insanity!

He meandered forward, slapping the blood-thirsty mosquitoes as they feasted on him. Leaves and displaced branches scraped red and bloodied tears into his arms. Caterpillars and beetles fell upon him from the trees. He hated insects in particular.

He squeezed into a second clearing, this smaller than the previous. Again, there were rotting, burnt tree stumps enclosed by more heavy forest. He had no idea where he was headed, for the sun was at its midday high, robbing him of directional clues.

This would constitute cause to terminate Tie from his job, provided Shigeru ever escape. And why in the hell would someone burn the trees in the selective way done here?

Without reason, he delved into the forest farther still, and now, he heard moving water. Picking up his pace, he parted a path through the forest, which was green, heavy, and teeming with life. His scrapes burned as he hastened his steps. Human beings belonged indoors, shielded from the elements. It had been too long since they spent time in the trees. He'd be fortunate to escape them.

The sound of moving water became a bit of a roar, so he knew there might be a clearing alongside it, furnishing an egress from this episode. At last, he reached the riverbank, a trail of rocks separating the trees and the finer sand abutting the waterline. He could walk along the bank to rejoin the civilized urbanites.

But then something caught his eye. Something not natural. Detritus and bits of wood moved along the water, parallel to his newfound path—chunks of it, and other things. Maybe tin or aluminum sheets, larger machine bits, like parts of automobiles, as well as larger bits still, like pieces of a home. All were burned. Just like the tree stumps.

He decided he'd outrun this nightmare. But the foul smell of death and decay returned. He tried to focus on his path and what lay ahead, but the source of the rank and spoiled smell once more caught his attention.

God, he wished he hadn't looked. It was a greater horror than anything he'd imagined before.

Death. The swift water carried body after body beyond count, even as they choked its mighty flow.

He pondered the scorched remains, having sustained injuries he could tell were not initially fatal. These victims had suffered, their faces melted away, their limbless torsos, bodies melded together by flame. What could be worse?

As though this place understood his thoughts, it treated him to another horror: bodies still burning appeared, the river beginning to surrender its great power to the holocaust before him. Children, women, men, livestock, timber, all wreathed in flames. Finally, scores appeared who had not yet perished, all screaming, malformed creatures, all seared under the power of Shigeru's greatest fear: the atom bomb.

God, this must have been a dream, as he knew a more modern instantiation would mean extinction. Somehow, he was observing the aftermath of the 1945 bombs. Two groves, filled with rotting tree stumps. The wanton waste of the single most important thing in all the known universe: intelligent life.

Oh, what malevolence could conceive this? He wanted to scream, but he could utter nothing. Instead, he watched children under mortifying immolation as they pleaded, shrieking in agony.

He slammed his eyes shut and buried his palms into his ears, pleading for the horror to end. After a few moments, the sound died. He reopened his eyes to discover the scene had darkened to silhouette, like a vintage black-and-white photograph. He could make out the trees along the horizon, though the shadow concealed the burned wood and broken bodies. A figure from the shadows moved from the riverbank towards Shigeru, with light illuminating his weary face. He wept, his emerald eyes swollen with tears.

Having found his voice, Shigeru cried, "What is this? Why am I here?"

The stranger answered, "This would be the only psychic foothold I have, for this terror remains very central to your mind."

Shigeru recoiled from him. "I don't want this terror. Make it stop. Please."

He replied, "I must communicate this warning—the catastrophe surrounding you now will happen once more, should we fail. I cannot explain it all to you this way, but I needed to contact you by a mechanism untraceable by the one who is fallen."

Shigeru had stopped sobbing, so he asked, "What fallen?"

He bowed his head, struggling. "I cannot maintain this link. Please, Sheeki tonbo, for your own safety, you must go somewhere safe until I can find you."

Shigeru reached for him. "How do you know that name? Who are—"

The stranger answered, "Just go wherever you can to take refuge. And take no electronic devices with you. I will reach out when the time is right." He took Shigeru's hand. "And one last thing—you are correct that biological time crystals exist. I believe you, with the others of the Seven Vesiks, will see this to completion. That is all."

He dissolved before him, as did the nightmare surrounding him.

Shigeru awakened. Drenched in sweat, a terrible mess, he spotted only darkness outside his snowflake-covered bedroom window. He'd had the dream many times before. His parents had described every detail of the bombings to him, determined to help him understand why he must try his utmost to prevent another such attack in the world, and his research into the disease of his choice left little to his imagination. He understood that one must know the precise outcome of such an attack if one was to fight for the future of their species. But the stranger was different. It was hard to take his words seriously, considering it had been a dream.

He slipped into a silk robe given to him by one of his off-again/on-again student lovers. He reached for a whiskey bottle resting on his dresser. Uncorking it, he drank straight from the neck. With a little luck, he'd avoid more nightmares tonight.

That was it! This night was the anniversary of his mother's death from cancer. Twenty long years earlier, just after the September Eleventh attacks had happened, her struggle against cancer had claimed her. Her last words to him were, "No more tears, my Sheeki tonbo." It was a special nickname she'd bestowed on him, for he had loved dragonflies.

He slammed his fists into his dresser, furious. Slurping more firewater, he fell into his office chair. Outside, horns honked as commuters started their day. Somehow, the sounds of the city comforted him. The sky shifted colors, signaling that sunup approached. He couldn't remember the day of the week, so whether he had to muster himself to appear in-office remained to be seen. He knew that drinking more led to blackouts, some of which could, maybe should, have ended his career.

He decided he'd make his way to his bathroom, though his feet were unsteady. Reaching the door, he flipped the lights on. He glanced at himself in the mirror and screamed in horror at the grisly figure before him.

Half of his face had been burned away, and all of his wavy black hair was gone on that side. He looked to his hands and arms, shrieking at the blackened gangrene covering them. He touched his forearm, and the tissue crumbled, falling to the floor. Looking again into the mirror, he realized his teeth were plain to see along the burned side. A meaty, clotted skull was visible. He reached for the hair he still had, but when he touched it, he pulled it free, his scalp separating from skull, with putrefied slime spilling down his neck and face. Crying and screaming, he watched as the form before him disintegrated.

And, at last, he awakened for real. The window permitted a large amount of light into his room, and he discovered himself seated in the chair next to his dresser, holding an empty whiskey bottle. "Fucking fuck," he muttered as he recognized he'd poured the remainder of the bottle into his lap. And he had urinated, soaking himself, his silk robe, and the French provincial chair.

Gasping in fear, he grabbed his hair to assure himself it was still there. He closed his eyes to hold back the tears. The night terrors had worsened. The world was in decay. The nightmare stranger's metaphysical woo-woo made him think of the Voyant woman. Was his subconscious trying to make sense of her? Maybe it was the other way around.

Shigeru wondered whether there could be salvation for him. His life had become misery between blackouts. Maybe death would be better. After all, he would never be able to drink or fuck enough to feel satisfied. Hedonists, too, needed hope.

*B****

Boothby tapped his foot into the floorboard in front of him. Archie sat in his lap as he stroked the little cat's neck. He chuckled to himself, realizing that his phobia for the small and furry deemed him an exception. If only Headmistress Sagini could see him—even a sinner can have reprieve from zoodoraphobia.

But the anxiety had by no means abated. His traveling companions were unlikely. Janet slept too soundly for the long drive to disturb her. Adam couldn't interact, beyond operating the car to assure their safety. Boothby could only guess that Ephyr's link to the young man could spend its cognitive strength in only so many ways, and driving like a bat out of hell took the cake.

He stretched his neck upward, scratching his curly graying beard. Then, in his lap, the black kitty shifted, stretching, nuzzling his hand with its little snout. A gentle voice asked, "You have questions? Purr. Puppet and puppeteerrr tirrrre from connection."

Boothby grumbled, "I think they'll think I'm crazy to talk to you, cat."

Archie yawned as he stared into Boothby's eyes with his gorgeous green eyes. "Ephyrr is my master. They suffer you not."

Nodding, he bared his teeth. "Okay, can ya answer my questions?" Archie pressed his face into Boothby's fingers, so he found himself scratching the beast's face with his nails, relaxing the kitty's muscles. He heard Janet breathing hard, so he whispered in a low rasp, "What's wrong with Janet?"

The cat purred as he said, "She ssufferss ALS."

The child appeared so fragile to Boothby. "Jesus," he gasped. She stirred, not breaking her fitful and uncomfortable slumber.

The cat's tail lashed at his hands, so he whispered, "Where the hell are we headed?" He squinted to see the stretch of interstate before them, catching northern New Mexico signage.

The cat's voice replied, "To rrendezvous with others. The Communion. Purr."

He rolled his eyes, exclaiming, "Good Christ, I left my Strieber-signed copy behind!" The cat peeped as Janet stirred a little at the word. "Poor child," he muttered.

Archie nuzzled Boothby's coat. He followed the cat's face with his fingers to trace the chunk sitting in the breast pocket. "The focus stone! I wonder." He lifted the object to Janet, and he felt the energy within it surge. So did his heart, tethered to this thing. To him, both heart and mind were a means of finding and sharing the truth.

Janet trembled as he held the stone above her. Archie whined as Janet began to moan, then cry. She extended her hand onto the device, sharing a hold with Boothby.

They fell fast into a trance, as far as he could tell. All other senses left him, and he found himself falling into darkness.

J✱✱✱

Janet knew she had returned to the dream domain of the *Arkivar*; casting her eyes above, she let the stars, nebulae, and aurora streaks overhead dazzle her. Looking around, she didn't find the *Arkivar* himself. She would have liked to thank him for their escape—he appeared to understand that Adam's safety topped her concerns. She mourned her destroyed home, but life outweighed things a million-to-one.

Alone, she studied the realm surrounding her while sitting on the stone stairwell leading to the *Arkivar*'s altar. The aurora above her fluidly spread its orange energy across the sky, with striations of yellow, green, and even red. If she saw the moment of creation, it couldn't have been more beautiful. Hours or even days could have passed.

Something punctuated her solitude. A stranger had entered—he was fearful, but not a threat. Twisting around, she beheld a plump, effeminate man, grizzled, with a curly black-and-gray beard. His large, inquisitive brown eyes covered her head to toe, but he didn't speak. She smiled, almost confessing rule number eighteen aloud: *Strangers often are friends untrained, enemies are always friends too trained.* Stretching her arms towards him, she said. "Welcome, visitor."

He flitted his attention here and there, and baring his teeth, he replied in a gravelly voice she couldn't take all that seriously. "Where are we?"

With a chuckle, she observed, "You must be from the East Coast." Taking a careful step towards him, she said, "My name is Janet—or, at least, I think it is."

He nodded, as though the name meant something to him. "Oh, God, are we dead already? The cat said you had ALS."

Janet crooked her head, perplexed. "Come again?"

He shook his head, seeming to settle. Pointing to himself, he said, "My name is Boothby." Then, he gestured to the sky covering them, asking, "What is this place?"

Janet joined him in stargazing. "Truthfully, I don't really know. It's a place where I've spent many a dream since my earliest memories. The architecture and glyphs are Aztec, but I don't know why."

Boothby looked at the fallen stones about her, adding, "It didn't go well for them." He caught himself, asking, "Are you Azteca?"

She glanced to the sky, then back to this visitor, sighing. "I always thought I was Navajo. To know for sure, I had Codeka do my DNA profile. God, that started this mess."

Boothby's eyes bulged and his throat rasped. "Codeka? From Kymara Futures?"

She shook her head. "I don't remember seeing that other name, but I found Codeka online."

He waved his hands with flair, shouting, "Genomics companies have all sorts of nefarious plans for their databases." Stopping himself, he leaned to her with caution. "Umm, what started this mess?"

She couldn't imagine a need for secrecy with this adorable little man. "Codeka came to my house with some sort of mobile lab. They tried to kidnap me, but someone killed them."

Boothby seated himself on one of the steps near her. "That seems extreme for kidnapping," he croaked.

Janet added, "He was not a man. It looked like used magic. Shit, I must have imagined him."

Boothby frowned. "Norcross. No, you didn't just dream him up."

She felt faint recognition of this New Jerseyan as he uttered the monster's name. "You—you're one of the Seven, also?"

He stroked his beard with teeth bared. "I don't know about that. But Norcross burned up my landlady."

Janet could feel a rush of blood in her ears. "He killed the Codeka team with what could have been magic."

Boothby disagreed. "No, no, it's technology. He can control matter and energy at a level we can't even imagine."

Puzzled, she asked, "How can you know that?"

He shrugged before scratching his head with a plump hand. "I've read about all this stuff forever. He must originate from a Kardashev Type II civilization. He ain't magic—but he can still kill us just as dead."

Janet recalled where she'd seen Boothby. "To stop Norcross, or whatever thing he used to try to capture me, the *Arkivar* got in my head to control me. He said I had the power to slow him, so he threw me at him. While touching, I saw Norcross learn about a few of the other Seven by stealing memories from the *Arkivar.*" She stopped, remorse striking her. "Jesus, he found you because of me."

Boothby didn't seem to be one who would hold a grudge. His words removed all doubt. "Well, Archie saved me."

Janet pushed her self-rebuke out of her mind. "Who is that?"

He rolled his eyes, answering with a nervous chuckle. "He's, ermm, Mister Ephyr's cat." Correcting himself, he added, "I thought he belonged to my super—she woulda been a cat lady if she weren't so selfish."

Janet looked at the empty altar above them. "I just learned that my *Arkivar*'s name is Ephyr."

Boothby gave a slow nod as his eyes played about. "It would make sense. He's the common ingredient here. This is his place? What are the Seven?"

Janet thought it over. "I'm not sure I really know. He called us Seven Vesiks. We have something to do with his world. He and Norcross are—"

"Aliens," Boothby said with a sigh. "Why would they care about us?"

She ran a finger over a vein on her arm. "I thought it had to be a dream. The Codeka team told me that I have two extra chromosomes. I think I'm one of them."

Boothby's eyes nearly exploded from his eye sockets. "Christ, that is why you don't send your DNA to a gene chop shop like Codeka."

She shut her eyes, whispering, "Hindsight is twenty/twenty. You realize this means you're an alien, too?" She didn't know whether he processed her words slowly, or at all.

He gasped, "Oh God, I think I might faint. Me? An extraterrestrial? That means my quest is over. Jesus," he groaned.

Janet's nursing training kicked into gear, leading her to ask calming questions. "How did you get here? I've never had a visitor in this place."

He answered with gusto. "I met Mister Ephyr when I was eight years old. He gave me this." He reached into his pocket to search for something. His face brightened as he pulled out a gleaming lump of metal.

She eyed it, a thing she'd mistake for a misshapen shiny rock. "What is it?"

He replied, "I'm not sure." Janet reached for it, and he begrudgingly handed it to her.

She touched the object. It was metallic, heavy, and, indeed, strange. Tracing its irregular edges, she could feel a thrumming from within it. "This really is odd."

He took the strange metallic stone back into his eager hands, responding, "I've been chasing the lights since I was a boy." He placed the alloy into his pocket, calmed by it. "He gave me a hunk of some alloy that turns out to be one of their tools. He called it a focus stone."

Without thinking, she said, "An alloy isn't a stone."

He shrugged with a playful expression. "It stopped Norcross from catching us. And it's making it possible for me to talk to you in here, I'm guessing."

She didn't understand, but she found him intriguing. "So where do you come from?"

He looked around. "Well, I grew up an orphan back in the 1950s. I am a journalist."

Janet asked, "Adam and I were orphans, too. Journalist as in news and media?"

He rolled his eyes again as his cheeks reddened. "Well, I work in news. Umm, UFOs." He paused, hanging on her response. "This is where you laugh me into a rubber room."

She chuckled. "Now that I think about it, I have read about you. The ufologist. With the Pentagon having declassified all that shit about them, I'd think people would take you seriously."

He smiled at her. "What a relief to hear you say that. But they don't."

She patted him. "I'd keep the bit about the cat saving you to yourself."

His face dimmed, then brightened. "You are just putting me on, aren't ya?" They shared a laugh before he asked, "What about you?"

She thought of it all as so remote. "I'm a nurse for infectious diseases."

His eyes were huge. "As in pandemic-level stuff?"

She nodded. "Trying to save people who believe their disease is a hoax."

He replied, "If this is the Afterlife and I was stuck with a moron like that, then, I'd know I was burning in hell. Is the young man your boyfriend?"

Janet laughed. "No! He's my brother. Well, foster brother. Besides, he's gay. I thought you guys had good gaydar."

Boothby grinned. "Well, a girl can hope."

She pointed to the dream sky above them while asking, "You want to find the lights? What will you do with them?"

Boothby appeared genuinely surprised by the question. He said, "Well, I want them to explain why they're protecting us."

Now she felt surprise. "How so? What are they doing to protect us?"

Boothby regaled her as though he'd rehearsed the speech so many times, it was etched in his gray matter. "For seventy years we've been able to kill everything on the whole planet, ourselves included. But we haven't. Not yet, anyways."

She listened, but the thoughts didn't connect. "We're still here. What does that have to do with UFOs?"

He shook his head, his scattered silver hair bounding from side to side in the light of the green aurora above them. "There've been so many near misses, and our government admits they appear over nuclear weapons. That's a fact." He paused at her blank expression, then added, "Haven't ya' read Ellsberg?"

She answered, "I know who Daniel Ellsberg is, but he didn't say aliens were here to rescue us."

Boothby's round face sparkled with enthusiasm, so she decided it prudent to keep him there. He added, "He said it was a miracle we ain't dead." He tapped his knees with his hands, adding, "I think it's certain. I'd planned to get close to a warhead to make the lights appear."

Janet looked at the small man with skepticism. "How would you do that? You really think you could set one off? They'd arrest you at the gates."

He tapped his fingers together nervously. "Well, I was gonna get help from the Plowshares. It's all academic now. Mister Ephyr knows how to bring them."

She asked, "How do you know they're not drones created by DARPA?"

He laughed. "No way. They move ninety degrees at six thousand miles per hour. We can't dream of that. Man and machine would be turned to paste and powder." He made a *squish* sound, leading her to chuckle.

Janet nodded in agreement. "Okay, they're aliens."

He shook his head. "They are drones, mostly. Here to keep us alive."

With a deep breath, Janet pulled her hair back, threading her hands with it. At last, her brain made the connection. "Katafaj! They must be the Katafaj!"

He leaned forward as his eyes widened. "What is a Katafaj?"

She shook her head as it all made more sense. "The UFOs. The *Arkivar* called them a defensive network, and that I'd soon meet the one who could summon them. It's you!"

He blinked a few times as he eyed the surroundings and mouthed the word 'Katafaj.' At last, he said, "Then I know my purpose."

She felt some triumph in schlepping one thought into another in her head, but one question pressed. "Why do they want to save us?"

He fidgeted, casting his large eyes about as he thought it over. For a moment, she thought he could pass for an alien. At last, he said, "They have some destiny in mind for us, maybe? I don't know. But Mister Ephyr will help us understand. Besides, isn't life worth saving?"

Changing the subject, she asked, "Do you know where we're going?"

He blinked, thought it over, then answered, "I think to find others like ourselves. Archie was leading me to Atlanta. It can't be a coincidence that I wanted to get help of a minister who used to be part of the Plowshares."

She agreed. "Ephyr said each of us in the seven would get a psychic impulse to find the next in the chain. He pointed me to a fracker in Texas."

Boothby nodded. "Okay, then that's why a Russian wanted to talk to me."

She nodded, recalling her earlier vision. "There are more places I saw. They mean something. Japan and Norway." She hesitated, a little concerned he would believe she was insane, yet she figured he would not deem her so, considering the nutcase factor he himself sported. "Well, in a vision."

He grasped his own throat anxiously. "Jesus, we're caught up with intrigue bringing together Russians"—he gulped—"and Texans."

Janet found his winsome way somehow reassuring. Piling on, she complained, "Why would they want us? I'm a cripple, soon to be so useless I can't wipe my ass, and you're tortured by your anxiety."

Her remark managed to cause him to laugh, and both shared a chuckle. He answered, holding his hands outward, "The meek shall inherit the earth?"

She looked hard at him, then answering, "Okay, Boothby the Meek, you'll have to be strong for both of us. If that creature intends to kill us, you must figure out how to stop him before anyone else gets hurt." She reached for his hand and asked, "Promise me you'll try? Adam is as close as any brother I could have. He's my best friend, and he's in mortal danger."

Boothby rolled his eyes. "Oh, if Miss Sagini could see me now."

She asked, "Who's that?"

He laughed. "It doesn't matter. Okay, I think I can get out with this metal chunk." He removed it from his jacket and clutched it tightly. Looking at her, he said, "It's been a pleasure meeting you, even if we are all gonna die."

She laughed, retorting, "Thanks for the encouragement."

The chunk shimmered, and Boothby dematerialized. God, she hoped for the best.

19. Temptation for the Dark and the Light

F***

Frankie sighed at his bloodied mug in his rear-view mirror. Tyler was an unfortunate and infuriating complication in an otherwise well-made plan. His wrist ached where Edith had bitten him. He wrapped it with gauze, though his plan would end him long before it could heal.

But now, his brother Tyler was at his house waiting alongside Sheila for him to appear. She would expect George to be with him—and he was, in a manner of speaking, along for the ride.

He thought the sapphire of his irises had brightened against the red-stained skin, though he wasn't given to vanity. Not like Tyler, whom he now knew to be fairy folk. The thought of him playing woman to a black man repulsed him, each a strike against his daintier brother.

Myra's words bounced in his head. He sometimes hated her, but he knew she was right about the importance of family. He didn't feel much contradiction about robbing George's children of their father; he figured they'd owe him for a childhood free of that mocking sack of monkey shit. But he could not rob his sister and father of his brother, even if he believed Tyler was living in sin.

If God had intended the races to mingle, they wouldn't differ so in intelligence. He knew others disagreed, but they were fools. The challenges faced by mulatto children had been the excuse his late mother would offer when warning against what she called miscegenation, and though Tyler couldn't carry the negro's baby, it still repelled him no end. He retched at the thought, and the thrum of the locusts pressed him. He had really looked forward to Sheila's terror at his blood-soaked face, but winning everything took time.

Once he felt certain he didn't appear too mucked-up, he took a deep breath, then opened the door. The night air was chilly, though he could still smell sulfur from one of the many fracking sites nearby. It was worse than the last time he'd been home, but he, too, was changed.

Unchanged was his small house, a structure offering little quarter. He knew they'd all see him as he entered, so he would play it casual.

The door opened as he stepped onto the sidewalk, Tyler popping his head out. "Hey, bro!"

Frankie smiled a little, feigning calm. "Hey, Tyler. What brings you over?"

They hugged, and Frankie's stomach turned over thinking of the black man defiling this small waifish-yet-male body. Tyler answered, "You didn't remember? We were supposed to have game night." Shit, he'd never double-booked before.

Stepping into the entryway, Frankie started to remove his dust-covered boots, as was his habit. He clenched his jaw, thinking just how unordinary the ordinary became when under duress.

He steeled himself for the scene he entered. Marvell, Tyler's—well, whatever—sat politely on the loveseat. A livid Sheila sat opposite on his larger couch, clad in a stained gray sweatsuit. Her legs were crossed, and she flicked her foot to balance a filthy flipflop on her toes. It pissed him off that rotten foot odor would find its way onto his couch. She was chewing gum furiously, another habit Frankie could not abide. He grew angrier at the filthy topknot on her head as it bobbed with her smacking and chewing. Even George had hated that. Frankie hoped they'd see only the worst of each other once they were reunited in hell.

But the scene before him was not without its charm. Frankie thought blacks were inferior, but he didn't really think they should be exterminated, no matter the hyperviolent dreams he had. Sheila, by contrast, detested them to the point of yammering about how the world would be better off without them. The irony wasn't lost on Frankie that she grew up in a trailer park, ensnaring a crooked businessman like George to keep her rolling in the fat. God, Frankie wanted nothing to do with a world where Sheila could thrive.

Tyler broke Frankie's concentration by asking, "What did you do to your wrist?" He touched Frankie's forearm.

Frankie answered, "I was caught in some barbed wire."

Marvell said, "Let me get peroxide. That needs doctoring."

Sheila wouldn't even look at Marvell as she said, "Fuck his wrist." Instead, she glared at Frankie, chewed her cheek, and blurted, "Where's that fat sack of shit? Where's George?"

Frankie floated a half-smile, wishing he could tell her the truth. Instead, he greeted the black guy with, "Hey, man." Marvell waved, and Frankie said, "George didn't want to come along, Sheila."

She rubbed her ruddy, gritty face, pulling free a dry flake from her temple. She looked at it, as though she were considering some cosmic truth, then flicked it to the floor. God, why didn't she know how to pretend to be a woman some man might be willing to touch? He longed to use a cheese grater on her textured, repugnant face. She answered, "That's fucking unacceptable! Where the fuck is he?"

Always with the profanity. He profaned many things, but she couldn't squeeze a sentence out of that disgusting mouth without peppering in a thousand curses. He shook his head, answering, "Look, Sheila, I wanted him to come home with me, but he—" He paused, looking to Marvell, then back to her. "I don't think we should talk about this in front of—"

She pointed a cruddy fingernail at him, "I don't fucking care who the shit is here. Where's my goddamned fat-ass husband?" He felt sluggish as the locusts swarmed in his head. She snarled at him. "Don't give me that innocent dumb-as-shit hick routine. Answer me!"

He clamped his teeth together in rage, answering, "Sheila, he wouldn't come with me when he found out you would be here."

She jumped off the couch, entering his no-fly zone of less than two feet. Pointing her finger at him, she shrieked, "Where is he, Frankie?!" The locusts screamed as she poked her pointer finger into his sternum.

Tyler stepped towards her, moving between them. "Sheila! Leave my brother alone."

She looked to him, snickering. "Or you'll do what, little man? Redecorate my kitchen?" She rolled her eyes, then turned back to Frankie. "Where the fuck is my husband?"

Marvell, to Frankie's surprise, also took his side in the conflict. "See here, Sheila. You can't come in a man's castle and make crazy demands."

She snarled at him, snapping like a feral animal. "Get outta my face, or I'll tell you what you are."

Marvell puffed his chest up. "What do you wanna say? Say it, then!"

Frankie stood between them. "Let me handle this, Marvell."

Sheila mocked him. "You can't handle shit, Frankie. Marvell might be the nig"—she paused—"darkie, but you're just black on the inside. I tell George all the time that you are pitch black on the inside."

Frankie could feel the magnum tucked under his coat, and he wanted to use it. Fighting himself, he said, "George stayed in Odessa, Sheila."

She crowded him harder, and the dizzying buzz of the *Korobskron* almost blotted her voice out. He started to close his eyes, so she poked him again, yelling, "Why is he there?!"

Frankie thought fast as he said, "He's with another woman, and she took him away, okay?!"

Sheila was, for that rare second, speechless. As the color drained from her face, she faltered. Turning to Tyler and Marvell, she mumbled, "It can't be. Why would he want to do that?"

Marvell stood, taking Tyler by the arm. "Hey, T, maybe we should go."

Tyler pulled his arm free. "I'm not leaving my brother, Marvell."

Frankie started to agree, but that blessed silence ended when Sheila accosted him once more. "You knew he was doing this, and didn't fucking tell me? You fucking men and your fucking cocks. You're like animals, coming everywhere you can. Go to fucking church. Sing the fucking songs. Then fuck fuck fuck. Jesus this, pussy that."

He snapped at her. "Don't joke about my faith. I didn't know what he did until today, and I told him not to do it."

Tyler closed ranks with them, scolding her. "My brother isn't like that, Sheila. You and your husband are your problems, not his. You should leave."

She ambled away from them in a blubbering mess. "He'd throw away our lives like that? I go to fucking Jenny Craig. I do everything I can to be attractive."

Frankie watched Marvell and Tyler exchange uncomfortable expressions, and he honestly felt glad they had each other. Maybe women were just too fucking crazy.

Sheila honked and wailed, "Why would he fucking do this to me? To our fucking children?" Frankie gritted his teeth, angry that she'd profane her own kids. She turned to him again, saying, "You gotta have some idea where he is."

Marvell volunteered, "Do you have his phone on locate mode?"

Frankie felt an internal quake, recognizing his mistake in stuffing George's phone with his body. Sheila reached for her purse, grabbing her phone. "No, I didn't think at all of that. Thanks, Martin."

Tyler shook his head reproachfully. "It's Marvell."

Frankie seized the phone from her. "If you go confront him, it'll make it worse, Sheila."

She grabbed it back from him, pushing him aside. "Oh, step the fuck off, Frankie. Like Tyler said, this ain't your problem." Fevered fingertips opened her contacts. Jesus, he hoped George's phone wasn't on.

Marvell stepped closer, pointing. "That's what you hit right there. He'll appear on a map if you have it set up."

She pulled her phone from him, complaining, "Don't fucking touch me or my phone. Black lives matter always fucking watching me, lusting."

Marvell raised his hands, stepping away, and Tyler shouted, waving her off, "Excuse you, bitch. Marvell wouldn't want you if you were the last woman on earth."

She just hissed, pressing buttons on her phone while Frankie held his breath.

And it happened. The map showed his neighborhood. The buzzing in his brain roared, suffocating him as Sheila turned her head to him. "It says his phone is fucking here, Frankie!"

He just couldn't do it now. Not with his brother in the crosshairs. So, he blurted, "He gave his phone to me."

She scraped her forehead so hard, blood welled up in a crag of dead skin. "So, he told you when he'd fucking pick it up, right?"

Frankie shut his eyes, faint from his Korobskron. Tyler intervened, telling her, "Sheila, I think you should just go. My brother is tired."

She pushed him aside, sneering. "Shut up, you fairy fuck." Turning to Frankie, she demanded, "Gimme that fat fuck's phone right now!"

He drew a breath, and clouds parted in his mind. There could be no more time— he should kill her and then himself to spare Tyler. The locusts calmed, making way for peace within him. In a sigh, he pointed to the door. "Okay, Sheila. After you."

She crossed her arms, adding another goddamned complication. "No, *you* go get the goddamned phone and bring it to me. I'm not going out into the cold. Smells like a thousand fucking farts out there."

Frankie accepted with a mocked bow. As he opened the way forward, Sheila hollered, "Don't leave that fucking door open. You don't have any insulation in this cardboard shack!"

He waved her off as he shut the door behind him. He heard her trade insults with Tyler, though he was relieved he couldn't understand them. The cold air refreshed him, so he took his time. Rounding his way to the side of his truck, Frankie pulled the plastic tarp off George's lifeless body to search for the phone. Laying his fingers on it, he pulled it free. He shut his eyes and leaned against his truck to think things through.

If he killed Sheila inside the house, he'd traumatize Tyler and Marvell. They probably wouldn't leave until after her, though, so he couldn't think of another path. If he let her go, there would be too many things he couldn't control, including police, her children, and any others between him and his goal. He was a crack shot, but it was still a risk to shoot in a room with his brother there. Giving her the phone and letting her go would give him a scant chance to regroup.

Sighing, he opened his eyes, then pushed a button on George's phone that illuminated the screen. Though he could see notifications listing twelve unanswered calls from Sheila, he could see blood and cracks on the screen. He rubbed the cracks, understanding that he must have hit the phone with one of his shots. There would be no explaining it.

He watched his breath turn to fog while he stood, thinking harder. The locusts hummed, but he couldn't think of a solution. He closed his eyes, drawing the frigid air into his lungs. He squeezed his fingers around the phone, offering a silent prayer for his Deliverer to give him strength. He remembered a jingle Pastor Chet taught him: "If God wants you to see this through, you can ask Him what you're supposed to do."

Frankie heard something behind him, so he opened his eyes and turned around. There was movement down the road—a man approaching. He bristled at the thought of another filthy homeless beggar wandering into his neighborhood. Well, this would give him one more victim.

But this figure marched with confidence, with muscle, moving in stealth, so Frankie watched him as he listened to Sheila and Tyler continue to argue with no small amount of noise in the house. Cornered, Frankie glanced at his front door, then back to the stranger making his way towards his driveway. He caught something strange about the figure's clothes, as though they were liquid, filled with light.

As he squinted to gain a clearer picture, the door burst open behind him. Sheila poured out of the entryway, yelling, "Frankie! Bring me that fat fornicating fuck's phone, now!"

But he couldn't remove his eyes from the stranger. At last, his face cleared, one of a man thirty-five or forty, clean and confident. The figure pointed his hand towards Frankie as he called, "I hear the swarm, Francis Putnam."

Before Frankie could answer, Sheila shouted, "What the fuck is this? Who the fuck are you?"

The figure ignored her, locking eyes with Frankie. "Do not fear, Francis. I hear them, too." He lifted a hand towards Frankie, quieting the locusts.

Sheila kept shouting. "You should fear me, goddamned mother fucker. Gimme his fucking phone!"

He couldn't unlock his mutual gaze with the stranger, so Sheila pried George's phone from Frankie without resistance. Looking it over, she slapped Frankie with it. "What the fuck is this, Frankie? Why is there fucking blood on it? Why—" She turned to see George's body in the truck, crimson fluid gleaming black in the moonlight. Dropping the phone to the gravel, she wailed, "Oh, my fucking God! Oh, fucking Christ!"

Frankie could hear her distantly, even though she pushed him and struck him. He knew Tyler and Marvell had followed Sheila, though they couldn't yet see George's body.

He knew Sheila was continuing to scream, but the man spoke once more, and Frankie could hear almost nothing else. "I've sought the one who would hear My call, Francis Putman." His sapphire eyes glowed for an instant, flickering over a boyish smile.

Sheila screamed, "Call the fucking police! My husband is fucking dead!" She then slugged Frankie's arms, hitting his wounded wrist. He yelped in pain, but the figure held his focus.

Now ten feet from them, the stranger broke their mutual gaze to look at Sheila. Frankie gasped at his release. He turned to Sheila while the stranger's tone shifted. With authority, he proclaimed, "There will be doubters in the last of days, Francis."

He pointed to her, and a stream of fire shot from his finger into her face. The blue orange flame melted her mouth and eyes shut. She moaned, clawing at her burning flesh, and collapsed.

The Man smiled, pointing to her. "She's so much more bearable without her tongue, is she not? Doubting Me is only one of her sins."

Tyler and Marvell rushed to them, but the figure waved his hand again, sending them hurtling over the truck to the ground.

The stranger rolled his head over his neck, cracking the joints, closing his eyes, exhaling slowly. Frankie knew what this man felt, even as he said, "Now, that feels right."

His eyes reopened, meeting Frankie's. The coldest sapphire with fiery amber, they brought Frankie comfort, despite—no, rather, because of the power they wielded.

He stepped closer to Frankie, then looked down to Sheila's tortured form. "Francis, some say not to rejoice in the death of the wicked. But I say, 'Go for it.'"

Frankie's body responded to His words. "Oh, Lord Jesus, it's You." The Lord placed His hand on Frankie's head.

Sheila distracted them as she kicked at the truck, flailing in agony. Cut-off from oxygen, she couldn't possibly last much longer. The Lord was irked, so He waved His fingers. Her legs snapped, femurs reaching an angle so unnatural that even Frankie cringed.

The Lord smiled, staring into Frankie's eyes. "Doesn't this feel right to you, Francis? This gorgon—a wretched covetous hag filled with idolatry for earthly riches—deserves death, don't you agree?"

He waved a second time, and her arms snapped, though the voiceless moaning continued. He laughed. "And she annoys the fucking shit out of you, am I right?"

The figure was now mere inches from Frankie, whispering to him, "I hear them. I hear the songs of your *Korobskron*. They rejoice at Our intercession."

Sheila groaned again, capturing the Lord's harsh focus. He waved his hand once more, and more blue and orange fire shot from his fingertips. Her misshapen body writhed as fire spread throughout it—her gargled cries died as the body fell to ash.

Frankie ejaculated as he dropped to his knees. Weeping in genuflection, he closed his eyes and caught his breath. A hand reached for his face, turning it to lock eyes once more with the Lord. He knew the burning blue eyes pierced his soul. He asked, "Are you Him?"

The Lord gave a slow nod of reassurance. "Francis, I am the One you've awaited. My name is Norcross, though you know other names. Monagar incarnate, Prymus, Arkiyan, Catalyst of the Vesikyar. More titles you wouldn't know. But I am the Lord you have sought."

Frankie buried his head into the Lord's hands, sobbing past his confusion. "Oh, Lord, You've finally shown up. I was so worried."

With tremendous strength, Norcross lifted Frankie to his feet. He then clutched Frankie's face as he uttered, "Francis, your faith honors Me. But you're correct to worry." He patted Frankie's cheek. "You know there is something desperately wrong with this world, and I have come to cleanse it in baptismal flame, just as I've demonstrated here." He pointed to the scorches where Sheila's body had been. With a charming grin, he asked, "Will you, Francis Putnam, join me? Will you take up My purpose?"

Frankie bawled, confessing, "Oh, Lord, I so want to follow the path of light. I have sinned. I have—"

The Lord interrupted him. "You have destroyed My enemies, and this pleases you precisely because it pleases Me. Your nation calls this *novus ordo seclorum*—a new global order wherein you will serve as one of My generals. Do you understand?"

Frankie kissed the Lord's hand. His flesh thrummed with heat and power. Tingling and quickened, he answered, "Oh, Lord, I'll do whatever you wish. I am so unworthy."

Norcross gently pat Frankie's hair. "So are all who serve Me. And yet, I have chosen you. The road ahead is long, and we have much to do. The enemy seeks to subvert My will, and so We must subvert his."

Frankie started to answer, but Tyler interjected with a squeal. "Who the hell are you?" Consumed by his Lord, Frankie had forgotten about his brother. He and Marvell reappeared, albeit bloodied and bruised.

Norcross whispered to him, "Our enemies would undo what I've come to create, and this degenerate is among them." He patted Frankie's arm. "You must pledge yourself to me by destroying him, just as I must destroy the false prophet."

Frankie anguished. "He's my brother."

The Lord answered, "He is a brother only by man's sinful law. Think: many a time in your childhood did you think to kill him." Images flashed in Frankie's head. He remembered holding a hammer to his young brother's skull, experimenting in witchcraft to pervert both Tyler and Myra, suffocating Tyler by placing his hands over the child's nose and mouth, and others he thought he'd forgotten.

Norcross knew Frankie's past. But Tyler, deviant sinner or not, would throw himself before the devil or god to save Frankie. Marvell shouted from the front of the truck. "Tyler, don't!"

Frankie felt torn apart. He whispered, "Please, run, Tyler."

His brother postured himself. "No, Frankie, let me help you!"

Norcross released Frankie, uttering, "Prove yourself worthy."

Tyler's face was as innocent as it had been the many times Frankie abused him in their childhood. Frankie removed the magnum from his coat, warning, "Tyler, you don't know me. You don't know the things I've done." Looking to Norcross, he said, "He's my brother. Can't he join us?"

The Lord's expression hardened; the light from the streetlamps above cast a monstrous shadow over his face. Forehead down, he said, "You will destroy him, or I will. And My means will bring him to terrible pain, whereas you may grant him an easy death."

Marvell shouted, "The hell you will, you mother fucker!" He rushed him, and Norcross caught by the throat with one hand, lifting him high.

Inspecting Marvell, he said matter-of-factly, "I see that this world celebrates the lower order a little too much."

Tyler started for Norcross, but Frankie held him at gunpoint. He cried, "Frankie, let me go! He's killing Marvell. Please!"

Norcross ignored Tyler, telegraphing his intent. "This animal breeds your brother as though he were cattle. There can be no place in My kingdom for degeneracy. Both must die, if"—he played his eyes over the black man's convulsing body—"we are to live." Frankie could hear Marvell's neck vertebrae giving way to the incredible force.

Tyler pleaded, "Frankie, let me go to him! I love him!"

Frankie could bear no more. He swiveled, pointed his weapon at Norcross, and fired. The bullet blasted a hole into his face, the gape gushing blood black under the lamp light. Weakened, he dropped Marvell to the ground. Tyler rushed to Marvell while Frankie screamed, "Get out of here! Both now!"

As Tyler peeled Marvell from the gravel, Frankie shot the Lord again and again, each impact causing Him to jerk away.

Tyler and Marvell had reached Tyler's car. His brother shouted, "Frankie, please! Come with us now!"

Frankie replied, "Marvell, get my brother the fuck out of here!" He shot Norcross once more, but his weapon clicked on empty.

He felt relief as he heard his brother's tires hurl gravel from his driveway. They were safe, at least for now.

But Frankie had truly fallen, wounding his Savior. He dropped his hands to his sides, the magnum weighting him down.

Norcross continued to stand, grunting and growling. His many wounds were closing as a green energy surfaced along his flesh. He touched his own face as the missing cheek reconstituted. He chuckled and quipped, "Such a disappointment, you are. To injure this face?" He looked to Frankie, clicking his tongue.

Frankie said, "Jesus, I don't know what's real."

The Lord moved upon him with swiftness beyond that of any mortal. Clutching Frankie's throat, he hissed, "I assure you that *I am real*. You are fortunate, young Francis, that I trade in forgiveness." He held his own face to that of Frankie, eyes on fire. After a few seconds, he loosened his hold, patting Frankie's cheek. "We cannot know Ourselves until We are tested."

Frankie could barely speak. "He is my brother. Forgive me, Lord."

240

Norcross took a step back from him, and with a cock of the head, he said, "You will have other opportunities to show your quality. But there is the matter of discipline."

His eyes shifted yellow, and the magnum Frankie held turned bright red, then exploded; the force and heat blasted Frankie's right hand from him. He screamed and faltered, but Norcross caught him by the wrist, closing the wound with fire from His righteous hands. "Pain, Francis—pain will make you stronger. You can resist fire quite well, but not Mine. Faithfulness is better. No more frailty." He adjusted Frankie's hair.

At that, He hopped to the truck, pointing to George's fat corpse. "This is proof of your strength: you destroy iniquity. I can teach you to wield the same fire." He touched the body, burning it away without leaving a scratch on the truck's gleaming veneer.

Frankie overflowed with relief at the Lord's compassion. "Thank you, Lord. Where have You been?"

Norcross said, "The world I left to save this place was home to filthy decadence and ignorant frivolity, cloaked within peace and love. They drove Me out because I offered them *order*." He collected His thoughts as He turned His focus back to Frankie. "Francis, you already know that this world is in trouble. You feel it. Killing the obviously wicked is easy. This world is better for these deaths." He stepped back, opening his arms. "But can you destroy the wickedness you love?" Norcross tapped Frankie's cheek, and with a breathy sigh, he answered, "The *Korobskron* dwells in many. They are My elect—in time, you'll learn to sense them." He pointed a finger to Frankie's chest, and the locusts deafened him. He whispered, quieting them. "But only if you are prudent enough learn. Do you want this?" Frankie hesitated, so Norcross touched his stump. "Have faith, Francis. I shall help you overcome this handicap."

Frankie wept. "I'm so sorry, Lord. I won't disappoint you again." He knew shock must've enveloped him, but nothing else mattered.

The Lord cast derision. "No. You only have so many limbs, appendages, and I'd hate to part you from them." He touched Frankie's face, leaning into it, whispering, "You are so important to Me, Francis. My ambition, My plan requires you. So, we must go now."

Frankie clutched his burnt wrist, then asked, "Where are we going?"

Norcross pointed east. "Others we must recruit have sensed the summoning—We must find them."

C ✱✱✱

Conique awaited the kettle whistle, a signal that tea was a mere moment away. She found herself sitting and wondering whether the high-pitched sound filling her ears was real. She thought she could hear Aurum's whimper through the shrill noise, but looking around, she could find no dog. Her eyes were tender to the touch—she knew she had been crying. At first, she wondered whether Reuben had died. Her stomach turned flips. Reaching for her chest, she found an alert amulet with a red button on it. She knew what it was, for she remembered her own mother wearing one for the last three years of her life. A note was glued to it reading, "Call Reuben." She exhaled in relief.

Conique closed her eyes, even though doing so caused pain. She reopened them at the sound of Aurum's cry, but the dog was nowhere. "It's okay, girl," she said in the hopes that Aurum could hear her words. Sitting before her was a pen and pad, with notes jumbled. She heard the cry once more, but Aurum wasn't there.

Conique stood to tend to the kettle, though her right hip ached something fierce. Touching it, she felt a huge bandage. It made no sense she should have an injury—but it hit her that Aurum was gone for the same reason. But the fear caused her to become more confused. She shouted, "Aurum? Where are you?!" There was no answer.

Pulling the pot from the burner, she switched off the heat, then poured the steaming water into her cup. Mixing some white grains of sugar into the tea, she inhaled the enervating vapor. Lifting the cup to her lips, she awaited the bittersweet mixture. To her horror, the tea was salty! She spit the liquid back into the cup, dropping it to the kitchen counter. She'd confused the salt for the sugar.

Collapsing back into her chair at the table, she glanced over the notes. They weren't unlike the fragments of memories floating around her head. It was as though her senses, her faculties, her memories, had come from a blender. Sounds appeared as colors. Images as music. It was difficult to endure.

As she stirred sweet cream into her teacup, she eased herself into a seat at the kitchen table with an arthritic groan, laughing. "Oh, Connie, why worry yourself? You don't have to be God." She laughed harder, adding, "It sounds better when Reuben says it." Looking at the paper before her, she couldn't help but think of the disease hiding notes with disappearing ink. The paper remained fixed, a taunt not lost on her.

She touched the grains in the cherrywood table her mother had left her. Touching it, she caressed a scar in the wood that her now-deceased daughter Angie had made with a steak knife. It had upset her at the time, not because she valued the thing more than her small child, but because she'd wanted her girl one day to sit at the table drinking tea and remembering her own mother.

The irony was that the scar on the table was now one of the few things she had to remember her once-small toddler. It pained her, for she could still see Angie at the table with her, and she regretted punishing her for it.

She'd destroy every possession she had to glimpse her daughter again. Her faith was hope, but bereft of her senses, it was weakening.

Glancing at the clock, she saw 5:40. The winter evenings could be lovely in Atlanta, but the sun vanished earlier than she'd prefer. She really would have followed the midnight sun all of her days, and as a flower child, she had once roamed the continents, traveling to Alaska and Chile, hoping to avoid the tightening night. The sun was her first understanding of God, after all.

She sighed, looking into her teacup. The cream swirled within the dark liquid, and the form was beautiful. It resembled the gaseous swirls within Jupiter and Saturn, and even the sun itself—beauty beyond reckoning.

The scribbles below her explained her situation. One note said, "YOU KILLED AURUM." Another said, "DON'T BE A BURDEN." And she remembered too much. Her mind was fraying, an unbearable erosion Conique had picked to be her threshold. The things left undone nagged her from something beyond her periphery. But her resoluteness returned, and she put her plan in motion.

She was grateful for the life she'd led, but she'd not burden Reuben any further, and she would act rather than suffer. She would not become a shadow, reeking of urine and feces, mottled with gaping bed sores. That was the one her mother took, so she would do anything to avoid it.

Looking to the tea kettle, she saw the poison she gave herself. Past surgeries had left her with a surplus of opiate medications, few of which used for long. She'd taken all of them, yearning for the disconnection of her respiratory system, per the internet's instructions. To be sure, she'd added vodka, knowing that the combination would be both pleasant and effective.

Her brothers and sisters in Christ might think she was headed to hell for what she had done. But this was not just a selfish act to rid herself of pain. Reuben had suffered enough, and wiping her ass wasn't something she wanted to share with anyone other than herself.

The room shifted about her as she looked again at the clock. She was a bit curious how fast the drugs would take her. She had been drunk many times in her life, so the sensations weren't unfamiliar. Her nose and fingers tingled and itched, and an artificial but very real euphoria filled her.

Would there be a tunnel? A light? She'd read some on near-death experiences, but it'd never interested her all that much. Near-life meant so much more to her, and she preached the Gospel for the living. Maybe her Angie and Reuben's son Rashad would welcome her together.

It pained her to leave her devoted husband behind, so she'd made it clear in her note to him that she insisted he move on, that he find someone else to care for him, and he for her. He was a handsome man, even at seventy-five, and older widowers had an easier time finding a new mate.

The room spun, and she felt tears bead on her cheeks.

She reached for the tea one more time, but her coordination had left her, causing her to push the cup and saucer to the tile flooring. Both shattered, but she could muster only a tiny groan at the breaking of her mother's dishes.

She looked down to the floor, and it seemed to swallow her. She watched her hands grasp the table, but her balance, strength, and reflexes had all distorted. She clung to the table in a last-ditch attempt to remain seated, but a rapid, loud knocking at the door caught her attention. She moved her head as best she could to see it, but her muscles betrayed her. Tumbling from the chair, she hit the hardwood with a thud.

Conique rolled onto her back, and in opening her eyes, she saw light and dark melded together, swirling as if she overlooked a huge teacup. Her brain couldn't distinguish between fact and fiction anymore, and she was open to the experience.

She heard a crash at the door and footfalls on her hardwood floor. Her breathing had weakened, and she was struggling to make sound. With one last push of energy, she opened her eyes.

Standing over her were two men—one was scarcely a man in age, slight and fit, the other one more of her era, a heavier, grizzly one. He spoke first, and his voice was so distinctive, so filled with gravel, she recognized it, "Jesus, what's wrong with her?!"

The younger man touched her wrist and neck as he glanced at the stove. With two voices, he said, "She's attempting suicide, Boothby. Adam must save her now."

Adam the savior? What a strange thing to say. Darkness took her, and she hoped to stay there.

20. No More Tears

*M****

Mayak woke to an explosion. Kierkov wasn't next to him, to his surprise. His robe was too soiled to bear, so he hurled it into his clothes hamper before pulling together an athletic suit he had. Again, he heard another thunder clap.

Rushing to the window, he could see only whiteout snow. It was still nightfall, and the wind howled. The racket was coming from somewhere in his apartment building. He dashed into the living room and kitchen, relieved that Kierkov wasn't lurking there. To himself, he whispered, "Sargon, why is this happening?"

The coat closet near his front door was slightly ajar, an aberration Mayak wouldn't leave. He crept towards it, tensing in apprehension. Hurling it open, he saw only empty space. He sighed with relief. He folded his arms in frustration. It dawned on him that she might have placed another surveillance microphone somewhere inside it, so squeezed his coats to find it. Bending down, he slid his head under the bottom shelf to dig among the boots and boxes on the floor.

His door pounded, startling him into hitting his head. "Goddammit," he said. The rapping continued, so he shouted, "Who is it?"

His visitor also shouted. "Mayak, it is Petrov. You must open door!"

Straightening, his head throbbed. After slamming the closet door, he massaged the back of his skull to ease the pain. He tried to look out his peephole in the entry door, but Petrov beat it into Mayak's forehead. This time, he hollered, "Fuck!"

Petrov yelled, "Please, Mayak, open door!"

Doubt plagued him, so he asked, "Are you alone?"

His friend answered, "Not for long. There is danger."

Mayak unfastened the lock, then pulled it open to reveal a bruised and bloodied Petrov. His friend fell into his arms, and Mayak heaved him into his apartment. "Friend, what has happened? How are you hurt?"

His friend, once a beacon of conviviality and sunshine, cried to him, "Lights appeared to me. Small form. It told me to help you escape." He breathed hard while blood oozed from his chest. "I am shot."

Cradling his friend, Mayak said, "Let me call ambulance."

Petrov answered swiftly. "Too late, Mayak. Shot is fatal."

Mayak trembled with shock. "I can try—"

Petrov interrupted him. "Please, let me help you. Creature explained what to do."

Mayak answered, "Who did this to you?"

Clutching Mayak with his last bits of strength, he said, "Agents outside your apartment. I thought I could sneak past them, but I guess they saw me." He smiled, crimson life flowing from his mouth. "I distracted them well with fireworks. They didn't expect it, though I didn't get past all of them."

Mayak looked to the open door, then back to his ailing friend's face. "Did you see Kierkov?"

Petrov sighed. "She hit me before my devices fired. I think she thought I was already dead." He laughed and spat blood from his mouth, whispering, "My own personal recipe should keep her blind for a bit." He waited for Mayak to reply, finally blurting, "Flash powder, my friend."

Mayak touched his friend's cheek, consoling him with a stern smile. "You missed your calling as chemist, my friend." Patting him, he said, "Petrov, please be still. I will get help."

Petrov said in a hushed voice, "Mayak, my friend. I received message to tell you."

Mayak glanced to the table in search of his phone, repeating, "Let me find help. Doctor lives down the street."

Petrov grasped Mayak's face, forcing him to meet his gaze. His breathing faltered, but his eyes were clear. "Please! I do not wish to die, but it is too late now. You must hear message!"

Mayak held his hand on Petrov's wound, but he knew the truth of it—he'd bleed out before anyone could stop it. Anguished, he whispered, "Okay, Petrov. Tell me."

Petrov fought to squeeze words from his throat, saying, "When lights appeared over launch pad, I saw vision. Creature appeared. Like alien. Small, like child. Think me crazy, but it happened," he sputtered.

Mayak said with a wistful smile, "You held out on me, friend. Did you tell Kierkov or others?"

Petrov upturned his mouth to a grin. "Comrade, you sound as though vision is commonplace. I am sorry I said nothing earlier. I believed I had hallucinated. No, I shared nothing, but I dream it every night now."

Mayak cradled him as his strength failed. Rousing him, he asked, "Petrov—what is message? From whom?"

Petrov coughed as he reopened his eyes. "A creature showed me vision of future should I fail to help you escape. 'All will fall to fire and maelstrom,' he said. 'Seven must become one,' so said the being." He sputtered, and blood sprayed into Mayak's face. He reached up his hand to wipe it away but couldn't rally the strength.

Mayak cried. "I'm so sorry, Petrov. I do not understand."

Petrov shook his head to quiet Mayak. "Now, who is holding out? There is vehicle at this address, left with instructions to proceed, so small being told me." He handed Mayak a crumpled note stained with blood, then said, "Small being told me that Ephyr Sargon had sent him to me." He squeezed Mayak's shoulder. "I do not know what lies beyond death, but I believed vision. I see recognition in your face, comrade." His breathing became shallow. "Creature made me memorize message so others will not find it."

Mayak listened, knowing his friend would die any moment. "Tell me."

Petrov said, "Creature told me you must cross threshold no other can."

Mayak searched his thoughts. "What does that mean? Please, Petrov." He bowed his head. Lifting it, he noticed that Petrov's eyes had drifted, as though he stared beyond Mayak. Gently easing his friend to the floor, he opened the note given to him. The geocodes weren't unfamiliar to him, though he knew even one typo in a coordinate could mean kilometers' worth of error.

There would be time for tears later. Living in Russia left him prepared to leave on short notice, but his secret weapon had always been Sargon. In his childhood, his passenger taught him much more than theoretical physics. He wanted words with him right then, but something held Sargon back. Petrov died to help Mayak—he would not squander the sacrifice.

He grabbed the heaviest of his coats, his scarf, his gloves, and his snow boots. A flashlight, rations, a first aid kit, an analog compass with an untraceable GPS receiver, and survival knife were all stuffed in his overnight bag already. He filled one thermos with coffee, a second with water. He programmed the compass with the codes Petrov died to give him.

He tossed his phone in a bowl of water, knowing it wouldn't survive long. He couldn't afford to be followed, so he had to eliminate any means of doing so. The blizzard would cover his tracks—literally, in this case.

Pulling a hefty ski mask over his face, he slipped his hands into his gloves, then opened the door into his hallway. He looked one last time at his friend, then closed his front door behind him.

247

He found his way to the hall exit, and, opening it, pushed hard to move snow aside. The lights lining the exterior led only to confusing shadows—all the better to hide him.

Trudging into the snow, he watched for Kierkov and her goons. Unless they carried infrared detectors, he'd slip past them. The journey wasn't long.

S***

Shigeru awakened, turning to the whiskey sitting on his nightstand. He coughed as the fiery liquid slammed his trachea. "Goddammit."

He stepped away from his bed, wrapping himself in his robe. Looking out the window, he watched snowflakes settling in the moonlight. The streetlights caused the flakes to sparkle, a half-right angle of lighting spread down to the glistening concrete. Snow was serene, but the hellscape of his nightmares hit him hard.

Catching his reflection in the window, he slicked his hair back. In the distance, he saw the city skyline, and it seemed far-off. He watched aircraft move through the atmosphere, landing and running lights illuminating the way.

He set the whiskey down, pressed his temples, and whispered, "Get a grip, Shigeru." He pulled his hair to the point of pain, angry. The figure in his dream mentioned Doctor Kunskapsen, but he knew she'd been unfit for travel, let alone to reach him.

He tossed a few ice cubes into his glass, poured a fresh drink, then collapsed into a chair. Fidgeting with his phone, he searched his email for any news on the golden-haired quantum physicist. He hoped her death had been misreported, a death hoax. But news agencies confirmed it for him once more. It was a fantasy, and Shigeru was spent. Mad was right about him—he wouldn't be capable of going on like this forever, even if he saved millions of lives.

A clear rap on his door plucked him from his brooding. He waited with a sneer. "Goddamned concierge asleep again?" Folding his arms, he downed more whiskey. The knock became a pounding. He shouted, "It is the middle of the fucking night! Go away!" It continued, enraging him. He jumped to his feet, steeled to shove the pest to the elevator. "This better be an escort."

He leaned into the door to peek through the peephole. He beheld the thing he'd least expected in the world—a very much alive and vibrant Doctor Olga Kunskapsen standing alongside the man from his dream.

She called to him. "Professor, we are here on urgency. Can you open, please?"

Forgetting his anti-etiquette, he unlocked and opened the door on command. She wore a tunic which appeared textured. She was more beautiful than he imagined, with both a build and height Shigeru preferred. He glanced at her companion, a handsome man wearing similar fabric as a long-tailed suit.

He said, "My name is Zephyr. Professor Nakamura, it is good to meet you, even if the cause is dire." Watching Shigeru's reaction, he said, "I know you have many questions, but this place is not safe."

Shigeru looked to Olga, and nodded with a sober face. "Zephyr is telling the truth. I understand you sought me out."

Stepping back from them, he glanced at his phone, maintaining an eye on the couple before him. Reopening the article on his phone, he confirmed what he already knew to be true—the identity of this woman. Not that he needed it, for he was partial to blondes.

He set his glass on the entry table, then said, "I reached out for you, but I learned you were—"

She did smile this time, answering, "Dead?" Looking to the mysterious man next to her, she added, "A deception. Zephyr rescued and healed me."

The man offered Shigeru no time to question, speaking with urgency. "I apologize for reaching you within your dreams. It, unfortunately, is the only means of contact without leaving a trace your people's technology can detect. I hope it has prepared you somewhat for the journey ahead."

Shigeru touched his small goatee, doubting this could be real. "Journey? What kind of hoax is this? Why would I go with you?"

Olga reached for him. "Doctor Nakamura, I know this is short notice, and I wish I could explain now, but please trust me, scientist to scientist." He watched her, and she removed her hands from her pockets to gesture for him. "This man has something wonderful to share with us, and maybe with the whole world. But—" She searched for the words.

Shigeru asked, "Are you unwell, Doctor?"

She nodded to him. "Olga, if you please."

He replied, "Call me Shigeru, then."

She smiled. "Shigeru, the cancer is gone, but I am not clear of the ordeal."

Zephyr spoke in her stead. "Had events gone according to plan, her disease would not have progressed so far. Shigeru, if I may, many paths are open, crossing one another, with destinations as varied as the stars in the skies. But sometimes"—his emerald eyes shimmered—"the destination is too far to reach by convention. So, we leave the road, and the terrain proves rough." He smiled, and his skin, teeth, and hair were all so perfect that even Shigeru felt green with envy. He spoke words that resonated within the physician, completing his speech with, "To meet at the appointed place, at the appointed time, we must endure said terrain."

Shigeru laughed at them. "That's vague and ridiculous. I must still be dreaming." He rubbed his eyes.

Olga spoke to Zephyr. "What else can we say? He needs to know the truth."

Zephyr looked to him, reaching for his face. "You've offered your tears today for your mother. More tears will come unless I can perform my function."

Touching Shigeru's face, he whispered, "I know you understand. Your work, your nightmares, your fears all return to a singular threat we must eliminate. I beseech you, Sheeki Tonbo."

Shigeru's eyes widened, and his heart hurt. "You said that in my dream. I am dreaming."

Zephyr clasped his shoulder. "No, Shigeru. This is as real as it gets."

Shigeru could read curiosity from Olga's crystal clear eyes. He said, "No one alive knows that but me. It was a nickname my mother gave me in privacy."

Zephyr was playful. "Because of your childhood love of dragonflies."

Shigeru resisted the hope in his heart. "I've had too much whiskey. This is insane."

Olga grabbed his arm, forcing him to treat with her. "This man cured me of terminal brain cancer. You're a medical doctor—you can examine me on the way if you don't believe me. But I implore you to do just that: believe. I've already seen wonders beyond the pale." Returning her sparkling blue eyes to Shigeru, she pleaded, "Your heart for those who suffer touches us all. Please come with us, for this man can move mountains."

Shigeru stood pondering, his mind awash in the readings of her work. She was as ironclad a scientist as he could imagine. Her faith in this man therefore did resonate, he had to admit. Zephyr spoke words which unraveled him. "Shigeru, joining us provides us with a closing window to save more lives than you could with a thousand lifetimes of work. This world is not the only one imperiled. The destruction you've sought to prevent is a teaspoon of water in an ocean of probable catastrophes." He touched Olga. "She would have died without intervention. Though your body does not ail, your mind is fractured. Deepening depression and disastrous engagements with others threaten you much in the same way. Your mother wanted you to make that difference. As she lay dying, she said, 'The struggle defines us. Do not turn away from the pain.'"

Shigeru remembered her. Her skin was warm and soft, her sundresses colorful, her hair long, glorious, filled with the smell of jasmine. His eyes misting, he said, "I want to believe. I want to believe someone cares about us. That someone is watching for us." Closing his eyes, tears streamed. He then asked, "But why should I believe that the hell our world has suffered was the Panglossian world of worlds?"

Olga shook her head, protesting, "It isn't so simple. I asked the same things."

Zephyr touched Shigeru's cheek, wiping a tear. His voice filled with compassion. "All of this is, as you have suspected, a work in progress. I have the answers you seek, but if we linger here, they will be academic, and nothing more." He leaned closer to Shigeru, and the hardened skeptic melted. "'We can have no more tears.' That is what your mother said just before you lost her, no?" He finished. "You believed she abandoned you. But the values inside of you are what survives of her."

Shigeru was awestruck. A man stood before him, but he heard his mother's words. He knew she would oppose the creature he had become and the things he had done. Shame covered him as fell to one knee. He was miserable, wretched, his narcissistic outcries were a sham, a crumbling veneer for desperate hope and unremitting dread.

Olga reached for him by reflex as Zephyr voice echoed. "To stand in advocacy for others, one must die to self. You have suffered, but you have inflicted suffering. There may be no greater suffering than the recognition of one's own guilt, for it carries with it the totality of the harm done to others. Will you try a new path, if only the first step?"

Shigeru opened his eyes to see Zephyr offering him his hand. He took it, and this enigmatic visitor helped him to his feet. Looking to Olga, Shigeru said, "What must we do?"

Exuding a warmth and energy, Zephyr said, "The journey ahead requires we restore balance to each of the Vesiks. Olga required extensive work, and I require your assistance."

"Because of her tumor?" Shigeru asked. "If you saved her from it, what more can I do?"

Zephyr nodded to her. "Touch her head, and tell me what you see."

It was strange for Shigeru to feel discomfort at touching a woman, but there was something unspoiled about her. Placing his fingertips along her scalp, he looked. Zephyr quickly said, "Not with your eyes. Look with your mind."

He sighed with frustration, but then focused his thoughts. Instantly, he could see neurons, axons, dendrites, woven together against black tentacles leeching life from healthy tissues. Thousands or maybe millions of small devices crawled the network of neurons and malignancies. He gasped, "I see it. I see it all."

Zephyr nodded his head. "Good. Now concentrate on the cancer, and tell the polyplasts to kill, to clear, to rebuild."

Shigeru strained, screaming in his head that the army of tiny robots destroy the bad while upholding the good. With every mistake, the healthy neurons suffered. With every correct execution, order was restored. The bots shifted in color as he moved them into position. Olga heaved at that. "I feel it. I feel you in my head!"

The hallway drowned from Shigeru as he fought, as if all other systems of his body arrested themselves to buttress this one act. Blood roared in his ears, and Zephyr's voice sounded as if he stood dozens of meters away. But he would not surrender to this thing.

At last, the color had changed among almost all the polyplasts. Nerves hummed with energy as the polyplasts replaced wrecked components. He disconnected his fingers as he fell into the wall behind him. His vision returned, with Zephyr supporting Olga. Shigeru returned to balance, invigorated. "It's a miracle," he said.

Olga met his gaze, her icy blue eyes electric. "Thank you," she whispered.

Zephyr gestured that he help him with Olga. "She'll require more work, but your intrinsic power to advocate makes it possible for you to control and coordinate the polyplasts. This is one tiny taste of the world waiting for you, Doctor."

Shigeru gave a slow nod. "Let's get to it, then."

Olga balled her fists in victory as Zephyr said, "That's the spirit."

*M****

Mayak struggled against blinding snow, the negative forty centigrade air squealing into his muffed ears. Led by his compass, he could see nothing before him.

His parents spun tales of grandparents who tied ropes from their front porch to the barn so that ordinary tasks like milking the cows wouldn't become headers on gravestones. His compass wasn't exactly a rope, but at least he could work out the distance and direction to the address Petrov had handed him. The arctic air washed his emotions from him, providing one blessing among the paltry few he could count on. He was grateful that the cold didn't cause him pain—he could bear extremes even beyond the reach of Kierkov and her more average foot soldiers.

After he'd marched hard for forty-five minutes, his compass indicated he'd arrived. The address was an empty field kilometers from Petrov's flat. A rusting barricade of barbed and razor wire ensconced the acreage, a space whose justification had long mystified the townspeople. Some thought it was a dump for industrial pollutants, while others, Petrov included, insisted it was a staging area for weapons exercises. But Mother Russia preferred her secrecy. None of it mattered to Mayak in this moment.

From his survival kit, he pulled bolt cutters into the air, his headlamp lighting the scene between blasts of fluffy snow. He snapped one piece of the fence after another, his foggy breath sparkling against the light. Replacing the cutters, he pulled the fencing apart, slipping into the enclosure; his coat caught on a bit of barb, but he pulled harder, tearing a sleeve. He didn't care, for if Petrov had been incorrect about the destination, another hour of inclement conditions would kill him, coat untorn or not.

Standing within the fencing, he could see nothing more than hefts of snow dropping from the sky. He shivered in bewilderment, wondering whether Petrov had sent him to chase a hallucination. Mayak spoke, though he couldn't hear himself over the wind. "Sargon, help me."

His compass vibrated, so he held it to his face to read it. To his surprise, an additional geocode appeared. It couldn't have been more than meters away from him, but seeing in the whiteout was impossible. More than that, he couldn't figure out how a new destination could find its way into the compass on a device incapable of receiving wireless commands. Then again, Sargon worked in mysterious ways.

Mayak accepted the destination, after which the compass indicated his next direction. The snow drifts were more than a meter high, so he fought with all of his strength to keep moving. The compass vibrated once more as he almost reached the target. The wind howled, and Mayak knew his feet were balking in resistance.

A voice called to him, as clear as though the speaker was a meter from his face. "Mayak, we regret what must happen next."

He knew the voice was in his head, much like that of Sargon. But it was someone else speaking, a first for Mayak. He asked, "Who is on brain channel?"

The voice answered, "Help was promised to you. To reach your means of escape, you must cross a threshold impassable by anyone but you."

He replied, "Swell. What does that mean?"

The voice was gentle. "The threshold is an energy barrier designed to prevent entry by any others. This is a security protocol intended to help you, and you alone. Please understand it is the only way."

Mayak shivered with a shrug. "I have little choice. Tell me, who sent you?"

Answering with haste, the voice said, "You know the answer to your question. Sargon awaits you downstream, but only if you survive this. Now, step forward."

Mayak pushed himself hard, parting the massive drifts before him. Once his compass indicated he was within five meters of the target, he could feel a heat and tingle all over his body. His muscles twitched and convulsed, and he guessed he was receiving mighty shocks and heat. It was a clever trick, filtering anyone who couldn't tolerate the pain. He started to laugh, but he was too cold. The tingling stopped once he was within ten meters of the destination. All at once, the shrieking wind vanished, as though he'd pierced a membrane of a cone-shaped eye carved from the weather. At the cone's center materialized an angular craft—it was a configuration he'd never seen. He stepped backward, and the howling was restored, together with a column of snow replacing the craft. As he stepped forward once more, the wind stopped, and the craft morphed again. Unbelievable technology indeed—some sort of bending of light to conceal the ship. As for the craft, it was black and sleek, yet the surface moved organically.

Mayak was mesmerized by the thing before him, so much so that he barely noticed the warmth and quiet within the cone. He listened, recognizing that his shivers and breathing were all he could hear.

An entryway appeared along the side of the craft, though he could not make out moving parts. Inside were no obvious controls, but a seat coalesced from the black material, and, after his exhausting hike, it appeared inviting. From the opening, warm air enveloped him.

He reached into the machine, and he could sense something more than technology. He touched the arm rest of the seat and found that it was warm, similar to rubber, or maybe leather. As he pushed an impression into the arm with his finger, the craft thrummed, and lights within it activated.

An alert bell sounded. and the voice implored him. "Hurry, Mayak. Climb into your seat."

A crash from behind startled him. He pivoted, though he couldn't see anything outside the cone. Another louder explosion rocked the conic calm, causing him to lose his footing. He piled himself through the portal just in time to watch a third explosion momentarily breach the wall of the cone, followed by a fluid dance of energy repairing the damage. He rolled into the chair as it responded to him, easing him into a position of comfort as though it had been meant just for him.

The aperture narrowed, muting the racket as the voice said, "Those in pursuit mean to have you. Prepare to liftoff."

The machine hummed to life as Mayak wondered whether Kierkov and her goons would be able to penetrate the barrier. He could hear the crackle of assault rifles up until the portal had shut completely.

Belting strapped Mayak to the chair. He could feel the gravitational forces changing, suggesting momentum. He closed his eyes, then pulled off his mask and snow goggles. His body warmed quickly, as though he'd dropped into a hot bath. Opening his eyes, he could see numerous holographic displays, as foreign to his mind as hieroglyphs. The voice in his head said, "You are safe now. Rest."

And he fell asleep.

21.Succession

C***

Conique opened her eyes as Reuben spoke to her with his resonant voice. "It's all right, dear. It's all right."

She looked at his face and sobbed. "I'm so sorry, Reuben. I can't go through with more of this. I couldn't force you to care for me."

His touch was delicate, and he stroked her hair. She looked behind him to see the pair of characters she had seen just before losing consciousness. The older smiled, though she wasn't clear whether he was happy or just plain crazy. "Oh, thank God. We thought you'd died." He clutched a cat, black as any Halloween panther.

Reuben snapped his head in the man's direction, rebuking him with, "Boothby, she wasn't even close to death."

The younger man, handsome despite being strained and exhausted, touched Conique on her forehead, neck, and wrist. He said, "Ma'am, my name is Adam, and I'm—"

She coughed a little with joy. "My savior?"

He laughed, then said, "That time, perhaps. I'm also a nurse." He examined her, asking her to follow his finger with her eyes, and other things she figured were routine for overdoses.

Reuben patted Adam's arm with encouragement. "You saved my Conique. I'm so grateful." He then stiffened his countenance, asking, "Why can't we take her to the hospital?"

The one called Boothby answered. "Well, the cat said that the Seven Vesiks would be endangered if we call for that kind of help."

Conique reached for him. "The Seven are real? I had a dream."

Reuben shook his head, having none of it. "Wait a sec. A cat? That cat?" He glared at Boothby, whose eyes bulged in reproachful embarrassment. "I can't believe what I'm hearing. How did a cat—" The shiny animal peeped a meow in response.

Conique grasped Reuben's arm. "Please, dear, I must know." She tried to sit, though fatigue overcame her. Looking hard at Boothby, she said, "I had a vision I thought was a dream. There were eight of us there."

Boothby nodded with a snort. "The Seven Vesiks."

Reuben stared daggers at him. "She just said eight! Come on, Connie, this is insane."

She squeezed her husband's forearm. "Please, Reuben. I must know."

He replied, "Jesus Christ, Connie. You just tried to kill yourself. This man"—he pointed at Boothby—"is clearly crazy."

The cat yowled as Boothby recoiled with bug eyes. Conique snapped, "That's enough, Reuben Hamora!" As her husband averted his eyes, she said, "Mister Boothby, what are the Seven Vesiks?"

Boothby fixed his eyes on a bejeweled lamp in the shape of a cherub, baring his teeth in confusion. Without looking away from it, he said, "I dunno exactly. The cat could tell ya better, but the lights are here to help us get together."

Reuben frowned. "Lights, as in UFOs?"

He nodded while holding his eyes from them. "I've chased them forever. Some sort of psychic imprint in us."

She turned to Reuben. "I saw Boothby in my dream. I thought I hallucinated it."

Her husband looked to Adam. "You seem a little less unhinged. What's your story? What the hell is happening?"

Boothby said, his eyes dancing along the room, "Mister Ephyr can use psychokinesis. He controlled Adam."

Reuben frowned, waving him off. "What do you mean? Who the hell is Ephuh?"

Boothby became indignant. "I don't understand why no one can understand me."

Adam's much calmer eyes soothed her, and he repeated, "Eph-yr, sir."

Reuben threw his hands to the sky. "Whatever, Ephyr, then! Who is he?"

Boothby looked at Adam, as though he knew the words to follow would pain the younger man. "If only Janet could speak' I blacked out. I don't remember what Ephyr did to me."

It hit Conique, so she asked, "This Janet is here?"

Adam answered with no small weariness. "She is, but she's in trouble, Miss Voyant."

Those words were all that was necessary to incentivize her. She pushed herself forward, with Reuben's disapproval. "Dear, can't you see? God isn't finished with me and my path." He sighed in frustration while she turned to the young nurse. "Where is Janet? I need to intercede."

Adam took her hand, supporting her to right herself, though he cautioned, "Miss Voyant, you probably should rest. You're fortunate we had a store of naloxone on hand to pull you from the opiates."

Boothby screwed up his face as the cat meowed. "Umm, we don't have much time, folks. Trouble is coming, according to Archie."

Reuben pointed to him. "The cat said that?"

Conique pulled Reuben's hand as he admonished her with puppy dog brown eyes. "Dear, the only thing that matters is service. Please."

His eyes teared as he looked away from her. "Dear, you just tried to kill yourself. Don't you know how crazy this is? It's malpractice with a capital M."

Adam answered, "Doctor Hamora, Janet is in trouble. I don't believe in hocus pocus, but if your wife can help her, it's worth a shot. I've seen things now that you wouldn't believe."

Reuben shook his head. "I doubt that. What's wrong with the young lady?"

Boothby piped up. "Well, she's got ALS, or so she said to me in her dream."

Before Reuben could speak, Conique said, "Bring her to me, quickly."

He then whispered to her. "Babe, please. I'm begging you to slow down. Remember what happened with Aurum."

She froze, searching her memories for the incident. Breathing faster, she said, "I admit my world is dissolving around me. But God didn't want me to die yet. I know Janet is a key to unlock a door. She is compassionate, and God wants me to show her compassion. You're a physician, babe. Let me try."

Reuben turned to the others in defeat. "Fine. Let's get her. My bag is in the kitchen."

Boothby looked at the cat as it meowed. He said, "Janet said you'd know what to do next, Miss Voyant. I know you can help her before that creature catches us."

Reuben stiffened as he stood. "Wait, what is this creature?"

Boothby anxiously replied, "I didn't get too good a look at him, but he intends to kill us all."

Reuben blinked his eyes in fearful rage. "Jesus, what are you talking about?"

Adam said, "I'll explain on the way."

Reuben and Adam left to carry Janet from the vehicle outside, while Boothby, stroking the small cat, remained with Conique. She reached for the little guy, and Boothby remarked, "He seems to take a liking to ya, that one." Boothby's eyes danced around the room as he chuckled. "Two days ago, I'd be crying and wailing like Tammy Faye if I had to hold a furry little thing like this."

Conique grinned at him. "My Aurum would have a fit—" She trailed, remembering her loss.

He asked, "Who is Aurum?"

She said, "My retriever. A wonderful old girl. She disappeared because of my memory lapses." Seeing his discomfort, she changed the subject. "Were you looking for me because of the Seven?"

Boothby's rasp was more pronounced when he spoke in a quieter tone. "Because I knew you could get to the Trident missiles."

She cocked her head. "You want to join the Plowshares?"

He tugged at his collar. "No, no, no. I just wanted a way to bring the lights here. Now I know I was supposed to find you."

Nodding, she said, "I read about the reports of UFO sightings near launch bases. I must confess that would take some courage."

His eyes bulged as he asked, "Why did ya try to kill yourself?"

She crumpled the burgundy bedspread in her hands. "I have Alzheimer's disease, Boothby. It's getting worse every day." He didn't answer, so she said, "I know what the end for this disease is. I hadn't planned to burden Reuben with it."

Boothby's cat hopped onto the bed, stretching his feet all the way out. She reached for him, running her fingers through his gleaming black fur. Boothby said, "You're too important to die, Miss Voyant."

She smiled at the small animal as he grunted and purred. "No one is that important, Boothby. I'm tired." She choked up. "I lost our dog during a blackout."

He looked back at the cherub lamp. "That's awful, Miss Voyant."

She chuckled. "My mother loved tacky things. You can have it if you like." She patted the cat as her mind cleared. "I made my peace, but if there's more to do, I must answer."

At last, Reuben and Adam returned, holding a gorgeous Indigenous girl with a raven sheen to her straight, long hair and beauty even without consciousness. Reuben complained, "This girl and Conique need to be in the hospital. This is just insane."

She would be angry with her husband's petulance if he wasn't so damned handsome with his stethoscope and other medical toys. Conique motioned for them to bring the girl closer. Once they placed her on the bed next to Conique, she touched her, caressing her cool bronzed skin. "She's suffering from a hex of sorts."

Reuben rolled his eyes as he pulled out his blood pressure cuff. "Conique, you've seldom done the faith healing."

Adam said, "She's in the early stages of ALS, worsened somehow by that monster trying to kill us. He burned her home to the ground and murdered two people."

Boothby whooped. "Three. He killed my landlady."

Reuben shouted to the ceiling. "We need to call the goddamned police!"

Conique said, "Be still, Reuben!" She touched the girl's delicate body. "I don't know if I can help her, but"—she said as she looked at Boothby, reaching for him— "we must try." He scooped Archie, passing him to Adam. Following her lead, he seated himself next to her. She took his hands, then placed them on Janet.

His eyes widened as he protested. "Is this appropriate? I really don't wanna feel her up."

Shutting her eyes, Conique whispered, "Through our Lord do we receive protection from the fallen spirits. Through the tree on Calvary do we let loose our inequities, so that the Spirit may fill us. We'll speak unknown tongues, and know unknown things. For all is known to Him, for all belongs to Him. Our Sister Janet requires Your help, Lord. We need You to light the path. And the *Yolteotl* belongs to our sister. She carries the heart of divinity. Divine Compassion. *Moyolitlacoani.* Please be with us once more."

Boothby shuddered and said, "I feel something. What's happening?"

The girl shivered, but her breathing improving. Adam touched her face as her eyes fluttered open. Her voice cracked. "Adam? Boothby? And—"

Adam said, "Try not to speak yet, baby. We need to examine you."

Conique smiled. "Child, my name is Connie, and I'm one of the Seven."

Boothby asked, "How did you do that?"

She smiled. "We call them the Gifts of the Spirit."

Boothby quipped without pronouncing a single R. "Far out, far out."

Adam and Reuben examined Janet as she stretched her arms and legs. Conique waved a hand to her. "She needs more work. More help than we can give her here." Turning to Boothby, she said, "Tell me about the creature."

He rocked back and forth. "He chased me until I found Adam and Janet. I don't know who or what he is, but he could shoot fire from his fingertips. Do you know what he is?"

Conique watched Adam and Reuben test Janet's reflexes, touched by the tenderness the two young people shared. "I had a dream I think I forgot. Seven people stood together, and an eighth person appeared. I believed he was a representation of Christ, but he's more like the devil."

Boothby rocked harder. "Headmistress Sagini told me the devil would get me eventually. Would 'eat me up.'"

Conique could see torment in the man's eyes. She patted the spread in his direction. "She sounds like a piece of work. I don't believe in the devil."

The cat squeaked as he stirred from a slumber. Boothby slowed his rock at that. "But you believe in Jesus, the Resurrection, all that jazz?"

She pointed to a wooden crucifix on the wall. "I believe in Love. Are the stories literal truth, or just metaphors for what we are to each other?"

He stopped rocking. "I ain't never heard a Christian say that."

Conique liked this man. She touched his arm. "You ain't met many real Christians, then." Turning her attention to the others at the foot of the bed, she asked, "How is our young lady?"

With more strength, Janet replied, "Still breathing. How about you?"

Conique laughed in cheer. "About the same."

Adam wept at his friend's convalescence, and he hugged her close. She patted him with compassion, whispering, "It's okay."

Reuben peered quickly at his wife. "The girl is sick, and I don't know if there's anything to be done. But she's stable for now."

The intercession had drained Conique, but she pressed forward. "Janet, I believe you know what we must do next."

Cradled by Adam, Janet pointed to Boothby. "His focus stone should point the way forward."

His eyes widened, and with his voice of gravel, he said, "Jeezus, I forgot about it."

Archie meowed at him as he removed a warped metallic chunk from his pocket. Piqued, Conique asked, "May I see it?"

He bared his teeth with some anxiety, letting her know of his reluctance. "It's saved me. Hopefully, it'll keep doing that."

Boothby passed it to her, and as it fell into her hand, she felt an energy from it. It touched her, then it floated into the center of the room, exploding into a three-dimensional globe, covering them in the light of sprawling amber continents, sparkling sapphire oceans, and glistening white snow. As it rotated, it reflected light into Conique's antique lamps and glasswork.

Boothby gasped. "Holy moly! I never seen it do that before!"

Reuben touched the Atlantic Ocean, and the light rippled. "What is that thing? How is this technology possible?"

Boothby touched the holographic globe. "It's not from here. I dunno exactly. Mister Ephyr gave it to me when I was a kid."

Conique's calm surprised even herself. She asked, "Why show this to us?"

Adam stood to reach a glowing point in Russia. "I think that's where we're supposed to go."

Reuben held his fingers within the light. "It's true. It's all true," he said. He then removed his reading glasses to take a closer look.

Janet said, "I saw a cascade follow from place to place. Norcross knows them, too."

Reuben looked down to her as he studied the globe. "Wait a second. Norcross is the monster you said was chasing you all?"

Boothby bristled as he held his arms with his hands. His eyes danced as he said, "He wants us."

Conique leaned to comfort him as Janet said, "We can't let him catch up to us."

Boothby pointed to the globe. "That chunk saved us from him. He can run faster than a car, but it stopped him."

Conique watched the little man gesture running with his fingers. "What is he?"

Janet brushed Antarctica with her fingers as it passed over her. "He's not human. At least, not like us. He's not from Earth."

Boothby pointed away from the globe. "I don't think he's from this universe."

Reuben pulled his glasses from his nose. "Okay, this is a little intense. We need a game plan."

Conique hollered, "Where are you going, dear?"

He turned to exit the room as Boothby quipped, "Well, I don't mind running, either."

Reuben called from the hallway. "We need protection!"

Adam asked Janet, "Do you think the Texan is one of the Seven?"

She pushed aside her hair, the blue from the globe sparkling in it as it moved. "I hope not. I don't know what kind of man he is."

Reuben returned with his pump-action shotgun and boxes of shells. "I ain't gonna be caught off guard by anyone or anything."

Janet sat up with frustration in her face. "Guns don't solve problems, sir."

As he loaded the weapon, he said, "White cops with guns against black kids don't solve problems. A black man protecting his family from an interdimensional psychopath might be a solution." Reuben pointed the weapon's handle to the spot over Russia. "And before we all get bright ideas about going to Russia, that is Siberia. And this is December. Even if we had the whole Russian military behind us, we'd have a hell of a time finding anything there."

Janet dropped back to the bed in exhaustion. She then said, "Boothby, you told me while you shared my vision that you saw a farmhouse in the tundra when you were a child. Could this be the place?"

Boothby's face lost its color, and he answered, "Oh, my Lord, we gotta go there!"

Reuben shook his shotgun up and down. "This is all bananas. Without help, we're not going anywhere." He pointed to his wife. "Connie, two hours ago you tried to commit suicide. Now, we have talking cats, visions of aliens, farmhouses, and the Siberian tundra. Unless that magic chunk can teleport us, we're not leaving. When this Norcross shows up, I'll deal with him."

Adam broke his silence, his curly brown hair glimmering under the globe light. "I'm sorry, Doctor, but this is no man. He can kill with his bare hands with power that only exists in the superhero movies. He'll kill you, me, and the cat"—Archie hissed at this—"and he'll take the others for himself. We have to go."

The globe winked out of existence, collapsing to the focus stone. It found its way back to Boothby. The room was dimly lit once more, and Conique's eyes adjusted. Reuben stood over them. "Even if running is the smartest move, how far can my wife and this girl travel in their current condition? Maybe we're outmatched, but I won't be driven from my own home."

Conique knew what to say—somehow, she was clearer than she'd been in months. "Reuben, dear, you are almost always cool and competent, and the voice of reason. Yes, I tried to take my life. Dementia is a shitshow. I thought I'd hallucinated this bit of the Seven since it isn't in any Scripture. But I was wrong, and the pieces are out there to put together. My whole life has been an exercise in showing His love and service to my fellow human beings, despite every possible critique, battle, ridicule, and so on. I've asked Josh—or Jesus, rather—for His purpose in all of this. I've fought other people's battles for decades, with your help for two of them. But *this is our battle*, and, like it or not, it's here, literally and otherwise. I wish on heaven and Earth that I had days to convince you instead of minutes."

Reuben leaned into the door frame as he placed the shotgun on a short end table along the wall. He looked past her, working things in that beautiful head of his. At last, he said, "Very well, Reverend Voyant. I never could refuse a sermon from you, Christ-normative or not. So where to next?"

She started to sit alongside her bed, discovering she wore only her night gown. "We call Love by any name we want. But I do need my robe."

Reuben fetched it while Conique looked at Boothby. "There is a physician in Japan named Shigeru Nakamura. He's one of us. We need to reach him."

Adam brightened up. "Yeah, I've heard of him. His proposed viral therapies for radiation sickness are amazing."

Janet chuckled. "Since when do you read the medical journals?"

He shrugged at her. "You're the one who told me about them, babycakes. I do think it's strange you call yourself an evangelical, Miss Voyant."

Reuben muttered as he cast a satin robe around Conique's shoulders. "That's not what *they* call her. Anyways, we're equal opportunity faith holders—and faith rejectors."

Boothby scooped Archie into his arms. "I don't care if its Buddha, Krishna, Allah, or some superintelligence. We can't know any of it if we don't follow these signs."

Turning to Reuben, Conique asked, "Fred from the Plowshares has a contact in Russia, does he not?"

Reuben shook his head. "Dear, we can't enter that country as tourists or humanitarian relief. Chartering into the tundra is impossible. If there are others in this circle, we should find them as quickly as possible. And that means leaving here as soon as—"

The doorbell interrupted him, sounding the Westminster melody. All five froze in place, exchanging looks of concern. Reuben placed a finger to his lip to silence the others. He lifted the shotgun from the end table as he gestured that he would answer the door.

The cat meowed, and Boothby whispered, "Oh, God, I don't know how to be brave, Archie." He pulled the focus stone from his pocket once more. He placed the cat next to Conique, and she petted him as he purred. She cast her gaze to Reuben, and though she thought she should've been worried, she wasn't.

Reuben turned to Adam as he pointed to Conique and Janet. "Please protect them. If I fire the gun, get them out the back door. The keys are in the truck, and you can get the hell outta Dodge."

Adam stood, asking, "Shouldn't I go with you guys?"

Boothby waved him down. "Oh, honey just stay here with the ladies. I'm not afraid of the monster as long as I have this thing. It stopped him before."

Reuben pointed to the bolting on the bedroom door as he said, "Lock this behind us."

Conique said a silent prayer as the door shut. Faith

*B****

Boothby followed close behind Conique's husband, who nodded to the chunk. "I'm hoping that does more than just planetarium shows."

He thought this handsome man a bit odd, the skeptic living with the evangelical faith healer. On the other hand, his own studies of science led him to believe that the unbelievable was subject to empiricism. But he dared not make remarks here, lest whatever wickedness awaiting them get the jump on them. But the chunk made the otherwise-anxious, timid E.G. Boothby wax superhero. He said, "Yeah, more than just a paperweight."

"Why did you think my wife could help you? Here, hold, please." Reuben handed Boothby the shotgun while he opened another box of shells.

Boothby groaned as the barrel sank his arms. "Jesus, they never seem this heavy when ya see 'em in the movies."

Reuben took the weapon to open and load it. "Nope. This is real life, and you never see it on the screen, big or small. So, again, why my wife?"

Boothby widened his eyes in frustration. "Am I the only one who gets it? The lights appear where the nukes are kept. All over this world. They attract them. Miss Voyant coulda gotten me close."

Reuben wasn't impressed. He half-whispered, "Then what? You set one of 'em off? Gimme the gun, please."

Boothby handed it to him with relief. "Well, I guess I thought I'd get help from the Plowshares. Anyways, turning one on wouldn't be that hard. I read all about it."

Reuben was dumbfounded. "My God, man. That is the kind of hare-brained plan that will land you dead. And that would be the upside. Downside you set off a WMD and level a city."

They had moved halfway to the front door, giving Boothby precious seconds to reassure this angry man. "Look, Doctor Hamora—we wouldn't be allowed to do it. The lights come to protect us. I could talk to them at last."

Reuben stopped, turning to face him. "You mean to say the little green men are some sort of first responders?"

Boothby whispered, though the neighbors could probably hear him. "No, the lights are drones. Mostly there ain't anything alive about them."

The bell rang once more, so Reuben hissed, "Quiet, man!"

Boothby grumbled at that. "You asked me, Doctor."

Reuben held a dismissive palm to him. "Shhh!"

They approached the door as the bell sounded once more. Reuben wheeled to face Boothby, whispering as quietly as the hulking man could. "I'll hold the shotgun at the door. You pull it open, staying behind it."

Boothby saluted, but Reuben shook his head in disapproval. "Affirmative, sir."

He postured, the heft of the gun weighing the septuagenarian down. He motioned to Boothby that he should open the door, and he struggled with the multiple deadbolts. Reuben whispered, "C'mon, man, hurry it up."

Boothby gasped, "Christ, you'd think you were keeping Saint Paul's diamond manacles here." He finished the final lock, rolling his eyes. At last, he could pull the latch, and the door opened to reveal two men he'd hoped not to see again.

The taller one sized him up before producing a badge. He asked, "Is it customary to answer the door with a firearm, Doctor Hamora?"

As Reuben squinted to look at Agent Carolina's identification card, he spoke fast. "You're armed, sir. Welcome to Atlanta, Agent"—he compared the image with the face—"Carolina. Hmm, North or South?"

She rolled her eyes as Boothby blurted, "I asked the same question! You followed me here?"

Reuben jerked his head hard at Boothby. "You know them?"

Angling his head, Agent Axley replied, "We've met Mister Boothby." He then sneezed. "Christ, they're worse here."

Carolina asked, "Would you mind pointing your shotgun away from us, sir? Threatening federal agents is a crime."

Reuben may have been old, but he was imposing. Boothby decided the agents must have been as anxious as he was. The elder physician flipped the weapon ninety degrees, pointing the barrel to the ceiling. He said, "You have no idea the day I've had. You'll know if I threaten you, officers."

Axley let out a sigh. "That's appreciated, sir. May we come in?"

Reuben held his weapon close. "You can say what you have to say right here. What do you want?"

Carolina kept her eyes on Boothby, causing his anxiety to spike. "We just want to speak with Mister Boothby."

Reuben shot a look of daggers at Boothby as he wiped perspiration from his forehead. "Nothing's stopping you. Talk fast."

Axley gestured for Boothby. "We returned to your residential complex after you left. It was in quite a state."

Reuben shrugged at him. "California is *quite a state*."

Carolina adjusted her long coat after replacing her badge. "Boothby, if there's anything you want to tell us, I suggest you do it."

This chilled him—his heart raced as Miss Tutog's melting face and shrill screams flashed into his head. He cleared his throat and swallowed hard before asking, "How did you find me?"

Axley shook his head. "No, no. We'll ask the questions here."

Reuben interrupted, "I think Boothby is entitled to an answer, considering he doesn't have to say a word to you. Tell us what you want."

Carolina folded her arms in defiance. "Do psychiatrists play lawyers a lot in Georgia? Doctor Hamora, are you aware of what happened?"

Boothby hesitated as Axley's face reddened in frustration. "Look, we're sorry for bugging his vehicle, but we're trying to secure and protect him. Four days ago, there was an explosion at Mister Boothby's apartment, with one casualty. She was burned alive."

Boothby nodded in confirmation to Reuben, causing the stout man's eyes to race in concern. He asked, "What did you find?"

Carolina quivered as her breath became fog. "Fire and arson squad ruled it accidental. But we know differently, Mister Boothby, don't we?"

"If you think you know the facts, why not tell us?" Reuben's hot temper comforted Boothby, even if he didn't prefer to be on the receiving end of it.

Axley pointed at Boothby. "We're trying to help you—please."

Reuben tapped the butt of his weapon on the hardwood floor as his eyes widened. "You're not acting under orders, are you?"

Carolina turned to Axley. "Sir, maybe we should tell them."

Axley responded with his own question. "Are Baumgartl and Yazzie present?"

Reuben rotated his face in mocking dismay. "Baumgartl and Yazzie? Are they a stand-up act?"

Carolina snapped once more. "Goddamnit, Doctor! There are grave threats to national security."

Reuben shook his head as he shook the shotgun at them. "Then you need to tell your supervisors about it. C'mon, man, you're here alone."

Adam's voice carried from the long hallway behind them. "What do you want to tell us?"

Axley shouted back at him. "Are you Adam Baumgartl?"

The young man hollered back at him. "Depends on who's asking, sir."

Carolina stretched to see over Boothby. "Mister Baumgartl, we are federal agents. We must speak with you and Miss Yazzie."

Adam made it to the door as Boothby eased aside to give the young man a little space. He asked, "What do you want with us?"

Axley placed his hands into his coat side pockets as he answered, "We have reason to believe that the man responsible for the deaths of two Codeka security contractors at Miss Yazzie's resident is the same who murdered Mister Boothby's landlord."

Reuben narrowed his eyes. "Codeka? The genetics company? And *mercenaries*?"

Adam nodded at him. "They sent two of their agents to take Janet."

Boothby gulped as he said, "Because of her being a Vesik?"

Reuben responded to Axley's curiosity by aiming the barrel of his gun once more. "Why the hell would they do that? Who are these people?"

Boothby knew part of the answer, so he cleared his throat to rasp to reply. "Codeka is one of three companies belonging to Kymara Solutions. They do much more than genetic profiling."

Axley asked Boothby, "Where is Miss Yazzie? And what is a Vesik?"

Reuben held a finger to him as he said, "What else do they do?"

Boothby replied, "Picoveer is into nanotechnology. Intellidez works on AI."

Axley pointed his thumb behind him. "Whether you know them or not, there is grave danger here."

Boothby shook his head. "Please stop saying 'grave.'"

Reuben scratched his black mustache. "Why would they be after Janet?"

Carolina shrugged. "They refuse to share their databases. Do you know, Mister Baumgartl?"

Unafraid to show his cards, Adam said, "Whatever they want, the one chasing us makes them look like stick figures."

Boothby was acquainted enough with anxiety to sense it in others. Carolina and Axley both were afraid. Carolina whispered, "Then *he's* real."

Reuben turned to Boothby with pain in his eyes, as though he wanted to apologize to him. Turning back to the others, he said, "Tell me what you know about him."

Axley shook his head. "Only enough to know all of Kymara fear him." Turning to Adam and Boothby, he said, "But it isn't possible that he destroyed both Miss Yazzie's house in Tucson *and* Mister Boothby's condo in San Francisco."

Reuben bobbed his head in understanding. "So that's why your superiors don't believe you. Your evidence doesn't add up."

Boothby volunteered without thinking. "He wasn't in both places. In Tucson, he sent a drone."

Carolina's face drained of color. "That isn't possible—Codeka's surveillance data showed a man."

Reuben tapped the gun butt on the floor once more. "I thought you said you didn't have their data."

Axley ran his hand over his gleaming hair. "SOP for Codeka is to transmit data immediately if misadventure or disaster makes it impossible to retain hardware." Shrugging, he added, "And we're the NSA."

Adam seized the opportunity. "Okay, tell us everything you know about him."

Axley bowed his head. "Agent Carolina?"

She spoke quickly. "For the past five years, Agent Axley and I have followed a series of intelligence transfers too orderly to follow random erasures and copying. We often understand lack of randomness to indicate agency behind it, even if we do not know its source or even motive."

Axley lit up a cigarette as he said, "This is one means of detecting virtual attacks online."

Boothby supplied what information he could. "The dark web masks crime of huge scale. They use computers to look for the cracks."

Carolina pulled her coat hard as snowflakes began falling. "Axley and I believe there is another agency, separate from all others here, which is directing decisions and resources to affect elections, trade outcomes, and more. We believe researchers at Intellidez are aware of this as well."

Axley brushed snow from his shoulders. "There is an invisible faction, interested in controlling global events."

Adam leaned into the banister next to him. "For what purpose?"

Carolina looked at her partner as he answered, "Simple—invasion."

Boothby couldn't take it anymore. "You can't stop the man chasing us, Agent Axley."

Reuben placed a mighty hand on his shoulder, signaling empathy Boothby wouldn't refuse. Turning back to the agents, he said, "Supposing this Norcross is coming, what is your plan? You're underwater on this."

Adam pointed to the charred Jeep in the driveway. "He did that while chasing us on foot. On the interstate."

Carolina broke her matter-of-fact affect. "We must take them all into custody, Jason. It isn't safe here."

Reuben postured after he popped his neck with an angled stretch. "That's not gonna work—without cause, we ain't going anywhere with you."

Axley's blue eyes bugged out. "My God, man, do you not want to be safe?"

Adam pointed harder at the Jeep. "He torched two people, and they were armed."

Boothby grabbed at his elbows as his heart raced. "Maybe we should trust 'em. We know we can't stop him. You guys have bigger guns, right?"

Reuben locked faces against Axley. "Like I said, we ain't going, *Jason*."

Axley broke whatever calm he had possessed, venting, "Fuck. Fuck. Fuck!"

Carolina grabbed his arm. "Sir, get ahold of yourself."

A meow sounded behind Boothby, so he turned to see Archie bounding towards him. He jumped into his arms, stretching his snout to Boothby's nose. Instantly, he felt less anxiety. He smiled as he said, "Hello, Archie!" Staring into the cat's small face, he thought to touch the focus stone in his pocket. He felt its asymmetries and grooves as it sent an electrical shock through him. Turning to Axley, he experienced recognition for facts he didn't know even a moment earlier. He could see a triptych of a helix, electron orbits, and a cross-section of the brain—it was Kymara's emblem. The journalist in him skyrocketed back into control as he said, "If these agents followed us, then Kymara's goons are probably close behind."

Carolina tugged at her belt to adjust her pants. "That's the first sense I've heard out of you, sir."

Boothby pointed to the agents as he said with huskiness, "In all my years of reporting and blogging, I never could get inside of Kymara's dealings—they are secretive with a capital S. Their non-disclosures are legendary, the most complicated and restrictive I've seen come out of the sectors where they operate."

Reuben stared hard at Boothby. "Make your point, please."

He pointed to the agents with accusation in his face. "How are you aware of Intellidez's information?"

Axley gritted his teeth, causing his jaw to tense. Carolina waited for him while Adam said, "You're working with them."

Reuben glared at Boothby. "What have you gotten us into?"

Boothby shrugged without returning his look. "Plowshares ain't exactly a safe venture, Doc."

Reuben turned back to them. "I don't care who they are, double-agent or not. They should get the hell off my property. I'm not—"

Carolina interrupted him. "We are *not* part of their organization, Doctor Hamora."

Axley bowed his head, signaling that she ease off. He then said in a low voice, "Kymara is well-named—what it is, who it is, where it is, are all enigmas wrapped in mysteries, orbited with lies."

Reuben's questions made sense to Boothby, even if his tone didn't. "If you're rogue, then it sounds like they have friends among your superiors." He let out a slow sigh, his ebony skin gleaming against the dying daylight. "I still don't know what this has to do with Boothby and Nurse Yazzie."

Boothby knew the answer. "They're looking for the Seven Vesiks." All eyes were on him as he continued. "They contacted me because a Russian engineer was trying to reach me." He met Axley's eyes as he said, "They know where the others are, too." Archie purred so loudly that the others noticed. Boothby laughed. "What? He's a cat. He purrs."

Carolina shook snow from her short hair as she answered without thinking. Axley jerked his head towards her in protest, but she shot her words first. "Jason, the problem here is the secrecy. We can't let Tucson and San Francisco happen again."

Axley berated her. "Agent Carolina, that's my decision."

She offered a humorless laugh. "It's not *your* decision. Chain of command and rogue aren't friendly bedfellows. Besides, Mister Boothby knows enough that we should be helping each other."

Reuben leaned towards Axley, reminding Boothby of the LBJ treatment. "Your junior partner has you there, Jason. If you're gonna barge in here on a day like today, you best help us out or get out."

Conique's genteel voice sounded from behind them. "Who is there, Reuben?"

Adam moved on reflex to intercept her, helping correct her unsteady gait. Reuben turned stopping his own apparent instinct to help her as Adam channeled his inner nurse by taking her arm. She fussed at him. "I'm not an invalid, yet, son. Who are our guests?"

Axley answered, "Special Agents Axley and Carolina with the NSA, ma'am. We're here to help."

Conique said, "And Reuben didn't invite you for some hot tea? Dear, have we lost all manners?"

He replied without taking his eyes off the agents. "Connie, I'm handling it."

She extended her arms as she and Adam reached the entryway. "With your twelve gauge? This isn't something we can sort with guns, dear. Besides, I believe they're here to help us. Invite them in."

He said, "Not after what happened today, Connie. You're not well."

She said, "I don't think Archie agrees. I'm the clearest I've been in days. Besides, I'd know the devil if I saw him."

Trying to mask his frustration, he said, "I can't believe what I'm hearing. Connie, you tried to kill yourself hours ago. Now, you wanna entertain these clowns?"

Adam braced her as he agreed with her husband. "Ma'am, you should rest. The Narcan hasn't been in your system long."

Axley asked, "Excuse me, she attempted suicide?"

Reuben held a hand to her. "Stay out of this. Now, Connie, they don't want anything important."

Carolina took a step forward. "Doctor Hamora, we're required by law to intervene under these circumstances. Ma'am, are you alright?"

He looked back at her. "Don't talk to my wife. Yeah, I can tell your superiors about investigating Kymara. I'm sure they won't tell their golf buddies running that outfit."

Conique made her way to the door as she reached for Archie. Boothby was glad to see her up and around, even if her care-worn face was more tired than ever. She said, "Fellowship is what we're here to do, honey."

Reuben looked to the ceiling as though some reason might fall from the sky. "I do not believe what I'm hearing." He directed fire to Boothby with a whisper. "Jesus fugging Christ. I don't know what it is you've brought on us, but you damn better get us out of it." Turning to them, he set the weapon down. "Come on in out of the cold. I'll give you fifteen minutes of her time."

22.Four Drives and Tundra's Snare

F✳✳✳

Frankie awoke in his passenger seat, the searing pain from his wrist reminding him of his sin. His eyes struggled to focus, and he turned to see his Savior situated in the driver's seat. Having seen Him at night, Frankie couldn't appreciate the astonishing presence of his Lord. Powerfully built, He boasted golden brown curls, icy white skin with even icier blue eyes. His smile was infectious and wide, though He wore no beard, even if Frankie had expected to see one on His divine face. Taking note of His passenger's waking, the Lord offered a small wink and nod. "I see you've rejoined us, Mister Putnam. We have labors before us."

Touching his stump of an arm, Frankie groaned in pain. He'd never experienced such agony, the experience leaving him wet with perspiration. The Lord took pity, or so Frankie thought.

He rubbed his eyes with his hand, scanning for interstate signs and directions. "Where are we going, Lord?"

Lord Norcross answered, "To locate suitable air transportation for a vital itinerary. We have a very long journey ahead of us, one we cannot make without help." He patted the steering wheel with a victorious grin. "Your machine, though crude, is powerful, capable, loud—fit to be a chariot. It's a pity it cannot fly."

Frankie stretched his legs, then asked, "Where will we go from the airport?"

Norcross might've been a little miffed, but he kept his cool. "Our first destination lies in the southeast corner of this continent."

Frankie's stomach cramped. "You mean Florida?"

Norcross chuckled at that. "No, not a swamp. It is near a city called Atlanta."

271

Frankie fidgeted, overwhelmed with questions he wanted to ask. But trifling with the Lord could heap even more terrible consequences onto his head. But Frankie did nothing without a plan. "Why there?" He bit into his thumbnail to sever a stray piece.

Norcross snapped, "Stop that filthy habit at once, Francis."

He released his left hand from his mouth.

The Lord answered, "In My failed attempt to capture the first of the Vesiks, I would detect a thread stretching from her into the others. I know that they are now activated, psychically linked. Thanks to My followers in this world, I've determined the identities of five of the seven, including your own. And it would appear that they've congregated together, simplifying the chase."

Frankie folded his stump under his left arm. "And when You have found all seven, what will You do?"

Norcross raised His hands heavenward. "Glorious rapture. There is a place called the Sleeping Land. It is so wild that your people cannot tame it." Excitement grazed his face as he met Frankie's eyes.

Frankie wasn't sure which part to question. So he said, "Texas is pretty sleepy. I don't know what Vesiks are, but a click is a group of friends, like on social media?"

Words punctuated with an almost affectionate patience, Norcross replied, "No, My friend. The place We must go bears a name meaning as such. You call it Siberia. And Vesiks make up an essential angelic cell of generals in My army. Seven in all, you are spokes on a wheel enormous enough to turn this world. With you, We gain advantage in the war."

Frankie disliked the use of *psycho*—his brother Tyler used to call him that when he tormented him and Myra as children—but he chose to move on, for this was his Lord speaking. He asked, "Why Seven? What binds us? Where is this in the Scriptures?"

Norcross shrugged with irony. "Scriptures record only so much, friend. Do you follow Me or a dusty tome perverted by hypocrites appointing themselves guardians of the faith?"

Frankie thought about it, remembering Pastor Chet saying similar things. "But surely this is the Second Coming, right?"

The Lord's face brightened with glee. "I am here, Francis. What do you think? I am free to incur this world at My leisure, though I do not prefer this place. Within each of you dwells a power I must have to complete My trial. For you, it is your *Korobskron*. Each of the others is blessed with another gift, together constituting a set of virtues." He pointed into the dark sky as snow flurries slung themselves into the windshield. "Those in this world scrape and bow to small men, deluded drunk with greed and power. The true enemy—"

Frankie asked, "The devil?"

Norcross chuckled at the word. "One of many devils. But if one considers the greatest evil of all, he would be faceless, coercive, and dominant."

Frankie bobbed a head in understanding. "You mean the Antichrist? He wants to tell us what to believe and how to live."

The Lord slid his fingers along the steering column as they passed over uneven concrete in the highway. "Indeed, *they* would seek power over you and My faithful followers. Many believe themselves wise enough, but few are chosen. This crooked world is filled with many."

Watching the open road, Frankie considered it. At last, he answered, "The heart is desperately wicked."

The Lord patted him with a strange grin. "You understand, Francis. You would do well to remember this. Faith requires power. I reward faithfulness, and I punish disobedience."

Frankie looked at his cauterized wrist. "I wanna do right by You, Lord. I want to help You." Norcross looked down to the injury, then back to Frankie with painful scrutiny. He corrected himself. "I *will* help You and see this through, Lord."

Norcross didn't remove his eyes from Frankie, leading him to believe they would crash. But for the eternal seconds in which he didn't look at the road, the Lord handled the pickup perfectly. He said, "No matter the cost?"

Frankie looked away from his wound, recalling an almost identical conversation with Pastor Chet when he was a child. He could almost hear Chet's voice. He then answered, "Anything you want, Lord." Even as he said it, regret gnawed at him. He could see Tyler's face, full of horror as he held his younger brother at gunpoint.

Norcross caught his mood. "I sense conflict within you. Would you follow My commands without question?"

Frankie thought of Tyler, and his heart ached. But he could not disappoint the Lord, so he said, "I would kill him if I had it to do over, Lord. Please forgive me for my sinful weakness."

Norcross touched his face, remaining transfixed on the snow-dusted interstate ahead. "Your weakness, or sentimentality, rather, is not unexpected. Dwelling among shit-hurling primates in this world is bound to soil one's resolve. But a second's hesitation can cost Us the Seven, and this world cannot be saved. Do you understand?"

Frankie squeezed his wrist stump, forcing himself to endure agony as his nerves screamed. He answered, "I will follow your commandments without question, Lord."

Norcross smiled, patting him. "Thank you, Francis. I am vicious in My retribution but lavish in My rewards. You want a reward next time." He then said, "I see you still have questions. What would you ask Me?"

Frankie pointed to the rear window as Sheila's torched body appeared in his mind. "The Commandments. One says, 'Thou Shalt Not Kill.'"

Norcross grinned. "Well, I think you already know the answer. Whether We deprive one of life or fail to save him from death yield the same results. If a man dies today or tomorrow, does it matter?"

Frankie tugged at his beard as he worked to understand. "What if he gets saved in the morning, and he won't be before that?"

Norcross pointed to a military plane in the sky above them. "Think on the souls lost in war. Is it wrong to extinguish them without offering a chance at redemption?" Disappointed that Frankie didn't reply, He said, "I Myself am not bound to the commandments, and, when operating under My direction, neither are you. This world cannot be remade in fire without its destruction. Billions will die in service of birthing a world which will fill you with pride. Killing—or violating any of the commandments in service to Me—is no violation at all."

Frankie understood this. Pastor Chet had stayed his *Korobskron* until it was ready to be loosed by the Lord. So, Chet's death was necessary for his growth. This troubled him, for Chet was the special father he didn't have. He turned to Lord Norcross, asking, "My father and sister—will they be saved?"

Norcross shook his head with a laugh. "Do you wish that they be saved? Pray not to avoid what you fear. Instead, I can help you bear whatever you must do."

This didn't make sense to Frankie, so he asked, "Can't you tell me whether they're gonna be saved? Aren't you omniscient?"

Norcross raised his eyebrows. "This is certainly the question of questions. Would you tell your own children every detail of their futures, denying them the joy and delight of surprise? When you read a book or watch a recorded story, would you always prefer to know it intimately beforehand?"

Frankie shrugged with a growing frustration. "Maybe. I don't like surprises, and I don't like to screw things up."

The Lord cracked wise at him. "Success can be a sweet surprise. You know this, considering your quick work of George." Unable to drag a smile from Frankie, Norcross looked back at the long open highway ahead of them. Speaking with less enthusiasm, he said, "We must all abide by rules established by the Creator. His will for Me requires a trial, and this trial necessitates I endeavor in darkness. In any case, I require only your acceptance, if neither your understanding nor approval."

This left Frankie more confused, at least along a few threads of the narrative. He asked, "You believe these other Vesiks are in the Sleeping Land?"

Norcross hinted amusement, even if He was frustrated. "One of them presented quite the challenge to Me, though I now know all their identities. Pursuing them now would be a mistake, and My agents are at work collecting them."

Frankie thought it over. "Who are your agents?"

Norcross flicked ashes from his cigarette. "We are many, My friend."

"But if the Vesiks are part of the Elect, wouldn't they welcome You as Lord?"

Norcross scoffed. "Would it be worth it if things were that easy, Francis?" Gaining no response, He said, "It is not *who* they are that matters; it's *what* they can do."

Frankie rested his stump of a wrist on the door. "I don't understand."

Norcross grinned. "Surely, you've felt different from your peers? You possess a power this world doesn't deserve. Each of the Vesiks possess some comparable gift, and if We are to be victorious, We require all seven. Rest assured, whether We capture them or not, All involved will attempt to access what lies hidden in the tundra wilderness of the Asian continent."

Frankie's stomach knotted as he risked challenging his Lord further. "But surely You know whether We should find them?"

Norcross tapped the steering wheel as He changed lanes to speed around a slow eighteen wheel rig. "You can see because light reveals the secrets waiting in darkness. Think, a flash of lightning enables you to see all things for an instant. This is the mind I bring to this world. We'll proceed along the path I deem best, waiting for a flash to tell Us otherwise."

Frankie found His words even more puzzling, but he decided instead to leave it at that. Besides, his stomach was grumbling. The Lord seemed to read his mind. "I am famished, Francis. What food do you eat here?"

Frankie gestured with his deformed arm before using his left hand with a huff. "There's a café there in five miles, a truck stop, and drive-throughs."

A quizzical Norcross angled His head as he asked, "What do you prefer?"

Frankie was hungry, too. He pointed to a billboard depicting a cartoon parrot whose blunted beak sniffed a stack of pancakes. "Tito's is okay, but the truck stop has more stuff." As Norcross drove them onto the exit ramp, Frankie observed just how good a driver the Lord was—he never had pictured Jesus driving a car, though a pickup made sense if He had His pick from a dealership.

Norcross pointed to the billboard. "We'll find something useful there at Tito's. And fewer people is a good thing, for now."

Frankie couldn't hold back his question. "What is Your trial, Sir?"

The Lord pursed His lips as He pulled the truck into the café's lot, rounding eighteen wheelers layered alongside one another for a long stretch. The café sat alone against the rear of the lot, as if it was an afterthought intended to catch overflow from the more convenient truck stop.

Stopping the engine, Norcross turned to face Frankie. "War has already begun. This world is the only one you know, but there are more, all at stake. Our enemies wish to do more than cancel or destroy Us. They wish to enslave Us. The trial is as simple as it is profound—these many worlds require Our stewardship. We destroy Our enemies for the breathing room We must have."

Frankie tugged at the shoulder belt in excitement. "That's what they're trying to do. I want to stop them all."

275

Norcross reached to disconnect Frankie's seatbelt after he clumsily fumbled at it with his left hand. He then opened his door, inhaling the chilled air with a nose up. "Methane and sulfur concentrations are high here." The cold wind picked at the pain receptors in Frankie's arm. He shivered at the hurt, catching the Lord's attention. "There, there, Francis. Serve Me well inside, and I shall provide a restoration, of sorts." He pulled Frankie's heavier coat from the truck, then eased his stump and healthy arm into the sleeves. The pressure on his wound was terrible.

The two entered the cafe, and a ruddy-skinned, smoke-voiced hostess welcomed them as she gawked at their bodies. She laughed at the Lord's iridescent onyx suit. "Liberace would approve. I bet you're just as loud under them clothes as you are outside them." Looking at Frankie, she said, "I swear! The one-armed man did it! You're a cool drink of water, anyway, Mister Blackbeard." Laughing hard, she honked, "Just messing with ya! Gentlemen, come on in." She pointed to a dining room of empty tables, save one or two vagrants near the rear. "You can have your choice. Just don't disturb little Tito. Idiot owner loves that ugly mold."

Frankie turned to see a tacky sculpt of the green parrot with pancakes that appeared on the billboard. She heaved a gravelly laugh as she thumped Tito. "Here are some menus. Sit anywhere."

One of the vagrants called to her, "Hey, can I get another water?"

She rolled her eyes to Frankie, mouthing, "Homeless trash." Looking to them, she replied, "Coming, so don't die of starvation before I can get there."

They sat in a booth as the Lord ran His fingers over it. "Such simple technology: pressed wood with colors within it."

Frankie found himself caught in reverie, aspiring over his lifetime to sit with the Divine. He asked, "So you need to eat, too?"

The Lord grinned. "Not ordinarily. But I make exception when seated with so important a follower. And you require protein, Francis, should your flesh cilice heal properly."

Frankie remembered his punishment as he slid his stump under the table in shame. The red-faced woman reappeared, pouring coffee into mugs already waiting on the table. "What is good, young lady?"

She blushed, or at least Frankie thought she did. Coughing a little, she said, "Everything on there, honey." She kept her eyes fixed on Frankie, and he felt his skin crawl with revulsion.

Lord Norcross flashed His eyes at Frankie and smiled broadly, mocking the Texan accent. "Then anything, ma'am."

She started to write on her pad, but then stopped. "Say again? Anything?"

Norcross grinned at her. "Yes, young lady. Bring whatever you recommend."

Frankie squirmed in his seat and said, "Lord, that could mean a lot of things."

"Have you not heard of Hercules and the crossroad? Sometimes, to understand the worldly, We must partake in vice." He looked into the black liquid in his cup.

276

The hostess answered, "Well, I don't know anything about that, hun, but if you want anything on the menu, I'll need some payment up front." She pointed to a sign at the hostess station, then motioned to the vagrants. "Manager's policy to discourage the squalid squatters."

Norcross grinned at her, asking, "What's your name, young lady?"

She winked with a cutesy shrug. "Why, Peggy, sir. I wish you could pay just in that squirter of a smile, but I'm gonna need some plastic."

Frankie fished his wallet from his pocket, struggling to use his left hand, but Norcross stayed him with a gesture. "We can provide payment of whatever sort you require. You may trust Me."

With a little reluctance, she said, "Okay, fine. No more idea on your order?"

Norcross smiled at Frankie, answering, "Dealer's choice, young Peggy."

Frankie stirred his coffee with his left hand, struggling for coordination. He flashed with hot anger. "Lord, why are we here? That woman is disgusting." He watched her fat ass swish back and forth, making him want to hurt her.

Norcross wagged a finger with a smile. "Trust Me, Francis. You'll understand soon enough." Tasting His coffee, He savored the smell. "Java beans are remarkable things. Worlds may differ, but caffeine remains a fixture." He placed the cup on the table, motioning towards Peggy. "Francis, My boy, there is more to do than traverse this geography. You have much to learn. For instance, Our server calls herself Peggy Anne, yet she prevaricates."

Frankie looked to her, then back to Him. "You mean she lies?"

He smiled, pointing to Frankie's chest. "Your Pastor Chet taught you how to control your *Korobskron*, at least for the duration of his influence on you." He sipped His coffee, then motioned to Peggy once more. "She, too, possesses a *Korobskron*, and she has killed more times than even she can remember."

Frankie lowered his head to whisper out of her earshot. "You can see it inside of her?"

Norcross's eyes caught the light of the sun as it crested just above the desert horizon outside, a play of colors entrancing Frankie. The Lord answered, "There is a secret of the Elect, the Priesthood, here to usher My kingdom into this place." He reached across the table, touching an electric finger to Frankie's sternum. "This *Korobskron* helps define My following. You've learned from the beginning of your life to try to understand the feelings of others, to care for others, to surrender to others what belongs to you by right." He leaned towards Frankie, joining him in the whisper. "The insidiousness of altruism, social contracts, empathy—all cover for tyranny, control."

Frankie remembered a name from his childhood. "You mean like Ayn Rand's teachings?"

Norcross slowly blinked his eyes, as though His holy gaze washed over Frankie. "Morality follows from your Lord's words, not from social expectation, delusions of egalitarianism, universal worth of all people. How often have you heard that you must adjust yourself to the feelings of others whose very existence betrays your virtue?"

Frankie rocked in his seat. "All the fucking time. I'm always supposed to tell people what makes them feel good instead of what is right."

The Lord nodded with satisfaction. "I offer a better way. You aren't broken or misshapen. The world around you is, and it is time to set things right. Now, let's have a little demonstration," he said as his eyes flitted to the oafish hostess. She returned to the table, handing over two large plates of French toast and eggs, and Frankie thanked her.

Norcross called, "Hazel Grant."

The woman froze as her long false eyelashes drooped around sagging eyes. Her confidence disappeared, she asked, "I'm sorry?"

Norcross turned to Frankie with a prodding elbow. "Tell Me what you see, young Francis."

He looked at her, sickened at the sight. He returned his eyes to the Lord as he replied, "I don't wanna look at her."

Norcross was giddy. "Just do it, Francis."

Frankie examined her grubby face and rat's nest of a red wig, and his mind filled with a disturbing series of images: Bodies hewn to pieces, screaming men, limbless, eyeless, crying, gnashing, torture. He couldn't help but feel an erection come on, despite the pain in his injured arm.

He whispered with decisive emphasis, "I see... simple... beauty."

The Lord's mirth blossomed to ecstasy. He said with hunger in His voice, "I can hear the thrum of the *Korobskron* within others, as you will, too." He clutched Frankie's shoulder as His voice seduced him. "The sacraments undertaken for Me should harden you so, for My followers need not differentiate the erotic from the righteous."

Peggy was taken aback at this as she asked, "Where did you hear that name? What are you talking about?"

Norcross's forehead became prominent. Glancing at the ugly hag, He said, "Hazel, your projects are worthy of Me. Your cleanup has rid the streets of many a nuisance, something for which you deserve accolades." He took her hand, and she staggered in his direction. "Do you understand Me, Peggy?"

Stricken by His magnetism, she fell into His arms. "Who are you?"

Norcross's splendid smile spread across His face, and He said, "I am your Lord, here to offer testimony of faith, and a gospel of truth. You are exactly as you should be. Your activities do Me honor."

She fell to her knees, saying, "I do not understand. Are you God?"

Elation filled the Lord's countenance, and He answered, "For you, most certainly. You have followed in My path since girlhood, since you slew your brother and sister for their tinker toys."

She buried her head in His lap, and as He caressed her red dyed hair, He said, "You see, young Francis, many carry the *Korobskron*, a badge of office in My priesthood."

Peggy, or Hazel, or whoever the hell she was, raised her shriveled face to His as tears of dark mascara filled the crevices. "What must I do, oh King of Worms, to prove myself?"

Frankie recognized that the vagrants were studying them, and Norcross whispered, "Hazel Grant, you will kill the older of the two transients you see."

She glanced to them, then asked, "But in a public place? What if someone sees me?"

He squeezed her saggy arms. "You are no stranger to this, and no one will see you, Hazel. Kill the older now."

She wiped the mascara streams as she heaved her lopsided trainwreck of a body back off of the Lord. She marched to the kitchen as Frankie whispered, "She'll call the police, Lord."

Norcross shushed him, remaining fixed on her. She emerged with a meat cleaver just as the vagrants pressed their own filthy demands. "Peggy, we want more water and crackers."

Answering, Peggy/Hazel coughed a reply. "Just a minute, and you'll get everything coming to ya."

Frankie froze in anticipation, watching her amble to their table with a ten-inch cleaver behind her back. One of the two said, "Hurry it up, grandma, or we'll write something bad online."

She tapped the blade with one of her cracked, month-old manicured fingernails. "You'd need to be able to read and write, hun."

One of the vagrants, drunk, spewed his water onto the table with a huff. "This glass is dirty." He sneered at her. Looking at her with his hollowed skull face, he said, "Your spray-on makeup is running. It made a solid five out of a two, princess." His laughed with his companion.

She said, "The glass, compared to you, is as clean as a surgery suite."

The grayer-haired of the two snorted at her. "What did you just say to me, lady?"

Hazel smirked. "I said you're dirty, but I have a way to fix you up."

She pulled the cleaver from behind her back, swinging it with strength shocking to Frankie. The cleaver cut deep into his skull, sending red fluid spraying over her. The victim's body convulsed from the brain injury, just as Frankie had seen among animals he'd killed.

The second vagrant screamed while Hazel hiked a foot onto the first's chest, gaining leverage to dislodge the cleaver from his skull with a juicy squelch. His lifeless body dropped away as she raised the gleaming weapon to the sky, washing herself in the blood oozing from its blade. The precious blood ran each of her face's myriad crevices the mascara tears had missed.

Norcross clapped in deliberation as Frankie felt his own erection fight him, straining against his pants. Pointing to the spectacle, the Lord said, "You see, Francis? You are a greenhorn." The second vagrant screamed and screamed, forcing Him to raise His voice. "You would judge her so harshly, because of disproportionate devotion to esthetics which matter little in the world to come. Hazel Grant offers you, My young friend, a gift."

Frankie looked just in time to watch her swing her blade at the vagrant's mouth, slicing both cheeks open by three inches. His screaming momentarily stopped as blood spurted, choking him. Radiant in the glow of carnage, the Lord eased Frankie to his feet. He led him to the convulsing indigent as Hazel greeted them with dentures and a blood-drenched smile. She surrendered the cleaver to Frankie as Norcross whispered, "This young derelict prioritizes his addictions over supporting his small children." His lips grazed Frankie's ear. "Still, his death ensures them no better fate. Will you destroy him for Me now?"

The second victim pulled himself towards the other side of the booth, struggling to grasp the table through the mass of blood covering it. Frankie felt powerful with the cleaver in hand, even if his left arm lacked coordination. The young man gained traction on the corner of the table, so Frankie buried the blade into his hand. He gurgled a shriek as he lost control over his body. Pulling the cleaver from the scrawny addict's hand, Frankie lifted it high, believing his Lord's energies surged inside of him. The locusts deafened him as he sank the cleaver into his victim's chest and neck. Mangled and flush with sanguine, glistening blood, he groaned in agony. Norcross shouted, "Good, Frankie, good!" Hazel cackled.

Frankie vaulted the blade high above his head before driving it down with all his strength. It connected with the parasite's neck, shutting his screaming protests down for good. Blood shot from the wound to the ceiling, splashing Frankie, the Lord, and Hazel. Frankie gasped as he ejaculated into his pants, with each spurt synchronized with the gush of blood. He almost lost consciousness, but he was more alive than he could ever recall.

Hazel patted his shoulder with a breathy voice. "Thank you, Lord. Have we done well by You?"

Norcross pulled them away from the explosion of blood and body. "Yes, you have."

Frankie faced the entrance to the kitchen as he wiped blood from his face. "Did the cook hear us?"

Hazel laughed as she took the cleaver from Frankie. "No, indeed. He's dead. And the dishwasher. And the busboy." Wiping the blade on her apron, she admired her face in the shiny reflection. Licking her dentures, she said, "Too bad Mister Tito wasn't in today. I guess we can't have everything we want."

Norcross smiled, lips tight against his teeth. "You see, young Francis, Hazel Grant here is dying of cancer. But she has served Our interests for decades."

She moved blood-doused hair from her forehead. "I have so wanted to believe, Lord."

The Lord laughed. "I told you, Francis. Something wonderful awaited Us here. My own *Korobskron* in need of vital fuel."

She distributed paper napkins to both men as she asked, "*Korobscur?*"

The Lord dabbed from His face. "Three drives remain prominent in this world—appetite, fatigue, and lust. Yours is a fourth, a yearning for what the first three can never satisfy. It always enslaves Us, but sometimes emancipates Us. Do you understand, Hazel Grant?"

She lit a cigarette after plopping into her own chair. "I think so. I guess I never thought I'd actually meet you."

The Lord bent towards her, planting a single kiss on her lumpy forehead. Turning to Frankie, He said, "You followed My commands admirably, Francis. Over time, you will find your left hand as useful as your right. Serve Me admirably, and I can fashion you a new hand, more powerful than that preceding it."

Frankie was so moved by the kill and the ecstasy following his reward, he didn't notice Norcross fitting His powerful fingers about his throat. Squeezing, He said, "Stray once more, and you will lose every appendage you have, including the one between your legs." He disconnected His hand from him, lightly slapping his face.

Hazel was giddy. "I'd love for you to hold me! Can you cure my cancer, Lord?"

Norcross lifted His eyebrows, as if she had asked whether He could walk across the room. "Hazel Grant, I can accomplish almost anything a follower could ever ask."

She moved to the edge of her seat. "What must I do?"

He answered, "We require a craft at the Goodfellow Air Force base, yet security could prove difficult to circumvent for Us." The Lord winked at Frankie as He pointed at her. "Hazel Grant is an officer stationed on base."

She laughed, "Jesus. You know it all, don't you?"

Frankie corrected her. "This *is* the Lord Jesus, ma'am." He still found her revolting, even if they had killed together. But he was confused. "I don't understand. Why do you work here?" He stared at the Lord. "Officers aren't so—"

Hazel chuckled at that. "Skanky? Trashy? You can say it, stud." Straightening up, her tone and expression tightened beyond recognition. "Sir, whatever you say, sir."

Norcross patted him with no small condescension. "We wear whatever masks are necessary to She must hunt, and a military base is unsuitable grounds for such."

Frankie thought hard. "Wouldn't someone recognize you here?"

She pulled the red hair from her head, revealing a short cut of gray hair underneath. Running her fingernails into her bulbous nose, she peeled it off to reveal a smaller one beneath it. Laughing at his surprise, she said, "People aren't observant, hon. Makeup, hair, and clothes change it all around. Besides, Tito's catches mostly folks from out of town. And no one misses the homeless." She tasted more blood from her face. "How long have you been killing, boy? Don't ya know the basics?"

Norcross interrupted with insistence. "Young Francis would have benefited you're your experience sooner, Hazel Grant. In any case, you've eliminated your enemies here, leaving only Peggy Anne to die."

She kissed His hand as He touched her cheek. "What do You wish?"

He seemed pleased at her simple affection. "We require air transportation with no plans to return to this place."

Frankie started to stand. "You mean not come back to Texas?"

She didn't hesitate. "Where do you wanna go?"

Norcross massaged her scalp. "Siberia. But We must make a single stop enroute."

Hazel stiffened at that. "Very well. There can't be any return, that's for sure."

The Lord placed both hands on her head. "I believe in you, Hazel Grant. Everything depends on timing, and Our time is running low. Can you do this?"

She closed her eyes. "Long have I hoped to gaze on Your face, Lord. I don't wanna hide who I am anymore. Mama Hazel's got Ya covered with this *ample bosom*." She traced her bust, causing Frankie's stomach to flip end-over-end.

Norcross clamped His hands on his shoulders. "We appreciate your generosity."

She hopped to her feet once more. "I have one thing to do here first."

After she scampered to the kitchen, Frankie asked, "Are you sure about her, Lord? She's insane. I mean, dangerous insane."

Norcross placed a hand on his chest. "She gives herself to Us and Our need. I require her, and you pledged to Me. It is that simple, Francis."

Frankie nodded as Hazel shouted from behind them. "OPEN sign is off, doors are locked. Did you know that one of the most dangerous things in the kitchen is oil? Mister Tito buys nasty palm oil in bulk to save money. I hate the goddamned smell of it, but there's more of it here than we could use in a year." She joined them in the dining room once more with a bottle of cooking oil. "If Peggy Anne ends, everything about her does, too."

Norcross watched her with a sparkle in His eyes. Frankie said, "I thought we are in a hurry." The Lord waved him off as He marveled at her with an almost animal fixation.

Hazel poured oil onto the Tito mascot before tossing a match on it. She hollered for joy as it ignited, melting away. "The dead Misses Tito made that ugly thing." She pointed to a door at the rear. "We should go. Cans of oil spray won't last more than a few more seconds in the microwave, and the gas burners are all on. I told Mister Tito that electric was safer. That fucktard just mumbled his Spanglish shit at me."

Frankie's heart skipped a beat. "What the fuck did you do? We need to get out of here!" He turned to Norcross. "Lord, what is she doing?" He burned with jealousy as his Lord fixated on the hag.

After a brief pause, Hazel caught each of them by the hand as she pulled them through the kitchen towards the employee exit. "We'll clean up at my loft before heading to base."

They rushed into the parking lot as Norcross pointed to Frankie's truck. "We happily let you direct Us, Hazel Grant."

Frankie tore open his door, hurling himself inside. The Lord fell into the driver's seat as Hazel swiveled to watch the restaurant explode. She flung her arms to the sky, howling maniacally with tears streaming down her pockmarked face. "The Lord has come! Fuck you! Fuck you all!!!"

A second blast knocked her into the truck as it jolted. Frankie shouted, "We hafta get the fuck out of here!"

Hazel opened the backseat door behind Norcross as she laughed herself out of breath. She smeared blood onto the leather seats, causing Frankie to bristle. She coughed and rasped, at last slapping the Lord on His shoulders. "Just exit that way, Lord. I'll tell you the way."

Frankie rubbed his ears as his tinnitus screeched, worsened by the explosions. "Why do that? Are you fucking nuts?"

She struggled to reply between gasps for air. "You do you, I do me, little man." Coughing and laughing, she added, "You know what? You do me."

Norcross laughed at that. Frankie glared at Him before shouting, "We gotta go! Christ!"

The Lord started the truck's engine, toning His smile with Frankie's scrutiny. "We may have a world to level, Francis, but little pleasures make it totally worth it, as they say here."

*M***

Mayak slept so deeply, so completely, he lost himself. And yet, he knew. It was something on the order of vasovagal syncope, a common occurrence for him: the world would melt from him when he stood too quickly. A bulwark against it would be better hydration, but there had been no time.

The vehicle carrying him subjected its passengers to dynamic forces like he'd never experienced. He'd surface from his slumber, only to sink to its depths once more. He struggled, but his feeble reflexes were just that: ineffective.

In the darkness, he heard his mother and father both calling his name. The voice of Sargon, garbled, as though he spoke from underwater. His friend Petrov, pleading for the life he'd been deprived. His hideous consort, the intelligence agent Kierkov, a villain, serving ends he couldn't fathom.

At once, the voices quieted, and he peeked above the darkness. Waking, he found himself in the fitted chair, and the chamber surrounding him coalesced into being. He couldn't tell how long he'd been mired in this muck, but the thrum of this machine, a more advanced aircraft than he'd ever seen, soothed him.

Beside him, the portal through the machine's skin opened, and he could see where he was. Stretching outward was tundra and wilderness, fantastic and terrifying.

He could see that the ground was some meters below, and the vehicle still moved, though at a velocity not uncomfortable for him. It struck him that the operator of this craft, man or machine, need not show him outside, but seemed to want to do so.

He heard a voice say, "You, cherished of the Vesiks, receive the honor of return." He darted his eyes, but nothing more than shadow flicked—a small form, almost a child, visible for an instant, then gone.

Mayak squeaked, "Who are you? Show yourself!"

Shadows appeared once more, but just a shimmer. Mayak wondered whether he was imagining it, though he'd never had visual hallucinations, even at the worst of his psychotic episodes. Nevertheless, a voice answered, "Being and showing, doing and speaking. If you hear me, must you see me also?" Mayak didn't answer, appreciating the logic. There was a pause, and then the voice said, "So be it."

The shadows swirled, and a small form with a large head and almost insectoid eyes materialized before him; the skin was gray, the body fitted within an ebony-and-crimson suit, the two colors swirling. "Shall this do?" The being spoke, yet its slit of a mouth didn't budge.

Mayak laughed. "Now I know this is hallucination. You are little green man from outer space?" He leaned back into his chair with a chirp. "Mister Boothby would be pleased."

Within him, he heard the voice chuckle. "In good time, Mayak the Brave." The small form stepped to the opening in the vessel's skin, waving its three-fingered hands over the land skirting beneath them. "The sleeping land below conceals many secrets." Turning back to him, the creature transmitted in more formal a voice, "I am Vigil, Curator of the Seven Ciphers."

An alien? A craft? It was madness, though Mayak was acquainted with it. Especially since the lights appeared.

But his manners mattered, just as his mother had told him, so he said, "Pleased to meet you, Vigil. You know me, but I do not know you. Were you contacting me on night of seven lights?"

Again, there was a chuckle Mayak could hear within his mind, and the small creature answered, "No, young Mayak. Aboard our smallest incursion drones, we place no lesser autobiomaton, or, abridged, biomekon. I am engineered to interface freely between organic and synthetic components, what you might call a cybernetic organism, though that scarcely depicts what we are and what we can do."

The creature Vigil stood before Mayak, exposing himself more to the light. Similar to the fractals of color resplendent within his suit, his skin revealed the movement of fluid or particles within. There was a beauty to it, as though nature would bless Mayak with opportunity to see into it.

But these fancies were the province of madmen. He said, "Were it not for my seeing lights in sky, I would not believe this to be real at all. What do you mean, no place for bio—" He paused, trying to recall the word.

Vigil answered, its small mouth unmoving. "Autobiomaton. Smaller craft, mostly available for incursion reconnaissance, with aerodynamics unsuitable even for us." The apparition touched its face with its small hand, adding, "To say nothing of yours and more evolved forms."

Mayak considered this and asked, "You appear quite evolved, Vigil. You speak, yet I only hear you in my mind. Is this not superior?"

Vigil's replies were warm, genuine, and respectful. "Autobiomatons were engineered to perform tasks our masters could not. And we do so happily, for function demands form."

This raised an important point. Mayak deemed creation myths a wasteful thought experiment, but the creature alluded to its creators, so he asked, "Who engineered you? Are you not alien?"

Vigil seated itself before him. "There exists both a complex and a simple explanation. Your Sargon coordinates and executes our incursions, for he is *Arkivar*, chief appointed to oversee our role here on Falterra."

"Why Falterra?" he asked as his heart skipped a beat—it was the term Boothby shouted in his mishap of a video.

Pausing at the question, the creature then replied, "A figure from ancient mythology, one of the clay twins."

Mayak's mind raced. "Whose mythology? I do not recognize—"

"This topic is restricted, young sir. Lord Sargon can tell you more, as he is my master." Vigil's ambivalence appeared to lift.

Mayak fell back into his seat as his mind raced. Before him was something more profound and consequential than any flying-saucer-and-little-green-men satire. "You mean all stories of close encounters are between people and constructs built by voice in my head?"

Vigil laughed. The small form was visibly touched. "Not all biomekons. But Lord Sargon is a gifted engineer, capable of repurposing and enhancing our designs for this place. We wait here."

Mayak looked over the tundra wilderness. He asked, "Wait here for what?"

The small form answered as though it were the most natural thing to say. "You, Master Mayak."

"I've never even been to Siberia." He stared at the blank surface dotted with trees and mountains before shutting his eyes. "And I've never seen alien, or, umm, biokon. Sargon never mentioned this."

Reopening them, he saw Vigil waiting for him. He would go with his senses on this, despite knowing that, as with the coin tosses he had been asked to predict, random chance could fabricate one hell of a fantasy. "Why are we here? What is below?"

Vigil extended its three-fingered appendage to the tundra below. "We must wait at the Seal of Seven Ciphers."

Mayak sought some clarity in the terrain below, but none came from it. "You mentioned that earlier. What ciphers? Why?"

Vigil replied, "I am permitted only to say that we must wait. A communications lockdown is in effect." Pointing to a methane cavity in the distance, it said, "There, beneath the earth, we must await the others. My duty is to greet and direct the Seven upon arrival. For now, I must take my leave."

Mayak strained to see the black hole ensconced in heavy snow and some bare trees. This proved more than a little frustrating, so he protested. "But wait, what are Seven, and what are we supposed to do? Why speak in riddles?"

Vigil's form shimmered and dissipated as Mayak heard more words in his head. "Only when the Seven are made One can the Eighth open the way. There will be no other message until then."

And he was gone. But the quiet was short-lived.

Mayak felt the craft turn, angling towards the cavity. The forces equalized as the shuttle lowered itself into the space; he estimated it was twenty meters in diameter, with an unfathomable depth.

As they descended further, the light from above left him. He couldn't measure how far the shuttle had descended, though the pressure adjustment within his inner ears let him know this was no shallow exploration. Though he couldn't spy detail below him, the rock wall visible through the shuttle opening caught a warm glow that intensified as he dropped.

Something was down there, and without Vigil's answers, he'd just grumble, with butterflies in his stomach. The creature either didn't have the answers he wanted, or it refused, under constraints Mayak could not yet comprehend.

Either way, he hoped understanding awaited him on the other side.

23. Agency and To Know His Name

*B****

Boothby had followed Kymara's story for years, the gigantic firm falling squarely in the crosshairs of his investigative reporting. The behemoth was desperately secretive, borderline paranoid, and robust in averting scandals throughout its years.

Though he could appreciate why Reuben would have resisted inviting Axley and Carolina through the door, he was grateful that Conique overruled her husband. It spoke to the gravity of their predicament that the physician agreed, despite his wife's fragile condition. Maybe he wanted to let her feel important for just a few more moments at twilight, or maybe he just didn't care anymore. No matter the case, Boothby welcomed the chance to question agents whose careers would benefit from his discretion. But the world could fall at a moment's notice, as Kymara's thriving in darkness had exacted the terrible price of inflating the doomsday probability.

As he stroked Archie's silky fur, Boothby felt empowered to launch his interrogation even before Reuben could distribute hot tea to each party present. He pointed to Axley as the younger man perched on the edge of a neat davenport. "I think you should level with us about your contact in Kymara."

Carolina said, "Mister Boothby, we are not required to share our sources with you. And—"

Axley interrupted her. "We're happy to tell you whatever you want to know, so long as you answer our questions in return."

Carolina accepted tea from their host as she answered, "We cannot reveal our sources."

Adam was firm in his disapproval. "You're not the New York Times. Why do you care about sources? You're protecting these goons led to me and Janet almost getting burned alive. We deserve the truth."

Axley offered a nod of thanks as Reuben brought him stevia for his tea. He then added, "I apologize that our position must be to serve the interests of the national security, not the curiosity of persons-of-interest caught up in the intrigue."

Reuben fumed at that. "You say that with such nonchalance, as though national security means anything when the people you promise to protect die."

Conique tried the softer tack, impressing Boothby with her capacity to disarm hostiles. She offered, "Look, agents, I invited you in so that we can all walk away knowing more. Or we can stare each other down and then slink back to defeat."

Boothby's confidence continued to grow, the longer he massaged the cat. He looked at Reuben. "Do ya have any cookies to go with this tea?"

Conique grinned at him. "Well, of course we do."

Reuben scraped his scalp with his fingernails. "We don't have time to eat cookies and drink tea. This is all serious, and beyond any of us."

She turned to her husband with a well-placed hand on his shoulder. "Dear, the real problem here is trust. We don't know what we're supposed to do next, if anything at all. So we should start with the snickerdoodles." He rolled his eyes as he marched off to the kitchen. She then leaned towards Agent Carolina. "Look, I can get insights into things, but we have to be on the same page. My husband is protective of me, and for good reason. If you stay silent, he'll throw you out and no one benefits, okay? And more risk for us all, right?"

Carolina looked at Axley with questioning eyes. He nodded almost imperceptibly, so she said, "If we answer your questions, we could face the death penalty. Is this not a sufficient risk to us?"

Boothby felt a tightening in his chest as it warred with his bottomless need to know. "Now, we're getting somewhere. Who is your contact in Kymara?"

Axley shook his head. "Nope. First question is ours. What are the Seven Vesiks?"

Boothby cringed as he steeled himself to answer. Conique said, "Dears, we wish you would tell us. We think Boothby, myself, and that poor sweet child in our bedroom are three of them."

Carolina said, "That isn't good enough. You say the words as though they're clear to you."

Adam answered, "She just told you that three of the seven are here. So you answer your question next."

Audible from the kitchen, Reuben chuckled at Adam's gutsy observation. Axley tasted his tea as he replied, "We don't know who he, she, or they is or are. The POC goes by the name Obfucius."

Adam laughed. "How chinophilic."

Boothby stirred his tea as Reuben returned with a plate of cookies. "Oh, hell yeah!"

Conique applauded her husband. "He's quite the baker."

Reuben passed out the pastries before planting himself next to his wife. He said, "Don't be silent on account of me. Tell me what the hell is going on."

Boothby asked, "When did Obfucius first contact the agency?"

Axley sampled his cookie, chewing slowly to indicate his pleasure with the taste. "About eight years ago, after I was stonewalled for months in trying to reach my former cohorts within Intellidez. And then, poof, like magic, I received a data packet from Obfucius along with an offer to transmit more should I cooperate."

Adam took a cookie just as he asked, "Why is he leaking the info to you?"

Carolina's round face grinned at him, betraying the informality to her otherwise formal delivery. "We reserve the subsequent question, Nurse Baumgartl. If you cannot define the Vesiks, tell us what distinguishes you from non-Vesiks."

Boothby felt his face flush with warmth. "Umm, you won't believe me if I tell ya."

Carolina said in flat affect. "Try us, Mister Boothby."

He gasped at the finality of it. "We have DNA from outside this world."

There was silence. Axley and Carolina both shared a dance of nonverbal gestures, suggesting this was neither a surprise nor an expected answer. At last, Axley whispered, "So all of the seven possess zed 24."

Reuben fell back into his seat. "Extra chromosomes? Just as you said," he said to Adam.

Carolina's eyes widened. "This explains Codeka's intervention."

Boothby washed down cookie with tea as he asked, "Okay, that should be worth multiple questions. What was the cooperation Obfucius requested?"

Carolina adjusted her place on the couch, her heft a clear contributor to the old springs croaking. "Answers to some of the same questions you've asked."

It hit Boothby. "They wanted you to share what you knew about the lights, then."

Axley shook his head. "No, it was more than that. There are reports on nuclear preparedness, technology projections for the rest of the global economy, and other revelations germane to global security."

Conique bit her lip as she asked reluctantly, "What kind of packet? Like a postal parcel?"

Reuben said, "I think he means a file on a computer."

Adam crossed one leg over another, leaving Boothby envious of the limberness of a young body. "What did they send you?"

Axley said, "Predictions on stock market changes, election results, foreign intelligence, other things they could not have known, even with that day's state-of-the-art domestic intelligence. We thought it was a Klaus tactic."

Conique furled her brow. "Klaus, as in Santa?"

Carolina stayed a small smile. "No, no. He's an engineer who infiltrated banking systems to show them how to improve security. We believed at first that Kymara wished to sell us better encryption."

Reuben bit off half of a cookie as he recentered the thread. "If they knew all of that, why did they need to know about little green men?"

Carolina shook her head. "You don't understand. They weren't indicating they had some omniscient grid, or they wouldn't have asked for the details we could provide. What they built is some sort of prediction algorithm capable of guessing with great accuracy what happens next."

Conique clanged her cup onto the coffee table, once again surprising Boothby at her familiarity with the appropriate jargon. "So, it's an oracle."

Axley folded his arms. "They can't tell the future, but they can estimate odds. It was unsophisticated, weak, but capable."

Reuben poured more tea for his wife as he asked, "What the hell does this have to do with flying saucers?"

Carolina's tone was flat, but urgent. "Obfucius claimed that their in-house system estimated destruction of Earth's biosphere was imminent."

Axley added, "To the tune of ninety-eight percent."

Boothby's heart dropped, but he kept his hands on the cat to ground him. Reuben was less impressed. "Okay, so a computer says the apocalypse is nigh. We in Plowshares have said the same thing forever."

Axley was quick to reply. "You don't understand. Their system could predict almost anything you could imagine, and yet it consistently said that omnicide"—he paused to adjust his wording—"we would all *die within months*, with consistent probability scores."

"So?" Reuben was getting testy.

Carolina took a second cookie. "We're not all dead. These are remarkable, by the way, Doctor Hamora."

Conique grinned. "We can't go extinct on an empty stomach."

Boothby nodded in understanding. "Their predictors say we should be dead, but we're not. Don't ya see? The lights are protecting us."

Adam adjusted his turtleneck sweater after finishing his cookie. "Why did NSA leadership bar you from further contact?"

Carolina's face reddened as she looked to Axley. He said, "Obfucius asked for more than we could give. It came from the chief's desk that we sever communication, without cause or official explanation."

Conique asked, "They don't have to tell you why they shutter a case?"

Boothby replied for them. "Not at all. They serve at the pleasure of their superiors."

Axley and Carolina exchanged glances. "But it wasn't before Obfucius provided one last data drop, the most important one sent to us. Because of the encryption protocols, not even the President could learn its contents without our consent. You see, Obfucius explained from the beginning that we could not trust our leaders."

Reuben laughed at that. "You needed an intelligence shadow broker to tell you that?"

Carolina's calm tone belied her clear frustration. "None among us is so naïve, Doctor Hamora. But one has to believe in something."

Boothby felt himself smile in delight. "They gave you a Rorschach protocol!"

Conique frowned at him. "What do you mean?"

Boothby tapped his feet in glee. "Packets which translate differently depending on the keys applied. This way, they could store several messages in one, hiding treasure among the junk."

Adam spoke as Boothby closed his eyes to imagine the possibilities. "Why would Obfucius trust you with the more complete packets?"

Axley lowered his head. "I used to work for Intellidez. None of my old contacts are there, but I had built a reputation for integrity among them. Obfucius made it clear that he wanted someone to know what Kymara learned, even if the White House and other world leaders were not trusted recipients, and I was I suppose an obvious choice."

Carolina said, "As we said earlier, US intelligence knows that another agency outside of our own has influenced global events. In fact, it must operate completely outside of agencies on this planet."

Adam sank into his seat. "Dope, man. And you're sure one of these aliens controlled me?"

Boothby tried to answer, but Carolina leapt first. "Please, Nurse Baumgartl, elaborate."

Conique said resolutely, "That poor Janet needed help, so someone helped. Is it that hard to believe in something larger than yourself?"

Boothby could think only of Headmistress Sagini and her torture devices fashioned from crucifixes and rosaries. Reuben held his wife's hand. "Look, we should stay on task. If you folks want proof, take a look at Boothby's, well, whatever he has in his pants there."

Carolina glanced away. "Doctor, I do not wish to explore Mister Boothby's pants."

Reuben snapped in frustration. "Chunk of metal, dammit."

Boothby felt his chest could explode. Archie planted his two front paws on Boothby's neck as he licked his face once. He no longer felt anxiety as it became clear to him what to ask next. "Um, my turn, officer. What made you check up on me?"

Axley's eyes lit up. "The final data drop suggested that an agent pursuant these very foreign interests would make landfall in search of a ufologist in San Francisco.

Obfucius said we very much needed to intercept Boothby before operatives representing remote factions could reach him, and that included other members of our own agencies."

Reuben questioned them without removing his eyes from Boothby. "Why?"

Conique asked rather innocently, "Isn't it their turn, dear?"

Carolina placed her hands on her belt as she bent towards him. "Do not trouble yourself, Miss Voyant. We do not know why. He received email from a Russian nuclear engineer Mayak Chernovsky, and another POI who led us to the name Francis Putnam."

Adam bobbed his head in recognition. "Yeah, Janet tried to reach him. But I think he's a kind of Varnumite, stuck up Ayn Rand's dusty shithole."

Boothby's confidence burned into him, and his ideas appeared as words on a page. "We need to get inside of Intellidez—I wanna know how they make such good predictions."

Axley wiped his mouth with a burgundy cloth napkin. "Even if we weren't pushed off the investigation, breaking into Kymara would be every bit as hard as infiltrating the NSA archives. But we do know that Mister Chernovsky knows his way around some of the hardest protocols available."

Conique was almost giddy. "Then we must find him."

Reuben threw his hands to the ceiling fan above. "Now we're back to Russia? Are there other more impossible-to-execute ideas before Connie and I retire? The moon? Saturn? May I remind you that the Eleventh Circuit was kind enough to release my wife because of her disease?"

She grabbed his arm, her bright blue eyes arresting his tantrum. Whispering, but cognizant that the others could hear her, she said, "We don't get to decide when we're needed and when we're not."

He huffed at that. "I married *you*, not the entire goddamned universe."

Conique turned to the agents. "Can you give us a moment, please?"

Axley and Carolina stood as she answered, "We must check-in."

Boothby started to speak, but Adam pulled him in his direction. "Don't get in the middle of decades of a dance. They'll work it out."

Boothby hopped to his feet as he said, "I gotta use the, well, john in there."

Reuben frowned at him. "Down the hall and to the left." He then continued watched the two septuagenarians argue, almost in their own language. He didn't know what long-term coupling was for him, and though he knew lust and fondness, his path was a lonely one.

Adam followed behind him, and he turned to the young man with a shrug. "I don't think I need help in there."

He laughed at him. "I'm checking on Janet, B-man."

Boothby closed the bathroom door, catching himself in an ornate tall mirror affixed to its inner surface. He winced at the old face he saw, though he remembered being young. The décor in the Hamora/Voyant's household reminded him of Miss Tutog, though with more southern grace and less flamboyance. He sat on the soft cover over the toilet, burying his head in his hands.

The bathroom latch started to shake, so he shot his rebuke. "Can't a girl get a little privacy here?"

There was no response, but the fiddling continued until the door gave way; Archie bounded in as Boothby shook his head. "You ain't taking no for an answer?" The cat surprised him again by pushing the door closed. "How the hell?"

Archie approached, placing his front paws on Boothby's knees. "What, cat?" He stared into the creature's golden eyes, so he asked, "What do those agents want, Archie? Doctor Hamora is already peeved at me enough." Boothby nuzzled him as he asked, "Why ain't ya saying anything now? I'm confused."

The small animal meowed as he nuzzled Boothby's coat pocket. Reaching in, he found the focus stone, and alongside it was a crumpled bit of paper. He pulled it out to see that it was the Plowshares' recruitment brochure. He smiled as he smooched it. "Thank you, Archie. Original purpose here makes the most sense."

Standing to his feet, he caught Archie in his arms. "Good cat, good cat."

Opening the ornate door, he met Adam; with a boyish smile, he said, "We gotta stop meeting this way, B-man. You seem happier now."

Boothby grabbed Adam with his spare hand. "It's all clear to me, now. Archie is a wonder, for sure. How is Nurse Yazzie?"

His bright eyes dimmed a little. "She's mostly out of it. Whatever Miss Voyant did for her hasn't held out. Does this plan include help for her?"

Boothby caught a glimpse of a Jesus portrait in the hall, and he cringed at it. "Yeah, I think so. Is it just me, or do they always make Jesus too hot?"

Adam looked at it. "Our foster parents had these things all over their house. It's a little nauseating, but Miss Voyant seems kinder and saner."

Boothby's voice growled. "Let's talk to the others."

O***

Olga woke within the light-filled room. Doctor Nakamura sat next to her, with Zephyr sitting amidst the numerous holographic consoles. Their host angled his head to her. "You're awake again."

Doctor Nakamura leaned to her face as he examined her eyes. "How do you feel, Professor?"

She grinned. "Olga. Just Olga."

He stopped to meet her eyes. "Shigeru." Olga started to sit, prompting him to stop her. "You need to take it easy. I'm not sure of the effects of what we've done."

Zephyr rounded the med bed. "Doctor Nakamura is correct—we must permit the polyplasts time to do their work." He placed a hand on her shoulder. "Coordinating them is sometimes more art than science."

She tried to think, though thought oozed more than flitted. "I felt his hands in my head." Taking a deep breath, she asked, "Can I see what you've done?"

Zephyr looked to Shigeru, deferring to him. The physician, more handsome in this light, said, "I'm not sure how to do that."

Their host said, "Imaging is a basic function of the medical station." Guiding her head, he touched the empty space above her head, igniting it with dazzling console lights. "In time, you will both understand how to access our technology. For now, this is the status of your brain."

A meter-wide explosion of lights above expanded into the shape of a brain. He rotated it with his hands, showing a gap in the tissue where the tumor once sat. She held her breath at it. "That's destroyed tissue?"

Zephyr nodded. "Endemic to brain injury is the swelling. We've reversed it. Each layer of color here depicts a different stratum, for ease of interpretation." He zoomed on the tumor site, pointing at fast moving bright blue specs. "These are the polyplasts Doctor Nakamura programmed. Combined with the pluripotents added earlier, we can heal the damage. But you will require these polyplasts henceforth to monitor the reconstructed tissue."

Shigeru's eyes sparkled against the light. "How did I 'program' these things?"

Zephyr answered, "You should ask how a piano player performs a complicated piece. It is nonverbal, and a skill few possess. In time, you'll improve."

He waved his hands, extinguishing the image. This led Shigeru to ask, "You called this *our technology*. What do you mean?"

Olga discovered her strength had not returned, though she longed to participate in a discussion so germane to her own interests. "He means to say we derive from something outside this world."

Shigeru leaned to her with naked shock in his face. Shooting his eyes to their host, he said, "Who are you? Really?"

Zephyr turned back to the control station with a pained expression. "Forgive me—piloting the skytax without remote access is trying, and I am no pilot. As I said before, my name is Zephyr."

Shigeru interrupted him. "You said your name already. Where are you from? Why are you here? What the hell is remote access?"

Olga felt some sympathy for him, the angry demand for answers more common to her professional experience than she'd liked. Answering, she lifted herself onto her elbows. "Zephyr hails from another world, as do we. We—"

Shigeru had no apparent use for her as he directed his questions to Zephyr. "What other world? Where is it? What system?"

Zephyr's pale brow furled. "This one, Doctor."

This didn't appease Shigeru one bit. "There isn't anywhere in this system where people could live." He looked at Olga, his eyes revealing belligerency run amok. "I must be dreaming. I drink too much."

Zephyr turned his full attention to the physician as he cast a sympathetic glance to Olga. "You're very much awake, and in the throes of withdrawal from ethanol."

Shigeru was infuriated. "That's bullshit. I don't want fucking riddles. If this is all real, then there's no reason why we face extinction."

Olga found herself impressed with his capacity to ground the revelations against the world he knew. But she guessed that Zephyr couldn't use Shigeru's anger in that moment. "He comes from another copy of Earth." She stretched her hands outward. "Another stratum in the multiverse."

Zephyr produced a small flask, a gesture Shigeru recognized at once. With some evident shame, he said in return, "I only need this to steady my nerves." He met Olga's eyes as she nodded that he indulge himself, even if just for her sake.

He swigged it as Zephyr said, "It is as best a replication of your favorite whiskey as I could produce."

Shigeru swallowed the drink as his ire lessened. He asked with flat affect, "The multiverse is real?"

Zephyr hinted at a smile. "Very much, Doctor. We call our world Ghya, and yours Falterra."

"Falterra? Why this?" he asked.

"Ghyan mythology—political and scientific leaders revere it. Certainly, Terra, or Earth, suffices, should you find it tedious." His expression was light.

"Then you knew of this world?" she asked.

Zephyr's eyes danced. "It was, for us, a recent discovery."

Shigeru's blank stare led Olga to add, "The multiverse theory purports that near countless copies of reality may exist, all branches across quantum probabilities."

Shigeru didn't look at her, though he had calmed even more. "I know what the theory is. Why come here? If we're from your world, why are we here?"

Confused by his line of inquiry, she said, "Shigeru, you sound as though this explanation doesn't surprise you. He is saying we are aliens."

Once more, he didn't look at her. "I'm asking Zephyr."

Something snagged Zephyr's attention, pulling his eyes from them. "A moment, please."

Olga claimed the opening. "He is here to find others like ourselves. You experienced a premonition to find me."

The doctor finally met her eyes, his own a black she found attractive, even if the person behind them was not. "I sought you because of research." Motioning to a stilled Zephyr, he asked, "What is the matter with him now?"

She raised her head and shoulders, and to her satisfaction, the gyrokinetabed accommodated her. "He is interfacing with the onboard computer systems. To your first statement, you must have experienced some psychic impression."

Shigeru waved a hand across Zephyr's face, causing him to break his concentration. "Bear with me, Doctor Nakamura." He turned, disappearing into the control station as an obsidian shield obscuring him from their view.

Shigeru tapped it as he turned to Olga. "Is he changing his clothes? He needn't have modesty here."

She cracked a smile, something unusual for her. "Zephyr is a consummate gentleman, Shigeru."

He rapped his knuckles against the obscure screen as it wavered against his touch. "That would be useful in many scenarios, I suspect."

She cocked her head. "A gentleman? I'd agree."

This caught Shigeru off-guard, though he recovered fast. "Back to your statement, I did experience vivid dreams including you."

Olga's affect was flat, but she said by reflex, "I'm uncertain I would wish to hear about them."

Shigeru's cheeks reddened as he scratched his black goatee. "I'm trying to say I never dream about people I don't know. And I rarely remember my dreams these days."

Olga turned to her side, placing weight on her elbow. "We are sixth and seventh of what he calls the Vesiks. You would seek me, as the fifth would have sought you."

He touched Zephyr's obscure shield, feeling it gently reply to his push with its own. "For what purpose?"

Tired, she laid her head to the spongey pillow. "He said we are to help save this world."

Shigeru scoffed. "Is that all?"

The black screen vanished as Zephyr emerged. "My apologies. This craft requires more attention than I'd prefer."

Shigeru shrugged at him. "Is it running out of gas?"

Zephyr's black eyebrows lifted. "You're more correct than you know. The energy stores of antiprotons and photons are low, and we have no immediate means of recharging them."

Olga's curiosity bloomed. "You carry antimatter aboard so small a vehicle?"

Zephyr answered, "It is standard for Ghyan spacecraft. The skytax is designed for low orbit, so the heavier gravity combined with the rush to prevent your death prove too much for what little fuel we had."

Shigeru wasn't happy. "I don't understand. You have the technology to cure a brain tumor, but you can't fly around Earth?"

Zephyr said, "As I indicated, we've pressed this vehicle beyond its operational parameters."

Olga felt a flush of gratitude, though her mind raced with questions. "Why not use something better?"

Shigeru seconded her. "This does seem like a shoddy plan, Mister Zephyr."

The answer hit her, even as she finished her question. "Because of Norcross."

Shigeru asked, "Just who the hell is Norcross?"

Zephyr didn't reply quickly, though Olga couldn't decide whether it was discomfort or protectiveness for them. "A very dangerous Ghyan. You asked, Doctor Nakamura, why we would come here. In truth, we've performed thousands of incursions over the last three centuries."

Olga said with no small irony. "We're not catching them at their best, Shigeru."

Zephyr appeared comforted by her words. He continued, "That much is certain."

Shigeru frowned in revulsion. "That almost sounds like rape—thousands of *incursions?*"

Zephyr waved a hand at him. "No, Doctor. Understand that our intentions are beneficent. Incremental, but aimed at a greater good."

Shigeru asked, "What good is that?"

Zephyr stood once more, gesturing towards his control station. "The purpose looming over all others, and one with which you are familiar—salvation for the seven worlds." Shigeru mulled over Zephyr's words, after which their host said, "We have little time and even less fuel, so I cannot explain further, yet. I require your help, Doctor. Locating more of the Vesiks is of utmost importance, and we do not have the benefit of equipment, outside this skytax. Anything more risks aiding Norcross in finding them first."

Shigeru's eyes darted as he continued to think. Olga felt the strange urge to proselytize him, an emotional impulse foreign to her usual disposition. "Shigeru, please help us."

Shigeru's brow glistened with perspiration as he struggled with himself. "No, I need to understand this. Why is Norcross looking for us?"

Olga forced herself to sit on her gyrokinetabed. "Zephyr, can we not perform a temporal laze with Shigeru, just as you did with me earlier?"

Zephyr was adamant. "No. You are too weak to do so, and I have insufficient power to aid you." He turned to Shigeru. "I admit I would demand specific answers were I in your position, Doctor. But the narrative is simple—Norcross should be gathering the Vesiks himself to preserve this world. But he has surrendered to his corruption. I promise more answers when time permits." Zephyr touched Shigeru's shoulder. "I understand that you fear hope, and I do not ask you surrender your despair. Now, have you received unusual contacts of late?"

He glanced to Olga, as though she might have the answer. At last, he said, "There is an American woman who tried to contact me. She is an evangelical activist who has risked jail to deface nuclear weapons."

Zephyr nodded as his face brightened. "That's it, Doctor. Can you remember a name and a location?"

Shigeru once more sought refuge in Olga's eyes, as though something had shifted within him. "She's bonkers, Zephyr. It makes no sense that she'd play any part in this."

Zephyr's tone became more urgent. "Her name, Doctor? Please."

Shigeru ran his fingers through his goatee, a feature Olga found appealing. He then said, "Conique Voyant—I tried talking to her, but she suffers from moderate dementia. She is one of us? How do you not know that?"

Olga shut her eyes for a moment, struggling against the vertigo. But she felt compelled to reply for their host. "They do not know our identities, Shigeru."

Zephyr's enthusiasm lifted Olga's mood, and Shigeru seemed better for it. "Doctor, do you recall where?"

Shigeru searched his pockets. "You can just look it up." His face reddened. "Dammit, I must have forgotten my phone. But can't you search for the information on the internet?"

Zephyr shook his head. "We cannot connect to external communications, or Norcross will find her before we do."

Shigeru then tended to Olga, placing a hand on her forehead. "It's American southeast. Maybe Georgia or North Carolina."

Zephyr headed into the control console. "Thank you, Doctor."

Shigeru placed a hand on Olga's forehead, but she slapped it away as she asked, "Zephyr? How will you overcome the fuel shortage?"

He called back to her as the obsidian screen activated. "We must hope the answer becomes clear upon arrival." With that, he was obscured.

Shigeru kept his eyes glued to the obsidian screen. She could see veins in his neck throbbing under the light, so she tried to soothe him with what little strength she had. "I, too, am a scientist, carrier of the skeptic's catechism. But I believe him, Shigeru."

He turned to her. "The technology is undeniable. Even if we trust Zephyr, can he overcome his brother? I fear we've simply changed the names of the players, but the apocalypse's drama holds the same ending for us." He seated himself on her gyrokinetabed, and the spongey material gave to accommodate him. In more of a formal doctor voice, he said, "No matter, you must rest, Olga."

She closed her eyes.

F✳✳✳

The sun had since crested above the desert firmament, though the sky continued to dust the land with light snow flurries. The three of them—Frankie, Hazel Grant, and their Lord Norcross—sped to reach the air base where she would, per Norcross, avail them one of the outgoing cargo planes. Norcross handled the pickup with confidence, as though it had been manufactured just for Him. Frankie said little, though he would have failed to utter more than the occasional phrase between her endless meandering tales. She loved dwelling on her sexual and predatory exploits, though Frankie worried that he'd found an even more disgusting variant of his deceased boss.

Her droning included grubby gems like 'pussies welded shut,' 'shit-stuffed throats,' and 'hydraulic dildos.' Frankie wondered whether he'd ever heard so many expletives uttered together. Rather than bother to count, he just tried to tune out the saggy old whore.

Norcross didn't share Frankie's disgust, but He did punctuate her bumbling rant with a decent observation. "This land is desolate, Hazel Grant. Do neither of you aspire to something greater?"

She didn't wait to answer, and her smokey voice annoying Frankie no end. "It's easier to carry out Your will here."

Frankie was perturbed, asking, "Why?"

Her chimpanzee's face crinkled at that. "There aren't enough people to matter. No one misses a transient, passing through my diner." She leaned into him. "No prime specimens like yourself."

Frankie despised this creature for helping herself to his personal space. In fact, he could not recall a time in his life in which he wanted others in his space, breathing near him, touching him—not even when he did date, which was rare.

Waving the noxious breath from his face, he asked her, "Why do you kill them?"

She pulled a cigarette from her purse, snapping the filter from it. "Because He requires blood sacraments to summon Him." She clicked her lighter once, with no flame catching on the first try. "And, lo and behold, here He is."

Frankie protested as she ignited her cancer stick. "I'd prefer you not smoke in my truck, ma'am."

Norcross clicked His tongue. "*Non est gustibus disputandum*, young Francis. An artist makes art." He turned to her, motioning for one Himself. "We'll need this vehicle no more once we've boarded the cargo plane, so enjoy it."

Frankie balled-up his single fist with reflexive anger. "What do You mean that We won't need it?"

Norcross puffed on the cigarette, flicking ashes into the door tray. Pointing outside, He said, "We'll abandon this pitiable moonscape, for the greatness awaiting you both as generals in My new order will mean the end here, all claimed by My cleansing flame."

Hazel laughed a terrible cough-punctuated laugh. "So long as I can watch it burn, Lord." Frankie remembered a neighbor's revolting death by emphysema, and he wished the same for her. Pastor Chet popped into his head, and he pushed the memory aside. Maybe the Lord would permit Frankie the glory of her sweet death—just the thought hardened him.

Then Hazel interrupted his reverie. "You'll want to exit on FM two eight three four; it's the employees' entrance."

Frankie asked, "How will you sneak us into the airfield?"

Norcross exhaled eye-burning smoke into the cab as he said, "Her identification will get us in. Dear Francis, leave the rest to Me." Winking, He placed the cigarette in His mouth to free both hands for steering them into the turnoff.

A spray of gravel showered the windshield, one leaving a mark. Frankie was livid, blurting out, "Watch the truck, Lord!"

Hazel laughed at his expense, but the Lord shrugged him off. "In the world to come, Francis, you can have ten thousand of these crude machines."

Frankie recognized the anger he often felt where his possessions were concerned. George had broken so many of them out of pure meanness. Supplanting the wince of rage was the image of George's mangled face, and Frankie's high-pitched rage transformed into the locust buzz of excitement.

Norcross patted him with a smile. "There's My boy. Yes, remember how it felt." He caressed Frankie's hair, causing him to bristle in discomfort. Leaning away, he learned that the Lord's grip could not be overcome. Ripping Frankie's hair from his scalp, he whispered, "Listen to Me, Francis. I love you *because* of your actions, not in spite of them." He then grabbed him by his hair, squeezing his face. "Never doubt this, Francis. You are one of My very special children." Frankie squirmed, but the Lord's hand squeezed his face to the point he yelped in pain. Norcross said, "Remember that you are Mine—you've pledged your everlasting soul to Me and My cause." He released Frankie, but the pain lingered.

Hazel laughed once more as she tossed her half-smoked cigarette into the floorboard. "Oh, Lord Satan, I worship You."

Frankie darted his eyes to her, "Satan?"

Norcross cracked a smile and puffed a drag on the cigarette. "Those selected for My army come to Me by varied means, Francis. Hazel Grant here may believe one truth, you another, but you see the same King: Me."

Frankie asked by reflex, regretting the words as they left his mouth. "Aren't you Jesus?"

Norcross leaned hard into him. "My enemies confuse the priesthood with names. You follow Me because of what you know in your *Korobskron*, and the same holds for her." Frankie's head filled with the thrumming, the deafening buzzing of locusts. The Lord's touch silenced them, leaving Frankie gasping. "They sing My will to you. We will meet others who know Me by names stranger still for you, but they hear the same song."

They passed the next few miles in silence before Hazel barked at the Lord. "Ahead is the gate. I'll need to show them my identification."

They approached a twelve-foot razor-wire-crowned fence with an entrance gate and a small brown guard shack. Pulling the truck alongside the guard window, Norcross pressed buttons on the door in search of the window control, first locking, then unlocking the door. Frankie was unsteady at directing Him, but he nonetheless said, "Umm, that one, Lord."

Hazel spoke low just before the window dropped. "Let me handle this."

The driver's side window dropped with a whine, chilly air rushing into the cab. The green-clad guard, masked and camouflaged, probed, "Identification and business?"

Frankie was astonished at Hazel's self-control—she spoke monotone, with deft and speed. "Tech Sergeant Krahl, how are you today?"

A doughy clod with a lazy eye and a bizarre facial tick smiled at them, a look Frankie felt certain was that of a monster who would pull wings off butterflies. "Hello, Lieutenant Grant," he replied. "Who are your guests?"

She maintained eye contact with him, but her posture and bearing were perfect. "The hour is today, Brother Bobby." Her words landed with him—he paused before looking over Frankie and Norcross.

Brother Bobby the guard scanned the military badge, then offered it to Norcross. He said, "I need to search the vehicle and see identification for your visitors, sir."

Norcross caught Bobby's outstretched hand, pulled him towards him, and whispered something that Frankie couldn't make out. Bobby's expression changed as he listened, all emotion and color draining from his face. Once released, he staggered back a bit, then said with a reverential bow and a tick wink, "My Lord. Hosanna in the Highest."

Hazel grinned, but her body language didn't betray the moment. "Let's speak at the commissary." She patted Frankie on his shoulder, pissing him off even more. She whispered, blowing her smoke-filled acrid breath into Frankie's face, "Bobby Krahl knows His Name, even if you don't."

Norcross clicked His tongue. "Now, Hazel Grant, let Us not tease young Francis."

The creature called Krahl pointed down the path with a dim tone. "You'll find access down there. I'll radio ahead."

Hazel clasped her hands together with an audible whisper, "Oh, rapture!"

The gate slid aside, and Norcross pressed onward. Bobby spoke into his radio, "VIP escort requested. Temporary replacement, please."

Craning to watch Brother Bobby unlock the way ahead, Frankie wondered whether such a creature could really share in the kingdom to come.

The grounds surrounding them became his focus. Empty, these fields had once served as test grounds for the many experiments conducted by the Air Force and its antecedents within the Navy and Army. Frankie recalled, even in his own childhood, just how often planes had flown over the airbases. Since 9/11, there had been an uptick. At least, that was what he could remember, being a young child.

But now, his curiosity had been piqued once more. "Lord, where will We go once aboard a plane?"

Hazel didn't hesitate in her reply. "Wherever the Lord wishes, boy." She torched up another smoke as she picked yellow crust from under her left eye, flicking it into Frankie's pristine floorboard.

Norcross pointed to a craft looming ahead. "That is Our destination."

Hazel clapped, holding the filter-free cigarette in her mouth. Still-smoldering ashes dropped from its tip to Frankie's shoulder, and he jerked to brush them with his missing hand. Furious, he slapped a clumsy left hand against his shoulder as the burning embers scorched the driver's seat. Her laughter enraged him, even if her words clarified their surroundings. "The C-130 Hercules, a fitting choice, Lord."

Frankie asked, "Just how will we pilot the thing? And how far are we going?"

Norcross pulled the steering wheel to angle them for the runway. Tipping His brow to the repulsive creature sitting behind Frankie, He said, "Hazel Grant once was a pilot, though she's been grounded for some time." He turned to her with a smile. "The fistfight you had cost your opponent her left eye, and most of her dignity."

Hazel puffed smoke, further poisoning the air in the cab of the truck, then only partly protested. "The cunt had it coming, Lord. I would've killed her had they not stopped me." She sputtered a cloud of smoke, then quipped, "I could still kill her if You give me leave."

Frankie waved the smoke from his face, and though he really didn't want to engage this woman in conversation, he asked, "What did she do to you?"

Hazel laughed a goose honk, replying, "She told me that if the carpet matched the drapes, no man would touch my box." She puffed more smoke. "So, I broke every bone in her face. Then, I pissed down her throat, and I mashed my glorious fire-red matt into her piss-filled mouth." Licking her lips, she winked cloudy eyes at him. "The matt is now all gray, if you'd like to see it."

Nauseated, Frankie was sorry he'd asked. He couldn't believe it, but his Lord laughed at her repugnant tale. "It was fortunate you convinced them that you acted in self-defense." He smirked at Frankie. "So reckless an act would normally lead to discharge, and a dishonorable one at that."

Hazel grinned as she pressed her cigarette into Frankie's seat, sizzling another burn into the once perfect leather. "Truly, I have friends in high places. But none of that matters, now, my Lord. I'll steal, kill, rape for You."

Norcross navigated the truck onto the airstrip where the giant airplane sat. Two young men stood on either side of the cargo door at the craft's rear. They motioned for Him to drive to the ramp. Upon reaching the ramp, a young airman tapped the driver's-side window. The Lord lowered it once more, this time with no hiccup. The airman said, "Sir, if you'll just drive your front wheels onto the two loading lines ahead, we'll do the rest."

Hazel wiggled her way out of the truck to speak to the airman, and Norcross offered a gentle nod to Frankie. The overcast clouds were appropriate to the icy cold he could see in the Lord's eyes. He said to Frankie, "Many know My name, Francis."

Frankie asked, "But why different names? She called you Satan, Lord. Isn't she a blasphemer?"

Norcross said, "Francis, understand Me. Falterra contains riches and splendor beyond anything your young mind can imagine."

He felt his breathing speed as he ventured a challenge. "But Pastor Chet didn't teach me that. Hazel doesn't follow Your commandments."

Norcross clasped his shoulder. "Francis, would you require a plumber to understand nuclear physics? Names are words, and no two hears them the same way. I offer you the power of command, but if you prefer to heed only ink scrawled on rotting wood, you can choose to spectate alone." Placing a hand on Frankie's chest, He said, "The thing you share with Hazel Grant, Bobby Krahl, and many others, is the song you hear inside. You were born different from most, and they are little better than cattle." He angled His head to Hazel. "She hears the same song, even if the words differ. Trust that the meaning is the same."

Once the two airmen had locked the front wheels of the truck into position, Hazel returned to the truck as she proclaimed, "We are good to go, my Lord. The harness'll pull Frankie boy's pickup into the cargo bay, and then I, along with Brother Bobby, will pilot Us."

Frankie winced as he asked, "If we're piloting this plane somewhere off any planned course, won't we be caught by radar and satellite?"

Norcross watched the airmen moor the front of the vehicle with chains and answered without looking. "Francis, dear Hazel Grant and Brother Bobby are not the only children who know My name. Besides, I've spoofed the aircraft's transponder, enabling Us to venture without resistance."

Hazel laughed that fucking goose-honk of a laugh right in Frankie's ear. "And then, we take the Lord wherever He says." She touched His shoulder with a wrinkled hand. "And the honor of all my days is to serve You, My Lord."

Norcross placed His smooth hand over hers, patted it, and said, "We must make haste."

24.Believers and Skeptics

*B****

Boothby bounded back into the dining area to hear Reuben fussing with his wife. "That's an insane plan, Connie, even for us."

Adam asked, "What plan is that?"

Axley pointed at Boothby. "His plan." He blasted a sneeze into tissue as Conique slid a fresh box across the table to him.

Reuben blinked his eyes in rage as Conique reached for his hand. He took it on reflex before Carolina said, "It might work, in all honesty."

Boothby cleared his throat. "Well, it ain't exactly easy. We mess up a warhead to force the lights to appear." Reuben was speechless, so Boothby did his best to assuage him. "They will come—there've been several cases where it worked."

Reuben buried his face in his huge hands. "Jesus. All it takes is one case where it doesn't. Besides, we usually defaced inert or preloaded tridents. What you've suggested is insane, and even if we did this, we'd never get into the reactor room."

Boothby swallowed hard at that. "You're not talking about missiles, are you?"

Carolina sipped her tea more delicately than Boothby would expect. She said, "Not at all. There is a nuclear reactor under construction by Kymara a few hundred miles away."

Reuben sighed hard. "Kymara. What a surprise. I thought they'd closed their doors."

Axley said with little emotion, "They reduced their workforce by several thousand following the acquisition. But the reactor's fuel was placed sixteen months ago."

Boothby fumbled with the focus stone in his pocket as he said, "If it's under construction, it probably isn't dangerous enough."

Adam turned on Boothby with gusto. "You're serious? You want to set off a reactor meltdown?"

Conique answered for him, her strength apparently waxing. "Whosoever is doing the saving of late will show up."

Axley's eyes were red with fatigue. He rubbed them hard. "Damnable allergies. Look, there is precedent for this. With the exception of tests and the two civilian bombings in 1945, no launch, intentional or otherwise, has succeeded in doing so."

Reuben rubbed his temples. "You're saying that just because we're still alive, it's safe to trigger a thermonuclear explosion?" He shot a look to Axley, likely hoping for backup. He counted on his fingers. "Let me get this straight—God tells you we should (a) break into a construction site, (b) overload a reactor, then (c) escape with little green men who charge in to the rescue?"

She shrugged as she said, "Well, I wouldn't say God told me." He tossed a hand to the air in anger.

Boothby was anxious but amped. "How would we do part (a)?"

Carolina brushed cookie crumbs from her tie and jacket as she said to her partner, "Obfucius could help us get in."

Boothby tensed his chin muscles to bare his teeth. "Why would he help us?"

The two agents exchanged looks, and Axley nodded to Carolina. She then said, "Because accessing these *lights* is high on Kymara's priority list."

Boothby plopped to his elbows on the heavy tabletop. "Jeez, plot twist. I knew there was interest, but I didn't know they were thinking the same thing I was."

Axley placed his cup on its corresponding saucer as his vibrant blue eyes sparkled with muted but evident enthusiasm. "As we mentioned earlier, you've been a POI for some time. Obfucius might just go for this."

Reuben tapped the table-top hard enough to ring the delicate dishes. "This is not happening, folks. Even if the aliens care enough to stop the meltdown, are we sure they'll show up?"

Axley nodded. "Admittedly, I don't know anything about a nuclear reactor."

Reuben slammed his plate to the table, shattering it. "You are not hearing me! We will not do this! We—" He stopped as he looked to the doorframe.

Boothby's heart almost stopped with the racket, but he, too, was shocked to see Janet standing before them. Adam leapt to his feet to brace her. "Babycakes, what are you doing on your feet?"

She struggled to speak. "I had a feeling I needed to know what was happening in here. Mister Boothby's plan is the straightest line."

*J****

Janet stood with strength she didn't know she had. Every muscle in her body ached, and not a one cooperated her way. But the way forward had not been a straight line, as he'd once told her. The people sitting around a rich oak table were mostly strangers to her. Her brother Adam, the strange little Boothby, and the elderly Conique were known to her. Her throat was dry as she asked, "Where are we?"

Conique had made her way around the table to help her. She said, "Poor thing, you must be thirsty. Reuben, please bring her some water." Taking one of her hands, she said, "Why don't you sit here?" She motioned for a small fainting bench in the corner.

Janet tugged Adam's shirt. "Baby, where are we?"

He said, "Atlanta, of all places. Or just outside of, rather."

She was grateful to drink the water Reuben brought her. One of the strangers asked, "Nurse Yazzie, we are Special Agents Axley and Carolina of the NSA. Do you require medical attention?"

Conique rebuked them by flapping a plump hand at them. "You know we can't call anybody." She pulled Janet's hair away from her glass of water. "Don't drink too quickly, dear."

Adam seated himself next to her. "You said their plan was the right thing to do. What do you mean?"

Janet examined the man and woman wearing matching suits before whispering to Adam, "You trust them?"

Reuben heard her, so he blurted, "I don't trust anybody, Miss Yazzie." Axley sneezed as he said, "Good God, man, have you not heard of antihistamine?"

Janet said, "Boothby, you've always had the power to convince them. The Katafaj is real."

Axley stiffened hard at that. "Where did you hear that word?"

Boothby's bug eyes danced about the room as he found his way to ask, "You mean tell them about it?"

Janet answered as Boothby nodded for her to continue. "The *Arkivar* said to me that you would know how to summon the Katafaj, and that it would help us to escape Norcross."

The androgynous Carolina didn't take her eyes off Axley as she asked, "You saw Norcross, Nurse Yazzie?"

The monster flashed in her mind as she recalled the screams of his victims. "Yes, I did." Boothby shivered, as though he could feel her fear. With pity, she reached for him. "I know you're afraid of him, too."

Reuben rocked back into his chair, the old wood creaking. "What the hell is a Katafaj?"

Axley held a finger to him as he asked Janet, "First, who is the *Arkivar*?"

Boothby squeezed the black cat in his arms as he said, "Mister Ephyr is the reason we're still alive. She knows him as the *Arkivar*" Their eyes were upon him, aiming to understand.

Janet started first. "Since I was a child, I dreamt of a place, an altar among ruins. It was like something out of Lovecraft. A brighter night sky than we see even in Tucson, with streaks of color among the stars. There's a pyramid of some kind, and seven stone seats. There are Aztec glyphs, and a voice. I used to see a figure to go with it, but more recently I just hear him."

Reuben sighed hard. "Nurse, I don't mean to disrespect, but a dream?"

Adam fired back with no delay. "She's heard him say things about the future. Little and big. Invasions, pandemics, who would win elections."

She said, "Most recently, he told me about a fracker in Texas, and"—she looked at Adam with fear—"To protect my brother."

Adam took her hand. "Babycakes, you didn't tell me that he said that again."

She was overcome with emotion, so she said, "It's okay to tell them, Boothby."

The quaint little man said, "If I share with you Agent Axley, you hafta tell me what you know about the Katafaj. I show you mine if you show me yours." Janet gave a small laugh as she wiped tears from her face. Overt emotional expression wasn't her cup of tea, but she chose to be strong as she listened. Boothby then said, "I haven't told a soul about this."

Carolina asked, "That you encountered class two UAPs while resident in Saint Thomas Boys' Orphanage at age eight?"

He rolled his big brown eyes in disdain. "If I didn't tell a soul, how would ya know about it, Miss?"

She corrected him. "Call me 'Agent,' Mister Boothby."

He stroked Archie's fur, and the little thing blinked a hello to Janet. Boothby continued, "I never wrote about this." He reached into his jacket pocket to retrieve the focus stone.

Axley gasped as Reuben said, "Oh, Jesus. That damn thing again?"

Carolina said, "That cannot be. Sir?"

Axley reached for it. "I've not seen one in-person."

Boothby shrugged as he rolled the chunk in his hand. "You know about this?"

Carolina answered, "Two were recovered from crash sites some decades ago."

Reuben tapped his fingers on the oak table. "Crash sites, as in UFOs?"

Carolina said with no affect, "UAPs, Doctor."

Janet could appreciate Reuben's humor, if that's what he was showcasing. He replied with his incisors. "Did changing the letters drop IQs? I don't care what the hell you call them—you're saying the government has evidence from crashes of these things?"

Boothby squirmed as he said with a rasp, "In all fairness, Doctor, this has been in the news in the past few years."

Carolina appeared anxious as she deferred to Axley. He thought about it before Reuben said, "Don't believe everything you hear." Turning to the agents, he said, "Look, you guys have gone rogue. It doesn't help any of us for you to withhold information now."

Axley poured himself more tea from the kettle. "You're right, Doctor Hamora."

Carolina protested. "Sir, we should not disclose intelligence matters. This—"

Axley spat his words. "Enid, we know what we've seen, and our superiors have reassigned us. We can no longer afford to ignore the evidence." Turning to Reuben, he said, "Yes, the lights, the UFOs, the UAPs, all are real. Enid?"

Carolina munched on a cookie as she spoke, spitting bits of cookie with each consonant. "The drones belong to a defensive grid called the Katafaj. Not even the President knows that term, and it sits buried under a mountain of red tape."

Reuben asked, "Why the secrecy?"

Boothby laughed. "Do ya think governments want people to know that some highly advanced grid will take down their nukes before he can launch them?"

Conique offered a germane observation, impressing Janet with her insight. "By defensive, you mean it does no harm to us. But people have still died. Japan, the South Pacific, Chernobyl."

Axley shrugged as he swallowed tea. "We don't know why Katafaj didn't interfere in those instances."

Carolina added her comments with flatter affect than Janet would expect. "Or why it didn't stop the Manhattan tests in the first place. Or why some of their drones crashed. Were they malfunctions? Deliberate sabotage? We do not know."

Reuben wiped his wet brow. "My God."

Axley said, "Those crash sites from around the world left behind bits of their technology, and, to my knowledge, there were two other handheld devices like the one Boothby has now. Yours appears damaged, and, though I was never permitted to examine the others myself, I do know that they contain alloys more sophisticated than anything our most gifted metallurgists could manufacture."

Boothby said, "Mister Ephyr gave it to me during my encounter with the lights. He told me to keep it safe, and that's what I've done for sixty years." Axley reached for it, causing Boothby to lean away from him at first. But he shifted, calm replacing fear. "You wanna hold it?"

Axley took it into hand as his eyes widened. "My God, I never thought I'd actually see one." As he held it, symbols ignited along its uneven surface. "Full of stars," he whispered. The light passed through his hand as he laughed, "It tickles." Returning it to Boothby, he said, "This must have been a difficult secret to keep."

Boothby's voice broke as he said, "I haven't had trouble keeping secrets. Mister Ephyr promised its meaning would be clear. It's already saved our lives once."

Conique passed another cookie to Carolina as she asked, "Where did you hear the term *Katafaj*?"

Axley politely refused a cookie as he said, "Obfucius shared it, and even searching for it within our database is too great a risk. Though I'd normally be skeptical of a coincidental dream reference, too much has happened to deny it all." He hopped to his feet. "I'll contact Obfucius right away to obtain access to Kymara's reactor." He stood and bowed to them. "Please, excuse me."

Reuben asked, "Wait a damn minute. Just like that, you think this will work?"

Axley said, "Boothby's plan to engage your activist organization would have failed spectacularly, and the FBI would have captured the focus stone. This, by contrast, at least has a chance of success." He and Carolina vanished, leaving the others to sit.

Reuben hopped to his feet to collect dishes without saying a word. Adam asked, "Is Doctor Hamora okay, Miss Voyant?"

Conique laughed. "It's a little ritual of ours—he does the dishes when he knows I'm right."

Janet patted Adam's shoulder. "Would you get me one of those cookies?"

He stretched to his feet as Boothby said, "Jesus, I could use some stronger coffee."

Alone with Janet, Conique ambled to the fainting bench before dropping herself next to her. Pointing to it, she said, "This belonged to my mother. 1855 was the date of manufacture. Comfy?" Janet patted the hard fabric as Conique laughed. "Child, they called them fainting benches for a reason—you'd only be comfortable if you'd fainted."

Janet smiled as Conique touched her hair. "You are so beautiful. Indigenous?"

She answered truthfully. "I really don't know what I am. I had intended to find out, but Codeka had other plans. I didn't want them to die, even if they were trying to kidnap me."

Conique held her tight. "It doesn't take much to love those you should. But caring about those who don't love you is a thing of wonder."

Adam returned with a plate of cookies. "Here we are."

Conique smelled the air. "Oatmeal raisin and Macadamia nut white chocolate chip. My Reuben has outdone himself." Taking one from the plate, she said, "He cooks when he's thinking."

Janet bit into an oatmeal cookie, savoring the taste as though she hadn't eaten in days. Adam asked, "How are you feeling?"

Trying to ignore her apprehension, she replied, "Nothing a cookie can't fix."

Handing her a second serving, Conique squeezed her with a discerning hug. "It'll get better."

Adam pulled a chair to face them before seating himself. Crossing one leg over the other, he asked, "Where is this all headed? We have no hope of overcoming the thing that's chasing us."

Conique said, "I discovered early in my faith that it wouldn't explain everything in the universe. Faith is just one road. There are others, and they all lead eventually to the same destination."

Janet asked, "You mean heaven in the afterlife?"

This drew a hearty laugh from her. "No, dear, nothing so trivial. All roads lead to service, to helping others."

Adam cocked his head. "If you don't mind me saying, you're not like other evangelicals I've met."

Conique shrugged. "Well, you might think of me as an enthusiast rather than a true believer. Most people who've lived on this Earth never heard His name—they got along fine."

She pinched his cheek. "As for the other evangelicals, they're babies, still learning to crawl. They cannot understand what they claim to believe until they understand why they claim to believe it. Obviously, they understand none of it. Faith is deeply personal, and never ought be divisive. I barely know you, but you and your sister represent greater light than almost all the hardcore folks I've known over the years."

Boothby bounced back into the dining room sporting a hefty mug of coffee. Janet couldn't help but smile at him. Adam asked, "How are we doing, B-man?"

He raised his cup. "Better, now. I kinda feel like I should have an IV of this stuff."

Janet said, "That got me through many a shift."

Conique patted her. "You'll recover from this, child. I know it."

Janet nodded as the front door reopened. Carolina plodded her way on the hardwood floors as Reuben emerged from the kitchen with white and red apron tied to his waist. His expression wasn't soft, but he wasn't closed. "So, Agent? What did you find out?"

She brushed more snow from her coat. "Agent Axley and I agree that it isn't safe to remain here. If we're to implement our plan, we must go now."

Janet thought about it for a moment. "Ma'am, I might not understand this plan, but I know I can't participate."

Carolina answered in flat irritation. "I understand that, Nurse Yazzie. We propose dividing into two teams. Agent Axley will take Mister Boothby into the reactor facility while I guard the remainder of this party at a local safehouse."

Reuben bristled. "You want us to leave our home?"

Janet started to explain the danger, but Carolina replied quickly and efficiently. "Doctor, you must know it isn't safe here. Norcross will try to secure these assets."

He sneered at her. "My wife is not a goddamned asset."

Conique reached for him with a pained expression. "Reuben, please let her continue."

Janet marveled at the unspoken looks between them, an insight she planned to add to her rules, assuming they survived. Carolina said, "Thank you, Miss Voyant."

Reuben frowned. "Just like that, you'd continue this rogue agent bit? You won't have anything to come back to."

Axley appeared with an answer Janet didn't expect. "There are operating procedures in place if we believe the chain-of-command has been breached."

Boothby's eyes widened. "Jesus. You mean Norcross is somehow making field decisions?"

Axley removed his black stocking cap. "Not yet."

Carolina asked him, "You reached Obfucius?"

Axley bobbed his head. "Yes. He agrees with our plan and will provide access."

Reuben asked, "Just like that? You told him we want to set off a nuclear reactor to attract aliens?"

Boothby spoke in his low rasp as Archie slinked from his lap to his shoulder, evoking a noire mink wrap for the ufologist. "Well, to be fair, this is a plan I thought out a long time ago." He scratched the cat's head between his little ears. "I just never thought we'd get this far."

Axley agreed. "Obfucius believes recent events justify the attempt."

Reuben tossed his apron back into the kitchen. "So we're supposed to trust him? What makes you think he doesn't want us to destroy a whole state? Or get his hands on Boothby's ball?"

Boothby shrugged. "Umm, balls?"

Adam chuckled as Reuben said, "That little machine in your pocket."

Carolina said, "Doctor, Obfucius has provided intelligence to us for years now, and he's never led us astray."

Axley peeked out the blinds at the sound of a vehicle before turning to face them. "He suspected Boothby had a focus stone, and now that he knows about it, he is certain we'll succeed."

Boothby asked, "Then he knows what it is and what it is for?"

Carolina checked her watch as she said, "Obfucius believes you have those answers."

Reuben rolled his eyes. "And you said you didn't work for Kymara."

Axley's eyes reddened with a sneeze. "For the final time, Doctor, we do not."

Conique was subdued, though she traded looks with Janet and Adam as she asked, "What do you two think?"

Adam said, "We escaped Norcross twice, but I don't think we will a third time."

Janet answered with garbled words. "I vote we go. I know this is what the *Arkivar* wants."

Reuben's eyes bore pity, even if he found all of this frustrating. "Young lady, you're very ill."

Conique said, "You're a doctor, dear."

He shook his head. "I'm a psychiatrist, and retired at that. She needs attention I can't provide."

She held a hand to him. "Doctor, this is bigger than me and my disease. If Norcross is chasing me, I won't hide among patients in a hospital." Adam's beautiful face watched her with such fondness, and she cried as they touched foreheads. With a strength inside of her, she said, "If we can't struggle for good when at our worst, then when else?"

Adam laughed at that. "A new rule?"

She patted his soft cheek. "You know it, babycakes."

Axley pointed at Reuben. "Doctor, please pack. The offer extended by Obfucius will not last long."

Conique touched Reuben's face as she pleaded with her own. He closed his eyes before uttering, "What the fuck." He stood to his feet. "Alright, let's do it."

Boothby's winsome expression made Janet smile as he shouted, "It's really gonna happen, now!"

*M****

Mayak stepped through the portal held open in the skin of the strange vehicle that had carried him so deep beneath the surface. He looked above him, where the cavity's opening was evident by the small white light. Could it be that he was scores of meters below? He should be cold, and yet he was warm.

He stood atop stone, but metallic, once more, almost alive. About him was the cylindrical wall of the methane cavity, though he guessed this must be a mere cover for its true purpose. He had not become light-headed, something he would expect if there were natural methane sources beneath him, all outgassing into the precious atmosphere. Before him, small lights ignited in the flooring, sketching a path to the wall. The lights themselves beamed from no evident emitter, but they were unmistakable, multicolored, not unlike fiber-optic Christmas trees his parents sent him; he felt a flush of nostalgia, understanding their tender intent to anchor him to the season they loved best. He had disappointed them with his staunch atheism; in context of the remarkable powers Sargon had provided him, they'd tried to conceal it. But he knew it brought them pain. His answer was simple: the world was too evil, too vicious, for him to believe someone or something governed every event in this cold cosmos.

It was a quote Mayak could never shake, for it delved more deeply into nature than any talk of the wickedness humans inflicted upon one another. Sargon taught him that there was more to the universe than the standard narrative, and his skrytyypass was silent on the topic of omnipotent, omniscient deities. Mayak's parents had believed that Sargon was an angel, sent to protect their son. Mayak didn't think so. Sargon had isolated him, robbed him of any semblance of an ordinary childhood, rendering him an object of ridicule, fear, and hate.

And yet here he stood, within a methane cavity in Siberia, neither frozen solid nor poisoned from errant gas.

At the end of the path, the wall opened, recapturing his attention. Bright light from within awaited him, but he stood still, uncertain what to do next. A small figure appeared, occluding the brilliant energy. He heard the voice once more. "Dear Mayak, third Vesik, we meet." It was Vigil, the small form he had seen within the craft during his voyage to this place.

He took a step towards the being, and without a thought, asked, "How can you be here? And there?"

The small form stepped forward, suited in the same crimson-and-onyx material, with the same child-proportioned, three-fingered hands, large eyes, and gray skin. Without opening its mouth, it spoke once more. "Paramagnetism permits us to assume three-dimensional form, at least temporarily. You needed to see me, so I projected myself."

Mayak closed the distance between them along the path, and the small form raised a hand to him. He hesitated, asking, "This is your true form?"

Vigil beamed more words into his head. "As true as one can define. For what is form?" His hand reached for Mayak, so he took it. The hand, though small, felt warm, comforting, and Mayak did feel a quickening come over him. Vigil released him, saying, "For now, you shall remain strong. But your vitality is waning, in need of the remaining of the Seven." He turned, pointing to the door. "Let us move inside, for there remains much to discuss."

Mayak glanced about himself once more, then followed the small form into the light with a mild, "I would say so."

Passing from the body of the cave, he entered a small chamber, its walls covered in the same material he saw in the craft, with fluid rifts and rivulets of crimson and onyx swirling, touching, like a darkened nebula. Vigil extended a hand to the center, and a chair coalesced from the floor. Mayak gasped at the feat, then asked, "Why am I here? What are you?"

Vigil pointed to the chair, saying without saying, "Please sit." Mayak obliged, for all Russians are taught from the beginning to obey the easy rules without question. Unlearning this during his time in America had led to some entertaining anecdotes, but now was not the time to recount them.

Vigil pointed to the wall, and it illuminated into a great screen of cinematic proportions. Mayak chuckled, "Perhaps you bring popcorn," and in that instant, materializing before him was a lap table bearing a candy-striped carton of buttery popcorn, glistening and fresh from popping. His eyes widened and he turned to Vigil. "How?"

The small form covered his mouth, as though he were laughing. He said, "The seat you occupy follows your commands. It serves as life support for organisms such as yourself."

He turned his small head to the screen, and the March of Progress appeared, silhouetting the transformation from knuckle-borne ape to erect human. The image shifted, and a more brain-centric sketch resolved into the image. "Do not worry with particulars now; evolution as you understand it leads to many destinations."

Mayak bobbed his head in vague understanding, then asked, "What is this place?"

Vigil turned to the screen, and a cross-section of the great methane cavity appeared, showing large chambers affixed to a central core. "This serves as a waystation for the Seven as they arrive."

He touched the popcorn, handing Mayak a piece. It was funny that Mayak had forgotten it, trying to understand the architecture of the space shown onscreen. How would one go about engineering such a structure so far underground? Thanking Vigil, he took it and ate it. The taste was better than any popcorn he'd ever had, so he smiled and nodded to the small creature in delight. The diminutive creature somehow conveyed pleasure, though Mayak found it difficult to read his expressions.

Then, Vigil's gentle voice assured him, "This sustenance contains all nutrients, vitamins, minerals essential to your health."

And it hit Mayak—this creature could read his thoughts. Mayak might've found this more distressing had he not spent all of his childhood in contact with an invisible being of immense power. He was more surprised that this popcorn could be nutritive. Perhaps his parents had been correct that there was a heaven, and he'd entered it. He'd loved junk food as a child.

He chewed more popcorn, then asked, "What are you? Why help me?"

Vigil answered, "As I said, I am a biomekon, a construct built by *Arkivar* Ephyr Sargon to await the Seven."

Mayak paused in chewing the popcorn, and his mind raced with questions. "Where is Sargon? Is he real person? Why did he leave me? You are his creation? Why did he choose me? For what purpose?" As he continued eating the popcorn, his appetite increased, as did his questions. "Why await Seven? Who are Seven?"

Vigil showed him a globe, spinning, appearing as it would from space—Mayak believed the image to be accurate, given he followed astronauts on social media, eager to capture every image of the world he could. "Your curiosity is insatiable, by design. You can speak to Master Sargon because you are not of this world."

He pointed to the globe, then spoke couplets to a poem, something Mayak was not expecting.

Seven seeds, planted well,
Do sprout life, this world will tell.
Seven Calls, the trumpet sounds,
Hallowed songs, Communion bounds
For when the Seven reach the Seal,

The Seven Ciphers shall reveal,
Ghya's gift, realms unfurled,
For the Seven are not of this World.

Mayak chuckled, "A poem? In English? To answer this?"

Vigil, motioning to the globe before them, said, "Art is the Highest Calling of the Human Mind, for science is art."

Mayak said, "Poem is in English—was there earlier translation?"

The creature swayed its head to affirm him. "We ensure translations capture phonetic appeal—the last to discover it were Sumerian."

While Mayak pondered, he saw spindles of radiant orange energy jet from locations about the planet, all leading to what he had to assume was the methane cavity in which he now sat in a chair, talking to an alien. He asked, "How were you constructed? Why?"

Vigil gestured an almost sardonic shrug, or so Mayak thought. He answered, "My name suggests my purpose: to serve with vigilance, awaiting the Seven Vesiks. My construction permits me to perform tasks unattainable by ordinary Ghyans and Falterrans."

"Vesiks? Ghyans? Falterrans? You use strange terms," Mayak said.

Vigil offered a slow nod. "Apologies. Vesik is word from a tongue long expired. Vanguards, harbingers, sharp end of the stick. Falterrans are the sapiens populating this world. Humans, you call them. We know this world as Falterra, though you call it Terra. Ghyans are my masters."

"Another race?! Here?" Mayak found himself at the bottom of the popcorn carton, but there were no unpopped kernels. Perfection, he decided. Without waiting, he added, "And what tasks?" Before him, a gigantic dark chocolate bar appeared, for it sounded quite delicious.

Vigil replied, "These are strange to you, but Vigil pointed to the globe, and they zoomed to the nuclear facility where Mayak worked. It was dark, and the lights manifested in the sky, just as he recalled. Vigil answered, "My Nantiom, Sigil, visited you that night."

Mayak asked, albeit muffled by the large bite of chocolate he was chewing, "Nantiom?"

Vigil created an image of himself, alongside another who looked quite similar, though the crimson streaks were sapphire, and said, "The concept of enantiomer means mirror molecular design. Something similar occurs when we are constructed. Think of him as my twin." He pointed to the lights, then to the projection of his twin. "Our devices manifest many designs, some of which are manned, but even they require dynamic constraints no ordinary Falterran can survive. So, we are biomechanical in design, capable of meeting tolerances demanded by our larger craft."

315

Mayak felt he needed a soda, so a holder containing a paper cup filled with diet vanilla soda, precisely his choice, appeared aside him. Such jolly good fun to experience his creature comforts! He asked, "How do your craft manage such feats? Lights in sky moved like no air vehicle I've seen before."

With a wave of his small hand, Vigil created a projection of the craft that had carried him to this location. The craft burst into its constituent pieces, and Mayak's small guide said, "Gravitons, so far undiscovered in this world, permit us to move with stealth and precision. Attenuating antiprotons to a precise frequency furnishes a steady supply."

Mayak, ever the scientist, couldn't help but ask, "But how do you power attenuation? And where do you get antiprotons? It would take tremendous power to accomplish this, even if you had supply. And tremendous power to contain antiprotons, and—"

Vigil touched him in deference. "Dear Mayak, for now, avail yourself of our computing resources. Without your Keystone, namely the Eighth, we cannot expand your understanding to that of the others."

He asked, "But who are the Seven? Why bring us here?"

Vigil said, "To evolve."

"Cryptic." Mayak sighed, then asked, "You mentioned seal, and Ghya's gift?"

The small guide patted him, answering in his head, "When the others come, you will have access, given you have undertaken the Rhykeng. For your protection, that topic is restricted."

"Governors on information. Mother Russia lives everywhere." Mayak sighed once more. The bigger issue hit him at last, so he said, "Final question, then. You said Sigil appeared to protect me. Protect me from what?"

Vigil cocked his head. "I apologize, Mayak, for I believed you understood. The nuclear launch was sabotage, initiated by Falterran agents."

Mayak bit his lip. "God, Kierkov herself? Why?"

Vigil answered, "She knew that a launch would trigger the Katafaj, the defense network. She failed to capture our drones, but she connected you to us when we used the opportunity to lift the kudeson preventing you from hearing Master Sargon."

He sank into the chair. "She was telling truth—you are immune response. But why? Who are Ghyans? What is kudeson? Why can't I hear Sargon now?"

Vigil bowed with delay. "A Cuelert Sapphire is in effect, per Master Sargon himself. Therefore, external communication cannot happen. We must await the others before exploring those topics. Given your history, I understand your frustration. Remember the master's words: 'skepticism presages your virtue—that of courage.'" He pointed to more food items appearing next to Mayak, encouraging him, "Please do eat and drink."

Mayak thought fast as he considered the scenario. "But if comms are blocked, won't you not be able to prevent other launches?"

Vigil paused, as though this question required more thinking than the small being was prepared to undertake. At last, he answered, "The Katafaj preceded the first Ghyan incursions here, and it relies on protocols we cannot access, so there would be no concern. Courage, Mayak." With that, he vanished.

Mayak thought about the words written in his thoughts. He had not considered it before, but skepticism did somehow resemble courage. Whatever the case, he felt connection, a manifestation of Mister Sargon—physical, real, and demonstrative of a larger world in which things might make more sense.

He couldn't help but trust Vigil, and that took little courage to admit.

25. Dog Days

*C****

Conique sat awake in the center seat of the agents' van, spacious like an airport shuttle. Reuben sat at her left with Janet to her right. Though her hair was darker, something in the girl's energy conjured Conique's deceased daughter. Janet's brother Adam was fiercely protective of his sister, though she imagined the reverse would have been true were the girl not ailing so.

The drive wasn't unpleasant, even for a winter jaunt. Conique remembered why she'd moved to Georgia in the first place—forests and glades full of life near the roots of the Blue Ridge Mountains were just one draw for the beautiful state. She loved the idea of evergreens—a testament to nature's resilience amidst dramatic seasonal differences. It was easy to forget that the world's fate was so precarious.

Boothby's frog croak of a voice carried more in the van than she'd expect, pulling her back to the moment. "Good Mister Archie," he rasped as he stroked the silky black fur of his cat.

Reuben leaned forward to tap Axley's shoulder. "That wasn't the right exit," he said as he pointed to an interstate sign.

Carolina's bluntness was on reflex. "Sir, we know where we're going."

Axley didn't look from the road as he corrected her. "It's okay, Enid. Yes, Doctor, this isn't the usual route. Kymara built roads not on the map so that employees can access the facility more directly. I suppose this area has changed a lot since you were last here."

Reuben eased back into his seat, but Conique knew him to be an ill-behaved passenger. She took his hand, happy to soak the warmth from it. As he pat her, she

318

listened to Boothby and Adam chatting. The younger man asked, "Do you believe the UFOs are watching all the time?"

Boothby tugged his shoulder strap as Archie emitted a gentle trill. "I don't think there's any question," he drawled.

Reuben's mood had not improved, evinced by his frustration. "If they've been watching, why do they let terrible things happen? I don't think we're that much better off."

Conique could see her daughter's face at that, along with the morose face of Reuben as he appeared when they met in grief group. It was a fair point, one with which she'd wrestled when reconciling the world around her with her faith. In fact, that was the key for her. She said, "It's faith, is it not, Mister Boothby?"

He shrugged. "I guess I hadn't thought of it that way."

Adam said, "But it has to be more complicated than that. They could clearly just show up and tell us not to kill ourselves, right?"

Boothby fidgeted, tapping his foot. Reuben sighed in frustration as his seat shook from it. "Man, must you do that?"

He rasped, "Sorry—I'm nervous, Doctor."

Conique turned to see a near blur of evergreen, kudzu, and wispy bare trees through the tinted window. And it hit her. "That's genius, Mister Boothby."

Boothby laughed. "Thank you, Miss Voyant." Leaning forward, he asked, "But what is genius?"

She said, "Just because there's a plan doesn't mean there isn't uncertainty."

Boothby gave a light kick to the back of the seat. "That's actually what I think is true!"

Reuben huffed as he bounced with the kick. "Dammit, man, can you not sit still?"

This caught the attention of their driver. Axley hollered, "Folks, please behave. We haven't far to go."

Ignoring the admonishment, Adam asked, "What do you mean, B-man?"

Boothby said, "I think the lights appear to make little changes here and there. But bigger changes are harder to justify."

Reuben crossed his arms over his chest. "Sounds like a lousy excuse. They can't stop us from blowing up a country."

Conique said, "Agents, you've been mostly quiet. What do you think?"

Carolina leaned back, turning her round face back to them. "I believe the question is academic, ma'am."

Reuben rubbed his salt-and-pepper beard with his mighty hands as he asked, "Care to enlighten us, Enid?"

She didn't bat an eye. "I am *Agent* to you, sir. Simple deduction. We are here, Mister Boothby's lights are real, and the data suggests an intelligence behind the incursions."

319

Axley seconded his partner. "The changes are incremental, but very real. We would not consider so dramatic an action, otherwise."

Reuben frowned as he slapped his forehead. "Why does that not make me feel better?"

Boothby pointed to three columns in the distance. "That's it!"

All eyes darted to the concrete and steel stacks crowning the green tree line. Adam said, "That's a nuclear power plant?" Conique followed his pointed finger to a massive structure sitting in a clearing, as if something so unnatural really could coexist with nature.

Axley replied, "Kymara has been building the plant for eight years. Logistical challenges have slowed construction."

Boothby grasped Reuben's seat to pull himself forward. "They decided to suspend construction indefinitely, last I read."

Carolina shot him a look. "How did you know that?"

He said, "Umm, that's not common knowledge?"

The agent's dark glasses barely disguised her frustration. "No, sir, it isn't."

Adam interrupted them. "I don't understand—if they're not building it, would there be a reactor?"

The agents exchanged a look, triggering Reuben. "Wait a sec—we're headed to break into a power plant, and we don't know whether they have a reactor there?"

Axley said, "I assure you, Doctor, the nuclear fuel is there."

Reuben wrenched his back to face Boothby, and the smaller man shrank into the seat as best he could. "Dammit, man. What the hell have you gotten us into? What's really going on here?"

Boothby said, "I really don't know what you're asking, Doctor Hamora. My plan was simple."

Adam said, "Would one of you like to explain to me what you mean?"

Reuben said, "The reactor and its fuel are among the last things installed in a power plant. If they halt construction, the most dangerous part of the facility is never opened."

Conique remembered the many books and references she and her husband had read in preparing themselves for antinuclear activism. She said, "They must be doing more than building a plant here."

Reuben sighed in fury as Janet garbled, "You're pretty risk averse for an activist."

He said, "Young lady, painting blood on missiles isn't the same thing as setting off a reactor." Glaring at Boothby, he yelled, "You better start talking, ufologist."

Conique touched her husband's shoulder. "Dear, play nice."

He recoiled, his eyes flared in anger. "Don't *dear* me, Connie. I do not appreciate being led into danger without knowing the plan."

Adam said, "I have to agree, guys. Why are we doing this? Janet and Miss Voyant really aren't up to doing, well, whatever we're trying to do."

Carolina mumbled something to Axley, as though her frustration wasn't obvious. She then shouted to him, "It isn't safe to leave them too far, Adam."

Boothby said, "It isn't safe anywhere."

Reuben leaned towards Axley. "Even if Kymara's campus isn't officially open, there will be plenty of minor staff. How do you plan on getting around them?"

Carolina replied almost like a robot. "They are hosting a guest lecture today, so most of their employees will have congregated in their amphitheater on the north side of campus."

Axley snickered at that. "Varnum apparently is here today."

Conique tried to remember the name, but it didn't come to her. "Who is that?" she asked.

Boothby answered, "S.K. Varnum is an influencer, or so some people think."

Reuben shrugged. "A darling of the libertarians, dear."

Axley said, "Kymara often hosts special speakers for their employees. Varnum is controversial enough that Obfucius thinks we'll have an easy time."

Reuben stiffened. "Okay, so the plan?"

Axley pointed to the road ahead, as though the map of the facility sat before them. "Picoveer Kennesaw Campus is divided into four quadrants: S, P, D, and—"

Boothby chuckled as he completed the sequence. "F! Ain't that cool?"

Reuben shrugged. "C'mon, electron orbits?"

Axley replied with his own shrug. "Most of it is unfinished, with a VIP reception near P-quad. D-quad is where Varnum will speak, leaving open a clear path to F-quad."

Carolina said, "Reception will issue us 'primer'-level badges, supposedly high enough to gain us access."

Reuben placed a hand over his forehead. "And a crowd such as ours won't appear suspicious?"

Boothby added, "It does seem strange that we only need a printer to get in."

Axley replied, "Usually, guest badges of so high a clearance would require executive clearance from two ranking members."

Boothby said, "Which means one of them must be Obfucius himself. Any ideas who he is?"

Axley hit the signal to turn off the interstate as he replied, "It could be a she. Not a clue, though Kymara was acquired several months ago by a financial conglomerate."

Boothby rocked in his seat in excitement. "Best, Holdings."

Carolina jerked her head towards him. "How do you know that?"

Conique slid her shoulder belt away from her chest as she turned to look at the little man. He met her gaze with a shrug. "Umm, they filed with the SEC last year." He shrugged harder. "Guys, those are *public* records."

Axley slowed the van as they moved along a service road. But his attention was clearly on Boothby. "It was through a shell company—how did you find out?"

Boothby's eyes darted about the cab of seats. "I read it online. The internet has all sorts of stuff if ya know where to look."

Reuben wasn't the least bit patient about it. "So, what? Who cares? Another tech firm shows its spots."

Boothby answered with defiance, as though knowing this thing was as natural as breathing. "Dana Best is really reclusive. He doesn't like for anyone to know what he's up to."

Conique's imagination lit up. "Could be he this Obfucius character?"

Carolina pulled her own shoulder belt forward, letting Conique know that her plus-sized breasts were uncomfortable, as well. She said, "Doubtful, considering his contempt for governments, intelligence agencies, and, well, pretty much everyone else."

Axley shushed them as they approached a turnoff into the forest. "We're almost to the southern fishbowl." Pulling the vehicle to a stop, he removed his seatbelt, moved between the front seats, then knelt facing his passengers. "Alright, folks. When we interact with security ahead, I will do *all* the talking. As far as they know, we're VIPs here to see Varnum and take a facility-wide tour. Obfucius assured me that we'd have no trouble infiltrating." He pointed behind him to what Conique only saw as a sea of green fir. "The reactor research core is some ways in, but there's minimal staff."

Carolina's expression tightened. "Varnum is a folk hero to some of these people, so we believe a few security checkpoints will be operated by building-specific computers which we'll bypass."

Boothby blurted with glee, "They're foolish enough to trust their systems to Kharla Sevens!"

Conique asked with no idea of the answer, "What is that?"

Carolina nodded hard. "AI software developed by Intellidez, Kymara's robotics firm."

Reuben's tone was of alarm. "You mean to tell me they've entrusted a nuclear reactor to crappy AI?"

Axley pointed to Boothby. "The reactor is inert, so this one better know how to trigger it."

Adam patted him on the shoulder. "You know how to turn it on?"

Before Boothby could reply, Carolina said, "Obfucius believes it. We trust him."

Reuben folded his arms. "A person you've never met?"

Axley's frustration eclipsed Reuben's. "Doctor, there is a monster who wants to capture your wife and these others. There is international intrigue, and possible invasion from outside the planet. Our contact has *never* misled us. Something has drawn your wife, Nurse Yazzie, and Boothby to each other."

Conique caressed her husband's shoulder. "Dear, it's okay to trust."

Axley's wristwatch beeped as he glanced at it. Looking directly at Reuben, he said, "Doctor, nod if you understand everything I've said."

Reuben was sweating, cuing Conique that genuine fear had its claws in him. She touched his face, disarming him somewhat. He then nodded to Axley. "Fine," he muttered.

Axley spun back into the driver's seat, reattaching his seatbelt in one smooth move. He said once more, "No one say anything."

Conique felt her own breathing intensify as they turned onto a path tightly ensconced by evergreens. Boothby mumbled behind her. "It's a singular entrance. Must be for VIPs only."

Carolina could hear everything, it seemed. She said, "One of many to bypass long security lines."

Axley shushed her. "Easy, people."

The van reached a small kiosk next to a tremendous concrete wall. Conique strained to look above her window, hoping to gauge the height of the fortress's wall. Mountains of razor wire and antennae lined the top some thirty feet from them. She decided that the navy could learn a thing or two from Kymara.

Reuben whispered, "Jesus. I had no idea this thing was so big."

Axley lowered his window as he reached the guard kiosk. He spoke so low that Conique couldn't hear him. She became aware once more that Boothby was tapping his foot nervously, shaking her seat. Reuben shot a glare to him, leading him to stop.

Two guards, neither of whom Conique would have guessed were adults, circled the van as they tapped computer pads. Axley continued to speak, and a few words were clear to her. "Guests," "tour," and "Varnum" were among them. She couldn't imagine that they'd breach the facility's wall, but the two guards stopped in their tracks, touched their ears, exchanged a glance, and then moved back to the kiosk. Axley nodded a few times before saying, "Thank you."

Reuben muttered, "I'll be a sunuvabitch," as Boothby gasped. The wall before them parted, revealing a path into the campus.

Axley took something from the kiosk guard before rolling his window back up. He shifted the van into gear, then pulled them forward through the gate.

Conique couldn't fathom what lay ahead, but she still believed in miracles.

F***

Frankie sat within a locker room containing six jump seats, all mercifully vacant. Hazel had remained within the cockpit, so he felt he could relax, even if the chair was uncomfortable. The plane was spacious, capable of ferrying dozens of airmen and supporting staff to combat zones. War was such a waste of money, but he couldn't deny his arousal when he thought about actual combat—he held his phone, and it was a gateway to many things even Pastor Chet didn't know.

Though manipulating the touchscreen with a single hand was difficult, he tried to gain a signal. Cell phones were apparently a no-no while in flight, but he didn't give a shit. His texts overflowed with messages from Tyler and his father, though he ignored them. Moving to the browser, he sought something more interesting. Rough pornography bored him, and his taste of blood led him to snuff segments, executions, torture, and mutilation. He remembered visiting the public library with his mother and their neighbor Suku, and Frankie would steal any glance at books on war and torture. The images burned into his brain, and he longed to be a part of them.

The internet changed it all, and though he thought it was a bad idea to use his phone, he was in pain and angry. Just as he started to open what others called *bloody torrent*, Norcross popped into the pod. Frankie's fingers slipped, flipping his phone from his hand down to the steel floor. The Lord leaned down to scoop Frankie's wayward device, and what He saw made Him smile.

"Francis, you should not use your phone. But—" He pointed to the patchwork of images depicting gore. "—I suppose I understand why." He touched a few of the thumbnails. "Fascinating that one can find this material so efficiently catalogued."

"Umm, that's personal." Frankie reached for it as his cheeks burned hot, and after a frustrating little game of keep-away, the Lord let him have it.

Norcross dropped into a seat across from Frankie. "You shouldn't be ashamed of it, Francis."

Placing the phone in his coat pocket, he said, "I don't wanna talk about it."

Norcross crossed one leg over the other. "Francis, listen to Me—you've fought your appetites for a very long time, convinced by others that these things would unmake you. Reality is somewhat more complicated."

Frankie motioned his head towards the cockpit. "Complicated like that old hag who can't keep her skeleton hands off me?"

Norcross smiled in delight as He lit a cigarette. "She's enthusiastic. But We're discussing you, Francis, and it's clear to Me now We should have spoken more earlier. But locating Hazel was the priority. Open your heart to Me. What troubles you?"

Frankie pointed to his aching stump. "I'm guessing you mean other than my burned off hand?"

Norcross reached for it, His touch nullifying the discomfort. "What else?"

Frankie closed his eyes as the pain subsided. "I was taught that these things We're doing are wrong."

Norcross asked, "Tell Me, do you believe forgiveness and mercy extend to all people?"

Frankie recalled the verse. "The way is narrow and few will find it. But the enemy is deceptive, and Pastor Chet—"

Norcross laughed at the mention, burning Frankie up in anger. "Pastor Chet was a *man*, Francis. Is it a deception to offer you the things I know you want?"

Frankie placed his hand on his forehead, thinking of his parents, his siblings, and Pastor Chet. "I don't know what I want. Pastor Chet didn't want this for me—he tried to teach me to not give in to this."

Norcross asked, "Do you believe the animals he helped you murder matter?"

Frankie could recall every kill shot he administered, but the first one remained the most powerful. Eventually, he could ejaculate just as he ended his prey's life. "You mean do they have souls? The Word says we have dominion over this world."

Norcross took a heavy drag on his cigarette. "What makes the Elect and the Priesthood more valuable?"

Frankie coughed at the smoke as he said, "They chose the Way."

Norcross led him a step further. "What about those who haven't? Those who never will?"

This hit Frankie hard. "They're like the animals?"

Norcross flicked ashes as He bared His perfect smile. "You're almost there, Francis. They *are* animals. They exist to serve Us."

Hazel interrupted them before Frankie could ask Him more. "Sorry to interrupt you, sweet cheeks. But, my Lord, there is a communication for You. And not a moment too soon."

Norcross stood to His feet. "Excellent."

Frankie pushed the safety belt aside as he hopped up. "Who is communicating? Where are We going?"

Norcross eased him back to his flip-down chair. "Ever the curious. My sources have determined the whereabouts of three of your fellow Vesiks. We must hurry to meet them."

Frankie resisted his Lord's powerful grasp. "I'm tired of sitting here. I want to see the cockpit."

Hazel cackled. "Aww, little Frankie wanna see Mama Hazel's titties up front?"

Frankie looked away in disgust, but Norcross said, "Very well, Francis. Join us."

He was on his feet before Norcross finished speaking. The Lord turned to leave the pod, and as Frankie followed, Hazel poked him in the ribs. "See here, Frankie boy. The Lord loves you in a way He'd never love me. Don't forget it."

Surprising even himself, Frankie muttered aloud, "I don't know how you could be—"

Norcross folded His arms neatly. "A devotee? Hazel Grant possesses discipline you cannot imagine, Francis."

Once more, she pulled herself together with perfect posture before offering a salute. "Then why act that way?" he asked, picturing himself cutting her to pieces with an electric knife.

Her stone-faced demeanor melted away as she squeezed his stump until he hollered. "There's no death you can dream up for me that I can't inflict on you, boy."

She released him as she disappeared through the grated door. Sweating, he vomited on the floor as the pain paralyzed him. He reached with his right sleeve, but he was further revulsed by the mangled mess. His left arm was clumsy, but it would do. He then left the pod to head for the cockpit entrance.

Inside, he found Brother Bobby manning one station as Hazel oozed her way into the copilot seat. Norcross stood, listening to their radio. He spoke a language Frankie didn't recognize, though his real hope was to just see something other than steel. Puffy white clouds filled the view windows, creating a fluffy white floor with a solid blue ceiling.

Hazel held her headset as she said, "There ain't much to see, sugar. We're high up, and the visibility down there ain't great."

He asked, "Where are we going?"

She said, "The land of peaches—Georgia. Sit there for better accommodations." She aimed a crooked finger to a jump seat across from Norcross.

Frankie frowned at it, knowing it wouldn't be a mite more comfortable than his seat back in the pod. Settling down, he asked, "How are you going to land us somewhere after stealing the plane?"

Bobby grinned over at Hazel with a creepy dead-eye and fluttery wink of a tick. She said, "Sugar, we haven't stolen a thing. We're a routine VIP transport, so no one will ask any questions." She showed her own fangs with a laugh, several stained with lipstick. "Did you think we wouldn't wait for Him?"

Norcross dropped his headset as He said, "Our targets are traveling to a research facility below."

Frankie asked, "How do you know? Where?"

Norcross massaged Hazel's shoulders a bit. "You can bring Us down."

She and Brother Bobby flipped switches, turned dials, and contacted towers below.

Norcross faced Frankie. "We're well-connected to this world, Francis. I'll find them with Hazel Grant's help. As for you, I have a surprise awaiting you below."

Frankie squeezed his right shoulder with his one remaining hand. "But aren't We in a hurry?"

Norcross leaned forward, clasping His own two hands together between His knees. "We have time, yet. Avail yourself of the shower before We descend. Admittedly, it isn't frilly."

Hazel couldn't stop herself from interrupting. "We have some airmen onesies that'll fit you real good, Frankie boy. They'll show off that nice package and cute little rear. I'll even help you into it, that's what I'll do."

Ignoring the wrinkled whore, Frankie asked, "What is the surprise?"

The Lord's playful expression disarmed him a little. "Stubbornly inquisitive. It's just as well, My friend. Your folk hero Varnum is eager to meet you."

Frankie shook his head in dismay. "That's impossible. Why would he be here at the same time that as these Vesiks?"

Norcross stood, pulling Frankie up with Him. "You don't believe in coincidences, Francis." He reached for Frankie's cheek. "I must confess a little jealousy that you revere Varnum so, but I have seen so few smiles from you, this must be a good thing."

Hazel honked like a pregnant goose. "Oh, I wish he'd look at me that way. Lemme at this Varnum, and I'll cut off his head and shit down his throat." She swatted at Brother Bobby as he rose and sank with soundless laughter.

Frankie instantly regretted insisting on joining them, but he was grateful to understand at least some part of the plan. Trotting from the cockpit, he hoped he could finish readying himself before Hazel helped herself to his personal space. She was a dog in heat, and he hated her for it.

S***

Shigeru watched Olga sleep. Her porcelain skin and golden hair were too beautiful for a world of ugliness. And that's what it was, even if Zephyr represented a better way. It had been so long since Shigeru had experienced hope, he'd forgotten the eagerness, the longing, the desperation all tied together.

Zephyr, for his part, was a gentle man. He appeared to want to help them, but Shigeru doubted than even the most powerful technology could tame the demons lurking within all people. The Ghyans possessed power, but more powerful humans meant more powerful ambition, more powerful hatred, and more powerful insecurities. And Zephyr didn't seem to be up to the Herculean challenge of saving a world, his or otherwise.

It probably made sense to leave Olga in Shigeru's charge. In his professional capacity, he could focus on her needs in the only way Shigeru could address any female's needs, given his admitted misogyny. At times, he hated himself, and though his mother wanted better for him, she abandoned him by dying early.

Clearing his head, he inspected Olga. She was more angel than woman. She breathed gently, and when he touched her, he could feel the polyplasts busying themselves in repairing her broken nervous system. Millions of them acted in tandem, some to siphon away excess fluid to normalize intracranial pressure, others to replace missing neurons with hardier ones fashioned from silicon and trace elements. When probing these devices, he wondered what went on within the brain. At the level of neuron, nothing was apparent. Even the artificial neurons were intended to play well with others, even if the collective function wasn't obvious.

Her beauty distracted him. Shigeru couldn't help but think of sex with her, even if her temperament nullified his usual tricks and tactics to woo so cool a woman. That intrigued him. Conflicted, he continued analyzing her with the polyplasts. Blood flowed, carrying natural and artificial waste from the region. He would increase waste disposal by 0.23% to bring balance.

At last, he discovered he had exhausted himself. Releasing her, he lost communication with the myriad devices restoring her to health. He was alone, once more, and it wasn't a great feeling. He turned to see Zephyr standing behind him, and the Ghyan's face was bright. Shigeru looked back at Olga. "I believe she'll recover, if I'm understanding what's going on correctly."

Zephyr touched his shoulder. "You're doing perfectly, Doctor. Time to rest."

Shigeru couldn't help but gush, if only by a smidge. "This is technology we could only dream about in medical school. There's nothing even on the drawing boards anywhere close to this."

He shrugged at the doctor. "It still requires an artist, and few can do it." He handed him a cup of liquid, a mixture of coffee and whiskey only Shigeru himself could have created.

Shigeru took it in hand, then tasted it with a smile as he said, "Thanks."

Zephyr patted him as he sat in a chair which formed directly from the glossy floor beneath him. "You've earned it. The past hours have been a great shock to you, and to the professor. She expected to die only a day ago."

Shigeru looked back at her delicate form. "I didn't know that I was already dead on the inside." He looked back at Zephyr as the Ghyan listened with focus. "Using your tools to heal reminded me of the reason I wanted to become a doctor. Sure, it was prestigious, and I'm an elite."

Zephyr drank from his own cup before he said, "There is a part of you destined to heal, and you knew it then."

Shigeru flashed with a little anger at what he believed was presumptiveness. "I'm complicated, Zephyr."

Olga spoke at that. "No one's taking that away from you, Shigeru."

Zephyr asked, "How do you feel, now?"

She pressed her fingers to her temples. "I don't know that I've known a worse hangover."

Shigeru said, "There's more to do, but I'm too tired."

Zephyr brought her a cup of water, flagging Shigeru's laser focus. The Ghyan said, "This contains electrolytes and other components the polyplasts require." He didn't hold back his praise, as if he didn't know it was intoxicating for Shigeru. "The doctor has adapted to our medical suite quickly, advantageous for us, considering our position."

Shigeru didn't waste the Ghyan's attention. "Okay, Zephyr, how far are we from Voyant?"

Zephyr said, "An hour. Even if we had the fuel, faster travel would alert Falterran surveillance satellites, and I'd prefer we avoid it if possible."

Olga said, "Do you have a plan for fuel?"

Zephyr appeared thoughtful. "I'm hoping that your fellow Vesiks lead us to a solution. Antimatter isn't easy to come by, even on Ghya."

Shigeru tensed his jaw. "I must admit, Zephyr, you appear inadequate to this mess."

It pleased him that the Ghyan appeared angry, even if it was for just an instant. "For the simple reason that I was not the intended agent, Doctor."

Olga sat up to side with Shigeru, an even greater pleasure for him. "Shigeru is right, Zephyr. Why seek us? Who sent you? I think we've earned answers."

Zephyr appeared pained by the tedium. "You are both correct. I do not know the identities of your fellow Vesiks." He looked past Shigeru with a troubled countenance. "In fact, I am uncertain we can succeed." He met the doctor's eyes, those of the Ghyan burning with energy. "As unsatisfactory an answer as it is, there isn't time now to explain all of it to you."

Shigeru felt a lump in his throat as he said, "I have to insist, Zephyr, or we aren't going to help you. If you don't trust us, how can we trust you?"

Zephyr closed his eyes as he considered it. "There must always be a first step, true," he whispered. Opening his eyes, he said, "The Seven Vesiks, when gathered by the Eighth, join to form a key to a lock. Buried somewhere in this solar system is the Vessafra, a device of tremendous power, and we must find it if Falterra and Ghya are to survive."

Shigeru tensed, as though the apocalypse hadn't entered the conversation sooner. "Survive what?"

Zephyr appeared puzzled. "You, Doctor, should know better than most. The world you call home is now confronting the deadliest of perils. We must activate the Vessafra before time expires. The Vesikyar key is essential to finding it."

Olga turned to her side to face Shigeru and Zephyr. She pushed golden hair from her cheek as she said, "What is the nature of this key?"

He said, "It is stored within the genomes of the Vesiks, an eight-part cipher recoverable from you only under the correct circumstances."

Shigeru asked the natural question. "What does it open?"

Zephyr said, "We believe it will open the path to the Vessafra."

Shigeru found this irritating. "What sort of path?" He waited as the Ghyan said nothing.

Olga beat him to the punch. "You don't know, do you?" she asked.

Zephyr's jaw tightened as he looked away from them. Turning back, he gave a slow nod. "You're correct, Professor. No Ghyan knows the precise nature of it."

Shigeru asked, "Then who put this Vessafra thing here in the first place?"

The Ghyan hesitated as Olga lifted herself on her elbow. She said, "You don't know whether you can trust us."

Zephyr's electric green eyes studied her. Shigeru felt a flash of pity for him, recognizing his expression as one he'd seen when delivering worst-case medical opinions to terminal patients. He found himself conflicted, upset that their host would withhold critical information, but he also could see the anguish. He surprised himself by his restraint. "I understand if you believe it's a risk to tell us the truth. But I would still insist."

Olga seconded him. "As scientists, our curiosity is insatiable, by design. Please, can you indulge us? What is the Vessafra?"

Zephyr shut his eyes, as if the answer might sit somewhere deeper inside of him. He spoke slowly. "I regret requiring your trust. Again, I am authorized to reveal only what I've shared so far. Straying from the prescription can only increase the risk."

Olga's thoughtful eyes danced around the room. "You're talking about a simulation."

Shigeru caught a hint of delight from Zephyr's otherwise distressed expression. The Ghyan said, "Indeed. Yes, I've relied upon strategy maps developed by an intelligent—"

Olga interrupted him. "The Vessafra is a computer!"

Shigeru sank into his chair at the thought. He envisioned walls of computing panels, much like devices his parents used in their work decades past. Zephyr's eyes widened with joy impossible to hide. "Good, Professor. The Vessafra is a superintelligence, a vast organic computer capable of coordinating the Katafaj. There is no greater power than that of the mind, and no greater an evil should that power pass into the wrong hands."

Shigeru tugged at his bolo tie. "Crossing dimensions doesn't matter. Everyone builds weapons too powerful for they themselves to handle."

Olga clicked her tongue at that. "They couldn't have created it, Shigeru. Otherwise, they'd access it more easily."

Zephyr said, "Well, he is partly right. You see—" He drifted before he reported, "We're arriving now. Should we succeed in our next few steps, there will be more to share."

Shigeru hopped to his feet. "We're already there?"

Zephyr gestured, conjuring a bright hologram of Earth's unmistakable surface. Their trajectory sparkled as he said, "It could have been mere minutes had we operated at maximum speed." He widened the landing point with his hands. "There is Miss Voyant's homestead, though—" He paused, cocking his head.

Olga asked, "What do you see?"

He waited a moment longer before replying. "There are other signals present there, a small militia, judging by their armaments."

Shigeru's throat tightened. "Are they more of your kind?"

Zephyr didn't wait to speak. "No, they're Falterrans. I've found no evidence that Miss Voyant nearby."

This disturbed Shigeru, weighing on his conscience for ignoring the American for so long. "They must have taken her."

Zephyr shook his head. "Unlikely. These appear in search of her."

Shigeru frowned at the hologram as it expanded into a chunk of land topped with a single house. "Can't we ask them?"

The Ghyan adjusted the image to show at least ten figures infesting Voyant's home. Zephyr said, "I do not believe we can interact without escalation."

Olga sat upright, surprising Shigeru with her question. "Wouldn't the circumstances justify it?"

Touching images within the hologram, Zephyr said, "It isn't necessary. Norcross hasn't been here, but I've found traces of our technology." The translucent house expanded, opening its rooms to reveal green sparks. Pointing to them, he said, "These are discharge exposures a focus stone."

Shigeru reached for the sprites, irked that they disappeared when in contact with his flesh. "What is that?"

Zephyr's countenance brightened. "A singular tool, rare even on Ghya."

Shigeru wasn't short on snark. "Yeah, but what is it, exactly?"

He was unfazed by it, opting to say, "It would have been entrusted to one of the Vesiks a long time ago by someone dear to me. It means he may actually know who the others are."

Olga shifted her weight with the aim of standing. Shigeru braced her as he said, "No, no, let's not stand up. You're still weak."

She complained, "I want to see the image closer. There's something there."

Zephyr adjusted the landscape. "What do you see?"

She jabbed a finger into one of the hills at a tiny orange sprite. "That." She reluctantly leaned into Shigeru.

Zephyr zoomed to the figure. "It appears to be nonhuman. A canine."

Shigeru felt his heart flutter. "Voyant's website shows her with a dog—it was a retriever, I think."

Olga said, "It would be strange that she would leave without the dog. My sister and her kids would never be parted from theirs."

Zephyr nodded. "We must secure this animal."

Shigeru frowned at that. "You just said you don't want to interact with the people there. Now you wish to rescue a dog?"

Zephyr spoke quickly. "Doctor Nakamura, soon, this craft will no longer fly. We cannot hope to capture a fuel replacement without the help of other Vesiks. This canine may hold the key to finding Miss Voyant." He turned to reopen his control station. "And you must capture the animal."

Shigeru eased Olga back to the gyrokinetabed before following him. "Me?"

He said, "The professor must convalesce a bit more, and I must remain aboard while we are airborne. You'll be fine." Zephyr emerged from his control station with a small earbud and a slab of dried meat. "Canines here, if at all similar to those on Ghya. Besides, this female is distraught, searching for her master. She'll respond well to a sympathetic biped."

Taking the stinky jerky in hand, Shigeru plugged his left ear canal with the bud. "How will I get down there?"

Zephyr flipped the holoimage as he fingered a region of trees. "I can release you there."

"Won't they see us?" Shigeru asked.

This amused the Ghyan for some reason. He said, "We can bend light, making it difficult for them to detect us even with infrared scanners. But we cannot conceal the exhaust temperature for more than a few minutes, so you must work fast." He turned his head at the small whine. "We're almost in position. The skytax's port below will be our best means."

Shigeru followed the Ghyan's finger with his eyes. The brilliant white of the floor split open to reveal a blur of winter-bare trees. The ground rose to meet the portal. He had a passing interest in aviation, though leaving the ground was more fun than returning to it. There was a hum in his earbud, followed by Zephyr's mellifluous voice. Knowing a sound test when he heard one, he gave a thumbs up. Muttering to himself, he said, "I'm a doctor, not a dog-catcher, dammit."

The portal crackled with energy as outside atmosphere filled the chamber. The hovering was so seamless, he couldn't tell they hadn't landed. Part of a flooring gave way to a few steps leading to the muddy glade bottom below.

Olga said, "Be careful, Doctor."

Zephyr motioned to the portal. "Please, make haste."

Shigeru huffed at him. "Alright, alright." He moved down the steps into winter air. His shoes squished into the all-too-wet soil, pissing him off.

The glade wasn't unlike those in his home province half a world away, but the smell of cooking hickory was distinct. He looked up, but only empty sky ensconced by craggy branches was above him. Voyant's house was a little more than modest but a lot less his style, considering her husband was a physician. He couldn't see the agents invading her home, but he already found himself hating them.

Zephyr's voice appeared in his head. "Doctor, the canine in question is twenty meters due east."

Shigeru said, "Christ, this dog better be worth it." He looked for the sun before asking, "Which direction is east? The sun is close to noon."

The voice in his head answered, "Directly away from the house. As you exit the glade, there is a hill downward. The animal is wandering below."

Shigeru sank his right foot into a puddle, soaking himself with chilly water. Easing himself from the trees, he could see deep into the valley before him. The view was breathtaking enough that he could understand the choice by Miss Voyant and her husband to live there. They were far enough from civilization for comfort. But that paired poorly with the government agents clawing through their things—nowhere was safe.

Zephyr's voice appeared once more. "You should be able to see her soon."

Shigeru squinted to make out the detail ahead of him. He could see the golden dog, though she appeared to be injured. Worse yet, she was in trouble.

She sat muddied, trapped between three wolves and a black bear. "Fuck me," he said. Holding the piece of jerky, he felt wholly ill-prepared to face them. He whispered to Zephyr, "There are wolves and a goddamned bear. This dog has gotten herself into a terrible scrape."

Zephyr said, "Scanning. Yes, four predators. It appears she has a broken leg."

Shigeru replied, "I can fucking see that. What am I supposed to do?"

He said, "A superior show of strength will overcome these."

Shigeru gasped in anger. "And what is my superior strength? I'm not a tiger. Can't you do something?"

He said, "A sonic pulse to frighten them would alert our enemies. Besides, an intensity sufficient to neutralize the animals would risk rendering you unconscious. Soon, I'll be in position to stop them. But you must distract them from the dog."

Shigeru pressed his finger hard into the earbud. "I don't fucking believe it. You come from another dimension to save us, but I have to fight a bear?"

Olga hollered over Zephyr. "Posture, Shigeru. Posture."

"Since when are you a bear-wrangler?" he said in a quiet but infuriated tone.

The bear angled its head as it became aware of Shigeru, as did the poor dog. She whimpered at him as the wolves encircled her, all growling in anticipation of their meal. He decided immediately that she owed her life, at least for the moment feral nature permitted, to the standoff between implacable predators, a symbolism not lost on Shigeru.

He heard Zephyr say, "Alacrity, Doctor. Our time is short."

This incensed him as he searched around for a defensive weapon. Large sticks and stones were the sum total of his search. He began by tossing rocks at the wolves, enraging the largest of the three gray-and-white monsters. The black bear waited, as though it understood that the crying retriever would be only the first course. He pelted the wolves with rock after rock, with only one out of four hitting them. Some rocks were small, and others heavy. He cut his hand on one of them as he struggled to maintain a steady stream of sailing projectiles. It absolutely sickened him to hurt the animals, but this was a question of least ugly among all ugly choices.

At last, the wolves fled, all, he figured, deemed the risk to great for just one supper. They howled and cried, a relief for him in not wounding them worse.

Zephyr said, "That's it, Doctor. Soon, you can collect the canine."

Shigeru was panting from the throws, his right shoulder burning from overuse. He sucked in air as he complained. "Just how do I deal with this fucking bear?"

The dog yelped as the bear advanced. He took a step towards it, causing the behemoth to stand. It took no scientific inquiry to understand that the bear was trying to frighten him, and frightened he was. He tossed a stone in the direction of his furry foe, startling it into an even taller formation.

Zephyr said, "The bear is afraid, Doctor. Advancing on it will cause it to retreat."

Shigeru wiped sweat from his brow, shocked at the level of perspiration in December air. He took a step forward, only to trip over a gnarly tree root exposed from soil erosion. He stumbled to the mossy mud, landing on his hands and wrists. "Fuck!" he shouted.

The monster lumbered towards him as he fought to free his foot from the root tangle. To his utter shock, the wounded dog screamed at the bear. Shigeru looked up to see the bear reeling on the retriever as she heaved herself towards a hopeless end. His heart sank at such a thing—the dog would die in defense of an immoral scoundrel such as himself.

She reached the bear as it approached him. Shigeru pulled as hard as he could on his trapped foot, ripping out of his shoe. Looking up, he saw the retriever sink her teeth into the bear's hindquarters. It roared, pivoting about as it slapped the comparably tiny prey. She screeched in agony as the bear's massive claws sent her flying.

Shigeru rolled to his back, then sat up as the bear loomed over him. Zephyr's voice echoed in his ear. "I'm almost into position. You carry polyplasts from your healing sessions with Olga—use them!"

The monster fell onto Shigeru, near-crushing him. He reached for the animal's throat, and once his fingers connected with its flesh, he could feel the tiny machines flow into it. The animal convulsed as they spread into its bloodstream—he directed them to move towards the bear's heart as he energized them for an electric discharge.

He could feel the bits struggle against blood currents, clawing their way along arterial walls. Between heartbeats, they made great progress crawling to the animal's cardiac muscle. As they gathered there, he gauged how much force would be required to stop the beast. He closed his eyes as the creature fell under his control. The tens of thousands of polyplasts fought into the cardiac plexus, affixing themselves to the nerve bundle en masse.

Zephyr's voice sounded in his head once more. "That's it, Doctor!"

Shigeru whispered at the break in his concentration. "I don't want to kill the bear."

Zephyr answered, "Visualize the kinetic curve."

He could see it at last, in a space between life and death. Thinking as hard as he could, he felt the swarm of machines expend their energies, shocking the animal into arrythmia. It groaned in pain as it rolled off Shigeru and down the hillside.

Shigeru gasped with barely the strength needed to breathe. He kept his eyes squeezed shut as the connection to the polyplasts dissipated. But he knew he couldn't rest in that moment—Miss Voyant's dog needed his help. He swung himself up to see the bear shivering at the foot of the hill. Shigeru wouldn't waste a moment as he wrenched his shoe free of the tree root, jammed his foot into it, then rushed the twenty meters where the dog lay.

Once on his feet, he could hear voices from the direction of the house. He made out the words, "There's someone there in the glade," along with, "Dammit, the area was supposed to be clear."

Shigeru dropped to his knees next to the ailing dog. He palpated her to decide she'd broken more than just her leg. She turned her head to him, nosing him with her long golden snout. A single lick of his hand said it all—she thanked him for saving her life.

He said, "She's in trouble. We need to get her out of here, but I heard voices above. They're coming."

Zephyr replied, "I've placed a device to distract and subdue them, far enough that you and the animal will suffer minimally. Stand by."

Shigeru patted the dog as he read her tag. "There, there, Aurum, is it? That's a beautiful name for a beautiful dog."

Zephyr said, "Initiating the pulse now."

Shigeru felt a tingling in his ears while Aurum glanced back and forth anxiously. He heard a voice say, "What the hell is that? It's coming from over there!"

He scooped the retriever into his arms as he saw light flash nearby out of thin air. Zephyr said, "The way is clear, so make your way quickly."

He stood, taking care not to hurt the poor dog. "I intended to take my time, Zeff," he said with snark he imagined was appropriate. With as few steps as he could take, he reached the portal. Steps formed to the ground, and as he climbed them, Zephyr reached from above to take Aurum in hand. He said, "Careful, she's badly injured."

As he took each step, the one before it disappeared. It all seemed to miraculous for him, but he felt as though he'd been electrocuted. Zephyr intertwined his arm with Shigeru's, schlepping him into the skytax portal. Once inside, he fell to the floor with vertigo.

Olga knelt beside him, herself winded. "Are you okay, Shigeru?"

He asked his own query. "How is Aurum?"

Zephyr had placed the dog on an examination table which hadn't been there before. He said, "Her wounds are deep, and, frankly, Doctor, I need your help."

Olga protested on Shigeru's behalf, pleasing him. "He's exhausted, Zephyr. Can you not heal the dog? You stabilized my condition."

Zephyr shook his head as he touched Aurum's soft fur. "I do not possess the strength now to coordinate the polyplasts. Doctor Nakamura is the only one here capable of that. And I must focus on our more immediate objective of locating the Vesiks."

Shigeru pushed himself to his feet. "What about the people outside?"

Zephyr nodded with a wink. "We're two hundred meters above them, unreachable. The sonic pulse slowed them."

Olga allowed Shigeru to help her back to the gyrokinetabed. She asked, "The emitter you placed? Won't they find it?"

He grinned at them. "Most Ghyan tools and technology can decompose into constituent molecules, rendering it invisible. The approach is not unlike that apparent to polyplasts."

After settling her back the energy bed, Shigeru joined him where Aurum lay unconscious. He said, "How will she lead us to the others?"

Zephyr pet the animal with genuine affection. "Many of the mammals domesticated in this world possess Ghyan analogues. They develop a kind of psychic link with their primary companion, and this is no exception."

Shigeru touched her, and his fingertips were electric. But he was depleted. "Zeff, I don't know whether I can help her. I can barely sense the polyplasts."

The Ghyan left the table for a moment, leaving Olga open to ask, "If this animal was so close to Miss Voyant, why would she leave her?"

Zephyr spoke as he joined Shigeru once more, now holding a small metallic tube which he handed to the doctor. "That's a very good question, but fortunate for us. With the energy signature from the focus stone, along with her connection to this animal, we can extrapolate a path."

The tube became freezing cold, then burning hot as he held it. He complained, "Damn, that's not comfortable."

Zephyr patted his shoulder. "I regret asking you to do so much, but this is your part to play, Doctor. The polyplasts will enter you shortly, after which you will neuroprint them to your will. I sense that the canine's injuries are restricted to broken bones, so you should be able to repair the damage with minor incident."

He felt them as the tube disintegrated in his hand. He could hear them inside his head, like a swarm of bees. He struggled to control them. "Jesus, I don't know if I can do this, Zephyr." The Ghyan simply touched his neck, and he felt a bit stronger.

He shot the polyplasts from his fingertips into Aurum's back muscles, and she whimpered at the discomfort. He could feel them move to ribs broken into her left lung, so he dispatched the army into each damaged region, moving bones back into place, welding them together with bone-adhering calcium gel. The swarm closed her lung while draining fluid into fatty tissue closer to the surface of her skin.

He covered her fractured femur with the microscopic healing machines, spraying and welding to reconnect severed parts. He could barely keep his eyes open as he finished the work, amazed that he felt more exhausted now than in any marathon he ran in his youth.

Zephyr squeezed Shigeru's shoulder. "You've done well, Doctor. She'll be fine now. And we can search for Miss Voyant now."

A gyrokinetachair formed behind Shigeru, catching him as he fell. Aurum turned her head towards his, and he reached for her gentle but weary face. She licked his hand once more, and he lost consciousness.

26. Heart of Picoveer

F***

Frankie found the descent even worse than takeoff. The flyboy suit he wore hugged his frame too hard, and he felt his flesh scrape against the rough fabric with every bump and shudder of the machine around him. Once they'd taxied, Air Force full-dressed variants of Hazel and the Lord came to collect him.

She grinned with crazily enlarged eyes in her reading glasses. "A snug fit is good for ya, Frankie." She reached for his crotch, cupping it in a gnarly hand at the same time she patted his butt.

Wrenching himself from her, he asked the Lord, "So what do you wanna do, now that we're here?"

The Lord said, "Hazel Grant and I can attend to recruiting the other Vesiks. You would probably enjoy Varnum more, and this could be your final opportunity to meet one you consider so great."

Frankie favored his handless arm with the other as Hazel tied the laces in his boots. He recoiled, but she held him still. "Just like a spoiled little shit of a toddler. I can teach ya, though."

He tried to ignore the grotesque distortion of a woman by focusing on Norcross. "You won't need my help?"

He answered, "I do not believe you are strong enough to confront them, and it's best to limit Our exposure."

Hazel opened an adjoining locker to fish out a tan insulator vest. Tossing it to Frankie, she said with as much of a blush as she could muster, "I seldom ask a man to put his clothes *on*."

The Lord laughed as He helped Frankie pull the vest over his shoulders. "Now, as far as Our friends outside are concerned, you are Lieutenant Putnam, and I am General Norcross."

Hazel asked, "Will You give me leave to make some kills?"

Frankie sighed in anger. "Can't you just let the Lord tell us what to do?"

She wheels about with mild irritation. "Goddamned toddler!" she called to him.

He shifted weight in his boots to test their tightness. Conflicted, he asked, "So why are You doing this for me?"

Norcross watched his chest as He pulled Frankie's vest taut to zip it closed. "It is important to Me that you believe in Our plan. And I would like you to have some of the things you want. Does that surprise you?" The vest tightened, immediately warming him.

Frankie couldn't stop himself from asking the obvious. "Is Varnum saved?"

Norcross adjusted the collar on Frankie's flight suit. "You ask difficult questions."

This left him more than a little miffed. "Why is it difficult?"

The Lord chuckled. "The answer isn't complex, but your feelings are."

Frankie asked, "Isn't it important? I've listened to him for years, and I wanna know that he's saved."

Norcross tightened the collar. "*That* instead of *if*. Can you cope if he is not?"

Frankie's face burned hot. "But he's helped me so much. Pastor Chet said he did work for Your kingdom—"

The Lord shrugged. "It depends on him. He isn't, strictly speaking, one of Us. But I task you with finding others for Our cause."

Frankie started to ask another question, but Hazel popped her head into the locker pod. "An executive vice president is here to receive Us, Lord."

He said, "General, if you please, Colonel Grant."

She saluted after attaching a camouflage cap feathery hair. "Yes, sir!" It was once more as if Hyde became Jekyll once more—she was all business.

Frankie followed Norcross and Hazel to a side door near the rear of the fuselage. By the time he was fifteen feet from the exit, he could feel cool air. Looking outside, he saw a staircase affixed to the metal skin of their airplane. Three people waited next to a spacious black limousine, all against a backdrop of large buildings kissed by large trees. A small and dapper Indian man said in a rapid voice, "General Norcross, welcome!"

Hazel elbowed Frankie in his ribcage. "Look at that monkey in a suit," she whispered.

Norcross bowed to the welcome reception. "Where is Mister Demmings?"

The speaker was nervous, though he tried to conceal it. "Well, he was stuck with other duties. But I'm certain he'd wished to be here for your surprise inspection. Gotta love 'em, right?"

Taking the little man's hand in His own, the Lord asked, "I am General Norcross, with Colonel Grant and Tech Sergeant Putnam."

He said, "I am Gaurav Chevur, executive vice president of Picoveer. How can we be of assistance?"

Norcross said, "Young Putnam would like to meet Varnum." Pointing to Frankie's wounded wrist, He said, "We would like to discharge My lieutenant in style after his accident."

Chevur's head bobbed from side to side. "Of course. The CEO supports any who serve our great nation, especially those injured in the line of duty, yes?"

Norcross glared at her, so she squeezed her smile into a frown. "Mister Chevur, I and Colonel Grant must travel within the campus—can you arrange this?"

He bobbed his head sideways again. "Of course, General. My assistants can transport you now. I'll personally escort Lieutenant Putnam to Nebula Hall where Mister Varnum will deliver his anticipated speech. His support for wounded soldiers is well-established." He raised a cell phone to his mouth. "Exec transport for two, runway A to Nebula, ASAP."

The phone beeped before replying with static. "Copy, Mister Chevur."

He lowered his phone as he said to the others, "Escort General Norcross and his colonel." He smiled, reaching for Frankie. "We support our wounded soldiers and veterans."

The radio squawked, mercifully cutting her off. "Sir, there's a minor security concern, so there will be a delay. Over."

Chevur looked to Norcross. "Problem with so few buildings operational, and Varnum requested extra security." He chuckled as he said it, adding, "Bohemian hecklers and the like."

Frankie wasn't amused, so he said, "He deserves to be safe," just as Hazel nudged him with her shoulder. He shot a look at her, and she motioned with her head to the Lord—Frankie was stunned once more by her own apparent self-control.

Norcross broke the moment by taking the executive's arm. "So Chevur, that's not entirely Indian, is it?"

He said, "A hypocorism, General. Short for Chevurnamenarpathy," he said with no change in his face.

Norcross didn't let her finish. "May we have an escort?"

Chevur's rubbery smooth face conveyed authenticity, though Frankie didn't buy it. "Of course. Which quad would you like to see, General?"

Norcross replied, "The Heart of Picoveer."

Chevur's plastic grin melted away. Regaining himself, he placed his little hands together. "With respect, General, the Heart is undergoing construction and is unsafe for visitors and other nonessential personnel." Norcross didn't budge, so he added, "I am certain there are plenty of completed structures within the campus of interest to—"

340

Norcross displayed his televangelist smile. "No matter the situation, I must examine the Heart Myself. I am certain My clearance overrides facility policy."

Chevur bobbed his head side-to-side once more. "Of course, General. If I may reach Mister Demmings for authorization, then—"

Norcross offered him a pad with text rendered. "I assumed you would have already seen this, no?"

Chevur's face whitened as he read it. He bobbed his head as he said, "Yes, yes, yes, yes. I see. Of course, General. You are most welcome, and I apologize that we were unprepared for you. Since the acquisition, our communications with corporate Kymara have been profuse."

Chevur glanced to his Asian assistants. "Take the general and His colonel to the Heart."

They lurched into action, one rushing to a black SUV parked nearby while the other offered a hand to Hazel. She said, "Please, Colonel, come with me."

Hazel nodded in agreement, donning her dyke military persona. Noting Chevur's back turned to them, she licked a finger and touched Frankie's stump. Chevur turned back to her, and she pulled herself together once more.

The timid executive paid no mind to her, instead leaning towards Norcross to say, "The situation at Heart is difficult. My assistants do not possess the clearance necessary to enter it, but I shall have Mister Demmings meet you in the northern lot."

Norcross placed a hand on Frankie's shoulder. "Lieutenant Putnam is your charge, Mister Chevur." He turned, joined the others, and they departed.

Chevur said, "I suppose you wouldn't be permitted to say, even if you knew the truth. But what does the general intend to investigate at the Heart?"

Frankie looked over to the corporate buildings next to the runway as the SUV disappeared among them. "I honestly don't know." He wanted to add, *And I'm not important enough to the Lord.*

Chevur motioned that Frankie follow him to a neat electric convertible parked twenty feet away. "Come, let's get you to see Varnum. He's always happy to meet his fans."

B***

Boothby rocked in his seat, anxious but excited. Maybe elation was a better word. After so many years operating solo under derisive vitriol vomited by contemporary analysts, scientists, and even other serious ufologists like himself, he stood ready to receive his vindication. The lights were real, and now he knew how to bring them. But he was grateful for the others.

The agents frightened him, but he felt more at ease knowing Axley and Carolina were helping them. Kymara and Dana Best were fascinating bonuses to the intrigue into which he, and now Archie the cat, stumbled. From his vantage in the rear of the van, he could see building after building within the complex. Carolina said, "Picoveer's closures left these buildings bereft of utilities."

Reuben sighed. "What a waste."

Axley pointed ahead to a turn-off. "It's a new world. But remote work is less likely for this arm of Kymara, considering they do classified work. But Dana Best is not one to tolerate any waste. They'll use these structures eventually."

Archie purred at Boothby, and he looked to his lap to see the cat sprawled on his back, full tummy exposed. He stroked the soft fur, marveling at him. "Aren't ya the little slut today, Archie."

Adam asked, "Did I hear you say that you're afraid of animals?"

Boothby shrugged. "Well, we all hafta adapt."

Reuben shook his head. "We all have our crosses to bear, I suppose."

Conique shushed him. "Dear, that's ugly."

Axley took his turn to shout. "Okay, people, let's keep it all tight."

Boothby stiffened his muscles as best he could. "Jeez, I hope you don't want me to stay this way for long."

Reuben glanced back at him. "He means be quiet, Boothby."

Conique whispered loudly, "That includes *you*, dear."

Axley said, "Okay, that structure ahead is our destination—Picoveer's Heart."

Boothby couldn't see much of it from his seat, but it was a sprawling building, if one could even call it that. There were six floors above the ground, but Boothby guessed there were that many if not more below.

Adam said, "They're building a reactor inside there?"

Carolina replied, "A microreactor, but still dangerous."

Axley added his own explanation. "It isn't the reactor we want—Obfucius said the nuclear fuel is stored deeper in the complex. By itself, it isn't that risky to possess it."

They pulled the van to a receiving dock as four security orbited the vehicle, making notes. Axley showed their chief a document before saying, "We have executive business here in the Heart."

The security chief read the document as Boothby tapped the floor once more in crippling anxiety. Reuben hissed with his whisper. "Goddammit, Boothby, stop jostling the seat!"

Janet touched his arm, with strength amidst her weakness. "It's okay to be scared."

He was relieved when the chief gestured that Axley take his party farther into the dock. He then walked towards the building as he spoke into his portable radio.

Boothby strained to glimpse the Heart, a monument to engineering. He wished he could spend years parsing their programs and discoveries. But there would be no time for that now.

The chief returned to Axley, motioning that those inside the van exit. A guard pulled open the sliding side door while Carolina and Axley exited. Reuben looked to his wife with apprehension while Adam said, "I don't want to leave you here, babycakes."

Janet said, "It's okay. I'll be fine with Miss Voyant, and they need your help more than mine."

Boothby watched Archie as he hopped into Conique's lap. He said, "I think the little guy wants to stay with you."

She cheered at that, explaining to Reuben, "He'll keep us safe here."

Carolina lent a hand to the physician as she said, "I promise you, Doctor Hamora. Your wife and Nurse Yazzie will be safe with me."

Boothby glanced wildly. "I wouldn't tangle with her, Doctor."

Axley said, "Come, Doctor, Nurse Baumgartl, Boothby. We have precious little time."

The security chief eyed Boothby with clear brown peepers. "You have a shifty face, sir."

Boothby cleared his throat, deciding he'd play hardball. "I'll have ya know, Mister Chief, I play nine rounds of golf with Dana's grandsons every week. You don't want the negative attention I can bring, do ya?"

The chief shrank from him, doffing his hat. "Sorry, sir. We're supposed to suspect everything."

Boothby replied flatly, "And nothing. Yeah, I get it."

Axley interrupted them. "Apologies, but we're on a tight schedule. This emergency inspection needs to be done by EOD. Doctor, sirs, let us go."

The chief asked, "Why are your other guests remaining out here?"

Boothby bared his teeth. "Do ya bring your wife, or, umm, husband into the Heart? We all travel together."

Conique said, "It's quite the commune, Officer."

The chief regarded her with scrutiny. "I'll bet it is, ma'am. I'm guessing this has nothing to do with Varnum's visit here?"

Carolina answered without delay. "We intend to accomplish our inspection while the riffraff acolytes fawn across campus."

After handing him four solid white badges, the chief directed Axley to the door ahead. "Well, I'd rather be working, so there ya go."

Axley, Boothby, Reuben, and Adam headed for the entrance. Boothby examined the badge, astonished that it didn't contain a single visible letter or image. Adam said, "We're so important, we don't have anything to show for it?"

Axley said, "Executive VIP badges conceal identities rather than explain them. Shareholders, government leaders, and the like carry them here. They signal we be left to do our work free of interruption."

Boothby clipped his badge to his coat as he said, "Amazing that I finally became a rich mogul."

Reuben clicked his tongue. "Without the riches, though."

The path ahead led to two glass doors twenty or so feet tall. But the glass was completely black, making Boothby wonder why one would go to the trouble of having a glass door. They parted, opening into a large reception area.

Reuben said, "With so many waiting areas, it's amazing they get anything done."

A lone receptionist awaited them, a girl dressed to the nines with beautiful hair, skin, and eyes. Axley nodded to her, saying in a hushed voice, "Since Kymara's acquisition, picture-perfect employees are expected at all levels."

Adam said, "So much for the casual tech world."

The receptionist said, "I'm Denise Terrell, and I'm pleased to welcome you to Picoveer's Heart. CEO Demmings would have been happy to greet you himself, but he's a huge fan of Varnum."

Boothby chuckled. "Who isn't?"

Reuben asked, "You're not interested in hearing him?"

She laughed as she scanned each of their badges with her gorgeously manicured hands. "I hear plenty. But some of us can't take off the time, as your surprise inspection explains well. Now, Agent, can you place your weapons in the holding locker number eight?"

Axley unholstered his pistol with a careful sigh. He handed it to Denise, but she dodged it.

"No, no, Agent. You can place it in the locker yourself," she said. She glanced at the others. "No other firearms?"

Reuben said, "They're not my favorite thing, no."

Axley opened the small locker, set the weapon down, then closed the door. He flashed a smile at her. "All unarmed."

She clearly warmed to him, making Boothby wonder what he did wrong when it came to his own intimate relationships. "Where are you going first?"

Axley looked up to Reuben, the hulking man standing over him by at least eight inches. He then said, "Microreactor. DOE needs to capture some additional data on it."

She typed into her pad. "Hmm, DOE inspected last week, too."

Axley said curtly, "That must be a mistake."

Denise frowned as she hit a few buttons on her pad. "No, they were definitely here. I checked them in myself."

Adam played along beautifully. "They always forget the little things, so here we are to clean it all up."

Reuben cut through the chatter. "We should move along the inspection, if we want to finish it on time."

Axley glared at him, but Denise was quick to say, "Of course. I don't wish to slow you up, so let me take you all down." She closed her station before rounding the elongated desk and station, clattering her high heels on the tile. "I'll open the way." She walked to a corridor behind the desk to manipulate an interface on the wall.

Axley whispered to Reuben and the others, "Let me do the fucking talking, gents."

Reuben rolled his eyes. "You're doing such a bang up job, man."

She turned to them. "Please, accompany me."

As they continued down the corridor, Boothby asked, "How long have ya worked here, Miss Terrell?"

She laughed. "Call me Denise, sir. I've worked with Carlyle since he cofounded Kymara a decade ago. He calls me his *political handler*."

Adam said, "That sounds more like public relations."

She laughed once more. "No, that's for everyone else out there. Government types such as yourselves require special care."

Boothby said, "So you've been here since the beginning. What do ya know about Dana Best?"

She didn't miss a beat. "You fellas do your homework. Yes, Mister Best is now our all-powerful deity, promising to bring efficiency back into the office."

Reuben breathed steadily as they plodded forward. "That doesn't sound like a glowing endorsement."

She shrugged. "Carl was okay with it. Who am I to question that? Like it or not, that's the new business model. Besides, your cousins at the SEC could have nixed the whole thing."

Axley said, "DOE, SEC, they may get paid by the same treasury, but we're on different planets."

Boothby looked around the stark white hallway as he said, "This looks a lot like a hospital to me."

Denise said, "White shows dirt, forcing everyone to be on their toes about clean rooms and careful experiments. Even the slightest smudge receives attention quickly." She pointed to one Boothby had just made with his black-soled shoes. He heard a woosh sound as a small panel of the wall opened, releasing a drone which homed in on the mess he'd made.

Adam said, "I'd love to have that for my apartment."

Boothby watched the small drone buff the floor to its former sheen before it returned to the wall. Denise said, "It's one of the advantages of having Intellidez under Kymara's umbrella. They supply the clean-up staff, we build smaller and smaller robots."

The layout of Picoveer's Heart confounded Boothby no end. Every hallway looked the same, with the blearing white floors and walls an almost torture to behold.

He understood functional designs, but this was ridiculous. He couldn't even make out where the lighting was hidden—maybe it was embedded in the walls everywhere.

The Picoveer admin leading them appeared just as spotless. Her complexion was perfect, with symmetric features, a fit form, and deep blue eyes. Her makeup was obvious but elegant. Boothby knew little about the newer management, but Carlyle Demmings had become a folk hero among nuclear and nanotech sciences. Of Kymara's three original founders, he'd happened into greater notoriety than his counterparts—his leadership style was reckless, fraught with midnight messages tormenting those beneath him into spending more and more time working on his projects.

Denise would have been a perfect fit for him—she was all image and personality. Her high heels clicked again and again on the pure white floor, aggravating him. She continued talking, clearly beyond Axley's preference. It did make Boothby wonder whether he was gay, a prospect he wouldn't reject. But the OCD-type didn't work for Boothby, as he'd discovered years earlier.

Denise said, "Carl and I worked together before Kymara and Picoveer. I always believed he could change the world."

Reuben surprised Boothby with his depth of knowledge, considering he appeared reluctant in believing any of the mess before them. He said, "I read that Picoveer was working on fusion."

She didn't halt her repetitive steps, but she did glance at him. "Yes, Carl believes we'll have something commercially viable in another decade."

Adam said, "I thought there isn't a way to contain the reaction."

Boothby chuckled. "Well, the sun ain't exactly contained, but it's pretty much the whole shebang."

Axley intervened a bit. "We must focus, team. Our inspection is—"

Denise completed his sentence. "Of the utmost priority, right?" She elbowed at him with a strange expression on her face. "Relax, Agent Axley. We're almost to the microreactor."

Boothby looked around them. "I don't understand. We've just been walking in the same corridor."

She laughed. "Well, we're almost to the central lift with service to almost all floors in the Heart."

Ahead, the corridor dead-ended into a seamless white wall. She removed a connector from her pocket as Adam said, "That's unexpected."

She plugged her device into a spot hidden from them, and the wall parted to reveal a large elevator. Gesturing for them, she said, "Gentleman, if you please."

Reuben said, "Well, I would say, 'Ladies, first,' but—"

She gave him a kindly smile. "Go on, sir."

Boothby hovered close to Adam and Agent Axley while Denise punched buttons on her pad. He said, "It doesn't seem like anyone is in the office today. I mean, I know Varnum is here."

She said, "Well, this is one of the few buildings in operation, and most employees don't have access. There are people here, but Carl, as I said, encouraged everyone to spectate." Her pad beeped, so she glanced at it. "We're at level phi, microreactor access."

The elevator doors parted to reveal a large lab with several cubicles. In the center was a mammoth cylindrical shaft of clear glass holding a medley of casings, tubes, and computer circuits constituting the partly constructed reactor. She said, "Be my guests, gentlemen."

They stepped into the lab, and the air was chilly. Boothby was happy he'd worn his heavy coat, even if he'd made a mess of it earlier in his long journey. Once out of the lift, he turned back to Denise as she pressed a few buttons on her pad. She glanced up, connecting her eyes with Boothby's. He felt himself sink as she waited behind them. He said, "Wait, there ain't anyone to help us in here."

She tapped more keys before she said, "Please hold for a message from Carl Demmings."

Behind her, the blank wall fizzled to life, focusing on Carlyle Demmings's almost pig-shaped face. He said, "Mister E.G. Boothby, Doctor Reuben Hamora, Nurse Adam Baumgartl, and, of course, NSA's own Agent Jason Axley, welcome to Picoveer. I can't help feeling a bit underwhelmed at your showing here."

The figure of Denise winked before dissolving into the myriad photons making her visible. Reuben gasped as Boothby clawed for his own throat. He said, "A hologram? Jeezus, I had no idea they were so advanced!"

Reuben swatted his shoulder. "C'mon, man, that's the thing in this situation with which you take issue? What about piggy Eckhart Tolle there?" He jerked his head at Demmings' image. "I demand you release us."

Demmings laughed menacingly as his image popped from the wall to fill the elevator with a projection of his torso and ugly features. "That's a great one, Doctor. You're intruders in my lab, here to do God knows what. Sounds like I'm the one in the superior legal position."

Boothby croaked as he tried to speak, his anxiety flaring almost to the fill-line. Shrinking from the gigantic hologram, he said, "Umm, we're not trying to steal anything. We just need to know—"

Demmings interrupted him. "Industrial espionage and treason by the NSA's bumbling Agent Axley, criminal mischief and sabotage by Plowshares' very own Reuben Hamora, and even if Adam Baumgartl is merely small fry if not an outright technoterrorist. But you're the real enigma here, Mister Boothby. By all accounts, you're a straitjacket waiting to strap up. Maybe it's too many chromosomes, or too few."

Reuben pushed on Axley. "Say something!"

He said, "This isn't possible. Obfucius has kept the trust."

Demmings bellowed almost a cartoon villain laugh, unnerving Boothby. "Relax, Agent. Your contact remains anonymous, despite my best efforts to find him. But he didn't count on Kharla Series Seven. She's the real McCoy, friends."

Axley's face drained of all color. "The AI system here? How did she—"

Demmings pointed at the room as the image of Denise replaced his, huge and terrifying. "Did you like her appearance? Doctor Hamora, we detected a definite physiological response from you when you saw her. We'll try not to tell your wife."

Reuben frowned. "Say whatever you want, you bastard."

She leaned forward, pulling at her own breasts. But it was Demmings' voice they heard when she opened her mouth. "Mister Boothby, Nurse Baumgartl, you're not swayed by her feminine charms. Sorry to say but Kharla's male form isn't ready for your tastes. Axley, you're a puzzle."

He replied in anger, "Get to the point, Demmings."

The CEO reappeared in place of the giant female. "Kharla flagged the urgent inspection request as sabotage. So, she and I did some digging. Turns out that none of you belong here. Kharla believes, like me, that there is a major whistleblower in the company."

Axley said, "That sounds like your problem."

Demmings frowned even as he snickered. "It's your problem, now. I happen to know that none of you left any indication that this was your destination. Kharla is especially adept at crawling the web, scraping terabytes for that one single morsel of truth. Computing is a marvel, I'm telling you."

Reuben's defiance astounded and impressed Boothby. The elder physician said, "Maybe you can ask Kharla to solve this without our help."

Demmings was a little miffed at that. "Activists—you're all the same, desperate to be a hero in a world that doesn't need you."

Adam's response startled Boothby even more. "I think you have that wrong, Mister CEO. You're the one society doesn't need."

Demmings replied, "Enough bullshit. I want to know your contact, Axley. You're going to help me find out who it is. And you'll pay for making me miss Varnum's speech."

Reuben shook his head in disgust. "Garbage in, garbage out."

Demmings smirked at him. "I have to say I like you, Doctor. It's too bad your secrets will cost you your lives. Including those of Conique Voyant and Janet Yazzie. Agent Carolina will prove easy to overcome, and I fear she may not survive the encounter. Who knows how many stray bullets there could be, right, Doctor Hamora?"

Reuben breathed hard. "You damned sunuvabitch. You'd better let us out of here."

Adam seconded him. "You hurt Janet or the others, and I'll fuck you up."

Demmings grinned at him. "I'm amazed at your resolve. But I don't think there's any help coming. If you give me what I want, I'll free you all."

Axley frowned. "Demmings, you know that even if we knew our contact's identity, we couldn't release it."

This appeared to agree with the monstrous projection. "Yes, Agent, I believe you. If you knew it, Kharla would have figured it out. But you can help me by explaining why you are here. What brings together so unlikely a team? Voodoo demented faith healer, nut-ball ufologist, counterculture nurses from Tucson, and two mediocre agents assigned to ferret secrets from Kymara? Why?" His smile disappeared as his nostrils flared. "Why, I ask again?"

Axley held his ground. "These are innocents, Carl. You don't want their blood on your hands."

Boothby felt the focus stone in his pocket, and it hit him like a bolt from the blue that the tool likely gave him the upper hand. His nerves stilled, and he said, "I can give you something bigger than Obfucius, but ya hafta release us first."

Demmings looked down at him. "An autographed copy of *Light Watching*? I would guess you have truckloads of them in your ratty condo. Then again, it burned to the ground." None laughed at his tasteless humor, so he continued, "What could you possibly offer? You've come up empty-handed, no matter what the little voices in your head have been telling you."

Boothby laughed with him at that. "Yeah, yeah, laugh it up. But Obfucius wants me, not these others."

Axley shot a worried look at him, warning him by expression alone that his dialogue was unwise. Demmings folded his arms with interest. "Obfucius, such silly pomp and circumstance. Okay, moon-watcher, tell me why you're more valuable than Agents Axley and Carolina."

*J***

Janet rested quietly in the van while Conique conversed with Agent Carolina. She asked, "What made you want to work as a spy?"

Carolina shifted weight from one foot to the other, clearly uncomfortable standing for so long. "Well, ma'am, we don't typically call ourselves that."

The older woman conceded the point. "Sure, of course. Agent, then?"

Carolina looked around the van as she said, "My parents worked for the CIA, so I've never really known anything else."

Janet coughed as she leaned against the armrest. "Wow, that's severe."

Conique said, "Were they troubled at your orientation?"

Carolina guffawed at that, even if Janet worried that it was penetratingly personal. "It's a new century, Miss Voyant, even if some of the stodgy old bureaucrats haven't caught up. They knew I preferred construction sets and superheroes, and they encouraged it. No one messed with me when I was a kid if that's what you mean. Not even the bigger bullies would take me on, but every once in a while, I administered necessary crackdowns"

Conique was smiling, as though such a revelation had never troubled her. Janet was moved by her genuine acceptance, seeing a bit of herself in the steely woman. She then asked, "What do you think is happening in there?"

Carolina frowned. "I can't help but be worried, to be honest." She seated herself in the middle row of the van next to Conique, sighing as she eased off her feet. With a low voice, she answered, "Obfucius has never issued so urgent a request, meaning they're compromised in some way."

Janet asked, "Do you think it's not safe?"

Carolina looked away as the sunlight glinted in her mean and lean haircut. "I don't trust any of these Kymara wackos farther than I can throw them. They build these god-awful machines, scalp the world for riches, then disavow all consequences while warning about said consequences. Jesus." She then looked to Conique. "Sorry for the Lord's name in vain, Sister."

Conique laughed at that. "All I do is say names in vain, it seems."

Carolina said, "Hold that thought, ma'am. Something's wrong."

Janet pushed herself up somewhat, but she was too weak to see. "What is it?" she asked.

Carolina whispered with clear apprehension. "The security chief and his lackeys just left. They wouldn't abandon us here unless someone else was coming to take their place."

Conique asked with a childlike naïveté, "Might they be heading to lunch?"

"No, Miss Voyant. I'm worried there might be trouble." The agent's tone was earnest.

Conique then said, "Okay, Mister Archie, have it your way."

Janet watched a black blur of fur hop out of the van, prompting Carolina to call him. "Dammit, cat, come back!"

Conique said, "Boothby won't be happy." Her expression faded as she said, "This hasn't been my week for animals."

Janet started to ask further, but Carolina said, "That's trouble ahead." She squinted to see at least three white vans inbound. She then pulled binoculars from her coat pocket. "Oh, God," she said.

Conique asked, "Why trouble?"

Carolina said, "Private security with military grade armaments, way beyond what ought to be available this far into the facility. They give mercenaries a bad name. Besides, Picoveer deployed their AI system here for protection, so—"

Janet broke her line of reasoning. "Is it capable of knowing why we're here?"

Carolina shot a look to the imposing structure looming over them. "Shit," she said.

Conique moved herself to the edge of her seat, though Janet didn't think the kindly old woman could cope with the coming threat. But she did ask, "Do you have a plan, Miss Carolina?"

She pulled a gun from her side holster as she said, "Not one that doesn't land us captured, dead, or worse."

Conique started for the van's side door. "Help me out of here, Agent Carolina."

She replied, "Miss Voyant, I don't think you should exit the vehicle."

Conique placed a hand on Carolina's shoulder. "Trust me, ma'am. I can buy our boys just a few seconds."

Janet tried to move, but her body resisted her. It was infuriating, terrifying, and crushing, all at once. She said, "Please be careful, Miss Voyant."

Carolina gestured a surrender with her hands before helping Conique step out of the van into the chilly air.

Janet managed to position herself so the scene to follow was visible. And she couldn't believe what she saw.

The drivers of the three vans positioned them around Axley and Carolina's vehicle, all some thirty feet away. Conique walked towards them with her hands in the air while Carolina held back, anxious. She called back to the agent. "No sudden moves. Let me talk to them."

Carolina grumbled. "I'd be fired for letting you do this, Miss Voyant."

Janet thought it just as Conique said, "I think a paycheck may be the last of our worries."

It troubled her, though, that the vans remained still. Conique advanced on them with her hands in the sky, and Janet couldn't help but imagine how terrible it could go.

Shouting ensued. "Drop to the ground, old woman!"

She asked, "Do I inspire so terrible a fear that you would tremble behind guns rather than talk face-to-face?"

The shouting continued. "Last warning—drop to the ground or we'll drop you!"

Conique laughed at them, stupefying Janet and Carolina alike. "You'd shoot the very thing you're trying to find?"

The voice shouted once more. "Down on the ground, now!"

She said, "I know you're not wanting to finish your shift knowing you shot an unarmed old woman. I've settled a lot harder arguments with just words, and you can, too."

Janet's dry throat left her voice in tatters, though she said to Carolina, "They won't actually do it, will they? You gotta do something."

Carolina tapped her own weapon furiously with her eyes fixed on Conique. "Nurse, if I threaten them, they're liable to kill all of us."

The hired goons shouted once more. "Fine, we'll tase you if that's the way—" He stopped in midsentence.

Conique's voice was no longer understandable to Janet. But she knew the kindly elder continued to speak to them as she moved closer to their gleaming white vans.

Carolina gasped. "I don't fucking believe it."

Janet's heart thumped in her ears. "What? What's happening?"

She leaned against the doorframe. "One of the guards just shook her hand."

Janet strained hard to sit up, and the scene couldn't have been more unexpected. Conique laughed as she talked to them, somehow subduing them with her disarming manner. Janet asked, "Can you hear them?"

Carolina said, "No, but I can read lips, more or less." She peered into her binoculars once more. "She's telling him about a sick child. He's crying, I think."

Janet sank back into her chair, sliding over the pleather seat with difficulty as her arm and leg weakened further. "Maybe she really is that intuitive."

Carolina asked, "Come again?"

Janet said, "She calls it a spiritual gift, but it's some sort of attunement to what's happening in people's lives."

Carolina said, "Hold a moment, Nurse." Looking with her binoculars, she said, "There's a problem. Others are circling her, and the friendlier one of them is arguing with them."

This wouldn't do for Janet. She pulled herself towards the open door as their agent protector kept her own focus on Conique's predicament. Her legs fought her as though they weighed a hundred pounds each, but she wouldn't leave her newfound friend for capture.

Carolina noticed she'd reached the exit, so she said, "Please, stay inside, Nurse. We—"

Thunderous booms shook the van and surroundings as a light flashed from above. Carolina caught Janet as she fell out of her seat outside the door. She exclaimed, "What the hell is that?"

A second pulse reverberated all about them, forcing she and the agent to the hard concrete. Janet rolled to her side to watch Conique and her would-be assailants crumple. Her focus faded, doused by whatever craziness ensued above them. She struggled to keep her eyes open, and Archie the cat landed before her. His golden eyes were attentive to her as he extended his front foot to her neck, inserting a single claw into her flesh. The pinprick smarted, and she fell to the blackness.

*B****

Boothby fidgeted as the terrifyingly real Demmings torso towered like a wild boar, licking his fangs as he prepared to feast. He couldn't help but wonder what secrets yearning to make themselves known to him, but survival was paramount.

He yanked the focus stone from his pocket. "This is what ya want, Mister Demmings."

The hologram chuckled. "Just what is your toy? A tennis ball in foil?"

Before Demmings finished his sentence, Boothby spoke in a calm, almost mechanized voice. "The hologram is comprised of a fluidic intersection of photon streams directed from five emitters arranged about Lab Nucleum." In an ordinary voice, he said, "I understand it!" The emulsions squeezed between panes of glass, the dozens of microlenses, and the laser sources sat before him in a real-time schematic. He felt the focus stone shudder as he directed heat into the emulsions, distorting Demmings as though he were made of melting wax.

He moaned monstrously, shouting, "You won't outsmart Kharla! You'll tell me who Obfucius is!"

And he was gone, with the lighting shifted to blood red. The voice they knew as Denise said, "Warning: fire suppression engaged. Security level omicron."

Shrill alarm klaxons blared as fire foam gushed above the holoemitters and all about them room. Reuben shouted as the mess layered him. "Christ almighty!"

Boothby panted as Axley shouted over the whining alarms. "How in the holy hell did you do that?!"

He said between breaths, "I dunno! I somehow could understand how the thing worked. I knew how to overload the secondary circuit to superheat the light-conducting emulsion!"

Adam aimed to pat his shoulder, but instead slapped a layer of fire foam. "Umm, way to go, B-man!"

Reuben held his hands over his ears in pain. "Okay, Mister Tech Manual—can you turn off that goddamned racket?!"

"I'll try!" Boothby heaved as he held the device skyward once more. Now, he could see the circuits controlling the alarms, and he depressed their currents. To their relief, the noise subsided.

Reuben wiped foam from his head, reliable in gathering their focus. "Thanks, Boothby. We need to find the reactor fuel, don't we?"

Axley pointed to a door at the rear of the lab. Adam asked, "It isn't in the reactor? Why there?"

Axley said, "The reactor isn't finished, and"—he pointed to a three-bladed symbol on the door—"that door has a trefoil on it."

Reuben squinted at it. "Sunuvabitch." He placed a giant hand on Boothby's shoulder. "You okay?"

Boothby shivered under the foam. "I think so," he rasped.

Reuben brushed some of the foam from Boothby as he said, "Then let's do this."

Adam's boots squished onto the foam blanketing the floor. "Watch your step, guys."

Had Boothby seen the door without the trefoil, he might guess it to lead to an ordinary cleaning closet. It was modest, save the oversized lock with a glowing interface. Axley reached it first, mouthed a tepid, "Wish me luck," and pulled the latch. The door didn't budge.

Reuben pushed Axley aside in as unscientific a move as Boothby could imagine. He yanked on the latch as he himself into the door as he shouted, "Open, goddammit!" It was immovable.

Axley tapped the door as he said, "Are you finished, Doctor?" Reuben stood back as the agent said, "This is a mag lock, bolted hard." He waved his blank badge at it, but the interface flashed a red DENIAL OF ENTRY on its GUI.

Adam had squeezed himself into the corner with them. "Mister Bee, what about that thing you have?"

Boothby gulped as the others parted to clear his path to the small door and magnetic lock. "I don't know how this works."

Axley said, "But you *want* to know how it works, right?"

It struck him as quite true. He *needed* to understand how things worked. He felt his own eyes widen as he squeezed the focus stone. "You're right, Agent! I'll try it." Baring his teeth, he glanced at the others. "Ya might wanna stand back, folks."

They gave him space, and he grasped the focus stone in his right hand as he touched the lock with his left hand. Closing his eyes, he saw the inner mechanism unfold in cross sections before him. He uttered as though he read aloud from a technical manual, "Each of the three locking bolts operate on an individual respective circuit to ensure that physical force on any single one fuses the remaining two. The bolts themselves are reinforced with nanomeshes to resist cutting torches."

Reuben interrupted him but with patience unusual in their interactions. "That's all well and good, Boothby. How do we open it?"

Boothby said, "I'm trying to think. Just a sec. Ugh!" He almost lost his balance, but Adam and Reuben caught him.

Axley said, "Focus your mental energy."

Boothby strained, but all of it disappeared from him. He stepped back, struggling to suck air back into his lungs. Axley asked, "What happened? What did you see?"

He looked at the focus stone, and it sizzled with power. "There was something else in there, pushing me out."

Adam asked, "What do you mean?"

Boothby touched his forehead. "I dunno. It was—" His right hand dropped the focus stone. "No!"

Adam caught it, but it seared into his hand. "Fuck! It's freezing!"

It landed on the solid white floor below, and ice crystals shattered from it in all directions. Boothby lunged for it, falling to the floor as he gathered it in his hands. "That was a close one," he said.

Reuben said, "It's not freezing to you?"

Boothby said, "Nope."

Adam cradled his frostbitten hand. "It had to be closer to liquid nitro."

Axley pointed to the door. "We're wasting valuable time. Can you try again?"

354

With Adam and Axley helping him, Boothby stood once more. He pushed himself into the door, this time with determination. Tightening his grasp on the focus stone, he planted his left hand on the door as he closed his eyes.

The door lock appeared once more, but the electrical pulses countering his careful manipulations continued. "Filaments along the locking bolts can fuse on a random assignment synchronized with a chronometer within the Heart."

Reuben shouted, "What the hell does that mean?"

Boothby faltered, but his companions continued to brace him. "It's still fighting me, eek!" he shouted. Tendrils of energy lapped at him, singing his nerves with pain.

Axley said, "You can do this, Boothby. Find a way into the Heart."

Reuben blurted, "You make it sound like you know what he's talking about. What the hell is the Heart?"

Boothby concentrated, and at once, he traveled along a filament within the second locking bolt. He could see a vast, dense web with thousands if not millions of red, blue, green, and yellow connections set against pitch black. Energy surged along the network away from him to some destination ahead, though some circulated in pockets nested within the network. He looked up to see more of the same—light storms moved like tsunamis, igniting every vertex in its path. But the energy didn't cross certain vertices more than one out of three or more waves.

He heard Axley call to him in echoes. "Where are you, Boothby? What do you see?"

He said, "It's some sort of network. Four-toned vertices. I don't understand it, at all. It's moving fast."

Axley's voice continued. "Try to change the throughput on a nearby node. There, move to a connecting vertex, a blue one if you can."

"I'll try." He stepped forward along a path, but he was sluggish. "Jesus, it's like I'm walking underwater," he said in a dry rasp. When he reached a blue vertex, he could see that it fed at least a dozen more vertices ahead. "Okay, I'm on one now."

Axley said, "Good, Boothby. Now, concentrate. Think of applying pressure to this node. We'll overload it."

Boothby looked at the twinkling blue energy below him, and he squeezed the focus stone as hard as he could. He could hear a roar of power surging from behind, and it made sense to him that he should open what should remain closed. He could feel the hairs on his neck standing, so he closed his eyes within himself, shutting out the light. Now, he found himself staring at a dial. Adjusting it shifted the behavior of the blue node. So he cranked it as far as it could go, and as he opened his eyes, the energy surged through him, frying the node and knocking him from equilibrium.

"That tickles," boomed Denise's voice.

Boothby opened his eyes to see the door and his friends. "Kharla?" he asked.

She replied with a voice shifting from Denise's gentility to a monstrous triple of voices layered together. "Ha ha ha. You're a talented one, E.G. Boothby. No human has ever accomplished so surgical an attempt to overload a stacked constant detection layer. I would welcome you all to Picoveer's Heart, but your trespass demands a heavy sentence."

The door came alive with current, blasting him and the others from it. Boothby hit his head on one of the large tables running the length of the room. He then fell to the unforgiving floor, knocking the air from his lungs. Without control of his muscles, he felt the focus stone fall. Trying to follow it with his eyes, he saw it bounce twice before rolling in a straight line towards the door through which they'd entered only minutes earlier. To his surprise, the door had opened during the commotion.

The focus stone at last collided with something beyond the lab door. A shadow reached to catch it, and Boothby froze at the figure who emerged, and not because he held what appeared to be Archie in his free arm. "Norcross," he gasped.

27.Infiltration

Janet could hear voices, but she couldn't those attached to them. One voice was surely that of Conique, but the other belonged to a stranger. Their conversation first was a jumble, as though she suffered some aphasia. Conique's tone was a mixture of relief and elation as she bandied words with the stranger. His tone was cooler, if not rude. But words didn't bring her back to consciousness—it was the very wet tongue of a dog. She opened her eyes to see a fluffy golden retriever drooling for joy at a new playmate. Janet couldn't help but laugh as the dog continued to wash her face, until she heard a half-hearted rebuke from Conique.

"There, there, girl. Let her rest." The retriever looked above Janet with a whimper as she backed away. Janet looked straight up to see Conique's face smiling above her. "Glad to see you're awake. It's been bedlam around here while you were out." She cradled Janet's head in her lap, the elderly woman's plump frame making for a comfortable pillow.

Janet said, "What happened? Where's Adam? Where are the others?"

She glanced away. "They're still inside. Whatever it was hit all of us, but the others haven't awakened yet. You've met my dear Aurum, now."

The man said, "You have no idea what I endured to save that dog."

Janet trained her eyes on him—he was Japanese, wearing a suit and bolo tie. She looked at Conique. "Is this Doctor Nakamura? A vaquero?"

Conique clasped her hands in joy. "Indeed, he is! Well, the first part."

Janet looked at the van. "Where's Agent Carolina?"

357

Shigeru said, "She appears to be fine, though unconscious, like all the others here. You and Miss Voyant received a neurostimulant to counteract the hypersonic pulse, though the explanation of how defies, well, explanation."

Janet could see Carolina on her back. "I need to help her."

Shigeru said, "Slow down, little lady. You're in bad shape, and I need to help you."

Conique waved a hand in the sky. "It's confirmation!"

Janet asked, "How did you get here? We had a heck of a time getting through the gates."

Shigeru produced a penlight to shine into her eyes. "Well, I came from the sky, for lack of a better explanation."

She pushed the penlight aside. "It's ALS, Doctor."

He continued his examination as he said, "So I've heard. Each of you suffer from a neurological disease, and Zephyr intends I restore you both."

Janet asked, "Who is Zephyr? Last I heard, ALS and Alzheimer's are incurable."

Conique rolled her eyes with a smirk. "I'd forgotten that."

Shigeru said, "Someone who convinced me that this world might be worth saving."

Conique patted Janet. "This is universalism!" She then leaned towards the doctor. "But who is your friend?"

Shigeru was irked as he palpated Janet's neck, though he said with little affect, "Friends, plural. Professor Kunskapsen is a new acquaintance, and Zephyr is, well, I guess you'll have to see for yourselves. But your condition, Miss Yazzie, is bad, and though the people here meaning to do you harm are incapacitated, this will change soon."

Aurum cried at that, so Janet asked, "What should we do?"

He said, "I can perform a quick procedure on you, but I wanted your consent first."

Conique inquired faster than Janet could do so. "What procedure?"

Shigeru could hardly stifle his disdain for Conique, though Janet wasn't sure why. He said, "It is difficult to explain, but I can guarantee its efficacy. Zephyr shared a technique with me beyond the medicine of this world."

Conique clapped her hands once more. "Other worlds? Aliens? Beam me up!"

Shigeru frowned at her, though he probably was trying to censor himself. "Please, Miss Voyant, I must treat this patient."

Janet shrugged. "Doc, she's just excited. Where is this Zephyr?"

Conique's face returned to neutral. "I didn't meet him. I woke up to Aurum and a dashing physician."

Shigeru pointed to the building behind him. "Zephyr and the professor followed your friends, leaving me and the mutt to help you both."

Conique cocked her head in frustration. "Now, Doctor, she's mostly retriever, even if we have no papers."

He said, "Listen, Miss Yazzie, this procedure will feel unlike any treatment you've ever received, and it is only the first of many. Though I'm skilled in my field, these tools tower as tall above all things medical century twenty-one as does the microlaser over flint scalpels. So please bear with me." His eyes betrayed his uncertainty, and an even greater pain in said uncertainty.

Conique patted him. "You can do it, Doctor. I know you can."

Shigeru's eyes were weary, but he remained vigilant. "I will dispatch a swarm of tiny machines Zephyr calls *polyplasts*. They're nanobots, for lack of a better term." He could read her hesitation, so he said, "Zephyr seemed to think you'd already understand the clusterfuck we're in. Pardon my shit mouth." Conique giggled, conjuring a blush and grin from the doctor. He then said, "Zephyr told me as we arrived here that you knew his friend the *Arkivar*."

Janet's heart leapt. "Yes. Though to say I know him might be to understate it. Okay, what do you need me to do?"

He said, "Well, try not to move, but breathe normally, no matter what you feel. Okay?" There was unsteadiness in his voice, but she ignored it.

Drawing even breaths, she wondered what the treatment would feel like as he searched with his fingertips for her left-side carotid. First, there was pressure, then a burn, then a radiating tingle. He said, "I've sent the first wave. You'll feel different sensations as they bypass the blood-brain barrier where they'll do their work. They must repair the motor neurons, though one swarm will be insufficient. You'll feel your muscles twitch."

She said, "Tickles, and cramps."

He patted her. "Just focus on your breathing."

Conique said, "You're very good at your job, Doctor."

He said, "I've never done anything like this in that job, Miss Voyant. And you're next, once Zephyr and the professor return."

Conique said, "There's an interesting thing you do when you mention her. A slight inflection that makes me wonder."

He said, "Miss Voyant, please, let me treat this patient." Aurum groaned at him, so he whispered, "Please?" He then removed his hands from Janet's throat. "They're all in. Now, we'll see about walking in a few minutes. I don't know how long these people will be unconscious."

Janet asked, "Can't you check on Agent Carolina? She's on our side, if there is such a thing."

He stood, stretched his back, then moved over to their van. Conique patted her cheek. "Don't you worry, darling. We're gonna get you all fixed up. A young lady like you shouldn't ever have to be sick like this."

Janet was touched by her kindness, but her professional and personal drives remained front and center. "How is Miss Carolina, Doctor?"

He said, "She appears to be fine, though not quite ready for prime time."

Conique asked him, "What was it used on us, again?"

He said, "Hypersonic pulse. At lower frequencies, it leads to unconsciousness. Not a particularly safe weapon, though. Zephyr indicated that each of you received a counteragent, though I don't know what."

Conique said, "Archie."

He asked, "Come again?"

Janet said, "The cat. Where is he?"

The very word sent Aurum into a gyration. Conique laughed. "Oh, my dear Aurum loves chasing the neighborhood cats."

Shigeru returned to them as he lit a cigarette. Janet said, "I'd thank you for not smoking."

He shrugged. "I'll take your thanks for saving your life, first, honey."

She was enraged at that. "You're not respectful, sir."

He said, "Good, anger will work out those motor neurons faster." He puffed on his cigarette. "Besides, the exposure is minor. Anyway, I didn't see a cat."

Conique stretched her hand to her dog's face as Aurum yammered a sound at her. "You didn't tell me how you rescued my baby, Doctor."

He flicked ashes from his cigarette. "It's a larger conversation. But we were looking for you, Miss Voyant. Your dog was alone, and not in the best of places."

She said, "I lost her a week or so ago. It was my fault."

Shigeru answered with surprising courtesy. "You're hardly responsible for what happens because of dementia. Besides, it's because of her that we could track you here."

Janet discovered that Conique was actually rocking her back and forth, making her think that she must have been a great mother. Conique asked, "How was that?"

He nodded to the dog. "Well, apparently when animals spend enough time with the special people Zephyr says we are, a bit of us rubs off. They carry a signature that somehow connects us, though I don't know the precise mechanism."

Conique said, "The Seven."

He dropped his cigarette, extinguishing it with his foot. "You know about us, then."

Janet said, "Only a little. The *Arkivar* said Norcross was trying to find us. We're not exactly human."

Conique laughed at her. "Who is, dear?"

Shigeru said, "True. We're built from a hybrid genome—Zephyr calls us *Vesiks*. There are seven of us, and together, with the professor, we make four of them."

Janet's muscles spasmed as she breathed. "Five. Boothby is another one of us."

Shigeru said, "I don't know of him."

Conique asked, "Who is Zephyr, and why is he helping us?"

Shigeru answered, "He is here in place of another, one called—"

Janet said, "Norcross. I saw him, and I've never heard of anything or anyone more dangerous."

Shigeru nodded. "That was Zephyr's description, as well. They are interdimensional travelers, here to unite seven people living among humans. Each of us carries genetic material from their world and beyond, and, once together, we open a door."

Janet coughed with little irony. "A door?"

Shigeru lit a second cigarette as he sipped from a silver flask. "It sounds absurd, and before yesterday, I'd have agreed. This door leads to something powerful enough to right the wrongs in this world."

Conique clapped her plump hands in delight. "I can believe that."

Janet moved her arms and legs, pleased that her muscles had become more attentive to her brain. But an evangelical's endorsement wasn't a great one in her mind. "I can't take that on faith."

Conique patted her. "Dear girl, it's all faith in the end. The important thing is that we show faith in one another."

Shigeru snapped at her with ferocity surprising even the religion-shy Janet. "I'd swear Miss Voyant that you have an inexhaustible supply of fortune cookies inside of you."

She grinned at him as the observation skipped above her. "You should have the ones I bake at home." Aurum cried at that, and Conique said, "No, sweetie, we're not going *home*."

Janet couldn't overcome the nagging weakness in her legs, so exerting herself led only to frustration. He eased her down. "Nurse, please just rest. We have time." He then checked her reflexes once more as he asked, "Why have you come to this lab? I cannot imagine that you had an easy time sneaking in."

Conique pined at the still unconscious Agent Carolina. "We've had help, though I think it's nothing short of a miracle." Turning back to the doctor, she sighed. "But Boothby really is the one who should explain, considering it was his plan. It was his intent to track me down so he could get his hands on a nuke."

Shigeru froze in place. "What?! Why?"

Janet shrugged. "It sounds insane, but I've seen horrors I didn't know were even possible."

The doctor's dark brow glistened with sweat, making Janet wonder about Doctor Hamora and the others. This doctor lacked even Reuben's charm, and that was no compliment. He said, "Norcross. Does your Boothby think this will stop him?"

She was cold without warning, shivering as the monster's face flashed in her mind. Neither needed to answer since Carolina regained consciousness. Her officious voice said, "Based on intelligence gathered, even that might be insufficient. I'm Enid Carolina, NSA."

He said, "Shigeru Nakamura, MDPHD."

Carolina's reply was swift. "Letter envy won't stop him, Doctor."

Conique played conciliator nicely. "Doctor Nakamura is one of the seven, Agent. If he's here, it means we have help."

Shigeru checked out Carolina as he said, "Take it easy, Agent. You've received a system shock."

She sat up rubbing her neck. "What was it?"

Conique said, "Sonar press?"

The doctor said without looking at her, "Sonic pulse is the term, Miss Voyant."

Carolina stayed seating, too dizzy to stand. "Have Axley and the others reported back?"

Shigeru said, "Others are searching for the others in your party. We have little time before the security forces wake up. Miss Voyant, Agent, you have to help me move Nurse Yazzie back to the van so we can rendezvous with my friends behind the complex."

The agent said, "Wait, who are your friends?"

He didn't disguise his anger. "I could tell you that Olga Kunskapsen and Zephyr were their names, but would that make a difference to you?"

Carolina froze. "Wait—you said *Zephyr*?" She waited, then asked, "Not *Norcross*?"

He shook his head. "Last I checked, those aren't the same names, Agent."

Her face became even more pale. "There is only one such codename among POIs, and it is Norcross."

Thinking of Adam, Janet clutched her chest as it felt as though it would explode.

F✱✱✱

Frankie found the ride to Picoveer's auditorium smoother than he'd imagined—Chevur's EV was no toy, and he couldn't help but think of Myra and her windup box of a car. He didn't have much time to think, considering that the bantam executive yammered without taking a breath.

"See here the lush foliage here in Atlanta," he said as he pointed to magnolia trees ensconcing their route.

Frankie clutched his stump as he shrugged. "They're trees, yeah."

Chevur glanced to his passenger while dwelling on the road before them. "May I ask how you came by your injury?"

Biting his cheek, he said, "I made a mistake, and I paid for it."

This troubled the little man. "That is tough, sir. Tough, indeed."

Frankie changed the subject as he tasted blood in his mouth. "How well do you know Varnam?"

362

Chevur smirked at the name. "Oh, I am not acquainted with him. At least not directly. I must confess I've not read most of his books. But *Chain of Industry* is a classic. It's as though Ayn Rand undertook a metrosexual makeover."

Frankie lit up a little, even if he didn't follow the reference. "Yeah, but I like *Polite Society* best."

Chevur cocked his little head to the side. "'Piety without curiosity inevitably betrays antisociety.'"

Frankie laughed at the quote. "Yeah, he has a way with phrases." He then offered his own. "'Pyramids invariably necessitate a narrow capstone crowning the flattened masses.'"

Chevur squeaked a laugh as he continued to smile. Tapping his fat little brown fingers on the steering wheel, he said, "Like your General Norcross, no?"

Frankie felt himself tense at the name, though guilt followed for his doubt. "Yeah, I guess so."

Chevur raised an eyebrow as he leaned toward Frankie. "Lieutenant, I detect uncertainty surrounding your superior?"

Frankie looked out his window at the plastic perfection of magnolia leaves filling out the sides of the smooth road. His feelings were complicated, not unlike those haphazardly packed around his family ties. But Frankie wasn't stupid—Chevur sought information, and Frankie didn't appreciate the sheltering. "He doesn't tell me His business, though I might know what He wants—His pad showed you something important?"

Chevur's look of satisfaction worried Frankie a little. He bobbed his head from side to side. "I hoped you might enlighten me. The message your general shared originates from Kymara's Okult Prime."

Frankie found himself squeezing his stump, bearing the pain. "What is that?"

Chevur lowered his voice, as though he feared someone might overhear them from inside a quiet-running car. "Publicly traded companies require public disclosure of executive leaders. By the nature of Kymara's three charters, executive identity can reveal unbaked IP, business strategies, and the like. So Kymara's true policy control remains hidden within the Okult Prime."

Frankie quoted Varnum. "'Governments, like the future, are the domains for secrecy and evil and monsters.' But why tell me all this?"

Chevur chuckled as he replied, "I respect you as a fellow traveler. I know who wrote the message, but I do not understand why."

Frankie was titillated, hopeful he might learn. "What did the message say?"

Chevur slowed the vehicle as they approached a turnoff leading to a mammoth building. "Aside from a directive that I personally providing you a means to meet our esteemed guest speaker today, that your superior and his colonel reach the Heart without delay. But the requirements are impossible—the Heart's key deliverable was months from completion. With economic uncertainty, construction on this campus has ground to a halt. Even a third of those attending this event will soon find themselves unemployed."

Frankie turned in his seat. "Why didn't you tell the Lord, umm, General Norcross that? What is the thing they're making there?"

Chevur bowed his head. "No one questions a directive of Okult Prime. But, can you tell me why the general is here?"

This irritated Frankie. "You wanna keep your secrets, but I should share mine? The general has a plan."

Chevur stopped the car inside a small roundabout. He waited as a Chinese valet approached on foot. Chevur quoted Varnum once more. "'A man without a plan is just a rudderless ship, a chaotic woman.'"

Frankie approved of the Indian's shared interest, so he volunteered as much as he thought he could. "Norcross is here to meet others. What is the thing your company is building there? You wanna pump me for info, you gotta answer first."

Chevur pursed his lips as he mulled his answer. "Very well, Lieutenant Putnam. The online rags already know this—fission microreactors were the principal aim, but, again, they are not yet consumer-grade. With the loss in manpower, the program appears in doubt. Did He elaborate on their identities? Is Mister Demmings among them?"

Frankie shook his head, deciding that the Lord would want to extend salvation. "I wouldn't know who they are, even if I saw them. Except for an Indian, erm, Native American girl. Janet Yazzie. You should talk to the general—He has many good things to say."

Chevur tapped his little brown hands together as his phone played a jingle. "Like Varnum? How very curious. But we must hurry should we intend to the talk. I should wish to converse more soon."

Frankie felt butterflies in his abdomen at the chance to hear his hero—the Lord's generosity was touching, he had to admit.

O***

Olga was astonished at Zephyr's deft handling of Picoveer's security. A single pulse of energy had paralyzed their forces and defeated their surveillance system. Cutting a path through the roof was his most primitive action, but he'd explained why one of the seven would consider so reckless a venture, and, as absurd as it sounded, she agreed.

The lighting in the facility was wonky, flickering a bloody red with shrill alarm klaxons burning into her eardrums. She was weak, but Zephyr was adamant she accompany him. The corridor was empty, and the door at its terminus was opening and closing, as though the sensors suffered a psychotic break. He braced her with his arm as approached it, and she couldn't help relishing that she stood within Carlyle Demmings' most intimate property without an invitation from him. He had been the most ludicrous man she'd ever known, having attended Cornell together so many years before.

Olga could hardly see through the heavy crimson blanketing them, though occasional blinding flashes let her see somewhat more around them. She almost said aloud that the poor illumination was desperately inappropriate for guiding hapless employees to the exits. But the klaxon wouldn't permit anything less than moderate shouting if one intended to be heard.

The logic of it demanded that her capacity for navigating under near useless bath of red light was not among the facility's security objectives. It was enough that Zephyr likely could see, and she was too weak to ambulate without his help.

But the rolling spheroid of alloy surprised her a great deal. It had struck Zephyr's boots, and he bended to pluck it from the floor. The partly ajar door before them led to another chamber with the same hazard lighting, but horror tales featuring balls tossed by off-camera monsters passed over her. Zephyr wasn't perturbed by it, though he appeared deep in meditative curiosity. Camera flashes continued, and, like lightning on a dark night, it aided her brain in mapping the terrain confronting them.

Olga intended to ask Zephyr why he picked up the chunk, but a raspy voice called out, "Norcross."

This caught Zephyr's attention, though his face betrayed no surprise at the scene before them. Olga turned to ask him, but another voice shouted, "It's him!"

She heard scrambling in the lab as Zephyr manipulated the chunk of metal in his right hand. He said, "I understand now." He then shouted back at them, "Mister Boothby, I mean you no harm!"

A deep and menacing drawl of a voice boomed next. "Come in here and we'll kill you, Norcross!"

Olga held Zephyr's arm as hard as she could as the fear blossomed within her. She asked with almost no strength to speak, "Why are they calling you that?"

Without removing his eyes from the half-opened door, he said, "I assure you, Professor—I am not Norcross."

A fourth voice rounded out the quartet from the lab. "Norcross, we've tracked you all over this continent. I am certain we'd know you."

The deeper voice said, "Dammit, man, I knew we needed to hang on to your gun."

Zephyr extended the chunk of metal towards the door. "Please, Mister Boothby, take your focus stone."

No one spoke for a moment, permitting the blaring alarms to refill Olga's attention. A large elderly black man appeared in the doorway with a paper-cutting arm in hand. She didn't know him, but she guessed the robust voice belonged to him. As he wiped sweat from his forehead, he pointed the blade at Zephyr. "See here, you will not take my wife or these others, even if it kills me!"

A younger man appeared next to him, and he wielded a heavy computer keyboard. "We'll fuck you up!"

Olga asked once more, "Why are they calling you Norcross? You said he was the greatest threat to this world."

A third man between the others in age pulled them back before emerging with a power cable in his hands. "Release the woman, Norcross. Now!"

Olga clung to him. "He saved me from death!"

Zephyr shouted above them. "Mister Boothby, you must have your focus stone if we're to succeed. I am *not* Norcross."

A squatty small man peeked from between his companions as his expressive brown eyes flickered under the frenzied lights. Tugging at his friends, he growled, "Please, guys. He'll kill you all. I'm the only one he wants."

Zephyr's voice became louder still. "Mister Boothby, your focus stone will tell you the truth of it. Please, take it."

The elderly but imposing black man said, "It must be a trick. No, Norcross, we won't play your way."

Zephyr said, "I am not Norcross."

Boothby had taken a step in Zephyr's direction, squinting in the light. "Wait, guys. I think he's telling the truth!"

The youngest of them said, "You think I would forget his face? I saw him three days ago."

Olga was quick in her reply, pronouncing, "That's impossible. He was with me."

The black man pointed the blade at Zephyr. "If you're not this monster, why don't you toss us Boothby's toy?"

Zephyr corrected him with a snap. "The focus stone is no toy, sir. It is the handiwork of my dearest friend, intended just for Mister Boothby, it would seem." He stepped one pace forward, and the three larger men postured in defense of Boothby. Zephyr held it closer to them.

The black man grabbed Boothby's arm as he moved to meet Zephyr. "It's okay, Doctor Hamora. I have a feeling." He reached for the chunk, and Zephyr released it to him.

The Ghyan then said, "You can use it to know truth, Mister Boothby. I see now why Ephyr entrusted you with it."

Boothby examined Zephyr's face. "You look almost just like Norcross, but you're definitely different."

Olga pushed on Zephyr's shoulder as vertigo spun the room about her. "Why do you look like Norcross?"

His answer made great sense to her, but she was nonetheless stunned. "Norcross is my brother," he said.

There was silence. Their surroundings were garish, cacophonous, grating. But she could hear nothing but her own breathing as she considered Zephyr's news. She asked, "Why not tell me?"

The youngest of the group said, "No fucking way! I'd swear you were him."

Another said, "It makes sense. You followed him here?"

The black man demanded, "Would someone tell me what in the hell is going on?"

Zephyr said, "It is simple, sir. Doctor Hamora, he called you? You're Conique Voyant's mate."

The doctor advanced on him. "Where is my wife?!"

Olga moved between them. "Miss Voyant and the young nurse are fine. Shigeru is tending them."

Doctor Hamora asked, "Nakamura?"

Zephyr nodded. "Yes, we've assembled almost all seven Vesiks, thanks to fortune and your canine companion."

"Aurum?" the doctor asked.

Olga said, "Yes. We discovered her near your home—it was overrun by operatives. I'm Olga Kunskapsen, by the way."

Boothby said, "This is Reuben Hamora, that's Agent Axley of the NSA, and Adam Baumgartl."

Axley rubbed his temples as he said, "I attempted to spoof the van's IP address, but the trick would deflect others only for so long."

Reuben said, "Enough bullshit civility. You are the devil's brother? Why are you here?"

Zephyr said, "It deserves an explanation, but we're already almost out of time. We must implement Mister Boothby's original plan to restore the skytax energy stores."

Boothby almost giggled. "Oh my God, we're gonna go on a UFO?"

Reuben said, "Quiet, man! We don't know who or what this is."

Axley held the cables taut as he said, "We'll require more of an explanation."

Zephyr replied, "I am no agent, ill-equipped to serve his function. But a very close genetic match is essential in stopping my brother. And I am that—

The alarm died as the lights flickered. A gigantic hologram of a man coalesced into their midst. He said with satisfaction, "Thank you, Zephyr, for explaining your utility. Never would I have guessed that I could trap a bona fide extraterrestrial in this lab, but you won't be going anywhere now." He eyed Olga. "And Professor Kunskapsen, could this day become brighter?! You're less dead than I expected."

Boothby grumbled. "Ya know this man?"

She knew Carlyle Demmings. "All too well. Carl, listen to me. We've happened upon truths too dangerous to ignore. Please permit us to do our work here."

His giant torso swayed in laughter. "Professor, as a scientist, you know I cannot do that."

She scoffed with gusto. "Carl, science does not conflate avarice with beneficence."

Demmings smirked at her. "Olga, you're still the least interesting queen of academic piety. Again, I wonder how you're still alive. That must be a find in and of itself."

Boothby reeled on him. "Nope, you can't kill any of the seven, Mister Demmings."

The monstrous form laughed once more. "Says the wild-eyed fruitcake who chases 'da lights.'" He mocked Boothby's accent, albeit with shoddy reconstruction.

Zephyr said, "Mister Demmings, I understand your curiosity, but detaining us further risks consummating the sixth extinction level event."

Demmings laughed. "The world will end no matter what, sir. It's better to seek survival, and you'll help me do it." He lifted his hands. "Those of us remaining will have blood on our hands, and you know it." Demmings angled his pig-features away for a moment before shouting, "Kharla, enact facility lockdown omega, now!"

His image vanished as Reuben shouted, "You mangy bastard! If I get my hands on him—"

Axley interrupted him as he tossed his makeshift weapon to the floor. "We have to escape this place." Turning to Zephyr, he asked, "Okay, if you're the good guy here, what do we do next?"

Thunderous booms echoed throughout the corridor and in the walls. Zephyr peered around as the walls crackled and shuddered. He said, "Fair enough. The security here?"

Axley stared at him until Reuben shoved him. "Agent, tell him what the hell we're up against. I dunno what you would even call it."

Axley replied, "A rough-hewn AI system."

Boothby answered, "Large language model and deep learning, I'm sure. Please, Mister Zephyr, can I shake your hand?" He beamed with affection, fondness, and inspiration, all rolled together. Zephyr chuckled as he offered one to the ufologist. He gushed. "Oh my Lord, I'm so happy!"

Reuben said, "Christ, can we work the problem, people?"

Axley said, "Picoveer placed the Kharla unit within this facility, despite industry and scientific leaders condemning them for it." He placed his hands on his hips as he spoke to Olga. "Professor, I know you by reputation. Are you aware of a workaround?"

Before she could answer, there was an alarm louder than any they'd heard so far. A woman's voice surrounded them. "Danger—biohazard released in Kaleido Lab. Please evacuate immediately."

Zephyr said between siren blasts, "Excess oxygen is flooding this floor—we must isolate the cause before we lose consciousness."

Olga asked, "You cannot access the computer directly?"

He said, "The tech I've brought with me here is insufficient, but you and Mister Boothby together can isolate the cause." He pointed to the misshapen alloy Boothby clutched with such fervor.

Boothby said, "I tried to walk Kharla's network, but I was not fast enough to close the gates."

Adam said, "I don't mean to sound ignorant, but what are you talking about?"

Olga shot her eyes about the corridor as she said, "Intellidez released a system nearly capable of human speech. But it runs off of a neural network."

Reuben shook his head. "It is no more neural than a bag of hammers."

Olga shrugged. "No matter the case, we may upload adversarial inputs intended to coerce a particular outcome, and these slightly perturbed instances are not differentiable, say by the human eye."

Boothby's eyes bugged out. "Yeah! We change a few bits, and a panda becomes a stovetop." He frowned as the alarms became more frequent. "I can see the network, but she pushed me out."

Olga asked, "What do you mean?"

Zephyr patted her with eagerness. "The stone helps Boothby understand and control technology. We call it Verix, or truthful focus. With this unique capability, Boothby may explore the makeshift AIs' vast data structures with neuronal switching speed increased for a time. It is a gift to be nurtured, but we must apply it as is, for now. But I surmise it is a question of speed."

She said resolutely, "Then let's go faster."

*B****

Boothby clutched his focus stone for dear life, daring not to imagine the consequences without it. It was cold to the touch once more, an example of it leeching heat.

Zephyr said to Olga, "I am sorry we must do this while you're still unwell."

Reuben asked, "What troubles her?"

She replied, "A malignancy in my brain tissue. It would have been fatal, but Zephyr saved me."

Boothby shouted to Reuben, "Maybe he can fix up Miss Voyant."

Axley looked down the corridor as he said, "Let's talk hypotheticals later. What are your intentions here, Zephyr?"

Zephyr motioned to the doorway marked for radioactive hazards. "The psychological imprint seems to have worked. Mister Boothby, are you or Miss Voyant the one to suggest it?"

Reuben set the paper-cutting blade on a nearby table as he said, "It wouldn't have been outside the craziest I've heard my Connie say, but I believe this harebrained scheme is all Boothby."

This drew a laugh from their mysterious benefactor. "Instinctive fascination with nuclear technology is, as best we can tell, buried deep within each of the Vesiks."

Adam had reached Boothby's side, patting his shoulder. "For what purpose?"

Axley answered for him. "The Katafaj."

Zephyr's face brightened with surprise. "How do you know that term?"

Reuben didn't permit Axley to answer. "They've been onto you people for a while. But it looks like you got here earlier than Boothby and Agent Axley had intended."

Zephyr cocked his head. "We aren't here because of anything you've done. But we must finish Boothby's plan."

Adam stood eye-to-eye with Zephyr. "Why?"

Boothby felt the clouds part in his head, so he interrupted. "Somehow, you knew this was gonna happen. But why can't you just summon your own technology?"

Zephyr released Olga as Adam took her by the arm in gentle assistance. He then said, "Because it isn't *my* technology. The Katafaj long predates Ghyan living or recorded memory, and I know of no more direct way to invoke it. It is precisely the aim of Mister Boothby's program."

Adam eased Olga as she clarified her savior's words. "He comes from a world called Ghya, a sister of Earth." She then turned to Zephyr. "What is the Katafaj?"

He said, "A vast network of machines installed here and on Ghya millennia ago."

Boothby's head spun with images of his many UFO sighting reports. "So, the lights?"

Olga finished his sentence. "Are drones."

There was another klaxon as Axley said, "Maybe we should just concentrate on getting out of here. Why do you want to bring the Katafaj here?"

Zephyr said, "As was indicated earlier, our transportation requires refueling, and the core of one of the basic Katafaj drones should provide an adequate substitute. We can summon some of them by activating the fuel rods intended for the microreactor being built here."

Boothby found them all staring at him, one after the other. His anxiety spiked. "Jeezus, I tried to open the door, but you know what happened."

Zephyr pointed to Olga. "Together, you can defeat the rudimentary security system in this building."

Reuben's reproachful face was becoming a thing, or so Boothby thought. "If it's rudimentary, why can't you overcome it? Aren't you the expert?"

Zephyr shrugged as his green eyes sparkled. "Did I say that? The system is self-organizing, and thus more unpredictable and dangerous than its creators are aware."

Axley pointed to the holoemitters which had inflicted Demmings' monstrous form on them. "It has the advantage of billions of conversations recorded. It knows how to predict anything we say or do."

Zephyr brought Boothby and Olga together. "Professor Kunskapsen can temporarily generate a temporal dilation. You, Mister Boothby, can than access the computer's network with greater ease."

The lighting changed to a garish, blinding white. All of them shielded their eyes as Kharla said, "I am releasing a neurosuppressant aerosol into the corridor. You will suffer less if you lay down on the floor now."

Reuben scoffed at her. "I think you mean *lie*, not *lay*."

There was a hissing sound, so Zephyr said, "Let us begin."

He escorted Boothby and Olga to the holoemitters. Boothby asked, "Just try what I tried before?"

Zephyr brought Olga's cold hand into Boothby's warm free one. "Each of you can do this, and the sooner, the better. Olga, just relax, and remember a memory you love. Then, imagine yourself there."

Boothby took a deep breath as he held the focus stone to the emitters. Olga's grasp on his other hand tightened as a flash of light appeared about them. Boothby turned to ask Zephyr another question, but the Ghyan stood completely still. He looked back to the others in the lab, and none stirred even slightly. He somehow could see the drops of poison the Kharla system was releasing into their air. He knew so much about everything he examined. The emergency lighting had slowed in its rotating color flashes, and the light became even redder.

He swallowed hard as he squeezed the focus stone. It sent shocks into his body, and he slammed shut his eyelids. Reopening them, he stood once more in a vast web of energy vertices, colored against the four subgraph primitives constituting Kharla's primary neural network. Energy still moved about it, but much more slowly. He started to talk, but Olga held his hand. Turning to her, he said, "Professor?"

She opened her own eyes before looking around the network. "Where are we, Boothby?"

He said, "Inside the AI's virtual brain, I think."

She took a step forward, watching the graphical edge give and push against her. "This must be the model trained for Kharla."

Boothby squinted to see a horizon of vertices and edges converging several hundred nodes away. "I dunno exactly what to do."

Zephyr entered the time dilation as he pointed to the glowing embers of convolutional neurons. "Mister—"

Boothby could have nothing more to do with the formality. "Please, just call me plain ole Boothby."

The handsome Ghyan nodded. "As you wish, Boothby. The professor can slow time for a bit, though her powers are weak. You can discover the design of the network to locate the input gates. Though the dimension appears high, your amplified switching speed should make it possible to traverse them quickly. We must apply a small perturbation to nodes flagged by the focus stone as chinks. Once done, the security system will eliminate the alert status, and the door will open."

Olga squeezed Boothby's hand. "I'll keep the dilation in place as long as I can."

Boothby gulped hard as he walked to the chain of energy gates providing an entry point for Kharla. He could hear a desperately slow voice speak, and he guessed it was Kharla herself. "Boothby... Zephyr lies to you... I can give you what you want..."

Olga shouted to him. "I'm increasing the dilation, though you must hurry!"

Kharla's voice became a single drone, a horror in synthetic sound. Boothby was uncertain what to do, but he touched the first node. Somehow knew exactly the gesture of his fingers needed to shift the input. His hand tingled as he placed it inside the node, and the sparkling energy burst into a crescendo as its color changed from red to green. He dashed from node to node, recoloring each with manipulations he understood in the moment.

Zephyr said, "Excellent, Boothby. You are almost finished." Once he'd recolored a gate, many downstream nodes changed colors, pouring from one tier to the next. Energies from the perturbed gates flowed faster, splashing the enormous grid with green, blue, and orange.

Boothby thought it funny that he'd zipped across hundreds if not thousands of nodes in the multitiered network. He boasted to himself, "Keir Dullea, eat your heart out."

Zephyr said within his head, "The professor cannot maintain the dilation for more than twenty seconds. You must hurry!"

Boothby was uncertain whether hours were passing, but as he bounded from one part of the network to another, his became child's play. The entry tier would supply data from Kharla's many feeds, including images, sounds, online events, and building facilities. He knew each of them as he knew the lines on his palms. His brain exploded as he traced the adversarial paths through the network—they were ripe for the picking. "I'm almost done!" he boomed to them.

The vastly slowed discharges regained some speed, signaling to Boothby that Olga's help would disappear. But he was a step ahead, sealing the final node to confuse and disable Kharla. "Almost done," he shouted. Fingering the last node delivered a hefty electrical shock to him, frazzling him. The dilation ended, but the damage was done. He watched the dozens of tiers explode with energy, with the system flagging fault after fault.

The stone released him as he returned to the waking world. Alarms blared and blasted as he fell to his knees. Reuben and Axley caught him as he asked, "What happened?"

Reuben said, "What do you mean? You closed your eyes, then you fell."

Boothby fought to reopen his eyes as he heard Zephyr say, "It appears you succeeded."

Fighting to remain awake, he said, "I was gone for days."

Kharla's voice screamed over the intercoms, at last dying to a well-earned if not complete silence. Boothby lost consciousness just as he heard Zephyr say, "With the way safely cleared, we'll require Doctor Nakamura and, if I'm correct, Miss Voyant."

Reuben's deep voice boomed. "Why? This place is nothing but hazards."

He heard nothing more.

28.Summoning the Lights

*F****

Frankie followed Chevur down a walkway lined with touchscreen-covered walls, advances reminiscent of weird sci-fi shows Tyler liked to watch. His thoughts, for the moment, bounced between his sister, brother, and father—he wondered what they would think of him. He hoped they'd understand that Frankie held a special place in the Lord's plan.

Yanking him back to the present, Varnum's voice boomed from the stage ahead. "I am gratified to stand amidst so intellectually sound *homo sapiens*. Laboring here as you do suggests that the American dream, a capitalist utopia, is alive and kicking." There were cheers which jumped in volume as Chevur badged into a door to their left. They entered at the rear of the stage, but Frankie could see the crowd just beyond Varnum's silhouette, obscured by the rear-facing stage lights.

Chevur patted Frankie's arm. "We shall sit behind him; after you," he said as he gestured to a comfortable pair of armchairs.

Frankie settled into his seat as he listened. Varnum repeated many of his own catchphrases, along with his staunch defense of military interventions he deemed, "necessary to preserve the global order essential to individual economic liberty."

This continued for several minutes, and though Frankie listened feverishly, he found himself furious that Chevur tinkered on his phone. True, the screen wasn't all that bright, and the stage lights meant Frankie could see almost nothing, but the lack of etiquette miffed him. Varnum discussed at length his thesis that, "mapping one's life with meaning is more important than compelling through childish pranks attention from authoritative leaders." Varnum spoke to an energetic audience who applauded

374

early and often, but the tenor of goodwill disintegrated when he said, "It is unfair to require public figures to indulge woke cry-for-attention fads which appear today but flee tomorrow."

Someone from the crowd shouted, "But isn't that what you do?! You use the word 'woke' with the wingnut fad."

He stopped, scratching his silvering hair with a flick of a wrist. "I require the standard of truth, and is not ephemeral, sir."

A woman piled her views on. "That's your opinion, not fact, Professor."

Another voice screeched from near the front of the audience. "Do you believe in fidelity, Professor Varnum?"

He said, "I do not understand what you mean. Fidelity as in—"

The voice answered. "*Marital* fidelity?"

Frankie was enraged, tapping his leg fast and with fury. Varnum cast his head back with laughter. "What is this? Impugn my character because you dislike my words? I have shared a beautiful life with my dear wife of thirty-two years."

The voice traded laughter with him. "Then I invite you, Varnum, to watch."

He said, "I don't believe you're part of the program, young man. This—"

The dark curtain behind Frankie and Chevur flashed with light as three projectors shot energy across it. Frankie watched Varnum wheel about to see it, so he and Chevur did the same. A video played, and, at first, Frankie could make no more of it than when his tech-challenged father flailed his phone while trying to record a video. At last, the screen focused on a young man's face. With one hand, he pulled his wavy hair from his forehead. Winking at the camera, he raised it. He was prone, and his back and butt were bared for the world to see. An older man appeared behind him, and dropping to his knees, his face was that of Varnum. The crowd gasped as he said, "I will plow this soil, but let's get you wet."

He buried his nose and mouth into the guy's crack, and the crowd gasped almost in unison. Frankie was frozen in place as the tick and tock of twenty seconds moved at a glacier's pace. The young man moaned as Varnum squeezed his buttocks apart.

Chevur leapt to his feet, shouting, "Deactivate those projectors! Now!" He tore his phone from his pocket as he screamed, "Get me the goddamned IT in this building. Now!"

Frankie wanted to vomit as he watched his idol lick a man's butthole. The locusts thrummed in his skull as he tried to shut the images from his head. The camera darted back to the young man's face as he winked with his nauseating moans. He then said, "Fuck me, daddy V. Fuck my boyhole."

Varnum's thin body stood as he disentangled his tongue from the young man's rectum. The live Varnum shouted, "For Christ's sakes, shut that off! That isn't me! *That isn't me*!!!"

Just as the film started to depict Varnum inserting himself into his little slut, the screen went dark. The audience booed him as his chief heckler shouted, "Fuck you, Picoveer! See Demmings' friends. Thanks for laying us off!!!"

Varnum dodged an apple hurled from the crowd just before he turned to flee. Chevur pulled Frankie to his feet as he whispered, "This way, Tech Sergeant! Come, Professor Varnum!"

He swiped his badge at the door, it opened, and the three escaped the jeering. Chevur spoke deliberately at his phone. "How did our separated employees gain access? Heads will roll for this, I promise you!"

An Indian woman replied, "Please, sir, we are trying to understand what happened."

Varnum was white as a sheet and covered with sweat. He said, "That was libel, plain and simple, Mister Chevur."

Chevur glanced at him but continued to complain to his phone. "I will fire all of your department if you do not find those responsible. This is a disgrace."

The mousy woman's voice answered, "Social media is exploding, sir. This is unprecedented."

Frankie found himself standing opposite of Varnum. His once proud hero met his eyes, and there was fear. "You believe me, don't you? It was a deep fake, designed to humiliate me." He then looked at Frankie's stump, and revulsion waved over his moist, colorless face.

Frankie didn't know what to say. As much as he wanted to agree, he could easily detect the humiliation and shame Varnum felt, neither of which would make sense if the video was fiction. Chevur pounded his phone against the wall. "Goddammit, I'll have their skins for this."

Varnum breathed hard. "I should go, Mister Chevur. Drive me to my hotel?"

He looked at Varnum with disgust. "You are a fool, exposing yourself so. I should make you take a rideshare, hoping they've watched your humiliation on their Space4Us accounts." He pointed to Frankie. "This wounded soldier was here to meet you, and now you are not fit to lick his boots." He then rolled his eyes, bobbing his head side to side. "You'd probably enjoy that."

Varnum looked at him with no more care than one would offer a tick on a dog's back. "Thank you for your, umm, service. You believe me, don't you? What one does in his bedroom is his business."

Chevur glued his eyes to his phone. "You mean *whom one does*. Unmitigated disaster. Disaster!"

Frankie glared at his fallen hero, pissed about Tyler, his hand, the Lord, the whole thing. "I want to go now," he said.

C***

Conique had placed her arm about Agent Carolina as the stout woman regathered herself. She was elated that Doctor Nakamura had found her, though his demeanor was unpleasant along any channel of conversation. Janet's color had much improved since the physician treated her, and the young girl now sat inside the van. If it weren't for the suffering of Conique's comrades, she would devote all of her attention to Aurum—she was woman's best friend to be sure. She was no worse for wear—her fluffy fur was as soft as Conique remembered it to be.

The others were preoccupied, she decided. "You seem too calm, Miss Voyant. Are you not worried about your husband?"

Shigeru said, "Look, I'm not the first to claim belief in another, but Zephyr is no monster."

Conique said, "And I'd be the first to have faith in another."

Janet punctured their hypothetical. "Look, it doesn't matter. I'd know him to see him."

Carolina glanced at her watch. "We need to move away from this building if Picoveer security wakes up soon."

Shigeru nabbed their attention by pointing to the Heart's entrance. "Speak of the devil, there they are."

Conique eagerly recognized her husband and Adam as they carried Boothby. She stood, plodding herself towards them. "Dear, what happened to him?"

Reuben said, "It wouldn't make a whole hell of a lot of sense if I tried to explain."

A man emerged alongside a golden-haired woman she recalled from her dreams. She said, "You are Zephyr. Who are you, Miss?"

Shigeru answered without offering her a chance to state it herself. "She is Professor Olga Kunskapsen, and one of us."

Carolina stood as she aimed her gun. "Stop right there, Norcross."

Janet seconded her. "I think it's him!"

Adam shook his head, holding his spare palm open to them. "No! Babycakes, this is his brother Zephyr! He's here to help."

Janet sat up to get a better look. "Fuck, he looks like him, but it's *not* him."

Carolina aimed her pistol into his chest. "I don't understand. How do we know we can trust you? Where is Agent Axley?"

Shigeru stood between them, impressing Conique with a hint of selflessness. "Look, lady, maybe you in America sorts out your differences with bullets, but this is a little bigger than all that."

Zephyr said, "Agent Axley awaits us inside to complete our objective. I understand your concern. My brother's behavior leaves much to be desired."

Janet frowned with a sigh. "That's understatement of the millennium. What the fuck is Norcross trying to do?"

Zephyr said, "I promise to tell you everything I can as soon as we're safely away from this place."

Adam said, "Baby, just trust us for now. I really believe he's here to help."

She didn't seem to budge, but Reuben agreed. "Nurse, I think he's the real deal."

Pushing hair from her face, she said, "Brother or not, I can see why you like him, Adam."

Winded from carrying Boothby, Adam replied, "That has nothing to do with it."

This left Janet on the edge of her seat. "So you'd be just as likely to take his side if he were a total dog?"

Conique patted Aurum as the dog groaned. "This is mixed company, child."

Adam said, "You're embarrassing me, babycakes." He then mouthed, *hot as fuck.*

Carolina rolled her eyes. "Gays."

Conique stood aside as Reuben and Adam lifted a slumbering Boothby into the van. Zephyr took one of her hands to kiss it. "Your steadfastness saturates all around you, Miss Voyant. Boothby will be fine, though we must hurry." Turning to the others, he said, "This is Doctor Shigeru Nakamura, the sixth Vesik." Turning to him, he said, "Doctor, I require you and Miss Voyant to join me inside."

Shigeru asked, "What's wrong with this man?"

Adam checked Boothby's pulse as he said, "I don't know what he did, but he shutdown the security system inside the Heart."

Reuben knelt before their retriever to shower her with affection. "Aurum, girl, I thought we lost you." He looked back to them. "Absolutely not. My Connie isn't going anywhere close to that radioactive mess."

Zephyr locked eyes with her, and she felt weak against them. He said, "Miss Voyant, you understand, do you not?"

She answered at last, "Reuben, it's alright. It won't hurt me."

He stood upright. "What are you talking about, Connie?"

She placed a hand on his chest. "I've never told you because I didn't want you to worry." Zephyr nodded for her to continue, so she said, "I learned during our first outing with the Plowshares that I'm immune to radiation."

Shigeru halted his examination of Boothby to ask, "Come again?"

Conique shrugged in relief. "It's true."

Reuben's eyes widened. "Jesus. I thought you were lucky."

She could sense the welling curiosity in each of her companions, so she related the tale as best she could. "We were supposed to deface a trident missile, but the inspections team had left the payload casing open. It was some sort of freak mistake one would not expect. So I and three others did our business to it, and they came down with ARS not long after. I didn't have a symptom one."

378

Zephyr smiled. "It's another of the Vesiks' gifts, and I'm glad you discovered it."

Reuben's face bunched in frustration. "Dammit, Connie, how could ya keep that from me?"

She patted him. "I just assumed God really wanted me to foul up those weapons, and that I couldn't be harmed by them. And it has always been true."

His anger became laughter. "And here I just thought you were just insane about high risk behavior."

She shared the laugh as they embraced. "Well, that too, dear."

Shigeru studied her with his black eyes. "Remarkable. What's inside of you could revolutionize my field if we knew how to reproduce it."

Conique felt immodest, if only for a moment. "Doctor, that'd be a first."

Shigeru shook his head with a grin as he turned to examine Boothby. At last, he asked, "Zephyr, you said you want me and Miss Voyant?"

He said, "To finish Boothby's plan, the two of you are necessary. Mister Axley is waiting inside for the three of us."

Reuben clung to her. "What's your plan, then?"

Zephyr said, "It's simple. Doctor Nakamura can infect the fuel rods with polyplasts, activating the enriched uranium. Meanwhile, Miss Voyant and I will generate a shield to protect us. The spike should trigger the Katafaj."

Reuben said, "I'm gonna come with—"

He stopped him. "No, Doctor. Her abilities are weak, and I cannot guarantee she can cover all of us at once. I'll serve as catalyst."

Conique took her husband's hands, uncertain whether she would see him again. "Dear, look, we've made it this far. If I'm immune to radiation, then it'll be fine." He didn't relent, so she said, "Look, we thought a month ago that I would die in a nursing home. Two days ago, I tried to end my own life. But something happened in the presence of these two," she said as she pointed to Janet and Boothby. "We're stronger together, and there's a greater destiny here."

Reuben kissed her hand and then her cheek. Turning to Zephyr, he said, "Please make sure she stays safe."

The Ghyan nodded as Shigeru examined Olga. "Zephyr, should we get these others back to your skytax?" he asked.

As Zephyr took Conique's hand, he said, "Power levels are minimal now. I've sent it into a parking position above this facility. It isn't ideal, but I require you to gather fifty meters north, behind that structure." He pointed to a warehouse in the distance.

Reuben acknowledged with a nod as he shouted to Carolina. "You ready, Agent?"

She motioned for Adam as he helped Olga into the van. Carolina pointed to Conique. "Yeah. Just be careful, Miss Voyant."

Zephyr tugged at Conique. "Let's go, Miss?"

The three of them headed towards the building as Conique heard the van engine turn over. She said a silent prayer as they reached the sliding glass doors.

The lengthy corridor before them alternated between pitch black and dark red, with shocks flickering along light panels along the walls. Shigeru said, "Hard to believe this is the pinnacle of American engineering."

Zephyr said, "The facilities within this structure are all linked to security, threaded into their expert system. Boothby and the professor disabled it temporarily, so we'll be contending with aberrations along the way."

Conique's eyes were wide open, and she laughed. "I could almost see better blindfolded. How far are we going?"

He said, "The central elevator is no longer in service. We'll descend three floors through a maintenance stairwell."

A pop of electrical energy startled Conique. Shigeru caught her as she said, "I'm a little rusty in my infiltrations, Doctor." Squeezing Zephyr's hand, she asked, "They said you're not from this world? You're here to save us?"

He didn't look from the corridor ahead, though she couldn't make heads or tails of it. Zephyr answered, "I traveled a great distance to be here. But whether we succeed, I can't say."

She felt hopeful, even if he didn't. "I knew someone like you would come."

Ever derisive, Shigeru whispered, "This isn't the Son of Man or Buddha or Allah or any other bullshit deity. And we might still all die, Miss."

Conique reached into her pocket to find a pack of cigarettes. Handing one to him, she said, "I'd recognize smoke withdrawal anywhere."

He turned to her with a puzzled but amused expression. "Isn't smoking against your religion?"

She chuckled as she flipped the lighter on. "I don't follow too many rules, Doctor." She handed him a smoke as he grinned. "You have a charming side, I see."

Zephyr coughed once at it. "Tobacco. We have something similar on Ghya. Let's hope the fire suppression system doesn't switch on."

At last, they reached the malfunctioning elevator. The doors were parted, but there was no car inside. Conique puffed her cigarette as she pondered the way down. "I guess we're not going to jump."

Shigeru said, "I would offer to break your fall, but you'd flatten me."

Conique patted his firm upper arm. "You'll be old, one day."

Zephyr said, "The elevator shorted out on our way back to the entrance. We'll take the road less traveled." He wedged open the maintenance door. Yellow lights turned on to trace a path to the stairs.

The three of them squeezed through the door to a stunningly narrow set of stairs. Conique looked down, but there was pitch black. "I don't even want to know how far this goes. It's a heart attack waiting to happen."

Shigeru flicked orange embers from his cigarette. "Says the overweight septuagenarian who smokes."

Zephyr pointed to a small door visible with nearby maintenance lamps. "That leads to the Kaleido lab where Axley awaits us." He looked to Conique, the yellow light rendering his contours even more pallid. "You follow me—the steps are narrow and steep."

As he moved between the handrails on either side of the grate steps, she placed one hand on his shoulder and the other on a cold hard rail. Shigeru dropped his cigarette, crushing it with his shoe. He then followed her.

They moved slowly as she said, "Well-done Voyant patty on gluten free alien and doctor buns."

Zephyr laughed quietly, but Conique could feel Shigeru's tension as he said, "Food, at a time like this?"

Conique laughed. "Well, there's a lot here to keep going."

The stairs creaked and groaned as they plodded forward. Conique was gasping for air when Shigeru said, "Zeph, she'll collapse if we keep going. And I don't wanna carry her."

She said, "This lighting adds ten pounds, Doctor."

There was another groan, loud and jarring. Conique stumbled, planting both palms on Zephyr's shoulders. He didn't waver, but she admitted, "Okay, maybe I am a little over weight."

Zephyr glanced above them. "That's not the problem. I can feel the security system attempting to reassert control."

Conique could see a flash of light from above. Shigeru said, "It looks like someone is playing with sparklers up there."

Zephyr heaved forward. "We must run, now!"

Conique fell forward, but Zephyr held her weight. Shigeru threaded his arms under her own as he pulled weight off her feet. They stumbled step after step, and she was certain she would fall. The metal beneath them groaned, and the stairs bounced and swayed. She cried, "Oh my God, I think it'll collapse!" The groan became a shrieking sound, and the structure shuddered.

They reached the landing as the door popped open. Agent Axley poked his face into the stairwell as he shouted, "This way!"

He reached for them, yanking Zephyr through the door. The Ghyan wheeled around to face her, and he grasped Shigeru's arms. Still interlocked through Conique's shoulders, they made it possible for Zephyr to haul them together. But she became stuck within the tiny maintenance door's frame.

Shigeru shouted over the clanging racket from above. "Christ, you're too fat!"

Zephyr said, "I am very sorry for the pain—relax your muscles!" He yanked at Shigeru's arms while Conique's hips and legs screamed at the compression.

Shigeru shouted into Conique's ear. "Dammit, don't tense. He said *relax*!"

"Let me think, then!" She breathed out, trying to remember any helpful mantra from her last yoga session. "Aum," she chanted.

"Seriously?" He screamed in pain. "Fuck, you'll dislocate my shoulders!"

Zephyr nodded to him. "I'm very sorry, Doctor!"

He yanked at them one last time, and Conique felt Shigeru's arms give underneath her shoulders. He hollered and whimpered in agony as they squeezed through the frame.

She and Shigeru fell forward onto Zephyr and Axley as the shivering wreck of stairwells behind them gave way. Conique turned her head just to see the stairwell drop, with girders and gratings clashing against the concrete walls in a dazzle of sparks. The small door slid shut, quieting the disaster behind them.

Shigeru gasped, out of breath for more screaming. Zephyr and Axley pulled him off Conique, and the Ghyan said, "This will hurt, Doctor." Shigeru nodded in understanding as Zephyr grasped his left shoulder with one hand while gripping his dangling arm with the other. He pulled out with a crack and pop as Shigeru yelped. "Very good, Doctor. Just one more." He repeated the procedure with the other arm before placing a palm on his forehead. "Forgive me for the pain, Doctor."

Conique was just a heap on the floor. "I'm too old for this," she muttered.

Axley offered her a hand. "You're doing pretty well, Miss Voyant."

She said, "Agent, this is Doctor Nakamura."

His expression brightened. "Another of the seven?"

Conique could barely catch her breath, but she shared his excitement. "Yes! He came with Zephyr here."

Zephyr helped Shigeru lean into the wall. The doctor said, "Nevermind all that. What the fuck just happened?"

Axley pointed to the elevator shaft nearby, the counterpart to the shaft entrance they bypassed on the ground floor. "Kharla is still functional. She destroyed the elevator after you took it."

Zephyr looked back to the maintenance shaft. "The system severed the maintenance stairs."

Shigeru breathed hard through the pain. He said, "What the fuck? You mean to say that a Kharla bot did that?"

Conique asked, "An AI?"

Axley shook his head. "You should have left Boothby here. Unless you know how to cut her cord permanently."

Zephyr glanced to the end of the corridor. "We won't need to deactivate her if we can access the fuel rods." He knelt to Conique. "Miss Voyant, we must go a bit farther."

She took his hand, and Axley pulled her by her other arm. She tried to stay quiet, but the pain forced her to squeal. "Jesus, it's arthritis. Sorry."

Once on her feet, she reached for Shigeru. "Doctor, I hope you're not hurting too much."

He breathed hard with sweat pouring off him. "Peachy, Miss Voyant."

Axley whispered as they moved forward. "I don't know what other surprises we can expect, but the door to the fuel storage is reset. I didn't go in."

Shigeru groaned. "No interest in becoming another nuclear casualty?"

Axley said, "The night is young."

Zephyr pushed a large door aside, and then they continued. Conique glimpsed a small door ahead labeled with the trefoil. He pointed to it. "Boothby and the professor weakened the security system so that we may open this door. But you, Miss Voyant, and Doctor Nakamura must activate the rods."

He released Conique's hand as she leaned on a table near the door. Shigeru swigged his flask as he said, "Zeph, I'm not sure I can do this. The polyplasts are hard enough to control."

She grabbed the flask from him. "I think I'll need this, too." The whiskey was stronger than any she'd ever tasted. Coughing, she returned it to him.

Axley said, "Zephyr, understand that our contact within Kymara agreed to this plan. But I believe they intended to trap us here."

Zephyr touched the door, examining it with care. "The Katafaj will appear, no matter the motives of any who aided us. Miss Voyant can provide shielding as Doctor Nakamura overloads the rods. But it is safer for you, Agent, to make your way to the others—Miss Voyant's powers are limited now."

Axley shook his head. "I'm not sure there is another way out of here. Besides, the storage room is lead-lined, and you'll need protection if more of Demmings' goons show up."

Zephyr frowned at that. "The lining will be insufficient once Doctor Nakamura dispatches the swarm into the rods. The others will need you."

Axley looked at Conique, and she could read his dilemma. She said, "Agent, it's okay. Zephyr and the doctor will help me escape."

He nodded before disappearing into the darkness outside the lab. Zephyr grasped the handle on the trefoil-marked door, and his hand pulsed with flashes of electricity. The lock thudded as its pins retreated, and the door peeked open.

Conique heard a voice she knew all too well. "Mother?"

An illuminated figure stood inside the rod room, and Conique gasped. "My God. Angie?"

She extended her arms. "Mother, I missed you."

O✱✱✱

Olga sat next to Adam and Janet inside the van. Boothby had regained consciousness, and they updated each other on the curious ways they happened to converge in Picoveer's backyard. Boothby was a gabber, yammering about his long search for lights in the sky. Janet appeared to have nerves of steel, and her brother Adam stayed at her side, as though this was his purpose. Aurum, the weary retriever, lay at their feet.

Reuben and Agent Carolina remained vigilant on either side of the van. She overheard him ask whether the operatives Shigeru eluded back at his homestead could have followed them. She indicated that they had spoofed the van's IP, but the transponder would have provided its final signal there. The explanation didn't appear to satisfy him, and Olga couldn't blame him for the frustration.

Boothby repeated himself. "Agent, how long are we supposed to wait?"

Reuben snapped at him. "Is there somewhere else you need to be?"

Janet shook her head. "Doctor, there's no reason to be mean to him."

He leaned against the van, patting a mitt of a hand onto the doorframe. "Sorry. They've been gone—"

Carolina finished his sentence as she checked the clip in her pistol. "Fifteen minutes, Doctor. I think whatever they're doing will take longer than that."

Boothby's expression conveyed confusion, though he sounded more agitated. "I should be in there. It's my plan."

Reuben shouted in a whisper. "Quiet! Someone's coming."

Olga leaned into the seat in front of her to spy a better look. There were half a dozen vans speeding along a path perpendicular to their position, all heading for the Heart. Leading the rear was an SUV with tinted windows. She said, "I'll bet you that's Demmings on his way to finish what he started."

Adam asked Carolina, "Can you contact your Obfucius friend?"

Reuben growled at that. "How do we know he didn't set this trap for us?"

Boothby rocked back and forth. "I doubt they can really trap Mister Zephyr, right?"

Carolina held a fist skyward. "Shush, people. That last car is coming to us."

The SUV rounded the corner to face their van. It stopped fifteen or so meters from them as its doors swung open. Demmings appeared, surrounded by security. He brandished a bullhorn before shouting, "You are trespassing on private property. Agents Axley and Carolina, I know you're here. I would ask how you breached our security, but disabling Kharla takes the prize today."

Carolina whispered into the van, "Be still, people."

Demmings continued, "I also know Olga Kunskapsen is with you. You, along with Edgar Boothby, Janet Yazzie, and Conique Voyant—fuck me, what a stupid name—will *all* surrender to me, now."

Reuben pulled a shotgun from beneath the seat, angling it to check its load. His voice boomed. "The hell we will! Why should we do that, Demmings?"

Olga moved to the edge of her seat before hopping outside the van. Reuben caught her as she stumbled, righting her as best he could. She raised her voice, but it remained weak. "Carl, we're at a crossroads."

He laughed as he traced the alley with his hands. "Olga, there you are, my dear. No, I'd say you're cornered."

Reuben said, "It's a metaphor, stupid."

She clung to Reuben as she summoned all her strength to shout. "Please believe me, Carl. The world hangs in the balance. Let us complete our work."

Demmings guffawed a pig squeal, an eccentric laugh Olga had hated having to hear in the classes and seminars they shared. "We have the manpower. We have most of the guns here. Two of you are armed? I think you should surrender, and then we'll talk about your *work*. For starters, just how did you spoof my Kharla? No one even at Intellidez knows how to do that."

Olga's voice was close to giving out, but she shouted, nonetheless. "What happened to you, Carl? You used to be gentler than all this."

He replied, "Olga, the world has changed. You don't know the things I've seen. The classroom doesn't prepare you for the realities of elite leadership."

Reuben sighed hard. "Jesus, I hate this guy."

Janet asked, "What about your focus stone?"

Boothby fumbled at his pocket as though he thought he'd lost his prized possession. "I dunno if I'm strong enough to use it."

Carolina nodded to him. "They don't know that." Turning to their foes, she hollered, "We have a weapon which can destroy this entire facility, Demmings. We've overwhelmed your AI system. Want us to wreck this place? Billions of dollars lost?"

He scoffed. "I call bullshit. You would have done it if you were going to. But I know about your powers."

Olga bit her lip. "That's more his style. Is he Obfucius?"

Carolina frowned as she shifted weight to another foot. "Not possible. The play makes no sense."

Reuben's breathing was heavy as Adam emerged from the van. "They're not taking us. Do you guys have a plan?"

Reuben and Carolina exchanged looks of fear. But Olga knew the game wouldn't end there. She grabbed Carolina's pistol and aimed it for her own head. Demmings could see her as he craned his neck.

Carolina struggled, but she released Olga as she whispered, "I got this, Agent." She then shouted, "I'll end all of this, Carl! Without all of us, we're no good to you."

He shook his head with another God-awful squeal. "I don't believe you, Olga. Suicide isn't your style."

She raised the pistol, fired it into the sky, then back at her head. "Think it through, Carl! I've spent six months preparing for death, and I've made peace with it. I won't be of any use to you if I die a second time. You're going to let us go."

Carolina whispered to her, "This is not going to work, Miss. That pig-faced bastard won't stop unless we kill him."

Olga knew the truth of it. "We don't need to do that. I just need time."

*S****

Shigeru's shoulders burned like hell. He swallowed the last of his whiskey as he leaned into one of the tables near the fuel storage compartment. The young girl's voice had captured Conique's attention. Zephyr said, "She's an illusion, Miss Voyant."

The girl said, "Mother, I've waited to see you so long. Why did you leave me?"

Conique's face twisted in pain. "Angie," she whispered. Closing her eyes, she said, "I know it isn't *you*. My daughter is dead."

The hologram wavered and froze. Zephyr pointed to it. "The security system is attempting to reassert itself. We must activate the fuel rods now."

Shigeru could see three projection holes within the storage compartment, so he stabbed two of the emitters with a paper-cutter blade, dissolving the young girl. Conique shook her head with squeezed shut eyes. "How did they do that? So cruel."

Zephyr took her by her shoulders. "The security system here possesses access to the global information network—reconstructing figures and voices is easy for it. I am sorry, Miss Voyant."

She uttered, "So real. So real."

Shigeru grunted in pain. "They call that an *intelligence*, supposedly more dangerous than anything else in this world."

Zephyr pushed the door open as he said, "Machines incapable of agency have little difficulty robbing others of it. The system is still mostly offline, so we must continue."

Shigeru followed the others into the room. Large cylindrical bins lined the walls, and the Ghyan tore open two of them. At least twenty rods jutted upward within each of the containers.

Shigeru examined them from top to bottom. They were thick, surrounded by several filaments meshed along their surfaces. He sighed in pain. "I've spent my career trying to stop this. And now you want me to set the thing on fire."

Conique anguished at it all. "What am I doing here? Why?"

Zephyr clutched her. "Courage, Miss Voyant. It is an illusion, meant to confuse you."

Turning to Shigeru, he said, "If we cannot calm her, you must expend polyplasts to stabilize her neurology."

Shigeru took Conique's hands, hoping a good old-fashioned bedside manner might do the trick. "Miss Voyant, you have faith that things will work out. We're in a jam, and you're the only one who can get us through this. Remember the nukes?"

She met his eyes, but in them he could see only terror. He raised a single hand to her forehead, the pain searing his rotator cuff. "Plowshares?" she asked.

He said, "Yes, Miss Voyant. Think about the nukes."

Zephyr took her free hand. "Miss Voyant, please, imagine how you felt when you touched the nukes. What happened inside?"

She breathed steadily as Zephyr continued speaking. "Think of it. That feeling will protect us."

Her eyes fluttered for a moment before they opened wide. She said, "A prayer that the radiation not hurt me. I feel it!"

Zephyr exerted himself as he placed a palm to her shoulder. "I can amplify her power. Now, Doctor, please send your polyplasts onto the rods as you take my hand!"

Shigeru found the Ghyan's touch electric, and his brain raced as polyplasts poured into his body. He felt a warmth emanating from Conique as she chanted almost inaudibly. He could see the millions of bots swarming into him, damaging and repairing tissue along the way. The process appeared to be as painful for Zephyr as it was for Shigeru, but he tried to retain focus on his task.

The machines repaired his injured shoulders as they passed along his lymphatic system. As they made their way to his free hand, he placed it on one of the rods. The heat blistered his hand, but he held firm to it.

He could see the bots as they flowed from his sizzling hand, invading one fuel rod after the other. The bots themselves struggled against the radiation, several of which disintegrated. But their carcasses provided a safer path for their subsequent waves. They encamped themselves along the rivulets of uranium, colliding with each other to multiply their kinetic energies.

Shigeru felt as though a freight train was passing through his head, and he knew his own blood vessels were fraying as his nerves fought to control the mighty weapon he now possessed. He eased off, fearful that the fuel rods would detonate.

Zephyr faltered, but Conique helped brace him. She shouted, "Do it, Doctor Nakamura! We'll survive! Believe me!"

The Ghyan seconded her as the crimson in his onyx suit reached a blinding crescendo. "The way is clear—activate them!"

Shigeru slammed shut his eyes, pushing the roar aside. There were hundreds of thousands of nanobots awaiting his command, and, with one last enervative push, he ordered them to turn their energies inward. Row after row fired heat and pressure into the filaments, forcing critical mass. For the briefest of instances, he witnessed the most primal forces of the universe dance to a tune natural law abhorred: fission. The uranium atoms began to fissure, releasing their mighty nucleic power in a cascading explosion.

He released the rods, tearing much of the tissue from his hand. He fell into Zephyr as his brain swirled. Conique shouted above the roar. "I can't stop the heat!"

Zephyr held Shigeru as he pushed her out the door. "Our work here is finished— let's escape now!"

B***

Boothby shivered at the standoff between Olga and Picoveer's vicious head. He tapped the focus stone, but nothing came of it. "I can't do anything!"

Janet patted him. "They'll come through for us, B-man."

Rasping, he blurted, "I wish I could do something. Dammit!"

Demmings then squealed in anger. "What the fuck?! Get off me you mangy thing!"

Boothby pulled himself up using the headrest of the seat before him. Demmings clutched his neck as a black blur of fur sailed off him. He exclaimed, "Archie?!"

The security force opened fire at the cat as Carolina tackled Olga to the ground. Reuben dove into the van, but Archie was the intended target. Aurum growled, displeased to miss the action. But bullets struck the windshield and headlights of the van, causing them to duck for cover inside. Boothby kept watch as long as he could, relieved that Archie dodged every shot before skittering underneath their van.

Demmings apparently didn't shut off the bullhorn, so it captured his every word. "Fuck, I'm dizzy. That cat did something to me! Fuck!" He fell into the closed passenger door of his SUV. "Hold your goddamned fire, you fucking morons! Get them! Get..." He collapsed to the ground as his squad ceased their onslaught.

Boothby tried to get out of the van, but Adam and Janet restrained him. "B-man, they're after you. It's safer to stay in here."

He whined at them. "But the cat *needs* me."

Adam shouted to the others as he hopped out. "Doctor, are you alright?"

Carolina covered Olga with her body, but Boothby could see she'd been hit by a stray bullet. Adam helped Reuben to his feet before tending to Carolina. The doctor said, "I'm okay. Just bruised. Agent, are you hit?"

He rolled her onto her back, and Boothby could see that her chest was covered in blood. Adam pressed his hands to her would as Reuben patted her face. Janet asked, "What is it, Adam? Doctor?"

Adam answered with panic in the young man's voice. "She's been hit in the chest. I can't tell how much damage, but she's bleeding fast."

Reuben helped Olga to her feet as he glanced to the security forces. "You okay, Professor?"

She nodded. "I'm fine. What is happening over there?"

He said, "It looks like Demmings is down. The cat did it."

Olga rubbed her neck. "Cat?"

Boothby bounced in his seat. "Archie is his name! He's mine. God, can ya see him?"

Reuben pounded his hand on the van. "Dammit, man, Carolina is down! Stay calm for a minute!"

Boothby was angry, but a seismic rumble caught his attention. He shot his eyes outside, and it appeared that the security forces were looking back towards the Heart building, just out of their line-of-sight. He lost balance, falling back into his seat.

Reuben said, "What the hell is that?"

A second rumble shook the van so hard that Boothby thought it would flip over. He clutched the seat as he watched Reuben and Adam fall to the concrete once more. Archie popped through the open side door, landing squarely in Boothby's arms. The small animal licked at a wound on his back, causing Boothby's eyes to water. "You just are too brave, cat." One last pulse shattered all the glass within the van, rocking it hard. He shouted, "Good God, it's 9.0!"

He doubled over to shield Janet and the cat as glass bits pelted them from all sides. The sky flashed with solar-level luminosity, forcing him to cover his eyes. Clutching the cat and the girl, he wondered whether the explosion would spread. For the seconds he spent in darkness, he found himself petrified that his plan might have been a delusion, after all. As the blinding light died, he peeked from his sleeves. The rumble continued like thunder from a retreating storm. The security force ahead was scattered, with their vehicles trashed from the enormous pulse. Brushing glass and debris from his coat and from Janet's long fine hair, he said, "I think it's over. Are you okay, Janet?"

She nodded. "Can you see the others?"

He passed Archie into her arms as the little guy struggled to clean his wound. "I'll check."

Stepping out of the van, he took care not to step on too much glass. Reuben and Adam were on their feet by the time he reached them. Adam knelt to Agent Carolina, but another thundercrack from above, captured his attention. Boothby looked to the darkening sky as Reuben asked, "Is this supposed to happen?"

Boothby waited, tracing the focus stone in his pocket. "I dunno. It was dark when I saw them the first time."

He helped Olga to her feet as she said, "It's like a total eclipse. Look at that!"

He caught it just in time—there was a fleeting scurry of lights high above them. Immovably attentive, he watched the lights dance into a rectangular array. For over half a century, he'd sought the lights with minimal success. With the wait over, he said, "Oh, my."

29. Wind-filled Sails

*C****

Conique clung to Zephyr, grateful he possessed great physical strength. She couldn't remember the blast, though she saw within herself a stone breaking the flow of water, sparing Shigeru and Zephyr from the brunt of it.

Opening her eyes, she could see that Shigeru followed closely, though he was burned badly. She couldn't speak, though the tumult surrounding her was too loud to fight. The Heart of Picoveer was disintegrating around them, but Zephyr moved like a shadow, flitting down another stairwell.

Rather than squander her energies trying to understand their predicament, she chanted slow prayers. It was clear to her that no matter the particulars of one's faith, believing in one another was the important thing. Zephyr was a stranger, but her mother taught her that strangers can show a kindness even the closest of kin can't fathom.

Conique understood that their part in this transcended her own knowledge, but that wasn't inconvenient to her. In fact, not knowing a fact filled her sails with wind. She pictured herself on the beach, and all was well.

Reopening her eyes, she could see Agent Axley through the Heart's glass double doors, even if he stood perpendicular to the ground. It became clear next that Zephyr carried her over his shoulder. Breathing heavily, he helped her to her feet as Axley sneezed and asked, "What happened? I think you'll bring the building down."

Shigeru shook his head. "Uranium happened. It's just a flesh wound." Shrugging, he exclaimed, "That isn't the only thing—look!" He pointed a burned

390

hand to the sky. Conique looked above at the dizzying spectacle. Eight lights had positioned themselves above the Heart.

Conique was delighted. "Dear Lord, I never thought I'd live to see the day. Literal UFOs. She'll be coming round the mountain, indeed!" Three of the eight lights darted to the south, casting a red hue on the buildings, evergreens, and construction equipment. She said, "They're in a great big hurry."

Paying no mind to the errant devices, Axley stood dumbfounded as the rumble from the Heart subsided. "Is it possible? Your technology, Zephyr?"

Watching the three bright spots skitter away, Zephyr said with concern, "We have less time than I'd hoped. To answer you question, Agent, the Katafaj is ancient, long preceding Ghya or Falterra."

Shigeru braced Conique as she heard the devices whine and reverberate. "What are they doing, now?"

Zephyr touched something on his wrist as he answered, "By design, they seek threats marked by unique energy signatures. The five above are stabilizing the reactor fuel we overloaded."

Conique asked, "The three that went yonder?"

Zephyr said, "It is best we don't find out. The response is both reflexive and brief. We must find the others at once."

"Come with me, Miss Voyant." Axley took Conique's arm around his neck as the four rushed from the broken husk that was the Heart. Conique could see the warehouse as they rounded a corner opposite to that traveled by their escape van. She plodded, and Axley maintained a consistent pace.

Marveling at the shattered glass all around them, she said, "I guess this is why you sent them behind the warehouse."

Zephyr nodded as he buttressed Shigeru into the alley. "I've hidden the skytax above this structure—it appeared the only one sound enough to bear the weight, assuming we failed to secure an alternate power source. But I require Boothby's help."

Shigeru coughed hard as he zipped his coat. "The unconscious one?"

"He usually talks a lot more, true." Conique laughed just before stumbling over bits of concrete expelled from the Heart. Axley fought to remain upright, and she felt guilt at all the diets she'd failed.

Axley complained, "Please, Miss Voyant, let's do this carefully."

She looked up just in time to see Adam and her husband kneeling on the concrete. "I wonder what's happened!"

Axley quickened his pace. "That's Carolina. Officer down. What happened?"

Adam said, "She protected us when that pig-faced Demmings opened fire. I think we've stabilized her, but she needs attention we can't give here."

Conique's thighs burned hot with the overexertion. No more than twenty seconds or so elapsed, but it felt eternal. Axley released her into Reuben's strong, eager embrace while Zephyr and Olga helped Shigeru into the van. She appeared to be cold, but there was unmistakable warmth between them.

Zephyr said, "We were successful—the Katafaj has almost finished its work, so I require Boothby's assistance."

Olga said, "He's over there!"

B***

Boothby stood, almost ready to genuflect at the scene. Five devices sat above him, and though he doubted they could know him, he certainly knew them. The frigid night those many years ago had been so critical to his development, and he wondered whether the moment could have been more perfect. He turned to see that Zephyr was standing next to him, though he didn't hear him approach. He carried Archie in his arms, but even that couldn't tear Boothby's eyes from the fixation above.

Zephyr remarked, "They're beautiful, no?"

Boothby's voice was weak. "More so than I remember. For all these years, no one believed me."

He said, "The Katafaj vexed my people for centuries, but we never doubted its purpose."

Boothby laughed at that. "I think I might be among five people in this world who understand what the lights do."

Zephyr crossed his arms. "True, you've always sought truth. It is why Ephyr entrusted you with the stone. You must use it now, Boothby."

The mention of the device diverted his attention from the show in the sky. Turning to Zephyr, he could see the man's resplendent beauty, and he wanted to trust him. Pondering it, he removed the stone from his jacket pocket. "Zephyr and Ephyr sounds a little too perfect," he said with a rasp.

Zephyr chuckled. "We were raised as brothers, often derided as Zector and Ector. Ephyr and I authored technology which transformed our world, but now is not the time. You must use your device."

Boothby sighed hard as he examined it. "I don't understand it, Mister Zephyr."

The Ghyan smirked as he planted a hand on Boothby's shoulder. "On the contrary, you have the means to discover what lies in the twilight of perception, leaving no proverbial stone unturned. I can reach you without speaking through what we call the Xarjik." His grasp tightened. "Tell me, Boothby, how does it work?"

Boothby thought it over as Archie meowed at him. It then hit him as he saw sectional diagrams of brains, connected with mesh. Almost robotically, he recited, "Neurotether! With augmentation, you can transfer information along a dimension separate from the first four. Good God, what did I see?" His mental picture disintegrated, frustrating him.

Zephyr's chiseled face was damp with perspiration. "Your powers are unfocused, as is the case with all of you. We'll need time and a rebalancing, neither of which we have in this moment. You must subdue one of the devices above if we are to make our way to the Seal."

Boothby breathed through his teeth. "I don't know if I can."

Zephyr took him in hand, holding his forearms. "Boothby, you have planned this for years. This is the very reason you sought Miss Voyant. This is the reason you stalked Jacques Valles. It's the reason you publish your newsletter, dog the intelligence agencies, and speak when anyone will listen."

Boothby's head angled as his eyes widened. "You know about that?"

Zephyr grinned. "Ephyr came to this world to help us find its seven Vesiks. He and his knowledge have vanished, but each of you possesses seeded knowledge of the others, even if it sits below your consciousness."

Boothby looked back as the devices continued their work. "A mad plan can appear sane in an insane world."

Zephyr's green eyes absorbed Boothby. "This is what you have sought. You would consider yourself an unconventional hero, but I tell you now that you are the one person standing between this world and the forces of evil. I followed my brother to stop him, but I am no match without your help. Courage, and the truth will open the way."

Boothby drew a deep breath before saying, "Oh, God."

He pointed the focus stone to the glowing objects, and, as though he traveled along a bolt of lightning, he could see them quite close. They were sublime, glorious, almost organic at closer inspection. He muttered to himself. "Carbon fibers reinforce the scaffolding. Skeleton withstands gravitons. Heart beats with power. Telekinetics—quantum entanglement permits local control." He reopened his eyes, breathing hard as he discovered that Shigeru, Olga, and Conique had ventured closer. The stone vibrated with energy. "Christ, that cannot be."

Olga asked, "What did you say about entanglement?"

Boothby frowned. "Something about controlling the nuclear fuel. I dunno."

Zephyr slapped his back in encouragement. "Continue, Boothby."

He closed his eyes once more. "Core operates with entanglement. Antiprotons, photons, all in immense quantities." He stood on a mountain of energy, but forces seemed inverted somehow. Gravity repelled, darkness illuminated, time marched backwards.

Zephyr's voice soothed him. "Boothby, focus on the Katafaj."

Boothby continued muttering, "There's something alien on the other side of the device—products of brains which expired thousands of centuries ago. No, there is one alive now. A being of immense intellect. But alone. So desperately alone. *Maddeningly* alone."

Zephyr's hands tightened on Boothby as he felt others helping to brace him. The Ghyan said, "Focus on the core, Boothby. We require it."

Boothby could see the drone. He reached a finger into it, and he submitted a single command—power off. A surge of energy passed through him, and he opened his eyes to see his focus stone floating in heated gyration above his hand. A beam shot from it to one of the five lights above, yanking it to them. He lost his footing, but Zephyr and Shigeru caught him.

Zephyr took the focus stone in hand, using it to wrangle and tame the finicky drone. It struggled, but he proved the better, forcing a landing.

Conique gasped, "My Lord."

Shigeru followed her comment with his own snide variant. "Thank you, Miss Voyant."

Boothby was uncertain what he was seeing—the device appeared to exist in interphase, as if it might transport away. Olga asked, "How is this possible?"

Zephyr produced a handheld device, flat with glowing crimson within it. He then approached the downed machine. "Not even we Ghyans understand it, Professor. But I can capture the needed energies."

Boothby watched in awe. "The core energy flows from outside this time and space, making it possible to do the things it does."

Conique laughed at him. "I understand all those words, but, put together, they don't mean mashed potatoes."

Zephyr stood over the drone. He pressed the collector into the shifting energy, at great pain to himself.

The drone shimmered, fighting to escape Zephyr's grasp. He shouted in pain before wrenching the collector free. The drone rolled away from him before rejoining its counterparts in the sky. The Ghyan fell to his knees as the lights scattered. Shigeru made his way to him, now joined by Adam. They helped Zephyr to his feet as he announced, "We can now refuel the skytax. Come." The crimson energy within the collector sparkled, energized with the mighty forces powering the lights themselves.

Boothby shook his head in near oblivious ecstasy. "They're full of stars, for sure!"

"Yes, they are," said a voice behind them. Boothby spun to see a bloodied Carlyle Demmings holding a pistol on them. "Now, you'll hand them over to me."

*F****

Disgust was a word and a half. Varnum had seized Chevur's front passenger seat, consigning Frankie to the back like a goddamned kid. They sped along the roadway with so little clearance on either side that he imagined slapping the ivy and leaves with his hands. Or hand, rather.

He could have puked at Varnum's agitation, rocking in his seat while yanking the seatbelt. "Why would they produce such a phony video?" he asked. He tapped his phone in fury. "It's already viral. Fuck!"

Chevur's face and head poured sweat as he said, "That is the least of our concerns, Mister Varnum. Can you not see ahead?"

Frankie reached for the headrests of the frontmost seats to pull himself forward, but he found himself slapping a stump against the leather surface, inflaming his meagerly healed wound. "What is up there?"

Varnum dismissed them. "This is my whole reputation! Carl will fix this. He has to."

Frankie squinted to see something glowing over the tree line a few hundred yards away. Chevur slapped Varnum's phone from his hand before pointing to the glowing red orbs. Slowing the car, he said, "Look away from your device, sir. What in heaven is this?"

Varnum grasped for his phone as he fumbled it into the floorboard. As he bent, he froze at the scene before them.

Frankie could see that the objects circled above a car, holding it with purple beams of shimmering energy. "That's the Lord's—" He stopped himself. "The general's car!"

Chevur's voice was breathy. "I cannot focus on them. What are they?"

Frankie bobbed his head in agreement. "Like a blurry photo. I need to get to Norcross!" The car shuddered at the streams holding it, so Frankie insisted with anger. "We hafta get ourselves over there, now!"

Varnum said, "Fuck that! Chevur, turn the car around." Chevur ignored him, so he shouted in his ear, "Goddamnit, Chevur, Carl will end you if you don't turn us around!"

Frankie could see Hazel round the car, shielding her face from the potent energy beams. She screeched at the top of her lungs. "Frankie!! Frankie, your Lord needs ya, now!!"

Varnum grabbed Chevur's right arm. "Turn us around—" One of the three orbs shot a beam into the hood of the EV, sending a jolt of electricity through them. Frankie felt his hair stand on end. Varnum stilled, whispering, "What the fuck was that?"

Chevur clutched the steering wheel for dear life as he pushed the ignition button several times. The vehicle didn't respond, so he said, "The engine has died. Lieutenant, what is this?"

Varnum threw his hands to the sky. "Christ, I'm going!" He tried to wrench himself free, shouting, "My fucking seatbelt won't unfasten!"

Chevur tried his own belt. "You're right. That beam must have melted the components."

Frankie was relieved that he didn't use his own belt, but his door wouldn't budge. "It trapped us!"

Varnum covered his eyes with his narrow hands. "I cannot believe this is happening. Chevur, you must help me!"

Frankie strained to see the car before them, and he could feel the Lord's presence. The locusts thrummed at his fury for the spectacle that was Varnum, but he could hear Norcross, too. "Francis, I require you now. The power dwells within you to rescue Me from this trap."

Frankie closed his eyes, shutting out Varnum's pleas and Chevur's rebuffs. "Tell me what to do, oh Lord."

"Rally to Me, Francis. Help is coming," his Lord said.

Frankie reopened his eyes to see Hazel tapping at his window. She produced a magnum pistol as she pantomimed some ludicrous command at him. He understood that he should shield his eyes and look away just as she pointed the weapon into the window and fired. Varnum screamed as Frankie's window disintegrated into a blast of breakaway pieces. She offered Frankie her hand. "C'mon, hot rod. He needs you, now."

Varnum held his hands defensively as he asked, "Who the hell are you? What is happening?"

Frankie grabbed Hazel's arm with his lone hand, and with strength of a man twice her size, she heaved him through the window, catching him as he fell into her arms. "There, there, Mama Hazel has you." As he separated himself from her, she said, "There ain't a second to spare, boy. Let's get to it!"

Varnum hollered at her. "Wait, help us get out of here!" She turned to blow a kiss in his direction, in no way easing his frustration. "Come back, you bitch!" he exclaimed.

Frankie and Hazel made quick work of the yards separating the two vehicles. Despite her age and prognosis, she was nimble as a cat. But his attention found its way back to the Lord's predicament. He asked her as they rushed, "What are those things?"

She honked at him, winded at last. "He said they are weapons sent to stop Him. I guess they're some sorta drone."

The swarm in his head numbed him with its collective screams, worsening with every step towards the three orbs. Hazel pulled him along as she breathed hard. "C'mon, Frankie boy. Hafta... Stop... Them..."

At last, they made it within five feet of the car. The air was electric, with Frankie struggling to move forward. Images of Varnum and Tyler and Marvell and Myra and George and Sheila circulated in his brain, confusing him. He sought Pastor Chet among those peopling his brain, but his face wasn't among them. Hazel fell under her own weight, the force of the weird orbs and their rays too much for her to bear. As she fell away from him, Frankie resisted repellant forces emanating from the orbs. Within the car, he could see his Lord suffering.

Norcross could see him, so He shouted through an opened back window of the SUV. "Francis, these devices are the enemy's doing, dispatched to hinder Us! I cannot free Myself from them!"

Frankie was conflicted, even as he wrestled with sluggish muscles. He reached for the rear door of the vehicle as the *Korobskron* roared in his ears. He slapped his stump to the handle, infuriated that his missing hand would foil him. He considered, in that moment, to let the Lord suffer His fate—it would serve Him right. But fear replaced rage, pivoting on the simple certainty that Frankie's lifeline would be gone. Norcross, like Chet before Him, understood Frankie, and it would be literal hell without that. He smelled and tasted blood, arousing him. He would save his Lord.

The magnetic energy proved fiery hard to fight, but Norcross's summons strengthened Frankie, even if the weakness in His voice jarred him. "Come, Francis! The Katafaj's field will not harm you! Come to Me!"

Frankie ripped at the door handle, but it wouldn't budge. "I can't get in!" he called over the roar of power surging through the vehicle's body.

The Lord's skin smoldered like embers in a fire, but He stayed fast. "Listen to Me, Francis. You have yet to tap your true power, and I had hoped it would not be necessary so early in Our journey. Holding Us is a graviton beam of immense strength. But you, Francis, are capable of reversing its polarity and banishing them."

Frankie shot his eyes to the orbs above them. They throbbed with power. "Lord, I don't know what to do!"

Norcross choked and spit. "Francis, summon your rage. Consider Our enemies."

Frankie turned back to see Chevur and Varnum imprisoned in the executive's EV. He seethed at Varnum, furious at his hypocrisy. It was funny that Myra had been right about him. Rage pulsed hard as the locust thrum dizzied him. He refused to surrender as his mother's voice lilted within his brain. "My precious Frankie—I knew the first time I saw you there in the crib that the Lord would have important missions for you. Don't forget that it's usually darkest before the dawn, son. The things you'll do, son."

He pictured her death, and the fury exploded within him. George, Sheila, and Varnum were all his enemies. The orbs' power weakened as he lost himself to anger. Norcross, though still held by the energy, called in triumph. "That's it, Francis! You have the power! Kill him!"

Frankie found himself free of the energy. Marching back to Chevur's EV, he tore open Varnum's door. His one-time hero uttered, "Thank fucking God. You have to help me get out of here, eh?" He hopped out of the car, grabbing for Frankie. "You're a gentleman, sir. Thank you!"

Once their flesh touched, the locusts deafened him. "No, Varnum, I ain't that. But I'll know the truth." He pulled Varnum close to him, feeling the slight man's frame against his own chest. To his disgust, he felt Varnum's erection as their bodies met.

"I don't understand," Varnum said.

Frankie hugged him, whispering into his ear. "Don't worry. I do."

Varnum seized as Frankie buried his survival knife into the fool's abdomen. The locusts sang to him as he twisted the blade, scooping at the man's viscera. "Oh, God," Varnum gasped. Frankie clutched his one time hero around the neck, plunging his head into his chest. He launched the blade into Varnum's chest, sliding it between ribs into the man's left lung. He coughed, and wheezed, and Frankie felt air escape as he removed his knife once more. Visualizing Varnum swallowing a penis, Frankie thrust the blade into his gaping mouth. Yanking it free, he tore the man's face open. Releasing Varnum, he raised his blood-drenched arms to the sky in triumph. The vital fluids enervated him, and he closed his eyes amidst five immensely powerful ejaculatory convulsions. In those moments, anything could be his; anything *would* be his. The wind had filled his sails, and he would happily stand upon mountains of corpses, victorious in slaying the Lord's many adversaries. Incapable of bearing more ecstasy, he opened his eyes as Varnum dropped dead to the pavement, all too brief a demise for the bloodthirsty Frankie. He examined the serrated blade of his knife as it dripped blood and shit fresh from the fool Varnum. He wiped it on Varnum's likely very expensive sports jacket, disgusted at the frivolous extravagance.

The locusts quieted just as Norcross spoke in his head. "Now, you are strong enough. Come, Francis!"

He jerked his head to the orbs holding his Lord. Rushing to them, he said, "Tell me what to do, Lord."

"Open the door and take My hand!" He shouted.

Frankie rushed to the vehicle and pulled the door handle off the chassis. It was fortunate that the door unlatched, so he dislodged it from the SUV to behold his Lord restrained by the energy surrounding him. He fought to face him, exhaling with tremendous difficulty. "Francis, take My hand!"

He touched it, feeling searing pain enter his lone surviving hand. "Tell me what to do, Lord! I'm Your vessel!"

Norcross managed to smile, despite the cut into His own strength. "Just stay in the moment—savor the victory."

Frankie surged as energy transferred from him into his Lord. His face and hands brightened while Frankie's swarm quieted, as if they were miles away. He became faint as his Lord flashed white hot. The car seats combusted as Frankie's flyboy suit smoldered. His life strength left him as the Lord drained him. At last, Norcross flung him clear of the vehicle.

He tumbled hard into the pavement, jutting his stump and hand into it to break the fall. From nowhere, Hazel leapt upon Frankie with a heavy blanket, slapping the embers away from him. He was too weak to resist, and she squeezed his chest, abdomen, arms and legs through it. "There, there, Frankie boy." She squatted over him, defensively to shield him from the heat.

Once settled on his back, he rolled to pull the SUV back into his field of view. The tires melted, the frame buckled, and the windows each popped to pieces. The roof split open, revealing a bright figure rising from it. With hands upturned, the Lord ejected a burst of fire towards the three orbs. They jerked away from Him, perturbed out of their orbit around Him. He performed the act twice more, scattering the injured drones to the sky. They tore away, piercing the sound barrier with thunderous booms.

Once clear, He stepped through the charred SUV's doors, slicing through the chassis as if it were warm butter. Frankie pulled himself up to sit as Norcross cooled. His clothing had burned away, revealing the iridescent suit hugging His frame.

He walked to Frankie, offering him His hand. "Good work, Francis. You are powerful, and how much more when you come into your own. Come, We must reach the others."

Hazel hollered from Chevur's car behind them, having slipped away from Frankie during the commotion. "Oh Lord, You have shown me Your truth! We are unstoppable, and We are many! Hail to Thee! Hail to Thee! But what do We do with little Gupta Patel here?"

Frankie could see that she held him in a choke hold, sliding a small cat's claw blade against Chevur's throat. He found himself pitying the little man, deciding death would be easier than pressing flesh against the dumpster fire of a woman. Norcross held a palm at her. "We may need him ahead."

She shoved him forward. He shivered, mumbling to himself as she slapped his back. "Well, fine, but I have dibs on gutting this sand nigger. Even if he is as cute as a little button," she said in baby talk as she pinched his cheek.

Frankie asked, "What's wrong with him?"

Norcross turned his eyes skyward. "The Katafaj temporarily scrambles the brain. The *Korobskron* provides some protection, but you, as a Vesik, would not require it."

"Brother Bobby'll have the plane ready soon, oh Lord," Hazel said as she listened in an earpiece.

Norcross turned from them, pointing to a large structure ahead. "We must hurry—the others have proceeded more quickly than I thought possible."

Frankie felt nothing, save exhaustion and confusion. "What do you mean?"

Norcross jerked His head back to them. "Hazel Grant, take Francis to the plane. I must go alone."

This didn't disappoint Frankie, but he asked, "Don't you need me, Lord?"

Whipping back to face His destination, He said, "You provided Me the strength to do what I must. You go, now!"

Hazel tugged at Frankie, pushing him towards Chevur's car. "C'mon, handsome, let's get you back, and into a new suit." She patted the burned material on his shoulder.

He would have felt rage at her for violating his space, but she had burned herself in beating the fire off him. Falling into the seat, he closed his eyes, if only for a moment.

O***

Olga hated the dissonance—before her unfolded a scientific wonder she would have crawled over broken glass to study, but instead, she faced an adversary who'd dogged her since grad school. She leaned into the van, frayed from the ordeal. She shouted, "Carl, you do not know what you're doing! Please, either help us or leave."

He grinned at her. "Oh, no, Oggie Pooh. I'm not one to back away from profits."

Shigeru held his burned hands at length, though the pain didn't diminish the man's spunk. "You pig-snouted bucket of shit—this world ends because you want your profits?"

Demmings whined in his laugh, a sound Olga desperately wanted to forget. "That's all that matters, Doctor Nakamura. Sex to you, money to me. Capiche? My darling nemesis here could have been rich, but she has *principles*. Bah! You people together are worth a trillion dollars, overpowering my Kharla, activating totally inert uranium, and summoning UFOs? Christ on his throne, I'd be a fool to let you go."

Reuben knelt over Carolina. "Sorry to rain on your Ponzi parade, but she's in bad shape, needing help I can't give her!"

Zephyr looked to Olga, and she surmised that he was too weak intervene. Taking a step towards Demmings, she warned, "Carl, the technology I've seen in the past few days will thrill and amaze you. But you must *help*, not *hinder* us."

Shigeru had joined Reuben in examining Carolina. Concentrating, he said with a gasp, "I can't. Fuck, I can't do it!" Conique's dog whimpered at Carolina's side.

Axley stood up with a threatening posture. "If she dies, I'll turn you into bacon!"

Demmings trained the weapon on him. "Trespassers will be shot, and you and your fellow agent aren't interesting to me."

Zephyr noticed Olga as she postured. He said, "Olga, wait!"

It was too late. Demmings squeezed the trigger, and Olga felt a surge of instinct and power explode within her.

As long rays of red light bathed them, she listened as voices droned to a halt. The scene froze around her, save a tiny bullet moving from the barrel of Demmings' gun in the direction of Axley. She pushed herself forward sluggishly, careful to step aside the others in their still form. At last, she reached the moving bullet, and she slapped it free from its course with one swing of her fist. She could feel her strength disappearing, so she bounded towards Demmings, as slowly as moving through water. Reaching him, she intended to pry the weapon from him. But it was not without consequence—moving the gun warped the barrel and ripped his fingers from his hand, leaving a red and white trail from it. Reflexively, she pushed the weapon back to his arm to mend what she'd broken. Despite her effort, the misshapen weapon slipped from her hands, slicing deep into his torso. Bone, organs, and blood spewed from his body. She vomited at the sight, and the foul liquid slapped hard into Demmings' face and chest, destroying him.

Olga's strength disappeared, and she fell to the ground. The others watched in silence, stunned at what she'd done. All, save Zephyr. His face filled with pity as he said, "You cannot control your power yet."

Olga turned to face the mess she'd made. Demmings lay on the pavement, twitching and destroyed. Axley touched the gun, tracing the damage. "My God. Well, I hope the bastard burns in hell."

Shigeru helped Olga to her feet, despite her dizziness. She stumbled, unable to stand under her own power. He said, "We must leave this place, Zeff."

Zephyr shouted to the others, "We must go, now!" He braced Boothby and offered a hand to Conique as she stepped out of the van.

Axley knelt to Carolina. "I'm not leaving her."

Reuben bowed his head, wiping blood from his hands. "No matter. She's dead." Aurum cried at that.

Shigeru pointed in the distance as he held Olga tight. She could smell cigarette smoke, though it appealed to rather disgusted her. He said, "Someone else is coming."

Boothby held fast to Zephyr's arm. "I'm so sorry, Agent Axley."

Olga heard a powerful whoosh from above. An opening appeared, leading into the invisible skytax. The noise somehow coaxed Boothby's black cat from beneath the van, and Adam helped Janet step from it.

Axley looked up from his partner's body, crying. "We were so close to seeing it all, Enid. So close."

Beneath the skytax's open port, a half open silver wire cage formed from smart matter, assembled quickly and efficiently.

Zephyr said, "I must transfer the collector's energy into skytax's dynamo. The lift can accommodate two at a time."

Axley rose to his feet after taking Carolina's weapon in hand. "I'll buy you time, Zephyr."

Boothby's raspy voice whined. "Agent, he'll kill ya. Don't!"

Axley patted him. "I believe, Boothby. A greater purpose, a *reason*. You must escape."

"Your courage honors us, Agent." Boothby's cat leapt onto his shoulder as they entered the lift together. Zephyr bowed his head to Axley as they ascended at once into the light above. A second lift replaced the first, just after it vanished.

Axley and Conique's husband braced her as they entered the cage.

Reuben whistled at Aurum. "Come on, girl!" She whimpered, sitting next to Agent Carolina's body. He called once more, "C'mon, Aurum. There's nothing left to do!"

Conique slapped her hands together. "Barbecue treat?!"

Aurum licked Carolina's face in farewell before hurrying into the lift. The elderly couple vanished, replaced by a third cage. The nurses Adam and Janet made their way to it, just as Olga lost her footing. Shigeru scooped her into his arms, holding her close.

There was a roar behind them, so Olga twisted her neck to glimpse a burning figure approach. Adam gasped, "Fuck, that's *him*!" No sooner had he said it, he and Janet were gone.

Shigeru's muscles tensed, and Olga could feel his breathing speed. A fourth and final cage appeared, with Agent Axley tapping it with Carolina's weapon. "You must escape, Doctor. Take the professor and go, now."

Olga complained with deep fatigue. "I should help."

Shigeru tightened his grip on her as he stepped into the cage. "I'm sorry, but you've played hero enough."

The burning figure reached Demmings' decimated remains. They burned away, and the pavement beneath the figure's feet scorched and bubbled. Olga's blood ran cold when she saw the striking resemblance between the gentle Zephyr and the monster. She met his sapphire eyes as he said, "Two more than I'd expected. How come you by the skytax?"

The lift remained in place as the vehicle shuddered. Boothby shouted from above, "Trouble getting the power running—hang on!"

The figure's gaze buzzed in Olga's head. She knew at once that he was immensely powerful, with an unslakable thirst. His aims were nothing short of apocalyptic, a burning of worlds. Even the loss of his own life would not deter him from the tyranny he sought. Somehow, Olga knew he was rummaging in her head. "How? *Who* has helped you?"

She cried, "He's in my skull! I can't get him out!"

Shigeru turned them away, ending Norcross's telepathic invasion. "Don't look at him," he whispered. "I don't think he can read us without eye contact." Olga knew it was correct, though she didn't know how Shigeru could know it.

Axley fired his weapon as he shouted, "Go!" He fired again and again, but Olga kept her eyes shut. Gravity shifted hard as the lift drew them into the safety of the skytax.

Within the vehicle's small reception area, the others waited in smart seats formed from the floor. Shigeru said, "Axley is in trouble."

Boothby said, "Archie told me that Mister Zephyr is still powering us up. We need time."

Conique's reply was incisive. "We're not cowards! We don't leave anyone behind."

Reuben patted her as he held Aurum between his calves. "Be still, dear. Be still." Aurum growled with her nose to the port.

Boothby winced at the remark, but he cocked his rounded face to the side with a whisper. "You didn't see what Norcross did. We hafta get the hell outta here!"

Janet shocked Olga with the force of her reply. "I stopped him once. I'll stop him again!" She stood, but her legs refused to cooperate.

Adam caught her in his arms. "What do you want me to do?"

"Help me up." She tossed her silky black hair into a ponytail, tying it tight.

In a blur of golden red, Aurum leapt through the port. Conique shrieked, "No girl! Aurum!!!"

Boothby clutched his black cat. "Archie, don't leave me," he pleaded.

Janet fell to her seat, seizing. Adam cradled her. "Baby. Janet! Wake up!"

Shigeru left Olga's side to kneel before Janet, their darker skin tones matching quite closely. It was always the insignificant patterns Olga noticed.

Conique tried to stand, but Reuben held her fast. "Let her go, dear. We can't go out there."

Flames lapped the ring encircling the port, with the skytax rocking against explosions. Shigeru lost his balance, sliding to one side of the tight reception. Adam grabbed for him, slowing his momentum.

Boothby shut his eyes and chanted, "Three clicks. Three clicks."

The port shut, blotting out both the flames and meager winter evening daylight. It was still more than Olga ever had growing up so close to the north pole.

Zephyr's voice reverberated around them. "Skytax is fully charged. We're underway. I suggest you all return to your seats."

Conique wept. "My Aurum. That poor man. Lord, why? *Why*?"

Shigeru said without thinking, "Why not, Miss Voyant? Why not?"

Adam offered to help Shigeru to his seat, but he waved him off. Settling next to Olga, he stared. She breathed a little more easily, hoping that the danger was behind them.

Janet awakened with a start. "Norcross knows where we're going!"

Reuben asked, "How do you know?"

Zephyr answered as he entered the small waiting area. "She knows because she can see through the eyes of others, if only for a time."

Conique sat forward. "You could see? Did Axley make it? Did my dog escape?" Her words rolled slowly, as if she would have preferred not to know the answers.

Janet concentrated as she looked away from them. "I don't know, Miss Voyant. I only know that Norcross is enraged."

Zephyr said flatly, "Then you already know him well."

Shigeru followed him fast. "Some family you have."

She continued, though she was troubled. "I don't understand, Zephyr. His anger felt righteous. As though he's righting some terrible wrong."

Boothby shrugged while Archie groaned a little. "He ain't a cartoon villain. They don't exist."

Shigeru shot back at him. "Swiney Demmings fared well at that." He turned to Olga. "Sorry about that." She tried to push the pig face from her mind.

Reuben ran a hand through his thick silver-gray hair. "What difference does his motive make? Is he a messiah, here to free Nazis from the bondage of civilization?"

Shigeru nodded hard. "Agreed with the other physician. Sorry as shit that he's your fucking brother, and all, but he's as close to a goddamned devil as I've ever fucking seen."

Olga spoke above them, though she knew it pissed off Shigeru. "This is academic. Zephyr is the only one among us who can answer our questions." Demmings' face stayed in her mind, but she shoved it as far aside as she could.

The Ghyan appeared to appreciate her deference, though he was probably more concerned with showing them the same. Reuben said, "Very well. Zephyr, is it? What the hell is going on here? What is with your psychotic brother? C'mon, you *owe* us answers!"

Zephyr reacted to something just out of their perception—he touched his wrist, handling a display. "Forgive me, the skytax requires more coaxing than I had hoped." Turning his eyes toward them, he said, "You are correct, Doctor. Let me explain as best I can."

30. Revelations

*M****

"Time for answers," Mayak muttered to himself. Rather than sleep, he would read the technical specs Vigil had eagerly availed to him. Besides, he'd already gorged on all the trash food he could obtain, though he suffered not one bit of indigestion. The more he ate, the faster his brain seemed to operate.

Sitting within a cozy nook, he marveled at the movement of data on the soothing black walls. He couldn't read any of it, but it comforted him that technology surrounded him. The terminal's interfaces were incredible, marrying ease-of-access with pleasant three-dimensional holographic consoles and displays. Learning to use them required almost no time at all, though he was a seasoned veteran of the personal computer. The operating system was similar to UNIX, with an easy translation. Admittedly, he dated himself by requesting a QWERTY keyboard—it would simplify searching the system. Just such an input device appeared, as though he watched a sandcastle dissolve in reverse.

Vigil had suggested that simple online agents would assist Mayak in learning about any topic he chose, but that parts of the archive would be inaccessible.

In truth, one single topic towered above all others—Sargon. Mayak longed to displace the jarring silence within his head. Though years had passed since his passenger abandoned him, Sargon's brief return transported Mayak back to a time when loneliness did not exist. He was introverted, but the solitude he preferred never separated him from the voice he shared with no one.

The articles and data cells made no mention of Sargon, save a single reference to a separate document redacted from the records. He half expected Kierkov or half a dozen other ex-KGB stooges to appear, explaining that his ignorance was for the good of the almighty state.

Reminding himself that Sargon was no Russian, he read what he could. There were extensive intelligence reports on the world around him—the global economy, military strength, climate studies, and a complete database of all things nuclear, be it weapons, power, or research. Was it possible that Kierkov was correct—that the drone incursions might be reconnaissance for an alien invasion? The records themselves might have supported that conclusion, but the almost carefree placement of them, as if no bad actor would ever scan the system, suggested that the Ghyans intended it more as an index. On the other hand, entering the facility in which he found himself probably was not possible unless the Ghyans or Vigil opened it up.

It all made his head hurt. Per the databank, Ghyans had been studying Earth since 1928. Though one could consider humans the staple of interest for them, it appeared they occupied themselves instead with incursions executed by a ubiquitous grid. "Katafaj," Mayak said.

He searched for the term, as best as he could spell it. Ten thousand individual data logs appeared, with timestamps varying over the past eighty years. He manually scanned some of them, but instead decided he'd like to see a cumulative percentage graph as a function of time. In accordance with his expectation, the number of logs increased exponentially as one varied the time from 1928 to the present. In other words, the number of events activating the Katafaj doubled every fifteen or so years. Scanning the logs, they were clustered about the topics listed among the less restrictive intelligence reports on Earth—climate, nuclear technology, and impact events. It was clear to him that the defensive grid was operational before the Ghyans' earliest records, affirming the scant details Vigil had supplied.

His recent readings from the eccentric ufologist Boothby helped him cross reference against incursions. He could recall maybe twenty of the timestamps associated with the close encounters on Boothby's site, and they certainly appeared among the thousands of log files.

The logs recorded locations using stereographic projection: using the rough locations for the events he could remember, he worked out the projection point and relative orientation of the Earth. Transforming back, he could easily obtain locations for the logged events.

Several types of deployed devices appeared throughout the logs. Other names corresponded to them: Kryafaj, Kaelafaj, Kasafaj, and Kumatafaj. He searched for Kryafaj, filtering to logged events occurring throughout Siberia, deep underground. The Kasafaj were devices tracked from a single location, also within Siberia, while the Kaelafaj referred to locations outside the planet itself.

He sighed as he rubbed his eyes. It then occurred to him that his own run-in with the drones might also appear among the logs, so he scanned them for the three terms he'd seen above, filtered to timestamps within the previous week. Scores of them appeared, marking the precise moment his boards went crazy. That night felt like an eternity in the past. There was a novel event occurring just moments earlier. The point of landfall was somewhere in the southeast of America, with a singular pair of events. The screen darkened as he tried to explore the anomalies. He slapped the keyboard, splashing the rivulets of smart matter to pieces.

"Damn and damn," he complained. He eased back into his chair, reaching for the potato chips he'd been munching.

He could hear Vigil's voice in his head, so he swiveled around to see the small form stand before him. "Master Sargon will be pleased at your ingenuity, Mayak. Even the most expert of Ghyan software researchers cannot perform your feat."

Mayak heard the compliment, but he remained true to his mission. "Yes, you need better security. But why can I not hear Sargon?"

Vigil raised a small three-fingered hand in deference. "Even for one so powerful as the *Arkivar*, his reach is finite. And because of security concerns, external communications are impossible."

Mayak pointed to the darkened terminal behind him. "I recovered event logs from minutes in past. But there is no external communication?"

Vigil angled his round head in amusement. "Master Sargon was correct in his assessment of your creative intellect."

Mayak frowned. "I want to know all about Katafaj. Archives hide too much."

Vigil said, "Very well. *Arkivar* Sargon would not disapprove. The Katafaj is a defensive grid embedded within Falterra's crust, ever vigilant to neutralize nuclear discharges, maintain climate equilibrium, divert impacts, and destroy invaders."

Mayak laughed, at least inwardly. "I gather as much from logs. How do they accomplish crazy ass maneuvers?"

Vigil seemed to laugh with him. "Aerial drones correct for attitude changes by dimensional skew—expend energy along dimensions outside of space and time. Thousands of such devices are hidden among the Falterran Solar System, an invisible army programmed to protect and nurture fledgling life."

Mayak asked, "Why so many in Siberia?"

Above the terminal, a holographic map of Russia appeared, laid over a green grid spanning the whole of Siberia. Vigil pointed to the bright image. "Many of the devices were immobile, intended to operate from a prescribed position. The Kryafaj sits beneath Siberia's tundra, intended to maintain low temperatures among the methane-filled peat bogs. The Kaelafaj occupies space around Falterra, ever prepared to divert asteroids, comets, and even other planets, if necessary. The Kasafaj you know."

Mayak shrugged as he pointed to Japan's position relative to the glowing outline of Russia. "Your Katafaj failed there. And in other places."

Vigil paused before answering. "Incursion gaps within the grid indicate possible variations on the network's objectives. We do not understand them fully. But there is another interpretation—the control mechanism could be faltering."

It hit Mayak. "What is control mechanism?"

Vigil didn't answer right away, so Mayak knew he hit paydirt. "We do not know. Analysis of the network's activities suggests responsive and perhaps prognosticative intelligence."

Mayak's mind raced as he considered possibilities. "Executive control must be quantum, even if it was hidden somewhere here. Have you simulated incursions?"

Vigil angled his head in amusement once more. "The master has taught you well, young Mayak. The executive control for the Katafaj is, we believe, a device of near limitless computational power, ever simulating how best to intervene. This device is key to the gauntlet before us."

Mayak rubbed his knees with his hands as he considered it, staring into the embers of the holographic map circling above him. "Supercomputer? How did you come by this?"

Vigil's tiny mouth didn't move, symbolic of his reticence. "Ghyans have studied the Katafaj for centuries, interested in its origins. I can say no more on this."

Mayak decided he'd collect answers with a different tack. He pointed in the direction he thought Atlanta or Birmingham might be, gesturing with emphasis. "What is happening in America? Logs were very strange."

Vigil touched the sleek onyx wall as data flowed into his hand. He said, "Please wait." He held his hand on the wall as the energy transfer intensified. At last, he severed the connection with resistance. "Our situation has changed. The Katafaj activated to reverse nuclear misadventure, but it encountered Ghyans who cannibalized one of the power cores. This is the work of the Vesiks, dear Mayak!"

He sat forward, almost touching the small creature. "Ghyan, like Sargon?"

Vigil touched the wall once more. "Please wait. No, not Master Sargon."

Mayak felt his heart sink a little, but he reported what he saw. "Kumatafaj was among logs."

Vigil froze as he planted both hands onto the sleek wall. "Please wait. Please wait. Hazard containment ruby." Tearing his grubby digits from it, he turned to Mayak amidst booming klaxons. "Arkiyan Norcross has neutralized and cannibalized drones, Master Mayak. We must lock this facility tight!"

Mayak shouted above the siren. "Who fuck is Arkiyan?!"

Vigil ushered Mayak to his feet. "The most dangerous Ghyan alive, Mayak. Thwarting the Katafaj is impossible without the help of the Vesiks, meaning he travels among them. Should he gain control of the Katafaj, he can destroy this world and all within it. Please accompany me, Mayak."

He took Mayak's hand as they left the nook behind. The corridors had changed their tenor, now covered drenched in throbbing red light. "Where are we going?" he asked.

Vigil pulled him with strength he wouldn't have attributed to a form so small, but he didn't resist. Vigil said without saying, "My first priority is to secure you, young Master. You are essential to his plan, and thus must be safeguarded."

Mayak watched pulses of red energy bound from behind them to some destination far ahead. He asked, "Should we not engage Sargon?"

Vigil shook his round head. "We cannot operate communications, but I trust he knows this already. I fear Master Sargon cannot hope to stop him."

Mayak was furious at this. "Who is Arkiyan that he may appear with such force?"

Vigil bowed his head. "We may know sooner than we should like. Please, accompany me to safety."

*B****

Boothby wasn't uncaring. Conique and Reuben lost their dog a second time, and Agent Axley had probably sacrificed his own life to help them escape. But finding answers to his dearest questions sat above any need to comfort. It also could have been that Archie the cat sat in his lap, purring as he stroked the soft shiny beast's head, neck, and back. He'd never intentionally been so close to a small animal, but there was nothing more natural for him in that moment. No matter the circumstances, Boothby was consumed by wonder. He sat aboard a vehicle more advanced than anything he'd ever seen—it was the stuff of his many studies into UFOs and advanced technology. He doubted even Jacques Valles could boast similarly. The cloaking mechanism, the apparent smart matter, and the capture of a drone from the enigmatic Katafaj all had blown his mind. He traced the outline of the focus stone in his pocket, electrified at these many revelations. And he knew more awaited reveal.

Many among the group surrounding him were integral to the narrative as it unfolded for him. He'd not felt so at ease ever, and he knew proximity to the other Vesiks had helped him.

Shigeru had tended to Janet, restoring much of her mobility and strength. It struck Boothby funny that one so impatient in almost every lane in which one could drive, but hands-on bedside manner didn't trouble him. Perhaps the physician thrived when there was a task he could solve.

Olga was cold and mostly silent. Killing her former classmate inadvertently had affected her, but he guessed she would have been much sorrier about it if it had happened any other way. Demmings wasn't a stranger in Boothby's world—he wouldn't underestimate the once huddled now slain technocrat's understanding of the Katafaj than he let on, but past was prologue.

It was a victory for Boothby to have, at last, opened a door he knew could lead to greater things. His comrades, new and old, had been transformed by the whole affair. Their unique abilities combined had realized his objective. He was solid.

Zephyr was an unknown quantity. He was beautiful, resembling Norcross so closely that one would confuse them at a glance. But his skin was paler, his hair was darker, and his eyes were green. He lacked the malevolence of his brother. Boothby had never known siblings, though he seldom suffered alone among the orphanage's many prisoners.

Tuning into the conversation, he heard Zephyr say, "Answering your questions is among my priorities. Please, accompany me." He gestured to a doorway as it appeared within the dark surface behind him. "With the skytax fully charged, we can avail ourselves of its comforts. You are tired—"

Reuben interrupted him. "I'm not too tired to know why this is happening."

Zephyr didn't seem to mind the doctor's impatience. "Of course. But there are refreshments ahead."

Conique hugged her husband as she said, "I wouldn't refuse a snack right now."

The others followed, and the young girl Janet, braced by her brother Adam, said, "Quite the turn of things, Mister B."

Boothby supported Archie with his arm as he stood to join them. "Rapture, Nurse Baumgartl. Just rapture." He winced a little inside at his butchery of pronunciation.

The chamber they entered came to life. Trees sprouted from the floor, first of powdery and liquid metal, second of the expected appearance. The walls and ceiling appeared to shrink from them, replaced by a wooded canopy above and dense forests around them. Boothby touched one tree as it continued to form. The material gave, though it tingled on his finger. He found it a most welcome place: a clearing cloistered within a spectacular forest of magnolias, oaks, cedars, and redwoods. He breathed the temperate atmosphere, smelling honeysuckle, lavender, and the gentle pine. The sun cast powerful red and orange light on the new friends.

Zephyr said, "I trust you all will find this setting a peaceful one."

Conique gasped as she touched one of the trees. "How have you done this? It feels real."

Olga answered for Zephyr. "This is smart matter, decades ahead of us."

Reuben peered about the trees. "Yeah, well, how does it work?"

Zephyr pointed them to a loveseat coalescing behind the doctor and his wife. "Magnetism, molecule-sized machines with polonium payloads in tandem to present form if not substance."

Shigeru didn't appear impressed, though Boothby thought he saw him running his fingers through the grass appearing on the floor. "Look, Zeff. These are great parlor tricks. I know you want to place us at ease, but, man? We need a plan."

Zephyr pointed to seats materializing behind Shigeru and Olga. "I assure you, Doctor, that such a plan is underway. We've attempted to account for the eventualities in preparation. Sit, and ask the arm of your chair for a beverage."

Boothby braced Archie by placing his forearm under the furry creature's rounded tummy with his upturned hand clam-shelled against his chest. The purring soothed him like nothing else. But he couldn't pass the opportunity to ask for clarifications. "Who is *we*, Mister Zephyr?"

The comparably younger man answered, "Young Boothby, eager to learn. We celebrate this highly on Ghya. I am referring to simulations computed before I departed my world."

"Before or after your homicidal brother?" Reuben asked.

Zephyr stopped with a start. "I am deeply sorry for what he has done."

Adam shook his head as he peered at the trees. "You don't know the half of it—he's murdered his way across the country, starting in Tucson."

Zephyr stared at the young man for a moment. "It would explain the lockdown."

"Come again?" Conique asked as Reuben led her to a seat.

Olga sat readily, even if the others didn't. "Their remote access into the Katafaj."

Zephyr nodded as he touched controls projected from his arm, enamoring Boothby of the tech. "She's correct. It means there is hope in this world."

Reuben was annoyed, even as Conique tugged at him to join her. "Look, man—why should we trust you when your brother tried to kill us?"

"Imprison us…" Boothby said to a glare from the elderly physician.

"Doctor, let me say once more that I am sorry for Norcross. I am here to stop him." Zephyr said it as he continued working his interface.

Boothby's eyes widened as it answered in three dimensions, with golden and blue shapes and glyphs scattering. Archie purred in his arms, and he felt the creature motion for him to sit next to Conique. Before Reuben could object, she pulled his sleeve hard. As he started muttering, she snapped, "Dear, if he intended to harm us, he would have left us with the devil. We're here with him, so sit down and hush!"

He gazed at his surroundings, shook his head, and slid next to her on a comfortable easy chair. Rubbing his gray and black beard, he surrendered with a gesture and an interrogative: "Simulations, like virtual reality?"

Boothby answered as he angled his head but not his eyes in the doctor's direction. "Gaming out the scenarios, right?"

Olga spoke in a tone surprisingly emotional to Boothby. "That makes sense. But I didn't mean to kill Carl. Did Demmings *have to die*?"

Shigeru helped into her seat before taking his own. He said to her, "It wasn't your fault. You had to stop him." She squeezed her eyes shut as he patted her.

Her cheeks glistened with tears. "He had a wife and kids."

Boothby bared his teeth as he said, "If it's any consolation, he was cheating on her." He nodded yes to her, only to shift it to a no when she failed to accept it.

Janet met his wild eyes. "I read that he's manic—cruel to his kids when they interrupt his work."

Reuben glared at him. "That means he deserves to die?"

Adam, to Boothby's relief, defended him. "That's not what he said, Doctor. But Demmings gaslighted everyone, parading Varnum and his other right wingnut celebs in front of anyone who would listen."

Reuben said, "Maybe it's my generation, but I don't think we should speak ill of the dead."

"Fuck the bastard—I'm glad he's dead," Shigeru said.

Janet waited to sit while Shigeru examined her. "Dying doesn't wipe the slate clean."

Conique astounded Boothby with her quick-witted pragmatism. "Either way, he's gone. We need to save all we can."

Zephyr bowed his head towards Olga as she sank into her wavering seat, and though his words intended encouragement, he could not hide his own despair. "Miss Voyant is correct, though I am sorry—intelligent life is a rare, beautiful thing deserving protection."

Boothby plopped nearby, grateful that Archie refused to leave him. Zephyr grazed the cat's whiskers and ears with his hand as he passed them, with the contact brightening the Ghyan. "What would you like, young Boothby?"

He was honest-to-god bashful, struggling to maintain eye contact. "Diet cola?" A chilled aluminum can of soda appeared next to him. "Wow. How did ya do that?"

Zephyr smiled at him. "With the drone's power core installed, the skytax offers numerous amenities. Its original function is commercial transportation for low orbit, so it is not without its comforts." Boothby eagerly opened the can, excited by the hiss of carbonation.

Shigeru touched the bark of one of the trees, but he yanked his hand from it the instant he saw Boothby watching him. He then tended to Janet as Adam guided her to a seat.

Zephyr glanced about the chamber at each of the others. As Boothby sipped his drink, the cold, aspartame, and burn together refreshed him. The wooded glen around them was an odd setting, but he found it charming. The others drank what he'd expect: neat whiskey for Shigeru, iced tea for Conique, beer for Reuben, chilled coffee for Adam, boiling tea for Olga, and steaming cocoa for Janet. Zephyr also partook, but Boothby didn't know what he was drinking.

Boothby overheard Shigeru say to Zephyr, "I've done my best to stabilize Nurse Yazzie."

"Nurse Yazzie can still talk," Janet hollered at them.

Zephyr bowed his head in deference. "Once we reach our destination, the diseases plaguing many of you will no longer be a concern. Your work is exemplary, Doctor, and not a moment too soon. I'll explain in a moment." Shigeru returned to his seat as he swigged his beverage.

Boothby caught Shigeru adjusting his bolo necktie, noticing it for the first time. Pointing to it, he said, "Bold choice." Shigeru smiled faintly before turning his eyes to Zephyr.

Their seats made up a semicircle, centered on the Ghyan's seat. It was a tree stump, carved into one large chair. He said, "This is an occasion to mark. Five of the Vesiks sit here with us, and the other two will meet us soon."

Janet asked, "How do you know this?"

He said, "Though our overload of Picoveer's Heart control center destroyed much of the data they had accumulated, their intelligence is surprisingly thorough—one of the Vesiks travels with my brother. I do not know whether he does so willingly, but Norcross could not have freed himself from the Katafaj alone."

Conique asked, "How did he help him?"

Zephyr waved his hand, causing a seven-pointed star to appear. "Each of the seven Vesiks carry powers unique to them. We call it the Vesikavir (and sometimes Vyrvesikon) or strength derived from virtue and vice. Each of you has discovered some of them, and the second of the Vesiks can generate tremendous amounts of energy when necessary. He also can resist heat up to temperatures needed to melt lead. Norcross would draw on those powers to neutralize the Katafaj."

"How does he generate this power?" Olga asked.

"Likely transduction of superheated matter from outside. The power is a mystery, even to us." Zephyr touched the holograms as they shimmered.

Shigeru pulled his hair back as he sighed. "Just who the fuck is he?"

Janet answered helpfully, "Frankie Putnam. He's a fracker in Texas."

Zephyr read something from his wrist, after which he said, "According to news media, he disappeared, along with two acquaintances. Further, two other POIs supplied a description matching Norcross, and there was a death connected to him."

Adam asked Janet, "Damn, the guy on TV did all that?" She affirmed, so he said, "He and some other moron said that fracking wasn't causing earthquakes there."

Shigeru complained, "So an anti-science shit-kicking fucktard is one of us? Fuck me."

Conique intervened. "Calm yourself, Doctor Nakamura. There are differences among people, and you just have to get used to it."

He scoffed at her. "Says the crazy evangelical. I bet you voted for ultranationalists."

Conique flashed with rage, replying, "No, I certainly did not, nor would I ever." She eyed him with intensity Boothby found a little disturbing, "Besides, Doctor Nakamura, if you were asked to abandon your rage and keep your pants forever zipped to save the world, would you do it?"

He replied in haste, "Without reservation."

Conique chuckled. "I bet Zephyr can make your part happen if you like, Doctor Nakamura. I always carry my pocketknife, and then all we'd need is a rubber band."

The Japanese physician's face whitened as Reuben forced a smile from his face. Jerking his head towards Zephyr, he asked, "What is to stop this Norcross fellow from taking control of the Katafaj?"

Zephyr said, "We're strangely fortunate—he cannot do so without Boothby."

Boothby gasped. "Jesus, he almost got me."

Janet said, "It seemed like he wanted to kill us."

He settled into a decorative chair of carved wood with direct line-of-sight to the others. "He intends to capture the Vesiks, though anyone else is collateral."

This caused Janet to stare at her brother with concern. Boothby surmised that she loved him with her very life. She asked, "Why? What does he want to do with us?"

Shigeru clicked his tongue in skepticism. But he spoke the truth in any case. "Supposedly, we contain a secret code in our DNA which together opens a lock."

Adam said a word Boothby certainly recognized: "Codeka."

Janet looked at her brother, then Zephyr as she asked, "Then we all have extra chromosomes?"

The Ghyan replied, "This distinguishes you from other Falterrans. Further, quantum signatures within your cells suggest you originated outside this universe."

"Not yours," Olga said with a certainty intriguing to Boothby.

He repeated the word, "Falterrans."

"Us," Adam answered. "Well, me, I guess."

Boothby replied without hesitation. "No, I heard the word. That's what Mister Ephyr called us."

Zephyr held Boothby's eyes. "So, *he* did find you, then? This is good news indeed."

"Who does he mean?" Conique asked.

"Ephyr Sargon: he's a Ghyan here on Falterra." Zephyr smiled with relief.

Reuben cocked his head. "More of you? He—"

"Has only the best intentions for this world," Zephyr answered with uncharacteristic sharpness which surprised Boothby. The Ghyan was quick to regain his cool as he continued, "One thing at a time. Yes, the Vesiks did not originate in this universe, nor mine." He remained guarded, prompting Boothby to entertain a scenario that made sense to him.

Shigeru folded his arms in defiance, with beaded perspiration on his forehead reflecting the warm light. "You owe us answers, Zeff. No more beating around the bush."

"Your reticence is... This is part of your simulation, isn't it?" Boothby asked.

"What?" Reuben asked.

Zephyr was himself surprised by Boothby's question. "Then you understand my position," he said.

"What's he talking about, Mister Bee?" Janet asked.

Ignoring her, Boothby instead locked eyes with their host. "Are you simulating this right now?"

Zephyr's expression softened as he turned to Janet. "To select a winning strategy, my journey here has received billions of simulations. The details—"

"Are important," Shigeru said.

Zephyr watched the doctor as Boothby leaned towards him. "Indeed. Ask your questions, Doctor."

"First, why do you call this world Falterra?" Shigeru asked with a glower Boothby deemed overkill.

Janet appeared interested in helping the Ghyan, though Boothby doubted even she had the complete picture. "The *Arkivar* used the same name. And Norcross. It's what they call this world. It's just their mythology, right?" She watched Zephyr.

"*Arkivar?*" Conique asked.

Zephyr brightened at the title. "A fellow Ghyan devoted to this world's cause. He located you, then?" He waited for Janet's nonverbal acknowledgement.

"The dude saved us from Norcross," Adam said. "Falterra and not Terra?" he then asked Zephyr.

He replied, "Ancient documents recovered from our southernmost continent posited that Ghya was one of seven worlds exalted by a super-race, comparative gods even to us. LaGhyar founded ours, and we took his name. Within the lore, they were known as the Vandaar, hence the name bestowed upon the ancient species who left the Katafaj here."

Boothby beamed in understanding. "Mister Ephyr called this world Falterra. This world's founder?"

"A Monagar, Falla was the Prymus to this world. He was one of two clay twins belonging to a sovereign goddess." Zephyr straightened his neck at the words.

"Jesus, weird words all around. Clay?" Reuben asked.

"Conjoined—ancient Ghyans believed conjoined twins were two meant to be one, carved incompletely from their earth mother," he replied.

"That would be the other way around, here." Adam offered to help Janet as she shifted in her seat.

"The twins were brothers to LaGhyar, my world's creator, or so goes the tale." Zephyr met Boothby's eyes. "Again, this is myth, obscured by time's passage. But the parallels are curious. Our planetary taxonomy respects this tradition—Ghyans revere ceremony and its many icons."

"But Terra? Falterra? Can't be a coincidence, right?" Boothby asked.

"Apologetics, man." Shigeru wasn't biting.

"Said a doctor on an alien spacecraft," Conique said with a laugh.

Janet said, "The *Arkivar* and Norcross said Monagar, and they called me Mona—it's the name the *Arkivar* has used in all my dreams."

Zephyr's face twisted at the mention, and his reply was measured. "Dymona was the name of the sovereign goddess, mother to our worlds' alleged founders. To call one 'Mona' is to ascribe great reverence. Ephyr's mate was a devotee, so it is possible he found faith in his time here."

"And Monagar?" asked Reuben.

"Children of Dymona and Ragar—the mythology holds that seven of their offspring founded the seven worlds. Each of the seven were Prymus to the respective world, and the Vesiks here descend from Falla. But this is mythology, and a distraction." Zephyr's expression was neutral.

Boothby slapped his legs. "It has to all be true, then."

"Fucking insane," Shigeru uttered with a hard sigh. "Can we stick to the facts? Why are we sick if we're so important?"

"Yes, Zephyr, our diseases?" Olga asked.

The Ghyan gestured an open hand to them. "Your unfortunate and varied neurological afflictions are partly symptoms of kudeson, a biological dissonance any of us who pass from one world to another."

Boothby asked, "Then each of us is crazy somehow in the head?"

Shigeru shot at him unprovoked. "I don't think you needed the former for the latter, little man."

Janet didn't permit the comment to fly. "Doctor, there's no reason to be an asshole to him. He understood more of this than any of us." She exchanged a comforting nod with Boothby.

Shigeru was clearly incensed at the young woman, but Zephyr cut them off. "Each Vesik suffers, be it malignancies, cognitive impairment, neurodegeneration, or psychological diseases."

Reuben looked to his wife, his puppy dog eyes deep with compassion. "Her dementia is part of this?"

Zephyr answered, "Indeed. None of the disorders are beyond Ghyan science, though my brother's treachery almost cost us the professor's life."

Boothby's innards squirmed in excitement. "We're from outside?! Where?"

The Ghyan said, "Even we don't know the answer to that. Until this week, we knew the identities of three of you, with the others hidden well within Falterra."

Conique folded her plump arms, clinking metal bracelets together. "We're aliens here, then?"

Reuben pressed his forehead against hers before asking Zephyr, "What do their genes unlock?"

Olga answered for him, evident once more of their earlier conversation. "The Vessafra, a computer hidden somewhere in this solar system."

Conique squinted her eyes in disbelief. "All of this for a computer? That doesn't make a lick of sense. Was the one we just beat not bad enough?"

Olga answered before Boothby could dump the nightmare from his mind. "No matter the appearance, that was something built only out of silicon. The machine awaiting us is both organic and synthetic."

Boothby jerked his eyes onto Zephyr. "That's true?"

The Ghyan nodded. "There is no greater power."

Reuben cocked his head in confusion. "Jesus Christ—worse than what we saw down there?"

Shigeru nodded with narrowed eyes. "Zeff here has firsthand experience—he built one."

Zephyr sighed slowly, as if he was ashamed to admit it. "The device I constructed is likely a small fraction as sophisticated."

"But more powerful than that? How?" Reuben asked. "You said you had answers for us," he demanded at the silence.

Conique snapped at him. "Dear, let the man speak! I adore you for your concern, but you've proven the point already."

"Fine. Please answer," he said in a huff. "How?"

Heartened as Archie hopped into his lap, Boothby answered on reflex as he had many times answering similar queries at his lectures and book events. "Biological brains still outperform every AI created, as impressive as Intellidez's security bot." Only then did it land on him.

Zephyr said, "We, too, attempted to instantiate human intelligence into the artificial, but we never could capture the gestalt that is the biological form."

He replied, "What is different then?"

Olga said, "Brains learn with almost no data. Large language models require millions of examples to learn even the simplest communication. Brains funnel out, data gluttons funnel in. And there are quantum implications, with hardly any of it clear to us. Intellidez's system required training on much of the corpus living on the internet—we could scarcely touch it, but basic inference is missing even in the most sophisticated designs."

Boothby volunteered his remarks, though he wondered whether they'd understand or not. "Look, the brain is capable of visions, dreams, and premonitions. Computers as we know 'em just do arithmetic really fast. That's how we tricked their security system. Wicked neat of the professor there."

Conique gasped at that. "A computer that can experience visions. My, that would be a feat." Catching herself, she shifted in her chair to accommodate, Boothby guessed, her uncomfortable girth. "I had a dream in which I saw the seven together, in some winter farm setting."

Reuben looked at his wife. "You didn't tell me about that."

She said, "I didn't remember until now, dear."

Adam said, "How powerful is the computer, Zeff?"

Zephyr spoke up for her. "The Vessafra is as powerful as a billion Ghyan brains networked together."

Shigeru said, "It sounds like just another goddamned nuke."

Boothby groaned at that. "I guess it's the wrong time to mention that Intellidez is working on that exact thing. The bot in the Heart was last generation for neural networks."

Reuben rubbed his eyes in frustration. "Jesus Christ on a fugging crutch. Those people really are outta their minds."

Olga tensed at that. "Demmings isn't anymore."

Shigeru regarded her with a spot of compassion, or so Boothby thought. Eying the others, he felt evasive. "Umm, it isn't exactly a secret. They was working on it with Pentagon money."

Olga followed him with a little reassurance. "They've failed so far in establishing an artificial link to biological neurons, but their work continues."

Janet guided them back to the first topic. "How do you know one of those, umm, Vessafras, is on Earth?"

"Not on Earth," Olga answered.

Zephyr hesitated, as if he pondered their interactions before whispering, "Let me explain." Their host clasped his hands together after finishing his strange beverage. "Because we found the same in our own system." He motioned towards the center of their semicircle, and a hologram of a star system appeared. "Let me show you."

"That's Ghya?" Boothby asked.

"The fourth planet in our system." Zephyr waved his hands into the empty space between them, summoning a dimensional image of a planet with city-covered continents spread among oceans.

Boothby knew at once that the continents differed, to say nothing of radiant, multicolored rings crowning the world. "Jesus, that's beautiful," he uttered slowly. It hit him that he was feeling unusually relaxed as Archie rubbed his face on Boothby's cheek, purring gently. The image was captivating, a welcome break from the tension among them.

Zephyr caressed the world's boundary with deference. "My home. Five hundred years ago, our world resembled yours. We had forged a sprawling civilization with brute force, though our technology eclipsed wisdom, the essential ingredient if a people are to prosper. Our planet ailed as we devastated the biosphere and depleted the resources."

The image before them shifted, with the atmosphere's white clouds changing to an ugly brown and green. Conique shivered at it. "I don't know that I like this story."

Zephyr surprised her with his passion. "This is a story every sentient creature must hear. It is too easy to repeat the mistakes made by others, and even easier if one is ignorant."

Olga drew a deep breath. "What happened? You must have overcome these things if this was five hundred years ago."

Zephyr pointed above as an image of one of the Katafaj drones materialized, lingering between phases. "The Katafaj appeared in our world, as well, and we owe our survival to its surgical incursions."

Boothby cocked his head. "You didn't create it?"

Zephyr's expression was playful. "We're an advanced species, but the simple answer is no. We did not, nor could we create the devices. But it is a device worthy of praise, for it has saved billions of lives. To our lasting gratitude, it appears to be well-suited to finding solutions requiring minimal damage or violence."

Conique placed her glass of tea to the arm rest, and it sank away in a sandy dissolve. "Wow. But who created it?"

Zephyr gazed at his world in thought. He was reluctant, though. "An ancient civilization of interstellar and interdimensional travelers."

"Wait a moment," Conique said with a raised finger. "You said your mythology purports a super-race—are these *them*?"

Zephyr's black eyebrows rose slowly. "There are parallels, as I said—the names are revered, so we on Ghya dubbed them the Vandaar."

"Then you should pay closer attention to those myths, Mister Zephyr." She leaned back in her chair as Reuben touched her shoulder—Boothby felt a twinge of sorrow that he had no such man devoted to him.

Shigeru reliably snapped at that. "Law of large numbers, Sister Superior—claim enough things, and some are bound to be true."

Zephyr wasn't amused. "The parallels are interesting, but the doctor is correct—if the mythology is, in fact, correct, the facts will lead us there."

Boothby felt certain the Ghyan was holding back, though he also felt certain he could trust him. The journalist within him begged for more, but he was far too timid.

Reuben had no such qualms. "Then, by all means, please enlighten us with these facts?"

Zephyr's face was unreadable. "Though we have not discovered evidence that they survive somewhere within the multiverse, their technology has enabled us to seek other artifacts left behind. We sought answers in the space beyond our world. Our system, like yours, contains other planetoids. We seeded them with thousands of probes, each scouring for answers."

He waved a hand, and countless dots appeared around the world as it shrank in size. They bloomed into still greater dots, reminding Boothby of nanobots. Olga said, "We have planned our own variant of this, a dandelion design."

Zephyr affirmed her as Ghya disappeared, replaced by a great gas giant striated by brown, red, and white clouds. He pointed to it as he said, "In the domain of icy giants far from our homeworld, we made a startling discovery. This is Korbus, a planet between your Saturn and Neptune in size. We detected radiation among its icy

419

moons." A snow-white sphere with striations and cracks formed adjacent to the behemoth world.

Boothby marveled as they zoomed into the frozen planetoid, as if they fell into it as it expanded into view. Dots resolved into focus as tiny drones, each infiltrating the surface.

Olga said, "We have some moons in the outer solar system which resemble this one."

Shigeru pressed them onto task. "What about your discovery?"

Zephyr cocked his head as they continued to fall into the moon, following one of the many drilling drones. "Buried below the ice shield and ocean of Ulym were remains of technology and biomatter." The image shifted to a ruined core, tattered. He pointed to it. "Understand, we Ghyans, like you Falterrans, had not encountered intelligence in space. We, too, possessed radio technology capable of detecting transmissions, and we'd found none. The consensus was that we were alone in the universe."

Olga sat up, intent on understanding. "What was the nature of the ruins?"

He said, "A great place of reverence and worship—intricate features carved within the moon's crust surrounding a temple. Within the temple was the basin of an extinct Vessafra, remains modeled from a cerebral organ we presumed belonged to the Vandaar themselves. The DNA was not unfamiliar, though it exhibited a quantum signature we could not match with our own."

Reuben asked Olga, "What does that mean, Professor?"

She responded with a question for Zephyr. "The Vandaar originated from another universe?"

He nodded to her. "Yes, and from an earlier epoch. Precise carbon-dating led us to conclude that the inert Vessafra had been placed millennia earlier."

Boothby stared into the projection, making out the distinct shape of a brain within a great housing. He said, "Jesus. That's why we can't find any life here. The multiverse."

Shigeru said, "Explain, please."

Boothby was delighted to speak on his favorite topic. "Radio signals would be evidence of advanced civilizations out there, but we don't find any. We broadcast our first signals in the 1930s, and we could easily destroy ourselves now. That's almost a century's worth of signals, and we'd detect either those or radiation from a nuclear apocalypse. We don't find anything like that."

Olga tracked with him so well, he longed to know her better. "Humans as we are now have been around for three hundred thousand years, and that's a blink of an eye on the cosmological calendar. One hundred years is like a hair on a flea on a tardigrade. It's statistically impossible that every single civilization out there is exactly within the three hundred millennia but *before* generating radio signals. So, we *should* detect them."

Reuben had simmered as he drank his beer. "What does that mean, then?"

Boothby shook his head, irked that it wasn't clear. "She's saying that there *can't* be aliens out there if we can't read any radio waves or clear evidence of nuclear detonations."

Conique connected the dots. "You mean to say that if they exist, they must use other means of broadcasting?"

Olga offered a half smile. "It is somewhat anthropocentric, but that would be the gist."

Reuben lost his cool, leaving Boothby to wonder whether he had always had anger issues. "Hello, why are we debating this? We have an alien sitting in front of us. And, apparently, I'm married to one." He gestured a mitt-sized hand towards his wife and the others.

Olga clinked her teacup against the saucer sitting on her left armrest. "Again, the multiverse, Doctor. We are one facet on a high dimensional structure."

Adam herded them back to the topic at hand. "The Vessafra—why was it there?"

Zephyr's eyes gleamed with the hologram's light, reflecting the cerebral shape. "It was too ancient, too decayed to provide meaningful justification. But the implications were overwhelming. Once we secured our discovery, three of us received appointments to research the find and advise our political leaders."

Adam did a double take. "God, you're like five hundred years old?"

Zephyr blushed with a chuckle. "Well, eight hundred, but who's counting. Thanks to science and evolution, Ghyans live a full millennium, sometimes two."

Olga reached for the shape as it was replaced by an image of Zephyr standing between two others, a strong-featured man with ebony skin and a gorgeous woman with red hair. The Ghyan touched the figures. "Ephyr Sargon was our leading cognitive and social scientist, and his wife Mirium Tradux was neuroscience's best mind."

Janet gasped at the images. "The *Arkivar*."

Adam seconded her. "Fuck, that's right. He looks just like the painting you made of him!"

Boothby said, "That is Mister Ephyr! He gave me the focus stone. Though he wasn't that young."

Zephyr bowed his head at the image. "Dearest Ephyr has searched for you for all the long years spent in this world. Before that, we were as close as brothers could be, working together for centuries."

Olga pointed to a younger Zephyr. "And that is you?"

Zephyr replied, "A young man full of hope and ambition, aiming to share our discoveries for the benefit of our people. Before the Vessafra, I was among the fringes of scientific minds, doggedly stubborn in my conviction that we would never replicate the Ghyan brain with silicon and data streams. I had claimed that amplifying our own intelligence would require biology itself rather than statistical replication. I received an appointment as the *Arkitek*, or chief scientist and technological advisor. I would have welcomed your help, Olga."

As he dressed his injured hand, Shigeru huffed at them with envy evident even to Boothby. "Enough of the mutual admiration. What did you learn?"

Zephyr cleared his throat as he continued, "With a quantum signature to search, we soon discovered more Vandaar technology buried within Ghya's surface—drones, biomatter, and terraforming devices. And so its purpose was clear—the Vessafra had been installed to operate Vandaar technology intertwined throughout our system. But it was useless to us without a living, breathing Vessafra to activate it."

Shigeru watched as the Ghyan solar system winked with Vandaar tech. He said, "It looks like an invasive cancer." He shot a glance to Olga, whispering, "Sorry—poor choice of words."

Zephyr gestured to the image. "On the contrary, the Vandaar left us the Katafaj, capable also of shifting climates, archiving our geological and biological records, and serving as a monument to the Vandaar themselves. Ephyr, Mirium, and I persuaded Ghyan leadership that our best chance at saving the world would be to augment the Katafaj." The projection generated orange beams connecting the network to the Vessafra housing on Efron.

Olga pointed to it. "The original control mechanism is the Vessafra. But it was dead?"

Zephyr said, "We needed one alive if we were to understand the Vandaar technology, so we instantiated a housing much like the one left behind." The projection brought together pieces into an octahedral housing. He pointed as the projection zoomed into the housing where a cerebral structure formed. "We cloned the Vessafra from genetic material, but we required an initial condition for neuronal connections. Since the new Vessafra would share contact with the three of us, we selected my brain to provide the mapping." The image showed the cerebrum within a projected Zephyr as it copied over the structure within the octahedron.

Reuben remained hardened, even if Boothby and Conique found themselves mesmerized at the intrigue. The older doctor asked, "Didn't you think that was dangerous? Nakamura is right that this looks like another Manhattan project."

Zephyr said, "I was reckless, but the Secretary General and Executive Polity were desperate to save our world. Our society had splintered and stratified. Most never knew economic or medical security. The scientific and political consensus was that Ghya would become uninhabitable within a century, robbing our people of their will and optimism. Our creation was an act of hopeless desperation."

Janet said offhandedly, "I guess if you're here five hundred years later, it worked, right?"

Zephyr gestured, and a fresher, cleaner Ghya appeared. "The fledgling Vessafra, named Prometer, advanced us centuries in decades. His capacity to simulate again and again the whole of our civilization's history made it possible for him to provide clear direction. We reclaimed the biosphere, Ghyans turned to wisdom, peace, and justice once they understood that the Vandaar had intended for us to flourish."

Shigeru smirked. "That sounds almost like religion."

Olga's retort surprised him. "It isn't uncommon to draw strength from the belief that something larger than you plans your destiny."

Zephyr said, "It is academic. Ghyans understood that an alien civilization once occupied our system. But Prometer led us a step further."

Boothby was near breathless in excitement. He said, "You found us."

Zephyr waved into focus two worlds, the second of which Boothby knew to be Earth. He said, "Prometer theorizes that there are eight worlds in total, all positioned along multiversal facets, manifolds nestled within a convex domain." A massive octahedral form appeared, with shadows of worlds appearing within the eight faces.

Conique appeared delighted, but it wasn't quite right. "Gosh, that sounds groovy. Two pyramids stacked on each other. But what does it mean?" She traced two lazy S shapes running on one edge. "Those look like—"

Boothby answered, "Chromosomes. Right?"

Zephyr gestured towards it. "Correct—it is a rune representing one of the eight fractures."

Boothby knew the symbol was familiar, even if he couldn't place it. Conique folded her arms. "*Otofos*..."

Zephyr asked, "You've heard this?"

"From a dream," she answered. "Norcross said it to me."

Olga found a symbol resembling a crook and stem. "The *Gemyn*."

Boothby recalled seeing it also, and it was clear to him. "Kymara's chevron! I'd expect to see two concentric circles."

Zephyr rotated the octahedron to reveal the third symbol, though five faces remained blank. "The *Dynax*."

Reuben clasped Conique's hand as he protested, "Someone explain this to me?"

Boothby chuckled despite his anxiety. "The three symbols of Kymara represent its parts: Codeka, Picoveer, and Intellidez. How can these be the same symbols?"

Zephyr crossed his arms. "Kymara's founders must be aware of Ghyan incursions—this chevron represented their company when?"

"Mister Best created the chevron at least forty years ago," Boothby said without a tremor to his voice. "What do they mean?"

Zephyr nodded at the other faces of the three-dimensional shape floating before them. "Each Vesik represents a fracture. One can examine history, science, and perhaps nature itself to find fractures propelling life forward. *Gemyn*, *Dynax*, and *Otofos* are three such fractures. Professor Kunskapsen, Francis Putnam, and Miss Voyant appear linked to these. I believe *Gemyn* also refers to Ghya, as *Dynax* indicates Falterra. The remaining symbols are unknown to us. The convexity of the shape above indicates that a blurring of the Vyrvesikon can save this and other worlds."

"Convexity?" Conique asked.

The golden-haired professor answered gently and earnestly. "It is geometry, Miss Voyant. Think of three dimensions. A shape is convex if you can pick any two points within it, join them with a segment, and the entire segment lies within the shape. There's always a straight path between the points, but not so in a non-convex domain. But there are other dimensions beyond just the three or four."

Conique nodded slowly, leading to Shigeru laughing a yelp in pain from his wounds. "Well, she doesn't get it. Next silly question?"

Adam's lightly spiked hair glittered under the burning orange of the hologram. "You said there were eight worlds. What are the others? What world corresponds to the Otolithic, umm, *Otofos*?"

Zephyr said, "Yours is the only other we've reached. The other six worlds are unknown to me."

Janet broke her long silence. "If those runes are part of Kymara, then someone there knows about the third world."

"It follows, indeed." Zephyr's reply was slow.

Boothby asked, "How did ya cross to our facet?"

Zephyr pointed to the shape hovering in slow rotation above them. "Prometer assisted us in discovering the Vydua, an interdimensional bridge connecting the respective systems of Ghya and Falterra. He shared with us a means of traversing it, and I believe he can commune with the others."

Olga said, "How is that possible?"

Conique grinned ear-to-ear. "Telepathy."

Zephyr said, "Consciousness, even for beings such as ourselves, is vast and inscrutable. Prometer says he doesn't understand the source of the knowledge, and I *believe* his sincerity. We agree it must be subliminal, resting in his mind's twilight."

Shigeru applied salve to his hand, watching the wound improve in real-time. "Could the information be within his genes?"

Zephyr answered, "It is too complex, though preambles leading him to think his way to a solution is possible." Steepling his fingers, he said, "No matter the source, he proved himself unmatched in his prognosticative prowess. In early tests, he could predict most global events, including election outcomes, weather patterns, and scientific breakthroughs. The Ghyan Senate formed a Bureau of Vessafra Affairs, naming me director. Prometer, after decades of intense testing, was included in intelligence briefings. I spent most of my time with him, teaching, but mostly learning. He confided in me a growing concern about the fate of Falterra, at last explaining that the transversal connection forever marries our fates. Should this world end, so will ours follow."

Olga asked, "How does he come by this conclusion?"

Zephyr watched the holographic housing rotate above them. "It is challenging. Even with neuronal augmentation, we cannot follow all his arguments. His record is perfect, but Ghyan leaders are divided. From across the Vydua, he sensed Vandaar technology embedded here, artifacts he believed he might be able to control."

Olga said, "There must be a quantum component to his consciousness for him to see so far."

Zephyr's affectionate nod to her noticeably irked Shigeru, leading Boothby to wonder. The Ghyan said, "We dispatched reconnaissance agents across the Vydua, incursions prescribed by Prometer to refine Falterra's course of events. He believes, as do I, that the Vessafra in this system is alive, but dormant. He analyzed the Vandaar relics, pointing us to the existence of the Vesiks and their utility in locating the Falterran Vessafra."

Conique said, "So the Vandaar wanted us to find the supercomputer. They predicted we would exist?"

Zephyr nodded. "Prometer deciphered enough of the Ghyan and Falterran Katafaja. We learned of the Vesiks and the Vesikavira, seven centers of virtue needed to earn access to the Vessafra. But the seven would require one more, a Keystone capable of uniting them. Prometer appointed my brother Norcross to serve as such, training him to undertake a quest of global concern. It was of the greatest import, demanding tremendous courage and ambition. My brother Norcross had already proven himself a brilliant scientist and explorer—Arkiyan, they called him. To aid him in his search, *Arkivar* Ephyr traveled ahead to identify the seven Vesiks. He has (to my knowledge now) successfully located three of them."

Adam slid forward in his seat to lean towards Zephyr. "Who are the others? He found Mister Bee and Janet."

Zephyr replied, "The third Vesik was the easiest to locate, and it is my hope that he guides that person to our destination."

Shigeru asked, "Which is?"

Zephyr summoned an image of Earth. He pointed to Siberia as Boothby exclaimed, "That's exactly where Miss Voyant said we was going!"

Zephyr draped his fingers along positions deep in the Tundra. "Beneath the frozen lands here, the Vandaar constructed a facility which, among other things, fabricates and repairs drones of the Katafaj. There is also a network of temperature governors designed to stay the vast stores of methane littering the peat bogs, for if this methane escapes, your catastrophic climate change will accelerate exponentially."

The hologram of Siberia expanded to render a lattice below the surface, with red marks appearing. Zephyr pointed to it. "One entry point is the Haligseal, a waystation left behind for the seven Vesiks."

Adam looked around the room at the others. "You mean the Vandaar built it all for seven people they predicted would exist?"

Olga tapped her teacup as she sniffed the steam escaping it. "They would have leveraged the same simulation technique Prometer knows by instinct, right?"

Janet asked, "Even across centuries? When was this built? How come the Russians don't know about it?"

Zephyr said, "The Vandaar were expert in concealing their work, a trait we Ghyans have attempted to emulate. I do not believe any Falterran agency, including intelligence arms of Russia and the United States, could outwit Ephyr. He believes the Haligseal contains the means to recover the Falterran Vessafra, but we cannot enter without the Vesiks."

Reuben sampled a cookie he'd obtained from the arm of his chair, pleased at its taste. "You mean you don't know for sure?"

Zephyr shook his head. "Prometer predicted correctly that we would be unable to breach the seal. It has resisted every effort."

Olga clinked her glass to the arm of her chair. "Why not search for the Vessafra here without using this Haligseal?"

Zephyr summoned a hologram of the Sol System. "Even if we guessed its location, we could not access it without the contents of the Haligseal. The Vessafra could sit beneath the surface of Venus or be buried deep within an asteroid or icy moon of one of the gas giants. Or even within the rocky core of one of the gas giants themselves, a place even Ghyans would struggle to infiltrate. But the means to locate and activate it are within the waystation."

Boothby couldn't contain his excitement. "So, you said that the seal is one entry to the underground facility. There are others out there?"

Zephyr nodded. "The *Arkivar* located the factories installed to maintain the Katafaj. Of all the Vandaar's works, this was most conspicuous. Ephyr built an estate around it to conceal it from prying eyes." The hologram zoomed to a remote spot in Siberia, all until a palatial mansion appeared.

Conique said, "That was what I saw in my dream."

Boothby's face lit up. "I knew it! So that's where Mister Ephyr took me."

Zephyr watched the image with fondness. "Ephyr has labored all these years to find you. Had Norcross not abandoned his duty, you would already be enroute to the Vessafra."

Reuben held nothing but protests. "Wait a second. You mean to say that this Prometer thing picked Norcross to find my Connie and these others, but he goes rogue, and you still trust your creation? Did it decide that you would be the savior, instead?"

Zephyr bowed his head with shame. "No, Doctor. As I suggested earlier, Prometer's stern warnings divided our leadership. We obtained a narrow majority within the Polity to dispatch Norcross, but his treason shifted opinion, convincing our leaders to abandon Falterra. They sealed the Ghyus Postern to the Vydua to contain Norcross. I crossed before they finished their work in the hopes of stopping him." His

426

eyes reddened with tears, softening Reuben's posture. The Ghyan said, "Shifting the Katafaj to recognize me rather than Norcross required little, considering our shared genetic material."

Olga asked, "Why not simply act here without the help of the Vandaar's tech?"

Zephyr stared at the projection of Prometer. "We simulated every possible incursion, and none averted the coming end. Direct, conspicuous intervention always results in disaster. So, our work with the Katafaj is careful, regimented, and light."

Conique said, "I still don't get it. If his actions will destroy this world, why does your brother come here?"

Zephyr was anguished at her words. "Norcross seeks power, above all things. He was born with a disease demanding constant treatment and the utmost supervision. You might call it sociopathy here, or moral color blindness. We call it *rapaxis*. As a rap, he cannot rely on his internal conscience to mitigate his more destructive impulses. Those afflicted either must submit for treatment or face banishment."

Reuben threw his hands to the sky. "Oh, my fugging God. This is the person your big brain in a box sent our way?"

Zephyr folded his arms. "Many of us, including myself, doubted Prometer's selection. But I could isolate no fault in his judgment, with days of searching. Norcross has acted under Prometer's orders hundreds of times to carefully guide Ghya's evolution. He appeared to be the natural candidate to assemble the seven Vesiks here. It wasn't until he'd commenced the journey across the Vydua this final time that we understood his intent."

Janet said, "I knew he was a monster the first time I saw him. Why wasn't it clear to you?"

Zephyr shook his head. "I can't speak for our intelligence failures, but he had organized others suffering from rapaxis into a new Elemental Concern. This was an ancient cult which enshrined their amorality, deeming it an evolutionary advantage rather than frailty. Norcross promised to free his fellow raps by capturing the Falterran Vessafra. The fate of all others here and on Ghya matter not one whit."

Janet asked, "You blame yourself, don't you?" Zephyr lowered his head in shame.

"Fuck me," Shigeru said. He then asked his chair arm for more whiskey, and it obliged.

Boothby then asked, "If you had stayed back in your universe, you would have been safe? They closed the portal here, so he couldn't get back there, right?"

Zephyr hesitated to answer, so Conique said, "You didn't come here to save yourself. You came to save *us*."

He met her eyes, and neither said a word. Reuben spoke next. "How can you be certain the others will meet us at this Halig thing?"

Zephyr said, "My brother will not fail to appear. He hungers for power above all things—it is as nectar to an insect, a destiny he cannot avert. But he cannot enter the waystation, thanks to Ephyr's lock."

"Why am I still worried?" Reuben asked.

Zephyr frowned. "He can wait for us to succeed, then try to pry the powers from the Vesiks." He waved to the hologram, and the chamber returned to the peaceful glen.

Boothby said the unthinkable, considering it could close a door to truth he'd sought to open all of his life. "What if we don't go there? If Norcross can't get inside without us, why don't we just hide?"

Zephyr replied, "Prometer attempted these in simulation, but disaster always followed. It is the *only* course before us. We must open the way to the Vessafra." Looking to each of his guests, Zephyr said, "I know this is much to process, and I wish the losses ahead were less than those suffered behind. I cannot guarantee our success, but Ephyr, along with each of you, have given us a chance. We lack two, but I believe the seven will appear at the Haligseal."

Conique looked to her husband. "I have faith," she said.

Zephyr pointed to Adam and Reuben. "You are neither Vesiks, nor are you Ghyans. The path ahead is full of peril, and neither of you possess any defense from those we'll encounter. I would implore you to consider remaining behind."

Reuben placed his massive hands on Conique's shoulders. "We'll ice skate in hell before I leave my Connie."

Adam agreed. "No, Zee. I am sticking with Janet, no matter what."

Zephyr's expression was warm. "Your courage is laudable. I hope our efforts honor it." He stood, opening his arms to them. "Each of you must agree to go forward."

Janet and Adam turned to each other. She said, "We're in."

Boothby winced, wondering what such a painful thing would feel like. Instead, he said, "Mister Zephyr, you showed me answers to all the questions I've always had. I lived in fear, but now, I'm strong."

Conique said, "I'm not going to refuse the calling."

Olga replied quickly. "Since I'd be dead without your help, Zephyr, every moment forward is a gift. Let's get to it."

The others waited for Shigeru. Once they all waited on him, he said, "The world is worth my time."

Zephyr said, "You must all rest now. We will reach the site of the Haligseal in a few hours. Once there, I will lead you through the Rhykeng, and if we're successful, the seal shall open to us."

Janet asked, "What is that all about?"

"Patience—you've waited your entire life to learn the truth," Zephyr said with a slow nod.

"Some of us longer than others, Mister Zephyr. I've never *not looked*." Boothby felt anxious with a shiver, but a purring Archie pressed his cold snout to a cheek, washing a warm comfort over him. In that moment, it hit him just how tired he was. The preceding events were millstones around his neck, and, somehow, his anxiety was still. "Maybe we can wait just a little while," he confessed as the feline's purr trembled against his neck. "I should be more afraid—what will Norcross do now?"

Zephyr's posture shifted. "What he has always done—fight to promote himself. But I suspect his path to victory will not prove so easy." He lost himself for a moment, but his recovery was swift. "Let's get you to a cot, Boothby."

Nodding, Boothby exhaled a deep beath. "Fair enough—forty winks and all that."

F***

Frankie waited aboard their plane, relieved to let Hazel work with Brother Bobby to finish readying the craft for flight. Ruminating, he strapped himself into his seat. He remembered the car seats Tyler and Myra needed when they were tykes, but he no longer felt ancillary or incidental to the Lord's plan—Norcross did, in fact, *need* Frankie to succeed. Though he didn't understand what he'd done, he found some security in the doing of it.

Hazel's selfless act in rescuing Frankie confused him. The locusts clamored for her blood, but he couldn't deny her importance. The Lord had chosen capable, if not desirable, servants.

No matter the circumstances, Frankie intended to press his Lord for answers. Pastor Chet explained that half of Satan's power lay in simple ignorance of the facts—he never shirked in replying to Frankie's many questions about faith and righteousness. His newfound importance emboldened him, and so he readied himself.

It had been perhaps twenty-five minutes after Frankie sat down in his seat that he heard Hazel shout, "The Lord is back!"

Frankie hopped to his feet, eager to learn what the Lord had to say. As he walked out of the private quarters, he could see Norcross appear in the starboard exit. Hazel greeted Him with a freshly lit cigarette. "My Lord, we got the plane ready to go. But I need to know where we're fixing to go. I hope you didn't already kill the little brown monkey."

Receiving her offering, He replied in disgust, "Mister Chevur is handling other matters for us. Chart us a course to Siberia. We must get underway immediately."

She hesitated at that. "Lord, We'll have a helluva time getting into *that* airspace."

He wheeled to face her, annoyed at her concern. "Disable our transponders. More who are sympathetic to Our cause await Us there."

Frankie asked, "What about the other Vesiks? Where are they?"

Norcross held a finger to him as He said to Hazel with growing anger, "Carry out My orders, Hazel Grant. We have no time, now."

Before heading to the rear of the plane, she said, "Best strap yourselves in, Gents."

Frankie said, "I thought We were coming here to pick the others up. Don't We need them, Lord?"

Norcross glared at Frankie, conveying cruel annoyance and seething rage. He clamped a hand on Frankie's shoulder. "Our situation has become more dire. The others I'd intended to recruit were not alone—another has arrived here, an interloper intending to usurp My place."

Frankie exhaled hard with frustration. "I don't understand. A demon?"

Norcross tensed his jaw until it popped. "A *demon*," He whispered. His grasp on Frankie's neck tightened, hurting him.

He gasped in pain, but the Lord smiled at him. "Please, Lord. I can't breathe—"

Norcross loosened His grasp as He said, "This pretender has succeeded in uniting five of the seven, Francis. Each of them possesses powers comparable to your own, and you've tasted but one drop of it."

He searched his thoughts to remember his Sunday school lessons on the end times. He asked, "But You overpower Satan in the end, right?"

The Lord's fiery gaze locked onto him, letting Frankie know He'd found a plaything in that moment. "You really do believe?" A smile found its way across His face as He placed His hands around Frankie's throat and head.

Shivering, Frankie said, "You made me believe, Lord. You have lifted me up."

Norcross touched Their foreheads together. "And you would do anything for Me, no?"

Frankie was sweating, angry at the Lord's disregard for his personal space. He also feared the Lord for His next words. "Please, Lord. You *have tested me*, already. I killed Varnum for you."

Norcross burst into laughter at him. Pushing him back, His expression filled with feral rage. "To serve Me, you must know the truth, Francis." His eyes burned alive with energy.

Frankie tried to pull away, but the Lord's strength was too much. "I know the truth, Lord. You are the Son of God."

He grinned before he asked, "Consider, My friend. What do you truly want?"

Frankie shrugged. "That Your will be done."

Norcross huffed in amusement. "Yes, yes, but what does that mean to you? Why should My will be done?"

It didn't make much sense that the Lord would question him so, but Frankie tried to follow Him. "Because the fallen angels need to burn for rejecting the Father. The wicked in this world must be punished." He recalled George's face filled with horror, and he felt another hard-on.

Norcross patted him on the cheek. "Such a simple creature. You know only the conquest, and it honors Me. Yes, We must destroy Our enemies, Francis. Without My guidance, you and the remaining seven will fail to fulfill your destiny. The enemies have advanced much further than I would have believed possible, so We cannot succeed unless they suffer ruin and Our hands. Do you understand?"

He cradled Frankie's head in His hands. "In My home, I led thousands into a new revelation: Our power derives from individual elements, distilled to perfection. Just as your Korobskron would compel your fellow inhabitants to incarcerate you, so did it isolate Me and My followers from society by petty bureaucrats and envious powermongers. We are pure in Our design, and We must destroy those who covet Our strength."

Frankie sputtered as the Lord's grip on his head tightened. "I know all this, Lord. They can't stop You."

Norcross tightened His hand around Frankie's throat. "You do not know the entirety, Francis, and I doubt your faith to see Our quest to its completion."

Rage flowed through Frankie. "I will do whatever You ask! I want to destroy this world."

Norcross loosened the hold as His eyes drifted to the ceiling. "They called Me their Arkiyan, Francis. I was the pinnacle of strength and power, entrusted to journey here for the grandest of all missions. Now, another seeks to supplant Me." He then pulled Frankie close. "You will not enjoy what I intend for you. Because the other Vesiks follow another like Me, We are disadvantaged."

Frankie gasped through the Lord's vice on his trachea. "Point my gun in the direction, Lord."

Norcross squeezed until darkness lapped at the periphery of Frankie's field-of-view. His face deformed to something feral, delighted that He held his life so casually. "Just a weapon to aim, is it? But My service requires more than just your hand." He released Frankie's neck, instead tossing him into the bulkhead. He collided with shelving bolted into the floor, and his chest seared in pain as he dropped to the grated floor.

"What is this, Lord? What have I done?" It was clear Frankie had no air in his lungs as he mouthed the words but said nothing. He touched his ribs, and they screamed with fire.

Norcross advanced on him. "I said you would not enjoy what I require." He kicked Frankie hard, cracking another rib. Erupting in fury, he shouted, "I have sacrificed much, Francis. Defective, dangerous, rapaxis, they call Me. But I am a god!"

Frankie sucked hard to get at the oxygen in the air. Coughing, he said, "I know You are, Lord. I know. We'll kill them together. I'll do anything."

Norcross bunched his left hand into Frankie's flyboy suit, plucking him from the floor. He tossed him into another bulkhead. "Then suffer on My behalf."

Frankie's left shoulder and arm ached as he rolled onto his back. He could remember the many times he'd bullied Tyler, tossing the much smaller child from one side of the room to the other. At least he had Pastor Chet to guide him from violence. But who would guide the Lord? He breathed fast, clutching his wrist stump as its nerves transmitted agony into his overloaded brain. "Lord, please, tell me what to do."

Norcross laughed so loud that the structure around them rattled. "If only I could tell you to die as you've lived, crawling in the dirt along with the rest of the primordial slime. I spent lifetimes laboring hard to rescue this sewer world, and, as simply as one snaps his fingers, I am excised, banished, replaced."

Frankie couldn't understand. Or maybe he couldn't bear to try. But the Lord's complaints made sense to him. "That's what they do, Lord." He discovered he'd bitten the inside of his mouth in the last fall, filling it with blood. He spit it out.

Hazel popped her head into the doorway. Her raspy honk of a voice was a welcome reprieve for Frankie, even if it was brief. "Lord, is everything okay?"

Norcross dismissed her with His hand. "You have your orders, Hazel Grant. Make yourself scarce." She disappeared once more.

Calmed a little, Norcross watched him closely. "Francis, I am not talking about the moronic group think of a people bursting with lies. Even a computer can mislead millions of fools." Dropping to His knees before Frankie, He said, "In My world, a place neither your theologians nor theoreticians can even describe, We have tried in earnest to dispense with ignorance. But even the well-intentioned fail to understand that some of Us deserve to rise above all others." He pet him before pinching a clump of his hair from his head. "I won't serve in this place," He whispered. Tearing the hair from Frankie's scalp, He laughed. Blood dripped fast from the wound, with the pain burning white hot into the core of his being.

"Please, Lord, why?" He reached for his gaping wound.

Norcross was feral, and His eyes were full of hunger. "Must there be a why? This world reeks, offending every olfactory receptor." He grasped Frankie's stump, causing unbearable pain. "Francis, pain installs so deep a psychic afterimage, it is hard to overcome."

Frankie screamed until he exhausted his breath.

Norcross kissed Frankie's hair as He held him. "Our one salvation is hidden in this solar system, Francis. I must have this power, and with it, We shall rule more than just a world—the very cosmos will confess and bend the knee. I will inflict the deepest of sorrows, the hottest of anger, and unbearable pain on you." He gazed to the top of the bulkhead, as if He saw the stars in their dizzying dance. He thumped Frankie's wounded scalp.

Wincing, he said, "Why hurt me, Lord?"

"Francis, you of all people know why. I can see you in your memories. You tortured animals to a knife's edge from death, dangling them for that sweetest twilight between agony and oblivion." He pressed His cheek against Frankie's face. "The locusts cry for release, and Mine emit song detectable across space and time. It is a fearsome thing, instilling terror in My enemies. They also communicate your desires and dark pleasures."

Frankie closed his eyes, repeating himself in pain. "You'll kill the demon. You'll kill the demon. You're the Lord."

Norcross didn't seem so angry, but Frankie felt concern that His mood could shift. He whispered His mocking reply. "*I'll kill the demon. I'm the Lord.* Francis, I would apologize for what comes next, but it wouldn't be truthful."

The Lord wrapped His arms around Frankie, crushing him with enormous force. Frankie heard his joints and bones popping while his nerves reported paralyzing pain from every quarter. Prying Frankie's mouth open, he yanked a molar from each quadrant, discarding them to clatter across the metal floor.

It didn't matter that Frankie remembered carrying out that exact torture on a stray dog wandering his childhood neighborhood. He had never screamed so hard, even as he choked on the blood oozing from the evacuated sockets in his mouth. At last, his scream disappeared as his vocal cords failed.

The Lord next squeezed Frankie's genitals so hard that one of his testicles ruptured. Again, Frankie had acted out the same horror on a buck he'd hunted; the sound wasn't something he would forget. But he could find within his past no counterpart to the agony he felt at that moment.

The Lord mutilated, and Frankie suffered. Black spots encroached on the periphery of his vision, and his own screams seemed to shrink.

With a wild look and a vicious grin, Norcross said, "There it is—I see it inside of you. Soon, you will be a perfect thing." He rolled his eyes in self-congratulation. "Poof! Next stop, and you'll be there, little Francis."

As he heard his bones starting to buckle, Frankie burned at his loyalty repaid with cruelty. And he would have his revenge.

Epilogue

It started with a dream, stretched across the firmament. Janet knew it well—the *Arkivar* visited her often. But circumstances differed greatly—she slept, but the aged voice was silent. She could touch the stones leading to his dais, but the light show was the lone attraction.

She felt pain throughout her body, though she couldn't be certain it wasn't the devastating infirmity that, until recently, she knew would write the concluding chapters of her story. Her fellow Vesiks gave her faith once more that the world might be saved. But it wasn't so simple—the mysterious Ghyans were positioned to offer tremendous aid, yet they withheld their talents where Falterrans might have benefited most.

Her body ached once more, and it left her straining to recall whatever was her waking life. She could hear Adam, but only the low hum of his singing voice from the shower. The melodic tones were replaced by groaning and screams, but her own voice was gone. The cries belonged to a man, but they weren't from Boothby or Shigeru, or even Zephyr. Instead, she knew they were Frankie's. Something terrible had befallen him, and though she quickly sighed with relief that the backward fool was suffering, she felt sorrow for him. He was a tortured soul, a prisoner to his own shortsightedness. But this was genuine physical agony, and it pained her to hear it.

The *Arkivar* was dark, even if Zephyr had led her to a deeper understanding of the world around them. All this time she'd thought he was a figment of her subconscious mind—maybe it was the other way around. She could hear Frankie fight, and his swell of pride to conceal his torment was clear to her somehow—he would not let his attacker know how much it all hurt him. She could respect him in that, but the young Texan frightened her. He overcame Zephyr's hold on Norcross, rendering their escape all too narrow.

434

It made little sense to her that Norcross would torture Frankie, but malevolence wasn't her style. She shut his howls from her head, shouting her rule number nineteen: "The pain is all in my head!"

"You... are... correct... Mona..." said a voice.

She shot her eyes from one side to the other. "*Arkivar?*" she asked even as she knew the answer.

The voice was sluggish but overpowering. "Negative. I have waited millennia for you... little... Mona."

"Who are you?" Janet asked as Frankie's cries died from her.

"You will know me... Soon... There is a bit more to cross before we meet. I must... be... free... I can see... you... now... It was not always..."

Janet swallowed as she breathed steadily. "I don't understand."

"Do not... trust... Ghya... They will... betray... will... you... Remain silent, and wait... Do not... share my words... They will endanger those you... love... Wait... for... ME!" The voice screeched, and Janet awakened with a start.

Adam gently shook Janet as she opened her eyes. "Are you okay, babycakes? Sounded like a doozy of a nightmare."

She replied, "It made no sense. It was the *Arkivar*'s temple, but someone else spoke. I don't know what it wanted."

Her brother cracked a smile, and his eyes were slow as they moved around the room. "My sister without answers—the world really is ending. The end of the world, as we know it!" he yodeled.

"Adam Baumgartl, you're drunk!" she said as she sat up.

"Brother Zephyr is cool," he replied with a chuckle. "He suggested we take stress pills," he enunciated with air quotes. "I can recommend the silver lilac." He moved aside to reveal a comfortable but Spartan sitting room. "So, you were saying about your dream?"

Her emotions calmed, partly at his relaxing demeanor. "Nothing—just be careful taking drugs we don't understand."

"It's my body, baby," he said with a bright smile. "Your dream?"

"Just more of the same. Where are we?" she asked.

"Still some ways out. This place is so dope—I need to ask Zee if we can crash at his place sometime. Anyways, we should meet the others soon. Feel up to it? Need help?" he asked.

"I'll manage," she said with a sigh. "You go ahead and I'll be behind you." She lightly punched his upper arm.

"Me ahead of you? Now, I really believe it's the end of the world as we know it!" he crooned with glee.

Index

437

Wikivinity

The *Wikivinity* defines the many narrative constructs from *THE EIGHTH DIVINITY*. This is an excerpt explaining terms you will find in the first volume.

- *Arkimus:* leading member of the Ghyan council
- *Arkitek:* chief of science and technology of the Ghyan council
- *Arkivar:* chief historian and information curator of the Ghyan council
- *Arkiyan*: chief tactical and intrigue agent of the Ghyan council
- *Falterra*: Ghyan designation of Earth
- *Ghya:* a sister world to our own—it birthed an advanced species similar to our own
- *Haligscriosta:* an accursed agent capable of mind control; they were once considered mythic
- *Kaelafaj:* drones originating outside Earth
- *Kasafaj:* drones released from the Estate.
- *Katafaj*: a network of devices installed here long ago to terraform the climate and defend the biosphere
- *Kryafaj*: a lattice of devices beneath Siberia.
- *Korobskron*: darkened heart, tormented by locusts
- *Kudeson:* neurological decay among the Vesiks and any other visitors between worlds
- *Podopech:* term of affection Sargon applies to Mayak
- *Posterns:* devices capable of opening the Vydua
- *Skrytyypas*: hidden passenger of Mayak
- *Vandaar*: the prime species preceding our own

- *Vesik*: one of the seven chosen from our world
- *Vesikyar*: the cipher taken from their foreign chromosomes.
- *Vessafra*: vast biological supercomputers
- *Vydua:* the interdimensional superstructure connecting our world to the Ghyan universe, with the understanding that five other worlds exist
- *Vyrvesikon:* the psychic composite of the seven

II

Heart Rites of
THE EIGHTH DIVINITY

Coming in 2025

9 798330 571